FIREBALL

Robert G. Begam

FIREBALL
A COURTROOM DRAMA

McGRAW-HILL BOOK COMPANY
New York   St. Louis   San Francisco
Toronto   Hamburg   Mexico

1 2 3 4 5 6 7 8 9 D O C D O C 8 7

ISBN 0-07-004308-6

LIBRARY OF CONGRESS CATALOGING IN PUBLICATION DATA

Begam, Robert G.
  Fireball.

  I. Title.
PS3552.E37R4   1987   813'.54   87-4153
ISBN 0-07-004308-6

BOOK DESIGN BY PATRICE FODERO

Acknowledgments

I thank Charles Einstein for his active participation in the writing and editing of this novel—and for thirty years of joyous friendship.

Dan Weaver's editorial counsel is greatly appreciated.

For her prodigious effort and remarkable skill at the typewriter, the word processor, and the computer, I am grateful to Evelyn Dotson Ness.

Finally, and eternally foremost, I thank my wife, Helen, for her daily inspiration.

—R.G.B.

In the summer of 1973, in the town of Kingman, in the northwest corner of the State of Arizona, a railroad tank car filled with liquid propane caught fire and exploded. A dozen or more leaders of that small community were killed. They had been called to the scene of the fire in line of duty as members of the volunteer fire department. The tank car then ruptured and they were consumed in the resulting fireball.

In its basis, therefore, this novel may be said to be historically true. However, all of the characters, the events, the principal locations—even the immediate cause of the accident—are fictitious.

This book is dedicated to the memory of those courageous men who died in Kingman.

Contents

Prologue

The only thing that can be said for sure is that the meeting did take place, somewhere, during the mid-1960s. It was by telephone invitation only—nothing in writing. There was no printed agenda. There were no minutes. Tape recorders were not permitted in the room. Indeed, everyone agreed that there would be no notes taken.

There was some speculation afterward that this gathering of the top executives of the largest oil companies and railroads in the United States had taken place at the luxurious Camelback Inn in Scottsdale, Arizona, under cover of a golf tournament. This rumor stemmed from inadvertent references, overheard during the ensuing years, to the Camelback Conference.

But, wherever it took place, the business was deadly serious. For two decades, since World War II, profits had been eroded by interstate truck and pipeline competition in the transportation of petroleum products. The railroads were hurting financially—and what was bad for them was bad for their cousins, the oil barons. Moreover, the oil companies didn't want to do business with the Teamsters. They much preferred the railroad unions, appropriately called the Brotherhood.

Everyone agreed that the old-fashioned little black tank cars were no longer cost-effective. The man from Phillips Petroleum brought with him a model of what he called the tank car of the future—shiny and white and better than three times the size of the little black car.

The hooker was safety. The little black cars were encased in 4 inches of steel-jacketed rock wool insulation. Over millions of miles for the better part of a century they had an unparalleled safety record. They transported the most volatile, highly explosive product manufactured by the oil companies—and never had there been a catastrophic explosion, even when the cars were subjected to the ever-increasing incident of derailment.

The big white uninsulated car was at the outer limit of heaviness for the rails. To burden it with the weight of steel-jacketed rock wool would be unfeasible from an engineering standpoint.

So the focus was on the grisliest cost-benefit study ever conducted in the history of American industry: would the profit generated by using the big car offset the actuarially predictable deaths and burn injuries and property damage that would result when it was involved in an accident and exploded?

The study plugged in figures for loss of product, damage to equipment, and legal fees for defending wrongful death and personal injury claims. The estimates of what it would cost to settle these claims with widows and orphans and burn victims were deliberately on the high side. The numbers argued an eloquent case. The profit potential dwarfed the cost of destruction.

There were a few somewhat tentative dissents, mostly couched in terms of public relations damage—adverse publicity that would result from the new tank cars' wiping out small railside communities. But it was the observation by one of the senior railroad executives that carried the day. He reminded those assembled about all the things that made American industry great—what made our country great—what enabled us to realize our manifest destiny.

He told them that he was on the board of the company that built the Empire State Building, and the same bleeding-heart arguments were made that to build a skyscraper would predictably kill a dozen or more construction workers, but, by God, they decided to "let 'er rip." And now there it is—towering over the New York skyline—a symbol of American industrial might.

The vote was unanimous.

PART 1

Jumbo Nellie Nellie

1

Trans World Airlines Flight 430 was a Boeing 727, of the 200 class first put into service in the early 1970s. It flew nonstop, St. Louis to Washington, departing at 12:55 p.m. central time, arriving at 3:35 eastern. Today, the first Monday in May, it was on schedule and halfway there, flying at its assigned altitude of 33,000 feet. There had been some choppy going—the day was extra hot for that time of year, temperatures well into the nineties from the Wabash east—and for a brief time the flight captain considered asking the air route traffic control center at Indianapolis for permission to seek a smoother trough higher up. But things were not that bad, and he doubted higher up was that much better.

On the wide-sweep radar screen at Indianapolis Center, the blip with the transponder label TW 430 edged its inching eastward course. The controller knew there was weather—they were four days into the heat wave now, with little relief even at night—but today for the first time he felt comfortable with it. At last somebody had seen to it that the air-conditioning in the radar room was working properly. Besides, before the day was out it might rain. The buildup was there.

Aboard TW 430, passengers looking out the windows saw nothing beneath them but a layer of cloud, quilted from white to dirty gray, here and there a thin snake tongue of lightning. In the right-hand seat in the flight cabin, the copilot lived the recurrent fantasy that he was a rainmaker, to the Ohio sky what Johnny Appleseed was to the Ohio earth, the contrails from his jet aircraft sowing the clouds below. So too would the contrails from the other airliners over this same cloud bank: American 181, approaching from the northeast on the New York-Louisville run, and United 84, coming from the south, nonstop Atlanta to Cleveland.

In the southernmost dewlap of the state of Ohio, the temperature on the ground had reached 100 degrees—just over 100 in the little town of Florian, population 1,874 by the 1980 census, even slightly fewer than that by now. The place was known for one thing: the Florian intersection, whose direction from the town was straight up. It was in the sky over Florian that the routes of those three main airways crossed. Not that there was any danger from that: flying each at a different altitude and reaching the intersection at a different time, the TWA, American, and United planes could be converging, as they were now, at comparatively close quarters and still have a space of 800 cubic miles in which not to collide.

In the radar room at Indianapolis Center, the controller viewed the three blips without alarm. His direct responsibility went to the control of even-numbered aircraft—those headed north and east. Seated before an identical display on his left, another controller directed the odd-numbered west- and southbound flights over the same territory.

TW 430 would be first through the intersection today: it was ten miles, less than a minute and a half, away. Both Florian and Indianapolis were on eastern time. The digital clock on the control console read 14:46—2:46 p.m.

At that moment, the flight engineer aboard the Trans World plane happened to glance at his weather radar screen. He blinked and looked again. "Say, doctor," he said, addressing no one in particular, "this x-ray shows a tumor."

Looking straight ahead, the copilot saw the giant, upward-thrusting pole burst through the overcast. As it shot upward, the umbrella opened. The fabric of the unfolding parasol seemed, at once slowly and instantaneously, to fill his vision with blackness. But the pole itself boiled with color, ornamenting the exterior of some barbershop or candy factory gone mad. There were the whites and reds, but also the terrible greens and purples, racing even higher as though regulated by some monster clock timed to have it reach the height of the oncoming planeload of passengers in the deadly perfect moment of intersection, an apocalyptic meeting in the sky.

To the copilot's left, the flight captain whispered, "Holy Mother of

God!" From his sideways seat, the engineer turned his head and looked between their shoulders through the windshield. *"Turn! Turn!"* he screamed. But even before the words, four hands had hit two wheels, two right feet had jammed two rudder pedals to the floor. Plastered against their seats, the three men could almost orchestrate the sounds from the passenger cabin beyond the door: first the clattershot of the whiskey miniatures, airborne from the serving cart in the aisle, then the voices, suddenly screaming full in their ears as the door sprang open.

On the ground at Indianapolis, the controller stared incredulously at the screen in front of him. He shook his head, and into his wire mike he said, "TW 430, I have you in an unauthorized ninety-degree right turn. Over."

There was no answer. The blip that was TW 430 now pointed head on at the approaching United 84. "TW 430," he repeated. "This is Indianapolis Center and I say again we have you in an unauthorized turn. United 84, target approaching you at twelve o'clock, thirty-three thousand feet. TW 430, maintain thirty-three thousand. Do not descend. Repeat, do not descend. Over."

Again, no answer. But the controller to his left heard a voice: "Indianapolis, this is American 181, turning right forty-five degrees. Weather emergency. Repeat, weather emergency. American 181."

And then another voice: "Indianapolis, United 84. Request immediate permission ninety-degree right turn."

The first controller took in the screen. He saw the American plane alter course; now, even before his permission, so did the United.

"Son of a bitch," he yelled, and put up a beckoning arm. The nearest supervisor came over. "They're all turning right," the controller said. He pointed a finger at the Florian intersection. "All three of them in emergency turns."

"Why?"

"Weather."

"What kind of weather?"

"Haven't said yet. But they don't want to climb. They don't want to descend. They just want to turn."

"Have you talked to all of them?"

"Not the first one."

"Which?"

"TW 430."

"Try him again."

The controller nodded, then said, "Here he is now." The voice in his headset said, "TW 430. Right turn to evade weather. We're checking the extent of passenger injuries."

The men at the screens looked up to see their chief coming toward them. "All right," he said. "All right. What the fuck's going on?"

"Something with weather," the supervisor said. "We're trying to find out."

"Well, the airport at Huntington's on the phone," the chief said. "They want to know."

"What the hell can we tell them?" the supervisor said. "Why don't they tell us? They're there."

"All they know is they just cleared a small plane for emergency landing. Pilot was damned near hysterical."

"About the weather?"

"No. They say he was talking about an atom bomb."

2

At 2:50 that afternoon, a man by the name of Joseph F. Purcell—many called him the best trial lawyer in the country—went into a used-book store on Fourth Avenue in New York City, just below 14th Street, and paid 14 cents for a slim paperback novel that had been published as a Dell Original in 1956. He was at that moment totally uninterested in the practice of law.

"Anything else?" the bookseller said to him.

Purcell shook his head. "Not unless you've got another copy of this one."

"If it's the only one you saw, then it's the only one. But I got fourteen thousand other books."

"They wouldn't interest me."

The bookseller gave him a dime and a penny in return for his quarter. "I make a fortune in rare books," he said.

3

By three o'clock, ambulances were en route to Florian from four communities in the Tri-State area—from Huntington in West Virginia, Ashland in Kentucky, Portsmouth and Mundelein in Ohio. There was no interstate highway on the Ohio side of the river, and the only federal highway, U.S. 52, hugged the riverbank. The only state route, the north-south Ohio 93, lay west of Florian, so you got there by using secondary back roads through what they call the knob country—great mounds rising to tops up to four hundred feet above the surrounding area. Mundelein, the nearest community of any size, was no more than nine crow-flying miles south of Florian, but by the most direct paved roads it was seventeen.

Tom Glass was driving those seventeen miles now. Born and raised in Portsmouth, he had attended college in Mundelein and now worked as a reporter for the daily paper there, the Mundelein *Beacon*. "In Your Beacon," he said aloud now to the ancient driver of the Plymouth he had just passed. In Your Beacon was the title the paper used for its front-page index of features. One of the features was County News. What he read in County News was the sum and substance of all that Tom Glass knew about Florian. He had never been there before.

He did suspect, though, that he was ahead of the ambulances. The paper was down for the day; as a moneysaving measure it no longer awaited the final Dow Jones from New York. And Tom Glass was leaving the office, passing just beneath the squawk box on the wall of the city room, when the state police call sounded. The one relevant word that Glass caught was "explosion."

Don Mittauer, the city editor, also gleaned no more than that. He said to Glass, "Your car downstairs?"

Glass nodded. "Camera too."

"This could be a big one," Mittauer said. He said that about drunk arrests and the removal of mattress tags. But not after hours. There was a quality, a strain, to the voice on the squawk box this time. Mittauer said, "You know how to get to Florian?"

"I'll find it," Glass said.

In fact, he found it before he realized it. The broken macadam road took him into a left turn, then straightened again, parallel now with the Gallipolis branch line of the Mid-Central Railroad. A lumberyard on his right bore the name JOHN STEWART—BUILDING SUPPLIES, and Tom Glass had seen the Stewart advertisements in the county pages of the *Beacon*: the ads, like those for other Florian establishments, gave no street address. "Down on Railroad Avenue," the Stewart ads said, and even that was fulsome.

So if that was John Stewart Building Supplies, this must be Railroad Avenue, all not quite two lanes of it, and thus it must be Florian, though its center had to lie farther on, for the lumber office was the only building in the vicinity. Tom Glass slowed down, hunting some evidence of unusual activity—any activity—and when he saw the three men by the side of the road to his right, he stopped. At first, his purpose was no more than to ask for information, but as he leaned across to the passenger window, the exterior trim burning to his touch so he pulled his fingers back, he found the sight curious, and he let the car move forward again, onto the shoulder of the road, and stopped and got out and walked back to join the three.

The object of their attention, the thing that had caught Tom's eye as he drove up, resembled a free-form sculpture in whitewashed steel. Streaked here and there with new black, both rectangular and convex in overall outline, its edges in a random pattern of smooth to ragged to saw-toothed, it emerged from the ground like a grotesque monument, a sheet of metal set on edge, perhaps 13 feet across at the base and 7 feet high. The absence of any regularity in the design seemed itself a form of discipline, accentuated by great black letters and numbers in perfect stencil blocking. The borders and streaks and rips and curves gave one life to this sheet of metal, but the sign on its side and its placement, the letters and numbers precisely perpendicular to the earth on which it rested, gave it totally another. NN 1462, said the letters and numbers, the sculptor's statement for a torn pane of steel.

One of the men nodded toward it, as though he were the artist. "What do you think of that, young fella?" he said to Tom Glass. And the two other men cackled. "I was standing there," one of them said, pointing, "not twenty feet away."

Glass said, "You were standing?"

"Right there. Like I say. Not twenty feet away." The man's face and work shirt were sopped with perspiration. "When she landed."

"Landed?"

"Never saw it coming, never heard a thing till after," the other said. "Whisssh! And there she was."

Tom Glass said, "Wait right here. Don't go anywhere."

"Who's going anywhere?" the third man said. "Bill here, he come busting in the office like it was a crocodile snapping at a nigger. Three of us didn't come out of there till just before you drove up. That right, Bill?"

Glass was at his car, taking a pencil and some folded blank paper from the front seat, then opening the trunk to get the camera. He rejoined the men, and the first one said, "What are you? *Herald Dispatch?*"

Tom shook his head. "*Beacon*. When was it this happened?"

"Half an hour ago, maybe. That right, Bill?"

"I wasn't reckoning what time it was," the one named Bill said. "You going to take a picture? How do you want us to stand?"

"Away from it. I just want the thing in the picture. No people."

Abruptly, it occurred to Tom that the only film he had was what was in the camera.

"Funny thing," the third man said. "We heard the fire horn before the fire."

"The fire?"

"Hell, lit up the whole sky when she blew."

"When what blew?"

"Damned if I know. This thing here's a piece of a railroad car from down the track, but don't ask me what got it here."

Tom saw it with recognition now. Yes, it would be a piece of a white railroad tank car. Puzzled, he said, "You heard the fire engine before the fire?"

"Not the fire engine. Too far away for that. Good mile from here to the center of town. No. The fire horn. You know: for the volunteers."

"But that was before the fire?"

"That's what I said."

"How long before?"

"What would you guess, Bill? Twenty minutes?"

The first man said, "Maybe it was two different fires."

"Then you don't know what actually happened," Tom said. "All you know is the thing here came flying through the air and then you saw and heard the blast."

"Can still see the smoke from it," the first man said, and peered into the distance. "Leastwise, you could a little bit ago. Looks like it might be raining to center of town now."

The third man said, "You fixing to go on over there and see what it was?"

Tom Glass nodded. "Let me get your names. You work over here?"

They gave him their names and watched as he wrote them down. As he did, he heard a siren behind him, and the first ambulance from Mundelein cruised past him, purple and low. It occurred to him that in the time he had spent with the three men at the side of the road, there had been no sound or sight of life from the center of Florian, and the ambulance was the first vehicle he had seen going toward the town.

4

As purple as the ambulance headed for Florian was the hearse that carried Saul Gutman to his final resting place on Long Island, almost to the Suffolk county line. The cortege included two automobiles containing faithful customers of Gutman's Delicatessen, on Manhattan's Ninth Avenue, between 22nd and 23rd, and among them, by the skin of his teeth, was Herman Molle. He lived just around the corner from Gutman's, but he had not learned the news till just this morning, when he went there for a tongue sandwich and a cream soda and found the place padlocked, with a printed death notice, framed in black, wedged between the security grating and the door. Too late for the funeral service, Molle still was in time—just in time—to hitch a ride to the cemetery.

The heat wave of southern Ohio still had not reached New York, and Herman Molle was, in any event, one of those older citizens who wear overcoats in May. The car was crowded enough with mourners without those extra layers of clothing. Molle was short, fat, and harsh-featured. As he opened the rear door to enter the car, the overcoat sleeve pulled back, revealing a section of his jacket sleeve pulled back to reveal the long green sleeve of his sweater, a color cutaway advertisement for a length of pipe.

"You're not hot?" the driver said to him.

"I'm just right," Molle said. They did not know each other. "Long Island is always cooler than the mainland."

"Manhattan is the mainland?"

"The temperature is always the same," Molle said. "I speak as an engineer who used to specialize. Gutman and I had our arguments in those days. But who was the specialist? I was."

"Don't put the heat on," the squeezed man next to Molle said to the driver. The driver nodded and started the car, and they rode in silence, two in the front seat of the Chevette and three wedged in the back. Finally, to make conversation, the man in the middle in the back seat said, "What did you argue about?"

"It was years ago," Herman Molle said.

"You don't remember?"

"Carbonation," Molle said. "In the old days there was lots of carbonation in the bottles. The Coca-Cola, the cream soda, the Canada Dry. You should have seen that Canada Dry."

"Not anymore," the man in the middle said.

"That's what I told Gutman."

"He should have known it."

"He did know it."

"Then what was the argument about?"

"It was a long time ago," Molle said, and the car fell silent again.

But he could remember it as though it were yesterday, the day the mailman brought the letter bearing the return address of the N. Nance

Company, Bucyrus, Ohio 48820. He had it in his pocket as he entered Gutman's Delicatessen—1966, his mind told him now. February 1966. The first week of February.

"A tongue on rye, Mr. Gutman," Molle said, "and one bottle of the cream soda."

"You always take out the bottles one at a time," Gutman said.

"Some day soon I'll stop taking even one altogether," Molle said. "The carbonation is down."

"I know," Gutman said. It was litany by now.

"It's the new bottles," Molle said. "Thin. Composition. No deposit. Throwaway. Only they explode on the shelves."

"Bohack's," Gutman said. He used the name generically; no such accident would ever happen on the West Side. "Besides, that's not the reason they took down the carbonation. They took it down because it was going down anyway. They put it in cans and started using the bigger bottles, and that meant there was always some left over after you poured it, so the leftover would go flat. So they figured you wouldn't notice it so much if it was flat to begin with."

"That's your theory, Mr. Gutman," Herman Molle said. "I tell you it's because of the thinner walls of the bottles. The cans too, for that matter."

"Then answer me one thing," Mr. Gutman said. "This goes back to the thirties, when everything was in the thick bottles. But even then, Coke had more gas than Pepsi. Why? I'll tell you why: because Pepsi was in the bigger bottle. You couldn't drink it all at once."

"Canada Dry came in a bigger bottle than either one of them," Molle replied. "And it had the most carbonation of all."

"That was ginger ale," Gutman said. "You poured it at a party. So even if the bottle was bigger, you used it up all at once. So it didn't have a chance to go flat."

"I could use an extra piece pickle in with the sandwich," Molle said. It sounded like the next step in his argument.

"An extra piece pickle," Gutman repeated. "One bottle cream soda. For once you could buy a whole pickle. Pickles got just as much gas as always."

"You can't argue with me that the carbonation is down," Molle said. "I'm talking soft drinks, not pickles."

"I'm arguing why it's down," Gutman said.

"But I'm in a position to know these things, Mr. Gutman."

"I'm not? What do you think I'm in business selling? American Flyer electric trains?"

"You could get it in a letter from the president of Coca-Cola, you wouldn't believe it."

"He wouldn't admit it."

"Twist his arm, he'll admit it."

"I'll make a note. Twist the president of Coca-Cola's arm."

"Times have changed, Mr. Gutman. Nowadays they make the contents conform to the package they come in. Even the tongue in this sandwich. Sure, you still cut it from the real thing. But how many places are left that do that? Most of them now, what is it? A processed loaf, cut square. How many real tongues do you see in New York anymore? It's what I say: the package is more important than what's in it."

"If we were talking tongue I'd agree with you," Gutman said.

"We're talking everything."

"No," Gutman said. "Not everything."

Herman Molle shook his head, paid his money, took his lunch, and went back out into the cold. When he arrived home, he re-read the letter in his pocket and found himself thinking of what Gutman had said at the end: "Not everything." Typical of Gutman to have the last word. Yet Molle reflected he had only himself to blame. Of course he would buy the cream soda only one bottle at a time: the single bottles at Gutman's were cold from the refrigerator case, unlike the cartons of six on the shelves. Why hadn't he pointed that out to Gutman?

Not that it was central to the discussion. Refrigerated or room temperature, the carbonation was down either way. But he had missed a talking point. He uncapped the bottle now, to have with his tongue sandwich. The sound of the escaping gas was hardly audible.

A talking point. But why fret about it? Let Gutman have the last word; how often did Gutman get a letter from an important company like Nance? What was he selling, Gutman had asked, toy trains? Gutman should only know the Nance people made real trains. Indeed, how often did Gutman get to ride a train, or travel at all?

All that was nearly twenty years in the past now. Herman Molle was on his way to the cemetery to bury Gutman. "If I had your phone number," said the driver of the car, who did not know him, "I would have called you and said don't wear an overcoat."

"You couldn't do that," Herman Molle said to him.

"What makes you think I couldn't?"

"Because I don't have a phone, that's why." Molle cackled triumphantly. "Who needs one?"

5

Without extra film, Tom Glass could take only four pictures in Florian, and of these the first one, from the roadside just beyond the lumberyard, had the greatest impact of novelty. AP Wirephoto picked it up, and it appeared in many newspapers, more than a few of them giving it front-page display, the following day. The surrealistic NN 1462 was the sole identifying remnant of the tank car that bore that serial number, a car known in familial railroadese as a Jumbo Nellie Nellie. The Nellies stood for the two N's, which in less artful turn stood for the car's manufacturer, the N. Nance Company; but the Jumbo stood simply for size. Within the right-of-way's ultimate tolerance for turning radius and clearances, it was the longest and highest and widest freight car that was possible to construct, a monster cylinder on wheels, 66 feet in its coupled length, $10\frac{1}{2}$ feet in width between the grabs.

The Jumbo Nellie Nellie's design cargo of liquefied petroleum gas — LPG, burned by the consumer as propane—qualified it additionally for official classification by the Department of Transportation as a "Class I Hazardous Location." This too was honestly come by. Since the mid-1960s, when the Jumbos first went into operation, the record of tank car fires and explosions was a roll call of places that speckled the broad back of a continent with timetable names: New Athens, Illinois…Armitage, Ohio… Kingman, Arizona…Laurel, Mississippi…Crescent City, Illinois… South Byron, New York…Crete, Nebraska…Fairlee, Vermont…Waverly, Tennessee. Some, like Fairlee, were the product of the derailment of a moving train; others, like Kingman, accidental to the unloading process. And yet the accounts that followed could be nearly interchangeable: "A dispatcher at the (Name of Place) sheriff's office said phone callers told her 'it looked like an atomic bomb, with a big mushroom cloud going up in the sky.'"

Florian was unique. An explosion, yes. But no moving train, no derailment, no group of tank cars coupled together, no unloading in progress. The Jumbo Nellie Nellie rested by itself on a spur track in the yard area behind the single brick building of the Tri-State Gas Company, which vended propane by the bottle and tankful to the nearby area. One cast in vain for any speciality. This was only one of nearly two hundred thousand tank cars on U.S. rails to haul hazardous cargo. As for the weather, that hardly seemed to count for anything. The pressurization inside the tank car was supposed to hold the propane below its boiling point of minus 40 degrees Fahrenheit, regardless of the outside temperature.

But a letter to the Ashland *Independent* reminded folks that this was Derby week downriver, and Derby week always brought a heat wave.

As he told Tom Glass and other reporters afterward, Gerald Baxter did not even hasten his step when he walked the north shoulder of Railroad Avenue the eighty or so easterly steps it took him to get from the Cleo Trailer Park to the office door of the Tri-State Gas Company. Looking to his left, he could see the huge tank car parked out behind the Tri-State office, and what he saw too was a tongue of flame, shaped perfectly, as in an advertisement for a gas range, for a few moments, then reducing almost to a state of absence, then pealing upward 100 feet or more again. The flame came from the dome centered atop the tank car, and accompanying it was a respirator sound, a sigh that sank as the blue tip sank, then announced itself anew when it soared again.

"I thought it was the safety valve," Baxter told the newsmen, "and when I got inside the office they told me I was dead right, it was the safety valve."

"So you didn't think anything was really wrong?"

"Not at that point in time, I didn't. The two of them in the office there, they went out back and had a look, and when they got back in the office they was having some kind of a discussion about it."

"You mean an argument?"

"I guess you would call it that," Baxter said. "The one of them wanted to call the fire department and t'other didn't. He said that's what a safety valve was for. Then the first one said that's what a fire department was for too and he went ahead and put in the call. Now I tell myself that first fella's probably the one who had it right, because a safety valve there, it's supposed to let off steam, but there's not supposed to be fire there too. I mean, now that means something wrong. You know."

"But you're the one who told them about it."

Baxter nodded. "Far as I know, I was the first one saw it. There was a colored fella around the side with a hose, but he was splashing his face with it. I don't know if he noticed it or not."

"But that's why you went into the office? To report it?"

"No, I just kind of mentioned it. You know. Like I say, didn't hit me as anything that peculiar at that point in time. No, I went in there to use the phone. Never did get around to it. First they called the fire department, then they decided they wanted to call their main office and tell them about it. I just cut out. Fire truck was there, and then Billy Harrelson drove up, and he saw me, and he wasn't about to get out of his car to watch any fire, not with his asthma and the weather being this hot and the smoke and all. Funny, the smoke didn't smell. Anyway, Billy rolls down his window and tells me come on get in, and I figured I can't pick up none of those TV dinners at the market and then walk it home in this heat, so I knew that's where Billy was going since he told me so, so I went with him. Made my phone call from downtown. So things worked out all right. You know."

Tom Glass said, "Do you know how long it had been burning before you saw it?"

Gerald Baxter shook his head. "Wouldn't want to swear to it."

"What time was it?"

Baxter's mouth shrugged. "Two-thirty. Give or take a stretch in and around there."

One point in time was a matter of record. It was 2:26 when Wayne Hopper logged the telephoned alarm from the Tri-State Gas office. Hopper, the only attendant on duty at the old firehouse on Center Street, pushed a button to activate the rotorcycle tape that would sound three blasts of the air horn, repeated four times at intervals of 15 seconds. Then he ran outside, chalked the name Tri-State Gas on the blackboard alongside the entrance, and came back and climbed into the driver's seat of the fire truck, not bothering to don fireman's coat or hat in the heat-locked mugginess of the afternoon. He set the truck siren to wailing even before he started the engine.

The horn activator was one of the few pieces of modern equipment belonging to the Florian Volunteer Fire Department, and even that was the simplest of its kind. A costlier model could encode not one tape but many, so that the number of blasts not only announced a fire but located it as well. But the Florian area was too spread out and thinly populated to warrant that extra expense.

And the word would spread in any event, particularly on a weekday when the center of town was active, and so today there was no undue delay in the response to the alarm. Within three minutes of the phone call, Hopper and the fire truck had reached the scene, and three of the volunteers, having heard or seen the truck en route, drove up close behind. And more kept coming. They were a prideful elite, the Florian volunteers. Their ranks included Owen Merritt, the mayor; Elliott Thoms, principal of the Union District High School; and Charley Middleton, branch manager here for the Bank of Mundelein, and by common assumption, in his case correct, the richest man in town. Fifteen days earlier, at the annual VFD barbecue, Middleton had accepted the red hat which proclaimed him Chief of the Volunteers for the coming year. A framed photograph of the occasion rested on his desk at the bank, and the helmet itself on the floor beside his chair, the proudest possession of his fifty-seven years.

He had been wearing it as he spoke by telephone from the Tri-State Gas office to the headquarters of the county sheriff. The old railroad clock over the desk read 2:35.

"Boys don't know quite how to handle this one," Middleton said. "There's some literature on it here in the office. They're looking for it now. We thought for a minute we had it, but she started up again, and this time the flame is in sheets like, and coming down over the sides of the car. Kind of waterfall-like, instead of going up."

The sheriff's man at the other end of the line said, "What does your full-timer say?"

"That's Wayne Hopper," Middleton said. "He said he's seen some literature on it. Got some, back at the firehouse. But he says—"

"Well, did you ever drill in it?"

"That's what I'm trying to tell you. Wayne says it's not just technique, it's equipment too, and we don't have the right equipment."

"To put the fire out?"

"No. I mean to drill. I mean, no real point in it. Wayne says they talk about shields and helicopters and approach platforms and the courthouse only knows what else."

"They've got a helicopter at Portsmouth," the sheriff's man said. "Use it for forest fires. Want me to ring them up?"

"You might do that. Tell them the situation first."

"Let me get this straight," the sheriff's man said. "How many tank cars is it?"

"Like I told you, just one."

"I mean how many in the train?"

"No train. No other rolling stock anywhere around. Just this one tank car, right in the yard out back. They were talking about going to unload it tomorrow."

"Unload what? Propane, right?"

"Right. Problem is, the damn thing's too hot to get up close to. And maybe that wouldn't be smart anyway. It might be a protection situation."

"Protection situation? You talking about evacuating the area?"

"I was going to ask you about that. I can send some of my men out now, for the surroundings rightabout. But there's traffic too, on the road. I think we could use some help."

"All right," the sheriff's man said, and rang off. His first radio transmission reached not only all mobile units of the sheriff's department but the cars of the state highway patrol as well. "Fourteen thirty-seven," the message ended, giving the time. It was 2:37 p.m.

Three miles to the west of the fire, a yellow bus turned toward it onto the washboard county road that would become Railroad Avenue, homebound with younger-graders from the Dixie Elementary School. The bus driver, Janet Brophy, decided she would lead off this afternoon with the Ohio song:

Round at the ends and high in the middle,
What's the answer to this little riddle?

But not all of the children were joining in. Janet left off the song and spoke to the rearview mirror. "Too hot for singing? Well, maybe we'll get some rain. Rain always cools things off, doesn't it?" Ahead and just off to the left, there was a flash of lightning. "Everybody count to four," Janet said. "Quickly. One-two-three-four." They did, and the sound of the thunder came.

Rosa Crewes saw the lightning too, from the spare bedroom upstairs in her frame house on Railroad Avenue. She had heard the blasts of the fire horn, and it appeared logical to her that wherever the fire was, lightning had started it. But even when she heard the fire truck go past, she did not leave the rear bedroom to investigate. The young man from Chicago who had rented the room would be here any time now—young man: he was barely a boy, all of twenty years old, so Dr. Nicholson had told her. Rosa herself was forty-seven. She wanted the bedroom to be as nice as possible. Would she tell this boy she was afraid of thunder? Thirty years ago she had told that to another boy, on a day that was so much like today, and held him very close, imprisoning his palm with her thighs sufficient to sweeten the freedom that followed. Sweat stood on her brow and throat now, and when she heard the ringing of the telephone her lips moved silently with the words "Let it be him," not certain who the him might be.

But the caller was Effie Livingston, from Dr. Nicholson's office. "Our young friend show up yet?"

"Not yet," Rosa said.

"Well, he was supposed to be leaving Chicago at dawn," Effie said. "But if he hasn't shown up yet, that's just as well. He was supposed to come over here when he got in, but he'll be tired and Doctor's going to close up early. Only three appointments the rest of this afternoon, and two of them canceled. Too hot. So tell him not to worry about this afternoon and make it tomorrow morning instead. 'Kay?"

"All right," Rosa said. "I'll tell him."

Effie giggled. "That way you'll have him all to yourself."

"I wouldn't worry about it," Rosa said smoothly. "It's like you said. Too hot."

Effie giggled again. "You're a one," she said. "Well, as I say, you shouldn't have too long to wait. Bet you he's there by three."

"Lord, it doesn't make any difference," Rosa said. "I'm not going anywhere." She said good-bye and hung up and went into the kitchen, took a pitcher from the cupboard and a can of frozen lemonade concentrate from the freezer compartment of the refrigerator. "Bet you he's there by three." By the kitchen clock it was 17 minutes till then.

Sixteen minutes before three, said the clock on the dashboard of the blue Cutlass. Stephen Coblenz had the windows up, the air-conditioning on maximum. Up ahead of him, he could see the stopped police car, orange hazard lights winking in off-sync, red roof-light revolving. In the center of the road stood the police officer, beckoning to an oncoming Pinto, waving it on past. Coblenz put a foot to the brake and saw lightning that was not lightning but something else, his windshield and world filled in this instant with light that was stark light beyond light, white beyond white, and crossing in front of him, as if it had come from the driver's window of the approaching Pinto, there flew a plank topped by a Halloween mask. And Coblenz knew his own car was moving, not forward but in one massive broadside thrust to the right, over the embankment beside the road and rolling top-over-bottom to the base of the gully beyond. Now he heard the thunder that was not thunder but something else, sound beyond sound. The Cutlass came to a stop upside down, Coblenz's hands welded to the steering wheel inside. He knew he was alive. He thought he was unhurt but did not want to move. His mind formed a testimonial to Body by Fisher, grateful and concrete, but understood nothing else. The air conditioner still blew, but it was as though someone had moved the control to maximum heat.

With no reference to the passage of time, Coblenz stayed that way, head down, held by his seat belt in the driver's position. The heat made his palate throb. No sound from anywhere: the world gone still. The only sign of motion, the left front wheel of his car, pointed violently outward from his reflex twist of the steering wheel when the force first hit him. He saw the tire spinning idly, silently, endlessly beneath a sky transformed into a ball of fire.

6

Victor Cuneo came into the room in bathing trunks and T-shirt and said, "Goddamn, Louise, this better be good."

"I'm sorry," his wife said. "Sorry if I spoiled your afternoon in the sand with Mrs. Price."

"Mr. Price," Cuneo said. "Not Mrs. Price."

"Oh? She wasn't there?"

"I'll tell you later. What is it now?"

"What I told you on the beeper phone." Cuneo's wife stood by the UPI teletype in the corner of the bedroom that served as her husband's office. "I tore the first bulletins off. They're on your desk. And there's more coming in now."

"It better be good, that's all," Cuneo said again.

"Ohio state police say at least eighteen dead," his wife said. "And more to come."

"It's not just dead that counts," he said.

"They counted pretty good with that DC-10," she said.

"And nothing decent since." Cuneo was at his desk, palms flat on its surface as he read the wire service copy. He was in his late thirties, not overly large but trim and darkly handsome, with the walk of a fast pigeon. He looked up and said, "Florian? Where the hell in Ohio is that?"

"I had trouble with it too," Louise said. "The Rand McNally road atlas doesn't show it. I had to get the foldout map. It's all the way down in the southern tip of the state. Near Huntington, West Virginia."

"Yuh, yuh, Huntington," her husband said. "Says here ambulances from Huntington. We got the phone book from there?"

"We should have. May not be this year's, though." She tore off the new take of the story, slugged

BULLETIN ADD 2 FIREBALL

and brought it across the room to him.

"Doesn't have to be this year's," he said, not looking up. "Find it and do the yellow pages. Gardeners. And Dress Designers. Or Custom Apparel Designers or however they have it. You know the drill."

His wife recrossed the room, this time to a wall of books whose two lowest shelves comprised a curious registry: the telephone directories of well over one hundred U.S. cities, most of them in the 60,000 to 80,000 population range. Victor Cuneo called it his "from there" file: places like Gainesville, Chicopee, Fort Smith, Anderson, Bellevue. The most you were apt to know about such places was somebody who was from there.

But a quick way to learn about them, Cuneo had discovered, was through the classified pages of their phone books. Miami, where he lived, was heavy with listings for window screens; Honolulu had none: the yellow pages described even the insect life and the climate. The financial climate too, and this was to Cuneo's purpose. A city where there was money would have a demand for professional gardening and custom dress design. You could graph its tastes in recreation and food in a rising straight line: more meat markets than bowling alleys, more travel agencies than meat markets. And what the classified listings said about a city would hold true in almost every instance for its surrounding area as well.

"You find the book?"

"Yes," she said. "I'm looking."

"Gardeners? How many?"

Louise Cuneo looked up, puzzled. "There aren't any."

"Dress designers? Or apparel?"

She turned pages. Again she shook her head.

"None?"

"None."

"Oh, for Christ's sake, give me the phone book, Louise." She came across the room with the Huntington directory and he slapped it down on the desk and began looking for himself.

"Oh, shit," he said. "More bowling alleys than meat markets." He flipped a swatch of yellow. "And more meat markets than travel agencies." More searching, and a short laugh. "And four times as many clergymen as dentists. Nobody in that fucking place is going to rub anything but his keys together." He sighed and handed the book back to her. "Sure. Appalachia. What do you expect? And look at all the injuries here. Never mind deaths. If this was before a Chicago jury instead of Hicksville, just think of a number. Millions, Louise. Millions! Make that DC-10 look like a Piper Cub." He was looking at the news account again. "Of course, that's the bad news. The good news is that's quite a railroad, the Mid-Central. Quite a railroad! Nice big target defendant. Even a jury in—what is it? Florian—even a jury in Florian might take it in its mind to sock the Mid-Central around a little bit. Especially when it's their own kinfolk that got blown up."

He was reading now from the latest take of the story. "Or," he said, as if to himself, "or—Jesus, Louise, give me the phone book back!" He grabbed the directory from her. "Tri-State Gas," he said. "Tri-State Gas. That might mean—yes! Look!" His finger jabbed at the heading that said Gas-Liquefied Petroleum-Bottled & Bulk. "See?" he said. "The one in Florian's just a branch office. The main one's in Huntington!"

Louise said, "Am I supposed to ask what that means?"

"Yes," he said. "You're supposed to ask what that means. And while I'm telling you what it means, you get the Airlines Guide and see what's the fastest plane'll get me here to there. Miami to Huntington. Huntington, West Virginia. Those are the key words, Louise, those last two: West Virginia. You know why?"

"No," she said, "but you're about to tell me."

"Right. I'm about to tell you. It's because of what West Virginia isn't. And you know what it isn't? It isn't Ohio, that's what it isn't. So Tri-State Gas isn't an Ohio-based business, and the Mid-Central Railroad isn't an Ohio corporation, and you know what that means? We're in federal court with this, Louise, federal court in Columbus, Ohio, and the best of both worlds. Close to where the money is and close enough to where the victims are." For the first time Victor Cuneo sat down. "Did I ever tell you you've got a nice ass?"

"Only when you're drinking," she said. "Do you want to look up lawyers in Huntington?"

"That's the best idea you've had today," Cuneo said to her. "Why not? A little drink never hurt anybody. Especially when it's by way of a celebration. We've got time. But I want to see the news at six. See what they've got on this. I'll make us a drink. What do you want?"

"I don't think I want one," she said.

"Ah," he said, "Louise is sore on account of Janie Price. But Louise has nothing to be sore about. Louise has a nicer ass than Janie Price."

"This has been going on two weeks with her," Louise said. She was as tall as he was, and a natural blonde, the kind of woman a jockey marries.

Cuneo stood up. "Nothing has been going on with her," he said. He moved toward the portable bar. "It's the husband I'm after. He's a lawyer,

Louise, and in case you've forgotten, it's my business to get to know lawyers. Do you remember the DC-10? You've been spending off it ever since."

"Well," she said, "are you going to look up lawyers in that book?"

"Why would I do that?"

"You said it was the best idea I'd had today."

"Oh, I meant the drink," he said. "No, the last thing I want or need is a lawyer in Huntington, West Virginia. Which reminds me: when you call the airline, rent me a car at the Huntington end. A luxury car, Louise. I have to look fine. Remember that."

"I know," she said. "First choice, Cadillac."

"Come get your drink, sweet-ass. Except from what that phone book tells me, ain't no Hertz or Avis going to have any Cadillacs lying around that town. I don't know what to tell you. Take your best shot, is all. Not for Christ's sake one of those Cavaliers. Maybe a Mercury."

His wife came over to the bar. She said, "But you're going to have to have somebody. Some lawyer lined up."

He handed her a martini. "It's interesting," he said. "If you want to be serious, there's only one law firm in the country I'd really like to have on this one."

"Who?" Louise said. "Have I heard of them?"

"Ever hear of the A&P?"

"What does that mean?"

"That's them, that's what that means." He had made the martinis with ice cubes, mixing them directly in a pair of thick-bottomed old-fashioned glasses that had gold-encrusted heraldry, two lions rampant on a petal field: the Cuneo coat of arms, so he had told her. One of the lions was flaking, he noticed now. He shook his head. "Can you imagine? A city the size of Huntington and only two travel agencies in the whole damn burg? And one of them's Triple-A. That barely counts. Did you see their ad, Louise? 'Airline tickets the same price as at the airport,' it said. What does that tell you, when you have to spell something like that out for people."

His wife took her drink back to the wall of shelves and located the book of airline schedules. She said, "I'm surprised you don't rent a plane and fly it up there yourself. I mean, if you really want to impress somebody."

"Not worth it," he said.

"But those other times—"

"Those other times I could stick people in the airplane and fly them to wherever the lawyer was. *That* impressed them."

"But not this time?"

"No, not this time. This time the survivors are where the accident is. They're not going to be flying anywhere. Those other times, we're talking about plane crashes. Fine. You come down in a cornfield someplace, where are the relatives? Six hundred miles away, two thousand miles away. What's the first thing they think of? Insurance, that's what." For the first time in three years, Cuneo found himself wishing he had a cigarette. "And when they're thinking insurance, they're ready for somebody to come along and talk damages to them: damages they'd never dreamed of. Drive up the next day, tell them your airplane's waiting, you're going to fly them to Chicago or L.A. and sit them down in front of the best lawyer in the business. Oh, that works, Louise. Yes, that works. But here—" The bulletin bells rang on the teletype, and he crossed to where it was. "Here they're right there. They've got to bury their dead. More than that, they've got to take care of the living. Half of them are probably burned themselves. Here you've got survivors who aren't just survivors of the victims. You've got survivors of the accident too. It's a whole different —well, Christ, listen to this."

He began reading aloud from the unrolling paper in the teletype console:

```
BULLETIN SECOND LEAD FIREBALL
     FLORIAN, O.--A RAILROAD TANK CAR FILLED WITH
PROPANE EXPLODED "LIKE AN ATOM BOMB" IN THIS SOUTHERN
OHIO TOWN TODAY, KILLING AT LEAST 20 PERSONS AND
INJURING SCORES OF OTHERS.
     A NUMBER OF SCHOOLCHILDREN WERE AMONG THE
VICTIMS OF THE BLAST, WHICH LEVELED SURROUNDING
BUILDINGS AND PRODUCED A FIREBALL OVER A MILE IN
DIAMETER.
     TRACKS OF THE MID-CENTRAL RAILROAD WERE TWISTED
AND UPROOTED, WINDOWS WERE SHATTERED IN SURROUNDING
COMMUNITIES, AND ONE FRAGMENT OF THE EXPLODING TANK
CAR LANDED A MILE AND A HALF FROM THE SCENE OF THE
BLAST.
     EYEWITNESSES SAID THE TANK CAR HAD BEEN ON FIRE
BEFORE THE EXPLOSION AND SEVERAL VOLUNTEER FIRE-
FIGHTERS WERE AMONG THE DEAD. ALSO LISTED AS DEAD
WERE EDWARD PETTIT AND GORDON ESTERDAY, EMPLOYEES OF
THE TRI-STATE GAS CO., A PROPANE RETAILER, ON WHOSE
PREMISES THE EXPLOSION OCCURRED.
     MOST OF THE SURVIVORS TAKEN TO HOSPITALS AS FAR
AWAY AS HUNTINGTON, W.VA., AND PORTSMOUTH, O., WERE
SEVERELY BURNED. A NUMBER ARE NOT EXPECTED TO LIVE.
MUNDELEIN COUNTY SHERIFF'S DEPUTIES SAID THE CAUSE OF
THE INITIAL BLAZE IN THE TANK CAR WAS UNKNOWN. "AS
```

FAR AS WE KNOW NOW, IT WAS JUST SITTING THERE," ONE
OFFICER SAID.
   A NUMBER OF THE VICTIMS WERE RESIDENTS OF A
NEARBY TRAILER COURT DEMOLISHED BY THE BLAST, AND A
CROWDED SCHOOL BUS ALSO WAS IN THE PATH OF THE
EXPLOSION. POLICE SAID A NUMBER OF ITS PASSENGERS
WERE "BADLY BURNED." IT WAS NOT KNOWN IMMEDIATELY IF
THERE WERE ANY FATALITIES ABOARD THE BUS.
   (MORE)

Victor Cuneo looked up from the teletype. "Oh, it gets lovelier by the minute," he said.

His wife said, "Earliest you could get to Huntington would be eleven-forty."

"Tonight?"

She shook her head. "Tomorrow morning. You change planes at Atlanta."

"All right," he said. "Tomorrow's soon enough. They'll still be busy dying. Besides, a little celebration might be in order for you and me tonight, don't you think?"

"You'll have to look at those children, won't you?" she said. "With the burns and everything?"

"The more they're burned, the more money it'll take to keep 'em alive," Victor Cuneo said. "In the DC-10 case, everybody was killed. What's a school kid worth dead? Nothing. But if he's got sixty more years to live, burned down to where he's a vegetable, has to wear a mask because nobody can live with the sight of his face, medical bills, a dozen skin-grafting operations—you begin to see what kind of money's here?"

"But the *sight* of them," his wife said.

"And don't forget," he said, "Ohio's not one of those states that passed any tort reform. No caps on damages for pain and suffering, or punitives or contingent fees. No, don't worry about me, Louise. The man to worry about is the president of Mid-Central."

"I wish I understood that better," she said.

"Wish you understood what?"

"I know it's the railroad you want to go after," she said. "But it doesn't say they're to blame for the accident."

"It doesn't have to."

"Then how do they come into it?"

"Simplest thing in the world," Cuneo said. "It's their tank car. They put it there."

7

From the headquarters of the Mid-Central Railroad in St. Louis, the general freight manager, Winston McHale, put through a telephone call to a trial lawyer in Chicago named Arthur Hawkes.

Hawkes came on the line and said, "Hello, Winston. What's the bad news?"

"How do you know it's bad news?"

"Come on, Winston," Hawkes said. "This is Arthur you're talking to. Remember me?"

"All right," McHale said. "We lost a big one. A Jumbo Nellie Nellie."

"A who?"

"LP tank car. Built by N. Nance—2 N's, so they call them Nellie Nellies. Propane. Exploded. Just standing there on the unloading spur and blew up."

"When?"

"This afternoon. At one forty-five our time."

"Where?"

"Florian, Ohio."

"Spell it."

McHale spelled it. At his desk in Chicago, Arthur Hawkes blocked the name in capitals on the legal-length ruled yellow pad before him. He said, "Whereabouts is that?"

"Southernmost part of the state," McHale said.

"You have an office there?"

"No. We've got a freight agent in Mundelein. About ten miles away. That's the nearest one."

"Oh, for God's sake," Hawkes said.

"No, Arthur, listen. There's twenty people dead. Killed by the explosion. So far. And I don't know how many burned. Sixty. Seventy. Maybe more."

Arthur Hawkes laid the earpiece of the telephone against the center of his brow, as if in pain. Then he took up the conversation again. "How did it happen?"

"Caught fire at two twenty-five. That's their time: one twenty-five our time."

"PD?"

"What?"

"Property damage?"

"No estimate yet."

"So you don't know."

"I don't know and I don't want to know," McHale said. "Those things go up like an H-bomb, Arthur. They say the fireball was a mile wide."

"What's it like?"

"What's what like?"

"The place where it happened."

"I don't know. It's a small town, Arthur."

"For a small town, that's a pretty big casualty list."

"Listen," Winston McHale said, "there are some answers I don't have, Arthur. Not yet, anyway. And I'd better tell you we're all upset down here. It's not like those other times."

Hawkes angled the earpiece downward and stared at it. Into the mouthpiece, he said: "Those other times?"

"Oh, these tank cars catch fire, Arthur. It's the nature of the beast. This is our first one where the public was involved—I mean, dead and injured. Other lines have had them, but not us. We've had them, but they were crew, not public. This is why I'm getting in touch with you. The rest of them, we could handle down here."

"I see," Hawkes said. "A Mid-Central first."

"I'll tell you another Mid-Central first," McHale said. "It may be a first for anybody. We don't—"

"Wait a minute," Hawkes cut in. "You said there was a fire first. Before the explosion?"

"That's right. That's the way it usually happens. Starts burning, heat builds up, bang, she blows."

"Then let me ask a stupid question," Hawkes said. "When you have a fire like that, what happens?"

"What do you mean, what happens? I just told you what happens."

"You mean bang, she blows, every time?"

"Oh, hell, no, not every time," McHale said. "Sometimes it just burns off. Especially when they're emptier than this one was. The pressure relief valve. That's what it's for."

"You mean that's the part that was on fire this time?"

"That's right."

"Well then, another stupid question," Hawkes said. "Actually a simple rephrasing of my first stupid question. Does anybody ever try to do something about it?"

"Do something about it?"

"Well, you said sometimes they burn off and sometimes they explode. In between times, does anybody ever try to put the fire out?"

"Oh, of course," McHale said. "That's part of the answer to your question about why so many casualties. The whole volunteer fire department was there. That's happened before, too. Fighting these things is tricky business. But those fires can be put out, Arthur."

The pen of Arthur Hawkes became busy again. "They can be put out?"

"Sure they can."

"But this one wasn't."

"I wouldn't be on the phone if it was. The fire didn't hurt anybody. The explosion was what did it all."

Hawkes was looking at his notes. "You're not telling me there were ninety firemen here—twenty dead, seventy injured."

"No, no, no, they were just part of it, Arthur. Hell, there was a trailer court next door. There was a school bus."

"A *what?*"

"Arthur, it's a bad one," McHale said. "It's a bad one."

Arthur Hawkes took a deep breath. Then he said, "All right, Winston. Get back to ground zero. What started the fire?"

"I was in the middle of telling you that and you cut me off. You said it was a Mid-Central first, and I said it might be a first anywhere."

"Well?"

"I'm trying to answer your question. We don't *know* what started it, Arthur."

"Well, this is fun and games," Arthur Hawkes said. "If you don't know now, you will when you investigate."

"Will we?" McHale said. "How? By examining the tank car? There's not that much left of it to examine. By talking to witnesses? The news wires are quoting the witnesses. They say it just started to burn."

Hawkes wrote "WITNESSES." He said, "Who are they?"

"Just people," McHale said. "Everyday people."

"Nobody saw anything special?"

"Lightning."

"What?"

"Lightning," McHale said. "It was building up to a storm there. Interesting: That's why nobody saw the mushroom cloud."

"The mushroom cloud?"

"I told you. Those things go off like an H-bomb. But there was a very low ceiling. It was all clouded over."

"Well, wait a minute. You said people. Just everyday people. But you said the fire department was there."

"So were the two men at the energy yard where they parked the Jumbo Nellie Nellie. They're the area suppliers for propane. But if you're looking for professional witnesses, I don't know where you're going to get any."

"Why not?"

"They're all dead, that's why," Winston McHale said. "The only theory we've got to go on is that the car was hit by lightning."

"But those tank cars have got to be grounded," Arthur Hawkes said. "Don't they? I mean, are you telling me you're running cars around your rails that catch fire every time there's a thunderstorm?"

"No," McHale said. "They don't catch fire."

"Now we *are* back to ground zero," Hawkes said. "First you say lightning caused it; now you say lightning didn't cause it."

"You haven't heard me out," McHale said. "Lightning's just part of the theory. It was a hundred degrees in Florian today. It's a wild coincidence but the theory is the heat causes the LPG to expand and that opens the pressure relief valve on the Jumbo Nellie Nellie. Situation normal. The valve's there to get rid of gas if pressure builds up. At that moment, lightning hits. Now, lightning isn't going to set fire to the tank car and gas isn't going to set fire to the tank car. But lightning's going to set fire to the gas."

"Wild coincidence," Hawkes said, but as he said it, he was blocking three words on his legal pad: ACT OF GOD. "I can hear the A&P screaming now."

Winston McHale said, "The A&P?"

"Aranow and Purcell," Hawkes said. "Personal injury lawyers in New York. Best in the business for this kind of case."

"But they're in New York," McHale protested. "Why would anyone call them?"

"I'm in Chicago," Hawkes said. "Why are you calling me? All I know is, every lawyer in Mundelein's got their phone number." He looked at his pad. "You had a fire going for twenty minutes before the explosion, right?"

"Maybe not to the exact minute," McHale said. "But right around in there, yes."

"Mm-hmm," Hawkes said. "And you had professional firefighters."

"*We* didn't have anything, Arthur."

"I mean there were professionals there."

"I don't know. Are volunteers professionals?"

"You were the one who used the word professional," Hawkes said.

"Well," McHale said, "I was including the people in the energy yard, the retailers. You know, the distributorship. I'd call them professionals too. But they're dead. They're all dead."

"You're not getting my point," Hawkes said. "My point is this: If these fires go on, and then they get to a certain point and you get an explosion, then there must be a formula."

"A formula?"

"Yes."

"A formula for what?"

"For fighting the fire. And for what goes with it. In this case, is there a formula for evacuating the area?"

"I don't know," McHale said. "I suppose there might be."

"Did they follow that formula?"

"I don't know," McHale said again.

"Find out," Hawkes said to him.

McHale said, "Maybe they were starting to and didn't have enough time."

"Find out," Hawkes said again. "And there's one thing else you've got to do. And right now. Got a pencil or a pen there?"

"Yes."

"All right. Write this down. Do *exactly* what I tell you. Ready? Look up the phone number of the Mundelein *Beacon*."

"I've got it. The Mundelein *Beacon*. What is it?"

"It's a newspaper."

"How would you know that?"

"That's why I said, 'For God's sake,' when you said Mundelein," Arthur Hawkes said. "I just finished trying a case there against the A&P."

"For God's sake," McHale said. "I hope you won it."

"I guess you could put it that way," Hawkes said. "The jury came in for me. Six to two."

"Six and two is eight."

"Eight-man juries in Ohio."

"Is that good?"

"Forget whether it's good or not and write this down," Hawkes said. "You direct-dial the *Beacon* right now and you give them a phony name and tell them you're from someplace else. You got that? I don't care where else. Make it—make it San Jose, California. That's a nice place."

Winston McHale said, "I don't know what you're driving at."

"Just write it down, that's all. And you say you've heard about the explosion in—where is it?—"

"Florian."

"Florian. And that you were on the local disaster committee when the chemical plant exploded two weeks ago, and you want to give them the benefit of what you did."

"What did I do?"

"Keep writing; I'll tell you what you did. You went to the local press and had them start organizing an emergency relief fund for the victims. All the people who were burned. It was a positive thing, something a whole community, a whole area, could get behind. Are you writing this?"

"Yuh," McHale said. "Yuh, I'm writing it."

"And then you follow up on it," Hawkes said.

"Well, we're leaving for there tomorrow," McHale said. "A bunch of us."

"Good."

"I'm wondering if maybe you ought to come in there too, Arthur."

"I'll have to," Hawkes said. "I've got no choice. But the follow-up is going to be this: Let the newspaper get the fund going. Then the Mid-Central Railroad contributes to the fund."

"I get you," McHale said. In his mind's eye, Hawkes could see him nodding into the phone at his end. "But why all the cloak-and-dagger, Arthur? Wouldn't it be even better if we started the fund ourselves?"

"If the explosion was your fault," Arthur Hawkes said. "Think about that."

"Oh," McHale said.

"Yes, oh," Hawkes said. "In fact, don't you be the ones to make the offer. Where's your division manager nearest to the accident? In Mundelein?"

"No, we've just got a freight agent there," McHale said. "Our division man would be in Gallipolis."

"Fine. That's better yet. Let him be the one to subscribe to the fund."

"I've got it written down," McHale said. "That's beautiful thinking, Arthur."

"Wait until you see my beautiful bills." His eyes roamed his notes. "And one other thing."

"What's that?"

"What does one of those tank cars look like?"

"I've got the specs right here," McHale said. "The Jumbo Nellie Nellies are 33,500-gallon capacity, noninsulated. Length 52 feet, $4\frac{1}{2}$ inches over the truck centers, 63 feet, 4 inches over the strikers, 65 feet, $11\frac{1}{2}$ inches coupled length. The payload is at 63.338 percent filling density, which is the weight of gas divided by the weight of water total at 60 degrees Fahrenheit. Width of the cars 10 feet, $6\frac{1}{2}$ inches over the—"

"I'm not writing any of this down," Hawkes said. "Not for now anyway. I'm just trying to get a general picture. You say Jumbo Nellie Nellie and it sounds like junior birdman code for something. But I guess you didn't mean it that way."

"That's what they call them," McHale said. "I'm just trying to answer your questions."

"Well, you've answered them," Arthur Hawkes said. "You going to be there for a while?"

"Yes."

"Then if I have any more questions I'll call you back." Hawkes hung up the phone, clasped his fingers at the base of his skull, and leaned back in his chair. His law office was a precise extension of his personality. His chair was straight-backed and matched the Italian antique inlaid walnut burl and marquetry table that served as his desk. He was tall, almost ascetic in looks and bearing, the rimless eyeglasses and steel gray hair putting on point a face that was not pointed to begin with. From his Turnbull and Asser shirts to the shoes handmade in Florence, he was impeccable. His three-piece suits, all custom tailored in London, all black, charcoal, or navy, draped his lean frame with perfect elegance. To his schoolmates in college he was the Hawk—quick, ruthless, devoid of sentiment, always to the jugular with his sardonic wit. But by the time he was graduated from law school, he defied nicknames. He became, simply, Arthur, and as his reputation in the courtroom grew and he became generally recognized as the top specialist in the country in defending large manufacturers, railroads, airlines, hospitals, and their insurance companies in lawsuits brought by people injured by them, or, as was so often the case, by the survivors of people killed, he became Mr. Arthur Hawkes for the defense.

An act of God, he said to himself. One second the weather liberates the gas—the next second lightning ignites it. He shook his head. It would mean the A&P. For Max Aranow, God was a target defendant. Aranow the dreamer, Joe Purcell the gunner. Purcell's mocking face in that Mundelein courtroom when the jury came in 6 to 2 against him. Purcell, whose mother had no stupid children, knowing he had built in a foolproof appeal. Aranow and Purcell. The A&P. And now this case, the enormity of disaster admixed with act of God. That school bus. Why that school bus at that place at that time? *The Bridge of San Luis Rey*, Arthur Hawkes said to himself, by Thornton Wilder as told to Max Aranow. And, he told himself, I'll never even see Aranow. I'll see Purcell instead. What Aranow wrought Purcell wreaks. And he owes me one. I stuck it into him in that bush-league county courthouse in Mundelein, Ohio, and now Aranow's going to spoon him twenty dead and seventy injured. From medical malpractice for one individual to ninety victims and half a town laid flat.

His clasped hands came up to the top of his head. His eyes closed. It'll be the A&P against God, he said to himself. I'll be a bystander.

No I won't, said another part of his mind. Maybe Aranow likes acts of God. Why shouldn't I like them too? Like them better than he does. If they intrigue him, they indemnify me. How does a jury find against me?

But one thing bothered him, and now he picked up his telephone and placed a call back to Winston McHale at the Mid-Central Railroad in St. Louis. When McHale came on the line, Arthur Hawkes said to him, "One thing—about your Jumbo Nellie Nellie."

"What's that?" McHale asked.

"Those specifications you read me."

"Well, hold on a minute here," McHale said. "No, here we are—What I said was 33,500-gallon capacity, noninsulated. Length 52 feet, $4\frac{1}{2}$ inches over the—"

"Stop, stop," Hawkes said to him. "I don't want to hear them. I just want to know one thing."

"What's that?"

"Who approved them?"

"Who did what?"

"Approved the specifications."

"The Department of Transportation," McHale said. "You can't build a railroad car without DOT approval. You know that, Arthur."

"I just wanted to make sure," Hawkes said.

8

The explosion severed power and telephone lines, a fitting overture for the violence of the thunderstorm that followed. And then a long, quiet rain broke the heat wave and put out the last of the fires that lit the wrecked surroundings, smudge pots for a prehistoric landscape. A portable generator, brought in from Portsmouth, pump-whined in the night five miles from nowhere, lighting the gymnasium of the high school as for a dance, and high on the gymnasium wall the pictures of the star athletes of the past smiled from among trophies, forever young, one of them smiling at his older self who now lay among the blanketed dead aligned before the long bench opposite, the duffel bags of the visiting team. An older self and yet at once younger, being so much smaller, no larger than a charred fireplace log with a belt buckle and a class ring and a child's jaw fenced with an adult's teeth; all black, but the blackest of all the holes where the eyes had been. This was Elliott Thoms, the principal of the high school and one of the volunteer firefighters. The school was too far from the firehouse for him to hear the horn alarm, but he had arranged with Charley Middleton at the bank for a phone call if one happened during school hours. Middleton lay next to him now, alongside Owen Merritt, the mayor of Florian, and for being mayor, Merritt would share celebrity status with Thoms in the late newscasts and the morning papers. But from the wall across the gym, Thoms smiled impartially upon himself and others one and all, here Elliott Thoms, the class of 1946, middle-distance medalist for the United States at the Olympics at London in 1948 and again at Helsinki in 1952, and from a sports columnist in New York to a track coach at UCLA, tonight Thoms's praises rang. "For he that runs it well, runs twice his race." So read the inscription underneath the picture.

The charcoal hunks on the floor, minitrunks with minicrowns and minibranches that were faces and arms and legs like the terrible trees taking human form in the Snow White ride at Disneyland, were of no recognizable gender. God would do the recognizing if relatives did not, and if neither then the job would fall to other hands, and the hardwood of the basketball floor rang hollowly to the arriving tread of the dentists of Mundelein County. No need to tell the unlistening to open wide, for mouths do open when the weather is hot, and for these the weather in Florian in one exquisite flash point tried to rival the surface of the sun. On the floor now they waited like laughing pirate flags for their charts, and the laughter was neither male nor female but in every case gargantuan; neither rich nor poor but in every case immense.

For the poor had their dental charts too. A man named Harry Wright had seen to that. He was a sixty-year-old attorney from Mundelein who was in charge of setting up the WIC—Women, Infants, Children— program for the depressed families of the area under a captioned title of enabling federal legislation to that purpose. The program included dental care, and Wright had the two enlisted dentists in the back seat of his six-year-old Volvo when he drove toward Florian.

At nine o'clock, Rosa Crewes came to the high school. The force of the explosion had propelled her through the open back door of her house, the empty can of frozen lemonade concentrate still in her hand, and she lay there underneath a wildly spinning clothes pole in the yard, watching her house burn to the ground, wondering dumbly what she would do with her young man now when he arrived, her mind framing apology. How long she lay there she did not know; she was without urge to do anything else. When the rain began, she sat up and cupped her hands to welcome it, then pressed it as a lotion of love against her face. After a long further time, she stood up, smoothing her dress, touching her hands to this morning's pageboy hairdo, and walked away from the house to the next street behind, where Dr. Nicholson had his office. Some one there, or in the vicinity, told her the doctor was at the high school, and so she began to walk there, not hearing the thunder, not seeing the devastation all around her, but only walked, physically unhurt, letting the rain envelop her in its own sealing warmth. At last, in full darkness by now, she saw the high school ahead of her, alone alive with light.

She did not locate Dr. Nicholson at once but did see someone else who served her purpose even more closely. The someone else was Harry Wright, the attorney from Mundelein. He was the man who had arranged that the young visitor from Chicago come to stay with her. Wright was small and chubby, with a chipmunk face too young for the rest of him. He was huffing at his eyeglasses, then wiping the lenses with his necktie, as he talked with an elderly couple in the hallway that fronted the gymnasium. Then he noticed Rosa standing there and he said, "Rosa. My God, look at you. Are you all right?"

She put her hands against her face again, then took them away and said, "He didn't come."

Harry Wright frowned. "He didn't come? Who didn't come?"

"The young man," she said. "The young visitor you were supposed to send me."

"You're soaking wet," Wright said to her. To the elderly couple beside him, he said, "Excuse me," and he came over and put a hand on Rosa's shoulder, leading her to a bench against the hallway wall. "Sit down," he said. "You say the young man I— oh, I know. The premed from Chicago. The one who was supposed to work in the program with Dr. Nicholson. What was his name again?"

"Coblenz," Rosa said. "Stephen Coblenz."

"That's right," he said. "Well, when was he supposed to be here?"

"Today."

"And he didn't come?"

She shook her head.

"Well, he was going to be driving from Chicago, wasn't he?" There was no alarm in Harry Wright's voice. "Was there any set time he was supposed to be here?"

"Today," Rosa Crewes repeated, tonelessly. "Dr. Nicholson said so. Effie Livingston said so."

"Well, he could have gotten held up," Wright said.

"No," she said.

"Why not?"

"If that was it, he would have called."

"Oh, well, no," Wright said, and reached down and squeezed her shoulder. "At least since this afternoon, the telephones haven't been working."

"Not in my house," she said, "but—"

"Not in anybody's house," he said. "They've just now got them working out of here. He could be—"

"My house is gone," Rosa said.

"Gone? I don't understand."

"Burned."

"Oh, Rosa," he said, and he looked intently down at her. "Are you sure you're all right?"

"I'm all right," she said.

"Let me take you to the cafeteria," he said. "You can use some coffee. I wish there was some brandy. You could really use that." He held out his hand, and she took it and stood up. "Your house? Burned? Totally?"

She nodded, letting him lead her.

"Well, come to think of it, I've got brandy at home," he said. "I'm going to be leaving here very shortly. Why don't you stay at my house?"

"I don't know," Rosa said.

"Then come with me. Jenny hasn't seen you in a coon's age. Just for tonight, anyway. Brandy beats coffee anytime."

"But what about him?"

"Him? Oh, the premed. Coblenz. I don't think you have to do much worrying. The sheriff's got a list here. We can check, just to make sure, why not? It's a lot less confused than I thought it was going to be, really. Remarkable, really, the line they've got on everybody. But we'll check. And they've got some dry clothes down in the girls' dressing room. You ought to get out of those things."

"What if he's dead?"

"Oh, Rosa, now don't go thinking that. It's ten to one he wasn't within fifty miles of here. And they already know who's dead. Identification's complete with everybody."

"I can stay with Effie tonight," Rosa said.

"Effie's here," Wright said. "But she's working with the doctor. They may be a while, Rosa. Why don't you come along with me? Really."

"No," she said. "He may come tonight. I'd want to be here if he came tonight."

And nothing would change her mind, so she stayed in Florian that night. And Harry Wright drove his two dentists back to Mundelein, leaving them off at their homes, then went home himself. When he got there, he said to his wife, "I could use a brandy. Really."

"Was it bad?"

"Like nothing I've ever seen."

"Was there any—"

"Really, can I have the drink first, Jenny?"

"I'll get it," she said, and went to the kitchen cupboard where the brandy was. Over her shoulder, she said, "There's a phone number in Chicago you've got to call."

He followed her into the kitchen. "Chicago? Who in Chicago?"

"It was what I started to ask you," his wife said. "I was asking was there any sign of a Stephen Coblenz. At the accident."

"*Coblenz*," Harry Wright said.

"He said it the other way."

"Who did?"

"The father. He's the one who's been on the phone. Called twice so far."

"Well, there isn't any sign of the boy," Wright said. "At least not out at the high school there, and that's where they've got the list. It's a hundred to one he just didn't make it."

"His father said he left Chicago at five o'clock this morning." She poured from the fifth of Christian Brothers and handed him the snifter. "If he wasn't going to make it he would have called."

"Maybe he did call. All the phones are down up there." He drank from the glass. "Did you tell the father that?"

"No," Jenny Wright said. "I didn't think of it. Besides, he sounded upset."

"Well, you can't hold that against him. Really."

"I mean *upset* upset," Jenny said. "Said if anything had happened to his son, he was going to sue anybody and everybody. Starting with you."

"Me?" Harry Wright said. He stood against the refrigerator, his back and the raised heel of his right foot bracing off it, and swirled the brandy in his glass, then drank again. "Why me?"

"Because you're the one who got the boy into this. You're responsible for bringing him here."

"Oh," Wright said. "Well, it's what I just said. He's upset. It's under-standable."

"You're sure he's not on the list up there."

"Yup. I checked it."

"For his name?" Those phone calls from the father had got to her. "His name in particular?"

"Yes, as a matter of fact. His name in particular. Rosa Crewes was wandering around out there and she was asking about him."

"Why would she want to know?"

"He was going to stay at her place. She had a room for him." Again he sipped from the glass. "When I say had, I mean *had*. Her house got burned down."

"Rosa's?" Jenny Wright put a palm to her throat. "That's awful. Is she all right?"

"She's one of the lucky ones. Didn't harm a hair on her head, and she's got fire insurance."

"I've had the television on in the bedroom," Jenny said. "It's all awful."

"I know," he said. "In a minute I'll be ready for a refill."

"You're not going to call Chicago?"

"Maybe after I've had another drink. It's an hour earlier there anyway." He finished the glass and handed it to her. "Don't you be upset."

"Well, I don't know," Jenny said. "I don't understand people like that. I mean, what kind of a man can that father be? The first thing he talks about is suing."

"Well, don't overreact to that," her husband said. "It's the language of distance."

"I don't understand."

"The father's in Chicago," Wright said. "Chicago's a long way from Florian, and the farther you're away, the more helpless you feel. You want action, and you don't know how to get action. So you threaten. It's the human thing."

"But people are going to sue, aren't they?"

"Oh, you'd better bet your life they're going to sue." He took his first sip from the second drink. "There's the dead, and there's the injured, and on top of both of them there's the town itself. You ought to see it, Jenny. Really. When the tank car blew, there was a Texaco station that blew with it. Anything one of them missed, the other one got."

"But there's insurance," Jenny said.

"Yes. Fire insurance for somebody like Rosa Crewes. And the energy yard would have insurance."

"Energy yard?"

"The gas company. Tri-State. Where the explosion happened." He put a hand to the small of his back and arched against it. "Lordy, I'm tired. Really. But they'll carry so much insurance and that's all, and I can't even think how big the claims here are going to be."

"Will you have some of the cases?"

"I won't be able to avoid it," Wright said. "They know me through the WIC program and two of those people are dead and at least six of the kids that I know of were on the school bus. It's business I don't even want, but inside of three days I'll be up to my ears."

"You *do* want the business," Jenny Wright said hotly. "Here's an oil company blows up half a town. You know what the oil companies have done to the people here. And now there's a chance to go after them."

"Really," he said. With one hand he removed his glasses; the other lifted his brandy again. He laughed without laughing. "Would you believe it, I hadn't even thought of that."

"Of what the oil companies have done?"

"No. I mean that an oil company would be involved here. I thought of the railroad, of course, and the people who make the tank car. But really, till this very minute when you said it, I hadn't thought of what was *in* the tank car."

"Well, isn't propane oil? Or an oil product?"

"It most certainly is."

"You know who I'd call?" she said. "First thing in the morning?"

"Yes," he said. "Joe Purcell in New York. Nobody in the country can handle something like this the way he can. Max will love it too. It's classic A&P. Little guys against the big guys."

"It's what you're all about too," Jenny said to him. "That's why you referred that malpractice case to him."

"Maybe not why I referred it to him," he said, "but certainly why Joe took it. You're right."

"And why he'll take this one," she said.

"I know. Little guys against—"

She held up a hand. "No, I don't mean only that. I mean the special stake he's got. If I know my Joe Purcell, he's just aching to get back here. After the way that malpractice turned out, if there's anything on this God's green earth Joe Purcell wants, it's walking out of that courtroom a winner. Harry, that's what you can make happen for him."

"Other people can make it happen for him too," he said. "I don't think we're the only ones thinking of Joe Purcell tonight."

"But you're going to be getting cases. Cases you can refer to him."

"I'd have to think so," Harry Wright said. "Can you imagine Purcell with Whizzer Thoms? Did you ever meet him?"

"Whizzer Thoms? I was trying to remember earlier. We saw him play, though, didn't we? Was it football or basketball?"

"Probably both," Wright said. "He did everything. That's going to be some funeral they throw for him, Jenny. Really."

9

```
To: A&P
From: BK
Re: Florian Fireball

Harry Wright called again from Mundelein at 8:00 a.m.
today. He's been approached by a third widow and feels
he's in over his head already and needs help. He wants to
have P fly out--or at least call--immediately.

He confirms what the Miami investigator told me when he
called. The fireball from the explosion was like an atom
bomb. Over a mile in diameter--everything and everyone
incinerated--24 dead, several more maybes--more than 80
injured--p.d. in telephone numbers. It's stupid to say JP
is too busy to call him. What do you want me to do?


To: BK & MA
From: JP
Re: Fireball

Call Harry and tell him we practice in New York. I've seen
enough of Mundelein and their goddamn juries to last a
lifetime. Tell him that the directory shows 1,241 members
of the Ohio Academy of Trial Lawyers. Tell him to pick
one. Mostly tell him to get off my fucking back.
```

Max Aranow winced. He was salt-and-pepper suit, narrow beige tie, the build and gray-white hair and flattened nose of a retired welterweight. "Let me tell you the truth, Bert. I would hate to be Elizabeth and have to transcribe Joe's memos."

Bert Klein slumped in a blue leather club chair, crossing one leg over the other, a Gucci buckle twinkling below his pants-leg cuff. "Don't worry about Liz. Working for Joe has made her a big girl."

"According to this memo of yours, Harry Wright called at eight o'clock today, meaning yesterday."

"Yesterday. That's right."

"And this reply from our concerned friend Mr. Purcell—it was written when?"

"I don't know."

"Was he in the office at all yesterday?"

"Nobody saw him if he was."

"But you must have been in here by eight in the morning yesterday. To get the phone call from Harry Wright."

"I was."

"And you were in here what time this morning?"

"Same as yesterday. A little before eight."

Max Aranow leaned back in his chair, an act that framed his face at level with wife, daughters, son, grandchildren all displayed on the oak credenza behind him. "And needless to say, nobody's seen him today either."

"Not that I know of."

"Then when did he dictate his memo?"

"Dunno," Bert Klein said again. "Might have been after hours last night, might have been before we opened this morning. All I know is, he came in, left it on the drum for Elizabeth, and took off again."

"Came from where? Took off to where?"

"Points unknown," Klein said. "I did call his house in Westport and the Yale Club. No sight, sound or smell of him."

"I need one extra full-time investigator to keep in touch with my partner," Max said. "Speaking of investigators, what's with this guy in Miami—"

"Cuneo. Victor Cuneo."

"Ah, yes. Cuneo."

"I told you about him, Max. Day before yesterday. When he called."

"Yes, I remember," Aranow said. "Made a commotion, did he?"

"That he did. Insisted on talking to Joe direct. Said he had burned children left and right and there hadn't been a case like this in twenty-five years."

"And you said?"

"I said I'd give Joe a memo on it. I didn't know what else to say."

"That's all right, that's fine," Max Aranow said. "No point ruffling the feathers of a man you don't even know. Just so long as you didn't give him any encouragement."

"I didn't. But I didn't think that kind needed encouragement."

"They don't. I assume he's called back again since."

"Has he ever. But trying to get Joe each time. Didn't bother with me. Maybe that's the best proof I didn't encourage him."

"Good," Aranow said. "In his racket, he can't afford to wait it out. He'll try other people and leave us alone."

"But," Klein said, "Harry Wright's a different animal."

"Oh, by all means," said the senior partner of A&P. "By all means."

"Then how can I do what Joe says in this memo and phone Harry Wright and tell him to piss up a rope?"

"You, can't." Aranow stroked his chin with his thumb. "Tell you what: leave this one to me. I'll call Harry Wright." He sat forward, and Bert Klein uncrossed his legs and stood up. "The flat rule, of course, is that we have nothing to do with Cuneo."

"Right," Klein said.

"The funny thing is," Aranow said, "he may have put his finger on it."

"What's that?"

"That there hasn't been a case like this in twenty-five years."

"Oh, it's something, all right," Klein said. "Harry Wright was telling me some of the things. You wouldn't believe them."

"Well," Aranow said, "first thing on the agenda is to find our wandering minstrel."

Bert Klein headed for the door. "If he turns up, I'll let you know. You going to be in the rest of today?"

"Not all of it," Max Aranow said. "But—oh, one other thing."

Klein looked back. "Whatever."

"What is this thing Joe's got on Mundelein? Wouldn't this case be in federal court in Columbus?"

"I thought about that, too," Klein said.

"What did Harry Wright say?"

"I didn't ask him about it. It didn't come up. The explosion wasn't in Mundelein, you know. It was a little town near there, called Florian."

"Oh, I know that," Max Aranow said. "That wouldn't make any difference anyway. I'm just wondering what Joe knows that we don't know."

"He always knows something nobody else knows," Bert Klein said. "In this case, though, I just think he's got Mundelein on the brain. After what that jury did to him, I'm not sure I blame him."

Aranow grunted and waved a hand, and Bert Klein went out. The older man sat there for a time in his empty office, then got up and went to the window and stared down at the westbound traffic on the street fourteen floors below. It always startled him how many people—native New York-ers—were unaware of the subway stop at Fifth Avenue and 53rd Street. You could take that subway and connect to anywhere. But where he was going, no connection would be necessary. The "E" train from Queens would take him direct to Eighth Avenue and 23rd, just five short stops away.

That was the journey he made now, first telling his secretary nothing more than that he would be gone, perhaps for the rest of the day. When he came up into the afternoon sunshine he walked east on the south side of 23rd Street to the great old granite hotel in the middle of the block. He chose not to announce himself downstairs as a caller for Ms. Marcy Beall, but instead took the elevator direct to the fifth floor, where her apartment was. It was an apartment, someone had said, that once belonged to Thomas Wolfe. Even before he pushed the bell, he could hear the music coming from within, the sound of a Gershwin piano.

No response to the bell; the piano kept on. Max Aranow pushed twice more, hearing the buzz-rattle result, and now the piano stopped and he could hear footsteps within, and the door was swung open by a tall, slender man in jeans and a faded green T-shirt that had GENERIC T-SHIRT written across the front in maroon block lettering.

"Ah," said Max Aranow. "You will want to know who I am. I am Nestor, came to woo the sulking Achilles in his tent."

"Not Nestor," the man in the doorway said. "It was Patroclus, I think."

"But Patroclus put on the armor of Achilles," Aranow said. "If you think I've come here to put on that T-shirt, you're out of your head."

"Come on in, Max," the other said. "Why didn't you call?"

Aranow shrugged. "Is Marcy here?"

"She's not here daytimes. You knew that, didn't you?"

"And when you're here and she's not and her phone rings, do you answer it?"

"Nope."

"That's why I didn't call," Aranow said.

"My partner," Joe Purcell said. "Mind like a trap. Did you close the door behind you? There's something I want you to see." For a moment, he seemed lost to view, blotted by the darkness in the tall, narrow hallway. He keeps disappearing, Max Aranow said to himself.

But the hallway gave way to the living room on the left, and as Aranow reached that entrance he could see Purcell, two-stepping an imaginary partner across the room to the 7-foot Knabe grand. Then he released the lady, bowed to her, and all in one lithe, perfectly conditioned move—

avoiding all surrounding objects: music stand, microphones, tape decks, a card table piled with pencils, composer's scorepaper, and notebooks, and everywhere wires, plugs, console lights and an unmatched pair of furrowed old gooseneck lamps dirtied by 60-watt bulbs—he slid onto the piano bench, hunked it forward only slightly, and hit a series of rising sixths.

Aranow had been here once, maybe twice, before, but had never seen the great high room like this. If it's nighttime and there's rain and lightning out the window, I'm getting the hell out of here, he said to himself. Otherwise I got to hold up a cross in his eyes and then pound a stake into his heart.

The top of the piano was down, and on it, surrealistically set upon separate lace-trimmed rose-colored doilies, were a half-gone quart of Walker Red Label Scotch and two wide-rimmed glasses, from a set tinted slightly green. Max Aranow came and leaned on the piano top and nodded at them. "You were expecting me after all."

"Not a thousand percent," Joe Purcell said. "One was a spare for ice. I was going good. But pour yourself a belt."

"Ordinarily I don't," Aranow said, and poured himself a drink. "Touch more for you?"

"Why not? We're celebrating."

"Are we? I didn't know. Silly me."

"Here," Purcell said to him. "Catch." And from the music stand he took something and skimmed it gently the short distance between them.

Max caught it and looked at it. It was a paperback book. A novel, it said. He did not recognize the author's name.

"*The Last Laugh*," he said, reading the title aloud.

"Symbolic, don't you think?" Purcell said. He reached and drank from his glass, then set it down and went back to the keyboard. Not looking up, he said, "Know what I paid for it? Five thousand dollars and fourteen cents."

Aranow had the book open. "Would you look at that?" he said.

"The fourteen cents," Purcell said, "was what it cost me to buy the book. Place on Fourth Avenue."

"For me?" Aranow said. "Joe, you shouldn't have."

"And five thousand dollars for a six-month option on the stage rights," Purcell said. "Closed the deal this morning. The guy's agent. They said don't worry about this agent, he couldn't book Lassie into a dog show. Now I'm not so sure."

"I never represent agents," Aranow said. He had an ever-changing checklist of types he never represented: morticians, retail florists, vegetarians, authors' agents (that was today's entry), insurance salesmen, Volkswagen dealers, hockey goalies, men or women more than once divorced, bill collectors, acrobats.

"It is just going to happen to be," said Joe Purcell, "one of the hit musicals of all time."

Aranow nodded, still looking in the book. "Don't tell me," he said. "Words and music by Joseph F. Purcell."

Purcell shook his head. "More than that. *Book*, music, and lyrics by Joseph F. Purcell. Nostalgia. Show business setting. The book's set in the early fifties, but I'm taking it back to the thirties."

"Ah," said Max Aranow. "One of those. In the first scene Flash Gorden meets Voltan, king of the floating city."

"Wrong," Purcell said. "The hero is a newspaperman."

"Perfect," Aranow said. "Live by the press, die by the press. The story of your life."

Again Purcell shook his head. "No. This guy's clean. He's entertainment editor for a wire service. Not your usual reporter scum. No better, maybe, but different. There's hope for him."

Aranow could feel the vibration of the piano through his hand and the glass it held. He stared at Purcell. "You want to know something?" he said. "We're partners how many years? Twenty-two? And I just this minute figured it out."

"What?"

"Who you remind me of. Know who? Elbie Fletcher."

The chord progression became a melody. "Thanks a million," Joe Purcell sang, "a million thanks to you, for..." His voice was baritone and on key, but nonetheless sandy, the color of his hair.

Aranow rode in on him. "Elbie Fletcher," he said, "played first base for Boston. Same height and weight as you—six foot, hundred and eighty. Same Mount Rushmore face: chiseled. Left-handed, same as you are. And had that elegant step of the prancing show horse. The knee action. You know?"

Purcell went back to the chords, left hand only while right hand reached for his drink. "But that was long ago. Right, Max?"

"What in this world isn't long ago?" Aranow said, and lifted his own drink. "I'm eighteen years older than you, Joe, and we're partners twenty-two years."

"No, Max." Joe had stopped playing.

Max closed his eyes, sighed deeply, and eased into the persecuted slump that he had carefully cultivated for New York juries when the judge over-ruled one of his objections. "What do you mean, no?"

"No to that tank car in Ohio. You want to try that case, you can go into that Mundelein courthouse and try it yourself. If you do, you'll be up against Arthur Hawkes for the defense."

"Who was talking about a tank car case?"

Max was now the pure innocent. Joan of Arc before the inquisitors. Joe's stare told Max that his performance was not selling. Max straightened up and Joe grinned warmly and went back to the piano.

"What'd you come track me down for? To hear me play the piano?" Max Aranow poured into his glass from the Walker Red Label bottle.

"Worse than that," Purcell said, "it'll be a case you can't win. And if you can't win it, God knows I can't win it."

"What makes you think it would be Hawkes?"

"Because he represents that railroad, just the way he represented that insurance company for the hospital when you sent me in there last time, Max. You said we were partners for twenty-two years. I accept the figure. And you hate insurance companies so you sent me in there. And you hate railroads, and I don't even know why you hate railroads, except they took off the dining cars. But twenty-two years is enough, Max."

"You have all the answers," Aranow said. "Also, you seem to know the case will be tried in Mundelein. That's county seat. State court. That's what you had in the hospital case. But what makes you think you'll have it this time?"

"What makes you think I won't?"

"I've done some checking," Max Aranow said. "Who are your defen-dants? The local energy supplier? They're not Ohio. They're headquar-tered in West Virginia. The railroad? They're not Ohio. They're head-quartered in St. Louis. The oil company? They're not Ohio. North American Petroleum. Delaware corporation."

"Oh," Purcell said. "I see. Without an in-state defendant it goes into federal court."

"Exactly," Aranow said.

"So we're not talking about Mundelein, Ohio. We're talking about the federal court in Columbus."

"Exactly," Aranow said.

"So we're not thinking of my having to go back into Mundelein to try a case in front of one of those American Gothic juries. And that judge."

"You're beginning to get it."

"Am I? You're forgetting who it was that manufactured the tank car. It's an outfit called the Nance Company. Look 'em up."

"They're a big company," Aranow said. "Fortune five hundred. But so are Mid-Central and NAP."

"Spectacular target defendants, all of them," Purcell said. "Except that Nance headquarters is in Bucyrus, Ohio, so you're in state court, not federal court, and you're throwing me right back into the county seat, that courtroom in Mundelein, and I ain't about to go, Max." Purcell reached for the bottle. "For three reasons. One, I can't beat Arthur Hawkes. Two, I can't win a case in that courtroom. Three, you're not going to win that case anywhere. Hawkes will play it was act of God and he'll win. Because that's what it was, Max."

Aranow stared at him. He said, "Is there any more Scotch after this?"

"How long you figuring on being here?"

"Not that long. I've got to pick up two herring for Sophie, to take down to Ambler with us." Aranow sighed. "But I thought I could use an extra drink. I have a fear of something."

Purcell took his right hand from the keyboard and reached down underneath the piano. What he came up with was another full quart of Walker Red Label. "Ask and thou shalt receive," he said. "You're opening up the place?"

"Yes. We're expecting you and Marcy, weekend after this."

Purcell responded with a wag of the bottle. "No question," he said. "Marcy's counting on it."

"The fear," Max said to him, "is compounded of two things. First, you lost yourself a lawsuit in Ohio and may be going up against the same people again, and second, you're launching yourself in show biz. This silly book you threw at me."

"What's silly about it?"

"You're saying it underwrites what I'm saying. What are you going to do? Lose one case and give up the law?"

"You just got it in one," Purcell said. "Except it isn't that great single one shining moment you make it out to be. If there's anything special about that tank car blowup in Florian, it's not that I'd be back in the same courtroom against the same opposing lawyer. It's just that you don't win a case like that, Max."

"I see," Aranow said. "In other words, you have no theory."

"What am I supposed to have in the way of theory? An act of God is an act of God."

Aranow drank from his glass. "There's always another way."

"Don't always 'another way me, Max. I did make one phone call on this. I talked to a heat transfer expert on the Fireball thing. Guy out in Kansas. Incidentally, I reserved him for you. Just in case Hawkes gets in touch with him, which I'm sure he will. If anybody's going to have theories, a specialist like that would have them. But he doesn't. He'll be glad to play let's-spin-a-theory for a hundred and fifty dollars an hour. He'll testify for twelve hundred a day. But I don't know what good he'll do us."

"I don't know either," Max said. "But there has to be a glory point. There always is."

"Then go ahead and take the case," Purcell said. "Just don't involve me in it."

Max Aranow turned his eyes up to the high ceiling. Then he looked back again at Purcell and said, "Was this piano here last time I was?"

"I don't think so," Purcell said. "Why?"

"I just wondered."

"If you mean, did I buy it for Marcy, the answer's yes. And the tape deck and the whole works. And did I buy this book property to write a show for her to star in, the answer's yes again. What else do you have to know?"

Aranow shrugged. "Nothing."

"Nothing," Purcell repeated, "except it would be a shame if we didn't take this Fireball case. It just won't wash, Max. Because after this case, there'll be another case. World without end." He reached over and slapped his partner's shoulder affectionately. "I started out as a piano player, old friend, and I'm going to wind up as a piano player."

"Well, then," Max Aranow said, "I would say this: that if you're going to go out the way you came in, you owe it to yourself to go out very well-fixed, and I have a feeling the Fireball can fix you."

Purcell stood up. "Come to the bathroom with me. Don't bring your drink."

Max followed Purcell into the old-style bathroom, tub sitting there on claw feet, in the apartment of Marcy Beall, an unmarried woman with whom his widower law partner from time to time lived. And to his further embarrassment, he saw Purcell reach into the medicine cabinet and pull out two cans, one a roll-on, the other an aerosol, but both Ban deodorant.

"Here," Purcell said. "Grab them." And he thrust the roll-on into Aranow's right hand, the aerosol into his left. "Now. What do you feel?"

"What am I supposed to feel?"

"Which hand is colder?"

Aranow did a take. His left hand did feel colder. Markedly so. He said, "My God, what's that?"

"Read it," Purcell said.

Aranow read the label on the aerosol. "*Warning:*," he said aloud, "*Keep at Room Temperature (not over 120 degrees Fahrenheit). Do not puncture or incinerate can.*"

"Interesting," Purcell said. "The colder it feels to the touch, the likelier it is to catch on fire. And in a hurry, which means an explosion. That's why they print that warning, and that's what happened to that tank car. It's a deodorant can—*a shaving can, an insect spray, a furniture polish*—on wheels. Just lay it on its edge and put something hot to it, and bang, she blows. And they live with those tank cars the same way you live with your deodorant or your insect spray. And that's why you don't have a case. That fireball in Florian is a fact of life, Max."

"Marvelous," Aranow said. "Now can I do something to get out of this bathroom?"

"Sure," Purcell said. "Demonstration complete. Except now you know, Max, not just why I won't take this case, but why you don't want it either."

"I don't know," Aranow said, steering himself toward the front door. "I mean, what *made* it blow?"

"Lightning," Purcell said. "The heat opened the safety valve—the heat of the day, I mean: it was a hundred degrees down there—and lightning hit the vapor, and thar she blew."

"Oh," Aranow said. He was at the front door now, and Purcell held it open for him, and Aranow moved slowly out into the marble outer hall toward the elevator.

"Wait a minute," Purcell said from the doorway. "I don't like that."

Max Aranow turned. "Don't like what?"

"What you just said."

"I said 'Oh.'"

"I don't like the way you said it."

Max grinned as Joe turned back into the apartment and closed the door behind him.

10

"I've got a crazy for a partner," Max Aranow had said, mostly to his wife, Sophie, on any number of occasions. Now, arriving home at their apartment in the old building on the northwest corner of Seventh Avenue and 57th Street, he said it today again.

In a bad year, Max Aranow earned $650,000. He had no sense of this.

It had to be said that he lived well. Certainly he rode subways as convenience might indicate, but he used taxicabs too, and at times the liveried Carey limousines—again as convenience proposed. He was sixty-four years old, owned no automobile, had never learned to drive one. Joe Purcell loved to point out, to anyone who questioned Max's life-style, that his senior partner paid less for transportation than some $30,000-a-year neighbor with a Toyota. He didn't have to buy the car, license it, garage it, operate it, maintain it, insure it. There were no bridge or tunnel or expressway tolls, no parking fees, no tow-away charges or fines of any kind, no speeding tickets, no pit-of-the-stomach feel when the cop sirened you over, no wondering what that strange rattle was, no risk of hitting someone or something when you were at the wheel. The guts of any personal-injury law firm had to be automobile accident cases, and Aranow had to be the world's worst lawyer in any such case. He never rode in the front seat.

"Did you get the herring?" Sophie said. Their daughter, Agnes, and her two daughters were part of the scene surrounding Aranow as he came through the door. "Everything today is too sudden," he said. "It closes in on me. I walk in my own door, I'm surrounded by females. Earlier today, I discovered something for the first time in twenty-two years. All this time I've had Elbie Fletcher for a partner."

Sophie said, "Elbie Fletcher?"

"Led the league in walks," Max said, "two years in a row, after the Boston Bees traded him to Pittsburgh."

The Carey limo was an hour away from coming to pick up Sophie and her daughter and granddaughters for the trip to Ambler to open up the house there for the summer. Sophie was small and spring-wound, like her husband. She said, "You got a call from Harry Wright in Ohio."

Max nodded. "It's understandable." To his youngest granddaughter, five years old, he turned and said, "First I have to get on the telephone. But you know what happens when grandpa gets on the telephone. He turns purple, and then he comes racing after little girls and chomps them with his furry tooths."

"You don't have furry tooths, grandpa."

"You've never seen them *turn* furry."

His granddaughter gave a little scream and fled away down the long corridor of the apartment. Sophie said, "Really, Max," but he was on his way into the parlor, where the phone was, and alongside it the pad where Sophie had written the number.

When Harry Wright answered, it was with a single question: "Max, what do I do?"

"Take your cases and file them. We'll handle this with you."

"What does Joe say?"

"Joe says no."

"I know why," Harry Wright said. "That licking he took on the Marlowe case down here—the malpractice. But you know whose fault that was, Max? Mine, that's whose."

Aranow said, "What what?"

"He got clobbered by one juror," Wright said. "I just found out today. And it's a shabby thing, a bleak thing. Because we'll never be able to nail it."

"Tell me," Max said.

"One of the women on the jury," Harry Wright said. "She was listed as a housewife. We ran the ordinary check and voir-dired the ordinary way. Today I just found out she got night work in a cafeteria. Two days after the trial started."

"So? The case was against the hospital, not a cafeteria."

"The cafeteria is also the one that operates the food service at the hospital," Wright said. "I know they got to her, and I'll never be able to prove it."

"Well, don't kick yourself around the block about it," Max Aranow said. "Those things happen."

"But Arthur Hawkes—"

"If Hawkes knew about it, the worst he'd do would be just let nature take its course. On every jury you find people whose interests may be similar to yours. The trick is to discover those interests, and the best man in the country for that, day in and day out, is Joe Purcell. Besides, if Hawkes had expected it he wouldn't have offered to settle the way he did. Unless there's something you haven't told me."

"No," Wright said. "She had this job opportunity, and Max, you have to understand—really—how lousy the job situation is down around here. And in the jury room she preached it out like Aimee Semple McPherson. What marvelous folks those hospital people were and what a genius of a job they did even keeping the kid alive. And the rest of them bought it."

"Does Joe know this?"

"You mean have I told him? No. I just got wind of it today myself. I could throw up."

"Good idea," Aranow said. "I suggest you do it in that shmecky cafeteria during the rush hour."

"So he says he won't take this one—the Fireball."

"That's right."

"But meanwhile you say A&P'll handle it."

"That's right."

"Well, who can try this case if Joe doesn't?"

"Nobody."

"Really," Harry Wright said.

"I have a feeling," Max Aranow said. "I had a session with Joe just this afternoon, out of the office. He kept saying no, but it kept spelling out a different way. To begin with, he knows more about the case than either you or I do. He knows why Ban aerosol feels colder than the roll-on. He knows—"

"Why the Ban what?" Wright said.

"—the best heat transfer expert in the country," Aranow said. "Already been in touch with him. He knows that Hawkes is taking it for the defense."

"I just found that out this morning," Wright said. "At the funeral for Elliott Thoms. Whizzer Thoms. You remember him, Max? Principal of the high school. Medal winner in the Olympics. It was a magnificent funeral, Max. People from all over the state. All over the country. The widow asked me to take her case."

"Hawkes was there?"

"Oh, yes. He was there."

"Did you talk to him?"

"Uh-huh. He said he was taking it. For the railroad, but the other defendants would close together and have him carry it for them too. Incidentally, I saw him talking to the judge and I'm sure it was about the case."

"The judge?"

"Well, he was at the funeral too, Max. Everybody who's anybody was at the funeral. Really."

11

It might have bothered a Harry Wright that Hawkes and the judge had talked about the case, but none of it bothered Max Aranow. Hawkes arguing his case at the funeral was merely Hawkes acting naturally. It was his creed that all creatures great and small—particularly the wealthy and the powerful—were entitled to their day in court, and those were his clients—from giant railroad to giant insurance company, all with legal staffs of their own, of course, but shrewd enough to reach out for Hawkes to handle the big ones. He was, like Joe Purcell, the best of the hired guns. The only difference was that if Hawkes lost the case, he got paid anyway. He even got paid for going to funerals.

Harry Wright had been wrong in a couple of his assumptions. He assumed Hawkes had shown up at the Whizzer Thoms funeral as something of a social necessity, but to Arthur Hawkes it was more intricate than that: it was a part of preparing his case. Many months down the road he could tell that small-town mid-America jury that he had been among them when they buried their dead. A touch, perhaps, but it was the touches that won cases.

And Wright thought Hawkes had met the judge at the funeral, but Arthur Hawkes was not about to leave that encounter to chance. Instead, at five minutes to nine that morning, he left the General Dexter Hotel, and in the remarkable pleasantness of the spring day—the heat wave had broken, the rains had gone—he walked the three short blocks to the Mundelein courthouse. This being Mundelein's, it yet was every small town courthouse and every courthouse square, the same two-story building, the same cupola gone green with weather and memory, the same two Civil War cannons flanking the main walkway. A sign in an unseen corner said, Do Not Spit in Unseen Corners.

Arthur Hawkes rather enjoyed the place. His talents as a persuader had a way of working well in climes like these. He downshifted with ease into home-folks talk, even though he himself headquartered in Chicago, and if occasionally the small of his back felt the derision in Joe Purcell's eyes, as in their last trial here, the Marlowe malpractice case, they still paid off on how the jury went, and the jury had gone 6 to 2 for Hawkes and the defense.

He had Purcell on his mind as he climbed the broad steps, a half flight to a landing, then the reverse turn to either of the narrower sets of continuing stairs to the second-floor balcony. Like Purcell, Hawkes's only previous association with Mundelein was the Marlowe trial, but perhaps they had more in common than that. For one thing, they both were patricians, in life-style and in education. Purcell was Yale, Hawkes was Virginia. In his mid-fifties, he was at least ten years older than the courtroom ace of the A&P, but that difference was no difference. At his home in Lake Forest, north of Chicago, hard by the Onwentsia Club where he golfed, Hawkes kept a chess set—an ordinary, almost drab set of worn pieces, except that they once belonged to the international champion Emanuel Lasker. And he had long since memorized what Lasker said about himself:

> I have stored little in my memory, but I can apply that little, and
> it is of good use in many and varied emergencies. I keep it in order,
> but resist every attempt to increase its dead weight.

And as he reached the top of the stair rise to the balcony in the courthouse, today in Mundelein in the wake of Jumbo Nellie Nellie and the fireball, Arthur Hawkes sighed and turned left. Along the east wall of the building on the second floor, as he approached it, were three facing doors: the jury room on the left, the courtroom in the center, the judge's chambers to the right. Hawkes went to the rightmost door and opened it and found himself in the little reception area where the secretary sat, but at this time of morning she was not yet there, so he went to the inner door and rapped on it, and a voice from inside said, "Come," and he went in. "Hello, Junior," he said.

The judge of Mundelein County, Junius Bohr, Jr., looked up from his desk and said, "Hello—why, it's Arthur. Arthur Hawkes. For God's sake, come in! Sit down!"

Hawkes went to the straight-backed armchair that fronted the judge's desk and seated himself, giving off the reverse effect of a carpenter's rule in the act of unfolding.

"Junior," he said, "how are you?"

Junior liked to be addressed as Judge instead, but Hawkes was not about to do that outside the courtroom itself. If he did that, there would be no contrast. One had to show respect, but one had also to show selfconfidence, and if people called this man Junior, he brought it on himself. He had run for election that way, with his campaign posters plastered against phone poles and trees throughout the county. JUNIOR BOHR FOR JUDGE, the signs all said, with the great red fronting "J" covering Junior and Judge alike, and in that familial territory the campaign won, ousting the generational alcoholic who had occupied the same chair for two decades.

As a result, Bohr had become the county judge at the age of twenty-nine, and the wire services out of Huntington carried a box on his election that called him the youngest judge in the country. He may have been.

Junior took it all with agreeable humility. Framed on his desk was the message of Brutus:

> As Caesar loved me, I weep for him; as he was fortunate, I rejoice
> at it; as he was valiant, I honour him; but as he was ambitious, I
> slew him.

He had come by his post honestly enough: Mundelein born and bred, Ohio State educated and degreed, more than four years in the county attorney's office before he ran for judge. And by now he was accustomed to being the youngest lawyer in his own courtroom. "Arthur," he said, "how the hell are *you?*" It was fat face and fat body to go with it, and no robes to cover, for he sat behind his desk in a short-sleeved white shirt with black tie, to go with the black suit he would wear to the Thoms funeral. Fat hands, too, and he reached one of them for a cigarette, then held the pack forward to Hawkes.

Hawkes put up a hand of his own. "Not me," he said. "I used to, but no more."

"I wish I could quit," Junior Bohr said. "When did you? How'd you do it?"

"I quit more than twenty years ago."

"For good?"

"For good. Never went back."

"But I do three packs a day, Arthur. You have no idea: I've never told you, how I'd sit in that courtroom while you and Purcell were having at it and be dying for that cigarette, and there was no way—"

"I noticed you never opposed a recess," Hawkes said.

"But you licked it," Bohr said. "My question is, how?"

"A case I had."

"Lawsuit?"

"Yes. I was part of the defense in the first cigarette cancer case in New Orleans. The plaintiff was dying of cancer and sued the cigarette company."

"He didn't win, did he?"

"No. He lost, and he died."

"I remember that," Junior Bohr said. His voice was a baritone in some way not in sync with his body. "It was a landmark. The big victory for the tobacco industry."

"Big victory, yes," Hawkes said. "Landmark, I don't know. That was the forerunner of the surgeon-general warning on all the packs and in all the ads. We won it, yes, but maybe we lost it too."

"You have an interesting side of the law, Arthur."

"Do I? You may be the first person who ever said that."

"Yes," Junior Bohr said, "I think you do." He was using language free from epithet, though when he had an actual case before him his words in chambers went foul: a defense mechanism, it seemed to Hawkes, designed to mask his youth. "Defend a murderer," Bohr said now, "and it's a one-on-one commitment, you to the client, and everybody understands it. But defend the telephone company—"

"Or the Mid-Central Railroad," Arthur Hawkes said.

"Or the Mid-Central Railroad," Bohr said, "or—"

"North American Petroleum," Hawkes said.

"The NAP, right," Bohr said, "or—"

"The Nance Company," Arthur Hawkes said.

"Nance, right, or Tri-State Gas, and you—"

Hawkes said, "Nobody's here to defend Tri-State Gas. They probably have nothing more than a million in coverage, if that. My bet is they just pitch it in and walk. Not that I can see that they did anything wrong. It's just a case where it'll be cheaper for them to pay than defend."

Bohr nodded. "That makes sense. And the accident did happen on their property."

Arthur Hawkes smiled. The judge had said it for him. There was no question of what mission had brought Hawkes here—it was the Florian fireball and they both accepted it unspoken. Far more important, the judge had used the defense word: "accident." The A&P was not going to come in there calling it an accident. "Explosion," "catastrophe," "holocaust," "disaster"—those would be Purcell's code words.

The young judge stared at Hawkes and tried to remember whether he had ever seen a smile on that face before. Without smiling back, he said, "Arthur, can you settle it out?"

"Why? You don't want it in your courtroom?"

"Damn right I don't want it in my courtroom. I didn't want the last one."

"This one isn't the last one. This one's front-page news all over the country. Make a big man out of you."

"Do what?"

"Make you famous, Junior."

"In other words, you won't settle it."

"Probably not."

"Why?"

Hawkes played not the ace and not the king, but a dulcet spade queen. "Because there's no liability, that's why. After all, who did anything wrong?"

"In other words, you may not offer much."

"Not in other words. In your own words."

Junior Bohr drew deeply at his cigarette. "You know," he said, "you may be right."

"I know I'm right. You start taking a careful look at the liability here and Junior, I've got to tell you, I'm damned if I can find any."

"You still sound worried, Arthur."

"A little. I called up an expert on the phone so he could be a potential witness for me and you know what he said? He said Joe Purcell had already called him."

"Oh, no!" Bohr crushed the cigarette angrily into an empty coffee cup. "I've got a fucking rematch on my hands. And this one will be like World War Three! Why don't you two bastards go tangle assholes in New York or Chicago. This is a nice quiet little town—with one fat, happy, and dumb judge who likes to rubber stamp a few default divorces and uncontested wills and then go fishing. Suddenly I've got the Super Bowl every year." He lit another cigarette and leaned forward, his tone now conspiratorial. "Arthur, tell me something else: who's Victor Cuneo?"

Hawkes blinked. "Cuneo? He's a case-steer operator out of Miami. But only the big ones. He circles disast—accidents like a vulture. On the carcass before it cools off. Are you telling me he's been working this one— Cuneo?"

"Oh, yes, I'm telling you just that," Junior Bohr said. "He spent like two and a half days here, and kept striking out when he tried to make that confirming phone call, so you know what he did then? He got in his rented car and drove to Charleston."

"Am I supposed to ask what was in Charleston?"

"Whether you ask it or not," Junior Bohr said, "I'll tell you. He picked up the dregs of the accident."

"In Charleston? I know a piece of the tank car flew through the air a mile, maybe more, but Charleston?"

"A TWA plane landed there," Junior Bohr said. "It was St. Louis-Washington, but apparently when the fireball went up the pilot was right there, right over Florian, and he went ape at the sight of it and turned the plane so violently he picked up some sprains and strains in the passenger cabin, so he emergency-landed at Charleston to off-load them. I'd call that rather secondary, wouldn't you?"

"I sure would," Hawkes said. "That sounds like small-potato stuff for Cuneo."

"Unless that's all he could come up with."

"Even if that's all he could come up with. He's got to have something else in mind. Like getting his dirty little foot in the door."

"Are you beginning to see why I don't want this ball-buster in my courtroom?" Junior Bohr said.

Hawkes shook his head. "You know," he said, "I was in Florian yesterday. With the cinder dicks."

"The cinder dicks?"

"Railroad detectives. Investigators."

"I thought you said it was pure accident."

"It was."

"Then what was the purpose of—"

"Automatic," Arthur Hawkes said. "You have no idea, Junior, how these people come in and take over. Spoil a crate of tomatoes, they're there."

"And what did they find?"

"Nothing."

"What were they looking for?"

"Anything," Arthur Hawkes said. "If a tank car explodes, and it's just sitting there at the time, one wonders why. So they look into it. They look into everything. Something had to set off this explosion."

"Everybody says lightning," the judge said.

"And everybody's right," Arthur Hawkes said. "It was lightning. But the cinder dicks came in to check anyway."

"For what?"

"They just came in, that's all. For example, they checked to see if there was a passing train with sparks from a journal box that could have jumped to the tank car and set it off."

"And they didn't find that?"

"Didn't find it? It's a branch line, Junior. The last passing train, with or without sparks from a journal box, was three days earlier. I tell you: they found nothing."

"Joe Purcell will love to hear that."

"Joe Purcell is going to hear that."

The young fat baritone face laughed for the first time. "And it won't convince him."

"No," Hawkes said. "It won't convince him. In his world, nothing happens by accident. *Accidents* don't happen by accident."

12

"As a matter of policy," Max Aranow wrote in an officewide memo for the A&P, "our adversary letters should be signed off 'Yours Truly' while letters to clients should carry 'Yours Very Truly.' Always remember, the four letters making up the word 'love' can be extracted from 'Yours Very Truly,' but not from 'Yours Truly.'"

"Max is right as usual," wrote Joe Purcell in a follow-up memo. "Love is an anagram."

In the wake of Aranow's departure from Marcy Beall's apartment, Joe Purcell stood in the windows on the northern wall of the living room, looking down on 23rd Street. It had begun to rain, complicating the late afternoon traffic rush. Streetlights and headlights came on prematurely because of the darkening sky. The damp black pavement mirrored the incandescent glare.

Joe closed his eyes. He recalled how the streets were also dark and wet with rain that morning long ago. During the ten-minute drive to Sky Harbor Airport from the Adams Hotel he couldn't remember a single word he exchanged with his beautiful young wife. Had they made love the night before? Did they have coffee in the room after the early wake-up call? What kind of lawsuit was he trying in Phoenix that January how many years ago? Did he win or lose?

How many hundreds of times had he reviewed in his mind that last hour before depositing Celia at the makeshift check-in shed for the scenic air tour of the Grand Canyon? Why had he wanted to talk her out of it? He had said something about the weather being lousy for sight-seeing.

"It'll burn off as soon as that Arizona sun comes up." She laughed, pecking him on the nose. "I kiss your nose," she said, and scampered through the light drizzle into the shed.

And the most vivid memory of all—total recall—as he sat behind the wheel of the Hertz car, adjusting the rearview mirror to wipe the little smudge of lipstick from the tip of his nose.

News of the crash reached his New York office first, giving Max the job of calling Joe at the federal courthouse in Phoenix. Joe hated that courtroom—it was vast and lacked intimacy, and local rules mandated that lawyers stand at a podium when interrogating witnesses or addressing the jury. "Great place for the defense but the pits for plaintiffs," Joe had told Max after his first appearance there. "It's the only courtroom in America where it looks like it's going to rain any minute."

The defendant's insurance company lawyer was cross-examining Joe's medical expert when the bailiff passed a note to the judge, who then immediately called a recess. As the jury filed out the judge told Joe to take the call from New York in his chambers.

No "the cat's on the roof" bullshit from Max.

"Joe, there's been a plane crash."

"Celia?"

"No survivors," Max said. "Our investigator is on his way to Flagstaff."

What makes men different from animals is that men laugh and cry, Joe had often told juries. Joe did both, but he didn't laugh out loud until three weeks after the funeral when Max brought the investigation report to Joe's room at the Yale Club. "Weather wasn't a factor," Max said. "It was a defective fuel tank selector switch. The suit is against the manufacturer."

"What suit!" It was a statement, not a question. "Will a goddamn lawsuit bring Celia back?"

"No," Max said. "And as your partner and your best friend and as a suddenly old man who loved Celia like a daughter, I suggest you forget about the lawsuit. Wrongful death of a childless nonworking wife. In Arizona, maybe worth $300,000, at the outside."

"Max, stop, please," Joe said.

"Okay. After all, by not suing you're donating $300,000 to Trans-Continental Insurance Company, which insures the aircraft manufacturer, and everyone knows that Trans-Continental is a great charity. Personally, I prefer the UJA, but then I didn't go to Yale."

It was then that Joe laughed and a few months later Max settled the case and all of the money was contributed to a basic science research institute in Israel—the Celia Purcell Memorial Laboratory was established.

A year later Joe and Max flew to Israel for the dedication. Afterward, the elegant world-class immunologist who served as president of the institute shook hands with Joe and thanked him.

"Don't thank me," Joe said. "Thank Mr. Aranow. It was his idea."

"Thank Trans-Continental Insurance Company," Max said. "This is the best thing they've ever done."

The rain had stopped now but not before dulcifying the May evening in a way that Max Aranow would say was peculiar only to New York and Philadelphia. Doubtless it was his background, but Aranow was the only man in America who could see those two cities as one and the same. On the street below, a westbound panel truck bore the legend EASTERN HUMAN HAIR GOODS CO. The smaller print said NEW YORK——PHILADELPHIA. He knows, Purcell said to himself.

What doesn't he know? That was the next question. In a bad year, Purcell earned $1,000,000: half again as much as Max. It had not been ever thus. When they started out together, 22 years ago, the partnership split had been the other way, and violently so: 5 to 1 for Aranow. But time and case load and the miniki—the miniki was the private word Aranow and Purcell had for the younger associates in the firm, an acronym for mick/nigger/kike—had asserted their claim. The miniki comprised Sheila O'Hara, Catholic University; Willie R. Blake, Princeton and Rutgers Law; Bert Klein, Harvard. Beyond that, the change in the partnership split took into account Purcell's emergence as chief trial counsel for the firm, and the ever-increasing amounts of time Aranow was devoting to *pro bono* work for the Legal Aid Society. "We are the blueprint for every law firm," Max Aranow said proudly. "The 'now society.' I, as senior partner, am the only downwardly mobile member of the outfit."

"Hang on," Purcell advised him. "I get myself my first hit musical on Broadway, it's bye-bye baby."

What was it, the way music possessed people? Whatever it was, it was five times that much if you *wrote* the music. Joe Purcell had to believe that. In one hand, as he stared out the window, he held the glass of Scotch. In the other was the lead sheet he had written for the best song in his show— soon to be, he knew, his first Broadway show —*The Last Laugh*. The lyric was simple enough:

> We have met before somewhere, when the world was green,
> Sometime in the springtime, in my dreams I've seen
> Your face at some familiar door somewhere, when the world
>   was new,
> We have met before somewhere, somewhere there was you.

You're a capable songwriter, Purcell said to himself. Better than that, maybe, you're reasonably honest. You don't go around rhyming "fine" with "time" or "dreams" with "New Orleans." He drank from his glass of Scotch, looked down again at the lead sheet in his other hand. You're more than a song, he said to the piece of paper. You're a passport. "And when I tell them," he sang to the piece of paper, "how beautiful you are, they'll never believe me...

"Oh yes," he said aloud. "They'll believe me. This time they'll believe me." He looked through the open doorway to his right, and from where he was he could see a part of the double bed, which Marcy had made up before leaving for work that morning. Seated on the pillow, its back against the wall, was a stuffed elephant, gray except for overlay pads of red at the ears and feet. "Hey, Caldwell," Purcell called to the elephant. "Do you believe me? I'd offer you a Scotch, but you don't drink." Purcell went to the bedroom doorway and leaned in. "Did you hear what Mr. Aranow said when he was here, Caldwell? When he said I was left-handed? You didn't know that, did you, Caldwell? Mm-hmm. Left-handed. The left hand is the dreamer. Always remember that, my friend."

Then he blinked and saw Marcy standing there, framed in the hallway across the room.

"Good God, lady, you came in quiet," he said.

"No quieter than other times," she said. She came and kissed him on the forehead. "It's just that you and Caldwell were having such an intimate conversation." Then she kissed him on the mouth.

After a moment he broke away, sat down at the piano, and said, "Hey, turn your back for a minute."

"Surprise?"

"Do what I say."

Marcy Beall did not turn her back. Instead, she closed her eyes and turned her head, a singer's gesture with a swirl of her shoulder-length chestnut hair. Quickly, Purcell at the piano bench turned to the card table behind him and scrabbled among the papers there. Then he said, "Here. From me to you with love," and she took the legal-looking printed document from his thrusting hand and said, "What's—oh, Joe, it's the contract!"

"Took out the option this morning," he said happily, and his hands were back at the keyboard. "Congratulate me," he sang. "Step right up, shake my hand..."

And Marcy, singing too: "Your baby told you that she loves you..." And she clutched the contract, and for the quickest moment in time her gray eyes went black, as eyes of any color will do, given the moment. Psychiatrists—optometrists, for that matter—call that black the evidence summoned in the emergency of fright or flight, but Masters and Johnson had seen the same thing in the emergency of sex. It was enough, in any case, to make Purcell's hands stop on the keyboard, and when they stopped, she said to him: "Hello, Sam."

Responding, he played Dooley Wilson to her Ingrid Bergman. "Hello, Miss Ilsa. Ah never expected to see you again."

"It's been a long time," she said.

"Yes, ma'am," he said. "A lot o' water under the bridge."

"Some of the old songs, Sam."

But he shook his head, and suddenly his voice changed. Now it was comic German gutteral. "No!" he said. The music had stopped. "You vill be the vun who sings! Ve have enough of zese inti—inhi—"

"Inhibitions," Marcy said. "But, Professor—"

"Inhibitions!" he said. "Exactly! From now on, ve—"

"But I don't know what to do."

"You know exactly vat to do. It is the closing—zese garments you vear. From zese come your intibitions."

"Inhibitions."

"Ja, inhibitions. Vat the closing means is intibitions. I have told you before. Only ven the closing comes off vill the voice come out. Seventeen years at the Inshtitute in Shtuttgart I have taught zis vay und Professor Kohlmeier before me."

"But I don't understand—"

"Vich vord didn't you understand? Come now! Off with the closing!"

"Oh, don't make me, Professor. I'll die if you make me!" Her fingers went to the buttons. "But you are going to make me, aren't you? Then just this? Will just this be all right?"

"Not for your intibitions."

"I'll sing like a bluebird."

"Caldvell the elephant vill sing better. I tell you halfvay is nossing. I tell you all the closing—every stitch, und mach schnell. Und then, my little shtudent, ve vill sing."

"Ve?"

"Of course ve." Purcell pulled at his T-shirt.

"But who will play the piano?"

"I forgot to tell you. Today is *a capella*."

"Lying down on the rug?"

"I forgot also to tell you. Today is lying down on the rug."

Marcy giggled, and then he reached for her and pulled her down and she stopped laughing, until, at completion, fully underneath the piano, she laughed again, and he with her. But neither of them sought to move.

She propped herself on an elbow, her forefinger tracing the sharpness of his cheekbone and jaw, and said, "How long was the agent here?"

"For the contract? He wasn't here. I went to him. His office. This morning." He opened his eyes. "What made you think I'd have him here?"

"I just assumed."

"Why?"

"The two Scotch glasses on the piano. Both of them've been used."

"Ah," he said. "*J'accuse*. Inspector Beall of Interpol is here."

"Well, it is a little strange."

"Not strange at all. Max was here."

"Max?"

"Aranow. The A in A&P. I'm the P in A&P. My name's Purcell."

"No names, please," she murmured.

"Right," he said comfortably. "No personal checks cashed."

"But why would you have him here?"

"I didn't have him, as you put it. He just showed up. Uninvited and unannounced."

"Am I supposed to guess why?"

"You know why. That case I told you about. The tank car that blew up in Ohio."

"He wants you to take it." It was a statement, not a question.

"Boy, does he want me to take it."

"Did you tell him about the musical? *The Last Laugh?*"

"Told him more than that. Threw the male menopause shot at him, like twenty-two years of fighting his battles for him was enough."

"Well," Marcy said. "I hope you weren't nasty about it. They were your battles too."

"No," he said. "I wasn't nasty. Matter of fact, it was a love feast. But it always is with him and me."

She smiled. "Did Max understand?"

"I don't know."

"You don't sound very upset about it."

"What's to be upset, lady? If Max understood musicals, he would have handled that case in Los Angeles that time and you and I would never have met."

"I mean, did you tell him? Did you really tell him?"

For a moment Purcell looked up at the underbelly of the piano. "Let me put it to you this way. The minute he walked in here, I threw a copy of the book at him."

"Then what?"

"Then I poured him a drink"

"The whiskey was very handy, I'm sure."

"What's that supposed to mean? Of course it was handy. You think I spent the whole day underneath the piano balls-naked like now?"

"All right," she said again. "And then?"

He sighed. "Then I told him how much it cost to buy the option. And I told him this was my passport to freedom and a new life."

"And he still asked you to take the case?"

"Of course. That's what he was here for."

"And you told him—"

"I told him no. No way. *Nada.*"

"Does he understand how much time it takes to put a musical together? Everything that goes into it? How you have to go out and audition the show for backers so you can raise money?"

"I already told you, lady. Max doesn't understand the first thing about musicals."

"Oh," she said.

"Oh," he said.

"You don't have to mimic me."

"Well, you have a sound in your voice like I didn't do enough."

"Did you?"

"I did everything I could."

"But somehow it comes out that Max doesn't know that."

"He knows it. If anybody knows it, he does."

She shook her head. "That's not what I meant."

"Then what do you mean? Spit it out."

Again she shook her head, and moved out from under the piano, and stood up. "I've got to put something on," she said, and he watched her from the rear as she moved through the living room to the bedroom door.

"Tell Caldwell everything's all right," he said from underneath the piano.

"You tell him everything's all right," she said.

When she came back, wrapped in a white terry cloth robe, he was standing barefoot in his Levi's, pouring himself a Scotch. "Drink?" he said to her. "We'll need some more ice."

She was tying the matching cloth belt to the robe. "Did Max Aranow go out of here understanding there was no way you'd take this case?"

He saluted her with his glass, then sipped at it. "Why, no," he said. "I can't say I'm sure he did."

13

In the old red-to-white brick building across the street from the courthouse in Mundelein, a stairway with timid bannister led to the second floor, and to the office there of Leonard Gough, chiropractor, and Harry Wright, ATTORNEY AT LAW—so the gold-leaf lettering across the several windows, facing the street, proclaimed. Finally, more than a week after Jumbo Nellie Nellie blew, Wright made contact on the phone with Joe Purcell.

"I've got a total of six cases in the office so far," he told the New York lawyer. "Seven if you count Rosa Crewes."

"Who's Rosa Crewes?"

"Just a woman who lives in Florian. But her house burned down when the fireball hit."

"Dead?"

"*Dead?* No. Not dead."

"Burned?"

"No."

"Then what?"

"I don't know what. You'll have to see what for yourself when you come down. We've got dead people. We've got burned people. We've got paraplegics—well, no, wait a minute. I said that wrong. The right way to say it is we've got one quadriplegic, but we don't have him. Terry Malloy in Chicago has that case."

"Is he coming in with us?"

"I don't know. Really. I don't know."

"Well, get back to where you were," Purcell said. "What about this Rose—"

"Rosa."

"Whatever-her-name—"

"Rosa Crewes. I don't know how to classify her, Joe. She's an old friend, and she ties in with this case Malloy has, but I don't know how to classify her. You have to understand that funny things happened when the fireball went off. Oh. And I think we have pictures."

"You *think* you have pictures?"

"Yes."

"We've already seen pictures."

"These are motion pictures. Movies."

"Movies? Of what?"

"The fireball."

"Before it happened? During? After? What?"

"After. But immediately after. Some guy in his car had a movie camera and started shooting."

"What do they show?"

"I don't know. I haven't seen them yet. I think he tried to peddle them to the television networks, but he may have wanted too much money."

"And he wants to sell them to us?"

"Really. I'm not even sure of the law on it. Seems to me he can sell the commercial rights, but if it's used as evidence he has to give it over."

"Well, get to see what he's got. That's numero uno. If there's any value in the pictures, we know how to be friendly about it."

"All right," Harry Wright said. "But I'm wondering something else."

"What's that?"

"Which case do I file first? Or doesn't it make any difference?"

"Beats me," Purcell said. "That Olympic champion who was principal of the high school—"

"Whizzer Thoms."

"Yuh. The Whizzer. He sounds like your biggie. But this isn't a horse auction where you put the best one up first and it jacks up the price on all of the others. Come trial time, yes, but not now. You could file them all together. Or you could file one a day, the old Chinese water torture technique, and get more press coverage that way, maybe attract more cases."

"That's a thought."

"Maybe it is, maybe it isn't. The bottom line isn't which way you go, but how little difference it makes. Hell, you could start off filing one of those school bus cases."

"That's another thought," Wright said. "We do have the bus driver. She was killed. Young woman. And left four children."

"Were any of them on the bus?"

"No. They're too young."

"Four preschool children? When'd she get time to drive a bus?"

"They live with the grandparents—her parents—here in Mundelein," Wright said. "So it works out. As for the kids, they're two years apart— the oldest is five, and then there's the twins—they're three—and a one-year-old."

"Sounds good. Anything else?"

"You want the whole rundown?"

"Not really. What's the box score?"

"As of now," Harry Wright said, "twenty-four dead, maybe two more to come."

"Injured?"

"That's harder to tell. Somewhere in the sixties, I guess, but who knows?"

"Are they all worth processing, or are there some hangnails?"

"No hangnails. But your friend Cuneo was in Charleston and found four cases of people hurt when an airplane turned out of the way."

"You mean that's all he came up with?"

"Apparently, and he was here first. Really."

"I know it. Climbed the phone wires hand over hand trying to interest me."

"And every other lawyer he could think of, after you said no. I think he's sore, Joe."

"What lawyer did he finally get?"

"I don't know."

"I can see it now. Junior Bohr will go for one of those airplane cases as the specimen and I'll be in court arguing how somebody's false teeth flew out five miles over the explosion. We'll get Dr. Santoniowiscoatovich, credit dentist, walk up one flight and save, no appointment necessary, same-day service for out-of-town patients. He'll be our chief expert witness."

"That reminds me," Wright said. "How much do we pray for in damages?"

"For the false teeth? Twenty-six dollars and fifty cents. Plus ten million in punitives for the insult."

"No. I mean really."

"I wouldn't put a figure in the complaint," Purcell said.

"Well," Wright said, "we have to put down something."

"The hell you do. No law says that."

"But I've never filed a damage suit without citing a figure."

"You'll never be able to say that again, Harry," Joe Purcell said. "I honestly think on this one we're better off not specifying an amount."

"This whole business of a specimen case is new to me," Harry Wright said.

"Actually, it's fairly new in the law," Purcell said. "But when you have a lot of cases resulting from one disaster, like this one, you consolidate them for discovery and trial. The damages might be different for each case, but the liability's the same, and you can't try a hundred damage cases before the same jury. So the judge picks one, and that becomes the specimen. On liability and punitives, it controls all the others."

"I know," Wright said. "Sort of a class action."

"In the sense that they were all victims of the same disaster, yes," Purcell said. "If the specimen case loses on liability, then nobody gets anything. But if you win, odds are the other cases will settle without trial. Those that don't will have a short trial—anything from a few hours to a day or two, on damages only. But that's with a new jury each time, so no juror has to sit for months or years."

Wright nodded. "And the amount each case gets from the punitive damage total would be pro rata what they got in compensatories."

"You've got it," Purcell said.

"No, I had a general idea of the structure of it," Wright said. "It's just, like I said, that I'd never actually been involved in a case like this before. Meanwhile, you say we don't specify an actual amount in the complaint?"

"That's right. No amount. Okay?"

"If you say so. But what's your thinking? Really."

"My thinking is I can't think of a number. But if I could, I wouldn't use it. There's going to be lots of ink on this. The goddamn newspapers always put the prayer in the headline. Some asshole sues for three million, then fifteen months later he settles for fifteen hundred. It demeans the whole process, Harry. And makes us look like greedy bastards trying to profiteer on a tragedy."

"Then what do we pray for?" Wright said. "Reincarnation?"

"Not a bad idea in this case," Purcell said. "But no. Just pray for such damages as an impartial jury deems fair and—"

"Reasonable," Wright said.

"Not reasonable," Purcell said. "Make it fair and just. Reasonable sounds like cheap—Good Food, Reasonable Prices. 'Just' is better."

Wright said doubtfully, "You're sure that's the way it should be?"

"Yup," Purcell said. "Also, I want to see the look on Arthur Hawkes's face when he gets hit with eighty different claims in the same case and not one of them sets a price."

"Then you're serious."

"Damn right I'm serious. You can always amend a complaint, Harry."

"Does Max think that too?"

"Max bids no-trump. He's walking proof that the Jews didn't kill Christ: they worried him to death. That's the only reason I'm taking the case. He gave me those goddamn sheep eyes."

"Well, I'll file any way you want," Wright said.

"Good," Purcell said. "And the faster you file, the faster it'll be printed in the newspaper and the more cases you'll get. It's in for a penny, in for a pound on this one. I'm not going to lose this like I lost the last one. This one I want to lose big."

"I'll do what I can," Harry Wright said. "Oh, I started to tell you about Rosa Crewes."

"What about her?"

"There isn't a thing wrong with her. I mean not physically. She just isn't the same woman she was before the fireball happened. She acts strange. She talks strange."

"Oh, I like that one," Joe Purcell said. "The tank car blows and it drives people crazy. Throw in the false teeth from Charleston and it's the blue-plate special."

"But if she's crazy, she doesn't know it. And I don't think crazy's the word, Joe. Really. I think it's some kind of state of shock."

"That could be even better."

"Then what should I do?"

"Find a doctor."

"I don't think she trusts doctors."

"Then she must be sane."

"Well, all right," Harry Wright said. "I'll start drawing the complaints. Jenny sends her love."

"Give her a wet kiss for me," Joe Purcell said.

"When are you coming down?"

"I don't know. Next week, maybe."

"You've got to see Florian. The town. What it looks like."

"What are they going to do? Rebuild it before I get there?"

"I mean, get the feel of it."

"I guess," Purcell said. "By the way."

"What's that?"

"What are the people there doing these days for fuel?"

"I don't know," Wright said. "I hadn't even thought of that. I guess they must be getting it from somewhere."

"You might ask around," Purcell said.

"Really," Harry Wright said. And after he rang off he sat for a time with here's-the-church/here's-the-steeple hands held close to his face, then reached for his dictating machine to form the first complaint that would be filed:

```
IN THE COURT OF COMMON PLEAS FOR THE STATE OF OHIO
     IN AND FOR THE COUNTY OF MUNDELEIN
              C O M P L A I N T
        (Tort————Non—Motor Vehicle)
```

He looked at the notes he had taken before and during his phone talk with Joe Purcell. If he had never filed a complaint quite like this one, still the form itself was there, the comfort and security of ritual, and what he had feared as a challenging task became in fact a surprisingly simple exercise.

VINCENT J.BROPHY the surviving   )
spouse of JANET ELIZABETH BROPHY,   )
on his own behalf and for and on   )
behalf of ELLIOT R. BROPHY, LOUISA   )
D. BROPHY, KATHERINE G. BROPHY,   )
and DEXTER A. BROPHY, the surviving   )
children of JANET ELIZABETH BROPHY   )

                        Plaintiff,)

                vs.   )
MID—CENTRAL RAILROAD COMPANY, a   )
Missouri corporation; NORTH AMERICAN   )
PETROLEUM COMPANY, a Delaware   )
corporation; N. NANCE COMPANY,   )
an Ohio corporation; TRl—STATE GAS   )
COMPANY, a West Virginia corporation;   )
BLANK corporations I through XV and   )
DOES I through XV,   )
                        Defendants.)
_____)

        Plaintiff, for his cause of action against defendants
named above, complains and alleges as follows:

                    FIRST COUNT
            (MID—CENTRAL RAILROAD COMPANY)

                        I-1
        Plaintiff is, and at all times mentioned herein was,
a resident of Mundelein County, Ohio.

                        I-2
        On or about the date specified herein, at approxi—
mately 3:45 P.M. Eastern Daylight Time, JANET ELIZABETH
BROPHY expired as the direct and proximate result of
severe burns and injuries sustained in the explosion of a
liquefied petroleum (propane) railroad tank car in
Florian, Ohio, at approximately 2:45 P.M. on that same
date.
                        I-3
        Mid—Central Railroad Company is, and at all times
mentioned herein was, a Missouri Corporation, authorized
to do and doing business in the State of Ohio.

And on it went, for nine separate paragraphs: "the gross, willful, reckless
and wanton negligent acts of defendant...proximately caused by...
knowingly and willingly...foreseeable...agreed and conspired...all other

defendants named herein... death of JANET ELIZABETH BROPHY...
survivors permanently deprived of... love, affection, comfort, care, counsel, protection, advice, guidance, society, training, companionship... and
in the case of VINCENT J. BROPHY the consortium." Nothing was
omitted, not even the cost of funeral expenses, and it went on in the same
vein, with an additional nine-paragraph count for each named defendant,
with few and minor-seeming variations. There was the factor of interlock:
Nance had designed and built the Jumbo Nellie Nellie; North American
leased it and filled it with its explosive contents; Mid-Central hauled it.
The retail final distributor was involved, but even this early, Harry Wright
could sense that the big three were not only the only ones worth suing,
but the only ones with a true proprietary interest in the Jumbo Nellie
Nellie.

No question, the case had a strong sound to it. But all cases upon filing
have a strong sound to them, fortified by the printed accompanying
summons, as here reading:

```
TO THE ABOVE-NAMED DEFENDANTS:
You are hereby summoned and required to appear and
defend in the above action, in the above entitled
court, within TWENTY DAYS, exclusive of the day of
service, after service of this summons upon you, if
served within the State of Ohio, and within THIRTY
DAYS, exclusive of the day of service, if served
without the State of Ohio, and you are hereby
notified that in case you fail so to do, judgment by
default will be rendered against you for the relief
demanded in the complaint.
```

"... the relief demanded in the complaint." *What* relief? The thing ran to
nineteen pages, and nowhere anywhere did a dollar figure appear.

If Harry Wright was worried about money, it was on that account, in
and of itself, instead of any concern for himself. All cases of this kind were
on a contingent-fee basis: the personal-injury lawyer put out his own time
and the expenses of the litigation, and if he won he recovered for both.
If he lost, it was his loss, not the client's, where the outlay of time and
money was concerned. This was the American contingent-fee system—
a system under which the poorest farm worker or ghetto dweller could hire
the best lawyer in the country, not excluding a Joe Purcell.

Tell that to an Arthur Hawkes and he would gag over it. Yes, he would
concede, the contingent-fee system was the poor man's key to the court-

house—but only when the target was inviting enough to make it worth a Joe Purcell's while. Let an uninsured Mississippi sharecropper run over a pedestrian and try to get Purcell to take the case. Hit the same pedestrian with a car driven by a vice president of AT&T while on company business and Purcell would be the one helping the victim to his feet.

But no, a Hawkes would also concede, that was not fair. He had never known Joe Purcell to chase a case, and in fact the A&P, like other leading trial-lawyer firms, would use its very success against major defendants to afford to carry minor cases as well.

To a small-town practitioner like Harry Wright, it often seemed in truth that it was the Arthur Hawkeses, with their corporate clients, who concentrated most on the big cases—and who, as the system worked, got paid win or lose. But Wright's very state of remove from the big league left him somewhat innocent and occasionally confused. He knew, for example, that as a matter of standard application, the A&P took a maximum of one-third of the recovery in any case—but often, depending on the size of the case, considerably less. And A&P would share that fee with the Harry Wrights who referred cases to them but would exclude any such sharing with nonlawyers. In fine distinction this meant the A&P would have nothing to do with case-steerers such as Victor Cuneo of Miami. But what actual social harm, Wright wondered, does a Cuneo do in a case like the Fireball? Regardless of his sleazy motives, he is getting people to good lawyers and preventing insurance companies from stealing their claims for a fraction of what they are really worth. Be it that he was not a lawyer, still and all, what had he done in this case that was wrong?

But such musings were peripheral to the task at hand, and what bothered Harry Wright was something far more fundamental. His information about the Jumbo Nellie Nellie at Florian was far from complete, but he knew—he *knew*—the cause of the explosion. The cause of the explosion was lightning. A chance bolt of lightning no human hand had anything to do with bringing about. And no one, not even top dog Joe Purcell, was going to convince a jury otherwise. What indeed would a Purcell, a man of obvious reluctance and no illusion, even want or need with a case like this? "I have a feeling," Max Aranow had said. "He kept saying no, but..."

Now here sat Wright, with the first of the many suits he would be filing, one after another. The concluding language of the Brophy complaint set no price but asked for money five ways: general damages, funeral expenses, exemplary and punitive damages, costs incurred by the plaintiff in bringing the lawsuit, and:

5. For such other damages as the jury deems fair and just.

                    Respectfully submitted,

                    HARRY WRIGHT, ESQ.
                    420 Elm Street,
                    Mundelein, Ohio 45635

                    ARANOW & PURCELL
                    9 West 53 Street,
                    New York, New York 10019

Then Harry Wrightturned off the dictating machine and said aloud to himself: This is the craziest lawsuit I ever got involved in.

His mind said back to him: Also the biggest.

14

If Harry Wright did not know quite why Joe Purcell had decided to come aboard in the case of the Fireball, Purcell for his part did not always know quite what he was doing in the law at all. The son of a tobacco warehouse operator in Windsor, Connecticut, he was awarded a partial undergraduate scholarship to Yale, then a full-tuition loan to the law school there. Likely the loan had something to do with an undergraduate paper he had written in which, having fun, he compared musical annotation to printed legal forms, as for contracts and wills, and concluded there was absolutely no difference between an indifferent lawyer and a very bad composer. The notion amused Purcell's humanities professor, and at his suggestion, still having fun, Purcell took the law school aptitude test. He scored the second highest grade among all comers that year, and he entered the law school and—still not trying too hard—did brilliantly indeed. More than that, he enjoyed it. He made *Yale Law Journal*, was consistently in the top 10 percent of his class, and upon graduation he married Celia Landover and they moved to New York, where his record at Yale had gained him one of the most coveted and prestigious postgraduate positions: a year's tenure as clerk for a judge in the Federal Court of the Southern District of New York. Address: United States Court House, Foley Square, Manhattan. "There's only one test of a great lawyer," Joe said to Celia. "Sooner or later, he walks through the doors of that building."

"And you?" she said.

"I get to see them in action, Seal."

Purcell's initiation, his first day in the chambers of an owlish veteran of the bench named Hector Karras, came with the utterance by the judge of what by then had not yet become a known phrase in the language.

"Joseph," Judge Karras intoned. "What's a sonic boom?"

"A what, sir?"

"A sonic boom." With a hand whose third finger wore a University of Virginia class ring soldered closed by fat with the passage of the years, Judge Karras pushed two documents in the direction of Purcell across the desk.

"A sonic boom?" Joe said. "I don't know."

"Take these home with you," Karras said. "Read them. Then draft me an opinion."

Purcell drew the two sets of papers to his side of the judge's desk. He glanced at them only long enough to determine that the topmost of the two was a complaint, the other a brief in support of a motion to dismiss. He said, carefully, "Draft an opinion?"

"That's right. You know what drafting an opinion is, don't you?"

"It means you want me to say what I think."

"No. It means I want you to say what I think. It's part of your job."

"But I don't know what you think."

"Right," the judge said. "You don't. Gradually, you'll learn what I think. But I don't want to be the one to inhibit you. Take it home with you, read it over, and find your own reason."

"My own reason for what?"

"For dismissing the case. I don't want it."

Something told Purcell the subject was closed. He took the material home with him that night, to the walk-up studio apartment he and Celia had rented on West Ninth Street, and showed her his assignment.

"Well, do what he said," she advised.

"I intend to," Joe said. "There's only one thing that bothers me in the way this stuff is presented. The complaint here is not quite six pages long. The reply is two hundred and thirty-one pages."

"Did you bring that up with the judge?"

"I didn't bring anything up with the judge."

"Ah, Joe," she said. "You could have asked."

"Maybe. Something told me better not. Besides, there's one easy theory that might account for it."

"What's that?"

"The complaint was filed by a private attorney," he said, and flipped to the last page. "Guy named Max Aranow. The reply—" he hefted it with both hands " —is from the government and whoever invented the word 'brief' never heard of this government. They're all make-work lawyers: It's part of the rigid art form. Never use one word when you can use twenty."

"Well," Celia said, "maybe that's why your judge doesn't want to have the case tried. He doesn't want to be bored to death."

"He could have worse excuses," Purcell said. "Don't forget he's appointed, not elected. He doesn't have to answer to anybody. He's not about to crowd up his calendar if he doesn't feel like it." He lifted his mouth to hers as she came around behind him, back of the chair where he was seated at the kitchen table, and placed one of his hands against the straw-colored strands of her hair that stood against his face like a display-window waterfall. She was small of build, with ballerina calves; his other hand moved down and back to one of them, then slowly upward, and his fingers tapped a blues beat against her thigh. Then the kiss ended, and he said, "By the way."

"Mmmm?"

"Do you know what a sonic boom is?"

There was no rush on it, he knew, but later that night he left the bed of his soundly sleeping satisfied young bride and read until four o'clock, first the Max Aranow complaint, then the government motion. It was a wrongful-death action against the United States Air Force and the Department of Defense, brought by the respective parents of two nine-year-old boys buried and suffocated by a landslide as they played in a pile of dirt fill at a construction project near their homes on Staten Island. The cave-in had occurred shortly after five o'clock in the afternoon—past quitting time for the workmen—and so there were no witnesses, and the bodies were not unearthed till early the following morning, the consequence of a police search generated by the panic-stricken parents of the missing boys.

One detail, quite lost in the mundane recitation of the facts of the case the first time you read it, was Aranow's specification that the cave-in occurred "at or about 5:19 p.m." If nobody had witnessed it, how did he know what time it happened?

A second read-through made the connection. Beginning at 5:20, and continuing for the next four or five minutes, Staten Island police had logged a series of phone queries about a claplike noise and the rattling of windows and crockery.

The crux of the Aranow complaint was that these things, and the fatal cave-in too, were the product of a sonic boom caused by the presence of a military plane breaking the sound barrier as it flew at some then-unimagined height of 50,000 feet or more over the area. It had to be that high at least, for while it was a clear day, the fact was nobody had reported seeing a plane in the sky.

And that was the fact that led off the government's reply, moving for dismissal of the case. As he went through the government brief, Purcell could reduce its components to four assertions.

The first of these was that there was no supersonic plane over that area at that time on that day.

In almost amusing haste came the second point: If there was a supersonic jet, it wasn't American.

The third and fourth points took up by far the most space in the government's bulky brief. Deep with citations and cross-references, point three sought to prove that this kind of sonic activity could not cause that kind of damage; the fourth and final point, equally heavy in annotated precedent, urged that the government could not be held liable for damages in any event for the actions of the military.

The impact of the defense presentation was overwhelming. One section of it alone—the question of whether a sonic boom could cause a cave-in — quoted scientific authorities in such a plethora of detail that the sheer weight of their opinion had to obliterate the plaintiff's case in and of itself.

And the citations as to government immunity were no less impressive. There was case law, for example, in three separate instances—one in California, one in Texas, one in Maine —and all of them in peacetime— where residents of private property close to air force bases had brought damage suits against the government because of the noise factor. All three suits were dismissed, and the dismissals affirmed on appeal.

The next morning, Purcell found himself yawning in the presence of the judge.

His Honor said, "Do I bore you?"

"No, sir."

"You were up late?"

"Yes, sir."

"How long have you been married?"

"Three months."

"Great God in the morning," Hector Karras said. "I've forgotten how it is."

"No," Purcell said. "I was reading about your sonic boom."

"Ah. And what'd you find out?"

"Why you don't want to try it."

"Good. Now the next thing to do is draft an opinion for me. Research it first."

"I won't have to go to the library," Purcell said.

"Why not?"

"Because there's nothing there."

The Karras owl eyes blinked twice. "How do you know that?"

"If there was anything there, one side or the other would have said what it was. There can't be any case law on sonic booms. This has to be the first one."

"Ah. So if I take it on, I'll be setting precedent."

"Yes."

"Do you think I'm in business to set precedent?"

"No."

"The entire structure of the law rests on what's gone before. You understand that, don't you?"

"Yes, I do," Joe said. "That's what makes sense about your not wanting to try this one."

"That, plus it seems pretty cut-and-dried," Judge Karras said. "The outcome, I mean. I don't know if you know this Max Aranow."

"No. I don't know him."

"Well, he's a good one," Karras said. "A crackerjack. But now and again he gets carried away a little. And he hangs on like a rat-catcher. That's why I need an opinion with some clout to it. Think you can deliver?"

"No, sir."

"What was that?"

Purcell put a thumb and forefinger to the lobe of his right ear and began to rub. "I said no, sir. I don't think I can deliver."

"Well why for Christ's sake not? You don't think Aranow's got a case, do you?"

"No," Joe said. "As a matter of fact, I don't. But you were talking about not wanting to set precedent, and if you dismiss this thing, I've got a feeling you'll be setting more of a precedent that way than by going ahead and letting him have his day in court."

"That's interesting theory, counselor. Stretch it out a little and you could say it about any case. We'd never have a dismissal. If there's no case here, as you say, why bring it to trial? Any reason, other than that precedent business? —which, incidentally, I'm not sure I buy."

"Well," Purcell said, "a couple of things. If it's a trial you're concerned about, I'm morally certain it won't come to trial."

"Why not? If the defense is that sure of winning."

"The air force," Joe said, "is going to have to permit the discovery process, and I don't think they want that. They filed more than two hundred pages in opposition, but in all that space, it's remarkable what they *didn't* say—what maybe they *couldn't* say—like, about the capability and range and points of origin of our military flights."

"I told you I didn't want this case."

"I know you don't want the case, but you do want an opinion, and I don't know how to give you one. If you deny the government's motion, you won't need an opinion. All you have to do is deny it. And I've got a hunch the government will settle."

"How nice for me," Hector Karras said. "And thank you, Joseph, for telling me how to go about my trade here."

Purcell put up a hand. "The point is, it had to cost the government more money to prepare that brief than it would to try the case." He drew a breath. "*Why?*"

Judge Karras looked at him. At length, he said, "I'm not sure I know why. It could be that the further you go into this, the more you encounter top-secret stuff that can't be talked about in open court. So they went all out to head that off at the very beginning."

"Yes, sir," Joe said.

Karras sat back in his leather pivot wing chair. "All right, Yale. You've got all the answers. Suppose you tell *me* what else."

"Well, it's only a guess," Joe Purcell said. "But I think they're going all out for this dismissal because they've got their eye not on this accident but the next one and the one after that. And it may be more than just the military. This jet stuff is fairly new. But it's only a matter of time before some passenger jet can break the sound barrier, so maybe private industry helped pick up the tab here to get some judge to knock it out from the word go." He breathed deeply again. "And if it turned out this Max Aranow had something here, it might not hurt you this time, but what would you look like if it turned out they started flying those real big things and really shaking things up on the ground?"

Karras put a hand to his eyes. "When I first met you—the interview we had—didn't you tell me you played the piano?"

"Yes, sir."

"Well, I just hope you play the piano well, that's all, because I'm going to do what you advise and refuse to dismiss this case. But if it actually comes to trial in my courtroom you're going to find yourself playing the piano for a living somewhere in Panama. I kid you not, Joseph. I kid you not." He saw Purcell smiling and said, "What are you laughing at?"

"I'm damned if I know," Joe Purcell said.

But he knew. Three months later there was a phone call for him, and when he took it the voice on the other end said, "This is Max Aranow. You don't know me, but I want to know if you're free for lunch tomorrow."

"I know of you by name," Purcell said carefully.

"I know," Aranow said. "You put a case of mine up on the board."

"That was Judge Karras' decision, not mine."

"In that case, you'd better be free for lunch tomorrow."

"I don't know what that means."

"I'll tell you at lunch. Can you make it?"

"If it's close to here."

"It's close to there. Arnold's. John Street."

Purcell found Aranow already at the table the following day. "I already ordered my drink," Max said. "Scotch and soda. Walker Red Label."

"I'd like that too."

"Like it because of you or like it because of me?"

"I could order a martini instead," Joe said, "but they make me sleepy."

"One martini makes you sleepy?"

"You said one. I said they."

"You want a double Scotch?"

"No, sir. I can space them out. While we talk."

"Talk about what?"

"Whatever it is you want to talk about."

"I was thinking just the other day," Max said. "We have no canned foods in our house. No frozen foods. With one exception: the tinned King Oscar sardines from Norway. And only one other import, and that's the Johnny Walker Red Label. We'll take certain packaged products, yes: salt and baking powder and flour. And of course the condiments. Tabasco sauce. But that's an American product, not an import. Ranks with the Underwood office standard typewriter and the DC-3 airplane. Nobody anywhere else in the world would even pretend to try to duplicate them, they're so good."

The waiter came, and Max said to him, "He wants the same thing you brought me."

"Red Label and soda," the waiter said. "Yes, Mr. Aranow."

Purcell said, "You come here often?"

"Often enough," Max said. "Are you going to want the porterhouse steak?"

"Yes. I think I'd like that."

"Once every year," Aranow said, "I get a shipment of porterhouse steaks. Not here in New York: it comes to the other house I have in Ambler. Pennsylvania. You know where that is?"

"No."

"Outside of Philadelphia. Not Bucks County; the next county down. But a nice place to be. The one rap against the porterhouse is that it's a juicy steak."

"Why's that a rap?"

"Because doctors say juicy steaks are bad for you. And doctors, incidentally, are crazy. They talk about this cholesterol that's supposed to be bad for you. Heart. But we've got some Amish in our county—the Pennsylvania Dutch—and I tell you, Joe, they eat butter and cheese and pork and lard like they're going out of style. And as a recognized class of people they have no heart disease. Absolutely none."

Purcell felt a swelling of warmth in his throat. Max Aranow had called him Joe. Called on to say something, he said, "You get a shipment of porterhouse steaks once a year?"

Aranow nodded. "It's part of my pay."

"Your pay for what?"

"For defending a man in a rape case. Successfully, I might add."

"You take your pay in steaks."

"I didn't have much choice in this case. It was Jag."

"Jag?"

"Judge Advocate General. JAG. The war. I don't know about you, but I'm having the herring first. They have the same recipe for it here that they have at Longchamps and Camillo's and McCarthy's. You ever been to McCarthy's? You can only get the herring there at dinner, not lunch. The outside is a showcase where they hang their meat to age it. Second Avenue and Forty-fifth. Southwest corner. You know the place."

"I don't know," Joe Purcell said. "I might have the littleneck clams on the half shell."

"Can't go wrong with them, either," Aranow said. "My wife, Sophie, makes herring. When you come to Ambler you'll taste a real herring." He signaled the waiter, this time to order. "Actually, Camillo's and McCarthy's are very close together. Lawton Carver and Mike Manuche run Camillo's. Carver's been the sports editor at the INS. There's some talk he may sell out his interest to Mike and maybe open his own place. It's a Texas deal. You know what a Texas deal is?"

"No."

"An interesting arrangement," Aranow said. "For when you split up a partnership. One partner specifies the price. The other partner has the option of selling or buying at that price."

"Fine," Purcell said. "You set the price, I'll sell."

Joe saw Max smile for the first time and he returned the smile, grateful that the older man had not been offended by his flip remark. Max drained his glass and chomped on a piece of ice.

"I've been a loner up till now," he said. "And it's had its advantages. But the load seems to keep getting heavier, and I'm starting to say no to cases that come in, just because there aren't the hours in the day to handle them. And if I get sick, everything stops."

"Let me get this straight," Purcell said. "With what you're saying, and that reference to when I come to Ambling—"

"Ambler."

"Ambler. Where you've got this house. You're not only telling me you want an associate, but you're asking me to be it." The waiter had set the clams in front of him without Purcell's noticing. "Why me? You don't know a thing about me."

"I know a great deal about you. Plus what I've learned in the last fifteen minutes, sitting here."

"Today? Here? *You've* learned something about *me?*"

"Sure. Now let me tell you something about myself."

"Oh," Purcell said. "All right."

"See this gray hair?" Aranow said. "See this face? What do you think?"

"You look like you refereed one too many Zale-Graziano fights," Joe said.

"I know," Max said. "It's just what I said: this is a nice piece of herring. You want a taste?"

"No. Want a clam?"

"No. The thing is, you see, I'm forty-two years old. But I started to reminisce at the age of five. O'Henry had a character: Caligula Polk was his name, and O'Henry called him a spokesman by birth. I guess that's me. I'm a people lawyer."

"A people lawyer," Purcell said. "I kind of like that."

"It hasn't even scratched the surface yet," Aranow said. "You know, I worked for the Truman committee."

"You did? During the war? I thought you were in the JAG."

"Not *that* Truman committee," Max said. "That was the famous one. No, actually this was before the war, and the chairman wasn't Truman, it was Senator Wheeler. Harry Truman was vice chairman. But Wheeler was never there. He was going around the country making isolationist speeches, so for all intents and purposes Truman ran the show, and he was the one who hired me as a summer intern, and for that matter it wasn't a committee, it was a subcommittee. And what it did was to look into railroad finances, and it came out writing the Transportation Act of 1940, and you never in your wildest moments dreamed that such pressures against you could exist. The problem was very simple. The presidents and vice presidents and chairmen of the boards of the railroads were stealing their own companies blind. I remember one point where Truman told me he never could feel comfortable around men who thought of money first, whose *business* was money." Aranow mopped the residual cream in his plate with dark bread. "But he also told me about Grover Cleveland: how Cleveland was a great president his first term and a lousy president his second. Because in the four years in between he'd worked for the Prudential Life Insurance Company, I think it was, and then as now the insurance companies were big-money people, as he put it, and that corrupted Cleveland. Just plain corrupted him."

Purcell said, "But—" Aranow put up a palm. "The insurance companies, more than anybody else in history, developed the art of spreading the risk; made a science out of it. And that's the basis of people law, Joe. When I say spread the risk, what do I mean? I mean you minimize the effect on any one person of having to pay damages. Something goes wrong with your Chevrolet. The mechanic who last fixed it had an obligation to fix it right. The dealer who sold it can have his obligation. But you have to *pressure* an obligation on the part of General Motors. Maybe the facts won't warrant it. But you have to be thinking that way going in. Because a civil lawsuit is a suit for damages, and the big guy doesn't feel it as much as the little guy. You hit a little guy with a ten-thousand-dollar judgment and you can bankrupt him. Hit GM with it, and that's tipping money for the vice president of the brake division. He pays more than that in country club dues and writes it off his taxes as a business deduction. You see what I'm saying?"

"I think so," Purcell said. "You're saying soak the rich. Only maybe you wouldn't put it that way. You have the more elevated approach."

The waiter brought the steaks. "Who has the more elevated approach?" Max said. "Me? Soak the rich is exactly what I'm saying." He smiled up at the waiter.

"Steak sauce, Mr. Aranow?" the waiter said.

"No way," Aranow said. "But a slice of raw onion might be nice. Joe?"

"I'm fine," Purcell said.

"You don't want steak sauce? Worcestershire? Ketchup?"

Purcell shook his head. "No. This looks fine, just the way it is."

"That settles it," Max Aranow said.

"Settles what?"

"I've been asking you if you want to come in with me. There are two hundred lawyers I could have asked, and you've never even tried a case. But you find a lawyer who wants to screw up a good piece of beefsteak with Heinz 57 and I'll show you a lawyer who'll get an overtime parking violation reduced to manslaughter. Come down to Ambler for the weekend. Bring your wife. Take off early Friday."

Joe Purcell said, "I don't believe this."

"I told you it was a good steak."

"That's not what I don't believe. There has to be something else. Why me?"

"Of course there is. When I called you up yesterday you lied to me over the phone. And I told you so."

"I was going to ask about that. What lie?"

"The sonic boom case."

"My God, I meant to ask about that," Purcell said. "How did it come out?"

"Oh, they settled. With the speed of light. Not the greatest price in history, but not the worst one either. What they couldn't stand was when I told them I was going after their secrets."

"Their secrets?"

His mouth filled with steak, Aranow nodded. "I had the discovery apparatus," he said, chewing. "I could go to an air base in Brussels and say give me the log of your flights that day. Because they've got the technology, and it's nothing for a plane from Brussels to wind up over Staten Island. And the base commander would say, No, we didn't send that plane up, but the United States has an air base in England, just outside of Bath, and I know the commander there and he's a shmuck. Ask *him* what he did with *his* planes that day. And the more you got into it, the funnier it would get, because you weren't just prying into classified military material —you were hitting these guys the way they love to be hit. The minute you tell a military man it's his legal duty to answer a question, it's Open Sesame for him to take a clout at some other military man he's hated for the last ten years. So the shmuck in Bath was going to tell me about the shmuck in Paris, and he'd tell me about a bigger shmuck in Verona, and the bigger shmuck in Verona would tell me about an even bigger shmuck in Copenhagen. And how do I wind up? I wind up as the one man in the world who knows the entire operation of the United States Air Force all over the globe that day. I know more than Kennedy knows."

Purcell laughed. "And spend what to find it out?"

"That's another reason why I want you to work with me, Joe. Because you'll see through it and ask a question like that." Aranow was still chewing. He gestured with his fork. "You cut it up and get to the bottom of it. I like that."

"And?"

"And what?"

"I asked how much it cost you. You said you liked that."

"I do. Oh, I see. You expect an answer. Well, nothing wrong with that, either."

"Wait a minute," Purcell said. "I'm not sitting here making demands on you."

"I know you're not. You haven't even said what you thought of the partnership idea."

"Partnership?" Joe said. "You really mean a partnership?"

"Not fifty-fifty, but fair. You'll earn your take. Do you like it?"

"Yes, sir. I do."

"Good. We'll talk the details out when you get to Ambler. And just to complete this, for your information, it didn't cost me one red cent."

"You investigated the entire air force and it didn't cost you one red cent?"

"Of course not. You're the one who pointed that out to the judge. Very clever of you. It was the government that spent money on this case, not me." Aranow, Purcell noticed, was a man who could cut meat without looking. "That was the basic lie you told on the phone."

"I didn't say anything like that on the phone."

"No, the judge told me. What you said over the phone was that the decision to deny their motion to dismiss was his, not yours, and that was the lie. A flat outright lie. The thing Karras wanted most in this world was to get rid of that case. You're his clerk, so you were loyal to him, and you said it was his decision. But it wasn't his, it was yours. So I found I admired you on two different levels. First for the loyalty, and I don't dismiss that as a commodity. But far more than that for seeing why this case deserved to go forward, with not a shred of precedent to go on. I went to the judge afterward and I said, I want your guy."

"What did he say?"

"He said for Christ's sake take him. What'd you think he was going to say?"

"And that was it?"

"That was it. Except I had to talk to you and see your reaction."

"My reaction's yes," Joe Purcell said.

"Aranow and Purcell?"

"Aranow and Purcell. Except, I have to tell you something."

"What?"

"I have other reactions. Like, I'm leaving something out."

"Leaving what out? Ask away. Unless it can wait till Ambler."

"It can wait till Ambler. It can wait forever. I have a feeling it *will* wait forever. You go past a point so fast, I find I want to ask a question about it, and by the time I get to it I forget what the question was."

"Good," Aranow said. "Learn it."

"Learn it?"

"You're going to be trying cases," Max Aranow said. "*Learn* to go by things fast enough so the other side doesn't ever get around to asking you about them."

"But what if *I'm* the other side? Do I let them do that to me?"

"You don't sound like it, no. Any more questions?"

"Yes," Purcell said.

"Fire away."

"I can't think of what they are."

"Well," Max Aranow said, "no harm done. After all. All we're doing is having lunch."

When Purcell got back to the Federal Building that day, Judge Karras said to him, "Did you make a deal?"

"Yes, sir. I'm going to be Max Aranow's partner. I gather you knew about it."

"Knew about it? I pushed the hell out of it. Though Max was the one who brought it up to begin with."

"You never said anything about it to me."

"I wanted to see how you got along when you met him in person. You like him?"

"Very much."

"And he likes you. By the authority vested in me by Moses and the state of New York, I pronounce you man and wife. And it's understood between you and Max that you finish out your one-year term with me?"

"Oh, yes. Has to be that way. I've got to take the bar exam first."

Judge Karras smiled. "Well, that makes it very neat, doesn't it?"

"Neat?"

"You've contracted with Aranow, but in the meantime you stay on as my clerk."

"Yes, sir," Purcell said. "But why neat?"

"Because," the judge said, "that means that for the remainder of this term I can recuse myself on every case that madman brings in here and use you for my excuse."

15

The great stone edifice, granite in a changing, face-lifting age, still stood within the financial gut of LaSalle Street in downtown Chicago. Once, from barely a block away, the Twentieth Century Limited and the Pacemaker and the Commodore Vanderbilt would pull steaming into the LaSalle Street station, completing the overnight journey from New York. And the trains of the Rock Island would come there too. And to other stations would come all the great passenger streamliners of the Illinois Central and the Burlington, and the Chief and the Super-Chief of the Santa Fe, and the Challengers and the City of San Francisco and the City of Los Angeles, and the Hiawathas from Minneapolis and Milwaukee, and that beautiful, beautiful train with the beautiful name—the Ann Rutledge. Pistons surging, they drove into that great heartland city. Yet they were only the trappings. What always counted more than passengers was freight. And in the switching yards where the freight cars were interchanged, one railroad to another, in numbers almost beyond counting, there were in any given single year, more than a million movements of petroleum tank cars alone.

So now if the passenger trains were no more, the freight trains still spelled the character of the town as they always had. And so in their turn did the old granite buildings. And to this old building, in May less than two weeks after Jumbo Nellie Nellie exploded at Florian, Ohio, there came three of the grittiest defense-law dinosaurs in the business. They came there at the invitation of Arthur Hawkes, whose offices were on the fifth floor of the building, except that they did not come there at his invitation, because "invitation" was not the word for it. Fun and games and all proprieties observed and then set to one side, they arrived not at Hawkes's invitation but at his summons. And they knew that. And he knew that.

He observed them sourly, assembled as they were around the meticulously antiqued walnut table in the conference room of Hawkes's office.

There was Herman Metcalfe, a dumpy Presbyterian of the type that seldom screwed for pleasure. Metcalfe had big tickets, there was no doubt of that. He was the house counsel for Trans-Continental Insurance. Law school: Boalt Hall, the University of California. But Hawkes could not hold that against him. Trans-Continental was the largest single insurance amalgamation in the western hemisphere, and among those it insured was the N. Nance Company, which had built the Jumbo Nellie Nellie.

Nance was a very large company. No question of that. But the other two men at the table facing Hawkes represented even larger companies — so large, in fact, that they didn't even buy insurance. Instead, they were big enough to insure themselves: the Mid-Central Railroad, represented here today by Ed Jamieson (Northwestern Law School—Hawkes could forgive that too), and North American Petroleum (Fordham Law—that, Hawkes would neither forgive nor forget). The NAP's lawyer was Tim Daly. The surname, Hawkes could accept, but to his codified thinking, the Tim was a bus driver's name.

It was to these irritations, big and small, that he addressed himself now—these and others. Among other things, the men seated before him, while experienced, even facile, in their offices and boardrooms, not only lacked even basic fundamentals in the courtroom; worse than that, they *whined* about it.

"Arthur," said Metcalfe of Trans-Continental, "they've filed the first complaint in this Fireball case and they don't even say what damages they're seeking. I never heard of anything like that."

Jamieson of Mid-Central: "What Herman means, Arthur, is that there's no money figure."

"I know what Herman means," Hawkes said. "The Ohio rules of procedure do not require specificity in the prayer for damages."

Daly of North American Petroleum: "Well, I've been around a long time and I never before saw a case where they didn't ask for a specific amount. Usually about forty times what they expect to get."

Everyone chuckled except Hawkes. He said simply, "Have any of you ever defended a case in a courtroom against Joe Purcell?"

"That isn't the point, Arthur," Jamieson said. "We're here today for one obvious reason: if none of us have defended a case against Purcell, maybe we won't have to defend this one either. Some interrogatories and requests for admission and we set them up for summary judgment."

"Save your breath," Hawkes said. "You're not going to win any motion for summary judgment."

"But they haven't got the slightest nuance of a theory against any of us."

Hawkes sighed. Each successive statement from these clowns served only to underscore further their ignorance of what went on in real life in cases like this. "What's established," Hawkes said, "is that a tank car blew up, and one of you built it and one of you filled it and one of you delivered it. I have to think maybe there might be just a nuance there."

Metcalfe said, "But it was *lightning*, Arthur."

"I think so. We're still waiting for the Labor Department on that."

"Who?"

"The Labor Department. OSHA. Remember?" Hawkes smiled. "You three play chess, don't you? Take a look at that board over there." He nodded toward a sideboard, with a chess set sitting atop. The men on the board were few—four white pieces and two white pawns, plus only the black king—and in the following arrangement:

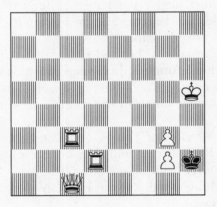

Hawkes stood up and fetched the chessboard to the conference table. "The problem is for White to move and mate in two. Anybody here see how?"

The three visiting necks craned down at the board. Here and again a hand moved out, moved a piece, then moved it back.

"You've always been a chess master, Arthur," Tim Daly said. "I've never beaten you."

"Ah," said Hawkes. "I'm delighted to hear that makes me a master."

"It's a fascinating problem, Arthur," Ed Jamieson said. "I wish we had the time to do it justice."

"How much time do you need?" Hawkes said. The phone on the sideboard buzzed, and he went to answer it. When he hung up, he turned to the others and said, "All right. I've got a call inside. Might take me fifteen, maybe twenty minutes. You wanted time? You've got time. Play with it."

And he left the room. Twenty-one minutes later he was back. He said, "Any of you get it?"

Herman Metcalfe shook his head. "Not yet," he said. "It's a fascinating problem, Arthur. Just beautiful. I can't remember seeing one like it."

"A fascinating problem," Hawkes repeated. "Everybody says that. Okay." He nodded and sat down. "And none of you solved it." He moved the white rook on bishop 3 to bishop 8. "Now all Black can do is have his king capture the pawn," he said. Then he moved the white queen to bishop 7. "And checkmate."

"Oh, my God, that's unbelievable," Metcalfe said.

"It's superb, Arthur," Daly said.

Jamieson nodded enthusiastically. "I've got to copy this down. It's the prettiest chess problem I've ever seen in my life. Almost worth the total cost of making the trip."

Arthur Hawkes said, "Almost?"

"Well," Jamieson said, "we were here to see how we were going to answer this first complaint —the one with this woman who was killed in the fireball and left the family behind—the husband and the four kids. And it's cute, the way they led off with this one ahead of all the others."

"Is it?" Hawkes said.

"I mean," Jamieson said, "that's what we were going to deal with, one way or another."

"Who told you that?"

"You did."

"I did?" Hawkes said. "When I summoned you here, I—"

"*Summoned*, Arthur?" Herman Metcalfe said. "*Summoned?* I thought I was invited, not summoned."

"Whichever you prefer," Hawkes said. "The point was to get the three of you here together in person, so that there could never be any doubt about one thing. That phone call I just took in the other room: it was a call I'd placed earlier to Washington. It looks like OSHA is going to be coming down on the side of lightning."

Jamieson said, "That should cinch it for us."

"Against some lawyers, maybe. Purcell isn't some lawyers. But the point is, I have to try the case my way."

Daly said, "Well, we know that, Arthur. We've always known that. Why do you think we want you on the big ones?"

"Sometimes," Hawkes said, "the big ones are the ones you don't have to try. Time and again on other cases, I've asked your people for settlement authority, and instead I get nickel-and-dimed."

"You complained about not having settlement authority in the Marlowe case," Metcalfe said. "We went to a certain figure and then we said try it. So you tried it. And you won it. And it was in Mundelein, Ohio. And it was against Joe Purcell."

Daly of NAP was staring out the window. Even from the fifth floor, one view carried unobstructed: northward, beyond the Loop, to the tracks of a freight-marshaling yard. And he could see, gleaming white in the sunlight, a jumbo tank car being pushed to coupling with another of the same. Easy, his mind told him. Easy, damn it!

Aloud, he said, "I met Purcell once. It was at a bar convention in Montreal, a couple of years back, and we got introduced, but it was only for a minute, because I was on my way into a seminar."

"You don't have to tell us you attend seminars," Jamieson said, winking at Metcalfe. "Every lawyer who goes to a convention does nothing but attend seminars. We all know that."

"Purcell didn't attend this one," Daly said. "He asked me what it was about, and I said constitutional law: the mechanics of getting an anti-abortion amendment into the Constitution. I'm very interested in the pro-life movement."

"Did you tell Purcell that?" Hawkes said.

"Matter of fact, I did," Daly said.

"What'd he say?"

"It was strange," Daly said. "He asked me if a fetus was a living person, and I said of course. Then he asked me if my family travel insurance policy paid off twice if a pregnant woman was killed in an air crash. Or three times if it was twins." Momentarily, he shivered. "I can see what you mean, Arthur, about not wanting to try a case against him."

"It goes one step further this time," Hawkes said. "This time, what I must insist on is that I want no interference. More importantly, I want no help. None of you will be sitting next to me. None of you will even be in the courtroom."

"Well, now, hold on, Arthur," Daly said. "We have our clients to represent and we can give you valuable input."

"Can you?" Hawkes gestured toward the chessboard. "There are three of you, and there are three key pieces on that board, and you had to move one of them or else it was stalemate. The solution is a part of what they call the Bristol Theme. I've used it before, in trying cases. None of you see what it is. If you'd seen it, you would have solved the problem while I was out of the room."

Ed Jamieson: "That's a little esoteric, Arthur."

"Is it? If I'm representing three defendants, then let me put it to you that they're accused of murdering a man and his wife and their dog. And I just might demonstrate the innocence of all three by proving that the dog is still alive."

"I think I understand this," Tim Daly said.

"Good," Hawkes said. "Call it the Bristol Theme."

"The Bristol Theme," Daly said. "That was just Arthur's way. To let us know that if you leave him alone he usually comes out all right." He looked around at the others. "I mean, when you come right down to it, if lightning caused the fire, then no one here's to blame. And Arthur here will tell us that's right. Right, Arthur?"

Hawkes smiled bleakly. "Right," he said. "The Labor Department finding, on lightning, hasn't come in yet. When it does, we'll all sit back and laugh. But Joe Purcell's going to be someplace on a tennis court in Westport, Connecticut, and when that news comes in to him, I'll tell you what I think: I think Joe Purcell's going to laugh too."

16

Another conference room, another meeting, the same number of actors: four. They were the miniki—Sheila O'Hara, Willie Blake, and Bert Klein—plus Felix Harding, a patent-leather man in his fifties who had been Max Aranow's bookmaker and now served as chief investigator for the firm. The room they occupied at this moment was just as tasteful as, but if possible even fancier than, Arthur Hawkes's conference room in Chicago. The walls were paneled in Kentucky walnut, brightened by the paintings of native Americans—Fay Zetlin, Sam Richards, Fletcher Martin, two Jamie Wyeths, a Bert Pumphrey. And it was a more private room than Hawkes had, for it was not reachable from the outer hall.

The A&P in fact occupied the entire fourteenth floor of that building, an L-shaped structure whose short end fronted on West 53rd Street just off Fifth, the long base of the L on 54th. The address was a 53rd Street address, but the lobby ran the length of the north-south block, and one might for convenience enter or leave as easily on 54th instead.

Again in the lobby, the building directory listed Aranow and Purcell, but that was all it listed for the firm. No individual names appeared. And on the fourteenth floor itself, again there were no names. One simply moved out of the elevator into a carpeted reception area with informally spaced armchairs and adjacent oaken end tables whose rack space held that day's *New York Times* and *Christian Science Monitor.*

"Why do we get the *Monitor?*" Aranow asked Purcell one day.

"I'm a son of a bitch if I know," Joe said. "First day I ever came to work for you it was already there."

"Well, who keeps renewing it?"

"Whoever ordered it in the first place, I guess. And the only one who was here in the first place was you."

"What you're saying is, I keep renewing it."

"I don't know if you do or don't. I know I don't."

"Then let me tell you something: I don't either."

"Maybe it just comes."

"Nothing just comes."

"Then call up J. Edgar Hoover and put him on the case, Max. One way or another, we'll find out."

Aranow shook his head worriedly. "I mean, who reads it?"

"I don't know. What are you after here? You want *Field and Stream?*"

"Those are gun lovers," Aranow said. "I won't have a gun lover for a client."

"I'm sorry I asked," Purcell said.

But there was a reason for the elegance, and each trapping of it, in the reception area of the A&P: a reason an Arthur Hawkes required not at all. For Hawkes's clients were by definition the very rich and the privileged elite, while the A&P could serve anybody. The essence of the imperious barrister, Hawkes could and did kick clients and fellow attorneys around, hectored them, insulted them, staged his sessions with them with an eye for what demeaned, an air of arrogance that would preset a chess problem none of them would solve. "Judge Landis was the same way," Max Aranow told Purcell one time, when they were discussing Hawkes.

"Who was Judge Landis?"

"The first commissioner of baseball. He had one ballplayer in there in front of him one day and he opened the window and told him to jump out and the poor guy almost did. Of course, in Landis's case he used it for protective coloration. He had the face and the bearing and the sense of the dramatic that went with his job, but the truth is he'd been a lousy judge. His law wasn't that good. Had one of the worst reversal rates— maybe *the* worst—of any judge of his time. Hawkes, on the other hand, deals from security, not insecurity. He's in a side of the business where an awful lot of bad lawyers occupy an awful lot of high positions, and the scorn just drips from him, it irritates him so. But one reason those bad lawyers occupy those high positions is that they know Hawkes is there to bail them out, so he can get away with murder with them. There's one story that he brought a lawyer for Bank of America two thousand miles to his office, then sat him down in the conference room and threw a ball at him and told him to catch it in his mouth, and he was going to keep throwing it at him till he did." Max laughed. "Were you serious, Joe?"

"About what?"

"About asking who was Judge Landis?"

"No," Purcell said. "Of course I know who Judge Landis was. It was just that the way you threw him into the conversation, with no identification or introduction or anything else, I thought maybe it could be another Judge Landis you were talking about. You have a way of doing that, Max. The other day, out of a blue sky, you said, 'She should have married the diver.'"

"She should have," Aranow said.

"Naturally," Purcell said.

But having different acoustics, Aranow and Purcell treated their people differently. The client sitting in their waiting room might be a man with a valid million-dollar injury claim, yet subsisting on hand-me-downs and food stamps. It was important to all that the initial impact be a touch of class. This involved furnishings and atmosphere, and it did no disservice to the image that the black-haired, dark-eyed Rita Guitterez, at the receptionist's desk, was one of the most beautiful women God ever created. And to the service of that image it was her rayon softness of voice that mattered most.

That softness impressed the man who sat in the waiting room now. Quite obviously he subsisted on neither hand-me-downs nor food stamps. The card he presented told Rita Guitterez he was James Price, Attorney-at-Law, Suite 875, Biscayne Towers, Miami, and if the plaid threads he wore did battle with his stocky build and after-shave face, still they were obviously well-costed. His mission, he explained to her in Cotton South twang, was "to see about associatin' my clients in that li'l ol' Fireball in O-hio." Rita's voice gentled him and reassured. Of course someone would see him, she promised, as soon as possible.

"Well, I've got nothin' but time," the man named James Price said. "And thank you for your kindness, li'l lady." What impressed him was the way she failed to question him. All he said was Fireball in Ohio, and evidently she knew exactly what case he meant.

For that was another thing the A&P made sure of. At any given point, the firm's selective case load in various individual stages of progress might consist of one hundred in number (most of them candidates for major six-figure recoveries, or even larger), in a range from medical malpractice to product liability, from aircraft disaster to toxic tort. But the rule was that whatever lawyer in the firm was first to know of a new case, Rita Guitterez at the desk out front would be second.

Thus now the lawyer from Miami, James Price, in the reception area, there to discuss the Fireball, while in the interior conference room the miniki sat around the large oval table discussing the same thing. Already they had parceled out the chief zones of responsibility: For Bert Klein, at thirty-four, it would be the facts of the explosion and the toll it had taken in deaths, injuries, property—all aspects of liability and some of the damage problems as well—in addition to which he would be second chair to Joe Purcell, sitting at his side in the courtroom when and if the case came to trial; for Willie Blake, the detailing and initial conferences and work-ups with new clients—those that came into the office by direct referral, such as from Harry Wright in Mundelein, or by association with other attorneys in recognition of the role Joe Purcell would eventually play as chief trial counsel; for Sheila O'Hara, part of whose everyday function was the administration of the A&P's finances, the coincident function here of supervising the cost of preparing the case, plus scheduling depositions, handling volumes of interrogatories, and supervising the legal research. The fourth person in the room, with lines to each of the other three, was Felix Harding—not a lawyer but an investigator, but no less essential on that account—who would be in charge of the field work, digging up answers to questions not amenable to normal research. It was he who had been doing much of the talking in the session so far. The miniki called him Nero, for Nero Wolfe—at once a reference to his girth and a compliment to his detective skills.

"The complications here are something," he was saying. "I would have given two weeks' salary to see the look on Max's face when Joe was explaining the explosion to him. I know what he meant—that LPG vaporizes at forty below, and then expands in a relative volume of three hundred and sixty to one, cubic footage. But it came out funny."

"Well," Bert Klein said, "in a way, Joe was making some kind of sense. I mean, in that cold snap in Minnesota a couple of winters ago there was an LP tank car—Sioux Railroad, I think it was—that derailed and over-turned, but it was sixty below zero so nothing happened. Except they had to evacuate the town, because if a heat wave came along and it got up to thirty below, the damn thing could have blown up." Klein was single, a womanizer, carefully attired. Today he was the guy with the profile in the Burberry's ad, only the raincoat was off and the tie loosened. "It's the shaving cream syndrome—the aerosol can. Anybody here know what Bleve is?" He pronounced the word to rhyme with "levee."

Sheila O'Hara said, "I know. It's two pounds of you-know-what in a one-pound bag."

"Wrong," Willie Blake said. For a black man, he was extremely black. ("Willie is the prototype of your UN ambassador from one of the emerging African nations," Max Aranow had said to Joe Purcell. "Always in the three-piece suit." Purcell nodded. "Sure," he said. "Coat, vest, and hat.") "Blevy is the American pronunciation. You're right about what it means, Sheila, but it comes from the English: Blivy."

"You're both wrong," Bert Klein said. "It's an acronym: B-L-E-V-E. Stands for boiling liquid expanding vapor explosion. That's what we're dealing with."

"Well," Sheila O'Hara said, "Nero's the one with the real point. The complications. I know one thing about this case already, and I've known it for a week: we're going to have to go on line with a computer—just to assemble and collate the data on what goes into a Jumbo Nellie Nellie. Let alone what contributes to the explosion. Did you know they even *fill* them by computer? And the minimum I can foresee is maybe two hundred thousand dollars for the total computer costs. And I'm the one who has to tell Max that."

Blake said, "Why don't you tell Joe instead?"

"Purcell? What good will it do to tell him? He'll sit down at the piano and write a song about it. Look, Willie," she said, "it's Max I've got to tell, and it isn't the two hundred thousand dollars that bothers me. It's the fact that I want to use a computer. I sit here at this table and say I like my job and I don't want to be fired. You remember what Max was like the day he found out the girls in the file room were using an electric pencil sharpener? You think I want to tell him we need a *computer*?"

"It's even worse than that," Bert Klein said. "Wait till I have to tell him he's got an oil company for a client."

Felix Harding said, "North American Petroleum. Take it from the top, Bert. They're a defendant, not a—"

"Who said North American Petroleum?" Klein said. "I'm not talking about NAP, I'm talking about Texaco. When the NAP tank car blew up, the Texaco station down the street blew up too. They're mad as a son of a bitch. Not to mention two dead on the premises."

Willie Blake said, "Well, the way to tell Max these things is the same way as always—you don't tell him. You just let them happen. The only reason the electric pencil sharpener became a thing was that somebody made the mistake of asking his permission in advance." He stood up. "Actually, it's *my* job to tell Max about Texaco being a client. You're overstepping your bounds, Bert."

"It always happens around here," Klein said.

"But in the nicest way," Willie said. "Here I've been mulling it over for a week, how best to go about it, and you just volunteered."

"Princeton leads Harvard at the half," Sheila O'Hara said.

"I don't know," Klein said. "This has got to be the only law firm in the country where a Harvard degree is like an eviction notice from the slumlord."

"No, no," Willie Blake said. "There are certain things only a Harvard graduate like you is equipped to do."

"Like what?" Bert said.

Felix Harding said, "Like how to tell Max about Texaco." He looked up at Blake. "Where are you off to? Meeting adjourned?"

"For me it is," Willie said. "You three dolls stay at it. I've got a man outside, wants to associate with us in the Fireball."

Sheila O'Hara said, "What case has he got?"

"Don't know," Blake said. "But cheer up. Maybe he's got a Gulf station."

He left the conference room and went to his office. It was another rule of the A&P—indeed unique as law firms go—that the associates had offices approximately as big as those of the partners themselves. At the age of twenty-eight, Willie Blake had an office of more than 400 square feet, furnished in total accordance with his own taste, and his taste ran almost perversely to Mississippi provincial, with bare wood plank floor, a rolltop desk, framed Old South daguerreotypes on the walls, and only a single hung credential—one that proclaimed the eligibility of Willie R. Blake, Jr., admitted to practice law before the Supreme Court of the United States. Against the wall opposite his desk were two antique brocade sofas, and centered in the room a circular walnut table with matching chairs, over which hung a bordello chandelier. The only aspect not within Willie's control was the telephone console—a starkly contrasting modern wonder of intercom, recording, voice-activated components established at the command of Max Aranow. Not that Aranow had that much use for such a system, but it was the product of a private communication service, not Ma Bell, and the opportunity to deny the phone company that equipment revenue was something Max had found irresistible. Willie Blake would always remember the first time he brought his mother and father in to see his office. The first thing they noticed was the phone system.

By contrast today, the first thing James Price of Miami noticed as he came through the door and viewed Blake's office was Blake himself. The moon-shaped black face knew it, and Price, realizing he was guilty of staring, looked quickly anywhere else.

His eyes lit upon the Supreme Court certificate on the wall. "Well," he said, and moved to have a closer look. "Well, if that don't beat all. You know, I don't believe I ever *seen* one of them before. You mean you been up there in front of the *Supreme* Court?"

"As a matter of fact," Willie said, "I have, yes."

"Well, don't that beat all?" Price said. He giggled. "They tell me they all fall asleep hearin' the arguments."

"Thurgood Marshall stayed awake," Blake said. He reached for a yellow legal pad. "Let's sit at the big table, Mr. Price, and we can go over what it is you have here."

"Well," Price said, "it's that li'l ol' Fireball in O-hio. See, let me level with you and tell it like it is. Onliest thing I know is real estate law. But I've been thinkin' of branchin' out, you see what I'm sayin'? And this one looks to me like it might be really somethin'."

Willie Blake's pen had not yet moved. "You've got a case in connection with the Fireball?"

"Four cases." Price smiled heartily. But Willie's pen still had not moved. Price moistened his upper lip with his tongue. "Not death cases, if that's what you're waitin' on. But interestin' ones: *interestin'* ones." The pen did not move; he moistened his lip again. "You know, when that tank car blew, there was an airplane in the sky right overhead. TWA. Full planeload. And up she comes like an atom bomb, and that plane had to take what they call evasive action—so evasive there were four people, passengers on that plane, had to be taken to the li'l ol' hospital when she landed—*emergency*-landed—at Charleston. Four of 'em: one dislocated shoulder, one collarbone, one whiplash, one back injury." Again the hearty smile. "And I've got all four of 'em."

Willie Blake nodded. "And you say you're a real estate lawyer."

"That's right. But like I say, I've been thinkin' of branchin' out."

"And you practice in Charleston?"

"No, sir. No way. Not me. That's Charleston, West Virginia. I don't even practice in Charleston, South Carolina. Strictly Florida. So far, that is."

"Then you what?—happened to be in Charleston that day?"

"No, no. Matter of fact I was out on the Keys that day. No, it was an investigator brought these cases in to me."

Again, Willie Blake nodded. "I see. Any particular reason he brought them to you? Forgive me for asking."

"Ask away," Price said. "That's what I'm here for: to answer your questions." He waited. So did the pen. "Oh," Price said. "The reason. Well, no mystery to that. This investigator's from Miami, same as me, and we're friends, you see, and he's the one been talkin' about helpin' me branch out."

"And he told you they were interesting cases?"

"Well, yes. You see, what he pointed out was in their case you've got an extra defendant."

"An extra defendant?"

"TWA," Price said. "Don't you see? The proximate cause in my cases was the airline and that plane careenin' around the sky that way."

Blake pursed his lips. "Well, now, that *is* interesting. Who is this investigator?"

"Victor Cuneo," James Price said. "Very well known in the field, I'm told."

"Well known enough," Willie said. "Did he tell you our firm doesn't take referrals from him?"

"He said there're a lot of people down on him and you might be one of them," Price said. "But like he pointed out to me, there's no reason for it. I mean, all he's ever tried to do is get somebody who's been done an injury and put 'm next to the finest injury lawyers in the country. And that's all I'm trying to do sittin' here now. Come all the way to New York for it. I mean, let me level with you, I've heard all kinds of preachments that it's wrong. But *why* is it wrong? Can't find nobody'll tell me that."

Willie Blake leaned back in his chair. He poised the pen like a spirit level, his forefingers pressing at either end. "Well," he said, "maybe I can suggest a reason to you. You see, quite recently Joe Purcell of our office tried a case in that very same courtroom down in Mundelein, Ohio, where this Fireball case will be tried—assuming it does go to trial. That very same courtroom, in front of the very same judge and against the very same lawyer who'll defend in the Fireball." Blake sighted over the ridge of the pen. "And Joe Purcell lost that case."

"Well," James Price said, "even the best of them can drop one every now and then. Ain't nobody bats a thousand in this business, not even Joe Purcell. And I don't have to tell you he's the finest there is. I've got to admit, it beats all, what you just said about him losin' an' all in the same place, same judge, same everythin', but that don't mean he's about to lose again."

Willie shook his head. "He may not have even lost the first one. It's up on appeal now. You see, he didn't localize one of his witnesses properly, and the other side objected and the judge sustained, so the witness never got to testify."

Price said, "Localize?"

"My word for it," Willie said. "It was a case, you see, of a little girl with an asthma attack, and when they got to the emergency room of the hospital, the people there didn't act fast enough and she wound up with permanent brain damage."

"Well, if they didn't act fast enough, how could Purcell have lost the case?"

"Oh, they *claimed* they acted fast enough," Willie Blake said. "Matter of fact, they put up the standard argument—that it was only their fast action that kept the kid alive at all. But Joe Purcell had this one witness, a very well-known New York doctor who's very familiar with emergency room procedures, and he put him on as a witness, only the other side objected that this doctor had never been to Mundelein before, so he couldn't testify as to standard practice in that location. That's what I meant by 'localize.'"

"I didn't know there was a law like that."

"There is. In Ohio."

"Didn't Purcell know that?"

"Sure he knew it."

"Well, why didn't he get a local doctor?"

"He didn't need a local doctor. He could have brought that same guy down from New York two days early, let him walk in one door of that hospital and out the other, and that would have satisfied the law on that point."

"Then why didn't he do *that*?"

"Because he's too good a lawyer, that's why. That witness wasn't that important one way or the other. Joe may have lost this one, but if he did there could have been another reason, like something in the jury room. The point is he set forth his case pretty good. But all the time he knew it was possible the jury would come in against him; that's always possible. So he deliberately set it up for that one witness to be challenged off the stand. That way he had grounds for appeal in case the result went against him. Now the appeal's been filed, and it's solid. It challenges the law on that point, and all the higher court's got to do is go along with most other states and agree it's a stupid law—maybe it wasn't always in the past, but in these days of standardization it certainly is—and bang! Joe Purcell's won himself a new trial."

"Well, if that don't beat all," Price said. "But great jumpin' God, a man's got to be confident to pull somethin' like that."

"He had reason to be confident," Blake said. "The other side had already offered him four hundred and fifty thousand in settlement. Not bad, for that part of the country."

"And he turned it down?"

"Advised his client—the mother of the kid—to turn it down, yes; and she took his advice. So same thing."

"My God, I would have settled," Price said. And he found himself looking down the barrel of the pen in Willie Blake's hand.

"So would Victor Cuneo," Willie said. "And that brings us to the answer to your question: What's wrong with these case-runners who steer lawsuits to the big lawyers? You just saw what's wrong. They don't want trials. All they want is settlements. In fast, out fast. Take the money and run. And they're always there, yammering it into the client's ear. What might be best for the client is something they never heard of. It's what's best for themselves—the quick score. That's all they're after." Willie dropped the pen on the table. "That's why case-runners like Cuneo make people like Joe Purcell nervous. You understand, Mr. Price?"

Price picked up the pen and looked at it. "I guess I do understand," he said at last. "But you have to advise me on one other point."

"Whatever," Willie Blake said.

"What do I do with these four cases? The ones from Charleston."

"Well," Willie said, "if it's advice you want, my first advice would be to forget about suing TWA."

Price inclined his head, in something akin to marvel. "If that don't beat all. Cuneo said TWA was the best thing about those four cases. Said they'd settle in a flash."

"They'll settle in a pig's eye," Willie said. "Your Cuneos eat settle for breakfast. I just got finished telling you that. Why in hell should the airline settle? They didn't do anything wrong; according to the papers they took standard evasive action, and that crew did everything right. People were praising them, not attacking them. No jury would go for an award against the airline. You'd just be fractionating your case."

"Then what do I do?"

"Well," Blake said, "one thing you can do is just file your cases against the defendants on the ground, like everybody else."

"*Me* file? How do I try a lawsuit like this?"

"Maybe you won't have to. In cases like this, with so many deaths and injuries, the judge is most likely to consolidate all of them and then pick out one case for trial. And Purcell will be the trial lawyer for the speci-men—that's what they call it, the specimen case—and in terms of the award he gets for the specimen, all the other cases will go to negotiation, where you work out a kind of pro rata amount, instead of each one of them having to be tried."

"Isn't that kind of risky?"

"Yup."

"I mean, what if Purcell loses and doesn't get anything. Like the time you just told me about."

Willie Blake stood up. "Well, put it this way," he said. "If he can't win, ain't no way you're gonna. He's got deaths; you've got hangnails."

James Price stood up too and extended his hand. "Well, I can't thank you enough," he said, "for givin' me your time and your counsel and everythin'."

"I hope you have other business in New York," Willie said. "It'd be unfortunate if you came all this way just to see us. You really could have phoned instead."

"Oh, not at all," Price said. "There's really two or three other things I can pick up on while I'm here, but even then, just gettin' to meet you and talk things over was worth the trip just by itself. I mean, it was *educatin'*." And as he passed through the door, Willie could hear him, still talking: "If that don't beat *all!*"

But when he got back to the Sheraton Centre, where he was staying, Price put in a long-distance call to Victor Cuneo in Miami. "It's just like you said, Vic," he said, when Cuneo came on the line. "They want no part of you or me or the cases. But it was still worth it, like you said it would be. Know what they did? They threw the house coon at me—I mean the *blackest* son of a bitch you ever *did* see—and he's like all the rest of them: they just love to talk and show off what they know. And he knows a lot, this one; I have to give him that. But maybe he talks too much for his own good. Or for Joe Purcell's good." Price had a high, clattering laugh. "Wait till you hear what he told me. God damn, it beats *all!*"

17

True to Arthur Hawkes's prediction, Joe Purcell was on a tennis court in Westport, Connecticut, when the news came. True also to the Hawkes forecast, he laughed when he heard it.

The tennis court was part of Purcell's backyard, and he was in the act of demolishing a neighbor teenager, 6 to 1 first set, 3 to 0 so far in the second, when Marcy came out through the sun porch and said, "Joe, your office was on the phone. Felix Harding."

"Nero? What did he want?"

"He said just to give you a message. Here: I wrote it down. The Department of Labor finding is that the fire in Jumbo Nellie Nellie—is that right, Joe? I had him say it twice—"

"Yuh," Purcell said. "I know what it is."

"—fire in Jumbo Nellie Nellie was caused by lightning."

"Sure," Purcell said. That was when he began to laugh.

Marcy said, "Something funny?" but when he laughed like that she did not expect to learn why. And she was determined to maintain an attitude of cool disinterest toward the Fireball case. Joe had brought her up to Westport the day before to convince her that he could do both—the musical and the case—and while she still wasn't convinced, she knew that further debate was pointless. Instead, she turned toward the well-muscled high schooler across the net and said, "Good morning, Christopher."

"Morning, Miss Beall."

"Giving him some trouble today?"

"'Fraid not. I can't handle left-handers."

"You can handle bad left-handers," Purcell said. Then to Marcy: "Twenty minutes more, then I'll be inside and change and we can take off."

"Let's take my convertible."

"All right," Purcell said. "Why not?" He went back to the baseline and waved ready-racquet at Christopher.

Coming into the house afterward—it had taken him only fifteen minutes, not twenty—he went directly to what had always been his own wing of the place, a large room furnished not totally unlike Marcy's apartment in the city, with piano, recording equipment, and acoustical tile save on one wall, which was given over to his library of books on music, record albums, and sheet music.

Purcell had designed this studio layout himself, as indeed he had executed the entire floor plan of the house when he and Celia had it built almost twenty years ago, their rise to Westport splendor financed by Joe's having brought in the first million-dollar personal-injury verdict west of the Mississippi. He had done the floor plan himself but had an architect do the exterior, which Purcell could visualize but not design, just as in songwriting he could write the notes but not the orchestrations, even though he knew how they would sound. But that was what architects and orchestrators were for. Even in his practice of law, Purcell was a creator, not a detail administrator. Now, with this morning's word from the office about the Labor Department finding, he was going to have to create something pretty good for the Fireball at Florian.

He had started a routine with his first jury trial shortly after he joined Max. Celia had been his sounding board. He called her his "average American jury." She was the first to hear his opening statements and his summations—usually propped in bed with a clipboard for note taking—while Joe paced in front of the bed-become-jury-box. Joe knew that Marcy was not an average American anything but he made a try at it with her when they were on their way to the Aranow place in Ambler.

"You see," he said to her, "this railroad tank car, loaded to the gills with liquefied propane, gets hit by lightning and catches fire. Twenty minutes later it explodes and takes half the town with it. Now—" he patted at the steering wheel for emphasis "—what shall we say was the cause of it?"

"You already know," Marcy said.

"Yuh," he said. "Lightning. An act of God."

"Then why are you taking the case?"

"I don't really know, Marcy. I fought it."

"Still," she said, "it could be an awful big one if you win."

"Sure," he said. "That goes without saying. But there's something else to it, and I'm damned if I know what it is. All I know is, it's *there*. And Max knows I know. Butter won't melt in his mouth while he sits there watching me break my ass on this one."

Marcy said, "Well, what is it, then?"

"I just told you: I don't know. The cause of the fire was lightning, right?"

"That's what everybody keeps saying."

"Oh, you can't contest it. We're going to have to concede that going in. Sight unseen, I can tell you that much."

"Then what else is there?"

"Just that the more people say lightning caused the fire, the more you think about it, because the fire didn't hurt anybody. It was the *explosion*, not the fire."

Purcell's right hand left the wheel and he began massaging his earlobe. They drove in silence for a while. "I'd have to guess," Marcy said at last, "that the fire caused the explosion."

He laughed his tennis-court laugh. "That's what I'd have to guess too."

"Then where does that leave you?"

"Back where I started."

They drove in silence for a time. Then Marcy said, "When do you think the case will come to trial?"

"Don't know. Take a long time in the preparation. On the other hand, that courthouse down in Mundelein, Ohio, doesn't have a crowded calendar. I wouldn't even want to guess."

"But longer than six months?"

"Oh, yes. Longer than that."

"And your option on *The Last Laugh*—that's for six months?"

"Yuh. But it's renewable." He looked questioningly at her. "Why? Where's the connection?"

"I don't know," she said. "You might know it more than I do. It's almost as if —" her hands groped for the right words "—as if you'd come to the fork in the road. Your law practice in one direction, musical comedy in the other."

"Why is it one or the other? Why can't I be equally interested in both?"

"I don't know," she said, "except that you seem to have committed to both of them at the same time."

He mulled that one. "As a matter of coincidence," he said, "you may be right. I decided to go ahead with each of them the same day."

"Some people reach the fork in the road," she said, "and don't know which way to go."

"Then stick me in the *Guinness Book of World Records*," Purcell said. "I went both ways."

"Without seeing the difference."

"*What* difference, for God's sake? I'm not going to go out to win one while I lose the other. If you asked Jimmy the Greek for the odds right now, the odds would be I'm going to lose both."

"But the odds of winning one or the other would be better if you didn't *do* both."

"Ah, that's a little special," he said. "That's the proof that says a good golfer can't also be a good surgeon."

"No," she said. "But a *great* golfer can't also be a *great* surgeon. And a hit Broadway musical takes greatness and winning this Fireball case will take greatness."

"You sound like the introduction to the Havemeyer lectures," Purcell said. "I won't buy it, Marcy."

"You won't face up to having to make a choice," she said. "That's what I'm saying."

"I still won't buy it," he said. "You talk about greatness; why don't we talk about luck? That enters into it too, you know."

"Which are we talking about? The musical or the Fireball?"

"Both," Purcell said.

"I wish I believed that," Marcy said.

"Now what does *that* mean?"

"Just that I think you've already got an idea in your head where you think your better chance is: where you're going to win and where you're going to lose."

"Ah," he said. "Then here it is: the good news and the bad news. Okay. The bad news first: Which one am I going to lose? The musical or the Fireball?"

"The Fireball," Marcy said.

18

The choice. The fork in the road.

Aboard U.S. Air Flight 201 from New York's LaGuardia to Huntington's Tri-State, Joe Purcell opened his dispatch case and started to take out the script of his musical. He had undertaken the story line, as well as the lyrics and music. It was slow going. But he liked what he had so far. He flipped through the manuscript, not reading it, but just to be sure that it was intact. He then replaced it carefully and took out a letter from an expert he had retained in the Fireball case.

```
Mr. Joseph F. Purcell
Aranow & Purcell
9 West 53 Street
New York, New York 10019

Dear Mr. Purcell:

The question can be raised as to what advantages could
accrue to an oil company, such as North American Petro-
leum, in switching from small insulated tank cars, such as
the 105A300W, to the jumbo uninsulated cars of the
112A340W type.

It can be shown that direct dollar savings were involved,
and that additional opportunities for improved profits
from an enhanced marketing position were involved in the
switch. It is instructive to begin with background
material on propane production and marketing.

Propane is used as a raw material for petrochemical plants
and as a general-purpose fuel. Propane sold as fuel is in
```

that portion of the market where rail transport is a significant factor. Propane is produced as a coproduct with other fuels in refinery operations, and as a co-product from natural gasoline operations. Thus, the output of propane fluctuates up and down in response to output of the primary fuel of the plant, which may vary in terms of location. A need exists to develop markets for propane produced coincidental to the major product line since only limited flexibility exists to change the ratio of gasoline to propane, for example, produced within the refinery.

Transportation costs are a large portion of the propane price structure. The first examination of ICC cost studies for large tank car shipments versus small tank car shipments indicated a typical 14% reduction in shipping cost per hundredweight for large cars per trip. Add to this the savings obtained by reducing the trips to deliver an equal volume of product by as much as two-thirds.

At the time of the Florian accident, lease rates for a 33,000 gallon 112A340W car were on the order of 260 $/month, while lease rates for 105A300W cars of 11,000-gallon capacity were on the order of 100 $/month. On an equal volume basis, a savings of 13% accrued for the larger cars.

The most recent survey, reflecting the period of not more than six months before the subject accident at Florian, O., reflects that on a 500-mile trip, shipping charges for LPG were on the order of one-third the F.O.B. refinery cost. For a 1,000-mile trip, they were on the order of one-half the cost at refinery.

Labor savings on loading and unloading operations would tend to be on the order 20 to 50% for 30,000 gallons of LPG when one jumbo car is used compared to three smaller cars.

From the foregoing, it may be observed that the switch to larger cars would produce benefit for the oil companies. On a bulk commodity like propane, even a small percentage saving in cost generates large total dollars in profit. Unfortunately, the profits have come at the expense of safety.

Very truly yours,

Purcell read the letter through, then gave it another, briefer scan, this time mainly for the underlining, most of which he had done himself. Then he put it back in the briefcase. The plane trip was bumpy only twice—coming into Pittsburgh and now again coming into Huntington. But it was on time: 1 hour and 12 minutes New York to Pittsburgh, 39 glorious minutes on the ground at Pittsburgh—no reason for that length of time other than the standard curse of being the connecting flight to an infrequently served next destination—then 43 minutes from there into Huntington.

It was raining when Joe came down the steps from the plane, briefcase in hand, garment bag over shoulder, and headed for the Avis counter, which gave him a Plymouth that he needed and a map that he didn't. His secretary, Elizabeth Frasciano, had booked him into the Western Motor Hotel in Mundelein, a place he had never tried or even noticed. But it was an exercise in elimination. The General Dexter Hotel in downtown Mundelein was out. "It's across the street from the tracks," Purcell said. "Those damn freight trains hit town at two o'clock in the morning and they make a rattling sound because they're all empties. I never saw a full one. I leaned out the window one night and counted two hundred and twenty hopper cars, all empty, all hitting through the middle of town at fifty-five miles an hour. You never heard a noise like that." He pulled at his ear. "And besides, Arthur Hawkes stays at the General Dexter and I'm sick to death of running into him in the lobby. It's bad enough I've got to see him in court."

"Well," Elizabeth said, "if you have a rented car you could stay out of town. There's a Holiday Inn and a TraveLodge or Great Western or something, on U.S. 52. Not all that far away."

"No," Purcell said. "I know that Holiday Inn. And the others. Not all that far away from Mundelein, as you say, but far enough. And besides, there are tracks there too. All you do is trade the Mid-Central for the Norfolk and Western."

Coming off West Virginia state route 75, the fastest route to Mundelein was to turn right on Interstate 64, then left before you got to downtown Huntington and over the ten-cent toll bridge that crossed the Ohio, and a straight run north from there. But this time instead Purcell continued past the Interstate to U.S. 64, then turned left, crossed the Big Sandy River marking the border between West Virginia and Kentucky, and found himself on Winchester Avenue in Ashland. At 13th Street he turned right and crossed the Ohio on the free bridge there. You see, he said to himself, in your old age you begin to get the smarts: you just saved ten cents.

He had never driven this way before but for him no map was necessary. He was headed north now on a two-lane Ohio road. The rain had stopped, but the huge trees beside the road, heavy with the burden of late spring, continued to drip great beads of water. Here and there to either side of the road would be houses, each one of them fronted by English-oval tanks bearing the sign TRI-STATE GAS: the residential propane users of the area.

It was a hilly, climbing drive, the countryside a dark, almost evil shade of green, proclaiming if only in worn memory the influence of the iron ore and coal below the ground. Then a right-hand T-intersection, and an arrow sign, pointing into the stem of the T, that said one word: FLORIAN.

And now the road ran parallel to the railroad track, off to Purcell's left as he drove. This he supposed would be the single-track Gallipolis branch of the Mid-Central, the one that ran through Florian. *He supposed*, but it was one of the few suppositions he permitted himself. Tomorrow, Harry Wright, the Mundelein attorney, would be covering much the same ground with him, taking him on a guided tour of the disaster area. Why then was Purcell doing it now on his own?

The answer lay, he guessed, in his own approach to the law: the impetus that was at work when fresh out of law school he advised Judge Karras to let Max Aranow's sonic boom case go forward. It was something Purcell kept to himself: If he talked about it, too many people would read it as self-serving, making him preoccupied with the show of it rather than any result; others would put him down simply as an eccentric. Result? He anticipated no result. But to him there was always the off chance that unguided curiosity might yield up a solution where the guided tour would not, that the ignorant beholder could sometimes see more for not being told where to look, that invention and inspiration belonged, more often than most would think, to the man without a body of knowledge to defend.

And the major effect of this approach would have to be, by any accounting, the number of times it didn't work.

But every once in a while it did. Ten or twelve years ago, before Celia's death, the wife of one of their Westport neighbors suffered a broken hip when a pyramid of soup cans collapsed and toppled on her in a local supermarket, and Purcell agreed to handle the case. It was mostly friendship, a little bit of *noblesse oblige*, and no realistic chance of actually winning. Among other things, the store had a witness ready to swear that the reason the cans collapsed was that the woman herself had driven into them with her shopping cart.

Some tortured theory might be mounted that in discharging its duty of reasonable care the store had no business piling merchandise that way in any event, and therein lay Purcell's only chance until, one Saturday afternoon, he simply went to the store himself as a customer.

No matter what aisle he visited, he could find nothing wrong with the way the goods were stacked. Not that they had changed things since the accident—he himself had shopped there before and detected no change. Indeed, all markets stacked their canned goods in the same manner: Short of an earthquake, any customer injured in such an accident had most likely to be in and of herself the prime cause of said accident.

What Purcell noticed instead on that innocent journey was something he might well not have noticed had he been guided merely and directly to the scene of the accident. What he noticed was a grocery stock boy with many pimples and a green apron, hefting a huge wholesale-size jar of Del Monte kosher dill pickles to a rear corner of the store where stood a large old-fashioned country-store pickle barrel. Except it was not a barrel. It looked like one, and the signs proclaimed OLD-FASHIONED PICKLE BARREL, but it was only a painted replica, constructed not of aged staves but of composition cardboard, and all but the top one-fifth of it was false bottom. That top part housed a shallow tray, into which the stock boy now emptied the contents of the Del Monte jar. The price posted for a pickle from the barrel was more than twice the price per pickle for the identical pickles in the retail-size jars on the shelf elsewhere in the store.

The following week, Purcell called the store's lawyer to discuss his client's case, except that he discussed very little of it. What concerned him, he said, was that the same stock boy who might have stacked the soup cans more carefully, who might have been on the spot to rescue his client when the cans began to fall, had his time taken up instead in busily defrauding the public at the pickle barrel.

Two days later the defense lawyer called back to offer Purcell's client a settlement of $35,000 for her hip.

"I don't know," Purcell said. "I never had a broken hip. Did you?"

"Joe," the other lawyer said, "I'd jump at that thirty-five if I were you. We've not only got a witness on this woman of yours, but we know something else—she's got a drinking problem. That's probably why she crashed into that stack of cans."

"You know," Purcell said, "if you were being charged twenty-five cents for the same pickle that goes for nine cents across the aisle, you might have a drinking problem too."

"Joe," the other lawyer said, "I was told that if you said no to thirty-five I could go to fifty thousand."

There were one or two conversations after that, as a result of which Purcell, by dint of one idle, unescorted visit to a supermarket, turned a probable zero recovery into $75,000 for a broken hip. "Very good," Max Aranow said, when Joe told him about it. "Sounds like you could have held out for more, but it pays to know when to quit. Leo Durocher explained it to me, years ago. Any time you argue with an umpire, he said, you have four reasons: First, if anybody's going to get kicked out of the game, you have to make sure it's you, not one of your players; second, you want your team to know you'll back them up; third, there might have been something worth arguing about; but fourth and most important of all, you're never just arguing that decision—you're arguing the *next* decision. Always remember there's a next time, he said to me."

"Thanks for the speech," Joe said. "I enjoyed every word of it. Now how about a word or two for the fact that it was pure asshole luck: my being there by the pickle barrel when the kid came over with the jar."

"But you were observant," Aranow said.

"I'm not going to say I wasn't."

"Then I'll say it for you," Max said. "You said it was Del Monte kosher dills, the large ones."

"Of course it was. I saw the label, then I went and checked the prices on the regular jars on the shelves."

"You saw the label?"

Purcell put up a hand. "You're on one of your things, Max. It's *What's My Line* time—blindfolds all in place, panel?"

"I said you saw the label."

"I already told you that. How could I have—"

"Did you read it?"

"Of course I read it. How could I have—"

"Where it said kosher dill pickles and how the ingredients were cucumbers, salt, vinegar, sugar, water, garlic powder, all the rest. Don't ask me how I know how it reads. That's how they all read."

"Oh, I'm setting myself up here," Joe Purcell said. "But I'll ask it anyway: What difference does it make?"

"Just that you should have thrown in Del Monte as a defendant," Max said. "Kosher pickles are made with dill, not vinegar. Del Monte calls it kosher and goes vinegar, not dill. *There's* your fraud: mislabeling. Right in front of your eyes and you never saw it."

19

Florian, Ohio: an old town, its history tracing back through the summer of 1862, when a number of slaves, encouraged by the abolitionist frenzy of Andrew Johnson, the Union war governor for Tennessee, fled the plantations south of Nashville and attached themselves, and their wives, children, dogs, diseases, to the newly formed Army of the Ohio. If any Union army was transport to liberation, as Johnson proclaimed, this one must be doubly so. It was moving north.

Don Carlos Buell, the major general in command, gave welcome neither to the fugitives nor to their hopes. He had it privately, from Grant and Halleck both, that no matter what the governor said, this trailing black flotsam was to be suffered, no more than that, entitled not to the food or medicines of the supply wagons, only to the protective dust. And that would mean more dust than protection, Buell reckoned, for the surrounding Kentucky countryside was sometimes hostile and everywhere parched, and if he was marching north, something else was even farther north: a Confederate army of 28,000 men, under the command of Braxton Bragg.

On September 17, Bragg's main force captured the Union garrison of 4,200 men at Munfordville, then swung northeast to join the rest of his soldiers, who under Kirby Smith already occupied the city of Lexington. From there, the blue grass carpeted an easy three-day march to the banks of the Ohio, and that could turn the war.

But the blue grass had turned to yellow, and as Smith fidgeted in Lexington, daily hunting water to drink, Bragg found his own progress slowed, and for the same reason. By the morning of October 8, he was still 40 miles short of the linkup, and advance units of Buell's Union force, their stores replenished temporarily from Louisville, had begun to irritate his flanks. The weather was unseasonably hot. In the past 48 hours, two tornadoes had touched down in central Kentucky, and each day started the same, with the early broiling effect of a layer of overcast that persisted till midafternoon.

Yet neither army quite knew the other's whereabouts or even its intent. What both knew was that there might be water enough in Doctor's Creek to merit investigation, and in that undertaking on that morning a Union cavalry group led by Brigadier General Philip Sheridan reached the creek, just west of the village of Perryville, and found there a lone black man who lay bleeding to death, his pancreas and groin stitched without pattern by Confederate bullets. They had taken him for a local Negro, and so did Sheridan, until the black man spoke. He seemed larger than he was, with a face that belonged on some ageless coin. He said two words: "General Gilbert." And that would only be Charley Gilbert, who wanted the troops to believe he was a major general but who was in fact still a captain.

Himself no longer a colonel, though he had not yet removed the patch of the 2nd Michigan from his sleeve, Sheridan appreciated rank to the nuance. The only people who would buy Gilbert for a general were the attached niggers from Tennessee. Gilbert's employment of them was adroit: they would discover, then guard, water holes for the use of officers only. Gilbert was regular army.

Sheridan was volunteers. He knelt lower: the black man was trying to talk during breaths, not between them. "I am Martin," he said. "My wife will tell you."

"Martin from where? Who was your master?"

"Sweet. Adamsville. The river."

"How many of them?"

"All of them."

"How do you know?"

"Same way you'll know. They're coming back."

Sheridan looked up. "Find Buell," he said. "We've got a fight."

"Fuck Buell," the nearest lieutenant said. "He's twelve miles away."

It would be a battle, Bruce Catton wrote, that the generals neither desired nor understood, but it was fought that afternoon. It came down as the Battle of Perryville, summarized in the words of one Confederate private: "Both sides claim the victory—both whipped." Before the month was out, both armies were back in Tennessee. The outcome disgraced Buell, who did not even learn of the battle until it was over, and his failure to reengage led to his replacement. Yet that day the South crested its high-water mark, and when Bragg withdrew the North had won the war.

That night, Philip Sheridan found his way through an intervening stand of sorry elm and birch to where the slaves were encamped, and spoke briefly with the new-mown widow of Martin Sweet.

"We'll bury him tomorrow," Sheridan said.

She shook her head. "Show me where he lies."

"You don't want to see him."

"I do," she said. It was as though she was trying to explain something. Her cheekbones cast upward shadows against her eyes in the resin light of the scrapfire; she could not have been more than twenty years of age. On the ground beside her the two children slept. With the news of Martin's death they had the place closest to the fire.

Sheridan said to her, "How old are they?"

"One walkin', one sucklin'."

"I'll send a blanket for you," he said, "and something to eat. But I brought you this. Do you read?"

"No, sir."

"It's for you to take with you. You can't stay here and you don't want to follow this army. It's going south again." He opened the folded paper. "Your safest way is east. The Kanawha country. Western Virginia."

"You write that down?"

"No. All I've written down here is the name of the place for you to go to. A place named Holderby's Landing. Also the name of a man there. Henry Eldredge. Can you remember that? Never mind, it's written down."

She looked away. "I want to see him where he lies."

"No," he said. "He'll receive a proper burial. A soldier's burial. He deserves it. That's why I'm here. But you won't go to see him. You'll pass safer through the whole state of Kentucky than you'll pass through this army tonight. You see this?" He held the paper down, and she turned her head and looked. "That says Philip H. Sheridan, brigadier general, eleventh division, Army of the Ohio. Ask the colored along the way who to show it to. They'll see nobody snatches you."

She looked down at the sleeping children. "I can't see him?"

"No," Sheridan said again, and folded the paper and pressed it into her hand. Then he returned through the trees and campfires to his tent, and told his orderly to get some food and a blanket to the Sweet woman. And he took a handkerchief and knotted it around some three dollars' worth of small change.

The orderly took the little sack of money and started out of the tent; then he turned and said, "What do I tell her to do with this?"

"You won't have to tell her anything," Sheridan said. "She's a bright one. She'll know who to show it to and who not. But make sure she gets the blanket. She has nothing to cover the children with at night."

The orderly said, "What was she doing up till now?"

"Using the shirt off her husband's back," Sheridan said. "That's why she wanted to go to the body."

"She told you that?"

"I could tell. The way she looked down at them while they were sleeping."

"Colonel," the orderly said, then caught himself. "General, I mean. That's an odd thing, what you just said."

"About her needing his shirt?"

The orderly shook his head. "No. About him being her husband. I mean, I didn't know slaves got married."

Sheridan laughed, all eyebrows. His division had made the difference against Bragg that day. "Maybe I just performed the ceremony," he said. "Oh, and find out what her name is. I forgot to ask her."

Her name was Anna. When she made her way at last to Holderby's Landing and located the man named Eldredge, she still had just over a dollar of the money from Sheridan. It was December then, and in the cold of the night Eldredge rowed her and the children across the Ohio, back-watering clear of the approaching lights he took accurately to be a very large river steamer. She was the *Lucinda Bell* and Anna had never seen such a grand sight, no less grand for the fact that this was now a hospital ship, moaning upstream, her gambling salon sodden with wounded.

The north bank of the river was the state of Ohio, the first safe stopping place for runaway slaves along the underground railway whose short route ran north-northwest through Columbus, Marion, and Toledo to Michigan and, just south of Detroit, the river crossing into Canada. But few of the slaves made it that far. Those who did not die en route found homes in the outbuildings of farms, a handy replacement pool for the men away at war. In the case of Anna Sweet, her journey ended barely twenty miles north of the point where she had crossed the Ohio, in hill country whose earth was for all seasons, hued with iron ore and limestone, fire clay and coal. There, in the town of Florian, Ohio, she came to work and stay in the house of Vivian Farnum, sister of Henry Eldredge, herself like Anna newly widowed by the war. Both the Farnum and Eldredge clans had migrated from southern New England, and both were fiercely antislavery. Anna would never recross the Ohio. That was Vivian Farnum's promise.

The promise was kept the following June. On June 20, 1863, the nearby Kanawha country entered the Union officially as the state of West Virginia. On that day, having nursed the influenza-stricken Vivian Farnum back to health, Anna Sweet died north of the river of the same sickness. Her orphaned children, the girl named Anna and the boy Martin, were too young to remember that Saturday, but both would remember the day eight years later when they recrossed the river. Vivian Farnum took them that day to be part of the celebration incorporating Holderby's Landing as the city of Huntington, West Virginia. For the children, it was the most enormous adventure of their lives. In the buckboard journey from Florian, they overnighted in the larger town of Mundelein, where they had slept that first night of freedom nearly nine years before, then next morning saw the great river and the city on the opposite shore. And the ferry tied up alongside the *Lucinda Bell*, in showboat grandeur once again.

But the most glorious sight of all had to be that of Philip H. Sheridan, home from his sojourn as guest adviser to the king of Prussia in the Franco-German war. The same Chesapeake and Ohio train that brought Collis Huntington, president of the railroad, for the christening ceremonies in his name that day also had brought not only Sheridan but his horse Rienzi. Few histories record that Sheridan was short, fat, harsh-featured; instead he is remembered inseparably astride Rienzi, and in that form he was a god, and hailed as such, still the most popular hero of the late victory over the Confederacy, when he rode as chief celebrant in Huntington's parade.

Young Martin and Anna got to meet the centaur—the Farnums and Eldredges saw to that—and Sheridan remembered them and their mother and most of all their father for, as the horseback general put it now, revealing the presence of the enemy at Perryville. "You know," Sheridan said, "when we drove Jubal Early out of the Shenandoah, Grant ordered a salute of a hundred guns in my name." The eyebrows went light with amusement. "All hundred guns aimed at the enemy. But he didn't pop a firecracker for Perryville. I saw him in the White House last week. I don't think he even remembers Perryville." He looked hard at the two children. "Someone should remember."

Someone did. There is a plaque that can be seen today embedded in the sideboard of a stall of shelves in the public library at Mundelein, Ohio. The shelves hold books, pictures, and other memorabilia of the underground railway. One of the photographs shows Henry Eldredge, Vivian Farnum, and the two black children standing beside the mounted Sheridan. The plaque is of native ore:

In This City
Martin and Anna Sweet
Children of Heroic Slaves
Found Liberty
December 17, 1862

20

Purcell drove his rented Fury through the sleepy Florian countryside. He slowed the car down to pass the district high school on his right. This was where they had brought the bodies and the walking wounded after the Jumbo Nellie Nellie disaster. Today, there was nothing in any way, shape, or form remarkable about the sight or scene of it. But having driven past the high school, Purcell resumed speed, and after a time something started ticking in the back of his head. The odometer on the Fury's dashboard kept clicking off the tenths of miles, with still no Florian in sight, and Purcell asked himself: why would they have taken them this far out of town? It was a nagging question, but one given solid substance by his conviction that

Arthur Hawkes must have already been over this route. The chess-playing son of a bitch'll make something out of this, Purcell's mind told him. *But what?* It's your job to find out, his mind told him. You know the one rule in this game: *No surprises.*

Now there was an intersection of another state highway, and more houses, a more built-up neighborhood, but there were no houses at the point where Purcell stopped his car and got out. What he had noticed was, simply, that the telegraph lines paralleling the Mid-Central tracks to his left suddenly had new poles. They were in and out, restoring the whole thing, his mind told him. He walked up a wet embankment to trackside and stared up at the new utility poles. Looking down the track, toward Florian, he saw nothing. After a time he slid-stepped his way back down the embankment and crossed the road back to where his car was. This time he caught his pants leg on a protruding hunk of wood and devoted all of his concentration to extracting himself without damage to the pants.

The escape accomplished, he smoothed his creases, got back in the car, started it up again, and, with a downhill bend of the road to the left, found himself in the presence of the holocaust. To right and left there were piles of black rubble, blackened foundations of houses, blackened fractions of houses still standing, and now, to his left, simply a blackened two acres of ground, totally leveled. He knew that this was the remainder of the Tri-State energy yard where the Jumbo Nellie Nellie had been parked— "spotted," if you used the railroad word for it.

And as he continued slowly toward the center of town, so did the desolation. Purcell's reaction was the same, if delivered tardy, as everyone else's: This place was hit by an atom bomb.

But he was prepared for it. The news stories the day of the explosion had said as much. What was surprising was the way life went on. People walked this street, cars drove it, as casually now as before. At the very epicenter of the blast he had noticed a parked petroleum tank truck with hoses extended, as if sitting there to dare another stroke of lightning.

Joe found the Western Motor Hotel without a false turn or even an uncertain touch to the brake pedal. He checked into his room, then drove the rest of the way downtown to Harry Wright's office. It was about 3:30 in the afternoon when he mounted the steps and came into the waiting room, a small, bare-walled area with no receptionist, only some chairs and a coffee table piled with *National Geographics.*

One chair in the waiting room was occupied by a not-too-young woman who had the chair turned so she could stare out the window, through the gold-leaf TA of the second word in ATTORNEY AT LAW, at the courthouse square across the street. She was not the first thing Purcell noticed when he entered; what he noticed instead was the card-on-a-string notice hanging from the knob of the door that led to Harry Wright's inner quarters: PLEASE HAVE A SEAT, it said.

Purcell sat down, and the woman turned and looked at him. "Well," she said. "It's you, isn't it?"

He put his thumb and forefinger to his ear, uncomfortable under her gaze. Aloud, he said, "Looks like the rain has stopped."

She had her brown-to-gray hair done up in a bun and wore a flowery print dress, blue on yellow, and had no makeup. It was impossible to tell how attractive she might be. But she stared at Purcell, almost like a steer buyer at an auction.

"It's you," she said again, and he, idiotically, said again, "Probably no more rain," then looked away.

"You should have been here at the beginning of this month," she said. "It was lemonade weather."

"That's what I heard," Purcell said.

"One of these days I'm going to make some more lemonade," she said, then turned her gaze back through the window.

Then the door to the inner office opened and the bespectacled chipmunk face of Harry Wright looked out and lit up and said, "Joe! You're here! Come on in!"

Purcell stood up and went inside. "Sit down!" Harry Wright crowed to him. "You look great, Joe. Really!"

Purcell sat down and said, "I shouldn't have—"

"I'm going to have someone come in here full time to help me," Harry Wright said. "Up to now I've been by myself, like you know, Joe; had a woman who came in part time to type stuff up and put out the billings, but it's getting out of hand with this Fireball."

"I was going to say," Purcell said, "whoever else it is out in the waiting room there, if she was before me, you should have—"

"Oh, she's not before anything," Harry Wright said. "She's just there."

"Just there?"

"Yes. Really. She's in here every day. Just waiting for news."

"News?"

"About her young man," Wright said. "She keeps looking down into the street. Waiting for him to show up." He took off his glasses and huffed into them. "But he's not going to show up. I told you about her."

"You did?"

"Yes. Her name is Rosa Crewes, and she had a house in Florian—oh, yes, I *did* tell you about her over the phone, and about the young man too."

"Tell me again."

"Well," Wright said, "the two of them tie together. She's a spinster lady. Rosa Crewes is her name. I've been administering this WIC program for the government, for medical assistance, and Rosa was going to give a room in her house to this young medical student from Chicago who was coming in to work in the program for the summer. *His* name was Coblenz."

"Was?"

"Is. He was the one who was hit by the fireball when it went off. Driving his car in from Chicago, almost on top of the place when it blew. Drove his car upside down off the side of the road, and he was that way when they found him. He's in the hospital now. Totally paralyzed from the nipple line down."

"Quadriplegic?"

Wright nodded. "I told you on the phone—it's Terry Malloy's case. Chicago. That's where the boy's from."

Purcell said, "Well, Terry's a good one."

"Really," Harry Wright said. "They're talking about moving the boy out of the hospital, maybe a week from now, and getting him back home to Chicago."

"Have you talked to him?"

"No, but Terry Malloy did. Flew down here with the parents. Malloy said he'd never heard a story like that—I mean, so vivid. The boy said he saw a plank fly in front of his face with a mask on it. And you know what that plank was, Joe? It was a railroad tie. And the mask a human head. And it belonged to the driver of the car coming the other way. The story checked out. They found that car more than a quarter of a mile down the road, still on the highway, with the driver still at the wheel, his hands still steering the car. Perfect steering. Except the driver had no head." Wright shivered. "Just thinking of it, I could use a brandy."

Purcell nodded and tugged at his ear. "Christian Brothers."

"With a splash of soda," Harry Wright said. "You remember that bar I took you to last time?"

"The one next to the movie house," Purcell said.

"That's the one."

"I remember. That was the good news. The bad news was the double feature at the movie: *Buffalo Bill* and *The Great Gatsby*. This is a hell of a town you've got here, Harry."

"Jenny liked *The Great Gatsby*," Wright said. "*Buffalo Bill* she could have done without. Even if it was Paul Newman." He removed his glasses once again, this time only to sight through them, a trifle sadly. "I guess by now you know we're small-town, Joe."

Purcell shook his head. "It isn't that, Harry."

"But it's not what you're used to."

"It is and it isn't. I had this feeling the last time I was here, only it's twice as bad this time. Do you know I drove up through Florian on the way here today? The great circle route. Over the bridge from Ashland."

"And then cut through the east side and back down here?"

"Yuh," Joe said. "That was it."

"Any reason?" Wright said. "I'm going to take you up there tomorrow."

"I know you are." Purcell's right hand remained at his ear. "No. No reason. Except the plane got in on time and I had time to kill and I did it. But the point is, I had a map in the car and I'd never been there before. Harry, I never even looked at the map."

"Well, that can happen," Wright said.

"And then I walk in your office and that woman out there turns and looks at me and says, 'Oh, it's you,' like she knew me, and I never before saw her in my life."

"Well, that doesn't even need explaining," Harry Wright said. "The thing with Rosa, you see, is that—"

"No," Purcell said. "What needs explaining is what I didn't even think of before today. How I was in here last time on the Ruth Marlowe case, and I kept locating things and knowing things no first-timer ever ought to know or locate."

Harry Wright shook his head. "No, Joe, you're over-thinking it. I remember my first trip to New York in 1964, for the World's Fair. And I found that somehow I knew where everything was. The only sign I was a tourist was that I kept looking up. But we were with a group, and I remember it was a Saturday morning, and we were at the Biltmore Hotel, and one of the guys in our group wanted to know where he could get a drink at nine-thirty in the morning on a Saturday and somebody said Grand Central. So he went out and got a cab and it was a seven-dollar cab ride, and it was only after he found the bar and had his drink that he found out what direction Grand Central was from the Biltmore: one flight down. But that never happened to me, Joe. I always had this sense of direction—built-in, you might say. Really."

"Sense of direction is one thing," Purcell said. "But that woman outside recognizing me—"

Again Wright cut in on him. "What do you mean, recognizing you? Don't you realize that's our case?"

"Our what?"

"Our case. She was in her house when the fireball came. She was literally blown out of her house. Lay there in the backyard and watched it burn to the ground. Up to then, she'd been a working, functioning human being. Commuted to Huntington four days a week, to work in a department store there. Everything was fine. But she hasn't been back to her job since. She's staying with friends here in Mundelein. Every day she comes and sits in my office and waits for me to give her news of this young man she was expecting."

"Have you told her?"

"No."

"Why not? She'd read it in the paper anyway."

"No, she wouldn't. There was a forty-eight hour delay identifying him, and then his name was only in one of the Huntington papers—after all, he was out-of-town—the big news was the local victims—and she didn't see it, and I don't want to be the one to tell her. She comes here every day and from time to time I go out and say, 'No news, Rosa!' And that's it. I don't know what else to do. Her mind's gone."

Purcell's eyes ranged the other man's office, escape-minded. "Who else have we got? The mayor of Florian. He's one of our cases, right?"

Harry Wright put his glasses back on. He began to tick the cases off his fingers. "The mayor, yes: Owen Merritt. Of course, being mayor of Florian isn't all that important."

"Harry," Joe said, "you have an inferiority complex. Not that I blame you, what with what they show at the movies here, at the—what's the name of that theater?"

"The Gem," Wright said.

Purcell nodded. "But still and all," he said, "you have a life a lot of people would envy. You have nobody to answer to, your practice—"

"I screwed up that Marlowe jury for you," Wright said.

"No way in the world anybody could have foreseen that," Purcell said. "I mean, the idea that anyone would get to a juror that way."

"Who's anyone?"

"Hawkes, I have to assume. Who else?"

"Don't assume things like that," Purcell said. "Arthur knows how to stunt as well as anybody in the business, and if something like that falls in his lap he'll cry all the way to the bank. He's the one who started up that fund for the burned survivors this time."

"It figured," Harry Wright said. "Really."

"But a fund is one thing and a rigged jury is something else," Joe Purcell said. "Rigging a jury is one thing Arthur won't do."

"Sometimes I'll believe anything," Harry Wright said. "Why wouldn't Hawkes fix a juror?"

"Because the unethical son of a bitch has ethics, that's why," Purcell said. "We've been over this before."

The chipmunk cheeks of Harry Wright seemed to relax. He said, "I guess. Of course, the best case you've got is that quadriplegic. Coblenz. I'd love to see us bring *him* into court."

"That's Terry Malloy's case."

"But if the judge decided he was the Specimen?"

"Then I'd be lead counsel, so sure."

"Even if he wasn't the Specimen, he'd make a hell of a witness. Really. Imagine him in a courtroom, week after week—"

"No," Purcell interrupted. "Don't imagine him in a courtroom for more than a few minutes. There's a line you draw. Max Aranow explained it to me, years ago. He said that when Gulden's advertises their mustard, they make you see the hot dog the mustard goes on, not the mustard itself. Max is very authoritative on the subject of food. The quadriplegic would be a beautiful specimen for us, yes. But we'd have to come in around him, not with him. He's over the line: something you want a jury to visualize in their minds week after week rather than see with their eyes."

There was a silence, and then Harry Wright said, "All right. But you were talking about the mayor of Florian. The trouble with him is that he's older than I am."

"Is?"

"Was. My mistake. He was killed in the fireball. All the volunteer firefighters were killed. Funny, Joe, how you can have heroes in a case like this, but when you have a volunteer fire department completely wiped out, you have *heroes*. Really." Wright looked at a piece of notepaper on his desk. "Oh. But he's—*was*—older than I am, and his wife died last August, so he can't be your top case. And we have Charley Middleton, the fire chief, and he was the manager of the bank, but he was old too, with his family grown, so we don't want him."

"What about Whizzer What's-His-Name?"

"Whizzer Thoms. I was getting to him. Far and away our best case, in my judgment. Really. National reputation—Olympic star, principal of the high school, whole state of Ohio in love with him. And we've got two cases of children on that school bus who were burned—"

"Badly?"

"One yes, one very yes."

Purcell's eyes became restless again. He said, "And?"

"Wait a minute," Wright said. "I'm going down the list, Joe. And that woman who was the school bus driver, that you know about. Not that great on damages, except she was young, with little kids. Husband's a truck driver." Wright looked up for a reaction, got none, and went back to the list. He was on the fingers of the second hand now. "One state highway patrolman. One deputy from the county sheriff's office."

"What about local police?"

"Local police?"

"Florian. They've got a mayor. They've got a fire department. They must have a police department."

Harry Wright looked up, puzzled. He took off his glasses. "You're the first one who's mentioned that."

"Mentioned what? That they must have a police department?"

Harry Wright looked down again at his page of notes. "You know," he said, "I've lived here all these years and I don't even know."

"There was nobody in the Florian police connected with the fireball?"

"I don't even know if there *is* a Florian police," Wright said. "Lord knows, I can find out fast enough."

Purcell put up a hand. "No rush," he said.

"They do have incorporated communities without police departments," Wright said. "Tie into county services instead of municipal. It just never occurred to me."

"Well," Joe said, "you can check it out."

"Well," Harry Wright said in return, "I *did* check two things out for you. Two things you asked about: the movies and the fuel."

"The movies? I thought we just went over that: *Buffalo Bill* and *The Great Gatsby*."

"No," Wright said. "That passerby who took movies of the fireball. I got in touch with him and he brought his projector up to the office. Showed them on the wall right there."

"And?"

"Not much," Harry Wright said. "Some shots of flames shooting up and down, but —"

"Up and what?"

"Down." Wright blinked. "Why?"

"Damned if I know why. I just wasn't sure I heard you."

"But the point is," Wright said, "it's just pictures of a fire. Any fire."

"Can you run them again for me?"

"I don't know why not. The man who's got them had some delusion he was going to sell them to television for five thousand dollars, but the networks wanted no part of it."

"All right," Purcell said. "What about the other thing?"

"The other thing? Oh—the fuel. You wanted to know who was supplying the propane in the area after the disaster." Wright consulted his notes. "You won't believe this, but the answer to that is the same people as before. Tri-State."

"Why wouldn't I believe it?"

"I mean, from the same place," Wright said. "It burned to the ground in four seconds flat, but they have underground storage, so they've gone into the extra supply—"

"Extra supply?"

"The underground storage. What's so strange about that?"

"I don't know," Purcell said. "Come to think of it, I did see a truck out there today, with the hoses leading underground. Said Tri-State on the truck."

Wright nodded. "We've had a very warm month of May," he said. "Wouldn't be at all surprising if their reserve—given the reduced demand for heating—was plenty."

Purcell brightened. "Harry," he said, "let's go get that brandy and soda you were talking about."

Wright brightened too. "Aces high with me," he said. "Want to stop across the street first?"

"What for?"

"Say hello to the judge."

"You told me Arthur Hawkes was already here."

"He was." Wright frowned. "What's that got to do with anything?"

"And he stopped by and said hello to Junior."

"Yes?" Wright was waiting for the other shoe to drop. Purcell was playing him the way Aranow played Purcell. "Then if Hawkes did, maybe it'll be nice if I don't."

The two of them went out through the waiting room, and Rosa Crewes was still sitting there, looking out the window. Harry Wright smiled and nodded at her and said, "Back in twenty minutes, Rosa."

She turned her head. "I hope you enjoyed the peignoir, Mr. Farnum," she said.

Purcell said, "What?"—and felt the jab of Harry Wright's elbow.

"I won't compete," she said. "I can make lemonade. But what does that count for?"

Harry Wright nodded brightly at her. "That's all right, Rosa," he said, and he threaded Purcell through the doorway ahead of him and down the stairs.

Outside, on Elm Street, they turned right and walked under the marquee of the Gem Theater, now showing as its double feature *Skullduggery* and *The Fortune Cookie*. Two doors beyond was the saloon, and they found seats together at the bar and both ordered brandy and soda. Purcell said, "What the hell name was that she called you?"

"I don't want to hear about it," Wright said. "Really. It's just the way she is. The way she's become since the fireball."

"She needs a doctor."

Wright sighed. "We've been over that."

"Well, its like the fun house at the beach around here," Purcell said.

"You don't have to tell me," Wright said. "I already told you, Joe: I'm going to be getting full-time help in the office."

Purcell took out a $10 bill and laid it on the bar, to carry the drinks. Wright moved for his own wallet, but Joe put up a hand. The connection was manifest: a psychiatrist cost money, extra help cost money, drinks cost money. Joe said, "How's your phone bill running?"

Wright shrugged. "Haven't seen it yet. I guess this month'll be a good one."

The bartender, who looked like a wire coat hanger, brought the drinks. Purcell said, "Put it down in your mind to call Sheila O'Hara in our office. Tell her you and I talked, and I said we'll go pickup on the expenses."

Wright said, "Joe, that's not usual."

"We'll make it usual in this case."

Even at this moment, Purcell was on uncertain ground with Harry Wright. The lines were not that cleanly drawn: The bookkeeping could be impeccable—could be? *would* be—but when one lawyer associated with another, there was always a question of whose expenses belonged to whom. It was a problem magnified a hundredfold under the contingent-fee system that paid off only when you won. And what about the client? Purcell was thinking now of Ruth Marlowe, in the malpractice case he'd lost to Hawkes here in Mundelein. Sheila O'Hara, of the miniki, back in New York—she had to be the most aware money manager Purcell had ever encountered. She was twenty-eight years old, and Max had found her in the Wharton School of Finance at the University of Pennsylvania, with that degree to go with her law degree, from Catholic University, and she was a Gloria Steinem look-alike, with tinted glasses and a husband who lifted weights. But Purcell, who told her everything, never told her everything about Ruth Marlowe, because at the point where he told Ruth Marlowe she ought to turn down Hawkes's settlement offer, Purcell had given her cash to keep her going. And in the text of things, a lawyer who financed his own client, when he had a contingent interest in the outcome of the case, was violating the canons of legal ethics, regardless of how good his motivation was or how dire his client's financial condition.

Purcell watched Harry Wright order another round of drinks and then said mildly, "Any news on the Marlowe case?"

Harry Wright shook his head. "Appeal's still up."

"I ought to phone her while I'm down here."

"Well, she's moved to Cincinnati," Harry Wright said.

"Then what about dinner with you and Jenny?"

"That's taken care of too," Wright said. "Tomorrow night. Only you're not taking us to dinner. Jenny's making up a meal at home. You remember the goulash you loved that time, Joe? She's making it again. Really." The new drinks came and Wright hit his forehead with his palm and said, "Oh, thank the Lord I remembered."

"Remembered what?"

"The reason Jenny's having you tomorrow night instead of tonight."

"Does there have to be a reason?"

"There is in this case. Tonight is something else for you: you're expected."

"Expected?"

Wright nodded. "Sunrise."

"Expected for what?" Purcell said.

"Dinner."

"Let me get this straight. I'm expected at sunrise for dinner?"

"That's right. Dorothy Brewer's place. Sunrise is the name of it."

"Who's Dorothy Brewer?"

"Oh, now, you *do* know that," Harry Wright said. "Really. Dorothy *Brewer*. The Brewer newspapers. You've heard of them?"

"Oh," Purcell said. "She's *that* Dorothy Brewer?"

"That's the one."

"She lives here in Mundelein?"

"Not here in town, no. Sunrise is due east of here, overlooking the river. I'm surprised you hadn't heard of it. It's one of the great estates in America. *Life* magazine did a six-page spread on it."

Purcell said, "I still don't understand. Where's she got papers? Baltimore, Cincinnati, Louisville, St. Louis—where else?"

"About eleven other cities," Wright said. "Including, in case you're interested, Mundelein. The *Beacon* here. That's hers too."

"Why would she want this paper?"

"Because her father owned it," Wright said; then he added, almost with a note of ethnic pride, "and for a small-town daily, it makes money. Mundelein's the county seat, so the *Beacon* gets the legal advertising. She's heard of you, Joe. And it might not be a bad idea for you to get to know her. Can't hurt any if there's a trial here."

"It didn't help a hell of a lot on the Marlowe trial."

"That was different. That wasn't that big a case, and you had the hospital here—local defendant. But all in all, I thought the *Beacon* was fair."

"Who wants fair? You know the old line: never mind getting me justice, get me acquitted."

"Well," Wright said, "when I started filing the suits, the *Beacon* ran stories and printed my name and yours—the A&P, that is. And somebody at the paper called up and said she wanted to see you when you got to town."

"You mean I'm just supposed to drive up and announce myself?"

"Oh, no," Harry Wright said. "She'll send a limousine for you. You're being picked up at seven." Wright eyed Purcell's brown worsted. "Do you have anything besides a business suit?"

"I don't think so," Purcell said. "I left my dinner jacket with the Yacht Club Boys."

"Oh, it's not formal," Wright said hastily. "It's just that—"

"I'll wear my bathrobe and go as a flasher," Purcell said. "Is it going to be a late night?"

"I don't know."

"Well, what time are we going over to Florian tomorrow?"

"Can be any time you want," Harry Wright said. "If we don't do it in the morning, we could have a bite of lunch and do it after that. Outside of familiarizing you with the locations, there's really not that much to see."

"I found that out this afternoon."

"I mean, they came in and cleaned up in a hurry."

"Who?"

"The railroad."

Purcell nodded. "I can see Arthur Hawkes now, heading the work crew. He's probably the one who filled in the crater. There *was* a crater, wasn't there?"

"Oh, yes," Harry Wright said.

"Did you get pictures of it?"

"The newspapers all took pictures. We can get prints of all of them."

"Even the ones they didn't publish?"

"Yes. I already checked."

"And the television newsreels?"

"We can get prints of them too. And OSHA had their people in right away, Joe, and we can get their report."

"We already got it in New York," Purcell said. He shook his head. "Leave it to Hawkes."

"Well, I'm not sure there was an ulterior motive," Wright said. "After all, the railroad got its tracks ripped up, and it's only a single-track line. I can understand their needing to get it back in operation as soon as they could."

"It's a wonder they didn't bring in Astroturf."

"I will say they did a thorough job of it," Harry Wright conceded. "They even located every one of the railroad ties that had been blown loose and carted them away."

Purcell shook his head. "Wrong," he said. "They missed one—the one I tripped over when I got out of the car today. See that little streak of black on the pants leg? That little mother sailed a good quarter of a mile from the explosion."

"Are you sure it was the explosion?"

"Uh-huh. First off, it was blackened from the heat—you can see that. We'll stop the car same place tomorrow and you can see for yourself. But in the second place, what else would it be doing there?"

"Would it be useful as evidence?"

"I doubt it, unless you find somebody who noticed it at the time. For the plaintiff's lawyer to come along nearly a month later and just happen to get out of his car and trip over it might be a little much for Junior Bohr. It is evidence of one thing, though."

"What's that?"

"That I probably ought to change clothes for tonight," Purcell said.

21

The miniki had been meeting, screening possible new cases without sign of interest or animation. "Now my turn," Bert Klein said. "It's puzzle time, fans."

Sheila O'Hara said, "Fireball?"

Klein nodded. "I've been going through the railroad's interrogatories and I've come up with the damndest thing you ever saw. It starts with Joe telling me, kind of offhand on his way leaving for Ohio, that he wanted to know how those people in that area were being supplied with propane after the explosion."

Sheila O'Hara said, "Why'd he want to know that?"

"You know Purcell," Klein shrugged. "Don't ask. The thing that's much more fascinating is what I've got here." He opened on oaktag folder and shuffled a page or two. "Not how they got propane after the accident, but how they got it *before.*"

"What do you mean, before?" Felix Harding said. "Before the fireball they got it the way they always got it."

"Did they?" Klein said. "Let me read the numbers to you. The tank car NN 1462—that's the Jumbo Nellie Nellie that blew up—was delivered to the Tri-State Gas siding in Florian on April 29. This according to the record supplied by the Mid-Central Railroad."

Sheila said, "And?"

"*And*," Klein said, savoring the word, "it was filled at the refinery at Whiting, Indiana, on February 27. This according to the record supplied by North American Petroleum."

Willie Blake said, "So?"

"So why did it take two months to get there?" Klein said.

There was silence around the table, broken by the clearing throat and voice of Felix Harding. "Well," he said, "there must be more than that."

"Oh, there's all kinds of things, Nero," Klein said. "All kinds of things."

"Like what?" Sheila O'Hara said.

"Like I checked on how long it takes a freight car to get from Whiting, Indiana, to Florian, Ohio," Klein said. "And it turns out nobody can quite give you an answer. Because they take it from there up to their classification yard in Chicago, and there it gets separated from all the other tank cars in its train and becomes a part of a new train, going wherever it's going, so it can be in with box cars and refrigeration cars and hopper cars and cattle cars and piggybacks with automobiles or army stuff like tanks, but they're all going in the same direction. And nowadays they do this all by computer, so that's that. But the best they give you is a range: four days to ten days, delivery from the refinery through the classification yard to the final destination in Florian, Ohio. In fact, this one was easy, because the deal between North American Petroleum and the Mid-Central Railroad is that they run LPG cars only over the tracks of the Mid-Central. That way there's an operating rake-off."

"Well, wait a minute," Willie Blake said. "You said four to ten days."

"That's what I said."

"But this one took *two months?*"

Klein slid the opened folder to him. "Read it and weep. Out on February 27, in on April 29."

"Well, what do the other people say?"

"What other people?"

"The energy yard," Blake said. "Tri-State Gas. God knows *they've* got to have records."

"Do they?" Bert said. "Let me tell you something interesting about Tri-State: you've heard of mom-and-pop groceries? This place is mom-and-pop propane. They bill their customers every two months, but the billings are based on readings a month earlier than that. So the fact is the Tri-State office in Huntington—the main place they had—has no record of what went on in Florian, because everything blew to smithereens with the fireball. All they know is the billings and readings were normal for the period before that."

"Which means what?"

"Simply that people were getting their propane from the Florian distributor the same as they always did."

"From where?"

"Goddamned if I know! Wintertime deliveries from those jumbos are usually thirty days apart. This one went sixty, and they still hadn't even unloaded the car at the end. It was standing there full on the siding. What were they using to service their winter customers?"

Sheila O'Hara said, "Maybe they had a mild winter."

"I checked that too," Klein said. "It wasn't that mild a winter."

Sheila O'Hara said, "They could have faked the record."

Willie Blake said, "Why would they want to do that?"

"I don't know," Sheila said. "But Bert's right: it's strange. Here's a place in Ohio going two whole months in wintertime without any delivery of propane, according to the records, and still the customers are being served and when the tank car finally does show up, they don't even bother to unload it."

"Willie's question is still in place," Bert Klein said. "Why would they fake the record? Somebody's got to track this down, Nero. It doesn't make any sense."

Harding nodded sadly. "Tuesday, they start running in Belmont. And I'm gonna be tailing tank cars in Whiting, Indiana. God forbid, I should have a nice VW rollover on Queens Boulevard. You say Tri-State's no help?"

"They're worse than no help," Bert Klein said. "They're not even a defendant any more. When I said mom-and-pop, I meant mom-and-pop. Their insurance company threw in the towel. They were only insured for three hundred thousand, and—"

"Only three hundred thousand?" Sheila O'Hara said. "I've got a million-dollar umbrella policy just on my Chevette. Costs me fifty dollars extra a year."

"Which makes you what?" Klein said.

"Overcharged," she said.

Klein nodded. "And they've just thrown it into the pot," he said. "They've agreed to pay their limit. Hell, they're more victim than villain in this. You suck blood from the turnip if you try anything with them."

Willie Blake said, "Then who's left?"

"The three biggies," Klein said. "Nance, the tank car builder. And NAP. And the Mid-Central. And just between us girls, I'm damned if I know why any one of them—"

Blake said, "Have we heard from Purcell?"

"No," Klein said. "He just got down there this morning. Right now, he'll be in a bar drinking brandy and soda and bitching about hick town juries in southern Ohio. You know, for once, I think he's got a legitimate bitch."

22

The Ohio is in all ways a remarkable river. The claim has been asserted that it drains the richest agroindustrial basin in the world, in its descent of 450 feet along its 981-mile route from Pittsburgh, where it is formed by the conjunction of the Allegheny and Monongahela, to its linkup with the Mississippi at Cairo, Illinois. The Mississippi at that point already has been joined by the Missouri. And yet at Cairo it is the Ohio, not the Mississippi, that delivers the most water.

"They have a town along the river," Joe Purcell had told Max Aranow, "not really too far downriver from Portsmouth—the town of Ripley, Ohio. They hung a lantern in a window there when the coast was clear. The lantern was in the kitchen of a man named Rankin—John Rankin—and something like two thousand slaves crossed the river and through his kitchen to freedom. It was one of the stops on the underground railway."

Aranow nodded. "Civil War."

"And before," Purcell said. "In the war, yes, but as much as twenty-five years before that. One time the river froze solid and a slave woman crossed the ice with her baby, and a young white woman heard that story and it made her write *Uncle Tom's Cabin*."

"How do you know these things?"

"How do you know who played shortstop for Detroit in 1908? It's a great river, Max. You ever been there?"

"I've been to Pittsburgh, Cincinnati, and Louisville. Pittsburgh for a World Series, Louisville for a lawsuit, and Cincinnati for a World Series *and* a lawsuit."

"That doesn't mean you know the river. It does everything. It freezes. It floods."

Again Max nodded. "The great flood of 'thirty-seven."

"You're an expert in that too?"

"Yes," Max said. "That was the year the ballpark in Cincinnati was under twenty feet of water—Crosley Field—on opening day—and Lee Grissom proved it by rowing a boat over the left-field fence. History has a way of fooling us, you know. Check the books and they'll tell you it was Lew Riggs who rowed the boat. Not so. It was Grissom."

"Want to know something, Max?" Purcell said. "I was talking to a sister of mine and she told me some of our family, on my mother's side, migrated to that southern Ohio country from Connecticut, long before the Civil War."

Max shook his head impatiently. "You're changing the subject on me."

"*I'm* changing the subject on *you*? I'm talking about American history and suddenly you're back on goddamn baseball."

"Baseball is American history. Would you rather talk about goddamn soccer?"

And it was baseball, not soccer, that some kids were playing in a field next to the Western Motor Hotel when Joe arrived just before six o'clock. The sky over Mundelein was now cloudless, its blue still bright under the daylight saving time of late spring. He went inside and showered and shaved and changed to a Yale blue turtleneck with oxford gray slacks, black demiboots, and dark blue blazer, and just at seven o'clock the rap came at his door and he opened it and found himself staring at a liveried black man who wore spats and a gray mortician's vest: a small, thin man with a voice too deep for his body. He said, "Mr. Purcell, *sah*, I am Castor."

Behind Castor, drawn up beside Purcell's rented Plymouth, was a black Lincoln Continental. Joe blinked, uncomfortably. He had the feeling it was not an occasion to shake hands. At home in Westport or in New York at the Yale Club there would have been no incongruity. But this was Appalachia. Joe tried a light line. "Fine, Castor," he said. "I'm ready. Do I ride in the back of the bus?"

"Ride any place you like, sah," Castor said. "Till we gets to the gates of Sunrise. Then you gets in the back."

Purcell laughed and got in the back. Castor headed the Lincoln due east out of Mundelein. It was a two-lane country road that dipped down through dairy pastures, lush with wetness from earlier in the day, and Purcell said, "Will we see the river before we get there?" But he was only making talk: his sense of direction already told him the answer, and Castor's "No, sah" came as no surprise.

Still making talk, he said, "Is this a big gathering you're taking me to?"

"No, sah." True-bred as a professional chauffeur, Castor never looked in the rearview mirror as he spoke, "Miz Brewer tries to *avoid* big gatherings. Be just you and her and his lordship and his ladyship."

"His lordship and his ladyship?"

"They been stayin' at Sunrise."

Purcell had a sense about Castor. He had the capacity—Princeton had nearly bred it out of Willie Blake, back at the A&P in New York—of black trend-setting in language, so that when they meant "the only one" they said "onliest" and when they meant "her" ladyship they said "his" ladyship, which in its way did more for language because it conveyed more information.

More than that, however, Purcell had the victim's feel of being in the hands of a master replier. The more you asked, the less you wound up knowing.

He would have to tell Max about Castor when he got back to New York, and about that weird woman in Harry Wright's waiting room, who said, "Oh, it's you," and talked about lemonade and how did Mr. Farnum like the peignoir and how she wouldn't compete. Compete with what? It raised the hair on the back of Purcell's neck.

But he was still talking. "Tell me, Castor: you from around here?" That had to be the most inane question yet.

Castor said, "Yes, sah."

"Right here? Mundelein?"

"No, sah. Chesapeake."

"That's right across the river from Huntington. The downtown bridge, right?"

"Yes, sah. You sure knows your territory. Up Huntington, down Ironton, there ain't no foolin' you."

"I was here a few months back," Purcell said.

"Yes, sah. Miz Brewer said you tried a case in the courthouse."

Purcell grinned. "Did she tell you I lost it?"

"No, sah. All she say is you better not lose this next one."

Purcell's hand went to his ear. "What else did she tell you?"

"You done heard it all."

Joe grinned again. He said, "What's it like?"

"What's that, sah?"

"I mean, growing up in Chesapeake. I grew up in a river town. The Connecticut River."

"That a wide river?"

"Not as wide as the Ohio."

"I had people in my family move there," Castor said. "Went into war work about there. East Hartford. United Aircraft. Used to tell us about a great new bridge there. The Charter Oak Bridge."

"It was new then," Purcell said. "It's not anymore. But I've got to tell you something: those bridges you've got across the Ohio around here— they've got to be the *oldest* bridges I ever saw. I mean, when were they built?"

"Ain't nobody rightly knows," Castor said. "You cross the Ohio around here, you got to realize one thing: you ain't noplace when you start and you ain't noplace when you get there. This gotta be one place don't need no new bridges."

Oh, Purcell said to himself, that was a line he had to get in somewhere. Was there a place in the script of *The Last Laugh* for it? Or did it do something else, instead, which was to describe himself? You ain't noplace when you start and you ain't noplace when you get there. He looked out the window: the road was rising now, and turning to the left. Then suddenly there were iron palings outside the window to his right, and a great open-standing set of gates, and Castor swung the car between them and onto a curving graveled driveway, and the first thing Purcell noticed was a shed that parked a snowplow, just off to his left. But now the driveway swept between two rows of fat-trunked maple trees, and suddenly turned hard right, and the trees gave way to lawn on the right and, out to the left, a sudden cliffside view of the river, perhaps as much as 300 feet below. Here, east of Huntington, the river had made its northward bend, toward its source at Pittsburgh, and stood all by itself. The great steel works and oil works and coal-transfer works, in that industry-laden stretch of the river,

25 miles from Huntington past Ashland and Ironton and nearly to Portsmouth, always lit by night because the furnaces had to be kept up, resonant with the sound of jackhammers pounding the pins of the hopper cars as the coal was transferred to barges—all these were downriver and around the bend, and all Purcell could see was the supreme beauty of the river gorge, sweeter than the Shenandoah where it broadened to reach Harper's Ferry and its meeting with the Potomac, sweeter than the Mississippi at Prairie du Chien, or the Hudson north of Bear Mountain, the Columbia downriver from Portland, the St. Lawrence beneath Quebec. And Purcell, who had seen them all—and the Rhine, too—drew a sharp breath and said, "Oh, my God," while at the same time Castor, at the wheel of the Lincoln, said, "That is the Ohio, sah."

But the car did not stop, and Purcell did not see the mansion before they were upon it. Here the maple trees had given way to beeches, and set beyond was the house, the antebellum mansion separated from the South by the great, aware, working river. Not pristine, for thick strands of ivy clambered the great white columns and clutched like Kong hands at the windows.

Castor stopped the car short of the house and bounced from the driver's seat to open the door on the left-hand side for Purcell, and Joe stepped out onto a flagstone terrace, the full display of the river still to the left, and saw a woman and a golden retriever coming toward him. The woman wore a velvet pantsuit and held a martini glass. She had aviator-style dark glasses, and very yellow hair done in spit curls; small, with a good figure. He took her to be about his own age.

The dog bounded past him and melted away, just as Castor had melted away, and Dorothy Brewer said to him. "Welcome, Joe Purcell."

"You have to be Dorothy," he said, and held out his hand. It seemed as right as with Castor it had seemed wrong.

"Come out back with me," she said, and her hand held on to his. "There are some people here who know you."

"Who?"

"Lord and Lady Eddington. Tony and Vivian."

"I've had some day around here," Purcell said. "Everyplace I've been, there are people who know me. Except I don't know them."

"Come," she said, and led him beyond the side of the house to the area in back, where the patio swelled with balloon effect. There were steps leading down to a swimming pool, and inset against the house were a stocked bar and chafing dishes with little tongue flames beneath and set-outs of oysters Rockefeller, large hothouse mushroom caps bubbling with fresh crabmeat and white cheese, Gulf shrimp in Creole sauce. At the exterior of the patio, where it turned inland, great cemetery slabs of rock, fully four feet high and a foot thick, girded the crescent, the teeth of some extinct Brobdingnagian lower jaw. They seemed to guard the place, and in an official capacity, for some of them were engraved as if by a notary's seal.

Almost lost in the spectacular setting were two other people. The man wore a white dinner jacket, the woman a full-length gown. "Hello, old boy," the man said to Purcell. "You did me a great favor two years ago, at the Thames Club."

"The Thames Club?" Purcell shook the man's hand. "Two years ago?"

"Oh," the man said, and giggled. He was a large man, and too big-chested for his size even at that. The woman beside him was an asparagus stalk topped with black hair. "Not our Thames Club—your Thames Club. The tennis tournament there. For cerebral palsy."

"You beat our Bunky in the first round," the woman said.

"Good and proper," the man said. "I'm Tony Eddington. This is my wife, Vivian. Bunky is our son. He had some illusions about his prowess on the court, I'm afraid. He was twenty-one, and you beat him six-one, six-love."

Purcell nodded. "I remember the tournament. I don't remember the score. I can tell you the score in the second round. Harold Solomon cleaned my clock, six-three, six-love. I remember getting three games off him in the first set. The fascinating thing was that two of them were off his serve. I'm afraid I don't remember much after that." Looking beyond their shoulders, Purcell set eyes on one of the most beautiful women he had ever seen. She was black, and dressed in a French maid's uniform, and he heard the voice of Dorothy Brewer saying, "Hallie, see if Mr. Purcell will have a drink."

"We're all doing martinis," Eddington said.

"That would be fine with me," Purcell said. He saw Hallie smile at him, but the smile was special, because it came from the eyes, and the eyes were suddenly the same as those of the madwoman in Harry Wright's office. He forced himself to look away, through the gaps in the giant's jaw, and he said, "That's an interesting stone fence, Dorothy."

Tony Eddington said, "You'll never guess what those stones are, old boy."

"I should complete the introductions," Dorothy Brewer said. "In fact, I'm remiss. Lord and Lady Eddington introduced themselves. But you've heard of the Eddington newspaper chain in England. You're in the presence of unique nobility, Joe: two people who live in an English castle and don't have to conduct hourly tours to pay the rent."

Hallie brought him his martini on a silver server. Purcell had to pull his eyes away from her. He said, "How many guesses do I get?"

"I think he should have three guesses," Vivian Eddington said. "Don't you, Tony?"

Dorothy Brewer said, "Three it is."

Something tugged at Purcell's throat. He swallowed and said, "Do I get to look at them first? Close up?"

"Be my guest," Dorothy said to him. "On the ones where you see markings, look behind them on the other side, because you'll see other markings."

"Did you say three guesses?" Purcell asked, and moved toward the stones. But he did not examine them closely. He sipped his martini. "Then is it all right if I take all three?"

"You sound rather sure of yourself." It was Vivian Eddington who said it, but her voice held a puzzled tone.

"Well," Purcell said, "guess number one is that this is Stonehenge West."

"No," Dorothy said. She was looking at him closely. "What about guess number two?"

"Guess number two would be that you had them manufactured as a conversation piece," Purcell said. "Am I close?"

"Closer than you might think," Dorothy Brewer said. "Guess number three?"

"There's only one guess left," Purcell said. "These stones were stolen from the Mason-Dixon line. The line that separated Maryland from Pennsylvania. They were milestones, but every fifth mile the stones bore the seals of the Baltimores on one side, the Penns on the other. It was pre-Revolution, more than two hundred years ago."

Lord Eddington said to Dorothy Brewer, "He knows."

"Of course he knows," she said.

"But you told me the Mason-Dixon line ran through this house."

"Not quite this house," Dorothy said. "But the river, yes. Tell them, Joe."

"Well," Purcell said, "by straight extension the surveyed line ran logically west to the Ohio, and then was commonly taken to follow the Ohio to the Mississippi, and then on westward along the line of the Missouri Compromise, so that it came to mean what separated the slave states from the free at the time of the Civil War, except that wasn't its original purpose at all."

Vivian Eddington said, "Why did they call it Mason-Dixon?"

"Because of your guys."

"My guys?"

Purcell took a silver cocktail fork and lofted an oyster shell. "Charles Mason and Jeremiah Dixon were two English astronomers. They were imported to settle the Pennsylvania-Maryland boundary dispute. They even brought the milestones with them. But people kept stealing them. I'd say somebody around here wound up with a pretty good collection."

"Now I know why you want a crafty barrister on the premises." Lord Eddington chuckled, pointing an accusing finger at his hostess. "Pinching ancient stones, old girl, could land you in the clink for years."

"I hate to disappoint you, Tony," said Dorothy, "but the statute of limitations on stealing these stones expired before I was born."

Lady Eddington said, "Fascinating." Hallie appeared to refill her drink, and Purcell looked at the long net stockings—looked so long he had to justify it, and so gulped the balance of his own drink and held out the glass for more. "I've been telling the Eddingtons about the fireball in Florian," Dorothy Brewer said. "I had my Mundelein editor bring me a copy of the complaint you filed. Now I want to win that case."

"That sounds like a papal bull," said Joe.

"I don't care what it sounds like," she said. "I've never wanted to see a case won more than this one."

Eddington said, "You didn't tell us, Dorothy. Did you know any of the victims?"

"No," she said. "But I know one of the defendants. McKenna. Harrison McKenna." You could spit the word "McKenna," and so she did.

Vivian Eddington said to Purcell, "That's the second or third time Dorothy's mentioned Mr. McKenna. But we don't know what he did that was wrong."

"Move over; I'll join the club," Purcell said to her. "I never even heard of the man. We're suing corporations here, not people."

"That's what you think, Mr. Purcell," Dorothy said. "Who are your chief defendants?"

He shrugged. "Nance, NAP, the Mid-Central." To the Eddingtons, he said, "The tank car manufacturer, the oil company whose propane was in the car, and the railroad." Back to Brewer, he said, "Now: Who's Harrison McKellar?"

"McKenna," she said. "He ran for the United States Senate here one year. By 'here' I mean Ohio. The three chief financial backers in his campaign were Nance, North American, and Mid-Central. Ring a bell?"

"Who beat him?"

"That's beside the point. He lost in the primary, and the man who beat him went on to lose in the general."

"He sounds like a great target defendant."

"Didn't you hear me tell you who supported him?"

"Yuh, I heard it," Purcell said. "But if a candidate was to get corporate backing in this state, those would be a pretty logical three."

"Before he ran for office he was an assistant secretary in the Department of Transportation," Brewer said. "Does *that* ring a bell?"

"Nope."

"The railroad division of the Department of Transportation."

"Nope."

"And do you know what he did after he lost?"

"Nope."

"He became the first vice president of North American Petroleum," Dorothy Brewer said. "And in line to become president."

"Well," Purcell said, "if you're telling me the oil companies and the railroads and the tank car manufacturers are in bed with one another, what else is new? That goes back to the time they made John D. Rockefeller break up the Standard Oil Trust and the Union Tank Car Company was a spinoff. UTLX—they're even bigger than Nance."

Dorothy said, "You don't understand one word of what I've been saying."

"Maybe not. But if you're simply saying that the Department of Transportation regulated these people and it was fox-in-the-chicken-coop where the industries being regulated supplied the regulators, then so what? Those days were the height of that stuff. Every other admiral in the Pentagon was on the payroll of the companies they bought the hardware from. It's the American way." He turned to Eddington. "The English way too, Tony?"

"Yes, but we're not as good at it as you are," Eddington said. "Perhaps we once were, but I think it had something to do with the shrinking of the empire and the devaluation of the pound. Our problem is that to buy something, you need the money to buy it with. Also, you Americans have so much to begin with. The only thing you've really had to go out and buy in the foreign market in the past ten years was Péle, that Brazilian soccer player. So you bought him."

"Not me," Joe said. "If I even went to a soccer game my partner would disown me. And I'm not buying the McKenna connection yet, Dorothy. You started out with a clap of lightning about how I have to win this case because of one man whose greatest sin is probably he got the *Reader's Digest* to write him up. Where's your case?"

Behind them, great full-length glass doors swung open, and Dorothy said, "We can talk some more about it at dinner. It's duckling and artichokes. Will you buy *that*?" She turned and led the way, through the doors and into a lavish drawing room that featured a 9-foot Mason & Hamlin piano of black mahogany. Oh, I've got to get at that piano, Purcell said to himself. Of the big four—Steinway, Mason & Hamlin, Knabe, and Baldwin—the Mason & Hamlin gave off the softest touch, this at once its greatest virtue and greatest curse. The top of the piano was raised, and he stopped and looked in at the lyre, and the metal imprint, forged from below to raise the letters, told him the piano had been manufactured in 1924. The mahogany case must be so mellow by now the music would cut like cheesecake. And this one 9 feet—a concert grand. Dorothy Brewer stopped and looked at him. She said, "You play?"

"Uh-huh."

"Well?"

"What's well? They loved me in New Haven, if that means anything. Almost went into music instead of the law."

"What stopped you?"

"Nothing stopped me. I may still do it. Lead the way to the food, Dorothy, and tell me more about your passion for McKenna. It may be my last case. Even if it isn't, I need all the help I can get."

"I don't know when you're joking," she said.

"Neither do I."

"I don't even know when you're paying attention."

"Oh, I pay attention," he said.

"Yes," she said. "To Hallie's legs."

"And to law and music. Between lawsuits I'm writing a musical."

"A musical? You mean, for the stage?"

"Yup."

"You know how to do that kind of thing?"

"I think so."

"Well, you'll have to play something from it after dinner." The table was set in an elegant but smallish room. Sunrise had two dining rooms, the other far larger, with a long Hearstian oaken banquet table and cloths of heraldry flattened against the walls. Joe was seated with Lord Eddington to his left, Lady Eddington to his right, and Dorothy Brewer opposing him face-on.

"Now I'll tell you," she said, and her eyes bore straight on Purcell. "Our friend Mr. Harrison McKenna was a defendant in a lawsuit in Akron, and it concerned a land grab—real estate—and they got to the judge. And I have a paper in Akron, and the judge ruled my reporters couldn't go into the courtroom, so they found a way to pick up the news from inside anyway. And the judge asked them about their sources of information and they refused to tell him, so he sentenced two of them to jail for contempt— the two of them, plus the editor who printed their stuff. And the three of them spent seventeen days in jail, and McKenna won the case."

"By Jove," Lord Eddington said, "how could you permit that? You should have gotten Joe here to take the case for you."

"Joe's the last lawyer I would have got," Dorothy said.

"I was clowning," Eddington said. "But it would seem to make sense, wouldn't it? You've told me about him and his law firm. They're at the forefront of these rights issues in your country, aren't they?"

"Every rights issue but this one," Dorothy said. "Right, Joe?"

"Right," Purcell said.

"You see?" Dorothy said. "The man from the A&P admits it. They like every amendment in the Bill of Rights except the First Amendment. Did you ever hear of the First Amendment, Joe?"

"Did you ever hear of the Sixth?" Purcell said.

"Oh, my," Vivian Eddington said.

"The Sixth Amendment guarantees impartial trial," Purcell said. "The First Amendment guarantees freedom of the press. Sometimes the one can conflict with the other. It's something judges have to decide, and there are no magic answers. You have to take it on a case-by-case basis."

Dorothy Brewer's voice went tight. "The First Amendment says Congress shall make no law abridging freedom of the press. *No law means no law.* I'm quoting Hugo Black of the Supreme Court when I say that. He didn't even want to hear the case of the Pentagon papers. He said if there was no law, then what law were they supposed to rule on?"

"Well, then, why not take the case of your own paper here in Mundelein?" Purcell said. "When I lost the Marlowe case here, they printed my name. When a guy dies, do you print the name of his doctor in the obituary?"

"I don't see the relevance of that."

"The relevance of that is twofold: number one, it goes to impartiality, and number two, it means the press doesn't need any help from me or my law firm."

Lord Eddington looked up from his turtle soup and said, "Well, now, I started something. What I do want to hear is more about this tank car. Blew the center of the town to smithereens, so Dorothy tells us. Dead and injured all over the place. There must be a magnificent recovery in a lawsuit like that."

"Or no recovery at all," Purcell said. "The fire was started by a bolt of lightning. It's not easy to prove human responsibility for a thing like that. In fact, it's hard to prove anything to a jury in Mundelein. Did you know they have eight-person juries in Ohio?"

"Why eight?"

"Saves money. Actually it's nine—you have an alternate juror in case one of the others gets sick or something. But you never know who the alternate is. It's like Russian roulette."

Dorothy Brewer said, "I wasn't aware of that. Isn't the ninth juror automatically the alternate?"

"Not the way Junior Bohr does things," Purcell said. To the Eddingtons: "He's the local judge. The courtroom's so small that when you impanel a jury he sits nine people in the jury box to begin with. The rest of the panel sits in the spectator seats and stands against the wall. As one juror after another is excused or challenged off, others sit down and take their places, and then you question them, and eventually you wind up with nine jurors. But you can't point to any one of them and say he or she's the alternate."

Vivian Eddington said, "Well, you must find out sometime."

"You do," Purcell said. "The last thing before he sends them to the jury room to decide the case, after the closing arguments, the instructions, everything, one name is drawn by lot and the judge just points to that juror and says, 'Thanks very much, you can go home,' and that's it." He was aware of Hallie over his shoulder, clearing away the turtle soup. "Furthermore, in some states the first juror picked is automatically the foreman, but here the jury elects a foreman in the jury room after they retire to decide the verdict. So you can wind up with egg all over your face. You can spend the whole trial trying to get one person elected foreman, someone who you are convinced will be strong and sympathetic to your side. Every time there's a photograph or a document or an exhibit to pass around the jury you hand it to him first and ask him to look at it and then pass it on to the next juror. You address him by name—"

"Him?" interrupted Dorothy.

"Or her," Joe smiled. "It can just as easily be a woman. He or she becomes a natural favorite to win the foreman election. Then at the end your prime candidate gets drawn as the alternate, and your whole tactical approach is shot out of the water."

Lady Eddington said, "But you get a chance to challenge them at the beginning."

Purcell nodded. "Peremptory challenge. First, a juror will be excused for cause, as they say. It'll turn out he knows one of the principals in the case, or says he has an innate prejudice against one side or the other, or if it's going to be a long trial he can claim hardship, although that doesn't happen around here that much."

"Why do you say that?" Tony Eddington said. "Why would there be less hardship here than someplace else?"

"Because there's no money in this area," Purcell said. "People get paid for jury duty. It may not be much, but it's a few dollars and they can use a few dollars." The duckling came. "Besides, it's a good show."

"I thought you said there wasn't anything that glamorous about this kind of a case."

"Compared to what's playing at the Gem, it's glamorous. Also free."

"Especially glamorous, I'd say," Vivian Eddington said, "when the famous Mr. Joe Purcell comes to town."

"That part of it loses a little in the translation," Purcell said. "You'd be surprised how many people never heard of me."

"Oh, you're hiding your light under a bushel, old boy," Tony Eddington said.

"But especially juries," Purcell said. "They hear of my fame only one way: from the opposition lawyer. He prances up and down in front of them pointing at me and saying here's the high-priced lawyer from New York. I adore that kind of fame." The duck was excellent. "But to answer your question, yes, we do get peremptory challenges. Last time I was here we got three apiece. Three isn't a very big number, and it artificializes everything."

Vivian Eddington said, "Artificializes?" She made it sound like a man's name.

"The point is," Purcell said, "a peremptory challenge means a challenge without any stated cause. You can just point to a juror and say I don't want him or I don't want her, and they're excused, period. You don't have to tell anybody why. But—" he raised his fork "—when you only have three of them, it becomes cat and mouse. You may want somebody off that jury, but the other side may want him off too, so why give up one of your challenges if the other lawyer will do your work for you? And the same time you're doing that to the other lawyer, he's doing it to you. You're on the guess. So here's a juror named Jones, and he's the last man you want on that jury, but you tell yourself he's also the last man the other side wants, so you wait for the other side to be the one to challenge him, and after three go-rounds, they don't. All right. If you had a fourth challenge, you'd say the hell with it and kick him off. But when you only had three challenges to begin with, there ain't no fourth challenge, and you wind up with that son of a bitch in the jury box, staring you in the face and grinning at you."

"Joe makes it sound complicated," Dorothy Brewer said.

"It is complicated," he said.

"My point," she said, "is that Joe is a master of such complications. That's why he has the reputation he has."

"You're generous, Dorothy, but really, nobody's a master of complications," Purcell said. "In fact, if you want a complication, I'll give you a beauty: with twenty-five deaths and scores of injuries, no one will live long enough to try all of the cases one at a time."

"That is a complication," said Dorothy. "How do you handle it?"

"Well, the gut issues—who was at fault, was the explosion caused by a defective product—those issues are the same in each case. So the approach is to ask the judge to select one representative case—what we call a specimen. It's tried with the understanding that whatever the jury decided in that case on liability—those gut issues—will control for all the cases."

Dorothy said, "How does the judge decide which case is the specimen?"

"Same way he decides everything else," Joe said. "Each side submits briefs. We'll urge them to take one of the cases with big damages and heavy emotional impact on the jury. The defense will go for a small case with no sizzle. And the judge will probably cut the baby in half and pick some case that's the middle ground between the two."

"But if you win," Dorothy said, "how does the jury decide the damages? If all they've heard about is the damages in the specimen case?"

"They'll hear enough about the other victims to decide whether exemplary damages should be awarded, and how much. And they get all the damage evidence on the specimen, so they can bring in a compensatory award in that case."

"Then how about compensatory awards in all the other cases?"

"If we lose," Purcell said, "there aren't any. If we win, most of the other cases will probably settle, using the specimen verdict as an index. Those few that don't settle will get trials on damages only, which shouldn't take very long."

"And the other damages?"

"The punitives?"

"I thought you used another word. Exemplary."

"Exemplaries and punitives are the same thing," Joe said. "It means that in addition to compensating the victim for the actual damage he suffered, you award extra damages to set an example—to punish—to deter the people who were at fault from going out and doing it again. And for that matter, to set an example for other people who might cause similar injury. When Ford lost the big Pinto case, Chevrolet recalled its Chevettes. They hadn't had similar accidents, but they wanted to reinforce the Chevettes anyway, just to play it safe."

Lord Eddington said, "Well, suppose the jury did give you punitive damages. How would they be split up?"

"Well," Purcell said, "as you've sensed, a punitive award would be just one lump sum, for everybody. But then it goes on the same kind of index. Once everybody's compensatories are decided, whoever got the biggest percentage of the compensatory total will get that same percentage of the punitive total. And so on, pro rata, on down the line." A Grey Riesling wine had come with the duckling, and Purcell raised his glass.

"It's not an import," Dorothy Brewer said. "It's Wente Brothers. California."

"Max Aranow would love you," Purcell said. "I love you." Joe sipped the wine, which was chilled to perfection. "In any event," he said, "now that I've lectured you so unmercifully on complex litigation, perhaps you know why I'm thinking about giving up the law and turning to musical comedy."

"Then we'll take you into the drawing room after dinner and you can play for us," Dorothy said. "I think Tony and Vivian would like that."

"Like it?" Vivian said. "I think it'd be glamorous."

"It's what I was talking about before," Joe Purcell said. "Free entertainment has a way of being glamorous around here."

After dinner they did go into the drawing room, and Purcell seated himself at the piano, with a goblet of Remy Martin on a linen coaster atop the square-out of the music rack, and began to play. For the Eddingtons, he did Noel Coward and some *My Fair Lady*, and at one point Vivian Eddington asked him to do "When I Grow Too Old to Dream," and Purcell said, "You know, I met Oscar Hammerstein once, at Max Aranow's place in Pennsyslvania. Hammerstein had a place in Bucks County, not too far from there, and this was a Sigmund Romberg waltz, and Hammerstein wrote the words, and he told me it was one of his all-time favorite lyrics—except that for the life of him, he couldn't figure out what it was he'd said. 'When I Grow Too Old to Dream'—when do you grow too old to dream? I mean, think about it."

But after a time, Purcell lapsed into Gershwin, with cocktail piano modulation, and he said, "The greatest lyricist of all was Ira Gershwin. Bar none. Because he *grew*. And his best lyrics came after his brother was dead. He did the lyric for 'Long Ago and Far Away,' and that was his all-time personal favorite for a single song, but it wasn't George's music. It was Jerome Kern's." He played the song but spoke the lyric. "Chills run up and down my spine. Aladdin's lamp is mine." He stopped. "Oh, my God, what words to put to that melody."

Lord Eddington said, "Do you know anything from *West Side Story?*"

"Bernstein? Anything you want. It wasn't his most distinguished score."

"I was thinking of 'Maria.'"

"'Maria'? I just met a girl named Maria—Oscar Levant said Maria was a number of notes in search of a melody."

"But you were going to play us something of your own," Dorothy Brewer said. "From your musical. What's the story of it?"

"It isn't my story," Purcell said. "I'm adapting it from a novel nobody ever heard of, called *The Last Laugh*. I took an option on it. Yes, I'll do you a song from it." He played and sang:

We have met before somewhere, when the world was green,
Sometime in the springtime, in my dreams I've seen
Your face at some familiar door somewhere, when the world
    was new,
We have met before somewhere, somewhere there was you.

He did not look at the keyboard as he sang. Instead, his eyes were on Hallie, as she entered from across the room with the cognac decanter.

When the song was over, Brewer and the Eddingtons clapped their hands effusively, but Purcell's eyes still held Hallie's. She was at the piano now, refilling his glass.

Dorothy Brewer said, "That was wonderful, Joe. You have to give us more. Maybe you're right—maybe you did miss your calling."

"I don't know," he said. "Maybe I should quit while I'm ahead."

"Did you know that Hallie sings?" Dorothy said. "Maybe the two of you could do something together."

Purcell sized Hallie up, not for the first time, but for the first time with an excuse. He said to her, "What do you want to do?"

"I don't know," she said. "I'm not as good as Miz Brewer says."

"Neither am I," he said. "Make any sense to do any R&B with this crowd?"

She shook her head. "Ain't nothin' without the electrics."

"Thank God," he said. "How about 'How High the Moon'?"

"Don't know the words."

"I can feed you. One chorus that way, then scat-sing it. Just stay on top nice and easy."

That way they did "How High the Moon," and then "Gone with the Wind," and a wicked "All the Things You Are." It was an evening. At the end, Dorothy Brewer took him to the front door, where Castor had the Lincoln drawn up, and said, "When will you be back?"

"Don't know," he said. "I'll be in and out. No question of that."

"How long are you here for this time?"

"Hopefully one more day. Maybe two. We're associated with Harry Wright in the case."

"I know that."

"So I have to go over the case load with him, and then meet with other local lawyers who've brought actions. If I can clean it up tomorrow, so be it."

"Why don't you think of staying here next time you come?"

"I'd love to. But you're in and out too, aren't you?"

"Give me a little advance notice," she said. "We'll see what we can work out."

"All right," Purcell said, and kissed her on the forehead and went out and got into the back of the limousine. And on the ride back to Mundelein he made no small talk with Castor; rather he closed his eyes and thought of Sunrise and the terrace whose border was studded with those great Colonial milestones. Yes, you can have three guesses, Dorothy Brewer had said to him.

Three guesses, the lady said, and now in his mind's eye the Ohio countryside ceased to be, and the Lincoln Continental in which he rode became instead a taxicab heading west on Wilshire Boulevard toward Beverly Hills. It was perhaps two years ago, and that day he and Arthur Hawkes had reached a settlement agreement in a swimming pool accident, and that night Purcell would be going to the theater for a kind of production he had never seen before. The theater, grandly situated on a Wilshire corner, came with orchestra pit and stage, though in recent years it had been given over to first-run films. For these few days, however, it had been taken over by the Oldsmobile division of General Motors for a full-fledged musical review built around the new Olds models for the coming year. Admission to the performances was by invitation only, limited to Oldsmobile dealers and independent lessors in California, Nevada, and Arizona, together with their families. It meant morale and morale meant sales. "I'll leave a ticket for you," Nate Borowitz had told Purcell the previous week in New York. "I guarantee one of the greatest musical shows you ever saw. You float an industrial show like this, it'd better be *right*."

Borowitz was an up-and-coming conductor, still in his twenties, and to be picked for the touring industrial show was a plum. Like the American exhibit at a trade fair in Moscow, a production of this sort could not afford a single flawed performance. It had to be not only theater at its best but theater at its best every time. "It's a takeoff on *Anything Goes*," Borowitz said. "Changed the plot, changed the lyrics, cut the running time to a single act of ninety minutes, but kept the songs."

"Who's the star?"

"Marcy Beall. You've probably seen her."

"I don't know if I have or not," Purcell said. "But I know I've heard of her."

"We did a road swing of *Hello, Dolly!* together," Borowitz said. "She did the Irene Molloy part. You know."

"It only takes a moment," Purcell sang, "for your eyes to meet and then..."

"That's the one."

"That Jerry Herman schmalz is fine business," Joe said.

"Well, Marcy's a good one," Borowitz said. "She carries the show real good. And wait till you see the final scene. It'll knock your eyes out."

He was right. The curtains parted, and there was rip-roaring stuff going on onstage, a chorus number ended by the entry of the heroine, a tall, well-proportioned young woman in a blue dress with legs that were the kind that went all the way up, and shoulder-length chestnut hair, and— most remarkable of all, the Mary Martin/Helen Traubel syndrome so infrequently encountered—a voice that went with the rest of her. Not even Ethel Merman had that. All the others—Henderson, Cook, Andrews, Grayson—had voices you expected, but only after hearing them: The first time was always a startlement. But Martin and Traubel had it, and Marcy Beall had it.

The show entranced its audience. It *moved*—moved to a climax of Marcy cakewalking as she sang, weaving in and out of five gleaming automobiles, each revolving slowly on its own carpeted turntable, each turntable at a different height off the floor.

Purcell's heart sang for the show, sang for the showmanship, sang for the way Nate Borowitz sang the audience out of the theater at the end with the exit music. And at the end the theater was in half-light, nursed by prisms of maroon and gold from the upholstery, and after a time all the musicians were gone, but Purcell remained where he was, and Borowitz made his way through the pit to the percussion end and looked up and held out his hand.

"What'd you think, Joe?"

"Unbelievable. I mean it."

"Believe it or not, I was holding myself back," Borowitz said. "Marcy reamed my ass after the matinee today."

"You mean you were happier at the matinee than you were tonight?"

Borowitz nodded. "She said it was like trying to sing behind John Philip Sousa and the Fifth Dimension at the same time."

"Well," Purcell said, "if you were holding back tonight, that matinee must have been really something."

"It's zest, Joe," Nate Borowitz said. "*Zest.* Want to go up the block and get a bite to eat?"

"Why not?"

"We'll take Marcy with us. I'm waiting for her now."

"Oh," Joe said. "Is it a thing between you two?"

Borowitz shook his head. "No way. She yelled so much after the matinee, I said to her, 'Look, let's try it again tonight and then we'll get some coffee and you tell me what you think then.' Tell you the truth, Joe, it'll be a favor having you along. In case she's still mad."

Then Purcell saw Marcy Beall onstage, over Borowitz's shoulder. She wore a green street dress, which at Purcell's eye level gave him her legs once again. She said, "Nate, I'm ready."

Borowitz turned. "You have to meet Joe Purcell," he said. "The lawyer from New York."

"You need a lawyer from New York," Marcy said.

"I thought he could go with us."

"Why not? You were still fighting me, Nate."

"It may not be the musicians," Borowitz said. "It may be the score itself."

Marcy said, "Hello, Joe Purcell."

"Hello, Marcy Beall."

"It was better than this afternoon," Marcy said. "I'll say that much."

"Then maybe I can control it," Nate said. "I'll go back to the hotel and work on it tonight after we eat."

Purcell said to him, "Are you going to change?"

"No," Borowitz said. "I'll change back at my hotel, after we eat. Marcy here, she has the royal suite at the Beverly Wilshire. A dressing room backstage here at the theater. Me, I have to change into a tuxedo at the No-Tell Motel."

Marcy laughed. To Purcell she said, "Are you a lawyer for Oldsmobile?"

"No," Purcell said. It was his turn to laugh. "If you knew my partner, you wouldn't ask that question. Come to think of it, he won't even stay at the Beverly Wilshire. One time he was there and he asked them to chill his tomato juice and they put an ice cube in it, and from then on he's stayed at the Ambassador."

Marcy said, "The Ambassador is awful."

"I know it," Purcell said. "That's where I'm staying. We have one of the bungalows. But right behind it is the Windsor Restaurant, and that's what counts with Max. They have a curried crayfish bisque he likes."

"Max?"

"My partner."

"Joe knows an awful lot about show tunes," Borowitz said to Marcy.

"Does he?" she said appraisingly. "Does that explain why he was here today?"

"I'd never seen an industrial show," Purcell said.

"You haven't said what you thought of it," she said.

"I thought it was great."

"Then maybe you don't know as much about show tunes as you let on."

Borowitz said, "Now, Marcy."

"Let's get something to eat," she said.

They went out the lighted emergency door into the alley and cut to their left and through a parking lot to Junior's restaurant, where they got a wood-backed booth for three and Borowitz began chomping on the pickles and sauerkraut even before the menu came.

"Sometimes," Marcy said, "I wish I'd done what the professor said."

Purcell said, "The professor?"

She nodded. "That was seven years ago. I was twenty-two. And there was this German professor who gave voice lessons, and he said he could teach me to sing only if I stripped naked for him. I had to remove my inhibitions, he said, and that was the only way I could learn to sing from the stage. Do you want me to strip for the matinee tomorrow, Nate? Because that's the only way if you shout that brass at me."

"I told you I'd fix it," Borowitz said. He was sitting next to her. Purcell was across from them, staring into her eyes. His mind said, If she was twenty-two seven years ago, then she's twenty-nine now. The rule is a man's mistress should be one-half his age plus seven. She's close enough.

Marcy returned his stare, and Joe was the one who blinked and looked away. He reached idly for his glass of water and said to Nate, but more to Marcy, "Got a good settlement today."

"I knew you were here on a case," Borowitz said.

"Kind of interesting," Purcell said. "We were representing this man who dived into the water off the side of a motel swimming pool, a place where he shouldn't have dived at all, because it was marked only six feet deep, and the guy went and broke his neck—every way you can break your neck and still survive."

Borowitz said, "And they settled?"

"Mm-hmm."

"But why was it the motel's fault if he dove from the wrong place?"

"Because he thought it was nine feet, not six."

"But you just said it was six. And marked that way."

"Right," Purcell said. "But the markings were on the side of the pool across from where he dove in." He took a ballpoint pen from his inside coat pocket and sketched the pool. "He was looking at this six," he said, "the number in the tile coping. But from where he stood, what does that six look like?"

Marcy said, "A nine."

"If we were seated side by side," Purcell said to her, "we could play kneesies. But at least this way you see what my client saw."

Borowitz said to Marcy, "Have you heard of the A&P?"

"What does that mean?"

"This is the P of the A&P you're talking to. Aranow and Purcell. They're nationally famous for things like what Joe just told you."

"I don't understand," Marcy said. "Was this accident out here?"

"Yes," Purcell said.

"Well, if you're a New York lawyer, why was it your case? I mean, if he thought it was nine feet and not six, why wasn't there a lawyer out here who could represent him?"

"Because he didn't exactly think of that at all," Purcell said. "We were invited into it because the local firm out here needed some extra ideas."

"In other words, it was you who told him it looked like a nine."

"Didn't look like, lady. *Is* a nine. Look at it for yourself."

They were eating at that point, Purcell remembered, the waiter having come and gone—or was it a waitress?—and his memory had lost the fix on what it was they ate. But at the same time he could remember everything Marcy said.

She said, "Then you're clever."

"Oh, very clever," he said.

"Knows every show tune ever written," Borowitz said. "Try him, Marcy."

"Why should I try him?"

A touch of new color came to her face, a punch of adrenal, a flaring to nostril and lip. "'Put On a Happy Face,'" she said.

"*Bye Bye Birdie*," Purcell said. "Words by Lee Adams. Music by Charles Strouse."

"'Somebody Loves Me,'"

"Gershwin."

"Music or lyrics?"

"Music. George."

"Then lyric by B. G. DeSylva, right?"

"Half right. Lyric by B. G. DeSylva and Ballard Macdonald."

"He's good," Marcy said to Borowitz.

"I told you," the conductor said.

"But not that good," she said. "I'll get him if it takes all night."

"You won't take all night on my time," Borowitz said. He signaled for the check. "Oldsmobile's treat," he said. "And I'm off for the No-Tell Motel, to modulate tomorrow's music for Madam Tetrazzini. You kids can sit here and play as long as you want to."

"No," Marcy said. "I'm going too."

"I'll walk you down the street to the hotel," Joe said.

"Thanks, Mr. Clever Lawyer."

"You're welcome, lady."

They were out on the street, and said good-night to Borowitz, and then Joe and Marcy walked the short stretch to the corner of Wilshire, then catty-crossed to El Camino where the hotel was.

She said, "Do you want to come up for a drink?"

He said, "Yes, lady."

"They've given me a suite with a piano," she said. "It's only a spinet, but it's there. Can you play piano?"

"Am a elephant big?"

"Then you can play for me while I get into something comfortable."

Purcell tried to think of an answer and found none, and they mounted in the elevator to her floor in total silence. She did indeed have a suite with a spinet and a kitchen with refrigerator and stocked bar, then the bedroom and dressing area and bath beyond.

"Scotch?" she said.

"That would be nice."

"With what?"

"Soda, if you have it. Over ice."

"I assumed you'd want ice."

"Never assume I want ice, lady."

"Oh," she said. "Well, then, you do have the wrong idea. Because when I said come up for a drink, it wasn't code for anything else. And when I say I want to get into something, it's because I want to get into something comfortable."

"The truth of it is," Joe said to her, "nobody ever said these things to me before. I know they're supposed to be standard, but I've never been through them."

"Good," she said. "Then you won't be a problem."

"Problem?" he said. "What is that?"

"We could make a little test out of it," she said. "Just so you'll know where we stand."

I'll give you three guesses: Dorothy Brewer at Sunrise. "I'll give you three guesses," Marcy Beall said in her suite at the Beverly Wilshire. "And any fantasies you've got will come true for you. If you get it right."

"If I get what right?"

"'My Ship.'"

"What's 'My Ship'?"

"Just the name of a song, that's all," she said. "The bar's there. Make your own drink. If you haven't got it by the time I come back out, you go home."

"And all you're going to tell me is two words—'My Ship'?"

"Don't complain," she said. "The Scotch is good. Take it and sit down at the piano and take off."

"This is like Rumpelstiltskin," he said, "with the three guesses."

"You can leave now if you don't like the rules."

"My rule is I always like rules, lady."

"That doesn't mean you get four guesses."

"I can still have a free drink in the meantime."

"Of course you can, Mr. Clever Lawyer." And she left the room.

Purcell took his drink and sat down at the piano. His throat was very tight. He tried various chords and phrases, some melody lines. He drank from his glass. And then Marcy was back, wearing an orange floor-length wrap with a full-length zipper up the front.

"Lady, you're good-looking," Purcell said to her.

"You've got three guesses," she said.

"This is the ultimate put-down."

"It is, isn't it?" she said agreeably. "But I need my sleep. So take your best shot."

"It's a hornpipe," he said. "I know it: music by Carver, lyric by Lensinger. A very obscure thing. It goes: 'My ship sails the ocean blue, In search of pirate treasure, The sails and the mast are new, Its riches beyond measure.'"

"No," Marcy said. His hands came off the keyboard. "No, no, no. Two guesses left."

Purcell said, "Could we leave off this nonsense, and we just finish our drinks and I take you inside and make love to you?"

"It's what I said. You're down to two guesses. Unless you just want to give up."

"All I've got left is a tarantella," he said. And he played and sang: "'Whose is that ship out there? It's my ship—my ship! Whose is that ship so fair? It's my ship—my ship!'"

"Why don't you quit while you're behind?"

"But what happens if I get it right the third time?"

"You can do anything you want to me if you get it," she said.

"Anything?"

"Anything."

"You sound awfully confident."

"Maybe I am."

"But you don't blame me for trying?"

"I didn't say I blamed you. I was giving you a face-saving way of clearing out. After all, that way you can always say you had one guess to go."

"What if I'd like another drink instead?"

"You want another drink?" Marcy said. "I'll pour you another drink. But you're not going to draw this out just because you've got a drink you haven't finished." She took his glass and went to the bar. "We'll make it half a drink." She looked at him from across the room. "What's the matter? Clever lawyer from New York has nothing to say? Can't say the six looks like a nine?"

Seated at the piano, Purcell said, "I don't know. I'll settle for small favors at this point."

"Half a drink of Scotch?"

"Half a drink of Scotch, lady. And playing Rumpelstiltskin. With one guess to go."

She brought him the drink, and he raised the glass to sip heavily from it.

"Don't buy time with me," she said. "You've got your one guess left. Do you want it or not?"

He set down his glass. "I guess I want it," he said.

"I can hardly wait," she said.

"Neither can I," he said, his throat ready to explode. He set his hands to the keyboard once again.

"Good luck to you," Marcy said.

He took a deep breath. "All right. *Andante espressivo,* quarter note eighty-eight to the minute." His hands began to play, and his Scourby voice to sing.

My ship has sails that are made of silk,
The decks are trimmed with gold,
And of jam and spice there's a paradise in the hold...

He sang it all the way through. The left hand trailed while the right hand reached for her zipper. She said, "Oh, you dirty betraying son of a bitch," but he said, "You gave me three guesses, lady. Ira Gershwin's words. His favorite show of all time. *Lady in the Dark.* Kurt Weill wrote the music. Did you ever hear the instrumental Benny Goodman did on 'This Is New,' from the same show?"

"All right, you son of a bitch," she said. "Don't rub it in."

The limousine came to a stop and Castor said, "We are there, sah."

"Oh," Purcell said. He did not wait for Castor to come around and open the door, but this time he did shake his hand. "Thank you, Castor. I hope to see you again."

"Miz Brewer say you gonna."

"Then I'm gonna," Joe said, and fished for his room key and went inside, the glow of that night two years ago still upon him. Three guesses. You know, he said to himself, if you hadn't known that song she *would* have kicked you out. He took off his jacket and sat down on the bed, and for a moment his hand went to the telephone, but by now it would be too late to call Marcy and tell her what had happened. Instead, he stood up and undressed and got into his pajamas, then went to his dispatch case and took out his pocket tape recorder, its cassette already in place, and sat on the side of the bed again and pushed the "on" button.

"This one's for Nero, Elizabeth," he said into the grill mike. "To FH from JP. Re: Fireball." He turned the machine off and smiled, remembering again that night in Los Angeles. The way Marcy's arms stayed at her sides when he reached for her zipper. "How many moments like that do you get in a lifetime?" he said aloud. An exultant laugh escaped his throat. He turned the recorder on again. "There is a man named Harrison

McKenna, a vice president of North American Petroleum. Used to be with the Department of Transportation. We need to know everything there is to know about him. I mean everything."

23

To: Winston McHale, Mid-Central Railroad, St. Louis
From: Arthur Hawkes
Re: Fireball

Please arrange to be in my office in Chicago next Tuesday, one week from today, at 11:30 a.m., for a private luncheon discussion between us. It is a discussion I prefer not to hold by telephone or through the mails.

McHale, the general freight manager for Mid-Central, was there precisely at 11:30. He cooled his heels for 40 minutes, and then Hawkes came into the waiting room, tall, ascetic, clad in a hand-tailored summer suit of solid dark blue. "Winston," he said in greeting. "Is your blood pressure up again, or is it just that all railroad executives have those red spots on the cheeks?"

McHale had come energetically to his feet. "You always badger me, Arthur."

"Do I?" Hawkes made a noise in his throat. "I reserved a private dining room in the Calumet Club, on the tenth floor here. Have you ever been there?"

"You never asked me to lunch before," McHale said, trotting behind him into the corridor and toward the elevator.

"I may never ask you again," Hawkes said.

"Ed Jamieson said you're giving everybody a hard time these days," McHale said.

Hawkes said nothing.

"Jamieson," McHale said. "Our trial counsel."

"I know who he is," Hawkes said. "A chess player. Do you play chess, Winston?"

"I'm afraid not."

"That's what Jamieson should say. I had the three of them in my office and set up a problem with a Bristol Theme solution and not one of them could get it."

"What's the Bristol Theme?"

"It's the theme of this lawsuit, really," Hawkes said. The elevator left them off at the tenth floor. "The Fireball. In the Bristol Theme, the key move to victory is to take one very important piece and simply move it out of the way."

"Sort of a sacrifice?" McHale said.

"Sort of," Hawkes said, "but only sort of. Tartakower said it is always better to sacrifice your opponent's men." They entered the tall double doors of the Calumet Club, and a red-liveried footman ushered them to a small walnut-paneled room, with snowy table kneed by two King Arthur chairs and a sideboard set up for drinks.

"Irish whiskey, neat, Henry," Hawkes said. "And a glass of Perrier on the side. Winston?"

"A Manhattan," McHale said. "With two cherries."

"When you contract cancer from the red dye in the cherries," Hawkes said, "I know a law firm in New York that will represent you. The A&P. But they would prefer you die from it before they take the case."

They sat at the table and were served the drinks. Then Hawkes waved his hand and Henry the footman was gone.

"I'm glad we're going to have this meeting, Arthur," McHale said. "There's one thing that's been bothering me."

"What's bothering *you* isn't why I set up the meeting," Hawkes said. "But if it's only one thing, I'm delighted. You can go first. Tell me what it is."

"The insurance question," Winston McHale said. "I know that Nance has outside insurance. But North American Petroleum and ourselves, the Mid-Central—we self-insure."

"Why should that make a difference? Insurance is insurance, no matter who writes it."

"Some of the boys were worried that if it went to trial the other side could bring it up. I mean, if we insure ourselves, we don't even have any limits. The sky's the limit. And once the jury finds that out—"

"How are they going to find it out?"

"The other side could find a way."

"Yes," Hawkes said, "Joe Purcell can find a way if anybody can. But the courts are very strict on that point. The only time the plaintiff is permitted to mention insurance is on voir dire—that is, the examination of prospective jurors before the trial—and then only to ask them if they have any connection with an insurance company. But—"

"What do you mean, 'But'?" McHale said. "From what I hear of Purcell, he can drive a truck through that hole. He'll kill us, Arthur."

"Thank you for the exhibition of panic, Winston," Hawkes said. "As I was going to say before you interrupted, But—and the But is that they can only do that in the state of New York. We're in the state of Ohio, so we don't worry about it."

"I worry about it."

"Why? If Purcell mentions it in any way at any point during the trial, it's instant grounds for mistrial."

"What if *you* mention it?"

"I'll do my best not to," Hawkes said drily. "Although I must say the point doesn't bother me. When you have three giant corporations as the named defendants, the jury pretty well figures they can afford to pay damages."

McHale said, "But if—"

Hawkes put up a hand. "There's another point along the same lines, and this one should interest you even more. But the law is good for us on this one too."

Winston McHale retreated to his drink. "Another point?"

"The doctrine of postaccident repair," Hawkes said. "Between the date of the accident and the time the Fireball gets to trial, it might very well be that one or more of the defendants would revise the way these tank cars are designed or operated. Some kind of safety measure. Now, if something like that got into evidence in front of a jury, it could be made to look like an admission that they were trying to correct an admittedly dangerous practice. But the law saves you on that point too, Winston. Just like insurance, such evidence is inadmissible."

"I'm glad to hear that," McHale said. "Although for the life of me I don't understand how you can keep evidence like that from being told to a jury."

"The reason it can't be told to a jury," Hawkes said, "is that the law, supposedly, is not an ass. It is supposed to be an instrument of social policy. If you trip over a piece of carpeting in a department store and break your leg, and it takes you five years to get your lawsuit to trial, it might be a very good idea for the store to fix the carpet in the meantime. But if they thought that fixing it would be an admission of guilt they'd leave it the way it was, and God knows how many other people might trip and break their legs too. So the law says go ahead and make your repairs, and the fact that you made the repairs won't be counted against you when you get to court. And the way to make sure it isn't counted against you is to say it can't be introduced as evidence. That way the jury never finds out."

"Except that your friend Purcell—"

"Yes, he can get it in if anybody can," Hawkes said. "But again here I'm not all that worried, unless you know something I don't. Tripping over a carpet is one thing. Having something hit by lightning is something else. But I thought you'd like to know."

The waiter—not Henry the footman this time, and jacketed in black instead of red—came with the menus and, taking Henry's role, poured another round of drinks. And Hawkes waved him out of the room in turn.

"Before we order," he said to McHale, "I must tell you I have good news and bad news. I'll give you the good news now. The bad news can wait till you begin to eat. The working of the digestive juices will be helpful for you."

"You're a great kidder, Arthur."

"Am I? You think I brought you here to kid you?"

"Then give me the good news," McHale said.

"First let me explain what a specimen case is," Hawkes said. "Only one of the victims of the accident will actually have his case tried." He outlined the mechanics of specimen configuration, noting that McHale's red spots, hallmarks of his cheekbones, were heightened by the second Manhattan, unless it was the red dye in the cherries. Then he outlined the coexisting case for punitive damages for *all* the victims.

The waiter came to take their orders, then left again. "Now," Hawkes said, "the good news is that we have a very good specimen case. A black handyman at the trailer court next door to the Jumbo Nellie Nellie. Killed instantly. Blown to hell and gone by the blast. But he was sixty-two years old, single, no relatives anybody can find, and he had a nice cancer of the . colon. He'd been to a clinic, and we'll get the people there to testify that he had less than a year to live in any event. So where's the exposure? Dead zero, that's where it is."

"Oh, Arthur, I love it," McHale said. "You're beautiful!"

"Don't go off the deep end," Hawkes said. "I didn't say I can *get* that as the specimen. But I'm certainly going to try."

"Well, who names the specimen?"

"The judge. Both sides apply for the case they want the most, but he can pick any case that's been filed in his courtroom."

"Then what makes you think he'll pick yours? Out of all the others?"

"The element of punitive damages," Hawkes said. "I'll make that the core of my argument. What we have in effect here is double exposure—compensatory damages in the specimen case: loss of earnings, loss of a loved one, medical costs in the case of a victim still living, so forth and so on—and then punitive, or exemplary, damages for *all* the cases, in case the jury finds wanton or gross neglect."

"But how can they find that, Arthur? I mean, lightning wasn't *our* fault."

"I didn't say they would find it," Hawkes said. "But it makes my arguing point for me: simply that if I'm exposed to the risk of a punitive verdict, then on the specimen side I'm entitled to a reduced-risk sample case. Otherwise I'd be up for maximum risk twice. It's a theory I haven't had occasion to use before, but there's a lot to recommend it. I'm having my brief filed with the judge in Mundelein later this week."

"Well, I think that's handsome, Arthur," McHale said. "You're a man who does his homework!"

"Preparation is everything," Hawkes said. "Emanuel Lasker said, 'Do not permit yourself to fall in love with the end-game play to the exclusion of entire games. It is well to have the whole story of how it happened; the complete play, not the denouement only. Do not embrace the rag-time and vaudeville of chess'."

"And your friend Purcell?" McHale said. "What will he—"

"I wish you would stop calling him my friend," Hawkes said. "To answer your question, he will be doing in his brief the same thing I am doing in my brief, only for the highest damage specimen, not the cheapest. He will argue one hundred and eighty degrees away from me: namely, that the risk of the jury's *not* coming in with a verdict for punitive damages for all the victims entitles him to have the one specimen case he can try be the biggest of all for straight compensatory damages."

"And what are his chances?"

"As good as ours."

The waiter had brought the soup. McHale said, "After what you just said, I don't understand what's so good about the good news. I mean, there's no guarantee the specimen will be the one we want."

"I didn't say the good news was that good," Hawkes said. "What's good about it is that we even *have* a good specimen case to go in with. I was surprised, and pleased. After all, the town of Florian didn't come out of that fireball intact. Now I've got something I can press with. If I don't get this case, it may still influence the judge to give us a specimen with low exposure. The fact that I've got a chance to put in for minimum damages is just a bonus I didn't expect. It can influence the judge in our direction even if he rejects our specific case and names another."

"Oh, I didn't think of that," McHale said.

"You're not paid to think of it," Hawkes said. "I think the one thing we can count on is that Purcell's not going to get the specimen *he* wants. That's what the black handyman gave us, Winston. Do you understand?"

The waiter came and removed the soup plates. Both men had ordered salmon, and it was set before them.

"Am I ready for the bad news?" McHale said.

"I don't know if you are or not. But Purcell has a computer going. And they've already turned something up, Winston, and when I ask you about it, you'd better have some straight answers to give me."

"I don't understand," McHale said. "We've got a simple case of lightning that hit a tank car. Who has to put that on a computer?"

"Is it a simple case?" Hawkes said. "Is it a simple case when that tank car was loaded at the refinery in Whiting on February 27 and didn't get to Florian till April 29? What kind of madmen are you?"

McHale waved his fork vaguely. "I have no information to that effect."

"That's why you're here: to hear it from me. Ordinarily, you'd be the last to know. Where's your explanation?"

"I don't have any."

"Well then you'd better get one, mister," Hawkes said, "and you'd better get one as fast as you know how. What was that Jumbo Nellie Nellie doing those two months?"

"Nothing, Arthur."

"Nothing, Arthur?"

"I mean," McHale said, "it has to be a simple mistake. An error in the records. Obviously, if the tank car was filled, it was delivered."

"Oh, yes. We have records of its being filled. And being delivered."

"Then I guess somebody forgot to write something down."

"You guess somebody forgot to write something down. Do you want to leave it at that? Let me tell you something, Winston. As a lawyer, I don't like surprises. But I especially don't like surprises when it's Joe Purcell doing the surprising."

"It just doesn't make sense," McHale said. "I'm thinking of the railroad part of it. But the other part of it—the surprises—that doesn't make sense either. I thought that was Perry Mason stuff, where one lawyer could surprise another in court."

"It is and it isn't," Hawkes said. "You can introduce rebuttal and impeachment witnesses without tipping off the other side. If you anticipate that one of their witnesses will say something you can disprove, you can just file the name of your witness in advance with the judge. You put the name in an envelope. And the law doesn't require you to reveal this to the other side until your witness actually takes the stand."

"I didn't realize that," McHale said. "How often does it happen?"

"Not very. A good way to avoid it is simply by talking to your witnesses in advance and saying to them, 'Look, if you have any skeletons in your closet, don't keep them a secret from your lawyer just because they have nothing to do with the case. *Tell* your lawyer if you were being treated by a psychiatrist. If it's not material, the other side will never get a chance to bring it up. But keep it to yourself, and something in your lawyer's direct examination while you're on the stand may hit the nerve by mistake, and then you're fair game.'"

"I didn't realize that," McHale said, again.

"I did us both a disservice by even bringing it up," Hawkes said. "What I'm telling you, Winston, is that I think the records have been faked here. Or at least there's that chance. Two months for that Jumbo Nellie Nellie to get from Whiting to Florian makes no sense: That's number one. Number two is that Purcell's bird dogs are surrounding it like the Interpol. Number three is that he can go into that courtroom and take an act of God with no liability, like this lightning strike, and take this little bookkeeping error of this one Jumbo Nellie Nellie and turn the jury against me in five minutes flat."

"He's that good?"

"He's that good. Why do you think he's got the bird dogs out? For his health?"

"Well, I'll look into it, Arthur," Winston McHale said. "But I really think you're overreacting, across the board. There's been a little innocent mistake here, that much is apparent. Of course I'll look into it. But I don't see where the business of how long it took the tank car to get there has anything to do with a bolt of lightning, and as for why Purcell's investigating it, you did leave out one possible reason, Arthur. You really did."

"Did I?"

"Yes."

"What reason would that be?"

"Just that he's desperate, Arthur. That he has no case."

Arthur Hawkes sipped at his second glass of Perrier water. "I've already considered that possibility."

"And?"

"It may be the right one."

"Then what's the problem?"

"Just that I can't afford to assume it, that's all. And I have this stupid two-month gap staring me in the face. And I don't regard it with equanimity, Winston. If I regarded it with equanimity I wouldn't have called you up here today. And you overlook something else."

"What else? I came, didn't I? I said I'd look into it, didn't I? What else is there?"

"The Bristol Theme," Hawkes said. "I may literally have to kick one defendant off the board to win this case."

"Which defendant?"

"You."

24

Covering the walls in Joe Purcell's office at the A&P were framed reproductions of sheet music fronts. Show tunes, all of them. "Falling in Love with Love," from *The Boys from Syracuse*; "I'll Follow My Secret Heart," from *Conversation Piece*; "In a Kitchenette," from *The Gold Diggers of Broadway*; "But Not for Me," from Gershwin's *Girl Crazy*; "Am I Blue," from *On With the Show*; "Tea for Two," from *No No Nanette*. The lyric to that last was said to have driven Vincent Youmans, the composer, half crazed with astonishment: "Day will break and you'll awake and start to bake a sugar cake for me to take—What the hell is that supposed to mean?" Jackie Miles asked. "She doesn't even brush her teeth, already she's baking a cake?"

Purcell's office was notable also for the fact that it had no desk. It had a breakfront work shelf with telephones and drawers and cabinets, but otherwise it was furnished as a living room might be furnished, and in taking a phone call Purcell might either stand up or sit on the shelf itself, receiver in his right hand, the left hand free for taking notes. He was a pacer, with high knee steps—Elbie Fletcher, the old first baseman, so Max Aranow had finally diagnosed him—and on this morning Aranow sat in a blue armchair while Purcell paced.

"Yesterday the Yankees defeated Cleveland eleven to five in sixteen innings," Max said. "What does that tell you?"

"I don't want to hear about it," Purcell said.

"That's the same thing you said the time I told you no race horse could have more than fourteen letters in his name. Why aren't you interested in the world that surrounds you?"

"I am interested in the world that surrounds me. I told Dorothy Brewer the history of the Mason-Dixon line."

"I was going to ask you about her," Max said. "Nero said you told him she'd furnished a lead."

"Something else bothered me more than that while I was down there," Joe said. "This crazy lady in Harry Wright's office. A case of insanity growing out of the fireball."

Aranow nodded. "Willie Blake said something about *that*."

"What I didn't tell Willie," Joe Purcell said, "was one line she threw at the two of us—Harry and me—while we were leaving his office and she was sitting there. She—" He broke off and went to the intercom button and pressed it, and the voice of his secretary, Elizabeth Frasciano, came into the room: "Yes, Mr. P?"

"What's a peignoir, Elizabeth?"

"It goes over a nightgown," she said. "Supposed to complement it, sort of. Flimsy. Sexy. Maybe with buttons or little tie-strings. Sometimes you can wear it *as* a nightgown."

"Ah," said Purcell.

"Do you want to assign this to a particular case file?" Elizabeth said. "Or is it a question that just came up?"

"The indirect answer to that is save the sarcasm," Purcell said. "The direct answer is I don't know yet." He rang off and looked across the room at Aranow. "I didn't know who she was talking to, this woman in Mundelein, whether Harry or me. But what she said was, 'I hope you enjoyed the peignoir, Mr. Farnum,' or something to that effect, and it gave me the willies, Max, because that's my grandfather's name—my mother's maiden name—my middle name: Farnum."

"It's not all that uncommon a name."

"No? How would you like to be standing there and hear something like that?"

"Call up Alex Haley," Aranow said. "Maybe you have roots you don't know about. I'm more interested in the peignoir."

"What can I tell you?" Purcell said. "I have no recollection of ever seeing this woman before in all my life."

"You're sure you just didn't give her a little you-know last time around, when you were down there for the Marlowe trial?"

"Come on, Max. Fuck that noise."

"I might have intended it as a compliment."

"You haven't seen the lady. She used to work in a store. Now all she does is sit in Harry Wright's waiting room. Spooks everybody that comes in or out the door."

"Maybe she calls everybody Farnum. You yourself just said you weren't sure if she was talking to you or him."

"Yeah?" Purcell said. "Well, the first time we talked about this case I said I wanted out. That goes double for now."

"In that case," Aranow said, "the best I can tell you is you have to stand in line. Terry Malloy wants out too."

"Terry Malloy wants *out?* He's got the best case in the whole batch. A medical student, twenty years old, whole career and life in front of him, first in his class, now quadriplegic on account of the fireball."

"Exactly," Aranow said. "So Malloy thinks he can separate this case out and make it the one case Hawkes would be willing to settle. They're asshole buddies, you know. Both from Chicago. Eat lunch together at that Calumet Club in Arthur's building. Did you ever taste that goyishe fish they serve there?"

Why did I just go to Mundelein last week? Purcell asked himself. I come back to report to my partner, and everything I found out, he already knows. He drew a deep breath and said, "Max, can I ask you something?"

"You don't have to," Aranow said. "You're going to say, 'Max, why don't you be the trial counsel in the Fireball?' But you and I both know the answer to that one. For twenty-two years you've built your courtroom presence, and each one of those years mine has slipped a little."

"Quit the self-pity," Purcell said. "You appear in court three times as often as the rest of this office put together."

"Doing what?" Aranow said. "Representing poor people against the establishment? That's the easiest trial work in the world. They're not trials to begin with: They're hearings. More than that, you automatically expect to lose."

"Which is what I expect in Mundelein," Purcell said.

"Except that you have it in you to take on a big one," Max said. "I always lacked a little something in that direction. I could get away with making up in theory and preparation what I didn't have in a courtroom, but I was never the gunner, Joe. When I spotted you, I knew in one minute you were the missing piece. No, you don't see me taking on something when we're really leveling."

"Then where is this law firm going?"

"Under your direction it's going fine."

"I won't accept that," Joe said. "You're putting a burden on me I won't acknowledge."

"What burden? I came in here this morning to put this burden on you? It's been a fact of life in this office for fifteen years, and you know it. One of the reasons we do so well in court is that we don't get into court that often. The other side hears the A&P and the other side folds and settles."

"Hawkes won't."

"He has in the past."

"He won't on this one."

"He might for Malloy."

"Bet me."

"Ah," Max Aranow said, "then that's where I earn my keep. Because Terry Malloy is in town and I'm having lunch with him. There's nobody as skilled as I am to argue why Joe Purcell should try a case in court. If we don't get into court that often it's because we do so well in court, but Purcell is the one who makes that appearance in court, not Aranow. Aranow's job is to say look out for Purcell. It's been a glorious partnership, I must say."

"Did you see that memo from Bert Klein?" Purcell said. "The one that quotes the Department of Transportation figures on the jumbo tank cars?" His pacing took him to a pile of memoranda on his work shelf, from which he extracted a paper. "This is years before the fireball happened, but it's the latest figures they've got on the jumbo tank cars. 'During the 7-year period studied, there have been 519 112 and 114 pressure tank cars'—the one-twelves and one-fourteens are the jumbos, Max, so it means five hundred and nineteen of them—'in derailments of which 168 lost some, or all of their lading. These occurrences have caused 18 deaths, 832 injuries, and 45 major evacuations involving more than 40,000 persons.' So forth and so on."

"Now," Max Aranow said, "you see?"

"See what?"

"These things blow up all over the place."

"You missed my key word, Max: 'derailments.' Our Jumbo Nellie Nellie wasn't derailed. It was hit by lightning."

"Well, wait a minute," Aranow said. "That goes to the effects of the explosions, not just the cause."

"Not when it comes to finding somebody liable," Purcell said. "Who's the defendant here? The Acme Lightning Company?"

"There's always something you don't notice," Aranow said. "Like that baseball score I gave you: Yankees beating Cleveland yesterday eleven to five in sixteen innings. All my life I've been seeing scores like that, and just this morning I realized."

"I won't ask you realized what."

"Realized," Max said, "that that score also told me the game had to be played in Cleveland. Any game that goes extra innings, or even into the last of the ninth, the home team cannot win by more than four runs." He looked upward and back, reflectively. "Incidentally, do you know that James Price hasn't filed any lawsuits in the Fireball?"

Purcell had spent too many years with Max to miss the beat when the older man switched subjects. He said, "Price! Isn't he the lawyer Cuneo got to pick up the dregs—the airline passengers—when he got shut out of the big ones?"

"Exactly," Aranow said. "Willie Blake told me that apparently they're not even going to bother to file. Wouldn't one of *those* have made a great specimen case?"

"Speaking of Willie," Joe said, "he has a very persuasive argument for us to apply for Whizzer Thoms as the specimen. Olympic track star. National hero. Sole breadwinner for a family that's still young. Two of them still pre-college. Principal of the high school. Worked with Jesse Owens in the Atlantic-Richfield program for underprivileged kids. Did lectures. Held clinics. An irreplaceable talent and individual and now he's gone."

"Plus that he was one of the volunteer firefighters," Max said.

"Plus even more than that," Joe said. "Willie put his finger on something. Among all the volunteer firefighters, Thoms was the one case of extra response. He couldn't hear the siren when it went off. He was too far away— five miles away, at the high school. But he had a deal with Middleton at the bank to have him called if there was a fire during his working hours. So he came in response to a phone call, not a siren. He'd set it up in advance that he'd be there anyway even if he couldn't hear the siren."

"How long did it take him to get there?"

"Nobody knows. No witness survived who timed his arrival. But what difference does that make, Max?"

"None at all," Aranow said, "except that it makes it even better. Consider the twenty-minute time span between the start of the fire and the explosion. If somebody had seen Thoms driving up at the last minute, just in time to get blown up, that's one thing: it's kismet. All accident. But if he got there earlier, in time to start help fighting the fire or whatever, it says even more for him—that he went all out, not only setting it up that he'd be paged by telephone but the fast way he covered those five miles. Without any witnesses, any best side of that argument belongs to us. Incidentally, did anybody at the high school time when it was he left?"

"I checked that while I was down there. They say as soon as the call came he took off."

"So," Max said. "It gets better and better. Beautiful stuff to nudge a jury with."

"Yuh, I told Willie I liked it," Joe said. "It's a nice added touch. Extra response, as I just said."

"I love it," Max said. He rose from the armchair. "Okay. Now I go to pick up Terry Malloy at the Sheraton Centre and take him to lunch. Report back to you this afternoon."

Purcell said, "He booked himself into the Sheraton Centre? I don't believe it."

"No," Max said. "I booked him there."

"You're a traitor to your class, Max."

"What could I do?" Max said. "It's the perfect hotel, considering we're going to lunch. Joe's Pier 52 is right there and The Stage Delicatessen is right across Seventh Avenue." He moved toward the door and paused. "I need this whack at him myself first."

"You don't have to explain why I'm not invited to lunch."

"I'm explaining why Malloy is in the Sheraton Centre. Besides, you already have a lunch appointment." Aranow nodded. "See you this afternoon."

"I should be back by two," Purcell said.

"'Kay," Max said, and went out the door.

Within two minutes, Joe was on the elevator, exiting the building on the 54th Street side, turning right the few steps to cross Fifth Avenue, then north the one short block to the St. Regis, and when he reached the dining room there he saw that Marcy was already at the table. It was against the wall, and he moved in beside her and in the quickest of motions snuggled his tongue against her ear.

"You've been back a century since you went to Ohio," she said.

"You smell good," he said, "and it hasn't been a century. Have you been here long? I would have made it earlier, but I was fencing with Max."

"Fencing about what?"

"You."

"Oh, sure," she said. "Wait till Caldwell the elephant hears this one."

"He knows this is my last case," Joe said, "and he keeps running around the sides of it. That's one thing I meant when I said 'you.'"

"What's the other thing?"

"A woman I met when I was in Mundelein," he said. "Listen to this, lady: her name is Dorothy Brewer. Ring a bell?"

"Of the Brewer newspapers?" Marcy said. "I've heard of her at the agency. *Everybody's* heard of her. Is that the one?"

"One and the same."

"And you met her?"

"She lives there. Damndest estate you ever saw. Place called Sunrise, overlooking the Ohio. It was a command performance. *She* sent for *me*."

"Why?"

"I'm not totally sure. She wants to help me win the Fireball, but it's a personal vendetta between herself and one of the oil company vice

presidents, and who knows what this will do? I'd hate to place a bet on it."
The waiter brought them a Scotch old-fashioned and a glass of Chablis,
unasked. He knew Joe and Marcy. "I gotta tell you, it knocked my hat off.
She's got the perfect setup. A big room with a beautiful piano, and she can
reach half the money on the North American continent in that one room
at one time." He lifted his glass. "A toast. You and I can go down there
and audition *The Last Laugh* and collect enough in that one session to back
the whole show."

"Well," Marcy said, "what does she say about it?"

"I don't know. I haven't told her yet."

"Then why are you so positive?"

"Because I played for her, and did 'We Have Met Before,' and she
flipped. I told her I was doing a musical and she thought that was great.
So all systems are go."

Marcy lifted her glass without returning Joe's toast and sipped her wine
slowly. Finally she said, "Joe, I want to do your musical more than
anything in the world—you know that—but you've abandoned the Fireball case."

"What does that mean—abandoned the case? I'm making all the right
moves."

"Oh, I'm sure you are," she said.

"Marcy, I don't understand. Don't you *want* to audition in the right
place at the right time?"

"Yes," she said. "I guess I do."

She turned quickly and kissed him on the cheek. "I'm sorry. It's just
that I hate to see you in..." Her voice trailed off.

"In what?"

"In competition with yourself."

"I'm not competing with myself. Lawsuits take months, years, before
they ever come to trial. The Fireball isn't even the only case I'm handling
at this moment. We have more than one client. We don't consider that
competing with ourselves."

She nodded. "I suppose you're right. I guess maybe what was in my
mind was having the audition for the musical in the same place as the trial
for the Fireball. It gives me the shivers."

"Without the musical and the Fireball that town gives *me* the shivers,"
Purcell said. He flash-debated telling her about Rosa Crewes and the
peignoir, Mr. Farnum, but if she reacted the same way Max did, wanting
to know how many times he'd laid Rosa Crewes, he could do without that
kind of aggravation. He did tell Marcy about the Farnum part of it, though,

and Castor and what it was like with Dorothy Brewer and his lordship and his ladyship at Sunrise, and Hallie, too, but without overdescribing her.

And what Florian had looked like, and about young Coblenz, the medical student who wound up quadriplegic, and the headless driver steering his car perfectly down the road, and how the energy retailer, Tri-State, was still pumping the propane from its underground tank to service customers, as though nothing had happened. And all about Whizzer Thoms and what a good specimen his case could be.

They were eating now, both of them on the lobster salad, served onto their plates from a great wooden bowl. "Didn't Thoms have life insurance?" Marcy asked.

"Sure, he had life insurance. But that doesn't let the oil company or the tank car people or the railroad off the hook." He raised a finger. "If."

"If what?"

"If they were guilty of anything."

"I don't know," she said. "I've never seen you so pessimistic about a case."

"Well," he said, "I was pessimistic to begin with."

"But you're so—" she groped for the word ". . . . *articulate,* so vivid, when you talk about it. Everything enthusiastic except enthusiasm itself."

"You didn't let me finish," he said. "I was pessimistic to begin with. The more I get into it, then sure, the more vivid it becomes." He reached for his glass of Chablis. "And, lady, the more pessimistic I get."

After lunch they went outside, kissed good-bye at the southwest corner of 55th and Fifth, she headed east toward Madison and he the one block south to the A&P. It was 2:30 in the afternoon when he got back, but he still beat Max Aranow by half an hour.

When Aranow got there he came direct to Purcell's office, sank into the one armchair that agreed with him, and said, "You won't believe what's been going on."

"Likewise and vice versa," Purcell said. He was pacing—more fiercely, it seemed to the older man, than before.

"Let me go first," Max said. "To begin with, Terry Malloy has mixed emotions. He's got more doubts about liability than even you have. On the other hand, he's got just one hell of a case: a brilliant kid with a ruined future, a ruined life. He's fine about your being the one to try the case if it comes to trial. But he wants to probe Hawkes for settlement first, and he wants to do that on his own. You should see what he's doing, Joe: he's making a film, *A Day in the Life of Stephen Coblenz,* where this kid's lying there and can't do a thing for himself. Everything from morning to night—

dressing, washing, eating, therapy, even when they dilly his bowels, is in this movie."

"It's a good technique," Purcell said. "We used it in the Slattery case, remember?"

"It's new the way Malloy's doing it," Aranow said. "He's using a professional film crew. With titles and sound and Technicolor." He sighed. "Terry's under enormous pressure. He knows the Coblenz family personally, and the father is mean as a panther. He doesn't think we have a chance at trial, but he thinks Hawkes just might settle this one case."

Purcell said, "That makes absolutely no sense."

"I know it doesn't. Except maybe it does. When a case like the Coblenz gets into a courtroom, anything can happen. Damages like that make a jury bend over backwards to find liability somewhere."

"Not a Mundelein jury. The record verdict in that town so far is a dollar ninety-eight."

"Well," Aranow said, "Terry's going to be here in the morning. Here in the office. You can talk to him then."

"I thought he was going to come this afternoon."

"He went back to his hotel to recover."

"From what?"

"Lunch. I took him to the Stage. It was a shambles, Joe. He ordered a corned beef sandwich."

"What else do you order at the Stage? Are you telling me they were out of corned beef?"

"They were for him. He wanted his on white bread with mayonnaise. The waiter said he was too old to take that order. It took twenty minutes of arguing. So one of the problems I have with Malloy is he may never talk to me again." Aranow sighed. "Then I come back to the office and who do I run into in the lobby? Phil the Dip. Only suddenly he walks right past me with his hat against his face, as if I were a photographer and he'd been caught in a police raid. Only process server we've used for the past eighteen years, and he doesn't want anything to do with me either. The world is going crazy."

Purcell stopped pacing. He said, "Max, do we know an Irving Cohen?"

"I don't think so, no. Why? You want to find one? No problem. Go to the Bay Parkway station of the BMT at five o'clock in the afternoon and holler Irving."

Purcell shook his head impatiently. "Let me ask you something else. Have we ever had a case of legal malpractice?"

"Have we ever sued a lawyer?"

"Not sued. Been sued."

"*Been* sued? For legal malpractice? No."

"You can never say that again, Max," Joe Purcell said. "You know why Phil the Dip wouldn't look at you downstairs in the lobby? Because he was up here serving a summons and a complaint, that's why."

"For legal malpractice? In this office? Who?"

"Me," Purcell said. With an expert left-hand curl he tossed a folded set of papers across the room. Aranow, the old third baseman, made the perfect catch. The first thing he looked for was the name of the plaintiff's attorney. There were two of them.

"James Price," Aranow read aloud, "Miami." He looked up. "Well, that's Cuneo's man; we were talking about him before lunch. And Irving Cohen, New York. Oh, that's why you asked. Well, no problem there. My guess is, he's just a name in the Yellow Pages. Somebody who's licensed to practice in this jurisdiction, which validates Price's being able to file against you in New York. Which sight unseen he's doubtless doing because the verdicts in New York are so good. What's it for?"

"Three million dollars."

"There you are. Do you want me to read it, or do you want to tell me?"

"Nothing to tell," Purcell said. "The claim is I fucked a client."

"Since when is that legal malpractice? That's what any client claims any time you lose a case for him. Precisely half the litigants in the United States walk around saying that's what their lawyers did to them."

"I mean fuck fucked," Purcell said. "You know, the old-style kind, where you used to take off your pants."

"Oh," Max said, and then: "Who?"

"Ruth Marlowe. The mother of the asthma kid in Mundelein."

"And she wants three million dollars? Was she that disappointed?"

"There's a little more to it. She claims I seduced her in order to persuade her against her better judgment not to take the settlement offer when it came in."

"Somebody must have worked on her pretty good," Aranow said. "I mean, after you. To get her to sign this complaint now. She knows the verdict's on appeal. You did the right thing."

"Not if the appeal's denied, I didn't."

"The crazy thing is that Price would have his name on the complaint," Max said. "Considering the way he and Cuneo got turned away on the Fireball cases, it's got to be extortion. There's no way they can win this suit in court."

"Maybe they don't think it will get to court. Maybe they think we'll settle just to avoid the publicity."

"What publicity? There are nineteen million lawsuits filed in New York City every day. Who's going to even notice this one?"

"It's on file," Purcell said. "And once it's on file, they can make sure somebody notices it. The denial never catches up with the accusation."

"I'm glad to know there is a denial. I was just about to ask. You mean this didn't happen?"

"Of course not."

"You didn't have relations with her?"

"Oh, no, I did have relations—I hate that phrase, Max—with her: that part's true."

"But it wasn't connected with the settlement offer."

"Of course not."

"The settlement offer came in later."

"No, it came before."

"How long before?"

"That morning. I know it looks bad, Max, but—"

Aranow put up a hand. "Did you ever give her any money? At any time?"

"Yes, I think I did. Some cash. There's no record of it."

"Did you give her any money that day?"

"I may have, yes. She was hurting for money, Max. Her ex-husband was in San Diego or someplace, and he was slow on the support payments. Nothing really you could do about it: he'd been out of work—it wasn't one of those deliberate things. So I was down there doing the trial, and we were together, and it was a Saturday—I remember that, because I'd rested the plaintiff's case the day before, so it was a Saturday morning that Hawkes met with me and made the settlement offer. I didn't know he was going to make it. I told him I'd relay the offer to her with my recommendation that she reject it."

"And then you saw her?"

"Yes, but that was set up in advance. It was understood we'd spend the day and the night together. Her parents had come in from Cincinnati to take the daughter back with them for a few days. As to how many times I was with Ruth Marlowe, that was the only time. As to how much money I gave her, I don't even know. It wasn't a case of high finance. Might have been sixty dollars one time, seventy another, that kind of thing."

"Does she mention the money in the complaint?"

"The money I gave her? No."

"I wouldn't think so," Aranow said. "A woman wouldn't want to say a thing like that. Not to mention that it wouldn't help her case any. So at least you can breathe easy on that point. If they were going to use the fact that you were paying out money to your own client, they would have used it here."

Purcell's thumb and forefinger went to his right earlobe. "Then that gets me off that hook. What's left?"

"Quite a bit, I'd say," Max said. "What we know going in is that Cuneo and Price aren't out for revenge here—not primarily; at least not at this point. If they were out for revenge on the Fireball, they would have filed the suit in Ohio, where the offense took place, instead of New York where the defendant practices. That *would* have got you instant publicity, in that small town. So we can assume they're out for money. But if we act as if we won't pay the ransom, then they *will* go for revenge. As you say, they can find a way to publicize it any time they want. So we have to act on it, and act fast. That's number one. Number two is, we have to make them believe we want to settle out. That's the only way to keep them quiet."

"Strategy, ten," Purcell said. "Tactics, zero. How do you accomplish what you just outlined?"

"I haven't got the slightest idea," Aranow said.

"It occurred to me," his partner said, "I'm going to need a lawyer."

"Oh, you've already got a lawyer," Max said.

"Who?"

"Me," Aranow said.

25

The miniki met the next morning. Felix Harding held the floor. "That discrepancy about the Jumbo Nellie Nellie being filled on February 27 but not delivered till April 29," he said. "You'll be delighted to know the mystery's been solved."

"Don't tell us," Bert Klein said. "Let us guess."

"They faked the records," Sheila O'Hara said.

"No, it was just a recording error," Willie Blake said.

"It sat in the yard in Chicago," Klein said.

Harding smiled.

"Come on, Nero," Sheila said.

"Okay," Harding said. "They didn't fake the records. It wasn't just a recording error. And the tank car didn't just sit in the yard in Chicago. In fact, it was hooked up to a train and moved out only fifteen hours after it reached the classification yard."

"That's impossible," Klein said.

"No, it isn't," Felix Harding said. "Bear in mind, I didn't tell you what train it was hooked up to."

Blake said, "What does *that* mean?"

Harding was enjoying the moment. "Very simple," he said, speaking slowly. "The Jumbo Nellie Nellie—NN 1462—got lost." He semaphored the resulting chorus back to silence. "When I say lost, I mean exactly that. I don't know if you have any idea how many freight cars get lost every day. Percentagewise, it's very small. Numerically, it'd scare the socks off you. The next thing you know, a Belt Line switcher was there to pick it up— the computer fouled up someplace—and off our favorite tank car went, into the wild blue yonder, over somebody else's tracks."

"Not the Mid-Central's?" Sheila O'Hara said.

"Not the Mid-Central's," Harding said.

"Then who else's?"

"Ask me the tracks of the railroads it *didn't* go on," Harding said. "It's a shorter list. To this moment, I don't have the full list of them. I don't think anybody does. When I say lost, I mean *lost*. I can't tell you that on this date it was in Omaha, or on that date it was in Fort Worth. All I know is, somebody would notice that car didn't belong on that train, so they'd leave it off for somebody else to pick up. Meanwhile, they'd ask their computer to check on it, and they kept on getting link situations." Harding's great girth rolled as he spoke. "A link situation is the ultimate in today's state of the computer art: it's where one computer can check its findings against another by means of AT&T long lines. In short, the computers can talk to one another on the telephone." The girth shook. "But it's like two people talking on the phone when one of them's made a mistake. The one who made the mistake gets defensive about it. So one computer winds up lying to another computer, and the other computer isn't geared to detect the lie."

Willie Blake said, "So all that time—"

"The exact dates," Felix Harding cut in, "are these: Our Jumbo Nellie Nellie was loaded at Whiting, Indiana, on February 27, just as the record shows. It was taken to the Mid-Central classification yards in Chicago that same day, and left there the following day attached to a train of the Santa Fe. On April 25 it arrived back in Chicago via the CB&Q, after wandering the western half of the United States for nearly two months. Back in Chicago, it finally was located, and it left for Florian on a Mid-Central train April 27. It got to Florian late in the day April 29."

Bert Klein said, "But there's a big hole still left in all that."

Harding said, "What hole? I told you that was the best tracing I could do."

"I'm not being critical, Nero," Klein said. "I had something else in mind: Tri-State, the retailer in Florian. Remember that over that whole two months they still were serving their customers. The question is, where'd they get the propane to do it?"

"Oh," Harding said. "Well, I was going to get to that, Bert. That's the easiest part to answer. Our focus was so much on that one tank car —NN 1462—that it never occurred to anybody there's more than one Jumbo Nellie Nellie in this world. When NN 1462 didn't show up at Tri-State in Florian and they started to run low, they just picked up the phone and called Mid-Central, and Mid-Central just ran another Jumbo Nellie Nellie—NN 2877, if you want *its* number—into Florian. This was like the third or fourth week of March. So they off-loaded the propane, replenished Tri-State's supply, and everything was hunky-dory. The railroad turned up the record of that, because Tri-State's branch office in Florian was the one that did the ordering, not the headquarters in Huntington. The reason for that is that the Mid-Central serves Florian but doesn't run into Huntington. So Florian did its own ordering direct, and got billed by North American Oil and the Mid-Central. But the bills burned up along with everything else in the fireball, and that left Tri-State in Huntington without a record of that extra interim tank car. To make that long story short, the mystery there is no mystery."

"And the case is no case," Sheila O'Hara said. "Now that we know what happened, what use can Joe Purcell make out of it? We know our Jumbo Nellie Nellie showed up late, and now we know why, but what does that information do for our lawsuit?"

The conference room went silent upon that note, and in the silence the door opened and Max Aranow came in. "Got some Xeroxes of something for you," he said, and passed them out. "Take five minutes to read it. Then I'll be back and we'll discuss it."

In five minutes he was back, sinking into the chair to Sheila O'Hara's right. He placed his hands, fingers interlaced like a monk's, atop the conference table, and he said, "First off, I've talked to Joe, and I will tell you everything he told me, and what I said back, and what our thoughts are generally." His prizefighter face was tired. "Then I hope somebody has a bright idea."

Willie Blake said, "I've got an idea right off."

"I'd rather go first," Max said.

"No," Willie said. "I want to go first. My idea is that you should fire me from this law firm. I'm the one who talked to this James Price dude when he was up here, and he was asking what was wrong with Cuneo, and I explained it to him, and I used Joe's Marlowe case as an illustration—where an ethical lawyer like Joe would have his client's interest at heart, and so could turn down a settlement offer that a money-grubber like Cuneo would jump at. I didn't actually use Ruth Marlowe's name, but I did everything else. I gave him so much information it led him right to her. Then he went to work on her and this lawsuit against Joe is the result. You want to know who put the dagger in their hand, you're looking at him."

There was a silence; then Aranow said, "Are you through?"

"Damn right I'm through," Willie Blake said. His eyes were wet. "In more ways than one. I'm going to find Joe and try to apologize to him, if he'll let me. Then I'll clean out my desk."

"Sit down, Willie!" There was a snap to Aranow's voice that perhaps only Felix Harding could readily remember ever having heard in the past. "It was a good speech, and I enjoyed every word of it, and in your inimitable style, which we all admire and value so much, I found only one small flaw in your presentation. There was a second baseman for the Red Sox a number of years ago, and somebody said, 'Although he cannot hit, he cannot field either.' In your case, you simply missed the point."

"I can't hit *or* field," Willie said miserably. "And I didn't miss no point."

"You not only missed the point, you cry at card tricks," Max said to him. "To begin with, and to settle one question, if it is a question, Purcell did take her to bed. No moral judgment is called for: It wouldn't be Joe if he hadn't. So much for that." Somehow the eyes seemed less tired now. "What did you do by confiding in James Price? You say you betrayed Joe Purcell. I say the jury's out on that. The record is there for all to see in the Mundelein courtroom and the Mundelein newspaper that Purcell lost the Marlowe case, and if you hadn't given Price the idea, then the printed record was there to do it for him—a printed record that sticks out like a sore thumb in a town as small as that. And if Price hadn't thought of it, I've got a pretty good notion Victor Cuneo would have. He's bred that way. They all are. Net result: you didn't tell Price one damned thing he wouldn't have found out anyway."

Bert Klein said, "He's right, Willie."

"Thank you, Bert," Aranow said. "Now do you want to tell him the rest of it?"

"The rest of it?" Bert said. "I don't know the rest of it."

"Then let me say what the rest of it is," Aranow said. "The rest of it is that walking into this room, I didn't think Joe had a chance. I still don't. You've all read the Marlowe complaint. There's only one smidgeon of a chance. I haven't filled you in yet on everything that was said between Joe and me, but let me summarize in advance." His fingers began to flutter like aggravated sparrows. "I told him he was in trouble from both sides: liability and public exposure. He said he had to have a lawyer, and I told him I'd be his lawyer. But we may modify that a bit. Willie?"

Blake said, "Yes, sir?"

"How would you like to be Joe's lawyer?"

"No, sir," Willie Blake said. "No way."

Sheila O'Hara said, "Maybe you'll wind up firing me instead of Willie, Max, but I don't think Willie should be the lawyer and I don't think you should either."

"That's interesting," Max said. "Your reasons?"

"Simply that this has got to take a top man somewhere," Sheila said. "And certainly not someone from Joe's own firm."

"Why?"

"Because it's the roughest kind of legal malpractice case there is. It'll take an all-time gunner to get Joe out of it."

"And we don't have any all-time gunners in the A&P?" Max said.

Bert Klein said, "We have one all-time gunner, Max, and we all know it: Joe Purcell. But you're not asking that he defend himself."

"Then Willie Blake wouldn't be satisfactory to you?" Max said.

"*I* wouldn't be satisfactory to me," Klein said. "And no, Willie wouldn't. He's got even less time in the pits than I do."

"Well, then," Aranow said. "Just maybe we could come back to me. How would I do?"

"Oh, Max," Sheila O'Hara said. "All the years I've been here you've been saying to us—you've been *showing* to us—you don't want to get down into the pit anymore. It was always Joe in reserve, to take us into court if we needed it."

And again a silence came. Aranow looked viciously around the table. "Nero?" he snapped at Felix Harding. "You haven't been heard from."

"I wouldn't want it to be you, Max," Harding said. He did not look at Aranow.

Max nodded heavily. "Well, then," he said. "We've settled one thing. The consensus is against the old man."

Sheila O'Hara stood up and put a hand in front of her eyes and began to sob. "I don't want to talk about this. I don't want to be here in this room while we talk about this."

She turned, and the voice of Max Aranow came: "Sit down!" And she sat down again, her face buried in her hands.

"All I meant to do, which is what started all this," Max Aranow said quietly, "was to say that instead of my being Joe's lawyer, I'd like Willie to be his lawyer. Because everything here that Willie saw to be such an enormous disadvantage is in fact the only advantage we have. *Let* Willie Blake represent Joe Purcell. He's the one who actually talked to this fellow Price. He thinks he told Price too much. Well, if he thinks that, Price is going to think it too. What's the one way we have out of this mess? Price's overconfidence, that's what it is."

Klein said, "Max, how will that make anything better?"

"It ain't gonna make anything worse," Aranow said. "Now let me tell you everything Joe told me, and then I'm going to want to talk to you, Nero, about some follow-ups. And Willie, I'm going to need you for something else."

And he sat there and went over all the data. And then he took Willie Blake with him into his office and dictated a letter from Blake to James Price:

```
Dear Mr. Price:

Re: Marlowe v. Purcell

You will recall our good meeting here. I am writing to you
this soon again because the above-captioned matter has
been referred to me.

I do not propose to conduct a lawsuit through the mail,
and so I have no substantive comment to make. I do propose
the earliest possible deposition of your client, to be
taken in this office, so that we may be certain she
certifies the facts as set forth in the complaint. That
formality being observed, I am certain you and I can
discuss the necessity, if any, for proceeding to liti-
gation.

Very truly yours,
```

26

"Well, if that don't beat *all!*" James Price said, when he got the letter. "Read that, boy! Now, you *read* that!"

Victor Cuneo said, "What do you get out of it?"

"Just that they're so ready to give up and settle, they're using the house coon to handle the case, that's all. We're in the money, Vic, boy. You understand what I mean? I mean, *in the money.*"

"I'm looking for the trap in it," Cuneo said.

"You get 'em down in writing like this, ain't no trap," Price said. "He's just spelled it out. They're giving up! All I got to do is sit down with that black boy and we're home free."

"And you think you can handle him?"

"Did I handle him all right first time? Wouldn't be no lawsuit at all if I hadn't handled him right, right?"

"Actually," Cuneo said, "I incline to agree with you. The thing that worries me is that deposition."

"Don't worry me," Price said. "I may not be their kind of lawyer, but I've closed too many real estate deals not to know when the pork's to the high side of the fire."

"Fuck the pork on the high side of the fire," Cuneo said. "If they want her there it's because they've still got one shot left: to get back to her and get her to swing back to their side."

"They kind of resign themselves to that not happening," Price said. "Read it again, Vic."

"Maybe," Cuneo said. "Still, it wouldn't hurt us to take another run at her, just to make sure, before you take her up to New York. After all. Three million dollars is three million dollars."

27

In briefs filed with Judge Junius Bohr, Jr., the rivals argued which case among the ninety-eight—twenty-six deaths, seventy-two injuries—should be the specimen. Nobody surprised anybody else. The A&P put in for the case of Whizzer Thoms, the Olympic hero; Arthur Hawkes entered his black handyman case.

Also to the surprise of no one, Junior Bohr accepted neither one. Instead, after lengthy consideration, he cut middle ground and came down with his ruling: The Specimen would be the case of Janet Brophy, driver of the school bus the day of the fireball.

Junior complimented himself that this represented an equitable plus for each side: for Purcell and the plaintiffs, a dead heroine to work with; for Hawkes and the defense, a nonbreadwinner to contain any claim for loss of earnings.

What stunned Junior was the demurrer. In from the A&P came a furious brief, making the point of Janet Brophy's age—and therefore the

age of her young husband, healthy, whole, and an obvious candidate to
remarry, which for all practical purposes would minimize any claim of
loss. But to cap the judge's amazement, in from Arthur Hawkes came an
even more furious brief, livid with the expectation that this specimen was
an open invitation to Purcell to parade the burned children of the school
bus one after another on the witness stand, thereby enabling him to
inflame the jury as no other case could possibly do.

To these responses, Junior reacted the only way he could: he scheduled
a date for Purcell and Hawkes to appear before him for oral argument. In
this, Bohr was following the rules. It bemused him that he must be the
only sitting judge in the country who would have Purcell and Hawkes
going under his gavel two times hand-running, first the Marlowe malpractice case and now the Fireball. As a pragmatist, he took no particular
pleasure in the distinction. As an onlooker, the man who could tell his
peers he was there when Hawkes and Purcell went at each other, he could
perceive the celebrity status at its best, and in his heart of hearts he couldn't
knock it. Hawkes was the lean, spare defender—persuasive, convincing,
incisive. And Purcell: Purcell was dreamy, almost indolent—and at his
most dangerous when he barely heard what was being said. Your famous,
your notorious, your headline-grabbers, your politicized all to one side,
Junior Bohr knew, as judges knew from the Supreme Court in Washington
to a mock court at the newly formed law school of the University of Hawaii,
that when you had Purcell and Hawkes you had the big league. It was an
uncompromised joy to watch either of them work: the only mistakes they
made were deliberate. And to watch them work against each other!...

But a judge was no onlooker. He was a participant, a man who called
the shots. And in the case of the Florian Fireball, one side had ninety-eight
victims and a town leveled flat; the other side had no apparent liability.
The ingredients could not reconcile: they did not therefore lend themselves
to settlement. And on the civil side of the law, a case that cannot be settled
before trial might perforce be a case that demolishes the judge's leverage
and influence during trial. Junior Bohr could remember his predecessor
on the Mundelein County bench, who in November of 1963 dictated a
settlement on the spot, simply upon the news that President Kennedy had
been assassinated. Upon that news, that judge had only to call the two
lawyers before the bench and say, as he did, "I cannot continue this trial.
It will be a desecration if I do so. I am dismissing the jury for the rest of
the day, and the two of you be back in front of me tomorrow and tell me
you fixed it up between yourselves." But Hawkes and Purcell were not
about to fix the Fireball up between themselves. And Junior Bohr foresaw

no avenue in that direction. A judge who cannot contemplate the settlement alternative is a comparatively powerless judge.

Great complications on the one hand, lack of any of the usual leverage on the other, Junior Bohr devoutly did not want this lawsuit in his courtroom. Yet he could not think of a way to avoid it.

In his law office across Elm Street from the courthouse, Harry Wright held a different view. That he could not perceive quite how the case could be won was nothing more than an unsettled factor Joe Purcell would find a way to overcome: that was what Joe Purcell was for. But on the heavy side of the scale, it was the biggest case of Harry Wright's lifetime; beyond that, it was impossible for Wright to conceive that Purcell could lose twice in a row. "He sounds pessimistic," Harry told his wife, Jenny, "but Joe always sounds that way when a trial's in preparation. Besides, it's like we said before: the very fact that he lost to Hawkes last time is the built-in guarantee this time. Joe's a competitor. He plays tournament tennis."

"I don't know," Jenny said. "He seemed—I don't know how to put it—disturbed, or distracted, or something. When he was here for dinner his first trip in on the Fireball."

"You just watch him when he gets into the courtroom," Wright said.

"I hope you're right," Jenny said. "I just hope you don't build up your hopes to the point where any of your other work suffers. You're counting on a lot here. Sometimes I wonder if an A&P or a Joe Purcell understands how a small law office has to keep going anyway."

"They're being great about expenses," Harry Wright said. "Joe bent over backwards on that."

"That's just my point," Jenny said. "They can *afford* to be great on expenses. They can lay out a million dollars and never get it back and it won't affect their operation or their reputation one thin dime's worth."

"Well, they didn't get into that position by taking on cases they couldn't win," Harry said. "Really."

"Maybe not," his wife said. "But now that they are in that position, and they *can* afford to lose, then I still have the same questions that bother me. Maybe it's not enough to say Joe plays tournament tennis. You know he didn't want to take this case."

"Yes, but there's something else," Wright said. "Who was the one person who was most after him to take the case to begin with? I was, that's who."

"You couldn't help yourself," Jenny said. "People were coming to you and asking for legal help. All you did was refer it to a specialist. You certainly did nothing wrong."

"Well, nobody's done anything *wrong*," Harry said.

"I hope not," she said.

"Well, we'll see what Joe's like next time he comes down," Wright said. "But if he's still pessimistic, just remember that's his way."

And this appraisal was of course not inaccurate. It *was* Purcell's way, more or less; in this case more. Aranow had gone to Philadelphia and Ambler, and Joe was at his home in Westport trying to work on the musical, but thinking about the legal malpractice suit against him. That he had made love to Ruth Marlowe to get her to turn down Arthur Hawkes's settlement offer was so absurd as not to connect with reality. But that he had made love to her was reality, and it was too easy to take the one as evidence of the other. The best way to lose the most was to fight the charge at all. And the only comfort was to know that Max Aranow realized this.

In his music room, Purcell on impulse picked up the phone and put a call through to Dorothy Brewer at Sunrise. He was somewhat startled to find she was there. He told her about the oral arguments that had been scheduled and gave her the date, and she said, "How long will you be here?"

"I don't know," he said. "Just as a fail-safe, I've got to meet with the Specimen myself—the truck driver I told you about: the widower. Hawkes might want to depose him, and we have to get him ready."

"Ready for what?"

"The funny questions."

"How do you answer funny questions?"

"Truthfully is usually best."

"Then fine," she said. "I can be here those dates. And you can stay out here."

"If you think I'm going to say no, you're nuts. Why do you think I called?"

"Let us know what plane you'll be in on," she said. "Castor will meet you at the airport."

"You don't have to do that," he said. "I'll be needing a rented car anyway."

"You can use one of our cars," Dorothy said. "Castor will meet you."

"I'm taking advantage of your hospitality," he said.

"I have my own thing in mind," she said. "I'll arrange to have another house guest here. Somebody who might interest you very much."

They rang off, and now Purcell called the office and asked to be put through to anybody who was free. The anybody turned out to be Bert Klein. Purcell told him he would be scheduling himself into Mundelein for the orals and the interviews, if necessary, with the Brophy clan. It was a decision Klein was glad, though not surprised, to hear. There were trial lawyers who would let a local Harry Wright handle that entire part of it, even let Wright go up against Arthur Hawkes in front of the judge and sit in while Hawkes deposed the Specimen, but Joe Purcell was not one who declined to take on such routine chores. And his scheduled trip made Klein glad for another reason. After he had talked to Purcell, he called Max Aranow in Ambler, and Max said, "Good. Then make sure Willie schedules the Marlowe deposition while Joe's in Ohio. I want to save Joe the embarrassment of being on the premises while we've got that going on."

It came to pass then that on the morning Purcell left for Mundelein, one of the elevators at 9 West 53rd delivered James Price and Ruth Marlowe to the floor occupied by the A&P. They were shepherded immediately into the office of Willie Blake. "Well, if this don't beat *all*," Price said. "The privilege of meetin' with you here again in your office. This pretty gal here is Ruth Marlowe."

Willie shook her hand. She *was* pretty, he thought, even though she had dressed plainly, and without makeup, for the occasion. Cuneo probably thought of that, Willie told himself: no seductress she. But she had a pert body, her black hair worn in bangs, and even the effort to keep the smile tight failed to alter the softness of face.

Willie said, "Is Mr. Cohen coming?"

"Mr. Cohen?" Price asked. The infinite southernism made Cohen sound like Quinn.

"Irving Cohen," Blake said.

"Oh," Price said. "Oh. Well, no. He couldn't make it."

"Well, no problem with that," Willie said. He turned to the woman. "Would you like some coffee, Mrs. Marlowe?"

"No, thank you," she said. She sat perched like a robin on one of the antique brocade sofas.

"Tea?"

"No, thank you."

"This shouldn't take long," Willie said to Price. "We're just waiting for the reporter to get here."

"We may have been a wee mite early," Price said.

"Just as well," Willie said. "It gives us a little chance to visit first. The important thing is for Mrs. Marlowe to understand the deposition procedure."

"I already understand it," she said. "Mr. Hawkes put me through it in my daughter's case."

"Well, Mr. Hawkes doesn't work here," Willie said. "A deposition is just a discovery process. It's nothing to be afraid of, Mrs. Marlowe. As I'm sure Mr. Price has told you, it's not like testifying in court. There'll be no judge in the room, and when it's all over you'll get a copy of the transcript of it, and you're entitled to change that copy if you think it disagrees with what you said. And Mr. Price is here to help you if you have any questions, and I'll be in the room too if you have any questions you want to ask me."

"It wasn't any fun the last time," she said.

"Well, the last time may have been a little different," Willie said. "You had a situation with a trial that involved testimony by other people and experts and every what-not. Here it's a lot more clean-cut. The first time you were a plaintiff on your daughter's behalf, and this time you're on your own behalf. So it's a much simpler thing."

James Price smiled to himself. He had briefed and rebriefed Ruth Marlowe four times since the news came from Blake that the A&P wanted to depose her, and all flags flying said the wind was fair. "Mrs. Marlowe," he said, "all you have to do is just answer any questions, because those questions will just go to your complaint. Is that right, Mr. Blake?"

"That's right," Willie said.

"And Mr. Blake here is not about to play Perry Mason with you," Price said. "Is that right, Mr. Blake?"

"That's right," Willie said. "If anybody plays Perry Mason, it isn't me."

There was a buzz at the phone console, and Blake picked up a receiver, then put it down again. "Well," he said, "we're ready. We're set up in the conference room, Mr. Price. Can you and Mrs. Marlowe come with me?"

They went into the conference room, and Price, upon looking around it, said, "If this don't beat *all!*" Then all were seated, with the court reporter at his stenotype machine, and Price said, "You can start anytime you want, Mr. Blake."

Blake nodded at the reporter, who said, "Mrs. Marlowe, can you stand and raise your right hand? You swear everything you will say in this proceeding will be the truth and the whole truth, so help you God?"

"I do," she said, and sat down.

A silence ensued. Price said, "Well, Mr. Blake?"

"Just a minute," Willie said. As he said it, the door to the conference room opened and a small, wiry man in a gray jacket and blue pants came into the room and seated himself across the table from Ruth Marlowe.

"Mrs. Marlowe?" he said.

"Yes," she said.

"My name is Max Aranow," he said.

"I've heard of you," she said.

"Well, I thought I would conduct this deposition," Max said. "It's a little unusual in one respect. You're still our client in Marlowe versus the Mundelein Hospital, where the appeal is still up, as you know. So I thought I might participate here. Is this Mr. Cohen?"

"James Price is my name, sir," James Price said. "I'm not sure I understand this. I thought Mr. Blake here was going to—"

Aranow shook his head. "No. As I say, I'll conduct the deposition. I have an overview here that might help expedite things. We want to make it as brief as possible, Mr. Price."

"Well, I'm all for that," Price said doubtfully.

"Then let's proceed," Max said. "Has witness been sworn?"

From that point, the transcript would say it all.

MR. ARANOW: Your full name for the record, Mrs. Marlowe?

THE WITNESS: Ruth D. Marlowe.

Q.   You're single, married, divorced?

A.   Divorced.

Q.   And your address?

A.   Presently 178 Homestead Terrace, Cincinnati, Ohio.

Q.   And the charge here as I read it is that a Mr. Joseph Purcell of this law firm influenced you unreasonably to reject a settlement offer in a lawsuit where he was representing you?

A.   That is correct.

Q.   And to use the plain words for it, he did this by seducing you?

A.   That is correct.

Q.   In his hotel room?

A.   Yes.

Q.   At the General Dexter Hotel in Mundelein?

A.   I think that was it, yes.

Q.   You think that was it?

A.   Whatever hotel he was staying at.

Q.   Well, your complaint specifies the General Dexter Hotel.

A.   If that was where he was staying, that was it.

Q.   Could it have been the Holiday Inn at South Point, Ohio, instead?

A.   If that was where he was staying.

Q.   You now no longer remember where he was staying?

MR. PRICE: I don't know what this is. It seems to me to be badgering. The name of the hotel can make no difference.

MR. ARANOW: If you want to testify to that, Mr. Price, we can hold a deposition for you too. If not, then let me continue to talk to Mrs. Marlowe. I simply am trying to ascertain where the event occurred.

THE WITNESS: I suppose it could have been the Holiday Inn, if that was where he was staying.

Q.   Well, let us find out where he was staying. This was on a Saturday morning, is that correct?

A.   Saturday about noon. He called me up and told me he had received a settlement offer.

Q.   He called you up, or did he drop by your house in his car?

A.   I think he did both.

Q.   You had no previous arrangement to spend time together that day?

A.   Why would we have had that? I didn't know the offer had been made.

Q.   Well, how far was your home from the General Dexter Hotel?

A.   Not very far.

Q.   Walking distance?

A.   Yes.

Q.   Then why would he pick you up in the car?

A.   I don't know. I may be wrong that he was staying at the General Dexter.

Q.   We have the hotel records. He was staying at the General Dexter.

A.   Is that a question?

Q.   The question is why he would use his car to pick you up.

A.   I don't know. I don't remember. It may have been he wanted a more private setting and took me to the Holiday Inn instead.

Q.   But you don't remember any detail as to that?

A.   No. I thought it was the General Dexter. I suppose it could have been the Holiday Inn.

Q.   All right. Then you say he called you up.

A.   Yes.

Q.   To say what?

A.   That he had received a settlement offer and needed to talk to me about it.

Q.   In other words, you had no previous arrangement?

A..   I don't understand.

Q.   That the weekend was open for both of you and you had indicated to him you wanted to spend it with him.

A.   I have already said, he called me to tell me he had a settlement offer.

Q.   You say you had no previous arrangement?

A.   Why would he have called me if we had a previous arrangement?

Q.   He might have called you to report the settlement offer, or just to confirm the previous arrangement. Which do—

MR. PRICE: Now, if you're testifying, Mr. Aranow, you ought to take the oath.

MR. ARANOW: I was asking a question which you interrupted, Mr. Price. My question was, which was it? Or was it both?

A.   I am confused here.

Q.   I don't want you to be confused. Your complaint says the General Dexter, but you now say it could have been the Holiday Inn. Let me suggest that it was both: that Mr. Purcell was staying at the General Dexter, but there was a weekend arrangement that took you elsewhere. Is that possible?

MR. PRICE: There's no evidence to that.

MR. ARANOW: There's evidence up the kazoo, Mr. Price.

MR. PRICE: I'm not aware of it. You will have to talk to me about this instead of berating the witness.

MR. ARANOW: I will talk to you on the record. I say that the weekend was prearranged, and I say that when Mr. Purcell picked up Mrs. Marlowe in his car, they drove first to Huntington, West Virginia, to the Franklin-Marvin Department Store there, and there is a record in the parking lot of the license number of Mr. Purcell's car, as registered with the Hertz agency at the Tri-State airport. They then went into the store, where Mrs. Marlowe purchased a peignoir—do you know what a peignoir is, Mr. Price?—and held it up for Mr. Purcell's approval. There is testimony available from the saleslady involved, Mr. Price, as well as a sales slip itself. They then drove to the Holiday Inn, where Mr. Purcell left Mrs. Marlowe sitting in the car outside and went inside to rent a room, and that same confirmable license plate number is on that reservation, plus testimony we can produce that the room was reserved in advance by a woman over the telephone.

MR. PRICE: I am not here to listen to speeches. Why are you questioning me?

MR. ARANOW: I am not questioning you. I am questioning Mrs. Marlowe. Mrs. Marlowe, you have heard what has been said here. Will you answer as to these things?

A.   I do not want to answer.

Q.   I beg your pardon?

A.   I don't want to answer. I want to drop it here and now. I think I was misled by my counsel, but more than that I think I myself was wrong to have gone ahead with bringing this suit.

Q.   Then you have dropped the lawsuit and it is now null and void?

A.   Yes. I think I would like some coffee.

MR. PRICE: So would I.

THE WITNESS: I was not including you, Mr. Price.

The miniki met briefly that afternoon. Willie Blake said, "You know how the old man can't make it in the arena anymore?" His eyes went totally white. "Holy Mother of God, you should have seen him in there. And Purcell thinks *he's* the master!"

28

Castor was at the Tri-State airport with the Lincoln Continental to meet the morning flight from New York. The day in late summer was cloudy, the temperature around 80 degrees, but for no ordained reason the cloud cover broke as the limousine crossed the 10-cent toll bridge over the Ohio, and north of the river the sun shone. A case had come into the A&P against a group of insurance companies who wrote flood insurance for residents of one state, but not for people living across the river in another state. The concept that weather discriminated man-mapped borders was untenable, yet traditions and even laws could result from it.

Joe Purcell said, "Know what I forgot to bring, Castor?"

"No, *sah*."

"My bathing suit."

"No never mind," Castor said. "Miz Brewer got one for you. Tennis racquet too."

"She's got a court? I didn't see it last time."

"They's two courts," Castor said. "Down past the swimming pool. They even all lights up at night."

"The neighbors don't object?"

"What neighbors is that, sah?"

"Damned if I know," Purcell said. "I was thinking about back home where I live. Westport, Connecticut. It's on Long Island Sound. But I don't have much land."

"Miz Brewer don't believe in houses close together," Castor said.

When they reached Sunrise, Castor parked the limousine and said, "They's down by the pool. I'll take your things to your room upstairs," and Purcell walked the flagstones to the terrace with its Mason-Dixon teeth, then down the stone steps to his right to the pool area below.

Dorothy Brewer was in the pool, wearing a black bikini and a white bathing cap. She waved as she saw him coming and breaststroked to the ladder, holding on there and looking up at him.

"Say hello to Nancy," she said. "Nancy Gelardi. Our Washington bureau chief."

On the deck beyond the pool, face down on a dropped-to-recumbent webbed chaise, a woman in a one-piece bathing suit turned dark glasses toward him and said, "Hi." The suit was orange and her hair was red. Like Brewer, she was small, but perhaps ten or twelve years younger.

"Hi," Purcell said. "I'm Joe Purcell."

"I know," she said.

"Want a swim?" Dorothy said.

"I don't know," he said. "I've got to be in Mundelein later this afternoon. I might just stay dressed."

"Lunch, then?" She pulled herself out of the pool, removed the bathing cap, reached for a towel, and performed the standard ear-emptying dance steps. At the nearest umbrella table there were silverware and paper plates and tomatoes stuffed with chicken salad.

"Yuh," Joe said. "I might do me one of those." But he did not sit down; instead, he paced.

"Don't picket Nancy," Dorothy Brewer said. "She's here to help you."

He stopped and looked down at the other guest. "She is?"

"Of course," Dorothy said. "You have to investigate those tank cars, don't you? Isn't that part of what you have to do to prepare your case? And those things are regulated, and they're regulated out of Washington, so that's where you'll be looking, isn't it?"

Purcell pulled at his earlobe. "You get no fight from me," he said.

"Then that's where Nancy can help you," Brewer said. "When it comes to knowing where the bodies are buried in Washington, she can find things the best investigator you could hire couldn't find."

From the chaise, not looking up, Nancy Gelardi said, "Because I know where to look."

"And where would you look in this case?" Purcell said.

"Where I always look." Her voice sounded almost uninterested. "In your case it's tank cars. So I look for the people who don't like tank cars."

"You mean the congressmen?"

"Screw the congressmen. I mean the people with power: the lobbyists."

"Which lobby did you have in mind?"

"Give him three guesses," Dorothy Brewer said.

"'Kay," the uninterested voice said. "Three guesses."

Three guesses. His memory twanged, and he grinned. "I'd look for the people who don't like to see propane transported by rail."

"Like who?"

"The pipeline manufacturers," Purcell said.

"Wrong. The oil companies run the pipelines the same as they run the tank cars. Why would they care?"

"Then the highway lobby," Joe said.

"Wrong again," Nancy Gelardi said. "Don't you think the oil companies run them too?"

"Then I've got one guess left?"

"You get a big kiss if you get it," Dorothy said.

"From who?"

"For now, you can guess that too."

"In that case," Joe said, "I will tell you what my third guess is. My third guess is that the lobby most opposed to shipment by rail would be the Teamsters Union."

Nancy Gelardi raised herself on her elbows and removed her sunglasses and looked at him. Her face was heart-shaped and she had gray eyes, and she seemed very close and on impulse he bent coolly and quickly and kissed her on the lips. But they seemed as uninterested as her voice, and Dorothy Brewer laughed. "And now my turn?" she said.

"Why not?" he said.

"And then Hallie?" she said. "She's inside. But all excited by the news you were coming."

"Why not?" he said again. "To the victor belongs the spoils."

Nancy Gelardi said, "What victor? The famous Joe Purcell got three swings and struck out. What the hell do the Teamsters care if the railroads do the long hauls for explosives? They've been going piggyback on the trains for years. Even moving vans travel by train these days. And the more the track mileage gets reduced, the more the Teamsters pick up in delivery service to and from the railhead."

Purcell stared down at her. He said, "You're convinced of that, are you? God knows you've got all the terminology for it."

"Yes," Nancy said. "I'm convinced. Because I've looked into it. Dorothy asked me to."

"Well, then, I'm glad I didn't get four guesses," Joe said, "because the only antirailroad lobby that's left is the one for Flying Tiger Airlines, and somehow I can't see air freight competing for the pressurized propane business. So who else is there?"

Nancy said, "You're looking right at them," and pointed through the downhill grove of trees. "Right there."

He looked, and between the trees, at the base of the high bluff where Sunrise stood, he saw the river. Soundlessly headed downstream, a diesel-driven tug pushed a string of seven 1,000-ton barges, lashed together with steel tendons.

"That's where the fight for the freight tonnage is," Nancy Gelardi said. "The same fight it's been for more than a hundred years: the waterways against the railroads. The canals, the lakes, the rivers, the intercoastals, the dredges, the dams, the locks. Big business? You have no idea how big, mister. Do you know that just in flat-bottoms, with no deep water, the Ohio carries more freight than the Panama Canal?"

Purcell nodded as she talked. "I'm a blue-eyed mother," he said, "I never thought of that. They would fight the railroads, wouldn't they? And with a big lobby in Washington, too."

"And the railroads fight *them*," Dorothy Brewer said. "Think about the Houston ship canal or the St. Lawrence Seaway."

"Rails have taken away from water," Nancy Gelardi said. "Sometimes water's taken away from rails. But if you want a heavyweight matchup between Washington lobbies, you can just start with those two."

Purcell said, "And you've got somebody in the water lobby you can talk to?"

"One man in particular," Nancy said. "Been there a long time. And as they say in Washington, he married early."

This is Polly Adler sending the girl out, his mind told him. Yet the fact of life was before him: there could be something a Nancy Gelardi might learn her way that a Felix Harding, the best investigator in the business, would never get to know.

"Well," he said to Nancy, "I'd love to talk to you if you can help me."

"That's why I brought her here," Brewer said.

"Except," Purcell said, "I'm damned if I know what precisely to tell her to look for."

"Listen, Superman," Dorothy said, "that's not Lois Lane you're talking to. Nancy's the Washington bureau chief for the Brewer newspapers. If you don't know what to look for, it might just be she can get a notion or two on her own."

"As a matter of fact," Nancy Gelardi said, "it just might be that the famous Joe Purcell—"

Dorothy Brewer snapped her fingers. "Wait, Nancy. You keep saying the famous Joe Purcell, and I just remembered: I talked to the famous Max Aranow on the phone, Joe."

"You did?" he said. "When was that?"

"Today. Just now. Not ten minutes before you drove up. He had a message for you: said to tell you he'd had a personal conference with the plaintiff in that malpractice suit and she'd decided to drop it, so it's all over. He said you'd know which case he was talking about."

Purcell was expressionless, but unable to forfend the quick sigh that escaped him. "Anything else?"

"Only that he wanted you to call him at his place in Ambler tonight, so long as you called after midnight. But he said it wasn't important."

Nancy Gelardi sat up on the chaise. For the first time, she seemed animated. "Now *that* intrigues me," she said. "Call me after midnight, but it's not important. How do you reconcile *those* two instructions?"

"You don't know my partner," Joe said. "There's a full moon tonight, and when that happens his face gets furry and he turns into a third baseman. I have to call him and calm him down."

Dorothy said, "Where's Ambler?"

"Outside of Philadelphia," Joe said. "Actually, there's probably a Phillies game tonight at the Vet, and that's why he won't be home till midnight."

"Over and beyond that, though," Dorothy Brewer said, "we had a nice chat, Max and I—getting to meet for the first time, if only over the telephone. I asked him frankly, among other things, what he thought your chances were of winning this lawsuit on the Fireball."

"What'd he say?"

"He said you were the only lawyer in the country who had a shot at winning it."

"That and fifty cents will get you to the zoo on the streetcar," Joe said.

"Quit pacing and come over here and sit down and have something to eat," Dorothy said. "Nancy, you come too. Otherwise the sun will come and you'll get botulism and retain Joe to represent you and he'll put me out of business the way it happened to that soup company."

Purcell seated himself at the table, to Dorothy's left, and silver-handled a stuffed tomato onto his paper plate. Then Nancy came and sat down across from him.

"Take off your coat, for God's sake," Dorothy said.

He took off his suit coat and put it on the back of his chair. "I'll tell you the truth," he said. "We're months into this lawsuit by now, and I still don't have the faintest notion about my opening statement to the jury." He gestured with his knife. "The opening statement is each side's way of telling the jury what evidence they're going to present. The one fundamental rule to it is that you never promise them something you can't deliver."

Nancy said, "What's so difficult about that?"

"The trouble is that if I don't promise them anything I can't deliver, then I can't think of any opening statement to make at all. Usually by now I have a pretty good idea. But not with this one."

"Well," Dorothy said, "all I can say is, Max Aranow didn't sound worried."

"I never saw the day when Max Aranow sounded worried," Joe said. "Not about a lawsuit. The way the hot dogs at Howard Johnson's aren't the way they were in 1939—great eternal verities like that, he worries about. But when lightning hits a tank car, so there's no earthly liability because it was a fluke of nature that caused the explosion, that doesn't worry him at all. What's in the pitcher? Lemonade?"

"Iced tea," Dorothy said. "You can have lemonade if you want it. We make it fresh here. Aranow would love it."

"Iced tea will be fine."

"We brew that from scratch too. No tea bags."

"Then you're right. Aranow *would* love it."

"And you're not here for your health," Dorothy said. "What is it you have in Mundelein this afternoon?"

"A court appearance," he said. "Oral argument in front of the judge. No big deal, and routine in a sense, except for one thing: I'm not all that sure what I'm going to say there either."

And he was not that sure. Dorothy Brewer turned a Mercedes 380 SL over to him for his use, and he drove into Mundelein and first dropped in on Harry Wright before crossing Elm Street to the courthouse. Wright said he had a client coming in and could not make it for the hearing. Purcell said that was all right. Then Wright began to talk about Felix Harding. "He was down here," he said, "and the one person he wanted to talk to was Rosa Crewes. What interested him the most was that before the fireball she worked at a department store in Huntington. But he told me something fascinating, over and above that. Really."

Again expressionless, Purcell said, "What was that, Harry?"

"Something he found out about her," Harry Wright said. "I don't know if he got it from her or from somewhere else. But he said that when she called me Mr. Farnum—"

"She called *you* Mr. Farnum?"

"That day," Wright said. "That day, Joe, when you were first here your last trip in, and we were going out the door, you remember?"

"I think so," Purcell said.

"Well, Farnum is an old name hereabouts," Harry Wright said. "Goes back to before the Civil War, when the family came here from New England. But what Harding uncovered was that Rosa Crewes was engaged to a Farnum boy when she was still not twenty years old, and he was killed in Korea, and she never married, and that's one of the things the fireball drove to the surface when it happened, the way it affected her head. Isn't it something, the way things like that happen? Really."

Something moved in the pit of Purcell's stomach. "Yes," he said. "It's something."

Then he went down the stairs and across Elm Street to the courthouse, then up the stairs again to the chambers of the judge, Junius Bohr, Jr., and in the little outer office a pudgy bleached-blond secretary sat, and she put a hand to her hair and said, "Oh, it's Mr. Purcell! You can go right in. Mr. Hawkes is already there."

Joe said, "How about a wet kiss, Lenore?"

"You stop that," she said. "There's a court reporter in there with them."

"Then I can give him a kiss too, can't I?"

"It isn't a him. It's a her."

"So? Perfect. I just went straight."

Lenore scootered her wheeled chair so it locked her against her desk. "I'm just telling you to go in there. Don't you come close to me."

He stood back, hands in hands-off position. "Lenore!" he said reproachfully. "You have no thoughts for fulfillment as a woman?"

"You wanted to fulfill me at the Marlowe trial," she said.

"The only authentic desire is one that comes more than once," he said. "Jung speaks of it."

"Well, right now you're late," she said. "They're expecting you."

"Eat a peck of oysters tonight," he said. "Begin to build up your body. Improve your outlook." He raised a finger. "I shall return." And he rapped at the inner door, then opened it and went in.

The first voice to greet his entrance was that of the judge, seated behind his desk facing the door. "Ah, here he is," Junius Bohr, Jr., said. "Fashionably late as always."

"Goddamn, Junior," Purcell said to him, and waved a hand in midair. "What is that you've got there? Is there printing on them? What are they? Camels?"

Rodlike from a deep armchair, Arthur Hawkes said, "Hello, Joe."

"Afternoon, Arthur." They shook hands. "Judge." Purcell reached across the desk to shake hands with Bohr. Across the room a white-haired stenotypist sat, hands at the ready over the keyboard of her machine. The judge said, "This is Mr. Purcell, Mrs. Tree."

"Pleasure," Mrs. Tree said, in a voice as muted as her machine. Junius Bohr reached for a Camel and lit it. "We were just asking each other whether we really even need Mrs. Tree this afternoon," he said. "Arthur was just saying maybe we could talk preliminary-conference-like, and if something needed to go on record we could always set it up for tomorrow. Mrs. Tree has a chance to get in to the dentist this afternoon."

"I can't touch silver to my upper left filling without a shooting pain," Mrs. Tree said, sounding as though she were reading off the tape of her machine. "But what he did last time was put a filling lower left. So I have what they call sympathetic pain."

"Sue him," Purcell said. "All sympathetic pain means is pain in a healthy place. We have one time around on the face of this earth. The last thing we need is pain in healthy places." He seated himself in the other chair, beside Hawkes, facing the judge.

The judge said, "Are you saying yes or no, Joe?"

"To what?"

"To our letting Mrs. Tree go for the afternoon."

"Not if it costs her a payday," Purcell said.

"She'll get paid two hours' time simply for the fact she was here," Bohr said. "That's the law in Ohio."

"Well," Purcell said, "last time we saw each other I didn't know the law in Ohio then either, did I?" He turned to the stenotypist and smiled. "Get thee to thy dentist, Mrs. Tree. And bear in mind: sympathetic pain is often actionable."

Mrs. Tree looked uncertainly about, but the judge nodded and said, "Thanks, Mrs. Tree. If we need you tomorrow we'll let you know."

She stood up, nodded, and, lifting her console to take it with her, left the room.

Purcell watched her go. Then he said, "So, Arthur. You want this off the record. Why?"

The judge said, "Joe, don't walk in here and start bullshitting like that."

Arthur Hawkes said, "A toothache is a toothache."

"It's all right," Purcell said. "I already said okay. Tell me something, Junior. Do you really want this case? I have a feeling you don't."

Bohr's cheeks jiggled as he sucked at his cigarette. As usual in his chambers he was the worst-dressed man in the room, sitting in half-length shirtsleeves, his head reaching little more than halfway up the back of the chair he occupied. He said, "Joe, what makes you think that's up to me?"

"It's your court," Purcell said.

"Yes," Bohr said. "And I take the cases that come before it. If that weren't the case, I wouldn't have taken the last one with you two sons of bitches."

"This is *ad hominem*," Arthur Hawkes said. "I didn't come down here from Chicago to listen to this."

"Oh, yes, you did, Arthur," Purcell said. "Right back where you came from, in Chicago, you've got the perfect settle-out case, and Terry Malloy to hammer on the other side. You want to make a move? A nice pilot settlement? Why don't you talk to Terry?"

"I've talked to Terry," Hawkes said.

"And?"

"And I'm not here to be questioned by you about it. Terry Malloy's an attorney in his own right. Some people think his skills might just exceed yours."

"Whoops," Purcell said. "Speaking of *ad hominem*. You going to rule on this, Junior?"

"Ah, shove it up your ass," the judge said to him. "I'm the one who doesn't have to listen to this shit. You—" he leveled a finger at Hawkes "—I don't want you in my court because of the way you condescend to me. There's no law on heaven or earth says I have to put up with that!"

Purcell started to laugh. "And *you!*" Bohr said to him, and shifted the pointing finger. "You condescend to the whole state of Ohio. You're doing us a goddamn favor even showing up."

Purcell said, "Now, language, Junior, language."

"And fuck that too," Bohr said. "I am on perfect ground in picking that Specimen and both you fuckers know it. You're not in for a change, you're in for point-scoring. Why do you think I let that woman go? Because of her goddamn teeth?"

"I'm in for a change," Hawkes said. "You think I'm going to let him march twenty-three burned children up to that witness stand one after the other?"

"There won't be twenty-three and you know it," Bohr said. "I'll allow two, at the most three of them, and that'll say it all. And that's the law talking, not me. Arthur, you know the law on cumulative testimony. What are you trying to gig me on here?"

Hawkes said, "Am I to take that as a positive—" but Purcell cut in and said, "Then where does that leave me? The minus is you strip me of my witnesses. Where's the plus?"

"What plus do you want?"

"Some kind of equity, that's what. What's left for me?"

"A young woman school bus driver and one of the few deaths that was witnessed," the judge said. "What more do you want?"

"I want some dollar signs," Purcell said, "that's what I want. Look what you're giving me here: the one surviving spouse who's got Eligible Bachelor printed in big block letters on his T-shirt."

"Your Honor," Arthur Hawkes said —the way he said it, it came out worse than calling him Junior—"my learned colleague very well knows that evidence of remarriage is inadmissible. Hoyt versus Colgate: 394 Northeast 471. Supreme Court of Ohio 1957."

"Hoyt versus my ass," Purcell said. "You'll find a way of getting it in even if you have to whistle the wedding march every time you piss side by side with a juror in the can during recess."

"Wait a minute," Judge Bohr said. "Both you geniuses with research clerks from here to Harvard Law School have come in here word-poor with not a single thing to add to the briefs you already submitted. I looked at the precedents you cited. They stink. I had better ones going in when I picked the case, and I've got four more since then."

"I still don't want it even if it involves only two of those school bus kids as witnesses," Hawkes said. "If it's only two, Joe'll pick the two most grotesque burn cases of all. We all know that."

"He'll pick the ones who were best in a position to witness the business," Bohr said. "That'll be part of my order."

Purcell said, "I've never in my life before seen a judge who begged on his knees for a reversal like you're doing, Junior."

"I'll take my chances," Bohr said.

"And I still don't accept it," Hawkes said. "Those kids on the bus didn't witness just what happened to the driver. They saw it happen to a policeman too. You pick one Specimen, but they'll be up there on the stand testifying to two."

"No, I've anticipated that," Junior Bohr said. One Camel freshly extinguished, he lit another. "Joe, you're going to have the one Specimen case, and I will not let you enlarge it."

"Get off the Quaaludes, Junior," Purcell said. "I've got the punitives going too. All the other cases."

"Maybe," Bohr said. "But first you're going to have to convince me that there's enough evidence of corporate recklessness or gross and wanton misconduct, and I ain't convinced yet, and if you get over that very high hurdle, then, and only then, what's going to happen is that I will read the jury the list of all the victims and their vital statistics. I'll do it in a way that will get just enough information to them so they will have the entire picture in front of them. I can assure you of that, Joe."

"Up your kadoozi," Purcell said to him. "If it's my case, why can't I present it to the jury?"

"Because the wording has to be contained, that's why. That's the law."

"Suppose the wording *is* contained? It'll still be your flat-assed voice doing the reading."

"You see, Junior?" Hawkes said. "Joe wants the dramatic rights."

"It's my case," Purcell said. "Why can't I present it? It's a case in advocacy. Is a judge an advocate?"

"You can advocate all you want for the Specimen," Bohr said, "but I'm not about to expose a jury to your misty-eyed, choked-up inflections on all ninety-eight cases. It would be the same as if I let you bring all the school kids on that bus up to testify. It's just an open invitation to inflame."

"So you're stopping me from inflaming twice," Purcell said. "First with the limit on the kids on the bus, then with having you read the other victims to the jury instead of me. You haven't even stopped Arthur from inflaming once. But me twice. Somewhere in this world there must be something that still resembles equity. You tell me: why is the score two to zero? You screw me twice, and Arthur not at all."

"I'm thrashed by the phony punitives to begin with," Hawkes said. "I'm in a courtroom in the home territory of the victims, but nobody says a word about that. Whether Purcell gets over your hurdle on punitives or not, and with what was clearly an act of God he shouldn't, we won't be able to find a juror in the whole state of Ohio who doesn't know that Florian was wiped out. I can be dead in the water before the trial even starts."

"Well, you both can go piss up a rope," Judge Bohr said. A new Camel took its place in his mouth. "I've sat here listening and listening, and nowhere do I hear that you've done the basic thing any two lawyers would do. Neither of you likes my Specimen—then why not sit down together and take it out of my hands? Has there been one word on settlement between you?"

Hawkes stood up. "Generally my philosophy is millions for defense but not one cent for tribute. However, there are public relations considerations here. The people of Florian have suffered considerable hardship. It will cost my clients a lot of money to defend and win the case. If Joe wants to bail out I'll talk to my people and recommend that they give the estimated costs of defense to the plaintiffs and Joe can work out the distribution among his clients. I can't promise anything but usually responsible corporations like Mid-Central and NAP and Nance heed my advice."

Junius Bohr stared at him. "All right, Arthur," he said at last. "That's a start." He turned to Purcell. "Joe?"

"Arthur's generosity brings a tear to the eye," said Purcell's gravel voice. "He's prepared to abandon his basic philosophy and give us some modest tribute. Well, my philosophy is that charity begins at home. So I think Arthur should keep his charity as close to home as possible in a safe place where he'll always have it—preferably by rolling it in a tight scroll and shoving it up his ass."

"Okay," Bohr said. "You both would rather rattle your swords than talk reason. My decision stands. The Brophy case will be the Specimen."

"That's fair and square," said Joe. "It's a goddamn mismatch—widows and orphans against three of the biggest corporations in the country. They've got unlimited resources for investigation and research and experts —so you exercise your equitable discretion by making it the biggest mismatch since I played Harold Solomon on a clay court."

"Well, you guys are no mismatch when it comes to hypocritical bullshit," Bohr said. "You two will go to a fifteen-round split decision every time. If you want to express a meaningful reaction, express it."

"Oh, yes," Purcell said. He too stood up, and put his fingers to his ear. "I live from one day to the next so I can come to southern Ohio and express meaningful reactions."

"We can do this all over again tomorrow morning for the record," Bohr said.

"And that'll waste more of my time in southern Ohio," Purcell said. "No. I'll talk further to the point, but in another brief."

"So will I," Hawkes said.

"We may have encountered an infinite moment here," Junius Bohr said. "The two biggest gunners in America totally agreeing on their total disagreement. Where are you staying, Arthur?"

"General Dexter," Hawkes said.

"You, Joe?"

"Out as a house guest, this time. Over by the river."

"Well, see if you can stay away from me the rest of the time you're here," Bohr said. "I say that in the professional sense, not the personal. Personally, I'm a good ole boy who loves both of you. Now, if you don't mind, I've got some other work to do: a disputed will. Some guy died and left his sister cut off because the *sister* had influenced the *mother* to cut *him* off when *she* died. I'd call the guy a motherfucker except for all I know he actually was. But I get this awful feeling the same will is being probated twice, nine years apart." He smiled and went for another Camel, the short, fat fingers yellow with stain. "Like looking up and seeing the two of you back in my courtroom again."

Purcell and Hawkes exited together. Downstairs, Hawkes said, "My turn to buy?"

"First right thing you've said today, Arthur."

"General Dexter?"

"No. Let's go across the street. I've got my car parked here."

They went into the same bar Purcell had visited with Harry Wright, and sat at one of the three tables, so the bartender came out and around to serve them. Purcell ordered Remy Martin with soda. "Harry Wright goes for Christian Brothers," he said.

"I often wondered about that," Hawkes said. "The tax-exempt status of a religious order." But he went for a gin and tonic. The place was quiet except for the inevitable two men humping and slinging the dice cups.

"You know something?" Arthur Hawkes said.

"What's that?"

"Junior Bohr uses even worse language than you do. That's how he asserts himself."

"I'd assert myself the same way if I'd been listening to you, Arthur. Jesus Christ. You've fooled that boy out of his jockstrap. You want to sit here and fool me too?"

The drinks came. Hawkes went to his swizzle stick and said, "There's a chess master named Tchigorin, and he said, 'When I have the white pieces, I win because I am White; when I have the black pieces, I win because I am Tchigorin.'"

"Very apt," Purcell said. "I'll buy it. But Junior doesn't know those things."

"Have you gone into the Brophy case?" Hawkes asked. "The Specimen? We're going to have to take this up while we're down here."

"That's the case I'm talking about," Purcell said. "Now you have it for the record that you were the one who brought it up over a bar. And then I was the one who said no to the settlement."

"Did I just hear you say no?"

"You didn't hear anything. I didn't respond to the offer because you haven't set any offer in front of me. That act you put on for Junior first with your brief and now today—that's the most arresting stuff since Horace Heidt used to say good-night to his mother on television. Here comes Br'er Rabbit—Oh, you can stomp me, you can whomp me, you can shoot me full of holes like a cheese, but *please* donnnnn't throw me into de brambledy bushes! The way you opposed Brophy as a Specimen—you love Brophy as the Specimen and you know it."

"Joe," Hawkes said mildly, "you're becoming passionate in your old age."

"Am I?" Purcell said. "Tell me more about that. Some quote from the world of chess, or whatever."

Hawkes smiled and shook his head. "There's an old German saying: No fool can play chess, and only fools do." He dried his swizzle stick fastidiously with a paper napkin and set it to one side. "If the Brophy case is low on damages, there were plenty of them in this accident even lower than that. Terry Malloy in Chicago has the bell-ringer: that young medical genius totally paralyzed for life. That, plus the fact that he wasn't even supposed to *be* in Florian. Everybody else, one way or another, belonged there, but not Malloy's boy. He was on a mercy mission, going in to help the poor people of the area over the summer. Malloy's a very capable lawyer, Joe."

"He's all of that," Purcell said.

"And you know," Hawkes said, "if I could conceive of a way to recommend that somebody—the railroad or whoever—might help him out with his medical bills, with just the day-in, day-out cost of keeping him alive—without putting into anybody's head that it was an admission of liability on the railroad's part—why, then, I'd be the first to recommend that, Joe. I really would. The people at Mid-Central are good people. Not twenty-four hours after the accident happened, they were the biggest subscriber to the fund to help the victims. No liability. They did it because they wanted to do it. I know you've named Nance and North American Petroleum as coequal defendants along with Mid-Central, but they're not a part of the daily life of Florian. The Mid-Central is: they do business there and they pay taxes there."

You bastard, Purcell thought, that fund was your idea to begin with. Mid-Central's your weakest defendant, so you're setting them up. And reminding me that the Coblenz case is Terry Malloy's, not mine. Aloud, he said, "Well, what's the next step?"

"I don't understand."

"Which word didn't you understand, Arthur? Suppose you find a way to get some compensation to the Coblenz kid. Are you saying you want to talk with me about some way the philanthropy might be extended to include others?"

"Don't make philanthropy a dirty word, Joe. If that were the only reason, I wouldn't apologize for it. But I don't have to tell you there's another reason, and that's the cost of preparing and trying this lawsuit. It's so involved it may set some kind of a record."

"Shouldn't I be the one worrying about that?" Purcell said. "The bulk of the expenses on our side come out of our own pocket. You've got your corporate defendants to pick up your tab, win or lose."

"I thought you'd share my concern," Hawkes nodded. "But you don't have a total monopoly on it. If this goes through the investigation, full discovery costs, trial costs, the appeals process, I think from the defense outlook I may be talking about something approaching three million dollars. If something in that neighborhood could produce a settlement, I'd be remiss if I didn't bring it to my clients' attention."

"Which in our case, after fees and just the costs we've run up so far, would average out to about twenty thousand dollars for each victim," Purcell said. "Assuming you went for a full three million."

"I didn't say we'd go for a full three million," Hawkes said. "I do know that Junior Bohr doesn't want us in his courtroom, and you certainly have better things to do with your career than turn an act of God into a lawsuit."

"What act of God?" Purcell said. "I've got better things to do with my career than turn *anything* into a lawsuit. It's the kid's last fight. But what do I do with the other people? Like Coblenz—Malloy's quadriplegic?"

"I already told you I could conceive of unique merit there," Hawkes said. "But even there, unique is one thing—obligatory is quite something else."

"But if it goes to trial," Purcell said, "Coblenz won't be Malloy's case—it'll be mine."

"Not if it's not the Specimen."

"The facts of it will still come before the jury."

"Yes. Junior will include Coblenz on the list he reads to the jury. I don't know what mileage you think you're going to get out of that."

"Just enough mileage to wonder whether you might look again and see whether your costs might exceed three million dollars."

"I can answer that right now," Hawkes said. "The answer is no."

Purcell drained his glass. "Well," he said, "will you be taking the Brophy deposition while you're down here?"

"I was thinking of it, yes," Hawkes said. "If he's in town. I understand he's an interstate truck driver."

"He is. Matter of fact, he was in Indianapolis when the explosion killed his wife. Can you imagine having to get back here under those circumstances?"

"It happens," Hawkes said. "Coblenz's family was in Chicago."

Purcell stood up. "I'll certainly tell Terry Malloy what you said."

"He already knows," Hawkes said.

"Then I'll buy the drinks the next time," Purcell said. "You want a lift down to your hotel?"

"Three blocks on a day like this?" Arthur Hawkes said. "I'll just enjoy the fresh air. I wish you wouldn't make it hard, Joe."

"Am I making it hard?"

"In a way," Arthur Hawkes said. "As some grand master in chess once said, 'It is no easy matter to reply correctly to Lasker's bad moves.'"

29

They went outside, and Purcell got into his car and drove back to Sunrise. This time Hallie opened the door for him, again in uniform but this one less flamboyant than the *Casino de Paris* outfit she had worn the night of his first visit. The smile and the eyes were the same, though. She said "You gonna play piano again tonight?"

"If you'll sing."

"I'd rather just hear you play."

"Why? You sing great." He mounted the great stairs to the second floor, where his room overlooked the Ohio; then he turned and saw that Hallie had followed him and was standing in the doorway.

She said, "I unpacked your things. Miz Brewer said to. In the closet there and the drawers over there, and your shaving things in the bathroom. And you've got your own thermostat there. It's set at sixty-eight. I don't know if that's how you like it."

"It's great, Hallie. Thank you." The high-ceilinged square room had Colonial-weave oval rugs, and flowered wallpaper and a four-poster bed, and through the bathroom door Joe could glimpse an ancient tub crouching on claw feet like Marcy's tub; but, as in Willie Blake's office at the A&P, there was the contrast of an ultramodern telephone console, set into the side of the bed table.

"That button on the left is for your own private phone calls, with its own private number," Hallie said. "But it won't ring unless you give out the number to people. Otherwise, any calls you get will come in downstairs and we'll buzz you. But you can make outgoing calls anytime you want, on the private line or either of the other lines so long's they ain't lit up. And the one on the far right is for you to buzz downstairs if there's anything you need or anyone else in the house you want to talk to. Main thing is, no bell ever gonna ring at you 'less you want it to."

"Great," Purcell said. "Nothing to wake me up."

"I didn't say *that*," Hallie said. "Less'n it rains, we got something to wake you up. Quarter of seven tomorrow morning, daylight time." She laughed. "That's when you find out why they call this place Sunrise."

Purcell looked out at the eastern view. He turned back and smiled at Hallie. She was smiling too. He said, "Anything else?"

"If there is," she said, "all you gotta do is buzz for it." She left him with that. He spent fifteen minutes with the cassette, summarizing the meeting in the judge's chambers and the barroom talk afterward with Hawkes. Then he went downstairs and found Dorothy Brewer and Nancy Gelardi on the tennis court, playing enthusiastic oh-peachy-shot singles.

"Maybe later tonight we'll turn on the lights and you can take the two of us on," Dorothy said.

Turn off the lights and I'll take the... went his mind, but instead he said, "Is there a cocktail hour?"

"Ring at the box over there for Hallie and tell her what you want," Dorothy said. "How'd your meetings go today?"

"Terrible. The whole world is jerking my chain."

"Maybe you can order me a drink too," Nancy Gelardi said. Her tennis dress showed Gussie Moran lace panties. "A gin rickey."

You can take the two of us on. He remembered that Volkswagen billboard, the girl with the football pennant and all the guys in the raccoon coats, off to the game in the station wagon, and the caption was "I'll Take on the Whole Gang." It was a billboard that came down almost as fast as it went up, but a treasured milestone in advertising withal.

They did not play tennis that night. Instead, Dorothy Brewer told Nancy about Purcell's musical, and after dinner they went into the huge room with the Mason & Hamlin and he played and sang songs from the show, including one piece that had no words, which he called "The No-Name Waltz." One song, "We Have Met Before"—We have met before somewhere, when the world was green, Sometime in the spring-time, in my dreams I've seen your face at some familiar door somewhere—they could not get enough of that. He sang it four, maybe five, times. In between, he did some talking about the way musical shows came to be put together these days. "I know you favor small gatherings," he said to Dorothy Brewer, "but some day before I'm finished coming down here—not this year, but maybe next—I just want you to pack fifty people in this room. Fifty millionaires, preferably. You're the only person I know who knows fifty millionaires. Could I get you to do that?"

"Do I have to include Harrison McKenna?"

"That's right. He's the one I'm supposed to reduce to the pauper state. No. He doesn't have to come."

"I told you about McKenna," Dorothy said to Nancy. "Three of our people in Akron went to jail because of him in that contempt case. Refusal to reveal the source."

"Well," Nancy said to her, "you know fifty millionaires not counting him, don't you?"

"In a pinch," Dorothy said, "I wouldn't be surprised."

"And we'll audition *The Last Laugh* for them," Purcell said. "And then maybe you'd be willing to conduct the pledge."

Nancy Gelardi said, "The pledge?"

"Not to-the-Republic-for-which-it-stands," Joe said. "Not that pledge. I mean lining up the backers: getting them to buy shares in the show."

"I might invest a dime or two myself," Dorothy said.

"A dime or two?" Purcell said. "You're going to be the producer. A little hot New York news you didn't know till now."

"Citizen Kane," Nancy said to her. "Then all your papers have to give the show a good review. This boy doesn't miss a trick."

30

Max Aranow was in Pennsylvania that night, but not at the Phillies game. The Phillies were on the road. Instead, Aranow attended a dinner meeting in an old red-brick private house just off Rittenhouse Square. There were people there from the law school of the University of Pennsylvania, and from the office of the mayor and district attorney and chief of police of the city of Philadelphia, and just after dinner a large black limousine with a motorcycle escort drove up outside and the governor of Pennsylvania got out and went inside and up a single flight of stairs to the drawing room where the others were gathered.

But among all the celebrities, it was Aranow who held forth. He talked at length about the in-workings of legal aid, as it applied to the poor of New York City. "I have one ground rule," he began. "I don't want to discuss the theory behind this program. Not in what I say to you, and hopefully not in any questions you have for me. We all have feelings about law and order. All right: You represent the law, and just for tonight let me represent the order. I want to talk about what's actually being *done*—in practice, not theory. It's being done in New York. It can be done in Philadelphia." Though he was not a large man, he controlled the room. "Putting up a problem is one thing. What can be done with it is another. I'm a trial lawyer by profession, but I'm here without any of the props— no pictures, no blackboard, no figures, no charts."

And Max didn't need any. Whoever said a picture is worth more than a thousand words never heard the Gettysburg Address or the Sermon on the Mount or Max Aranow on the social necessity of legal aid.

After the meeting, he got the last train of the night on the Reading, and from the Ambler station he took a cab home. Sophie was waiting up for him. She said, "How was the meeting?"

"I think it went well," Max said. "I want to be totally honest with you. I could use a Swiss cheese sandwich with a little Gulden's on rye."

"I've got the cheese," Sophie said. "And I've got an extra for you: I did a fresh batch of cole slaw."

"Save yourself while you're making it up," he said. "I'll take it out here on a paper plate with a paper napkin."

"How long have we been married?" Sophie said. "When did you ever get a paper plate or a paper napkin from me?"

Max gave her a hug. "Sophie," he said, "you're good for the environment."

"I was good for the environment before there was an environment," she said.

She brought him his sandwich and kissed him and then went to bed. The timing was perfect. Just as he finished eating, the phone rang with Joe Purcell calling from Ohio.

"I'm in a bedroom with my own private line," Joe said. "They have it rigged here so the sun wakes you up. You think you've got a Spectrum in Philadelphia, you should see the spectrum here. There's three broads in this house—the proprietor, the guest, the servant. It's rigged: Any way I go, it'll turn out it was the wrong way—the most direct route to the inner ring of hell. Women clawing at my doors and I'm celibate."

"I trust your judgment," Max said.

"Don't be cynical with me, Max."

"What cynical? I've always trusted your judgment. It worked perfectly in the Marlowe case."

"Don't be sardonic with me either."

"Who's being sardonic? Did you get my message?"

"Of course. That's why I'm calling. Why else?"

"The only chance you had of winning was that you actually took her to bed," Aranow said. "The deposition lasted two minutes. That stupid lawyer she brought from Florida with her didn't hurt any, and afterward she and I actually went out to lunch together. I like Ruth Marlowe. But if you don't take her to bed, you're in a lot of trouble. Then it would just be a case of her word against yours as to whether you influenced her to turn down the settlement. This way Nero turned up with all the extra things we needed— the parking slips, the motel reservation, everything."

Purcell laughed. "Harry Wright still doesn't know what Nero was doing down here when he talked to that gal Rosa Crewes. The only thing Harry can figure is that it had something to do with the Fireball."

"Maybe it'll turn out it did."

"But she was the clerk in the women's department at that store in Huntington."

"Oh, I used that," Max Aranow said. "I used it."

"And remembered me because I reminded her of somebody else."

"Good," Max said. "Three running cheers. The point is, if you don't lay her, it don't count."

"Language, Max."

"Sophie's asleep. That's why I said call after midnight."

"Speaking of language, you should have heard Junior Bohr down here today."

"How'd it go?"

"Arthur Hawkes has him pegged right. I had a drink with Arthur afterward. Junior's on the defensive nine ways from Sunday. I wish I could say it helps us, but I don't think it does. He resents the big-time lawyers, he's scared of his own youth, he's totally frightened trying to figure out how his courtroom can even make physical room for everybody if the Fireball comes to trial. I can sympathize with him there. It's not that big a courtroom."

"Will he change the Specimen?"

"No."

"Did he ask you and Hawkes to talk settlement?"

"Yes."

"Did you?"

"Oh, it came up," Purcell said. "In fact that's all Arthur talked about while we were having a drink. I listened to him, and that was that."

"Did you sound interested?"

"Of course I did."

"But you're not interested."

"Of course I'm not."

"First tell me what Hawkes said."

"He talked about spreading three million dollars around to save the cost of litigation."

"In this case? That'd be twenty thousand per claim."

"I told him."

"Not even including property damage."

"I told him."

"Then how many stupid children does he think your mother had?"

"None. He had two streets to work. Number one, Junior Bohr's begging for settlement, so Arthur wants it on record he made the overture. Number two, he's trying the Battle of Salamis—divide and conquer. He sent me sixty-eight different messages that Terry Malloy's case could run on its own."

"That quadriplegic's the best case of them all."

"You felt you had to tell me that, Max?"

"If Malloy ever separated out, we could be in trouble."

"You felt you had to tell me that, Max?"

"How'd you play it?"

"I had one drink with him and came back here, that's how I played it."

"Then what happens now?"

"We're stuck with that asshole Specimen, that's what happens now."

"I should have had a little tongue," Max said.

"What did you say?"

"Oh, I was just thinking that a little tongue goes nice with Swiss cheese and Gulden's mustard on rye bread."

"Max," said Joe, "why don't you have a little Ovaltine in your Orphan Annie mug and get a good night's sleep. I'll check in with you tomorrow."

Joe hung up. He looked at the buttons on the phone. "Buzz downstairs if there's anything you need," Hallie had said. I wouldn't mind her tongue without the Swiss and rye, he thought.

He walked over to the window and looked down at the river. He could see lights on the canal barges moving slowly downstream. Railroads fighting canal boats for freight.

He went to his briefcase and fished through his files for his expert's report. He found it and put it on the night stand, undressed, put on his pajamas, plumped up the down pillows and began to read the passages he had underlined on the plane on his first trip to Mundelein. Transportation costs are a large portion of the propane price structure . . . switch to larger cars . . . benefit for the oil companies . . . profits . . . at the expense of safety.

He turned off the lights knowing that the process had begun. There would be no deep, peaceful sleep anymore. Every night, from now until the trial was over, he would be trying the case in that fitful half dream state that all trial lawyers know so well. Tonight pieces of the opening statement would emerge—but the pieces wouldn't fit.

He rolled over and tried to picture Ruth Marlowe's face and body and then Nancy and Dorothy and Hallie and Marcy—but the images were out of focus. Then he pictured a jumbo tank car exploding into a huge fireball, lighting the sky over the black waters of the Ohio River with the canal barges moving slowly downstream.

31

His name was Vincent J. Brophy, but henceforth he would be known to one and all as the Specimen. And Joe Purcell, who had to represent him, met him for the first time in Harry Wright's office in Mundelein and disliked him instantly. Vincent Brophy was one of those undeniable Irish bloods of black hair and Mediterranean face, of the kind that occupied every third cell in Dublin's municipal jail. Though larger and heavier, he still had the quality that makes showgirls marry jockeys, and was instantly identifiable as 5-foot-9 whether you encountered him sitting down or standing up.

In Wright's office he was sitting down when Purcell came in. Joe took one look at him and said to himself, Oh Christ in a basket. Harry Wright made the introductions, but Purcell remained standing, pacing in a small space fronting the window.

"You drive a truck?" he said to Brophy.

"Right," the Specimen said. "GVW nine thousand."

"What's GVW?"

"That's gross vehicle weight," Harry Wright said.

"Thank you, Harry," Purcell said, with a who-asked-you? look. To the Specimen he said, "Does that gross vehicle weight include yourself?"

"No weights include the driver," Brophy said.

"What other weights are there?"

"Payload. I can carry six thousand pounds."

"So overall they rate you as an eight-ton truck?"

"That's right."

"How big a truck in size?"

"Sixteen-foot van."

"What do you usually carry?"

"Depends."

"Depends on what?"

"Luck."

Another replier, like Castor. More you ask, less you know. Purcell said, "What about the day of the fireball?"

"I was in Indianapolis."

"All day?"

"No, en route from here to there. Picked up a load of patio furniture in Portsmouth for delivery to a mail-order house in Indianapolis. It's a run I get every three weeks or so."

"You're an independent?"

"Right."

"What kind of patio furniture?"

"Knockdown. The customer has to put it together."

"And when you deliver that in Indianapolis, what do you do then?"

"Turn around and come back."

"Empty or loaded?"

"Depends."

"Depends on what?"

"Luck." Brophy was dressed in a short-sleeved plain sport shirt and slacks of heavy gray drill held by a glistening macho belt of Indian weave. "That day I loaded in Portsmouth in the morning and got to Indianapolis about seven at night. I overnighted in a motel and delivered first thing in the morning. That was the first I learned about Janet. They had a message there for me."

"You didn't find out till the following morning?"

"No. Why would I?"

"Nobody knew where to reach you?"

Brophy shook his head. "Some trips I get there before closing same day I started out. So in case of any messages, that's the phone contact I always leave."

"You didn't have any TV in your motel room?"

"I don't even remember. If I did, I didn't turn it on."

"Why not?"

"I was tired, that's why."

"You don't like television?"

"Sure I like television. I said I was tired."

"Isn't that what television's for?" Purcell asked. "When you're tired you flop down on the bed in the motel room and unwind?"

Harry Wright said to Brophy, "Joe has to know these things."

"Why does he have to know them?"

"To help you."

"What's it got to do with my wife dying?"

Purcell's pacing increased. "Now, goddamn it, Harry," he said. To Brophy he said, "Is it possible you did turn the television on?"

"Why do you want to know?"

Purcell pressed thumb and forefinger against the sinus bridge of his nose. "Let's put it this way: You did not see the news on television that night?"

"I already told you."

"The next morning when you came downstairs: you had breakfast?"

"They've got a coffee shop in the motel."

"You bought a paper?"

"No."

"You saw a paper in the racks there?"

"I don't know if I did or not."

"The headline could have been underneath the fold," Harry Wright said. "That's the way Dorothy Brewer says it, Joe; I've heard her. The upper half of the paper doesn't show that piece of news because it's on the lower half."

"Many thanks, Harry," Purcell said. Again to the Specimen: "So you didn't find out till the day after your wife died."

"Right."

"And then it was only when you drove up to deliver your cargo to the mail-order house, and the message was waiting for you there."

"Right," Brophy said again. He had a crackly, nervous voice, the sound of an apprentice jockey complaining in the starting gate.

"And when you did get to the mail-order house and got the message?"

"I called home and talked to my mother-in-law."

"And she said what?"

"She said don't hurry."

"What'd she mean by that?"

"She said she'd seen the body of my wife at the hospital, and all they knew her by was her ring and the things the kids in the school bus said, making everybody know it was her, so there was nothing to come back to look at."

Purcell felt a chill in his spine. "And so you didn't hurry back. You didn't get on a plane."

"No," Brophy said. "I did what I always do."

"Which is what?"

"Drove back in my truck. I mean, if I fly back I have to leave the truck in Indianapolis and how do I get back to it again? It's the way I make my living."

"Was it making a living to drive back empty in the truck?"

"You mean go through deadhead and downtime? Who told you I did that?"

"Nobody. I'm asking you. What do you usually do?"

"Well, usually if I get to a place like Indianapolis and unload," the Specimen said, "then that next morning I'll call around —the mail-order house where I am, but the moving companies too—and anybody's who's got a load going back the other way, I'll pick that up too. When you've got a van as small as mine, you can deliver to the door. It can be a plus."

"And that particular morning?"

"I was lucky."

"Lucky?"

"Allied Van had a quarter-load they could subcontract to me, going to Ironton, so I drove over there and picked it up."

"Knowing your wife was dead."

"And knowing it didn't make any difference when I got home. Because she *was* dead. Meaning we couldn't have her salary anymore. Everything depended on me."

"I buy that," Harry Wright said.

"I hope the jury buys it," Purcell said. "Arthur Hawkes is going to zero in on that: the man who puts business first in his mind."

Brophy turned toward Purcell, and he said, "What would *you* have done?"

"I'm not about to talk to a jury about what I would have done," Purcell said. "Hawkes can put it up that you were business-as-usual with a dead wife and four kids who might have needed you when they found out their mother had been killed. He'll make the most of it. My job is to rehabilitate you."

"Rehabilitate?"

"Save you from the other side," Purcell said. "On the surface, it can be made to look awful. But maybe we can bring it off. Now tell me: When were you in prison?"

The Specimen stared at him. "Me? In prison? For what?"

"I asked you one question," Purcell said. "You replied by asking me three."

"I've never been in prison," Brophy said. "I don't know why you want to talk to me that way. If I had been in prison, what would that have to do with the way my wife died?"

"Arthur Hawkes will explain that to you in court," Joe said. "What the fuck do you think this is? Fun and games? Come on. Let's go." He moved toward the door.

The Specimen looked up bewilderedly from where he sat. He said to Harry Wright, "Where are we going?"

"Where Joe says," Wright said, helplessly.

"We're going to your place," Purcell said to Brophy. "Where you and the kids live. With your in-laws."

"For what?" Brophy said.

"So I can play the piano."

"How'd you know we had a piano?"

"I told him how musical Janet was," Harry Wright said to Brophy. "How she wrote songs and drew pictures and wrote books."

The Specimen stood up, proving he was still 5-foot-9, and said, "I don't see where that's got anything to do with anything either."

"Well, we have to see the whole picture. Really."

"The whole picture is do I collect or not," the Specimen said.

"I wouldn't put it that way," Wright said. "Would you, Joe?"

"Yes," Joe said. "I'd put it that way."

"Then Mr. Purcell here and I understand each other," Vincent Brophy said.

"No, we don't," Purcell said, and they went out and drove in Harry Wright's car to a small, old Mundelein street that had trees flanking the pavement, then sidewalks, then lawns in front of brick houses that had no garages or driveways, the street *was* that old. Residents used the alleys in back and separate out-built garages, not visible from the street, to park their cars.

In one of the houses there, Brophy lived with his four preschool children and his in-laws. The kids and the grandmother were home as they drove up, and the first thing Purcell noticed was the upright in the parlor. It was a splendid black piano that could have been bought, and was, for $20 during the depression.

> Louisa and Katherine love the animals
> Louisa and Katherine love the animals
> Every elephant, every pig,
> Animals small and animals big!
> Louisa and Katherine love the rhinoceros
> Not to mention the cockatoo!
> The hippo, the orangutan,
> The polar bear: It's true—
> Every animal in the zoo!

It was Purcell seated at the piano, inventing the song as he went along, singing to the cluster of Brophy's twin three-year-old daughters. The one-year-old, Dexter, was asleep upstairs, but his brother, Elliot, at the age of five, eldest of the children, heard the piano and came into the room, so Purcell had to fashion a bridge for him:

> Elliot says I don't like the music,
> Elliot says I don't like the words,
> Elliot says I'd rather have the lions
> Than the rhino or the monkey or those silly birds!
> But Louisa and Katherine love all the ostriches,
> The seals with their flippers and the panther too!
> Louisa and Katherine love the animals
> Every animal in the zoo!

"Now that," said their grandmother, "now that's the first time the piano's been touched since Janet went away from us."

"Again!" the children babbled, and Purcell had to do it again, stumbling over the newly invented words, but the children remembered where he did not, so it came out the same.

"That's Janet in the picture," her mother said, and Purcell stood up at the piano to look at the framed photograph atop it. It showed a round-faced, soft-eyed young woman with a plump smile and dark home-permanent hair. "You can't tell it in the picture really," the grandmother said, "but I was the one she resembled most."

Brophy said, "We got some in color someplace. Snapshots."

Purcell said to him, "How old was she?"

"When she died or when that picture was taken?"

"When she died."

"Twenty-seven. But the picture was taken a good two years before that."

"Vincent," the grandmother said, "you have to show Mr. Purcell the drawings and the songs and her book."

"What for?" the Specimen said. "She never sold any of them."

Purcell said, "Did she ever try to sell them?"

"Oh, sure. Spent half her salary on postage. Up to New York she'd mail the stuff, back from New York it came."

"Did she save her rejection slips?"

"Her what?"

"The letters or notices, or whatever, that came back from the publishers she sent to."

"I don't know," Brophy said. "It's all in one of the boxes in the closet. Take me an hour to dig them out."

"Take the hour," Purcell said. "We can always have some more songs. Right, you guys?"

The children chorused, and Purcell began to play again, this time improvising a number about a friendly snake with faulty vision. In the meantime, Vincent Brophy moved to go upstairs to locate the box of his dead wife's papers. Harry Wright went with him.

At the top of the stairs, the Specimen turned to Wright and said, "Where'd you find that queer?"

"Purcell?"

"Yes. Purcell. Is he crazy or what?"

"He may be the best trial lawyer in the nation," Wright said.

"Well, does he know what's on trial here? My wife gets killed in an explosion and he wants to see her poems and her rejection slips. And he turns to me and says when was I in prison? What kind of a question is that? And what's it got to do with anything?"

"That's just Joe's way," Wright said, himself not all that sure of the answer. "He throws out lines like that to test people. If he's going to represent you, he has to know everything about you. Things you wouldn't even think of."

"How do I know if I watched television that night in the motel?" Brophy said. "And if I did, I wouldn't have watched the news. I never watch the news."

"Look," Harry Wright said to him, "you're going to have your deposition taken tomorrow by the lawyer for the other side. It's better to have your own lawyer go over everything with you beforehand than try to guess what questions the other side will spring on you."

"You mean the other side can ask me if I was in prison?"

"Yes, as a matter of fact they can. It's admissible as evidence."

"Why?"

"Because something like that on your record goes to your credibility as a witness, and the jury is entitled to take that into consideration, when you get on the stand in the courtroom."

"When *I* get on the stand? What did *I* have to do with the explosion?"

"You're suing for the loss of your wife," Wright said to him. "Who can testify to what that loss meant to you if you don't?"

"Well, I have no prison record," the Specimen said, "and I don't know what those things in the box in the closet mean, and how can I tell him if I watched television that night if I don't remember? All I remember was I was beat-up, dead tired."

"Then when Hawkes asks you that— that's Arthur Hawkes, the defense lawyer—that's what you tell him."

"Why wouldn't I be tired?" Brophy said. "It was the hottest day of the year, remember?"

"That's right," Wright said. "I'd remember something like that too."

"The next day, driving back, wasn't as bad," the Specimen said. "The rain killed the heat wave."

"Well, you can go over all that with Purcell later today and tomorrow morning before the deposition," Wright said. "But for now let's find the stuff he wants to look at. Really."

The Specimen shrugged and led the way to the closet, and afterward he answered all of Purcell's questions, though many of them seemed to have no bearing on anything at all.

With that preparation, the chief surprise for Brophy came in the form of the deposition itself. Arthur Hawkes skimmed over his personal and marital history, covered only briefly his whereabouts the day of the fireball and how the news reached him, and concentrated mostly on his past and present earnings as a truck driver, plus his wife's earnings from driving the Florian school bus. And that was all.

After it was over, the Specimen's anger returned. "I like that Hawkes five times as much as this guy of yours," he said to Harry Wright. "Easy, polite, no sweat, stuck to the things that mattered. This after my own guy talks to me like I'm a Mafia hit man."

Alone with Purcell in his office later on, Wright told him what Brophy had said. "Actually," Wright said, "I was surprised too."

"At what?" Joe said. "How sweet and loving Hawkes was? Come to think of it, I was all choked up myself. He's got the Specimen talking ninety miles a minute about how they always wanted four children and how she took ten weeks off from driving the school bus so she could have the last one. But if they can afford to live like that, then they really didn't need her supplemental income that much, did they? That's what Hawkes was getting at with that poor-dear-boy shit, and as if that's not bad enough, the goddamn Specimen couldn't keep his mouth shut. He kept on volunteering."

"Oh, but think of what a loving family they were," Harry Wright said. "Really. *That* came out loud and strong."

"Tell me something," Purcell said to him. "What did half the town of Coventry say when Lady Godiva rode past sidesaddle?"

"I don't know," Wright said. "What?"

"Hurrah for our side," Purcell said.

32

The claims toll for the Florian Fireball was now twenty-six dead and seventy-eight injured. Only two of the latter were not burn injuries—Rosa Crewes, a classic case of traumatic psychosis, and Stephen Coblenz, paralyzed when the force of the blast blew his car into off-the-road overturn.

The Coblenz case continued to grow in force. For sheer horror, it could not match the case of the headless driver, steering the car safely down the highway. Indeed, for local glamor, Coblenz could not compete with Whizzer Thoms, the high school principal and renowned ex-Olympian. What Coblenz did that no headless horseman, no middle-aged celebrity, no Janet Brophy could do was to paint in vivid colors, his case above all others, the effect of a catastrophic accident as seen in the not-quite-dead. If his case were settled, Purcell would lose the linchpin of his courtroom scenario and be left with a Specimen who looked worse with every passing discovery.

One such discovery came to Purcell through Willie Blake, who got it from the investigation mounted by Felix Harding. Blake did not wait for a meeting in the conference room to bring it up. He barged into Purcell's office and said, "Ready for Nero's news?"

"I don't know," Purcell said. "Should I hear it standing up or sitting down?"

"Standing up," Willie said. "You get too nervous when you sit down." He himself sat in Max's favorite chair. "You asked the dude if he'd been in prison, right?"

"Mm-hmm."

"Why'd you ask him that?"

"He had the face for it," Purcell said. "But he denied it. You mean he *was* in prison?"

Blake shook his head. "No. But if thirty's the bull's-eye on the dart board, you get twenty-nine. He does have a felony conviction. When he was eighteen. Pleaded guilty and got probation as a first offender. But it's still admissible in court."

"What was the conviction for?"

"Statutory rape."

"Oh, great climbing Jesus in the morning," Joe Purcell said.

"Maybe you should have settled for that three million Hawkes offered you," Willie said.

"Maybe I should have jumped into a bathtub and slashed my wrists."

Blake's black face was doleful. "You know," he said, "my guess is you would have been better off with the black handyman case."

"If we had him for a specimen Nero would turn up three dope convictions and a bank robbery on him," Purcell said. "This horseshit case was doomed before we took the vows."

"Well," Willie said, "Sheila says to tell you we're going on computer. The depositions and the interrogatories and all the rest are just piling up too high and too fast to be handled manually."

"All right."

"It costs money."

"What does Max say?"

"We haven't told Max. Max isn't a big fan of computers." Willie crossed his legs. "But he is a big fan of your friend Dorothy Brewer. He thinks that investigation she's got her gal in Washington doing can be dynamite."

"What do you think?"

"I don't know what I think. The idea of the waterway lobby against the railroads is interesting, but last time I talked to Bert and Sheila we all thought it was a case of tunnel vision."

"Tunnel vision? Why?"

"Because," Willie said, "all it does is distinguish between one way and another of transporting fuel."

"What else is there?"

"The fuel itself," Willie said. "We keep talking about how you deliver it, but doesn't it go back beyond that?"

"Back beyond that to what?"

"To what the fuel is to begin with. Who ever heard of transporting coal in a tank car? Why wouldn't the coal lobby be our biggest friend in Washington instead? Coal versus oil: There's a real matchup."

"You and Sheila and Bert feel that way?"

"Yes."

"And you told Max?"

"Yes."

"And what did he say?"

"He said we were crazy."

"I agree with Max," Purcell said. "The coal people are in bed with the railroads. The railroads are in bed with the oil companies. They've got no separation the way the riverboats do."

Willie Blake sighed. "Then maybe my next piece of news will say something to you."

"Make it good. I'm thinking about killing the messenger."

"Nancy Gelardi, Brewer's Washington bureau chief, called you and Bert took the message. It was about the hearings the Department of Transportation held to approve the design of the Jumbo Nellie Nellies—the big tank cars."

"What about them?"

"Nothing."

"She called up to say that?"

"Bert said she was quite excited about it. Hearings on those things are routine. But in this case there were no hearings."

"When did all this happen?"

"Years ago. It goes back to the mid-sixties. Nance started building them in 1966 in accordance with a government regulation."

"Maybe the regulation was already in place."

"No. It was a design change, and the regulation was published by the DOT in March 'sixty-six."

"What about the files of the Nance Company?"

"Bert's filing request for production now."

"Well, what do you know?" Purcell said idly. "Silver Blaze."

"Silver who?"

"One of the Sherlock Holmes stories," Joe said. "The curious incident of the dog in the night-time." He could recite it from memory, and did: "'Is there any point to which you would wish to draw my attention?' 'To the curious incident of the dog in the night-time.' 'The dog did nothing in the night-time.' 'That was the curious incident,' remarked Sherlock Holmes."

"That's it?" Willie Blake said.

"That's it," Purcell said.

"The trouble is," Willie said, "it's like the way they lost the Jumbo Nellie Nellie for two months. We solve that mystery; now a new one comes along: There's got to have been a hearing, but we can't find one. So we'll solve that one too. And does that put us any closer to winning the case?"

Purcell laughed. "This particular Jumbo Nellie Nellie—when was it built?"

"You've got it there somewhere," Blake said. "But I think Bert said 1968."

"And it's been operating all those years?"

Willie nodded. "Safely."

"Until last spring it gets hit by lightning," Purcell said. "Where does that leave us?" He thought of Castor's words: You ain't noplace when you start and you ain't noplace when you get there.

"Just with a case that gets bigger all the time," Blake said. "That's the next piece of news: Cuneo hasn't given up. His buddy, James Price, went ahead and filed for those four people who were hurt when that plane saw the mushroom cloud and turned right. Didn't sue the airline—just the same defendants we're suing. So they're in with us."

"That's clever, not suing the airline," Purcell said. "I wonder who suggested that to him."

Willie swallowed. "I did."

"It figured," Joe said. His pacing stopped. "Just think, if we'd had one of those cases six weeks ago, we could have put it in for the Specimen, instead of Breaker, Breaker."

"Anyway," Willie said, "the box score is now twenty-six dead, eighty-two injured."

"All of them riding on an ex-convict and a bolt of lightning," Purcell said. "Is Max in his office?"

"Yes," Willie said. "But don't go in there."

"Why not?"

"As a favor to all of us. He's happy."

"He's always happy."

"Especially so now. I was in there with some good news."

"I'll happy him," Purcell said. "That no-good—" He stopped. "What good news?"

"I settled for a million eight in that plastic surgery case," Willie said. "And Sheila's got an offer in front of her for three million two for the three kids with the skateboards."

"Good God," Purcell said. "You mean we could go two seven-figure shots in the same week?"

"If Sheila settles. She's downstairs now walking around the block twice, to make it look like she's thinking it over."

"With the way our luck has been going she'll get mugged and blow the settlement."

"She was brilliant on the case, Joe," Willie said. "The skateboards today are what the trampolines were twenty years ago." He stood up. "You know something? The first day I came to work here you took me to lunch and told me how rewarding civil law could be. You said that the criminal trials got all of the headlines —the Patty Hearsts and the Charles Mansons and the Jack Rubys—but all they ever did was relate to law already on the books. It was the civil side, you said, that made new law. And I've never forgotten that. Consumer protection, environmental protection—even civil rights. More new law is generated in law offices like this one than ever starts up in Washington or any state senate or assembly."

"Well, I've got to congratulate Sheila," Purcell said. "And you too. Although in your case it was like shooting fish in a barrel."

"Damn, no," Willie Blake said. "I had problems and you know it."

"What problems? The surgeon started out with that woman telling her he could make her look as normal as himself."

"What's that got to do with anything?"

"The fucking surgeon looked like Lon Chaney, Jr., in *The Mummy's Curse*," Purcell said. "That's what it's got to do with anything." He brushed past Blake and tried the seldom-used connecting door between his office and Aranow's, opening it softly, and just enough to see Max alone at his desk. Then Purcell piled inside, slamming the door behind him.

Aranow looked up, startled. "Great horny toads," he said, "it's Elbie Fletcher, first base."

Purcell stormed to the desk, then began to pace back and forth.

"Will you stop that?" Aranow said. "You look like the target of Mussolini in the shooting gallery."

"Oh, great," Purcell said. "Just great. Willie was in here a little while back, right?"

"Yes," Aranow said. "The bearer of glad tidings. I sent him on in to you."

"Sure you did. You he tells a million eight for one case, three million two for another. Me he dumps on. Like my Specimen in the Fireball was convicted for rape. Why don't we put masks on our letterhead, Max? You be comedy. I'll be tragedy."

"You have to remember," Aranow said. "The Giants in 1951 lost eleven games in a row, starting the first week in the season. But they went on to win the pennant."

"You can shove your baseball up your ass too," Purcell said. "Some guy in a boat rows over the left-field fence in Cincinnati and with you that unlocks the secret of the universe."

"Did I tell you the left-field fence?" Max said. "Lee Grissom that time? I don't know what made me say that."

"Sometimes I don't know what makes you say anything," Purcell said.

"It was the center-field fence," Aranow said.

33

Chicago in December had never been Joe Purcell's idea of a good time. He had thought about sending Bert on this trip and now was really kicking himself when he discovered that Hawkes had not even ventured across town to cover the deposition personally. Instead he had sent two middle-aged subordinates, Steppenworth and Halsey. Joe had encountered them in the Marlowe case and had promptly dubbed them the undertakers because they both invariably wore three-piece black suits, white shirts, and black ties. Their primary function was to hand Hawkes documents and exhibits whenever his wrist snap-thrust a demanding palm. Steppenworth was a gaunt stork with a spot of red at the tip of his nose. Halsey was a squat bullfrog with spots of red on both cheeks. But what made them truly Dickensian was that, as far as anyone knew, neither man had a first name.

From 8:30 in the morning until just after noon, Steppenworth had deposed a registered nurse whose specialty was rehabilitation and care of quadriplegics. She had made a good case for the conclusion that it would cost over $100,000 per year, at present prices, to provide what she called an "ideal environment" for Stephen Coblenz. She detailed all of the physical and occupational therapy and state-of-the-art equipment he need-ed—hydraulic lifts on specially outfitted vans to transport him, electric wheelchairs, a specially designed house with wide doorways and ramps, temperature control with special filters to keep the interior air sterile, push-panel controls which Coblenz could operate for speaker phones, lights, TV, and an alarm system in the event of an emergency. On top of that, he needed a full-time live-in housekeeper to cook and clean and wash and shop, and a male attendant to assist him in all of his functions from morning to night, and part-time substitutes when the housekeeper and attendant had their usual days off and vacations.

Joe's favorite moment came when Steppenworth leaned forward, took a dramatic pause, and asked, "In all fairness, Mrs. Harris, might not one expect that some of these vital services could be provided by Stephen's devoted mother?"

"It's my understanding," she answered, "that because Stephen's inju-ries have essentially bankrupted the Coblenz family, Mrs. Coblenz is providing almost all of these services at the present time. Stephen's father has taken a second job, is now working fourteen hours a day, and helps his wife as much as he can. Stephen is a full-grown man and she is not able to turn him in bed every hour or so to prevent bed sores, nor can she transfer him to and from his chair. Her love for her son makes her life endurable. However, Stephen is exceptionally intelligent and sensitive, and watching his mother's life reduced to that of a full-time indentured slave is hardly what I would call an ideal environment for him. Moreover, Mr. Steppenworth, you must remember that actuarially we can expect Stephen to outlive his mother by thirty years or more. Who will volunteer to be his slave after his mother is dead?"

Steppenworth had a whispered conference with Halsey and, back on the record, told the witness he had no further questions and suggested a lunch break. Joe and Terry Malloy ran across the gray slush-covered street to a hamburger joint. The wind whipped off Lake Michigan, making the 100-yard dash seem like some kind of Arctic marathon.

They found a corner booth and ordered cheeseburgers with raw onion and hot coffee.

"If you think she was good," said Terry, "wait until you hear my guy this afternoon. University of Chicago, Ph.D. in economics, qualifies like gangbusters. He's done a ten-year projection for the city of Chicago and the city is basing all of its budgetary projections—tax structure—everything—on this guy's work."

"What's the bottom line?"

"Six and a half million. That's the present value of the net economic cost of giving Coblenz the ideal environment that Harris says he should have. And that's just the out-of-pocket expense. Add on his pain and suffering and loss of enjoyment of life—he'll never marry, have kids. He's got normal sex drives but can't have an erection—no way of satisfying his sex drive. No bowel or bladder control—and a high IQ so he can fully understand and cerebrate about his misery. Joe, I tell you, this is a bell-ringer. A jury, even in Mundelein, has got to give him at least ten million."

"Or nothing," said Joe.

"How's the liability preparation coming?"

"One step forward and two steps back. But your case has got to help. If I can find even a small peg, your case is so good that the jury's going to want to hang their hat on it."

"I can't understand Hawkes not showing," said Terry. "He sends over those two assholes and he just had to know that my experts would eat them up."

"You don't know the man, Terry. If he shows up, it means that he's concerned. That would be inconsistent with his position in two ways. One, he's going to tell the judge that Coblenz isn't the Specimen so none of this stuff gets before the jury. And while we'll get some of it in, he's ninety-five percent right on count one."

"What's number two?"

"You don't get ten cents, much less ten million dollars, for an act of God."

34

Now it was 4:30 in the afternoon. Halsey had been going with the economist for over three hours and was now on long- and short-term discount rates.

"But Dr. Bilyou," said Halsey, "if young Coblenz takes the 6-point-5 million you say he needs and puts it in ten percent triple-A rated bonds he'll have six hundred and fifty thousand dollars per year for the rest of his life and never have to touch the principal."

Halsey smiled at Steppenworth, who nodded approvingly. "And any investment counselor who advised him to do that should not only lose his license but be shot," said Bilyou.

"Why?" Never ask a killer like Bilyou "why?" thought Joe.

"Because it locks him in to a fixed income based on the purchasing power of a dollar today. Maybe he'll be okay for the first five or ten years. But we've got to give him a fifty-year program. Therapists who are getting thirty-five dollars an hour today were getting three-fifty an hour for the same service ten years ago. With medical inflation rates what they are, they'll be getting three hundred and fifty dollars per hour ten years from now. He has to have a diversified portfolio with sophisticated management that hedges against inflation. Let's put it this way. Fifty years ago this would have been a sixty-five-thousand-dollar case because hospital rooms only cost five dollars a day. Now they cost five hundred dollars per day and how long would ten percent interest on a sixty-five-thousand-dollar fixed fund last? Thirteen days, Mr. Halsey. And then he's out in the street for the rest of the year. Stephen Coblenz will not fare well out on the street. We're not talking about frills and luxuries for a quadriplegic. We're talking about life and death. You don't pinch pennies with a cripple."

Halsey turned to Steppenworth and they embarked on another whispered conference, with Halsey busily scribbling notes on his yellow pad. Malloy's secretary came into the deposition room and handed him a message.

"I hate to break this up when things are going so well for you, Mr. Halsey, but I have an urgent phone call. I'm sure a ten-minute recess will handle it." Malloy winked at Joe and left.

Steppenworth and Halsey continued with their huddle. The court reporter changed pads in his stenotype machine. Joe walked over to the window and saw that it was snowing again. He looked at his watch. Almost five o'clock and his United flight left at 7:45. He resolved to leave, even if the deposition wasn't over. He wanted New York and Marcy tonight.

The windows in Terry's modern office building were floor to ceiling. Joe stretched out his arms, palms and forehead on the glass. He looked down and could see the pedestrians thirty-eight stories below. The wind had to be howling by now because the snow was more horizontal than vertical. But the soundproof double-paned and insulated glass made it eerily silent.

He looked up at the suddenly dark and empty sky. He couldn't see the clouds but knew that they must be heavy and ominous. He thought that he'd better call O'Hare before leaving Terry's office to see if flights were taking off.

The glass was cold on his hand and face and a chill ran through him, causing him to back away and head for the coffeepot. Steppenworth was reading the *Wall Street Journal*. Halsey was reading his notes and the court reporter and the witness were talking about the futures market in precious metals.

Joe had known Terry for years but he never before had seen that expression on Terry's face as Malloy reentered the room, closed the door behind him, and leaned back against it, his eyes closed, fists clenched, and jaw muscles flexing.

Steppenworth put down his newspaper and stood in place. Everyone in the room was silent, all eyes on Terry's ashen, fixed grimace.

"Terry, what is it?" Joe asked.

"It's Stephen," said Terry, in a rasping voice that Joe had never heard before.

"What about Stephen?"

"He's dead."

"Dead?"

Terry Malloy crossed slowly and silently to the deposition table. He sank, even more slowly, into the chair he had been occupying all day. He put his elbows on the table, cradling his head in his hands, and stared at the Coblenz file, open in front of him.

"The cocksucker killed himself."

The court reporter slowly, almost reverently, folded his stenotype machine and packed it away in its black imitation leather case. He knew, as did everyone in the room, that there would be no more questions for the economist. The Stephen Coblenz case was now worth nothing.

35

Purcell's phone was lit as he walked into his New York office the next afternoon. He picked it up, and Elizabeth Frasciano, his secretary, said, "Bert Klein's here to talk to you."

"Send him in," Purcell said, and waited while Klein entered and sat in his customary chair.

"And?" Purcell said to him.

"Here's the best I can do," Klein said. "I traced this business of the hearing in Washington back to February 17, 1966. The routine was that if the DOT approved the specifications for the tank car, they'd write a regulation that incorporated that approval."

"But there was no hearing."

"Not that we can find out."

"Willie told you about Dorothy Brewer's gal in Washington?"

Klein nodded. He was open-shirted with a great gold necklace, the hair showing down to his midriff.

"When and if this thing gets to trial in Mundelein," Purcell said to him, "do us all a favor and show up in a shirt and a tie."

"What's wrong with what I've got?"

"You look like you're going on *Let's Make a Deal*. They don't take to that down there. By the way, did you know James Price has filed those four TWA passenger cases?"

"Willie told me," Bert said. "Price is associated with a lawyer in Mansfield, Ohio, named Samuel Wilding. Did we ever hear of Samuel Wilding?"

Purcell shook his head. "Same business as up here," he said. "He has to connect with somebody authorized to practice in the jurisdiction. Samuel Wilding is the Irving Cohen of Mansfield."

"Well, anyway," Bert said, "it appears that the hearings were scheduled for that date, February 17, 1966, and Nance sent out invitations in advance to three experts they always used—technical specialists in design, metal, stress, axle capacity, so forth..." He reached into his pocket and drew out three folded pieces of paper. "I've got the copies of the letters here." He put them on the table beside the chair where he sat. "For all the good they'll do us. These are the three outside people who were supposed to show up at the hearing. But that was for the show of it. They were all in Nance's pocket."

"What makes you say that?"

"Because I called them, that's why," Klein said. "Two of them, one in Atlanta and the other in Los Angeles, said they'd filed reports and couldn't make the hearings."

"What about the other one?"

"Far as I can guess, the other one's dead," Bert Klein said. "He was right here in New York." He leaned down and picked up one of the letters. "Herman Molle, downtown here, West 22nd Street. But he's not listed in the phone book and Nance had used him before but never used him again. So make it two experts and a dead end."

"Maybe he's not dead," Purcell said.

"They weren't going to use any experts who didn't agree with them," Klein said. "So what difference does it make?"

"None," Purcell said.

"Even if there wasn't any hearing."

"I know."

"And I know we have to cover all the bases and check these things," Klein said, "but how does it wind up helping the case when you're dealing with a bolt of lightning?"

"Beats the living kapok out of me," Purcell said.

"The only thing is," Klein said, "it's like the lost tank car. It beats up on you till you get to the bottom of it."

"Willie and I were talking about that."

"But then when you do get to the bottom of it—nothing."

"We talked about that too."

Klein rose and headed for the door. "I'm sorry I didn't have anything better for you, Joe, but I've run my course on this."

Purcell waved a hand. "Fine. Shut it off."

Murphy's Law: Whatever could get worse, would. Klein said, "I can check it to the last point—get a reverse telephone directory or put a trace on this guy Molle."

"Sure you can," Purcell said. "And you'd might as well."

"I'll do it. Tough break for Terry about the Coblenz kid," Klein said, and left the room.

Purcell punched a console button and told Elizabeth to get Arthur Hawkes in Chicago. Shortly, she buzzed back, and Purcell picked up the phone and said, "Arthur, how the hell are you?"

"Terrible," Hawkes said. "Do you have any idea what the cost of preparation is on this Fireball?"

"That's what I called you about," Purcell said. "We've got everything you've got and more, considering our position of having to lay out costs."

"Including the nickel for this phone call," Arthur Hawkes said. "What's on your mind?"

"I was sitting here thinking of Junior Bohr," Purcell said.

"You were?" Hawkes said.

"And about that town and about that courthouse and about our problems with financing this case."

"And?"

"And I've talked your three-million-dollar offer over with everybody here."

"And?"

"The answer is no."

"I'm sorry to hear that," Hawkes said. "That was some time ago."

"I gave it all the room I could."

"Then I guess we have no deal," Hawkes said.

"Maybe you do and maybe you don't," Purcell said. "The victim count is up to a hundred and eight now. Four new cases have been filed."

"I know," Hawkes said. "Four TWA passengers. The remove-from-the-remove-from-the-remove. And yet a clever sort of exercise. They go right around the carrier and attack my clients."

"You're talking merit?"

"Merit? Of course. Very shrewd. I ran a check on this man Price in Miami. That approach would never have occurred to him. Somebody else must have suggested it to him. Maybe somebody in your office."

"Then what do you think about it?"

"I think those four cases will lose the way the other hundred and four will lose. If Chicken Little was right and the world collapsed, those four cases from the airplane would be worth a gross of something around four thousand dollars. That's what I think."

"I happen to agree with you," Purcell said. "And we also have another problem. Knowing you, I don't have to tell you what it is."

"No, Joe. I'll tell *you* what it is. Your best single case just went and died on you—Stephen Coblenz."

"I heard it was suicide."

"It was. Very sad."

"Then tell me something, Arthur."

"What's that?"

"How does a quadriplegic commit suicide? Everybody around here just takes it at face value. But I've got to confess I'm curious."

"That was the same thought that crossed my mind when I heard it," Hawkes said. "You and I do think along parallel lines."

"Did you get an answer?"

"Yes," Hawkes said. "I'm told he was systematically undereating—starving himself. It took a while, but by the time they caught on to how much he wasn't eating, it was just too late. Don't forget, he was a medical student. He knew things they didn't recognize he knew."

"I'm a son of a bitch," Purcell said. "Then it *was* suicide."

"Yes, Joe, it was," Arthur Hawkes said. "And killed your case for good and all. And *that's* why you're calling me, isn't it? You want to settle."

"Did I say that?"

"I'll spare you the position of being the one to have to say it. I'll say it. Does that help you?"

"We talked it over," Purcell said, "and we turned down three million."

"What three million?"

"The one you talked about in the bar in Mundelein."

"Oh, no," Hawkes said. "You turned that down *then*. I made the gesture, but you said no, and so then and there it ceased to have any force."

"And in its place?"

"In its place is nothing. I grieve along with you, Joe, over the preparation costs of this lawsuit. I have no more passion than you have to go into Junior's court again. But I don't see that there's anything we can talk about. What do you think?"

"I think what you think, Arthur," Purcell said.

"I knew you would," Hawkes said.

They rang off, Purcell with knuckles white. Hawkes had him hog-tied. The clock told him it was time to leave the office and go down to Marcy's place, and so now he left, taking with him only the papers Bert Klein had left on the table: the three letters to the three experts that proved absolutely nothing.

But he took the subway down to Eighth Avenue and 23rd Street, and when he emerged into the daylight at street level, he consulted the address on the one letter, the one to a Herman Molle in the 300 block of West 22nd Street, and for the living hell of it he took it on himself to go there, and after all Bert Klein had said was totally astonished to find a little gray-haired man who answered the door there and did indeed identify himself as Herman Molle. No, Molle said, he did not have a phone. That explained that. Then Purcell explained why he was there, and Molle seemed to give way in astonishment. "Come in and sit down," he said. "I'm retired now, but I love to talk to people."

PART 2

The Specimen

1

Judge Junius Bohr, Jr., of the Court of Common Pleas for the State of Ohio, in and for the County of Mundelein, had for the past several months been letting his hair grow, in the hope that in full forelock and sideburn he might take on the auburn nuance of seeming to be older than he was. Gowned in his robes, he now looked more prelate and less choirboy, but what he wanted was to look mature and judicial. What he continued to resemble instead was the youngest sitting judge in the state of Ohio.

To an Arthur Hawkes, a Joe Purcell, the Fireball came to trial in record time: a bare seventeen months after it happened. For Junior Bohr it was a record delay: no case he had ever presided over had taken so long. His was river-country justice, and that justice was what the Constitution said it had to be: speedy. The crowded calendars in Cleveland and Cincinnati and Columbus could back cases up four, five, six years. The worst delay he had ever seen was in that previous Hawkes-Purcell matchup, the Marlowe malpractice case: nine months in that one. But even that was the fault of the case, not the court: it had taken time for definitive prognosis of the little Marlowe girl to come about.

And though he complained and berated and whipped both sides with increasingly onerous deadlines and cutoff dates, Bohr reluctantly conceded that the nature of the Fireball case justified an unusual amount of time for discovery—hundreds of depositions, thousands of interrogatories, production of tens of thousands of pages of corporate and trade association documents—a mass of paper that forced both sides to go on line with computers. Each had taken a separate room, Hawkes at the General Dexter Hotel and Purcell at the Western Motor Hotel, where hired paralegals could function at any time of day or night, punching into the system by modem to locate where in their endless piles of stacked documents any single needed fact might be.

Hawkes, with the seemingly unlimited resources of the defense, accommodated with tranquillity to whatever deadline Bohr imposed. If necessary he could, and did, send ten associates to ten different parts of the country to take simultaneous depositions.

But Purcell climbed the wall every time he saw another written order from Bohr setting another impossible timetable.

"If I get my hands on that hick-town asshole I'll kill him," he said to Max one day, throwing both the court order and the envelope it came in on Max's desk. "Just look at the bullshit on the envelope."

Max chuckled as he read the stamped legend next to the postmark aloud: JUSTICE DELAYED IS JUSTICE DENIED.

"Max, it's not funny," Joe said. "There's no way in hell that we can finish the AAR depositions in twenty days. We've got to go from coast to coast—Boston, Washington, Atlanta, Chicago, Houston, St. Louis, San Francisco, Los Angeles."

"What's the AAR?"

"The Association of American Railroads. We're deposing all the members of the AAR Tank Car Committee who attended any meeting at which there could have been a discussion about developing the jumbo uninsulated tank car. The meetings were held over a period of ten or twelve years, back in the 'fifties and 'sixties. We still haven't found a clue, much less a smoking gun."

"Why do you have to go to all of those cities?"

"The committee members who are still alive are either working for railroads or oil companies, or they're on company pensions, and they want their company lawyers present. We can't subpoena them to Ohio—so we have to go to them."

"Wonderful," Max said. "Do you realize every single one of them is in a major league baseball town? The great American sport grew up on the rails of the great American industry. The only thing that's hurting the game now is jet air travel, which puts most of the games under the lights and—"

"Max, please!" Joe interrupted. "I don't care if Abner Doubleday was screwing Cornelius Vanderbilt's sister. I've got a case to get ready and Bohr won't give me enough time. You'd think this shmuck has been around long enough to know that on the plaintiff's side we never want delay. Our clients don't get a nickel and neither do we until the case is over. The other side has the use of our money—and their goddamn lawyers get paid by the hour—not us. When railroads or oil companies or manufacturers or insurance companies ask for more time, a good judge should be skeptical—but when we ask, even a horseshit cretin like Bohr ought to know we need it."

Max walked around the desk and patted his partner on the shoulder. "Joe, take it easy. Maybe Junior knows more than you give him credit for. Maybe he's convinced that the Fireball victims aren't going to get that much out of another thirty or forty depositions. Maybe I'm not convinced he's wrong. A case like this can never be a hundred percent prepared."

"Max, I'll settle for twenty-two percent at this point. You know, this is not exactly a rear-end whiplash you've handed me. Call the cop and the chiropractor and argue pain and suffering to the jury. This is like World War Three, and I can't get ready in the taxicab on the way to the courthouse."

"Okay," Max said. "I'll send Bohr a copy of the *City Bar Journal* with that speech I made to the Young Lawyers' Section last year. Remember the part you liked so much? Delay in getting one's case decided is not a virtue, but it may well be a symptom of a calm, deliberative system of justice."

A week later Max walked into Joe's office with a note and envelope from Judge Bohr. "Junior sent me a note—just one sentence—thanking me for sending him the speech. But look at the envelope."

Joe did. It bore a new stamped legend: THERE IS NO COURT CONGESTION IN IRAN.

Joe never knew that the next day Max sent Junior a mailgram:

```
YOU WILL GO FAR IF YOU REMEMBER TWO THINGS. LET GOOD
LAWYERS TRY THEIR OWN CASE AND ALWAYS GET TO THE COURTROOM
AT LEAST AN HOUR BEFORE THEY DO.
```

On this particular morning, after a large glass of tomato juice, spiked with Worcestershire and Tabasco sauce, and a cup of instant coffee, Junior Bohr arrived at the courthouse at 7:30. Toby Ball, the night watchman, let him in the side door, and said, "I knew it was goin' be you, Judge."

"You're amazing, Toby," Bohr said. It was a routine they had, one that never varied. Toby would let him in the building, and there was a colloquy between them. It might concern the weather or a major news event or a ball game or, as was the case this morning, next month's local election.

In his chambers, Junior chuckled at the neat stack of documents that his secretary had left on his desk: fifty Xeroxed and stapled copies of the Fireball victims list, all 107 of them, other than Janet Brophy; first the dead, then the injured, in alphabetical order. What a simple solution to a problem that had taken up more pretrial wrangling, more hundreds of pages of briefs, than all the data put together for any other trial Junior Bohr had ever seen. Junior had ruled that these lists would be distributed to every potential juror as the first order of business this morning. As a matter of custom, the entire panel always were asked if they knew anyone connected with the case—lawyers, parties, witnesses—so by letting the jurors see the names in advance, he would not have to go through the tedious and repetitive act of reading the names again during the trial.

"We kill two birds with one stone," he had told Hawkes and Purcell. "We give them the list, ask them if they were personally acquainted with any of the victims, and then let those selected keep the list for future reference. That way we take care of both voir dire and punitive damage evidence at the same time, with one simple and quick procedure."

What amused Junior now was his recall of how his decision left Joe Purcell and Arthur Hawkes equally infuriated. From Purcell's standpoint, the descriptions accompanying the names were inadequate: they did give age, occupation, marital and parental status, and, in the case of the eighty-one surviving victims, a label covering the injuries sustained. That lumped the Cuneo-Price airliner victims in with everybody else—dislocated shoulder, broken collarbone, whiplash, and sprained back—to demean therefore the entire case. "All you left out was the common cold and the clap," Purcell had told the judge, to which Bohr had replied, "They're your cases, funny man, not mine."

But even worse for Purcell was Bohr's decision, in the case of the twenty-seven dead, not to list any of the detailed circumstances of death. "Dead is dead," he said, and his only concession was to list the dates of death, which was almost no concession at all, since among the fatalities only Stephen Coblenz had survived for any appreciable length of time. That the fireball had left him paralyzed, and driven to suicide on that account; that another victim had literally been beheaded at the wheel of his car by a flying railroad tie; that the elite of Florian, the volunteer firefighters, had to a man lost their lives—details such as those nowhere appeared. Purcell would have to do the best he could, within the rules, to bring such evidence forward and give it shape.

That fact in turn was what honed Arthur Hawkes's anger. That Purcell could find a way around that antiseptic list Hawkes never doubted, and for that reason the list itself became, in Hawkes's view, an extraordinary weapon in Joe's hands. Legally, the list was an exhibit in the trial. The jurors thus could take it into the jury room with them when they deliberated their verdict at trial's end, if they so desired. Arthur Hawkes sensed that Purcell might just suggest that desirability in his closing argument. It could be by then that what for Purcell was the weakest form of presentation would end up his strongest. The sheer roll call of the dead, let alone the injured, face up on the jury-room table, hour in and hour out, could carry an impact of final persuasion that Hawkes in all his brilliance of advocacy throughout the trial had no way of undoing.

Once again, therefore, Junior Bohr had ordained the ultimate in the art of judicial compromise: a directed action that neither side wanted. And how delicious and reassuring it was to reach a decision which each of these trial lawyers ranted and raved about with equal fervor.

In his chambers, caressing the Xeroxed lists like a painter with a new favored canvas, Junior Bohr leaned back and lit a Camel. Ordinarily he favored the great glazed deep-dish ashtray on his desk, with its frieze, maroon against the ceramic off-white, of skirted, spear-carrying pharaohs. But today that ashtray sat empty and pristine, and instead the judge used a standing ashtray, a miniature of the Seattle space needle, for the ashes of his young life. Less than two hours from now, robed by his secretary, he would exit by the direct door that connected his inner office to the courtroom. "All rise," the bailiff would intone, and Junior would mount the bench and commence stewardship of the biggest trial he had ever had to handle.

The door through which Bohr would enter the courtroom was to the left of the bench, as the judge faced the court. A similar door to his right led to the jury room. The jury itself would sit along the window wall to Junior's right, directly facing the public doors to the courtroom, and immediately to the right of the bench, raised but still one level down from the bench itself, was the witness box. If he looked straight ahead, Bohr would have in view the two counsel tables, the one facing him on the left the defense table to be occupied by Arthur Hawkes and his two undertakers, Mr. Steppenworth and Mr. Halsey; the one on the right, by tradition nearer the jury, by the plaintiffs: Purcell and Bert Klein, and from time to time Harry Wright too. Behind them, against the back wall of the courtroom, were two rows of spectator seats, which this morning would be taken up almost entirely by the pool of prospective jurors.

That pool ran to more than forty people, fifteen of whom would be seated at random in or beside the jury box, with the balance occupying the spectator seats. Modernized to air-conditioning and dark pine paneling three years ago, the room had space for a jury of nine—four in front, five behind—to bespeak the state rule of eight jurors plus one alternate. For jury selection, six extra chairs would flank the box, bringing the total to fifteen, since Purcell and Hawkes were entitled to three peremptory challenges apiece. But as any of the fifteen might earlier be excused for cause, their places would be taken by people moving up from the remainder of the panel in the spectator seats.

It had been an education for Judge Bohr to watch Purcell and Hawkes spar for jurors in the Marlowe malpractice trial, each of them having his own idea of who he did not want on the jury, yet each marking time, unwilling to squander a challenge on a juror the other lawyer might also elect to excuse. What made them a perfectly matched pair was their completely different techniques: Purcell paced the courtroom, tugging at his ear, yet every move a consummation of the blocking of the legitimate stage. On direct examination of a friendly witness, Purcell lay back, never interposing his body between the witness and the jury. On hostile cross, he would be so close to the witness the jury would have to strain even to see the person who was testifying.

And if the judge admired the technique, the fact was that so did Arthur Hawkes, but Hawkes was not fool enough to imitate Purcell and adopt the technique for his own. In examining a witness, friendly or unfriendly, Hawkes would simply rise in place and talk from the counsel table. No fireworks: it was a set, unimaginative, quiet approach—the approach of the Establishment. And all the more powerful in its effect on that account, because the courtroom itself was the Establishment. He had the sense that secretly Purcell envied him on that account, for Hawkes, by eschewing any sense of theater, had going for him the greatest sense of theater of all: *Hamlet*, I, ii. Everybody in motion except Hamlet himself. Therefore all eyes to the stationary target.

More in the tradition of melodrama than classic theater were three secrets attached to the case of *Brophy et al. v. Mid-Central et al.*, and the judge was the keeper of all three. Two days ago, there had gone into the safe in his office an envelope from Arthur Hawkes. Within that envelope was the name of a witness who might impeach or rebut the testimony of some earlier witness. Hawkes had the legal right to file this name with the court, without Purcell's knowing who the witness was, or even if such witness would ever be called to the stand. And yesterday a similar envelope had arrived from Purcell. He had the same kind of witness to use against Hawkes, or at least the sealed envelope suggested that. And on the part of both players, it could be no more than gamesmanship.

But there was nothing of gamesmanship in the third secret, which belonged to Junior Bohr alone—and not even he knew what that secret would be. For a third sealed envelope was going to go into his safe and that accounted for the empty deep-dish ashtray on his desk.

Junior stubbed his Camel in the space needle, lit another one, then took a blank sheet of paper and folded it twice lengthwise, twice crosswise, creasing each fold to a violent degree. Now the sheet of paper was divided by its folds into nine subsections, upon which Bohr wrote down the numbers 1 through 9. Then carefully he tore the page into the nine resultant blocks, folded and refolded each block, and deposited them in the ashtray.

Within twenty minutes, Mrs. Tree, his court reporter, would be in his office. She was augmented this time: two other court reporters, one from Portsmouth, one from Cincinnati, had been imported by Bohr for this trial. They would spell one another at the stenotype console, not so much to relieve fatigue as to have one reporter typing the transcript offstage while another was taking courtroom notes, so that at day's end—and at a price— each day throughout the trial both sides could buy and thus possess what they called "The Daily"—the up-to-the-minute transcript of all testimony.

But Mrs. Tree would have a more ceremonial function this morning. She would enter the judge's chambers, reach into the ashtray that contained the nine numbered folded slips, place one of them in an envelope, sight unseen, and hand it to Judge Bohr, who in turn would put the envelope in his safe. With Purcell and Hawkes bearing silent witness, he would light a match to the eight slips left in the ashtray and watch them burn.

And Bohr would not go to the safe for that envelope till the end of the trial. Then, and only then, he would fetch it from the safe and read off the number, and whichever juror sat in that numbered chair would be declared the alternate and would be excused, leaving the other eight to decide the case. It was the quintessence of anonymous and therefore unprejudiced disqualification of a juror. Both Purcell and Hawkes had seen Bohr work this stunt in the Marlowe trial, and both of them had recommended it to the legal trade, for neither had ever seen such a clever, totally impartial procedure for alternate-juror selection. A judge might be offended by the way a juror acted during trial, but that offense could commit that judge against one side or the other. Junior Bohr had found the way to get around this, by making sure in advance that he had no idea which juror might ultimately be excused. Even if he did not have the sense that the juror might favor one side against the other, a judge could too frequently acquire the feeling, during the course of the trial, that one person in the jury was emerging as the leader. It was up to both Hawkes and Purcell to spot that leader in advance—jury selection, after all, was their specialty, not Bohr's. And they would play to that leader. But if for any reason they missed that leader, and therefore did not play to that person, Bohr with his simple ashtray device could never be accused of playing to that leader either. "My theory on the alternate juror," he had said, "is don't know and don't want to know." And so the discharged alternate could be any one of the nine who sat throughout the trial. Purcell would not know. Hawkes would not know. Only the judge would know, except of course he did not know either.

But he was not surprised that lawyers of the caliber of Purcell and Hawkes found his unique system both agreeable and refreshing. Lesser attorneys, accustomed by rote to having the alternate juror identified as such before the trial began, sputtered and fumed over Junior Bohr's approach. "What's the use of picking out a pet juror and concentrating on him, then seeing him buy the bullet at the end?" Harry Wright asked Joe Purcell.

"The use of it," Purcell explained, "is that under the usual system your best juror might still be the alternate—except you know it in advance. And he knows it in advance. So what does he do? He sleeps through the whole fucking trial. I don't *like* talking to nine people when one of them's asleep."

"But the other side of it is—"

"There is no other side of it," Joe Purcell said. "Sure, I can single somebody out and take a chance with playing up to him, knowing he may be the one who goes. But it's eight-to-one in my favor it won't happen. I'll settle for those odds in a courtroom."

2

"I had an unbelievable dream last night," Harry Wright said to Bert Klein. They were in Wright's office, across the street from the courthouse. "I dreamed Purcell took all day voir-diring the jury and then it was Arthur Hawkes's turn and he stood up and said, 'I have no questions, but the case is over. I've won it.'"

"You might be at least half right," Bert said. "I've never seen more background detail on a jury panel." Haunted by his memory of the Marlowe verdict, Wright had done everything he knew to investigate the prospective jurors, but he had no feel of certainty. If a man was unemployed, was that good or bad for our side? It could be argued both ways: The man thrown out of work could hate the Establishment—and what greater Establishment was there than oil companies and railroads?—and thus align himself with Purcell. But by equal token his attitude could be if I can't make it, neither will anybody else—thus denying money to anyone, and making him as pro-Hawkes as otherwise he could be pro-Purcell. "Don't be surprised," Bert Klein said to Harry Wright now, "if Joe takes all kinds of time with this jury."

"I wouldn't blame him if he did," Wright said.

Klein shook his head. "No," he said, "it's not what you're thinking. It's not just a question of who the jurors are. It's a question of who the Specimen is. Joe's going to have to preempt. He's got to tell the jury going in that Brophy had a prior conviction."

"Why would he do that?"

"So they'll know it. Would you rather have Hawkes spring it on them later in the trial? I don't say it's ideal, but we're stuck with what we've got."

Harry Wright mopped his brow. "I don't enjoy the prospect of going into that courtroom. I have to confess that."

"Max Aranow doesn't enjoy the prospect of going into a courtroom," Bert said. "So you're in good company, Harry."

"But Joe enjoys it," Wright said hopefully. "Doesn't he?"

"I don't know what Joe enjoys," Klein said. "That's why I came down early from the motel. I had to get out of there. It was a scene out of *Don Juan in Hell*. I walked down the hall from my room, to the working suite we've got, and here was Perry Muncrief, one of our paralegals, sitting at the keyboard of the computer, doing a trial run on data retrieval. In the next room was Purcell, sitting at the piano—"

"The piano?"

"Yes. He ordered a piano. And he's sitting on the piano bench and playing and singing to a stuffed elephant named Caldwell, also sitting on the piano bench. He's got more music with him than we've got exhibits. Don't ask, Harry."

Wright said, "I don't even know how much he wants me in the courtroom."

"As much or as little as you like," Bert Klein said to him. "I know he wants you there today for jury selection. And you *have* to be there for the verdict at the end."

"I already know that part of it," Harry Wright said. "From the Marlowe trial. Purcell won't show up to listen to a verdict."

"He never does," Bert said. "It's evolutionary. Years ago, when Max Aranow hired Joe, part of the reason was that as junior partner, Joe would have to be the one to sweat out the verdict. Now Joe has become like Max and passed the job on to people like me and you. They're alike in that one respect: they can't stand the emotional attrition. If I advance through the firm, I'll get to the point where I'm the same way, and I'll pass it off to someone else. It's a luxury, Harry."

"Speaking of the devil," Harry Wright said. For the door to his outer office had opened, and Joe Purcell looked in.

"Show time, gentlemen," he said.

"Yes," Wright said. "We can go over to the courtroom now. We were just here waiting for you, Joe."

Purcell looked at Bert Klein. "Did you get me that copy of *Fortune?*"

"It's in the car downstairs."

Harry Wright said, *"Fortune?"*

"*Fortune* magazine," Purcell said.

"Joe's going to carry it into the courtroom with him, Harry," Klein said. "Face up. On the cover it says they have an article on the five hundred largest corporations. Which of course includes Mid-Central, NAP, and Nance."

"Oh, that's a great touch for the jury," Harry Wright said.

"I'm not doing it for the jury," Joe Purcell said. "I'm doing it for Hawkes and the judge. I just want to irritate the pricks."

Harry Wright stood up. "You won't believe the dream I had last night. Really. I was just telling Bert. Hawkes didn't ask the jury a single question, and he won the case on voir dire."

"Tell Arthur that when we see him in court," Purcell said.

"Speaking of Arthur Hawkes," Wright said, "I have some special news for you. Do you know he's registered for a chess tournament in Huntington next Saturday? Not a tournament, really—an exhibition. He's going to play eight opponents simultaneously."

"Well, yes, I did know that," Purcell said. "Arthur's an accredited master. He's conducted these exhibitions before. I might even go watch him myself."

Bert Klein said, "I didn't know you enjoyed chess."

"I don't. I enjoy Arthur."

"Actually," Bert said, "it might be fun. Watching him against eight opponents."

"Particularly in this exhibition," Purcell said. "Did you know he's going to do it blindfolded?"

3

Quarter-turned toward the American flag, limp, like a Dali watch, on its standard, the bailiff said, "All rise," and the room rose. "The-court-of-common-pleas-state of ohio-county-of-mundelein-is-now-in-session-the-honorable-junius-bohr,-junior,-presiding," said the bailiff, and the door opened and Junior Bohr entered the room. There before him were Arthur Hawkes, flanked by his two undertakers, and Joe Purcell, flanked by Bert Klein and Harry Wright, all with eyes upon the judge except Purcell, who was staring at the outer doors to the courtroom, as if seeing them for the first time. Bohr looked too. They're *doors*, he said to himself. What the hell is he staring at?

But Junior's eyes took in other things as well. He seated himself, upon which cue did all others, and the judge said, "Before we proceed, I would like to ask counsel to approach the bench." Hawkes beat Purcell to the bench by a full five beats. The judge waited patiently for Joe's arrival, then nodded benignly at him and said in a near-whisper, "You've got exactly fifteen seconds to get that copy of *Fortune* out of sight. You've already gigged Arthur with it. Now get rid of it."

"Not so fast," Joe said. "This is a serious First Amendment issue—freedom of speech, freedom of the press. Let's confer. Maybe we should hear this in chambers."

"Listen, Purcell," Bohr whispered, "there is no way you're going to sit there and wave inflammatory things at this jury panel. I tell you for the last time, get rid of it."

"We just got finished saluting the flag and already you're compromising me in front of the jury," Purcell said. "I can't start out in their eyes fighting with the judge. So I'll do what you say. But I'm going to log this against you."

"Log away," Bohr said.

"I'm only giving in," Purcell said, "because of your capacity to astonish me."

"What's so astonishing?"

"That you wouldn't want to take it into chambers and discuss it there. You can smoke in your chambers. Here you are, two minutes between cigarettes, and still going strong."

"Get back to your counsel table and do what I said with that magazine."

Purcell nodded amenably. "Smile, judge, you're on *Candid Camera*," he said, and went back to his table and flashed a finger at Bert Klein, and Klein took the *Fortune* and put it down into one of the open briefcases on the floor beside him. In doing so, he missed—but Purcell did not—the amused flicker of Arthur Hawkes's eyes.

"Now, ladies and gentlemen of the jury panel," Junior Bohr said— there were no microphones in the courtroom, not even at the witness stand: the room was small and had good acoustics—"you are being selected this morning to see which of you will be the jurors in the trial now before this court, of..."

As the judge droned on, Purcell turned around and nodded at the Brophy family—Brophy himself, the four children (marvelously well scrubbed and behaved: Harry Wright had seen to that), and their grand-parents, the father and mother of the dead school bus driver.

"I like number four," Bert Klein whispered. "And number eight: her I'd like to bang just to make it an even once."

"What about six?" Purcell whispered back.

"Not too shabby," Klein conceded, and that took care of the three women under the age of thirty-five who occupied the jury box forward left of the table where the lawyers sat. The nine permanent jury seats and the six extra chairs, three to either side in the back row, supplied at random those panelists to whom the judge was talking, but he was talking as well to the extra jurors in the spectator seats. He identified the lawyers, then the Brophy family in the first spectator row, asked the prospective jurors if they knew anyone involved. Then he distributed and explained the list of 107, and here there were some questions. A woman in the spectator section said she had *heard* of Whizzer Thoms, the famous Olympic athlete, and there were nods of similar recognition from other jurors, but Judge Bohr asked whether that might affect their judgment, and when they shook their heads he let them stay. Four or five others he excused for cause: one woman said her husband worked for the Mid-Central Railroad; another said a trial of more than a few days would wreak hardship on her; and so it went. But by happy accident it was jurors in the spectator seats, not those in the box, who were excused. The front fifteen seemed clean, and that would speed things along. Judge Bohr explained that the lawyer for each side was entitled to three peremptory challenges, then said, "All right, Mr. Purcell. You may commence."

Joe rose and walked before the jury box. "Ladies and gentlemen," he said to them, "the judge has already explained to you that this is a case in which while only one claim will be tried, one hundred and seven additional claims must be considered. The one claim to be tried is called a Specimen case, and it is for compensatory damages. That is for the loss to this family, the husband and the four children, of the young wife and mother who was killed by the explosion after she stopped her school bus and —"

Hawkes was on his feet. "Object."

"Sustained," Junior Bohr said. "You're selecting a jury, Mr. Purcell, not pleading your case."

"Thank you, Your Honor," Joe Purcell said. He turned back to the jury box and caught the semblance of a smile—was it a mocking smile?—on the face of juror number nine, a young black. Did Nine know that three of the dead at Florian had been black, Purcell wondered, or was he there on a screw-you-Whitey mission, contemptuous of both sides?

"I was trying to separate those facts," Purcell said aloud to the panelists, "because one of the plaintiffs in this courtroom, Mr. Vincent Brophy, has been in court before. As a young man in his teens, he was tried and convicted for the crime of statutory rape. He was not a rapist himself, but he was a party to what happened. And he has not been inside a courtroom from that day to this, and that was more than a dozen years ago. My point is that on that occasion he received a full measure of justice and paid his debt to society." Joe's voice was gravelly low. "I must now ask each and every one of you, is there anyone here who in his or her deliberation of this case will hold that prior conviction against Mr. Brophy? Or will you, instead, do for him now what that other jury did those many years ago— give him justice: justice—nothing more, nothing less?"

There was no response. Purcell began to tug at his ear. "Then let me assume that justice is the goal of everyone here. That is all, as attorneys for the plaintiff, we will ever ask of you in the course of this trial: justice. Because the defendants are three wealthy corporations, we are not looking for money simply on that account. Because twenty-seven people died and another eighty-one were injured, we are not looking for sympathy on that account. When it becomes Mr. Hawkes's turn to question you, he might very well ask you whether sympathy will play a part in your deliberations, or the multi-million-dollar status of these giant defendant corporations—"

MR. HAWKES: Objection.

THE COURT: Yes, Mr. Purcell, it is well taken. There is no foundation that these are multi-million-dollar—

MR. PURCELL: The North American Petroleum Company is not a multi-million-dollar—?

MR. HAWKES: No, objection on other grounds as well. I merely wanted to say, I am licensed to practice law and can present my own case without any assistance from Brother Purcell.

THE COURT: Either way, the objection is sustained.

Oh, Purcell said to himself, Arthur's going to use that Brother Purcell shit on me again this time. Aloud to the prospective jurors, he said, "I was only going to say that if Mr. Hawkes asked you questions like that, he would be completely right to do so. But I can ask you the same questions, and I am doing so now, and that is my right. Let me put it this way. There is no question that when you hear the evidence of the personal tragedy suffered not only by the Brophy family but by scores of others in this holocaust, you will be moved —you will feel sympathy. You would not be human if you didn't. The question is can each of you lay that sympathy aside when you render your judgment? Can you give us a verdict based on reason rather than emotion? Can you give us a verdict from your mind rather than from your heart?" He stopped and scanned the fifteen faces before him. No one moved. Not an expression changed. "I take it from your silence that you will all be able to do that," Purcell said to them.

At the plaintiff's table, Bert Klein husked to Harry Wright, "See? He's taking it away from Hawkes. There's no way now for Hawkes to get good jurors off for cause on the ground that they can't lay sympathy aside."

Purcell now was singling out jurors, to ask them questions about themselves, yet never once did he follow up with another question along the same line as its predecessor. One reason for this was that he was not particularly interested in the answer. Where juror thirteen, in response to Joe's question, said, "*I* have two children," and juror one, to the same question, said "*We* have no children," a Harry Wright would be weighing the difference between a parent and a nonparent. But in the priority of things, a Joe Purcell would first note the difference between the "I" of Thirteen and the "We" of One. It was the difference between a potential leader and a potential follower, and that was what Purcell weighed the most. He had only three peremptory challenges. And he did not propose to waste a challenge on a follower.

Nine, the only black on the panel, was interesting for the fact that his eyes kept shifting toward the spectator seats. George Proctor was his name: thirty years of age, and a bricklayer by trade, he said. More mottled brown than black, his eyes set wide in twin piers bridging flat nostrils, he was the most correctly dressed member of the panel, with quiet dark suit, terribly white shirt, narrow dull-red tie. In most cases of wrongful death and personal injury, the plaintiff's lawyer turned away from a juror who dressed too neatly: it bespoke precision, and the precise were the bankers, the bookkeepers, the accountants, the police, the engravers, the die-makers— those who wanted to account for every dollar, who sought absolute proof rather than merely the preponderance of evidence that a plaintiff required. And yet in George Proctor's case it might be the opposite.

"How long have you lived in Mundelein?" Joe asked him, and the reply was "Ten years, going on eleven. But my wife's people go way back." And with that answer, Purcell did not have to ask who it was Proctor kept looking at in the spectator seats. To serve on a jury was an event in George Proctor's life. And if he had to live in this town, and his wife's roots were so pronounced, then the priority was that they had to get along. The book told Purcell that this was the classic Uncle Tom. He would put up the great show of dignity and diligence, but once in the jury room, whatever the whites said, he would agree.

This therefore was the one kind of follower you might challenge off a jury, for his stake lay not just in following a leader, but a certain kind of leader. Proctor would follow the Establishment lead, and the Establishment was Arthur Hawkes's territory. This was the danger of having a lone black on any jury, and more was the pity from Purcell's standpoint, for minorities of any kind usually made for good plaintiff's jurors. They dealt more with emotion than the WASPs—laughed harder, cried harder, empathized with pain, and in the jury room balloted not from the purse but from the heart. Precisely, in short, the kind of juror Purcell wanted most—but would find least of all here in Southern Ohio. The Marlowe jury had been all-WASP. And of the fifteen finalists for the Fireball, all but two were the same, and one of those, being the only black, might be prone to curry the defense.

That left Fifteen, a roundish middle-aged man named DeSabitini, whom Harry Wright's research proclaimed to be an Italian carpenter. Purcell was pleased. Italians were warm, friendly, and emotional. And carpenters were, in and of themselves, excellent plaintiff's jurors. There was a subtle touch to that: change DeSabitini from carpenter to cabinet-maker, and he would change from pro-plaintiff to pro-defense, from the man accustomed to covering up his mistakes to the precision artisan for whom no mistake was to be tolerated.

But of course Arthur Hawkes knew that too. And, just like Purcell, he had three peremptory challenges, three jurors he would excuse with a wave of the hand, no reason necessary. DeSabitini's chances of remaining on the jury were not all that great.

At the lunch break, with Purcell still going strong in his voir dire of the panel, Harry Wright drew him to one side in the corridor outside. "I don't know how to say this to you, Joe," Wright said, "but the judge isn't happy with Bert."

"With Bert? Why?" Purcell was listening to Wright, but his eyes were on George Proctor, the black panelist, and his wife, a homely, almost severe-looking woman who obviously wore the pants in that family. To them, Purcell nodded benignly, but it was the woman whose eyes locked with his own.

"Well, he's—I don't know what the word is—*flirting* with a couple of the lady jurors," Wright said. "Really."

"Do you blame him?" Purcell said. "He's been down here two days. I've been down here three days and Nine's wife just looked good to me."

"No, I mean really," Harry Wright said. "You know how Junior is. There was that *Fortune* magazine to start it off and now this, and you know he has to stay in control. He knows he's the youngest lawyer in the courtroom, and he's going to take it out on you."

Bert Klein joined them. "Hey, I've got to pass my hotel key to number four," he said. "If she doesn't take it, then number eight for sure."

Purcell said, "Harry here thinks you should wait till the trial's over."

"Really," Harry Wright said. "I mean, things can get obvious."

"I *can't* wait till the trial's over," Bert Klein said. "For God's sake, I'm only human."

"I kind of like Six," Purcell said.

"That's what you said before," Klein said. "I think she kind of goes for you more than me."

Harry Wright said, "They have an oyster stew at the General Dexter. Do you want to go there for lunch?"

"Why not?" Purcell said. "All Bert needs is oysters."

"I get a rash from oyster stew," Bert Klein said. "General Eisenhower suffered from the same thing. During the invasion of Africa in World War Two. They flew in the oysters from Chesapeake Bay, and he loved them, but he'd break out into this rash."

My God, Purcell said to himself, this boy is going to make a great trial lawyer. Max Aranow has molded him into his own image, same as he did me. Spitting the nonsense, the absolute trivia, left and right, and yet every minute knowing exactly what he's doing. It isn't in any of the books. It isn't in any of the courses you take. It's instinct. And if you don't have it, Max doesn't hire you to begin with.

Steppenworth and Halsey were having lunch together at the General Dexter. There was no sign of Arthur Hawkes: he might be taking lunch in splendid isolation, upstairs in his room. Purcell did not see him again till the afternoon session in court, and Hawkes was already seated at the defense table when Joe entered the courtroom. Outside in the corridor he once again had come face to face with Mr. and Mrs. George Proctor. This time, Purcell whistled to himself and said, I will be god*damned!*

With the resumption of voir dire, Joe spent more than two and a half hours with the remaining jurors. He had taken the panel through a wearing examination, and when he finally turned to Arthur Hawkes and said, "Pass to you," there was a faint smile on the defense counsel's face.

Hawkes rose in his chair and said, "Your Honor, I don't have a single question to ask this panel of jurors. We are close to adjournment, and for all of this day, Brother Purcell has been raking these panelists over, with one extraneous question after another. Provoking, yes. Inflammatory, yes. Irrelevant, yes. Going to the point at issue in this lawsuit, no. I pass this jury for cause. I am totally satisfied with them."

At the plaintiff's table, Harry Wright felt his body go rigid with the adrenaline pump of fear. My God, he told himself, I dreamed last night he won the case on voir dire, and now he's gone and done it! To Purcell, he whispered, "Is he through? Really?"

"Not quite," Purcell whispered back, "but if you're wondering if your dream last night just came true, so am I."

Wright put a hand to his eyes. "What do you mean, not quite?"

"Watch," Purcell said.

Having resumed his seat, Hawkes now rose again. "Excuse me, Your Honor, I do have one question—just to address to the jury in general." He nodded amiably at the panelists. "Aside from any traffic violations or fender benders or the like, has any one of you been involved in any kind of an accident? Any kind at all?"

Juror eleven, a thin, sad man, raised his hand.

"Yes, sir?" Arthur Hawkes said.

"Four or five months ago, my house was hit by a tornado," Eleven said.

"I see," Hawkes said. "How bad was the damage?"

"Well, it was covered by insurance," Eleven said. Purcell grinned as the forbidden word came from the other side. "And nobody was hurt."

"I see," Hawkes said. "But what *was* the damage?"

"Well, there was a fire in the kitchen," Eleven said. "And some structural damage."

"And what caused that fire?"

"A rupture in the gas line that feeds the house."

"Feeds the house from where?"

"From the propane tank outside."

"I see," Hawkes said again. "And what did you do then?"

"I don't understand."

"Did you sue the manufacturers of the propane gas?"

"No, of course I didn't."

"Did you sue the manufacturers of the pipe?"

"No."

"Did you sue the people who brought the pipe into your house?"

"No."

"Thank you," Arthur Hawkes said. "Pass back to Brother Purcell."

"See what I mean, Harry?" Joe whispered to Harry Wright. "Your dream *did* come true."

"Oh, my God," Harry Wright said. "How could I have prevented that?"

"You couldn't," Purcell said to him, and rose to go before the jury. "Mr. Galt," he said, addressing juror number two, "I want to thank you for your time and diligence. We will excuse you from the jury."

He turned to Hawkes, who rose in place. "Mr. Lilly, you're excused. Thank you."

Lilly was Ten. Purcell had hoped against hope to save him. Like Brophy, the Specimen, Lilly was a truck driver. Purcell had not brought this out on voir dire, but Hawkes's jury research had of course turned up that fact, and the first element he would eliminate would be the identity generated by common occupation.

Purcell's turn again. This time it was Eleven—the man who had been hit by an act of God and hadn't bothered to sue about it.

Hawkes again: "Miss Watkins, thank you." And juror number four rose huffily and left the box.

Now it was Bert Klein's turn to grin, as Joe Purcell rose for his final peremptory challenge. "Mr. Taylor," he said to Fourteen, "thank you for coming. We excuse you."

And Hawkes, with his final go: "Miss Thompson, you're excused." Eight rose and departed.

Judge Junius Bohr rapped once with his gavel. "Will the jurors in the supplemental seats take places in the permanent jury box, please? Any place will do. Thank you." There was movement as the jury closed up the nine permanent seats. No longer known as Fifteen, DeSabitini, the carpenter, now would be known as Two. As Nine, George Proctor started to get out of his chair, then realized he should stay Nine the way he was. He threw a triumphant glance to his wife in back court. "Now, that will conclude the business for this day," Junior Bohr said, "and the jury is admonished not to discuss this case with anyone, even your own families. We will adjourn till ten tomorrow morning. Mr. Hawkes, Mr. Purcell, the court received this morning your filings on instructions. I will set a rule about supplementaries. I don't want them floating in on me every ten minutes."

Harry Wright turned to Bert Klein and said, "Eliminating that guy who'd been in the tornado I can understand. But why did Joe excuse the other two?"

"He didn't like their body language," Bert said. "I've seen him work so many times. When he gets that juror who folds his arms or leans away or puts a hand up to his face when he's answering a question, Joe's alarm system goes off."

"But he left the black man on the jury."

Klein shrugged. "He only had three challenges. Hell, Hawkes left DeSabitini on the jury. He only had three challenges too."

"Well, Hawkes I don't understand even more than I don't understand Joe," Wright said. "Really. I would have sworn those two women were pro-defense."

"Except for one thing," Bert Klein said to him lightly. "They both had fallen totally in love with me. You were complaining at lunch that the judge had noticed it. That means Hawkes had to notice it too. He had to use up two of his three challenges on libido." Klein smiled broadly. "As soon as we get back to the motel, I'm going to line up two dates on the telephone. You see how it works, Harry?"

Wright shook his head. "I don't understand how you can talk that way, Bert. This is the biggest case I've ever seen. And you talking the way you're talking."

Purcell turned to join them and said, "We saved Two—the Italian. That's about all I can say. The rest of it looks like Mount Rushmore."

"Two may be powerful," Bert said. "He's outgoing."

"That's the problem," Purcell said. "He agrees with everybody."

"What about Proctor, the black?"

"Mother Nine," Purcell said.

"Who?"

"Mother Nine. That's who he's going to turn out to be. Did you notice him in the hall outside just after the noon break? With his wife?"

"I think so," Wright said.

"And then just before we went back into session again for the afternoon? The two of them again outside in the hall?"

"Yes. They were there."

"And what was the difference?"

"Was there a difference?"

"She had a notebook," Purcell said. "A stenographer's notepad. That means they went and bought it during the lunch break. After he'd listened to me but before he'd listened to Hawkes." Joe turned to Bert Klein. "Did that Xerox machine get installed at the hotel?"

"Supposed to be installed today."

"Good," Purcell said. "I need it. We both have cars? We'll drive them separately. Harry?"

"I think I'm going to go home," Harry Wright said, "and have a brandy."

Purcell and Klein drove to the Western Motor Hotel, where together with Perry Muncrief, the prelaw paralegal, they occupied a first-floor total of five adjoining rooms: from left to right, a main reception-and-meeting room; a room that housed the piano, the Xerox, the computer teletype, and the files; and the Muncrief, Klein, and Purcell bedrooms.

Muncrief was in the sitting room in front when Purcell and Klein entered.

"You had a phone call," Muncrief said to Purcell. "From somebody named Castor. He said you'd know who he was."

"I do," Purcell said. "Castor is the last of nature's noblemen."

"They installed the Xerox," Muncrief said.

"Good. Did they install the bar or do we have to get room service for the ice?"

"I didn't ask them for the bar. I thought they might think badly of us." Muncrief was a smallish young man—enrolled at Rutgers, he had come to the A&P on Willie Blake's recommendation—with the look of a baby owl.

Bert Klein said, "They didn't think badly of us when we asked for the piano."

"Well," Perry Muncrief said, "we have the whiskey and the mix, and there's an ice machine just down the hall. If you want a drink, I'm ready for you."

"Scotch and soda," Purcell said. "What did Castor want?"

"He said you were expected at Sunrise for dinner and wanted to know if you had your tennis racquet. Otherwise, they'll have one ready for you."

Bert Klein said, "How can you have dinner at sunrise?"

Purcell put up a hand. "Everybody goes through that routine once. What is this? Cutty Sark? Goddamn it, Perry, didn't somebody tell you Walker Red Label?"

"Don't mind Mr. Purcell," Klein said to Muncrief. "He's always edgy the day he picks a jury."

"You call that a jury?" Joe said. "Perry, get me a cassette from inside. Christ, she gets me out there in October and all of a sudden it's time for tennis." He sipped at his drink and called out, "Perry?"

Muncrief reappeared at the connecting door with a cassette in his hand. "Castor said they also have a set of clothes for you to play tennis in."

"Sure they would," Purcell said. "You ought to see the way they dress Castor and the maid. It's the Eaves Costume Company out there." He took the cassette, switched it on, and closed his eyes.

"If you want to work," Muncrief began, but Bert Klein put a finger to his lips and gestured the paralegal toward an armchair. This is part of your education, his look said. Just sit back and listen. And enjoy.

"To Max Aranow from P," Purcell said into the grillwork of the cassette. "Re: Fireball. This recalls the time you tried to con me into hoping this would be tried in federal court in Columbus, and lord love a duck, Kingfish, here we is in Mundelein in that same state courthouse with that same Speedy Gonzales for a judge, and wait till you see the jury. Only one of them— number two—is worth a damn, being an Italian carpenter. His name is Rafael DeSabitini, and the only reason Hawkes didn't get rid of him is he used up his challenges on a couple of broads Bert was eye-fucking— that's E, Y, E, hyphen, fucking, Elizabeth. I kept thinking of that essay by Addison about the guy who was seized in the courtroom for staring suggestively at a lady on the grand jury and prosecuted under the statute of ogling."

Purcell switched off the cassette and said, "Somebody mix me another drink, so it'll be ready. I'm going to be dry."

Bert Klein said, "I'll get it. *The statute of ogling?* I never heard of that."

"I wish you were bi," Purcell said. "You could have ogled some of the guys too." He switched the cassette back on. "The rest of the jury is same as the Marlowe trial—all Baptist, including Mother Nine, who's black and is going to take notes, for God's sake. His wife bought him a notebook. When that television program *Soap* went on the air, there were fourteen stations on the ABC network that refused to run it, and the first refusal came from the station right here in Huntington."

Purcell was staring through a gap in the window drapes now, and again he turned off the cassette. "Bert," he said, "Perry—what are those two trees outside the window?"

Klein and Muncrief looked. "You don't know," Purcell said. "So I'll tell you." He sipped at his drink. "They're scarlet oaks. Never so right a name for them as now in October. And never so right a place for them, except maybe Birmingham, Alabama, because where you find coal and iron ore and limestone all together in the same place, that's where the scarlet oak is. Did you ever see a tree like that?" Turning on the cassette again, he said, "Mother Nine's a bricklayer, Two's a carpenter, and One works at the post office. She's one of four women on the jury. Name Lydia Herbert. Married. No children. Forty years old. Four is a real estate agent named Grace Cutter, mid-forties. Six is Jean Cartwright, thirty-four, wife of a milk farmer. Two children but nice. Bert ogled her too. So did I. Little in the way of return ogling. Seven's the resident grandma, Hilda Graysmith, late sixties, widowed, five grand-children, lives on a farm with one of her sons and his family."

Again Purcell went to his drink. "As for the rest of the men, Three is a baker, thirty-eight, name Gregory Sales. Five is a poultry wholesaler, Lucas Pointer, fifty-two or three. Eight's name is Leonard Still, works in a cannery, but it's seasonal and he's laid off for the next three months till a greenhouse crop comes in. Thirty-eight, if it matters. Anyway, none of the nine appears to have had anything to do with Florian. Didn't even go to the regional high school, or have any kids who did. You might call that bad news. But the worse news is that six of the nine—the last six covered—all belong to the same profession. Real estate, wife of a dairyman, grandma who lives on a farm, baker, poultryman, cannery worker—one way or another all six are connected with land or crops or livestock, and people who live off the land know what happens to them with flood or wind or ice. Or lightning. And they also know you can't go around collecting money for it. So Hawkes just plays this act of God at them with the Fireball, and you've got six people ready to buy it going in. The other three—One, Two, and Nine—I just don't know. I've already told you why I like Two and why we might be scared of Nine. It's interesting that One works for the post office. She has no leadership quality at all. But she puts me in mind of Arthur Hawkes's stationery. It gives his street address and then it says just plain Chicago and then the zip code. I think that's a tasteful touch, Max. The word 'Illinois,' let alone any abbreviation for it, is totally unnecessary. All it does is devalue the Chicago. So why the hell does our letterhead read New York, 'NY'? What's the 'NY' for? End of memo, Elizabeth."

He switched off the cassette, and for a time there was silence in the room. At last, Perry Muncrief, the paralegal, said, "Mr. Purcell?"

"What?"

"Can I ask you a couple of questions?"

"I don't know why not."

"Number one," Muncrief said, "is to ask you what it is I'm doing here, with my own room to sleep in and everything."

"That's in and out," Purcell said. "Yours is the spare room. We'll have witnesses coming down, or people from the firm, or whoever, and then you'll double up in Bert's room, whenever it plays that way, so we can always be able to offer a bed or two extra. As the need arises."

"But that wasn't what I meant," Muncrief said. "What I meant was that principally I'm here to operate a computer."

Purcell went to his drink one more time. "You'll get to see some of the courtroom action," he said. "Such as it may be. We'll see to that."

"*That* wasn't what I meant either," Muncrief said. "What I meant was, why do you need a computer at all? I just sat here listening to you dictating the whole makeup of the jury out of your head. No questions, no pauses, no notes. If you can do that, what do you need a computer for?"

"Because," Joe Purcell said, "if we didn't have one, I could be sued for malpractice. If the technology exists, we have to use it. I wish Max understood that better than he does."

Bert Klein said, "That answer you, Perry?"

"Plus," Purcell said, "there just might be a time when the computer proves useful. You've seen the data that's gone into this case. It isn't what you'd call uncomplicated."

"I was just impressed, that's all," Muncrief said.

"I wish I was," Purcell said.

"And then another question," Muncrief said. "You said it was interesting that juror number one worked for the post office."

"It is," Purcell said.

"Because it reminded you of the stationery."

"Partly because of that, yes."

"Partly? What's the other part?"

"I don't rightly know yet," Joe said. "I dare call nothing trivial when I reflect that some of my most classic cases have had the least promising commencement—'The Adventure of the Six Napoleons.' You remember your Sherlock Holmes, Perry? You, Bert? From there, it goes: 'You will remember, Watson, how the dreadful business of the Abernetty family was first brought to my notice by the depth which the parsley had sunk into the butter on a hot day.'"

"Oh, Jesus Christ," Bert Klein said.

"My thoughts exactly," Joe Purcell said to him. He stood up and reached into his pocket, bringing forth a folded piece of paper. "You say the Xerox is working, Perry?"

"Yes, sir," Muncrief said.

"All right," Purcell said, and placed the paper down on the bed table nearest to him. "Sometime in the next couple of days, run me off sixty or so of these, will you?"

He set down his glass and moved to the door and opened it. "Hi," he said turning back to Klein and Muncrief. "I'm Phyllis George. And my day starts with tennis. *And* my Osterizer Blender." And he went out, closing the door behind him.

The two young men left in the room said nothing for a time. Then Bert Klein said, "They only made one of him."

"I believe it," Perry Muncrief said. "What's that piece of paper he left? For me to Xerox?"

"I'm afraid to look. Go look for yourself."

Muncrief went to the table and picked up the folded sheet of paper and read it. Then he said, "Bert, you won't believe this."

"I'll believe anything," Klein said.

"Come here and read it for yourself."

Klein went over and stood behind Perry Muncrief, reading over his shoulder.

"I don't believe this," Klein said. And together they read a complete list of all the numbers, sets, and characters of the nine scenes of Act I and the six scenes of Act II in *The Last Laugh*, Book, Music, and Lyrics by Joseph F. Purcell.

4

Purcell was singing one of the songs from the musical to himself as he drove from Mundelein toward Sunrise. Most likely the surroundings prompted it:

Nothing has changed since I was so high
They're still writing songs about the moon in the sky.

"Nothing has changed," went the song. In what was left of the daylight, the woods lining the road raged with the colors of autumn, and nearly blood-red were the maples that guarded the graveled driveway leading to Sunrise.

Now the turn in the driveway disclosed the breathtaking gorge of the Ohio to Purcell's left and, gentler in the arriving twilight, the opposite palisade. He had brought a sweater, but the evening was Indian summer, soft and balmy. Parking his car in front of the great house, he walked the flagstone terrace around to the back. The golden retriever came to meet him like an old friend, and he heard voices beyond.

They were there on the patio: Dorothy Brewer in dress slacks and her friends from England, Lord and Lady Eddington, and Nancy Gelardi, the young woman from the Washington bureau of Brewer newspapers, and Hallie, who was serving drinks. The Gelardi gal was the only one dressed for sanity. Hallie was back in the French maid's costume, and the Eddingtons, lord in white dinner jacket and lady in full-length gown, precisely as Purcell had first met them nearly a year and a half ago. The thought attacked him: Those are the only clothes they own. But then he noticed something added: a tall, excruciatingly thin, amply pimpled young man wearing Bill Tilden tennis clothes—white ducks, V-necked white sweater with narrow red and blue collar piping—who leaned Raggedy Andyedly against the house like a Gatsby prop. And now Castor appeared in his mortician's cutaway, to torch the luau lights that fringed the patio.

Greetings were exchanged. "You know everybody here, Joe," Dorothy Brewer said. "Including Bunky. You must remember Bunky."

The puppet against the wall did not move. "Six-one, six-love you beat me," he said to Purcell in a high, nasal voice. "At the Thames Club. I'm *thirsting* for revenge."

Hallie, unbidden, brought Purcell a martini. "Good luck on your trial," she said to him.

"I'll need it," he said.

"No, you won't," she said. Her eyes mocked him.

"I must say I agree with Hallie," Dorothy Brewer said. "Everyone said you got off to a fabulous start today."

Purcell started in with his drink. "Who's everyone?"

"Tom Glass," Dorothy said. "My reporter. From the *Beacon* here. He was the first reporter on the scene when the accident happened."

"The defense calls it an accident," Purcell said. "We call it a catastrophe, an explosion, a holocaust."

"How many people did it actually kill, old fellow?" Lord Eddington asked. "I'm afraid I've lost track."

"Actually, it killed twenty-seven," Purcell said. "But, as a matter of law we have either twenty-six or twenty-five or perhaps fewer that are actionable."

"But the lawsuit says twenty-seven," Dorothy Brewer said.

"Indeed it does," Purcell said. "Courtesy either of a friendly defense or a smart defense." His left hand held his drink; his right tugged at his ear. "One of the cases committed suicide, months after the fireball happened, but he was driven to it by his injuries. The law differs from time to time and place to place as to whether you can claim that a suicide is a proximate result of a defendant's negligence, but we did and the defense didn't object. Then there's the case of all the firemen who were killed when the Jumbo Nellie Nellie blew."

Lady Eddington said, "The jumbo who?"

"Nellie Nellie. The tank car. Some courts have ruled that those deaths are not actionable. There's something called the Fireman's Rule—sort of like assumption of risk. The fireman's job is to fight fires, and the theory is that we can't have firemen filing lawsuits every time they think the fire was negligently caused. That might discourage homeowners from calling the fire department."

Lord Eddington said, "You mean the defense didn't bring that up either?"

"Nope," Purcell said. "Actually, it's a kind of complicated thing, because the rule might extend to paid firemen but not to volunteer firemen. There was a precedent case at Crescent City, Illinois, where they might have explored that, but for some reason they didn't. In any event, Arthur Hawkes, the lawyer for the defense here, could have played around with that, and for some reason *he* didn't. Not even against the one member of the Florian fire department—the driver of the fire truck—who *was* paid. So we wind up with twenty-seven dead. Official count."

Lady Eddington said, "This Hawkes doesn't sound very bright."

"No?" Purcell said. "He's only the best in the western world. You've got a huge sympathy factor here. These firemen were all local people, and if the jury gets the idea their cases are being excluded because of some fine-print technicality, that could backfire on Hawkes. Don't forget that in addition to twenty-seven dead, we've got eighty-one injured. You lose more than you gain if you make a thing out of trying to shave one or two off totals like that. Hell, I've even got four cases of minor injuries— sprained shoulder, stuff like that—from passengers in an airplane that tried to duck out of the way of the smoke. They came from another lawyer, and as lead counsel I'm stuck with them, and Hawkes is ecstatic about that.

He'll make it look like *I'm* the one going for the fine-print technicality. Here I've got a hundred and four serious and direct victims, and I'm throwing in four hangnails to make it a hundred and eight."

Dorothy Brewer said, "How long do you think the trial will last?"

"I'm not sure." Purcell grinned. "When are you auditioning my show?"

"Two weeks from Saturday."

"The trial will still be on," Purcell said. "Ordinarily, I doubt we'd wind up one like this before Christmas, but we've got Swifty Morgan for a judge."

"Till Christmas?" Nancy Gelardi said. "What would take that long?"

"The number of expert witnesses, for one thing," Purcell said. "Not to mention the lay witnesses, but experts have a way of taking their time on the stand."

"But how many witnesses can there be?"

"I think we've listed sixty-eight," Purcell said. "Experts and otherwise. The defense will have about thirty."

"Why do you have so many more than them?"

"Because the burden of proof's on us. By the way, did you ever come up with anything on that NAP vice president, the one who used to be with the Department of Transportation?"

Was it a warning look that Dorothy Brewer cast at Nancy Gelardi? Or was Purcell imagining what he saw? It was Dorothy who spoke now: "Nancy has no results yet. But it wasn't for want of trying."

Purcell turned to Dorothy. "Then maybe you can tell me why you said I'm off to such a fabulous start in this trial."

"I already told you. Because Tom Glass said so."

"And Tom Glass is covering the trial for you?"

"That's right. Needless to say, he's on your side."

"Needless to say, all that gets me is a mistrial. He's one of the witnesses I'm going to call."

Amiably, Dorothy Brewer said, "You can't have everything your way, Joe."

"I'm not talking about my having things my way. I'm talking about the courts having things their way. There's already been a ruling in this state that a newspaperman covering a trial can't also be a witness for one of the sides in that trial."

"I'm familiar with that ruling," Dorothy said evenly. "But that was a case where the witness was testifying to what he heard said. All Tom Glass will be doing in your case will be saying what he saw when he arrived on the scene. Besides, he won't even be getting a byline."

"That's one of those typical freedom-of-the-press lines," Purcell said.

"As if it changes anything. And you walk around claiming the press doesn't abuse its privilege?"

"According to James Madison in the Virginia and Kentucky Resolutions of 1790," Dorothy Brewer said, "some degree of abuse is inseparable from the proper use of everything, and in no instance is this more true than in that of the press."

"Tell that to Arthur Hawkes when he moves for a mistrial and Junior Bohr when he grants it," Purcell said.

Dorothy shook her head. "No. You're too close to the trial to understand what I'm saying. The reason Tom Glass isn't getting a byline is that in a trial this drawn out, this technical, this *dull*, there's only so much attention we can give it. That plus the fact that the *Beacon*'s an afternoon paper, and we only print one edition, so we'll miss that day's testimony in any event."

"You can review it the next day. The jury still reads your paper."

"There won't be anything in it to inflame them."

"You don't have to inflame. You can still influence."

"So I can. And you have a remedy for this?"

"Yes. The obvious one. Substitute another reporter for Tom Glass."

"What difference would it make? I told you the stories weren't going to be signed. You may know who's writing them, but the jury won't."

"It's still the *Beacon* covering, and the *Beacon* had the first newspaperman on the scene after the fireball."

"Then your solution is for us not to cover it at all. And to instruct our reporters in the future never to be the first ones on the scene of an accident."

"Catastrophe," Purcell said.

"Even better. If it's a catastrophe instead of just a plain old accident, *then* we hold back sending anybody to cover it."

"Three cheers and a bloody good hear, hear for all hands," said Bunky from his position against the wall of the house. "And what with the time we've taken here, in all this glorious conversation, we won't be able to get in our tennis match before dinner, will we?"

The words, Purcell sensed, were spoken with relief. "Well, now," Joe said lightly, "I'm going to be here from now on. And there's still time between now and when the weather turns cold. What was it I beat you by last time?"

"One and love," Bunky said. "But I've improved."

"And I haven't," Joe said. "That does create a problem for you, doesn't it?"

5

Bert Klein and Perry Muncrief were already seated in a booth in the coffee shop of the Western Motor Hotel when Purcell entered to join them for breakfast. He slid in beside Klein and said, "That reporter for the Mundelein paper the *Beacon*—Tom Glass. I don't want him for a witness."

"Why not?" Bert asked.

"The *Beacon*'s going to take our side," Purcell said. "If we've got a choice—nonpartisan on the witness stand or partisan in print—we'll take the print." Klein and Muncrief both had orange juice in front of them. The waitress came and Purcell ordered tomato juice. "Sure, I knew Dorothy Brewer wants like crazy to see us win—she's got her own axe to grind—but she kind of clued me in last night to expect extra-nice treatment. So the hell with putting Glass on as a witness. All his testimony will amount to will be to describe the aftermath of the explosion, and we can cover that with other witnesses and our visuals." He turned to Muncrief. "We've got the films ready to go, Perry? The TV news tapes and that piece of film that guy shot of the tank car burning?"

"All set." Muncrief did not look up from the menu. Nor did Bert as he said, "The Specimen called."

"Brophy? What the hell did he want?"

"He said the minute he saw you he was going to kill you with his bare hands."

"He's been saying that every day since Hawkes took his deposition. What set him off today?"

"This little beauty," said Klein. He reached down beside him and brought up the Huntington morning paper, folded back to display a three-column story at the bottom of page 2. The headline said:

Ex-Convict Plaintiff in Florian Fireball

Purcell's gut kicked at him, as he began to read the text:

MUNDELEIN—Selection of a jury in an accidental death case here was enlivened yesterday when the New York attorney for the plaintiff revealed his own client's prior conviction for statutory rape. J. F. Purcell, lawyer for Vincent Brophy, 32, a Mundelein truck driver, introduced the fact of the conviction against Brophy

14 years ago in an effort to learn if it would prejudice prospective jurors against Brophy's current claim, which relates to the death of Brophy's wife in a railroad tank car explosion at nearby Florian 17 months ago.

The dead woman, Janet Brophy, was the driver of a school bus who had left her vehicle to investigate the cause of a police road-block. . . .

The waitress came with Purcell's tomato juice. He silently handed the newspaper back to Bert Klein, held the wedge of lemon over his glass, and squeezed. "I'd like to get ahold of that reporter," Perry Muncrief said.

"What reporter?" Purcell said. "Maybe they're not covering it at all and just relying on Hawkes to phone it in. At least it didn't make the front page. They're probably reserving that for 'Fireball Victim Murders New York Lawyer.'"

"Don't make the funeral arrangements yet," said Bert. "I calmed him down when he called this morning by telling him we were looking into the possibility of going after the newspaper for libel."

"Libel?" said Purcell with genuine astonishment. "Hirohito had a better case against the *New York Times* when they accused Japan of bombing Pearl Harbor. What are you going to tell him tomorrow when he shows up with his Smith and Wesson thirty-eight?"

"The truth," said Bert. "That you did a terrific job of drawing the sting and how much worse it would be if you had waited for Hawkes to bring it out with bugles blaring."

Purcell gazed speculatively at his younger associate. "You seem wan this morning, Bert. What is it? This upset when the Specimen called you or lack of sleep? Did you score last night? One woof for yes, two woofs for no."

"Woof," Klein said.

"One of those women jurors excused yesterday?"

"Woof."

"You mean you made it that fast?"

"Woof. But I had some cooperation."

"Obviously. Last question: Do you ever say woof, woof to anything?"

"Woof, woof," Bert Klein said.

Purcell nodded at the newspaper on the seat beside them. "Actually," he said, "the press doesn't count for that much, one way or the other, in a case like the one we've got. The most natural reflex in the world is to dive for the newspapers the minute they come out, to see what they said about you, but in the end result, in this kind of trial, it counts for *bupkus*. Nobody gets the electric chair from this case. Nobody even gets jail time. It's a civil suit. There are only two sexy kinds of civil suits: divorce and libel. And even they have a way of coming to trial too long after the actual event." Purcell took a sip of his tomato juice and then stirred in a few shakes of pepper. "In short, we've got the worst of all possible worlds, when it comes down to exciting any public interest while the trial is going on. Memories are short, and asking the public to sustain interest over the time it takes to try a case of this kind is asking too much. Hell, two weeks after Neil Armstrong walked on the moon, they'd lost interest."

Perry Muncrief shook his head. "Then why were you so interested when we showed you the Huntington paper just now?"

"No particular reason," Purcell shrugged, "except the natural first set of juices that always flow when it's a case of your own the paper's talking about. That's something you can never cure. And the fact is that this is the worst death-and-injury toll ever caused by an exploding tank car."

"Then doesn't that disprove what you've just been saying?"

"No," Purcell said. "It proves it. Here's the opening day in a case of that scale and that importance and that much interest to the readers of the only morning paper covering the area, and it doesn't make page one. It made page two at the bottom. In the local paper here in Mundelein, it may make page one for two or three days, but then they'll start dropping it too. So much for newspapers. As for television, they hit it like hell for a couple of days after the fireball first happened. But you didn't see any cameras around the courtroom yesterday, and you're not about to. You tell me the Specimen's mad as hell about this story. Screw him. The man who's got a right to be mad is the judge. Junior Bohr has to run for election. And the paper didn't even mention his name."

Having his own breakfast at the Holiday Inn at South Point—an address that had occurred to him out of the Ruth Marlowe testimony against Purcell—James Price also read the Huntington paper, and left in mid-forkful to go to a phone booth and call Victor Cuneo in Miami.

"Vic," he said into the telephone, "if this don't beat all." And he read the headline and the story over the phone.

"Good," Cuneo said, when the reading was over. "Now get out of it."

"How d'y mean, get out of it?"

"Go to Arthur Hawkes and tell him you want to settle out the four TWA cases. Do it today. Right now."

"Do I see the sense in that?"

"Think about it," Cuneo said. "Purcell's out to throw the case. I understand he's got some outside interests. Whether he knows it or not, he's got a death wish."

"But how does that benefit us?"

"I'll tell you exactly how it benefits us," Cuneo said. "You go to Hawkes and say we're willing to settle out those four cases."

"I'm not sure what those four cases are worth."

"They're worth a million dollars, that's what they're worth. Maybe more. You take off those four cases, and the judge will have to announce that fact to the jury."

"So? Instead of a hundred and eight cases, that still leaves a hundred and four. And our claims aren't worth any million dollars."

"They are if you do it today. Right now. The jury will take it as an admission that Purcell hasn't got a case—four clients bailing out on him even before he has a chance to prove anything. He screwed himself blue with that rape business yesterday, and I guarantee you Hawkes is just looking for a way to punctuate that. And Hawkes will be very happy to pay extra for four little punctuation marks. Remember, the jury won't be told how much he paid to get those four cases out of there."

"Then Hawkes'll go for that extra dollar?"

"Hell," Cuneo said, "I heard he gave Purcell a firm offer of three million to settle out. If we can help him win, of course he'll go for it."

"Well, I know three million sounds like a lot," Price said. "But put all the cases together, and it doesn't come to that much."

"It does if it means Purcell can't win," Cuneo said. "That son of a bitch tried to screw me out of my living. I've had nothing but dribs and drabs ever since he took off after me when this case first broke. More than anybody else, he's marked me lousy in this business, and this business happens to be my living. Well, if he wants to screw me, I've got a few ways left to screw him. And what's the matter with you? You're a fucking real estate lawyer. Do you want a hundred-thousand-dollar score for yourself or not?"

"Now, you don't have to talk to me like that," Price said. "I have my own reasons to oppose Mr. Purcell. His law partner *demeaned* me in that deposition in New York, in the Marlowe case."

"Then go to Hawkes and do what I say," Cuneo said. "And if it worries you, then think of it this way: You haven't got a goddamn thing to lose."

"But do you know Hawkes? What if he says no?"

"I just answered the second part of that question. As to the first part, no, I don't know him. But it's hard for me to imagine him sticking up for Purcell."

"But what if he does?"

"Then we'll work on something else," Victor Cuneo said. "Just you think money, that's all. In this trial, that's all that matters to Purcell, and it's all that matters to Hawkes. Money! If it weren't for money, nobody would give a damn."

6

It was the first trial of this kind for James Price. Given the presence of outside lawyers, the perennial courtroom hangers-on in any town, the notoriety of this case, and the sheer number of interested parties, one could only suppose the foreshortened supply of spectator seats would be crowded to overflowing.

But if that was so yesterday, it was only because of the presence of extra prospective jurors. Today it was not so at all. Price found ready seating in the second row. Cuneo may have been right. Purcell and Hawkes were nationally famous for the opening statements they would put up, yet still the room was not overcrowded. It was Cuneo's bottom line: In a case like this, who gave a damn?

But Price had a special interest. The judge, with that fat neck and choirboy face extruding from his robes like a glob of toothpaste from a black tube, seated himself, bade the jury good-morning, and nodded briskly at Joe Purcell.

Joe nodded back and rose to his feet. He could feel the Specimen's eyes boring into his back. What are you going to accuse me of today? Vincent Brophy's eyes were saying. Sodomy?

"May it please the court, ladies and gentlemen of the jury," Purcell was saying, "I want to call attention to the fact that the four little Brophy children are not here today, and I think for natural reasons they will not be here most of the time during the course of this trial. Their father, Mr. Vincent Brophy, is here today, but as he is self-employed, with work that takes him away from Mundelein and often out of state, and because this work is his only source of income, he may of necessity be absent also from this courtroom as time goes by. But he will be here whenever possible."

"Quite reasonable and customary," Junior Bohr said. "Mr. Hawkes?"

At the defense table, Hawkes lifted his palms in assent. He wore an Oxford gray suit, with matching vest and off-white tie, but in deference to the rural environment he also wore what Bert Klein called shit-kicking shoes, of high-waxed caramel hue. Framed in black crepe by Mr. Steppenworth to his left and Mr. Halsey to his right, he had with him his courtroom spectacles—his own touch of black in their heavy rims.

Only recently, Hawkes had read an article in *Trial* magazine, the text of a speech delivered at a seminar by a prominent trial lawyer, and it went to the importance of the opening statement in a jury trial. The speech hammered home the significance of the psychological principles of primacy and recency. Primacy told you that the first thought, the first image, the first argument, the first word you hear is the one that has the most profound impact. The correlative doctrine of recency was that you have the best memory of the last thing you hear. So if you were to graph the impact of primacy and recency you would find it shaped like a 'U.' The maximum impact is made by the first thing you hear. The impact goes way down in the middle. Then it comes back up again on the most recent thing you hear. The whole middle section of any sequence of ideas that are transmitted has the weakest impact.

The speech, which had fascinated Hawkes, then discussed how you apply these psychological principles in ordering your trial presentation. And the conclusion was that your strategy is dictated by the strength of your case. If your case is strong you are better off using a *climax* order of proof—starting with the weaker points and building to a crescendo—a dramatic climax. The principle of recency would firmly implant in the jury's memory your strongest point.

But if your case is weak, you should use the *anticlimax* approach— start with your strongest point, your strongest argument, so as to grab instantly the attention of the jury, get them going your way right from the start.

If your case is strong, come on easy and build. If it's weak, lead with your best. I have the feeling, Hawkes said to himself, that you're going to lead with your best, Joe.

Purcell was standing at his table. "Mr. Purcell," Judge Bohr said to him, "you may now make an opening statement on behalf of the plaintiffs."

Magic time. The overture. Beat, melody line, rhythm, and theme. In his mind's ear he heard the opening notes of the overture to *The Last Laugh*. He looked at the jury and said, "The day they buried Janet Brophy, it rained. Janet was just twenty-seven years old. Her oldest child, Elliot, was there in the rain. He watched them put the casket in the ground. He told his little sisters—the twins, Louisa and Katherine—about it afterward. They talked about whether the water would get in the casket in the ground. They asked their dad about it, Louisa and Katherine did. Louisa and Katherine were three. Elliot was five. Vincent Brophy didn't bring the twins to the funeral, but he thought it was okay to talk about it. They still do. Dexter, the youngest, was only one year old when his mother was killed. He doesn't remember, but his brothers and sisters do. They tell him about her now. They all talk about her all the time."

Purcell's voice was low, but none of what he said was missed by anyone in the courtroom. Some phrases were whispered, but it was all heard and felt. Oh, there were others—twenty-six of them dead, another eighty-one injured—important people: Owen Merritt, the mayor of Florian; Whizzer Thoms, the great Olympic athlete—and they had been killed not just by the fireball but in the act of fighting the fire that led to it. There was no shortage of heroes in Florian that day. But there was a heroine too, and that heroine was Janet Brophy, who stopped her school bus in time to make sure that all the children aboard that bus would survive.

Purcell talked about grief, and at the defense table Arthur Hawkes stared down at his fingernails. A less adroit defense counsel might be seeking desperately to object and break the mood Purcell was creating, but Hawkes knew it was all perfectly proper: a groundless objection would be overruled peremptorily by Junior Bohr, serving only to underscore Joe's point and give him a reason for putting on that goddamn hurt look.

And Purcell talked on. Hawkes noticed that Mr. Halsey beside him was taking copious notes. "Stop that," Arthur hissed at him. "You don't dignify a tearjerker by taking notes." Janet Brophy, Purcell was saying: how she wrote music for kids, songs her children still remembered, what a wonderful mother she was, her affection for kids to the point of driving a school bus. And Grandma had come to stay because Elliot was afraid no one would take care of him and his sisters and his little brother now that Mommy was dead.

Now Elliot was telling the twins how Mommy had gone to heaven, and when they went to heaven they would all see Mommy again. Hawkes looked at the jury, which had its own grandmother, number seven, who had begun to weep. Number six, the farmer's wife sitting beside her, had her handkerchief out: she would be the next to go.

Hawkes caught the judge's eye and nodded toward the jury box. Junior saw the tears and looked back at Hawkes, who pointed to his watch. The judge leaned forward, almost apologetically. "Mr. Purcell, excuse me. I hate to interrupt your presentation of what the evidence will show, but time for the morning recess..."

Five minutes later, in chambers, Hawkes was fuming at the judge. "Damn it, Junior, this isn't an opening statement. It's *A Death in the Family*, by James Agee. How long are you going to let this go on?"

"Fuck it, Arthur," the judge said. He was on his second cigarette of the recess. "Do you want me to get the court reporter so you can make a record? Because I'm not telling Joe how to try his goddamn case."

Purcell, his coat off, was stretched out on the sofa. His eyes were closed. "Thank you, Junior," he said. "You're a brick."

"I wasn't talking to you," the judge said. "That's number one. And number two is, I don't know what the fuck Arthur's worried about. If you had any proof on who or what caused the fireball you would have told the jury by now."

"Between now and the end of the day I'll try to think something up," Purcell said.

"Shit," the judge said. "You *are* going to take all fucking day, aren't you?"

He did take all the day: the rest of the morning and the entire afternoon session. From Janet Brophy he went to other victims, from other victims to a portrayal of the holocaust overall. Then back to Janet Brophy. From Janet Brophy to the testimony that would be heard from expert witnesses. From expert witnesses to a charge of conspiracy among the three defendant companies, as to the manufacture of a tank car they knew was unsafe, and the entitlement therefore to compensatory damages for the Brophys and punitive damages for all.

The jurors, he reminded them, were the conscience of the community. The evidence, he was sure, would persuade them to bring in a large verdict, and a large verdict required courage—the courage it took to stand up to huge corporations, a kind of courage not everyone possessed. And back to Janet Brophy, and from her to the evidence of liability. The tank car should have been insulated. Had it been insulated, then even though it was struck by lightning and caught fire, it would not have ruptured and rocketed violently; the LPG would have had time to burn off harmlessly through the safety relief valve.

And from that argument of defective product to the peculiarities of interstate transportation, which were such that these things were done by committee, and the industries that control this committee were the railroad industry and the oil industry. Indeed, this railroad and this oil company had representatives on the committee that designed this tank car.

And from there as reconstructed into the fact that there had been a delay of two months in delivering this tank car, so that when they filled it they had done so for the expected ambient temperatures in the wintertime, thinking it would be delivered in the wintertime; but in fact, as a result of the combination of late delivery and an unseasonably warm late April, it wound up being delivered in summerlike ambient temperature. As a matter of greed, North American Petroleum stuffs as much LPG as it can into the Jumbo Nellie Nellie, in effect overfilling it, and the overfill becomes significant because of the heat, because there isn't enough vapor space to allow for the expansion of heated liquid, a problem aggravated because of the absence of insulation. If there had been insulation, the heat could have been kept out. And all of that combines on the day of the explosion to create a buildup of pressure that sets off the safety relief valve spontaneously, venting vapor into the air around the dome of the tank car, and lightning ignites the vapor. And all this the evidence will show.

And back to Janet Brophy, and it was past five o'clock when Purcell finally ended. "Tomorrow," he said to the jury, "Mr. Hawkes will give you the opening statement for the defense, and the question may arise as to why we're here at all, here in this courtroom. To that, I can tell you now: I'd rather not be here. If I had the power, I would simply point to the doors to this courtroom, those doors over there, and have them open and see Janet Brophy walk in through those doors, healthy and alive. Look!"

He turned and hurled a pointing finger at the main doorway of the room. And stood there, holding the pose, in the total silence of the courtroom.

The doors opened. A gasp, from jurors and staring spectators alike.

From the doorway, an ancient black man stared back at them. He carried a broom and dustpan, and his eyes cast about doubtfully, bewildered at seeing court still in session at this hour.

Purcell's surprise, as total as anyone's, hung for an instant. Then he recovered, dropped his finger, and turned back to the jury. "It wasn't Janet, was it?" he said. He nodded his thanks to the jurors and sat down.

In the car going back to the motel, Bert and Perry alternately laughed and swore over that unexpected ending. Purcell, in the front passenger seat beside Bert, said little. From the rear seat, Perry Muncrief said, "It was just a great recovery you made. Unbelievable!"

"Everybody in that courtroom was staring at that door," Bert said. "What a thing—everybody in the room!"

"Everybody except one," Purcell said.

"Who was that?"

"The Specimen."

7

"You wish to make your opening statement now, Mr. Hawkes, or reserve?" The judge on the morning after.

For an instant Hawkes became invisible, as the dark shoulders of Steppenworth and Halsey crossed in front of him in consultation. Then he parted the flaps in the black tent and rose to his feet. "No, we will make our statement at this time, if Your Honor please." He turned to face the jury, his gaze falling speculatively on Purcell en route. Then he removed his glasses and placed them on the counsel table in front of him, his right hand touching lightly against them.

"Ladies and gentlemen of the jury," Hawkes said—his voice was almost toneless, but it carried—"you sit in this courtroom as the triers of the facts in this case. And I stand before you as one whose mission it is to present those facts to you. That is all I am permitted to do, it is all I am able to do, it is all I will do. And about those facts I must first give you one piece of warning—and then one piece of assurance."

Against the outside wall of the room, last on the right in the back row of the jury, Mother Nine, the black juror named George Proctor, moistened the point of a bright new yellow pencil with his tongue and opened his notebook.

No question about it, Hawkes's technique lent itself to note taking. In the first row of spectator seats, Perry Muncrief wished he had a notebook too. This morning at breakfast, Purcell had interrupted the conversation to ask how long it was between the appearance of the Little Orphan Annie comic strip and its production as a stage musical on Broadway. Bert Klein had said, "Forty years, at least," and that news seemed to depress Purcell more than anything.

Perry Muncrief could not imagine Arthur Hawkes, at breakfast with Mr. Steppenworth and Mr. Halsey, giving vent to such irrelevance. Instead, the master of close-order drill was moving precisely as a timepiece as he spoke before the jury now. He had told them of a warning: the warning was there, and it was that a great mass of technical data—in chemistry, in physics, in metallurgy—would engulf this courtroom in the days and weeks to come. But he had told them also of an assurance: the assurance was there, and that lay in the simplicity of it all.

Lightning had struck the tank car. The plaintiff would concede that point. "You may have read in your papers or seen on television," Hawkes said to the jury, "episodes in which freight cars carrying various gases were derailed. But there was no derailment here. You may have heard at one point or another of some human factor—some human being who did something or made something happen, and an accident then took place, and the plaintiff may want you to think that way in this case. But lightning is lightning. We will show no human being came near that tank car."

In point of true fact, Hawkes went on, the reality was that lightning had *not* struck the tank car—or, if it did, that contact itself was immaterial. "The only thing that could have caused the fire that day was a one-in-a-million coincidence piled on a one-in-a-million coincidence: the lightning strike not only hit where it did but when it did, at a moment when the safety valve atop the jumbo tanker was releasing vapor because of the hot weather."

Did that make the safety valve at fault? Hawkes shook his head. "No. The safety valve was working perfectly. The plaintiff concedes this. The company that manufactured that safety valve is not a defendant in this case. There is your proof right there. When I said this was simple, I meant it, and you can see why."

And even at the point when the lightning ignited the gas, what damage had been done? "We will present to you factual testimony, based on overwhelming record and experience, that any properly trained fire department could and would have put that fire out. They had the time to do it. And they had been shown how to do it. We have a witness who will tell you that barely a year before the accident occurred, he made a special trip to Florian to brief their fire department on how to handle just this specific kind of eventuality."

And so: "The very worst— *the very worst*—damage that ought to have come from this would have been one burned, or partially burned, railroad car. With the loss, or partial loss, of its payload."

Now, Hawkes said, "Brother Purcell has made the point that somebody—he does not say who—put that piece of railroad track, where the tank car was parked, right next to a populated trailer court. We will present to you as a matter of incontrovertible fact that this railroad siding at the Tri-State energy yard was there *before* the trailer court was built. People came to the site of the accident; the site of the accident did not come to them."

And then to the question of conspiracy: "A conspiracy to do what?

Break the law? We will present to you as a matter of incontrovertible fact that none of these defendants broke the law."

To the question of money: "I cannot comment on money, other than to say it is something everybody likes to have, because as a simple matter of fact the plaintiff does not comment on money either. His prayer for monetary damages here gives us no dollar figure. And as a matter of fact, that is just one more place where we agree with the plaintiff. You have to establish that an accident of this kind is somebody's fault, in order to establish damages, but both sides here agree that lightning is nobody's fault. And therefore we agree there are no damages."

"Object." Purcell's voice was hardly audible. "Sustain," the judge said. "In the end, it is the jury who will reach that decision, Mr. Hawkes."

"Your Honor," Hawkes said, "is it not curious that there is no money figure in front of this jury?"

Not looking up from his seat, Purcell said, "Object."

"Yes," Bohr said. "Limit it to what you will present to the jury, Mr. Hawkes."

"I've already said what I will present to the jury," Hawkes said. "I will present them with the facts to show that this was an accident, pure and simple—an unavoidable accident for which no human being, let alone any company, can be held responsible. Lightning is lightning. It is an act of God."

"Object," Purcell said.

Hawkes stared at him. "You say lightning is *not* an act of God?"

"I'm saying that if that was all there was to it, we wouldn't even be here."

"That's all I want to hear," Junior Bohr said. "From either of you. Mr. Hawkes, have you concluded?"

"Yes. I believe so, Your Honor."

"Then we will have a ten-minute recess," the judge said, and rose to head for his chambers.

In the corridor outside, along the railing overlooking the well to the first floor, Purcell said to Bert Klein, "We haven't got all that much time left before the lunch break. What do you think?"

"Perry's got the tape and the film," Klein said. "Let's put them on and get them out of the way. Hawkes will stipulate to them, I'm sure. No wasted time to qualify."

"All right," Purcell said. "Then after lunch, we'll start with the Specimen. I want to get him on the stand and off, and out of this courtroom forever."

"I agree," Bert said. "Are you going to go far with him?"

"I'm not going to go anywhere with him," Joe Purcell said. *"You're* going to handle him."

Klein said, "Me? The Specimen?"

"Why not? You were in Harry Wright's office with me the other day when we ran the routine past him."

"Well, wait a minute," Bert said. "I thought I was going to take the technical side and you'd take the human beings."

"What made you think that?"

"Because the humans are what count."

"Mm-hmm," Purcell said. "And when I leave the firm after this case and you become the next partner, you remember that."

It came across Bert Klein's mind: My God, he wants *me* to take the burden of this case! Aloud, he said, "So I get to practice?"

"Sure," Joe said.

"On *this* case?"

"Why not?"

"Because it's the biggest case we've ever had, Joe, that's why not."

"Did you hear Hawkes inside? He just disagreed with you."

"And I don't have a feel for a two-tier case like this one, where you have a Specimen out in the open and all those other cases just waiting in the wings."

"Makes no never mind. Testimony is still testimony."

"And I don't have a feel for this courtroom. This judge. This defense lawyer. You've been there before. I haven't."

"Yuh, I was here before," Purcell said. "And I lost." They went back into the courtroom. Perry Muncrief had set up the tapes and the projector as best he could, but the product was grievous. There was the Huntington airport's voice tape of the small-plane pilot, in the moments directly following the fireball explosion, that he had been nearly blown apart "by an atom bomb," but the dialogue lacked clarity. Even worse were the television videotapes of news coverage of the explosion. Weather had kept camera helicopters from shooting the scene, so what was there was surface exposure and interviews, good as far as they went but in no way depicting the fireball itself. And least effective-seeming of all was the private photographer's film of the tank car burning after the explosion. Taken from a distance, it showed flames going up and down, and that was all.

Then it was time for lunch. Klein and Purcell walked to the General Dexter. Perry Muncrief lingered behind to pick up the first newsstand copy of that day's Mundelein *Beacon.* Then he joined them, and all of them read the unsigned story on page 1:

Fireball Trial

First Witness Today

A jury of five men and four women awaited the start of testimony today in a broad-scale damage action arising from last year's "Florian Fireball" tank car explosion which took the lives of 27 persons and injured 81 others.

At direct issue in the local courtroom of Judge Junius Bohr, Jr., is the case of Janet Brophy, the young school bus driver and mother of four who died a heroine's death after stopping her bus in time to assure the survival of the 22 young grade schoolers aboard.

Most of the youngsters suffered burns from the heat of the blast, however, and they too can be awarded damages if the jury finds gross negligence on the part of the N. Nance Company, which constructed the jumbo tank car, Mid-Central Railroad, which delivered the deadly cargo to Florian, and North American Petroleum, which filled the car with its volatile payload of liquid propane fuel.

Also among the claimants are survivors of the other death victims, whose number included Mayor Owen Merritt of Florian and Elliott "Whizzer" Thoms, principal of the district high school and former Olympic hero, both of whom were members of the volunteer fire department battling the blaze that preceded the explosion.

The tank car was positioned on an unloading track at the Tri-State Gas Company when the fire broke out.

(please turn to page 6)

The Purcell team was turning to page 6 when Arthur Hawkes appeared beside their table, smiling benignly down at them. He shook hands with Perry Muncrief, whom he had not met before, and said, "Don't bother reading the rest of it. It's just a rehash of your opening statement yesterday."

"My favorite subject," Purcell said. "You done good with your opener, Arthur."

"I don't know," Hawkes said. "Number two worries me. I should have challenged him off that jury yesterday. If I'd had one more peremptory, I would have."

Purcell nodded. "What's-his-name."

"DeSabitini," Hawkes said.

"I kind of like him," Joe said.

"So does the judge," Hawkes said. "Did you see the way they nodded at each other at the start?" He put a hand on Purcell's shoulder. "Can you meet me in the bar here at five o'clock? I'll have somebody I think you might want to meet."

Purcell nodded, and Hawkes went his way. Looking after him, Bert Klein said, "I didn't notice anything between the judge and Two."

"Oh, it was there," Joe Purcell said, "and Arthur picked up on it. But I don't attach much meaning to it, and I don't think Arthur does either. Two and the judge happen to belong to the same club."

"How'd you find that out?" Klein said.

"Just by looking at them. They're both fat."

Perry Muncrief said, "He seems pleasant enough. Hawkes, I mean."

Purcell ordered a Beefeater martini, very dry, over ice. "What are you looking for, Perry? Heroes and villains? Scott Fitzgerald said, 'Show me a hero and I'll write you a tragedy.'"

"It isn't that," Muncrief said. "It's just that there's got to be something wrong with somebody who *wants* to go through life representing those multi-million-dollar companies."

"All right," Purcell said. "Then instead of quoting Fitzgerald, I'll quote Anatole France: 'The rich man is just as entitled to sleep on a park bench as the poor man.' Arthur has very firm notions of equality."

Klein said, "What do you think he wants to see you about later?"

"Haven't got the slightest," Purcell said. "We can brood about it while we're having lunch."

They lunched and brooded, but no one came up with anything, so they trooped back to the courthouse, and to start the afternoon session, Burt Klein put the Specimen, Vincent Brophy, on the witness stand.

Purcell found himself pleased with the way the Specimen performed, and downright proud of Bert Klein. Gently, Bert led Brophy through the story of his courtship, his marriage, the settling and reforming effect his wife, Janet, had upon him, their love for each other and the four children, the income she brought in from driving the school bus, the possibilities her future held as a writer of children's books, the extra toll of grief for the fact that he was away from home when she met her death, was overnight in Indianapolis without even hearing the news till the following morning. And then:

Q.   But when you did hear the news, did you drive straight home?

A.   No. I stopped to pick up a payload at Allied Van, to be delivered in Ironton.

Q.   You did that, knowing that your wife was no longer alive?

A.   Yes. I always tried to do that— pick up a paying cargo for the return trip. Not only because it meant income, but because the business is competitive, and I didn't want some other trucker establishing his reputation ahead of mine, as somebody who could be relied on for hauls like that.

Q.   But on this particular day—

A.   On this particular day, it seemed even more important than ever.

Q.   You're saying that among your thoughts were thoughts of your children and how you could keep money coming in now that your wife was gone.

MR. HAWKES: Leading the witness.

THE COURT: Yes.

MR. KLEIN: Then I will rephrase the question and ask the witness to tell his reason in his own words.

THE COURT: Yes. That is the way to do it.

THE WITNESS: Yes. Well, my reasons were what you just now said. I could only think of what the future would be like for the children.

Q.   Now that your wife's earning capacity was gone.

MR. HAWKES: Same objection. Is the court going to admonish counsel?

THE COURT: The examination of this witness has been agreeable up till now. But Mr. Hawkes definitely has a point.

MR. KLEIN: Well, I think actually I have no further questions.

Hawkes rose to cross-examine. But the cross-examination was no examination. He had been nothing if not thorough with Brophy months earlier when he took his deposition, with particular emphasis on the extended 10-week maternity leave Janet Brophy had taken for her youngest child, with its clear implication that her earnings must not have been all that important. In the courtroom now, however, he dealt with that issue not at all. His entire exchange with the Specimen consisted instead of:

MR. HAWKES: You appear as a loving, faithful, and devoted husband and father, is that not right?

A.   Yes, sir.

Q.   Please understand, then, that the answer you just gave makes it difficult for me to have to ask this next question. But I have an obligation, a duty, to ask it, just as you, as a sworn witness, must do your best to answer it. My question is this: If you had lost your wife for some other accidental reason, would you automatically have sued for damages?

A.   I don't understand that question.

Q.   Let us say your wife was driving the family car to visit a friend, and parked in the friend's driveway, and had a sudden heart attack and died. Would you have sued her friend for damages?

A.   That's not what happened here.

Q.   I know. We are stating what we call a hypothetical. Put it another way: Suppose a friend of yours drove up to visit you and had a fatal heart attack in his car while that car was in your driveway. Would you consider yourself financially responsible for that death?

A.   Of course I wouldn't be.

Q.   You understand, therefore, that just because an accidental death occurs, in this case on your property, that does not necessarily make you responsible for that accident? You understand that?

A.   Yes.

Q.   You acknowledge the fact that things can go wrong which are nobody's fault?

A.   Yes.

MR. HAWKES: That is all. Thank you.

THE COURT: Thank you, Mr. Brophy. The ordeal of testifying in cases of this sort is always greater on those must closely connected to the event. The court appreciates this fact. You have another witness ready, Mr. Purcell?

MR. PURCELL: Yes, judge. But we will have an exhibit—a chart—to introduce here, and if the bailiff can set up the easel and the pointer, we would be glad of that.

Without a glance at Purcell, Vincent Brophy was on his way out of the courtroom. Purcell turned to the spectator section, and a small man clutching a large display board came to his feet and proceeded forward to the witness stand. He handed the display to the bailiff, and it was placed upon an easel facing the jury. Now Purcell rose in his place and began to qualify the witness, whose name was Carl Owens, a professor in the department of physical sciences at Marshall University in Huntington, specializing in meteorology.

The display on the easel was actually a graph. Its vertical lines showed the months of the year, its horizontals the temperature in Fahrenheit. Three jagged lines— the top one red, the middle black, the bottom blue— coursed their way across the chart.

"The black center curve indicates the normal annual mean temperature," Dr. Owens was saying. "The red curve above and the blue curve below indicate, respectively, the highest and lowest temperatures ever recorded in that month."

"And that shows us the temperature in Florian?" Purcell said.

"Well, in Huntington," Dr. Owens said. "But it is close enough. Huntington is a river bottom, and Florian is in hill country, but as far as recordings go, there is not one degree's difference between them over the long haul, at any given point in the year."

"So for all intents and purposes one can stand for the other?"

"That's right."

Q.   Then can you show us with that pointer, Dr. Owens, the mean temperature for the end of February?

THE COURT: You may leave the stand, doctor, and go up to the easel and use the pointer.

THE WITNESS: That is on this middle black line. It is 39 degrees.

Q.   And the top red line? The hottest it has ever been at the end of February?

And on they went, Purcell seeking to establish the mean and extreme temperatures for the end of February, when Jumbo Nellie Nellie was supposed to be delivered, and then for the end of April, when the tank car actually showed up.

It took a while, because Purcell wanted to know about deviation as well. "So," he asked as his final question, "if you had to plan ahead and allow leeway from the norm, you would plan greater leeway on the hot side?"

"Exactly," the witness said. "Records are there to be broken. So far the record is ninety-nine, but this coming year, or some other year in the future, sooner or later it's bound to go past that."

"Thank you, Dr. Owens," Purcell said. "Your witness, Mr. Hawkes."

There was a faint smile on the defense lawyer's face as he rose to cross-examine.

MR. HAWKES: Dr. Owens, you are here as a weatherman, is that correct?

A. What kind of weatherman? A weatherman on television? No, I am not that kind.

Q. You take offense where none was intended or offered. I meant simply that you are a student of the weather.

A. And a teacher of it as well.

Q. Yes, indeed. An excellent teacher, I have no doubt. Surely that is why Brother Purcell called you to the stand here today. And so, let me ask you this: Did he tell you why?

A. I don't understand.

Q. Did he tell you why he was employing you to testify in this trial?

A. I still don't understand.

THE COURT: I think the question is clear enough, doctor.

THE WITNESS: I am not clear. Am I to testify about what Mr. Purcell said to me away from this courtroom?

THE COURT: The question is in order. No obloquy attaches to it. Do you agree, Mr. Purcell?

MR. PURCELL: Anything you want. He can answer the question.

A. He told me the tank car was filled at the end of February and delivered at the end of April, and he wanted to demonstrate the weather picture on both of those dates.

Q. And he came to you as a weatherman— forgive me, a weather expert—to provide the answer to that.

A. That's what he said, yes.

Q. And you have done so?

A. Yes. There are many ways you can check the veracity of my chart.

Q. I have no need to do so. But tell me, Dr. Owens, do you

specialize in the capacity of certain and several compounds in the gaseous state to expand or contract in terms of temperature?

A.   Generally speaking, a gas expands when it is hot and contracts when it is cold.

Q.   Fine. I think the jury already knew that. The question is whether you can get any more specific than that?

A.   Are you asking me if Mr. Purcell discussed this part of it with me?

Q.   I wasn't, no. But so long as you bring it up, then did he?

A.   No. We didn't go into that part of it. Not except in that most general sense I just set forth. But it is a good overall rule.

Q.   Is it? I asked you before if you specialized in the properties of things in the gaseous state. Can you give me a yes or no answer to that?

A.   I suppose I would have to say no. I do have a body of knowledge that gives me an overview.

Q.   Does your overview extend to the paraffin or saturated hydrocarbon C 2, H 8, the third member of the series C nH 2n plus 2?

A.   I am not sure what you are talking about.

Q.   I have no further questions of this witness.

THE COURT: Thank you, Dr. Owens. Your turn as a witness has been completed. I must say something however to Mr. Hawkes, which is that this court, and I think this jury, are properly mystified by that last question. All those letters and numbers—can we be enlightened as to what they might be?

MR. HAWKES: Propane.

8

The bar at the General Dexter was the old hotel's finest room. Well-populated at five in the afternoon, it was hung in old oak and leather that worked together to deaden noise, and the privacy was augmented by darkness, the tables in the booths illuminated only by the muted red of chimney lamps.

It was so dark, in fact, that Purcell almost missed Arthur Hawkes entirely. A man seated in one of the booths, against the right-hand wall, looked like Hawkes, but he was alone, so Purcell looked elsewhere, then squinted back through the gloom and saw that the solitary figure was Hawkes after all.

Joe went over and slid onto the seat opposite the other lawyer. "I thought you said you were going to have somebody with you."

"I do," Arthur said. "He's in the men's room." For the first time, Purcell noticed a half-empty glass on the table in front of the space next to Arthur's. "He drinks Manhattans," Hawkes said.

"Red dye in the cherries," Purcell said, and waved at the aproned waiter. "Carcinogenic. I think we're splitting the press, Arthur."

Hawkes nodded. He himself was nursing a gin rickey, and when the waiter came Purcell ordered Red Label and soda. "You've got the afternoon paper on your side," Hawkes said.

"And you've got the morning. Big headline—Rapist Seeks Damages."

"What about the afternoon? Deadly Cargo. That's a lovely way to describe the contents of a freight car."

"Accurate, though," Purcell said.

"About as accurate as rapist," Hawkes said. "Speaking of which, wait till our friend comes back from the men's room."

"He's a rapist?"

"I don't know. I only met him twenty minutes ago, for the first time. I was talking about newspaper accuracy. He showed me a newspaper clipping that described him as a lawyer. I talked to him on the phone yesterday and again this morning, and now here in the bar before you came in, and if he's a lawyer, I'm sending a nasty letter to the Association of American Law Schools."

"Why do you bother with him?"

"He's your cocounsel, that's why. His name is James Price. You've heard of him?"

The waiter came and set Purcell's drink in front of him. "Yes. I've heard of him," Joe said.

"He was the one who went after you about the Marlowe woman," Hawkes said.

"Don't I know," Joe said. "Still never laid eyes on him, though. Max was the one who took him on."

Arthur Hawkes nodded. "I suppose it won't surprise you any to learn that deposition has become a collector's item. Enlarged your reputation."

"And Max's."

"His doesn't need enlarging. You're serious about quitting the firm, aren't you?"

"Quitting the law, not just the firm. You get tired in this business, Arthur."

"I don't need to be told that," Hawkes said. He sipped at his drink. "I get so sick of clients who won't give me sufficient settlement authority. The concept that it costs less to settle a case before trial than win it in court is one that just hasn't trickled down to them."

"In its way, it's a new concept," Joe said. "I can see why they hold you down. Besides, they like your track record. You offered me four hundred and fifty thousand in Marlowe, and if it had been six hundred thousand I would have told the woman to take it. As it was, I told her not to, and what happens? You win the case in court, and she collects nothing."

"No," Hawkes said, and shook his head. "Even that one wasn't worth it. You were right when you said it was a new concept, but it's there, and it's the inflation factor, and one runaway jury, like the Pinto case, and where are you?"

Purcell shook his head. "No, that's a bad example, Arthur. Sure, the jury brought in a hundred and twenty-five million in the Pinto case, but what happened then? The trial judge knocked it down to size." Latecoming notwithstanding, his drink was nearly finished, and together they waved to the waiter for a refill. "Where I think you're right," Joe said, "is the business of the actual cost of trying a case at today's prices. Not just the dollar figure, but the fact that it ties up money. There's an orthopedic surgeon in Los Angeles who's asking four thousand dollars a day, plus expenses, to testify as an expert witness."

Hawkes laughed. "Will you be using him in this trial? I'll have to ask him how much you're paying him, when he's on the stand."

"What's sauce for the goose," Joe said. "If you ask my witnesses, I'll ask yours. And my witnesses go on before yours, so I get the last crack."

"I'll take it under advisement, counselor," Arthur Hawkes said. In truth, neither he nor Purcell had a habit of parading witness fees in front of a jury: expert witnesses were paid to testify, and the more expert the witness, the more he was likely to charge. Indeed, there were cases—the Fireball was one of them—where it was a race for the same witness, as in the case of a heat transfer specialist this time, who had agreed to testify for Purcell simply because Joe's phone call reached him first. He could as easily have testified for the defense.

"Goddamn," Purcell said now, "what's he *doing* in the men's room?"

"I don't know," Hawkes said, "but from the way he talks, I've got a feeling he's going to tell us. Oops. Speak of the devil."

Two men reached their booth simultaneously. One was the waiter with the new round of drinks; the other was the stocky figure of James Price.

"Well, now," he said cheerily, and slid in beside Arthur Hawkes, holding out a Kiwanis hand to Joe Purcell. "You must be the famous Mr. Purcell."

Purcell eyed him. "You going to have another drink?"

"Well, now, I think I *will*," Price said, hoisting his glass for the waiter to see. "Though it's probably the worst thing I can do. Seems I got a case of what they talk about in the Pepto Bismol commercial— *distress in the lower* tract. But time for a celebration, I say, and there's nothing like a li'l ol' Manhattan cocktail when it's time to celebrate."

"Fine," Purcell said. "What are we celebrating?"

"Mr. Hawkes here hasn't told you?"

"I thought he should hear it from you," Arthur Hawkes said to him. "He's your trial counsel, after all."

"Well, right, you're a very logical thinker, Mr. Hawkes," Price said. To Purcell: "Mr. Hawkes and I have been in negotiation by telephone. About my clients, in this li'l ol' *Fireball* case."

"Yes, indeed," Purcell said. "Four of them, weren't there? The ones who were in that airplane? What was it again. One dislocated shoulder, one whiplash—"

"They were *hospitalized*," James Price said in a hurt tone.

"All treated and released the same day," Purcell said. "And the airline picked up the hospital tab. Am I right?"

"Don't matter under the law who paid the hospital," Price said. "They didn't waive their rights to further *re*dress."

"But now they have," Hawkes said. "Is that correct, Mr. Price."

"Yes, indeed," Price beamed. "I've talked to all four of them, and I counseled them to settle. And I'm glad to say they took my advice."

"All right," Purcell said. "So that's four fewer clients I represent. Did you have to get me into a saloon to tell me that?"

"Mr. Hawkes thought it would be appropriate," Price said.

"I did indeed," Arthur Hawkes said.

"Mr. Hawkes said it would be completely agreeable to him to have four cases fewer pending against him," Price said.

"I did indeed," Arthur Hawkes said.

"In fact," Price said triumphantly, "Mr. Hawkes agreed to talk to his companies—those defen*dants* that he represents in this li'l ol' trial—about settlin' out in these four cases."

"I did indeed," Arthur Hawkes said.

Purcell started to say something, then looked at Arthur Hawkes. The glint of amusement in the latter's eyes was signal enough.

"Don't let me interrupt you," Price said to Purcell. "You were going to say?"

"Nothing," Purcell said. "You go ahead."

"Well, not much else to tell," Price said. "I realize you may not think this is a helpful development for your case, Mr. Purcell, having it come out that your clients are startin' to desert you. But it was through me that you got those clients, and I'm still their personal and primary attorney, and I have to do what I think is best. I explained that to Mr. Hawkes, and he agreed."

"I did indeed," Arthur Hawkes said.

"And I just thought both trial lawyers in the case, Mr. Purcell and Mr. Hawkes together, should be present, here and now, so everything would be aboveboard," Price said.

Joe Purcell said to Arthur Hawkes, "I don't believe this."

"Believe it," Hawkes said.

Price looked from one to the other. A look of dawning came upon him. "Ah, now, hold on here," he said. "I know what Mr. Purcell's thinkin'. He's thinkin' this is all just an act of revenge on my part. I embarrassed him with a lawsuit I had to bring against him a while back, and he thinks I'm still out to embarrass him. Well, I'm sorry about that. I truly am. But talkin' across this table, we're just three lawyers. Just like the two of you, you'll go after each other hammer and tongs in the courtroom down the street, but after hours you can have a civil, social conversation together over a glass or a plate."

"I do not believe this," Purcell said again.

"Believe it," Hawkes said again.

To Price, Purcell said, "And you arrived at a settlement with Mr. Hawkes?"

"In a manner of speaking, why, I guess so, you might say that," Price said. "Isn't that correct, Mr. Hawkes?"

"In a manner of speaking," Hawkes said.

"And—" Price's voice hardened, in spite of himself "—I just thought it'd be the fittin' thing for you to be here to hear it for yourself." He raised his Manhattan in salute to Purcell.

"In other words," Purcell said to him, "you haven't heard the figure yet."

"I already told you," Price said. "I wanted you to be here for that. But Mr. Hawkes told me he'd talked to his clients."

"I did indeed," Hawkes said. "Briefly!"

Price said, "Briefly?"

"Briefly was all that was required," Hawkes said. "I told them you were ready to settle your cases and asked them what they thought it was worth. Speaking for myself, I thought they were worth thirty thousand dollars, to be split up any way you like. They agreed."

Price nodded expectantly, the smile on his face the same as before. "That kind of talk's to be expected, I know," he said. "But what's the figure you decided on?"

"Thirty thousand," Hawkes said.

"Well, now, just hold on here," Price said. "Vic told me to—I mean, I was thinking just an awful lot bigger than that. I mean, like seven figures. If you want to hear the actual figure, it's —"

Arthur Hawkes put up a hand. "I haven't any interest in hearing it. I've already stated the offer. Thirty thousand. That doesn't mean thirty thousand and one. It means thirty thousand."

"Well, I can't go back and tell my clients that," Price said.

"Then don't," Arthur said.

"Well, now, we're being frank and aboveboard here," James Price said. "I mean, thirty thousand for four injuries isn't even nickels and dimes at today's prices. But it's even worse than that. The point is, what it's worth to *you* in this li'l ol' *Fireball*, Mr. Hawkes, right at this juncture before the trial actually gets really going. I'm not sure you took that into consideration. I mean, bearing in mind all things, like the effect the loss of these clients is bound to have on Mr. Purcell here and the case he's tryin' to put on."

"I assure you," Arthur Hawkes said to him, "all things were taken into consideration."

"And all you came up with was thirty thousand?"

"Yes," Arthur said.

"If this don't beat *all*," Price said.

"There is one condition, actually," Hawkes said. "You have to tell Victor Cuneo he doesn't get one penny out of this."

"Ah, now, wait a minute," James Price said. "Even if I were inclined to accept your offer, how could I tell Vic that?"

Joe Purcell said, "Why not try it and see? The real lawyers of this world, no matter what side of a case they're on, want nothing to do with the Victor Cuneos. And you're a lawyer, aren't you?"

"And the less he gets, the more you get," Arthur Hawkes said. "Do you accept?"

"I accept your offer," Price said.

"Congratulations, Mr. Price," said Purcell. "You are one hell of a tough negotiator."

James Price leaned toward Purcell. "You," he said to Joe. "*You're* the one with revenge in his heart!"

"I didn't even know about it," Purcell said.

"I'm acceptin' the thirty thousand," Price said. "But I expect a modicum of gratitude to go with it." He turned back to Hawkes. "Didn't I explain to you how taking these four cases away would help you? How it would embarrass the other side?"

"You did indeed," Hawkes said to him. "Rats leaving the sinking ship, I believe was the way you put it."

Price stared at him. Then he looked at Joe Purcell and stood up and leaned across the table. "You *did* put him up to this," he said. "You whore-mongering, adulterous son of a bitch."

Purcell's left hand shot out and slapped the right cheek of James Price, so fast and so hard that the startled Price careened from the booth and fell to his knees.

Joe Purcell stood up. So did Arthur Hawkes. "You'll notice," Purcell said to him, "I used an open palm. You're my witness."

"Witness to what?" Hawkes said. "I didn't see anything. But if we're leaving..." He reached into his pocket, drew out a $20 bill, and placed it on the table. "My treat," he said. "For the drinks and the entertainment both."

"I'll get you even," Purcell said.

"Don't be ridiculous," Hawkes said. "I'm the one who invited you. Don't you remember?"

Still on his hands and knees in the gloom, Price watched them exit past him, one pair of legs to either side. Then another pair of legs showed up, and Price raised his eyes and saw the waiter looking down at him.

"Do you need help, sir?" the waiter asked. "Did you slip and fall?"

"*Slip and fall?*" Price said. "I was ass*au*lted!"

"Sorry, sir," the waiter said.

"Sorry, sir? You saw it, didn't you?"

"Saw what, sir? It's a trifle dark in here."

"That Purcell's got to be a certifiable maniac," James Price said, picking himself up. "Where's the telephone?"

"Out in the lobby, sir."

"And you didn't see a thing? You didn't see him assault me?"

"Mr. Hawkes wouldn't do a thing like that," the waiter said, taking the $20 bill off the table. "He's a gentleman. Stays here at the hotel when he's in town."

"Never mind Hawkes. What about the other one?"

"The other gentleman? I didn't notice him."

"Forget it," Price said. He pulled his suit coat smooth and went out into the lobby and got on the phone. "Vic," he said, when Cuneo came on the line, "wait till you hear this. If this don't beat *all!* . . . Well, no, the thing is it didn't work out. Not the way you said it was goin' to . . . Well, before you start on me, Vic, you have to bear in mind now that there are some things you don't know about lawyerin', you not bein' a lawyer and all. What I have is good news and bad news. The good news is that Purcell is all upset, just like you said he'd be, from hearin' that those four clients were desertin' him. You should have seen his face, Vic! . . . The other thing? Hawkes and the money? Well, that's the bad news. But I have to make it short, Vic. Either that or call you back. I've got this *dis*tress in the lower tract . . ."

Just outside the main entrance to the hotel, Joe Purcell turned and said to Arthur Hawkes, "Just one question."

"I know what it's going to be: Why'd I agree to pay him anything?"

"It does fascinate me," Purcell said. "I have to confess to that."

"Very simple," Arthur said. "Those four cases were the airline passengers, and TWA wanted out."

"But TWA wasn't in," said Joe. "Price didn't sue them."

"That's what I like about you, Joe. Your world's so different from that of all the Prices and the Cuneos. You can't even think the way they do."

"Help me," said Joe.

"Cuneo wouldn't let TWA off the hook. Win, lose, or draw, he knew that somehow, somewhere, he could nuisance them into a few bucks— at least the cost of defense—or blackmail them with the threat of bad publicity."

"But the suit against TWA is dead. The statute of limitations has run."

"Cuneo handled that. When Price filed his suit he told TWA that he would join them as a defendant if they didn't agree in writing to waive the statute of limitations. So they agreed. They figured being sued later was better than sooner, and somewhere along the line somehow they might get out."

"It's a new low even for Cuneo. Petty hijacking."

"That's a good name for it," Arthur said. "I'll use that in court some-day."

"Probably against me," Joe said. "So they were willing to pay thirty thousand dollars to avoid any more publicity from this."

"No. That's less than what I saved them. I've had seventy-five thousand in my pocket from them, to settle those cases, right along."

Joe Purcell grinned. "You're a master, Arthur. Another quick forty-five thousand saved for the stockholders."

"Yes," Hawkes nodded. "That plus the fact that I just got rid of the four tough cases."

9

The witnesses for the plaintiffs were a curious, disorganized group. "I hope you orchestrate your musical better than what we're doing with this crowd," Bert Klein said to Purcell during the second week of testimony, but there was no reproach in what he said. Much of the ordering of witnesses was simply beyond the A&P's control. And much of that, in turn, was the doing of the judge.

Junior Bohr had come down hard on Purcell's attempts to broaden the scope, and witnesses fell by the wayside, expert and nonexpert alike, including one of Joe's personal favorites, a professor of history who would testify to the interlocking consortium John D. Rockefeller had established so that Standard Oil controlled tank car manufacture and railroad rates as well.

"Forget it," the judge said to Purcell. "That was a hundred years ago. You're not putting that tweedy asshole on the stand in my courtroom."

"Was it a hundred years ago that Standard Oil also tried to control the press?" Purcell said. "Have you been reading the morning paper's coverage of this case? The jury's sure as hell reading it. You haven't put a ban on them."

"I never heard of Standard Oil controlling the press," Bohr said.

"There are a lot of things you've never heard of. A man named Frank Kellogg. A man named Melville Stone."

"You're right," the judge said. "I've never heard of them. Who the hell are they?"

"Kellogg," Purcell said, "was secretary of state under Coolidge. Before that, he prosecuted Standard Oil under the Sherman Anti-Trust Act. And Stone was general manager of the Associated Press." Joe took a sheet of paper from his inside coat pocket. "And Kellogg wrote the following: 'Melville E. Stone is controlled absolutely by the Standard Oil people. He will not, of course, send out any reports of the testimony that he is not obliged to, at least that is my opinion from all that I have seen. . . . It is astonishing that that concern can control the Associated Press.'"

"I see. And when was all this?"

"In 1905."

"And were the charges ever proved?"

"No. Kellogg retracted them. They did prove that one reporter was on the take, but couldn't prove that Stone was aware of him."

"Go away," the judge said.

"There's more," Purcell said. "There was a congressman named Sibley, from Pennsylvania, and he was a special friend of Standard Oil. And there was a man named Archbold, who was a vice president of Standard Oil. And—" reading from the sheet of paper again "—Sibley wrote to Archbold, 'An efficient literary bureau is needed, not for a day but for permanent and healthy control of the Associated Press and other kindred avenues. It will cost money, but it will be the cheapest in the end and can be made self-supporting.'"

"And that was in 1905 too?"

"That's right."

"Then what the fuck has it got to do with anything?"

"It establishes a foundation, that's what it's got to do with anything. You know my list of witnesses. I intend to call the public relations director of North American Petroleum. He'll be an unfriendly witness, but you can bet your robe that Arthur won't call him. And I'm going to have him testify to how much money they spend on influencing the press. What started out as a clumsy idea at the turn of the century has become a fine art, Junior."

Bohr nodded. "Sure, but why stop there? One of your clients is the widow of the guy at the Texaco station that blew up in the fireball. Why not call the man from Texaco? He'll be a friendly witness for you, not an unfriendly. He'll testify as to how Texaco decided to change its public image by sponsoring the broadcasts from the Metropolitan Opera."

"I can read that Huntington morning paper," Purcell said. "And so can the jury."

"And so can I," the judge said.

"Then you know they're doing nothing but presenting the case for the defense. Day in and day out."

"That's one way of putting it. Do you have any hard facts to back up a charge like that?"

"If I did, would you let me put them on?"

"That's another way of saying you don't. And if you did, no, I wouldn't let you put them on. That's the subject of your next lawsuit, not this one."

"You rule like that and how am I supposed to put on my case?"

"Badly, just the way you've been doing. If you've got a weak case, blaming it on the press isn't going to help you any. And if the Huntington paper makes it out that you're horseshit, it may be because you're horseshit. Up to this point anyway. If you think you can save yourself by putting witnesses like this on the stand, then go ahead and call the fuckers. And the minute they're sworn in, Hawkes will object to their being there and I'll sustain. So why go to all the trouble?"

"To make a record," Purcell said, "that you kept my witnesses off the stand. You did the same goddamn thing in the Marlowe case, and I lost it."

"I can always be reversed," Bohr said. "But somehow I have the feeling this isn't going to be one of the times. If you think you're going to get some jerk-off historian to cream all over John D. Rockefeller on the witness stand, you can go take a flying screw for yourself." He lit his fifth Camel of the conversation. "Don't let's take this any further, your bending my ear like this. Just go away."

Purcell stood up. He reached the door of the judge's chambers, then turned back. "Conspiracy is conspiracy," he said. "One day or another I'm going to get it in."

"If anybody'll find a way, you will," the judge said.

"And meanwhile the jurors are reading that newspaper, morning in and morning out."

"I don't know how many of them read the morning paper," Bohr said. "If anything, they're more likely to read the afternoon—the *Beacon* here. After all, that's the local Mundelein paper and they're all local people." He smiled. "And that's the strangest thing of all, isn't it? That dog-and-pony show you want to put on about how the press can be controlled. Funny, you haven't said a word about the *Beacon*. Can it be because the *Beacon*'s on your side?"

"Are you saying that goes to conspiracy?"

"Me? Perish the thought. The fact that you spend half your nights humping the publisher wouldn't even enter into it, would it?"

Purcell stared at him. "You're talking about me and Dorothy Brewer?"

"Yes, but totally without prejudice. I'm very broad-minded."

"But you think there's something between me and her?"

"I'm not the only one who thinks it."

"There isn't," Purcell said. "If there was, I wouldn't lie about it."

"Fine," the judge said. "Then that rules out sex."

"What else did you have in mind?"

"Conspiracy," Junior Bohr said cheerfully. "As you just finished saying, conspiracy is conspiracy."

"I see," Joe said. "And where would you have got that idea?"

"From Arthur Hawkes," Bohr said. "You think you're the only one who comes in here complaining about the press?"

And he waved Purcell from the room, loser in that battle. Other battles were fought. Purcell found himself losing those too. One was his attempt to introduce evidence about Stephen Coblenz, the quadriplegic whose suicide had been the most recent and most bizarre of the twenty-seven fireball deaths. Purcell had wanted the parents of Coblenz to testify so that he could get before the jury the dramatic nature of what had befallen the young medical student, the fact that he was a stranger come to town to help heal the sick, the point that the fireball produced not only death but the despair that led to death, all combined one with another to paint the mystic universality of the tragedy with unique impact. Judge Bohr would allow none of this. It went too far afield from the specimen case. Living victims of the explosion would, within limits, be permitted to testify, though only as witnesses to the fireball, not victims of it—a delicate dividing line that Purcell had already managed to obliterate here and there—but the only relatives of the dead to take the stand would be the relatives of Janet Brophy.

There was, Bert Klein pointed out, one lovely way to get the Coblenz story in front of the jury: use Rosa Crewes. She herself was one of the victims of the blast, one of the plaintiffs in the case—but she was also an eyewitness, who could testify to what she saw, heard, and felt that day. "And if you want universality, she gives it to you," Klein said to Purcell. "You've got all the burn victims, but Rosa Crewes wasn't burned at all. Her body stayed intact. But her mind went. Now: Coblenz is supposed to stay at her house while he's in Florian. She has the room all made up for him, she's got a thing in advance about having this fine young man under her roof, then the fireball hits, she finds out what happened to Coblenz, and now she's a case of shock."

"I don't think they ever actually told her about his death," Joe said.

"They didn't have to. That's in front of the jury already. He's on the list."

"It's tempting," Purcell said. "But we can't take the risk."

Klein thought for a moment. Then he sighed. "I guess you're right."

"You know I'm right. You don't put mental incompetents on the witness stand. You don't know what they'll get it into their heads to say."

What Purcell said was true as a general rule for all such witnesses. That made it particularly true for Rosa Crewes. If ever Joe Purcell had literally screwed himself out of potentially valuable testimony, it would have to be in this one instance. "I hope you enjoyed the peignoir, Mr. Farnum." That was all he needed. "They then went into the store, where Mrs. Marlowe purchased a peignoir—do you know what a peignoir is, Mr. Price?—and held it up for Mr. Purcell's approval. There is testimony available from the saleslady involved, Mr. Price...." Max Aranow at his best. And on the record. Even thinking of the Rosa Crewes courtroom potential in the Fireball brought a shiver to Joe Purcell.

Some of the plaintiff's witnesses were effective. The testimony of two ten-year-old girls, both of them passengers on Janet Brophy's bus, both with flaming facial scars from the fireball, was absolutely riveting. Vividly they told of the screaming and horror aboard the bus, of hair and clothing bursting into flame, of air so hot it could not be breathed. And both told of the way Janet Brophy had calmly instructed them to get under their seats while she alone fought her way outside the bus to investigate and to die. When Klein turned them over to Arthur Hawkes for cross-examination, the defense veteran in all common sense simply shook his head. "No questions," he said.

He was hardly so silent, however, with a witness named Eugene Meara, who had been the general manager of the Tri-State Gas Company at its main office in Huntington. No, he testified under direct examination by Purcell, they no longer had their branch operation in Florian. Their only postaccident activity in Florian had been to use up what propane remained in the underground reserve tanks.

Purcell pressed him on that point. How much fuel was in the tanks? Meara told him. Wasn't that a lot? It was a fairly good supply, Meara said. And yet there was a fully loaded Jumbo Nellie Nellie waiting to be unloaded as well, wasn't that so? Yes.

Q.   Isn't it a fact that your people in Florian didn't unload that jumbo right away because they had no place to put the contents?

A.   Yes. That can happen.

Q.   So there are times when these tank cars are used not just to haul this propane but to become in effect an auxiliary storage tank when they reach their destination?

A.   Yes. Until you use up the fuel you already have on hand. It has to be stored someplace. You can't just dump it on the ground.

Q.   You don't take that into consideration in timing your orders for more?

A.   You try to, but you can't always be exact. Better to have a little extra than to run dry.

Q.   And what they deliver is always a full Jumbo Nellie Nellie? You can't order a smaller amount?

A.   You could, but you get a better price break when you order by the carload.

Q.   In other words, you're encouraged to buy by the carload?

A.   I suppose you could put it that way.

Q.   And when you get more than you need? What do you do then?

A.   I told you. You can use the tank car for auxiliary storage.

Q.   No, that's when you get more than you can handle. My question was, what do you do when you get more than you actually need? That can happen too, can't it?

A.   Well, you're in business to sell as much of it as you can.

Q.   So you try to encourage consumption of propane among your customers?

A.   Well, one way or another. I mean, you certainly advertise and let people know you're there. Some things you can't regulate. The weather, for example. If it's cold, they use more fuel. If it's warm, they use less.

Q.   But there are other ways to keep a business like yours flourishing, aren't there?

A.   I wouldn't say we'd been flourishing. Not since what happened that day in Florian.

Q.   Yes, I think we can all appreciate that. But you mentioned advertising, and as I understand it, there's more than one purpose to advertising. On the one hand, you try to get people to use more of your product. On the other hand, you also try to increase the number of customers you serve, isn't that right?

MR. HAWKES: Object. I don't see how any of this is material.

THE COURT: Sustained. You're not showing any relevance here, Mr. Purcell. What difference does it make how they advertise?

Q.   All right. Then let me ask you this. When you say you get a price break, who gives you that price break? Is it the oil company or the railroad?

A.   I don't quite know how to answer that. Both of them, I suppose. Do you mean, how do we pay our bills? To who?

Q.   No, actually you've answered that question, I think. When you said both of them. Each of them obviously benefits from a full payload, wouldn't you say?

MR. HAWKES: Object. Leading and immaterial.

THE COURT: Sustained.

Q.   Well, if both of them set the price, are you aware of a historical pattern there?

A.   I don't understand.

Q.   Oil companies and railroads, going back a hundred years and more to the time of John D. Rockefeller, when—

Hawkes was on his feet. "Objection!"

"Sustained," Junior Bohr said. "Don't look surprised, Mr. Purcell. You know we can't have any of this."

"If the court please," Purcell said, "one of the central issues framed by the pleadings is the conspiracy between these defendant companies. The jury is certainly entitled to hear evidence on that issue, all of it, including the complete history going back to—"

"No, no, counselor. I've ruled. Spare us gratuitous speeches on the subject."

"Your Honor," Joe said, "this is incredibly unfair to all of the victims of this holocaust that could have been avoided by—"

"Mr. Purcell," the judge interrupted, "I don't think that the rules of evidence, which you have been bending, twisting, and torturing throughout this trial, are unfair at all. My ruling is based on those rules. If you prefer to think that I rule as I do because I'm the meanest man in town, that's your privilege." He reached for his gavel, anticipating the laugh that came from the jurors and several spectators, and rapped the tiny courtroom back to silence.

As if cued by the gavel, Hawkes was on his feet. "Your Honor, may I respectfully request that the jury be instructed that Mr. Purcell's unfounded accusations are not evidence and are to be disregarded."

"No, Mr. Hawkes," Judge Bohr said, "I feel like being mean to both sides today. Besides, I think the jury understands the rules of evidence quite well by now and is likely to follow those rules without further instruction, far better than Mr. Purcell and you, despite my instruction." Another laugh. Another gavel.

Purcell returned to the witness. This time, with laborious and time-consuming examination, he led Eugene Meara, the Tri-State man, through every phase of the ordering procedure, including the billings and the manner of payment. Two or three more times, Hawkes objected, and was sustained each time. There was, however, no further mention of John D. Rockefeller.

More than an hour later, Purcell turned the witness over to Arthur Hawkes for cross-examination, and it was as if the defense counsel, all this time, had been sitting in a different courtroom listening to a different witness in a different lawsuit. Not one question he asked went to anything Meara had said under direct examination. Hawkes had a totally new subject in mind, and he went at it mercilessly.

Q.   An energy company like yours—you have rules that go to the matter of proper handling of the product?

A.   Yes.

Q.   And the people in your branch office in Florian were supplied with those rules?

A.   Yes, of course.

Q.   And a number of those rules deal with proper procedure in the event of a tank car fire?

A.   Yes.

Q.   And who supplies you with those rules?

A.   Well, they come from all over.

Q.   You get recommendations and advisories from the tank car manufacturer?

A.   Yes.

Q.   And from the oil company?

A.   Yes.

Q.   And from the railroad?

A.   Yes. And from the fire underwriters, and occasionally the state and city or whatever. We always complied with the codes.

Q.   You complied with the codes. Do they call for periodic drills in fire fighting?

A.   I believe those are suggested.

Q.   Suggested?

A.   Yes. As opposed to mandated. Some of the drills you couldn't conduct if you wanted to.

Q.   Why not?

A.   Because your particular branch might not be of the size the manual is talking about, or you might find a manual talking about how to drill with certain equipment, only you don't have that equipment.

Q.   Why wouldn't you have it?

A.   Again, maybe the size of your operation wouldn't warrant it. Or maybe it's new equipment not yet being marketed generally. Or maybe it's available but you just can't afford it. Those things, as I say, aren't mandatory. It's like when you get a new car and the owner's manual that comes with it tells you all about the proper use and care of the air-conditioning unit. But if the car didn't come equipped with air-conditioning you're not going to sit there practicing how to set all the switches and vents.

Q.   So would it be safe to say your branch at Florian didn't have all the equipment mentioned in the various recommendations?

A.   I don't think any energy yard anywhere has all the equipment.

Q.   Well, let's take it step by step, from the beginning. Let's say a fire breaks out. What's the first thing your people were trained to do?

A.   What they did do.

Q.   And what was that?

A.   I believe they called the fire department.

More chuckling in the courtroom. A belly laugh from Rafael DeSabitini, number two in the jury box.

Q.   Did you mean that to be funny?

A.   No, sir. In fact, that goes to the whole point here. You can't just take an energy yard and set it down anyplace you feel like. The codes are very clear on that. When you deal with a flammable product like propane, you have to be within a certain maximum distance from a firehouse. And our yard at Florian was well within that limit.

At the plaintiff table, Klein whispered to Purcell, "Arthur slipped on that one." Joe nodded. The answer to the next-to-last question, about calling the fire department, had brought the laughter that broke the mood, and Hawkes's reproof of the witness—Did you mean that to be funny?—was more critical of those jurors who laughed than of Eugene Meara for making them laugh. DeSabitini and the other jurors would hold that against Hawkes: What brought their amusement was not a stupid answer but a stupid question, the defense counsel's own doing. Indeed, the witness's extended answer to that question made the question even more ill-conceived. Recovered from his momentary irritation, Hawkes knew he had slipped. What he would do now would be to make the most of the answer he got:

Q.   You make a good point, sir. Because firemen are supposed to drill too, are they not?

A.   Yes, of course. You expect them to be trained.

Q.   And you expect them also to carry certain equipment that would perform the same functions as some of the equipment mentioned in the various manuals?

A.   Yes, and that is another reason why we wouldn't have all the equipment on hand. It would duplicate things the fire department already has.

Q.   And knows how to use?

A.   Certainly.

Q.   Do you know for a fact that the Florian fire department was so equipped?

A.   I couldn't give you a rundown on what they had. You'd have to ask someone who was with the department.

Q.   I intend to. But, so long as you are here testifying now, do you know for a fact that the Florian fire department drilled in the use of that equipment?

A.   Again, you'd have to ask them.

Q.   Again, I intend to.

A.   Some things I can't talk about.

Q.   And some things you can. Your water supply, for example.

A.   Water supply?

Q.   Yes. Water. For fighting fires. Would you say your installa-
tion at Florian was up to code in volume and pressure?

A.   It passed the inspection.

Q.   What passes inspection can be one thing. What is adequate
is something else. What is in conformity with the code is something
else. What about your unloading racks? Did they have a sprinkler
system?

A.   Yes, they did.

Q.   On the day of the accident, was it in working order?

A.   I assume so.

Q.   You assume?

A.   Yes.

Q.   You don't know for sure?

A.   How can I know for sure?

Q.   That's right. How can you?

All the remainder of that day in court, all the following morning, and most
of the afternoon, Hawkes had Meara on the stand, plastering him with
exhibits—manuals and other literature—going step by step over each piece
of equipment, each recommended procedure. The impact was cumulative
and inexorable: Here was one thing after another that could have been used
or should have been done, in Florian left unused and undone. The
damage was deep and the witness needed rehabilitating, but when finally
Hawkes released him to Joe Purcell for redirect, Purcell waved a tired hand
and dismissed him. Nothing of real value occurred to him with which he
might now blunt the impression Hawkes had so indefatigably constructed,
and even if some remedial avenue of questioning were available, such
questions might just as shrewdly be left unasked. The jurors wanted to hear
no more from this witness, and for Purcell to prolong his testimony could
only serve to aggravate them.

Instead, for change of pace as much as anything, Joe put seven-year-old
Elliot Brophy on the witness stand.

Bert Klein would conduct the examination of Elliot. "He's going to be perfect," he told Purcell. "Remembers all kinds of great things about his mommy. And how he felt when the fireball happened and after she'd gone away to heaven. He even sang me one of the songs she wrote for him."

"Beautiful," Joe said. "Will he sing it from the witness stand?"

"You bet your ass. What'd you think I had in mind?"

All things that Klein had promised came true. Earnest and well scrubbed, innocently hesitant in his surroundings but responsive to Bert's gentle questions, the hairs on his head defiant of any brush that obviously had been taken to them, so that he looked not unlike a newborn sparrow, Elliot won spectators and jury alike. Even Junior Bohr was taken, and allowed Bert full range in a line of promptings that had all four women jurors weeping, as Elliot told how he would meet his mommy again in heaven.

"And," Bert said then, "do you remember what it was like singing songs with your mommy at the piano?"

Elliot nodded.

"Yes," Bert said, furnishing thereby the spoken answer that the court reporter's transcript would need, to indicate how the witness had responded. "And do you remember that she wrote special songs just for you and your sisters, and even how your baby brother would try to sing them too?"

Elliot nodded.

"Yes," Bert said. "And do you remember one of those songs that you could sing for me now?"

Elliot nodded.

"Yes," Bert said. "Which song would you like to sing?"

"The zoo song."

"How does it go?"

Elliot's voice was small, but the courtroom was very still, as he sang:

Louisa and Katherine love the animals
Louisa and Katherine love the animals
Every elephant, every pig,
Animals small and animals big!

At the plaintiff table, Purcell's eyes grew large. *Good Christ almighty, Bert, that's my song, not his mother's!* Not that Klein was anything other than innocent in this. Obviously, Elliot had remembered the song from the time Purcell first improvised it and the kids made him play it over and over again. And apparently Elliot had recognized Purcell that first day in court, seen him with Klein, then seen Klein again as the latter prepared him for his testimony, and when Bert asked him to sing a song, the boy thought Purcell's song was the one that was sought.

> Louisa and Katherine love the rhinoceros
> Not to mention the kangaroo!

Didn't I have it cockatoo? Purcell asked himself. Sure I did. And he's got kangaroo. And kangaroo's better. But now Elliot was finishing with a flourish: "Every animal in the zoo!" There was a ripple of laughter from the spectators, the laughter of delight. In the jury box, Two and Four applauded—DeSabitini and the lady realtor, Grace Cutter. Others in the spectator pews applauded too. From the witness chair, Elliot Brophy looked happily around. He drew a deep breath, raised his voice, and, to the further delight of his audience, let them know it wasn't over yet:

> Elliot says I don't like the music,
> Elliot says I don't like the words,
> Elliot says I'd rather have the lions
> Than the rhino or the monkey or those silly birds!
> But Louisa and Katherine love all the ostriches,
> The seals with their flippers and the panther too!
> Louisa and Katherine love the animals
> Every animal in the zoo!

This time all spectators and jurors applauded. Bert Klein, a proud and happy grin on his face, turned and gestured to Arthur Hawkes, who smiled indulgently back, then waved his hands. "No questions," he said.

"Well, young man," Junior Bohr said, the rolls of neck and chin rippling as he leaned downward toward Elliot Brophy, "we all want to thank you very much for being here with us today. You can go back to Grandma now, if you want to. And I think court can adjourn for the day. The jury will remember the admonition."

At their table, Purcell said to Klein, "Very nice. In fact, you went so well in practice that I think you ought to take over a hundred percent for tomorrow and Friday."

"No technical witnesses?"

"No. Who's next up?"

"The cop from Portsmouth. The expert on evacuation procedure."

"Put him off till next week. When are the two women testifying?"

"Monday. They're both flying in Sunday."

"Then make him wait till after them. Who can you put on for tomorrow and Friday?"

"What's left on the human side. They're the only ones I've prepared. The grandma hasn't testified yet, and we've got that dentist, with the testimony about identifying the bodies."

"Anybody else?"

"Bunch of other people who helped pick up the pieces."

"Put them on," Purcell said.

"Any reason for this switch? Other than that you're trying to get out of work the next couple of days?"

"That's not just *a* reason," Purcell said, "it's the *only* reason. I'm picking up Marcy at the plane in just over an hour from now."

"She's coming in tonight?"

"You sound surprised."

"The audition isn't till Saturday," Bert said.

"Yes," Purcell said, "but I figure some extra rehearsal time won't do us any harm. Don't worry: I'll be in court. But the only notes I put down'll probably be sixteenth notes. Do me a favor and make it as no-brainer as you can. And stay out of any fights with Hawkes."

"Sixteenth notes, hey?" Bert said.

"Musical notation," Purcell said. "A courtroom first."

"Maybe a courtroom second," Klein said. "Did you notice Mother Nine while Elliot was singing? All the while, he was writing away in his notebook."

10

There were no jetways at the Tri-State airport west of Huntington; rolling stairways had to be used instead, and tonight a cold rain was falling. Purcell thought it would be a nice touch, a symbol of love good for Marcy's morale, if she found him waiting at the fence outside nonetheless, bareheaded to the elements. Having thought that, he decided to wait inside the terminal building. Don't risk a cold, he told himself. You have to sing Saturday night.

"Good evening, sah!"

Purcell blinked and swung in the direction of the voice, and saw Castor standing at his elbow, black London Fog coat buttoned to the chin to battle the cold and rain.

"Ah," Purcell said to him. "Good evening. Meeting the same plane that I am?"

"Only plane they is."

Joe nodded his head, not so much in agreement as for the fact that Castor's logic made you nod your head. "Celebrities? Houseguests?"

"Celebrity. Ain't but one of him."

"Do you know him?"

"No, sah. Never laid eyes on him."

"I always wondered about that," Purcell said. "How do you go about meeting a stranger at an airport? I mean, if neither of you know each other, isn't it easy to miss connections?"

"No, sah."

"Why not?"

"I hold up a sign." Whining jet-engine noise from the outside came simultaneous to the public address voice announcing the plane's arrival. "Like this," Castor said, and unbuttoned his coat and took out a square of cardboard on which had been written, in black crayon capitals, a single word: ARANOW.

"I'll be a son of a bitch," Purcell said. "Is that my partner?"

"You have to ask *him* that when he comes in," Castor said.

Again the Castor-caused nod from Purcell. "But I'm a son of a bitch," he said again. "Why wouldn't he let me know he was coming in? We didn't get a room for him or anything."

"He's staying at Sunrise," Castor said. "Miz Brewer issued the invitation."

"She didn't say anything about it to me."

"You ain't meeting him. I am."

Doors slid open and arriving passengers began streaming in, dotted rather than wet with rain. Purcell saw Marcy and Max entering together. "Yours is the short one," he said to Castor, then went up to hug Marcy and punch Aranow's arm.

"Surprised?" Marcy said gaily.

"You didn't have to bring him, you know," Joe said. "He sings lousy."

"How's the trial?" Max said.

"Lousy," Joe said. "This is Castor. I didn't know you knew Dorothy Brewer."

"I don't. She called me up and made me an offer I couldn't refuse. Striped bass in a vinaigrette made with walnut oil. Served over endive. I haven't had walnut oil in thirty years."

"She wanted Max to be at the audition," Marcy said.

"Why?" Joe said. "As a potential backer? Forget it. Max has got deep pockets and short arms."

They were moving toward the baggage area. "Mundelein used to have a team in the Ohio Valley League," Max said to Castor. "Is that right?"

"You got a good memory," Castor said. "That was thirty years ago."

"Yes," Max said. "The last time I had walnut oil."

When the bags came, Joe had to hustle Marcy through the rain to the parking lot. The last thing he saw when he looked back was Castor driving up to the entrance of the terminal building, to pick up Max with a big black umbrella and the limousine.

"Why does this always happen?" he said to Marcy. "I make more money than he does and I don't even own a goddamn umbrella."

"Don't fret," she said. "Being cold and damp arouses me."

The heat and the windows were up, the windshield wipers sighed. It was cozy. "We've each got a metronome," Marcy said, as they drove.

"I'll start," Joe said, and keeping time to the swish of the wipers, sang Sam's chorus from "If I Had My Love to Live Over." Then Marcy sang Abbie's, and together they did the duet.

"I love all the music in the show," Marcy said. "And that one went beautifully."

"I wish we could have printed it and put it in the can," Purcell said. "It was as good as we've ever done it."

"People will be singing that one on their way up the aisle after the curtain falls," Marcy said.

"No they won't. They'll be doing 'We Have Met Before.'"

"You sound awfully positive."

"I am."

"How do you know?"

"I asked Abe Burrows about it once," Joe said. "I said, 'Can you tell in advance which song the audience is going to be singing as they leave the theater?' And he said, 'Sure: the one the orchestra's playing at the time.' And we're playing them out with 'We Have Met Before.' In fact, I'm going to use it in the entr'acte too."

"Not in the overture?"

"It never was in the overture. Always save one good one out from the overture. I learned that from the way Bennett and Lang orchestrated *My Fair Lady*. 'I've Grown Accustomed to Her Face'—that was entr'acte, not overture. Nice."

They worked at the piano in the A&P suite at the Western Motor Hotel till after 11:00 that night.

Then they took a break and Joe opened a bottle of Remy Martin while Marcy went to her room and changed into a robe of burgundy velour. When she returned Joe was seated at the piano playing "We Have Met Before," the open bottle and two empty snifters perched on the piano. Marcy poured more than a splash in her glass and sat next to Joe on the bench. She noticed that Joe had turned off all the lights in the room other than the small lamp on the piano.

"Book, music, lyrics, *and lighting* by Joe Purcell," she said. She took a sip of brandy and with a break-dancer move made a three-quarter clockwise twirl on the piano bench and came to rest straddling it in horseback fashion facing Joe.

He could see a faint flush in her cheeks. "Do you like the Remy?"

"It makes me feel warm and sexy."

"I thought cold and damp aroused you."

"Maybe it's you that arouses me," she said. "Have some brandy." She took some brandy into her mouth and swung around onto his lap and kissed him. As his mouth slowly opened she fed him the brandy from hers. They drank slowly and sweetly back and forth and then explored each other's mouths with their tongues.

Marcy stretched out across Joe's lap, cradling her head in the crook of his right arm. "Now, I'm really warm," she whispered. "My nipples feel hot and hard." She parted the top of her robe. In the dim piano light her jutting nipples seemed to match the color of her garment.

He cupped her breast with his hand, at first gently and then more firmly, and then began to caress her nipple as he lightly kissed her other nipple and felt its hardness with his tongue.

She reached down and felt his erection. "I want you," she said. "I want you now."

Joe swung off the bench and carried Marcy to her bedroom, still kissing her breasts as he moved slowly into the dark room and onto the bed.

Marcy slept in the next morning. Joe arrived at court a few minutes early to look for Max Aranow but there was no sign of him. Finally he showed up for the lunch break bearing copies of the Huntington and Mundelein newspapers.

"This must be some trial," Max said. "The morning paper says Defense Scores. The afternoon says Jury Weeps."

Both were stories of the previous day's events, the Huntington paper featuring Arthur Hawkes's cross-examination of the Tri-State Gas man, Eugene Meara, while the *Beacon* led with the appearance of seven-year-old Elliot Brophy.

"I said something to the judge about the coverage," Purcell said.

"Hawkes should be the one complaining."

"He complained before I did."

"What gets me," said Max, "isn't so much what they say as where they say it. Here in Mundelein you're already on page two. In Huntington you're on fourteen with the southern Ohio shorts."

"I hope we stay on fourteen. I thought Dorothy Brewer was going to keep us on page one."

"She's got a problem," Max said. "She was telling me about it last night. They're an afternoon paper, and by the time their readers sit down with it at home they can be thirty hours behind the news. She said her editor had asked you for an advance list of witnesses you were going to call each day, so they could update it that way, but you said no."

"I didn't say no. I just haven't been giving them the list."

"Why not?"

"Because I don't know who I'm going to call, from one day to the next. And if I don't know, how can I tell anybody else? It's that kind of trial, Max. And more and more trials are, nowadays. I'm getting out at the right time."

"You're too preoccupied," Aranow said.

"I'm not preoccupied," Purcell said. "I'm moonlighting."

Max was in court that afternoon and both sessions the next day, and afterward Purcell asked him what he thought of Bert Klein's work.

"Bert's first-rate," Max said. "The only thing that worries me is the way he plays to number two."

"I do it too," Purcell said. "He's our best hope on that jury. DeSabitini. I told you about him."

"Yuh, but you're playing Mundelein roulette," Aranow said. "Suppose Two winds up the alternate."

"Hell, Hawkes is doing the same thing," Joe said. "Haven't you watched him on cross?"

"Yes, I have watched him. But he's playing to a pair of them. Four and Five. Very clever, the way he hedges his bets. First off, they're liable to be sympathetic to him. Second, one's a woman and one's a man. Third, one's front row, one's back row. Fourth, one sits to the right, the other to the left. If either one of them is the one to go, he's got a backup."

"I was going to play to two of them," Joe said. "Two and—"

"The *schwarzer*," Max said.

"Mm-hmm. Mother Nine. But it's too much of a risk of backfire with the others. Plus the fact that no matter who winds up odd man out, at least six and probably seven of them are going to be WASPs. I'm already playing to the only Catholic. You want me to play to the only black too?"

"He's the only one keeping notes," Max said. "That might count for something."

"What it counts for is the risk that the rest of them resent it. They're eight white people in a courtroom, sitting with a black who thinks he's going to Johns Hopkins."

"That can work the other way too. They might fall back on his notes when they get in the jury room to deliberate."

"I said it was a risk, not a certainty," Purcell said. "But you weren't watching all that carefully. We've got a secret weapon at work."

"What's that?"

"Bert. He may be playing to Two, but he manages to let Four know he's got a letch for her. She's in her forties and she's flattered. That may be one of the reasons Arthur's playing to her. He doesn't want to lose her to a sex maniac."

11

Trial lawyers playing to jurors are not unlike writers of musicals playing to potential backers, Joe thought, as Dorothy Brewer introduced Marcy and him around the room. For the Saturday night audition at Sunrise, Dorothy had assembled an eminent group of some twenty-five people— not so much show business as money, which suited Purcell well. The Eddingtons were there, returned from Houston, and well-heeled types from Miami and St. Louis and Montreal, from Boston and Philadelphia and New York. The one full-fledged producer on the guest list, Carole Shorenstein, cabled her regrets from London, but she sent one of her lieutenants to sit in.

Playbook in hand, Purcell seated himself at the Mason & Hamlin, with Marcy standing over his right shoulder. Joe's ability to talk and play at the same time was manifest as he told his listeners about the plot of *The Last*

Laugh. Then: "The lights dim in the theater," he said, and as he said it, Castor—cued to a rheostat on the wall of the large room—dimmed the lights. Only the large floor lamp that had been moved beside the piano remained at full brightness, and Joe's hands struck up the overture.

All but a few lines of essential dialogue would be omitted from this presentation, and there would be no intermission. Joe's cover narration would introduce each number, and so essentially it was a procession of songs. But that was what a musical was. It could not be presented any other way.

He was three numbers into the show before there was applause; somewhat to his surprise, it was for Sam's first number, sung solo by Joe in his beery voice:

The last time I dreamed
The pastime that seemed to me
Extremely unfair
Was to be there
And to see
Taxicabs in the sky
Each last one of them passed me by...

The applause came, and quickly Joe and Marcy were into the rhumba, "Ten Points for a Spanish Dancer," a clever, fun piece with a good beat. The audience thoroughly enjoyed it. But on "If I Had My Love to Live Over" things went as badly as they had gone well in the car coming in from the airport Wednesday night. Joe's voice cracked and missed, and Marcy couldn't save him.

They did better on "We Have Met Before," and Joe thought he did extremely well with Sam's "Here Am I," the final song of the first act. But the number could not deliver the intended punch. The curtain for Act I would come down on Sam dancing, not singing, and Purcell had not figured a way to play the piano and dance at the same time. He covered it with explanation, and went out weak therefore.

The second act was shorter, and its build was good. The three final numbers—Abbie's solo "He'll Never Know"; the comedy reprise of "We Have Met Before," with Joe and Marcy in the character of senior citizens; and the finale, the ensemble reprise of "Abbie Understands"—moved the show to a fine conclusion, and when Joe played the exeunt chorus of "We Have Met Before" not only Marcy but, as she waved to the audience, at least half the people in the room sang along with him.

Afterward there were champagne and congratulations, though how much of it was the politeness enforced by the occasion Purcell could not guess. "Your face at some familiar door somewhere—I love that line," one man said to Joe. He was Leonard Kinder, a New York garment manufacturer who had backed some shows in the past and whose wife, Mary Ellen, had herself done some professional singing and acting, and been active in the Theatre Guild. "It has a feel to it." He sang the line: "Your face at some familiar door somewhere." He did not have the tune right.

One thing Dorothy Brewer had said she would not do. "I'll get the people here and make sure they have enough to drink," she told Purcell. "But I'm not going to conduct the auction afterward. In fact, I don't want an auction. I think it's out of place."

"Ah, give me a break, lady," Purcell said to her. "The time to sell points in a show is right after they've heard it."

"I don't think that's even true anymore," Dorothy said. "Your show is set in the past and so are you. The purpose here is to influence them to want to invest, not get them on the dotted line. Then they tell their tax accountants they've reached a decision, and *then* you get your backers. The only way they'll sign up right away is if they've got their tax accountants with them, and that you certainly don't want. You can't audition to a room full of bookkeepers."

Dimly, Purcell perceived she was probably right. The time of impulse spending was past: it simply cost too much today to float a Broadway show. He would have to wait.

What with champagne and supper and postmortems with Marcy back at the motel suite, and the marvelous feeling of relief that they had met the challenge of auditioning new and original material combined with the even more marvelous feeling of satisfaction that they had done well, followed by a round of joyous lovemaking, Joe did not get to sleep until after two Alka-Seltzers at five o'clock in the morning. At least he had had the foresight to make the audition a Saturday night: to face a session in court today would take him beyond his ability to cope.

He knew exactly how long he slept, for at 7:30 in the morning his phone rang. It was Leonard Kinder. Could Joe meet him for breakfast in the coffee shop in half an hour?

Joe could and did, and afterward he went directly to Marcy's room and rapped on the door.

It took her a while to come out of sleep and put on a robe and answer, and when she opened the door he forced a grin and strode past her to the window, then turned and said, "We're in business."

In mid-yawn she said, "What?"

"Kinder," he said. "I just had breakfast with him. He wants to back the show."

"Oh, my God," Marcy said. "How much of it?"

"All of it."

"*All* of it? Is he crazy?"

"I refrained from asking him that." Joe turned and looked out the window. There are no taxicabs in the sky this morning, he thought. "His wife's been talking about leaving him, and he figures this way he can buy her back. The money doesn't bother him. He figures he can make a *Springtime for Hitler* out of it and write it off if things don't go right."

"I don't understand," Marcy said. "Why would his spending three million dollars on a show win her back? I know she's interested in the theater, but she won't be *that* interested."

Joe turned slowly and looked Marcy straight in the eye. "She will if she stars in the show," he said. "She's been talking about making a comeback."

"Mary Ellen Kinder's going to do Abbie?"

"You got it in one."

"I thought I was going to do Abbie."

"You are."

Neither of them moved. Marcy was still in the doorway, Joe at the window. They stood there, talking across the room.

"I see," Marcy said. "We're going to have two Abbies. She does Tuesdays, Thursdays, and Saturdays; I do Wednesdays, Fridays, and Sundays. Who does the matinees?"

"Come off it," Joe said to her. "She's too old to play Abbie."

"She's in her early forties," Marcy said. "She's not too old to play it. Too old to play it well, maybe, but not too old to play it."

"Which is exactly what the critics in Boston and New Haven will say," Joe said. "If it gets that far, which it won't. Gets that far with Mary Ellen, I mean. Come here."

She took two steps toward him, then stopped. "No, that's far enough," she said. "We're going to talk this out."

"I just explained it to you," he said. "There's no problem. Kinder puts up the money, and it's the big gesture that wins her back. That's all he's interested in. If she's a flop, then at least he tried. He'll blame it on the show, write off his loss, and they'll live happily ever after. He gets what he wants, I get what I want, you get what you want. What could be more perfect?"

"You say you get what you want?" Marcy said. "How does that come about? Your show folds in New Haven. Is that what you want?"

"It doesn't fold in New Haven. Mary Ellen folds in New Haven. You step in and take her place."

Marcy shook her head, as if to clear it. "I do not believe this," she said. "I'm listening to it, and I do not believe it. What do you think this is— *Forty-Second Street?* Understudy goes on at the last minute, saves the show?"

"You're no understudy. I'm not getting through to you."

"Damn right you're not. First you tell me how Kinder will explain to his wife it was the show's fault it flopped, not hers. Then two days later it opens on Broadway with me instead of her and it's an all-time hit. Which is it? Either a show folds or it doesn't."

"You don't understand," Joe said. "I did say Boston and New Haven, yes, but I also told you it wasn't going to reach that point with her."

"How do you know?"

"Because I'll make sure of it, that's how I know." He pulled at his right ear. "Soon as this trial is over I'm quitting the firm. What does that mean? It means I'll have full time on the show. You and Kinder are the same— you keep forgetting it's *my show*. And it's going to stay that way. The final word on who's in the show rests with me."

"Oh," Marcy said. "I see. You're going to hire her, get the husband's money, then fire her."

"You're still missing the point. The point is, Kinder won't care. Lose money, it's a write-off; make money, it's a profit. Meanwhile he's saved his marriage—or at least he made a try. The way things are now, the marriage is dead. So what has he got to lose?" He forced another grin and sat down facing her on the twin bed nearest the window, the bed on which they had made love last night. He patted it gently. "Come here," he said again.

Marcy came over, but when he reached up she pulled away and sat on her own bed, next to the night table. "You explained all this to Mr. Kinder, I suppose."

"Of course I didn't."

"You don't think you're leading him on..."

"Who's leading who on? I didn't call him at seven-thirty this morning. He called me."

"But you had to agree to his condition."

"I'll tell you word for word what he said to me," Joe said. "He said, and this is a direct quote, 'I don't know if Mary Ellen will be right for the show. All I know is I've got to do something.' That's what he said."

"And when it turns out she's not right for the show, then what? What do you do for money?"

"Sell tickets, that's what. The sets will be bought and paid for. The lighting, the costumes, the orchestrations. Everything. That's where the money goes—for what you have to spend up front before there's any receipts coming in. Getting it off the ground is where the money goes. You know that."

"All right," she said.

Joe bounced on the bed. "I feel twenty years younger."

"So do I," Marcy said. "Back to the time with the braces when the dentist said it wouldn't hurt." She picked up the receiver from the telephone on the nightstand and punched the button for the front desk. When it answered, she said, "This is Miss Beall in Room 202. Will you send a bellman in twenty minutes for my luggage? And if there are no taxicabs, can you order one for me? To take me to the airport? Thank you."

She put the receiver back and stood up. "I'm going in the bathroom to dress," she said. If her voice had been shaky before, it was calm now. "I may also throw up. Either way, I don't want you here when I come out again."

She was past him now, taking things off hangers and out of drawers, to take to the bathroom with her.

"You know," Joe said, "someone watching your reaction might think you were more interested in your part than in my show."

Marcy spun around and faced him. There was a long pause as if she were counting ten to regain her composure. Finally, she said, "Joe, this may well be our last conversation, so listen good. I think you're probably the greatest trial lawyer in the world, and with a little training and a new wardrobe, who knows, I could be the world's greatest trial lawyer's wife. But you don't want to be a trial lawyer, and God knows, I've never heard you play the 'Wedding March' on your little Steinway. That means our relationship is you write the songs and I sing and dance and in between gigs we screw a little. But if someone else sings your songs that makes me nothing more than a broad you sleep with between trials or musicals or both—and that's not a job I'm applying for."

"Marcy, this doesn't—"

"I'm not finished." She cut him off. "On top of all that there's a little matter of ethics. You may know legal ethics, but you don't know Canon Number One of show business ethics. Holding out a plum to a backer's girlfriend is like tampering with a jury."

"She's his wife—not his girlfriend," Joe said. "And your analogy stinks. He's buying the show. Jurors don't buy trials."

"That's a lawyer's answer—not the answer of a legitimate producer. You're demonstrating what I told you a long time ago. You can't make it big in two careers."

"I don't want two careers," said Joe. "Just one."

"And now we've come full circle, Mr. Trial Lawyer—because that's all I want—one career." Marcy turned and entered the bathroom. The door closed behind her.

Joe sat there for a long time. If she's throwing up in the bathroom, he told himself, she's doing it very quietly. There were a notepad and pen on the night table. He took the pen and wrote I Love You on the top page, then tore it off, stood up, went to the bathroom door, slid the notepaper underneath it, and left.

Back in his own room, Joe sat on the bed and took from his pocket another slip of paper—one that Leonard Kinder had given him at breakfast. On it was written a telephone number. Joe punched long distance, then dialed the number. A woman's voice answered, and he said, "Mary Ellen? This is Joe Purcell calling from Ohio. Ah—Leonard already called you. Good. You already know the news, then." He lay back on the bed and listened.

12

Max Aranow flew back to New York, surprised for the second straight time to find Marcy on the same flight. He stopped at her seat and looked down. "We've got to stop meeting like this."

She looked up, but said nothing.

"All things considered, I thought it went all right last night," he said. "Your partner thinks so too."

That was all they said to each other.

The following day, Harry Wright showed up for the afternoon session in the Mundelein courtroom. He sat next to Bert Klein at the plaintiff table as Purcell introduced a new witness, a woman named Elaine Schlesinger who had a wen on her left cheek and an obvious sense of middle-aged solidarity.

Her accent was New York. So was her calling: she was the editor in charge of children's books at the Whitecliff-Hall publishing firm, and as such, she said, she had received material from Janet Brophy, who was trying to break into the field as an author.

"This should be a good afternoon," Harry Wright whispered to Bert. "Really."

"Anything will be an improvement over this morning," Klein whispered back. "We had a gas convection expert. The jury fell asleep during the direct and didn't wake up until he developed uncontrollable hiccups during the cross."

Purcell was taking the witness over the uncertain path of an author's potential income:

Q.   And how much money, in your judgment, could Janet Brophy have earned as the author of a series of children's books?

A.   The sky was the limit.

Q.   The sky was the limit? Can you be more definite than that?

A.   I'm not sure I can.

Q.   Why not?

A.   Because so much of it would have been up to her—up to Janet Brophy herself. Can I enlarge on my answer, Your Honor?

THE COURT: I don't know why not.

THE WITNESS: Essentially, we thought Janet was capable of doing more than one thing. She wrote stories, yes, but she also wrote songs, and I think the real reason she had not been published before was that she viewed her own talents as separate enterprises. At the time she died, we had just then convinced her, I think, that this was not the best way to go about it. We had been discussing a book that would combine her gifts all within the same package. We thought she should tell her story in book form, but by the same token we thought that among the illustrations for the book would be the sheet music for the song she had written to go along with it, or maybe more than one song. We were even considering bringing out the book with slipcases inside the front and back covers containing little cassettes, so the music could be played while the child was reading the book, or being read to.

Q.   And this was a new technique?

A.   Yes and no. Stories have been fitted to music before, and music to stories. In the children's field you have "Peter and the Wolf" and "Winnie the Pooh" and "Brave Cowboy Bill" and I don't know how many others. And there have been cases where books and records came packaged together. But what was most rare, I think, in Janet Brophy's case, was that she would have become one of the very, very few people in all history who did everything herself. The book, the music, the lyrics. That is most unusual, Mr. Purcell. You find it very seldom even on the Broadway stage.

Q.   Yes, I am somewhat aware of that. It would be fair to say, then, that Janet Brophy had a very special and unusual talent. Is that correct?

MR. HAWKES: Object. Leading. Brother Purcell loves to put his own words in other people's mouths.

THE COURT: No, I don't think so, Mr. Hawkes. Essentially, the witness had already said the same thing. You are being capricious.

MR. HAWKES: He does it all the time.

THE COURT: I will allow it this time. I've just said that, Mr. Hawkes. The witness can answer.

Yes, Elaine Schlesinger said, Janet Brophy had a very special and unusual talent. Patiently, Purcell continued to refine the issue. Finally, he brought the woman to a hard figure: "I think," Schlesinger said, "she could have earned at least fifty thousand dollars next year."

"Next year? Why next year?"

"Because," Elaine Schlesinger said, "in the ordinary scheme of things, production schedules and the like, next year would be when her first book would have been out there in the stores, in the marketplace, and we would be seeing the results of the sales. But of course she had future projects also in mind, more books, some of them with the same characters as her first book. That's why I said the sky was the limit as to what she could earn, down the line. If she'd lived to do it."

Q.   If she'd lived to do it. And you are certain of that?

A.   As certain as I can be. Yes.

Q.   Forgive me if I sound uncertain, or as if I am casting any doubt on your qualifications, but you understand that a lawsuit is by definition an adversary proceeding. That means that after I am done, Mr. Hawkes will cross-examine you, on behalf of the defense. And Mr. Hawkes is going to ask you—

MR. HAWKES: Objection.

THE COURT: Yes, I think so.

MR. HAWKES: Five minutes ago he was leading the witness. Now he's leading me.

THE COURT: Yes, Mr. Purcell. The court has no information leading anyone to believe that Mr. Hawkes is paying you to ask his questions for him.

MR. PURCELL: It is my question.

THE COURT: Then ask it. Don't predict what Mr. Hawkes is going to say.

Q.   Very well, judge. The point is, Mrs. Schlesinger, that you are talking here now about actual earnings figures, and obviously the jury is going to want to know how reliable and objective your testimony is. We are talking about projected income, or estimated future earnings, because Janet Brophy is no longer alive, and for that reason I have to ask you these questions. And the first question is this: What in your judgment would have stood in the way of Janet Brophy and the publication of her first book?

A.   Nothing.

Q.   Nothing?

A.   Nothing. As I said, the only problem was in getting her to put all the separate things together—the music, and the words to the songs, and so forth and so on—and she agreed to do this, and we all thought that was the way to go and that it was worth waiting for.

Q.   But suppose you'd been overruled.

A.   Who'd been overruled? Me myself? Who would overrule me?

Q.   You consider yourself master in your own house?

A.   I'm not sure I know what that means. As I said at the beginning, I am the vice president of Whitecliff-Hall in charge of children's books. The final publishing decisions rest with me.

Q.   Then is Whitecliff-Hall master in its own house?

A.   Of course. Oh, wait a minute. I see what you are driving at.

Q.   Whitecliff-Hall is owned by somebody else, isn't it?

A.   Yes. We are owned by what is called a conglomerate.

Q.   And at any point, that conglomerate owner can overrule you, isn't that right?

A.   No, it isn't right.

Q.   You can't be overruled by anyone? The president of your own publishing house? The conglomerate that owns your publishing house?

A.   In theory, yes. In practice, no.

Q.   When a small publisher merges with a larger publisher, that larger publisher has no say in what the smaller publisher does?

A.   We were not taken over by a larger publisher. There was no merger. As I say, we are owned by a conglomerate—a corporation that does many different things. They are diversified. We are the only publishing house they have.

Q.   And they aren't interested at all in what you decide to publish?

A.   Only in what they call the bottom line.

Q.   What is that?

A.   They want to see us make money.

Q.   And you're aware of that, are you?

MR. HAWKES: Object. Immaterial.

THE COURT: No, overruled.

Q.   What is your opinion on the effects of conglomerate ownership, Mrs. Schlesinger?

A.   I think it is terrible. You encounter a mentality that says either give us best sellers or don't publish the book. But I happen to believe a publisher should publish a book that may not make money. If it informs, if it instructs, if it edifies, if it elevates, then it has a place in the scheme of things. You cannot have a branch library somewhere, with twenty thousand books, consisting just of two thousand copies each of the ten current best-sellers. You told me last night you went to Yale, Mr. Purcell. Yale University has more than seven million bound books in its library. I would be surprised if one percent of them ever made money.

Q.   I do not mean to irritate you with my questions.

A.   Oh, yes, you do. I don't know why, and I don't know that much about the law, but you are treating me here as though I were a hostile witness under cross-examination. I came down here to testify for Janet Brophy, not against her.

MR. HAWKES: Objection.

THE COURT: On what grounds?

MR. HAWKES: I don't know on what grounds. I simply have the feeling this whole thing is being staged—prearranged in advance. For what purpose, I can't imagine, but I don't think Brother Purcell does these things idly.

THE WITNESS: If he's staging it, it's news to me.

MR. HAWKES: None of this line of questioning was disclosed in pretrial discovery, Your Honor.

THE COURT: I won't refuse it on that basis, Mr. Hawkes.

MR. HAWKES: Then why is he attacking his own witness?

THE COURT: I don't know. But I can ask him. Mr. Purcell?

MR. PURCELL: Judge, I said before I would sound like a cross-examiner, and you overruled me. This witness has said the sky is the limit when it comes to what Janet Brophy could have earned, and I am willing to play devil's advocate if that's what it takes to get the jury to believe her.

At the plaintiff table, Harry Wright turned to Bert Klein and said, "Is Hawkes right? Is Joe staging this with the witness?"

Klein shook his head. "No. He spent maybe six minutes with her last night. And it was all him talking to her about his musical, about how he wrote everything himself, the same as Janet Brophy did. He asked her to hang around while he played some of his songs for her, but she got a look of panic on her face and fled like a striped-assed baboon."

Wright studied for a time. Then he whispered, "Then what in God's name is he doing?"

"He must know something," Klein said. "There's something in this that wasn't in her deposition, something nobody thought of. He's setting a trap for Arthur."

"What trap?"

"I don't know any more than you do. It's my best guess, that's all. Otherwise, he wouldn't be acting this way."

Wright said, "But don't you think Hawkes realizes this?"

"Maybe he does. What good does it do him?"

Purcell himself had returned to direct examination:

Q.   So your ownership does have a say in what it is you publish, and yet for some reason you're telling us this doesn't involve you. You're not affected. Why is that?

A.   Because it wouldn't affect the children's division, Mr. Purcell. We don't produce translations of Latin poets or books on how the fungus blight attacks the leaves of rubber plants. My children's division makes money and always has. So they leave me strictly alone.

Q.   All right. Now pardon me for asking this, but if you dropped dead tomorrow, who would determine your successor? Your own publisher or the conglomerate owner?

A.   I haven't the slightest idea.

Q.   Could you find out?

A.   I could but I won't.

MR. PURCELL: Your Honor, is that a responsive reply?

THE COURT: I can't think of one that could be more responsive.

MR. PURCELL: There's an obvious lack of cooperation at this point.

THE COURT: That is your problem.

MR. PURCELL: Then I have no further questions.

THE COURT: Very well. Mr. Hawkes, you may cross-examine.

MR. HAWKES: Thank you, Your Honor. I think I can be very brief with this.

THE COURT: Yes. That is always a help.

MR. HAWKES: Mrs. Schlesinger seems to be upset.

THE WITNESS: I am all right. It is just that those questions from Mr. Purcell were not what I bargained for. As I've said before, I came down here to testify for Janet Brophy, not against her. This silly, meaningless business about conglomerate ownership, as it would have affected Janet, was something I just wasn't prepared for, especially coming from her own attorney.

Q.   We will accept the fact that you are owned by a conglomerate and leave it at that. And I for one also accept that you are master in your own house.

A.   Thank you.

Q.   Had your company, Whitecliff-Hall, ever published anything written by Janet Brophy in the past?

A.   No.

Q.   To your knowledge, had any other publisher ever published anything by Janet Brophy?

A.   I can cut this short for you, Mr. Hawkes. Janet Brophy had never been published by anybody.

Q.   So at best, nothing she published now would be a result of her past reputation.

A.   That is right. We thought we had something of value here. But there was no track record.

Q.   Which means, if I hear you right, that any speculation as to what her book or books might do would be pretty much just that— speculation.

A.   I guess the short answer is yes. But it would be informed speculation.

Q.   But it would still be speculation?

A.   Obviously.

MR. HAWKES: Your Honor, I said this would be brief, and it was. I have no further questions.

THE COURT: Good. We can now dismiss this witness. Unless you have something on redirect, Mr. Purcell.

At the plaintiff table, Joe Purcell rose, and husked to Bert Klein, in splendid imitation of Boris Karloff, "Watchth thisth one." Then he strode forward, to engage the witness on redirect.

Q.   Just one question, Mrs. Schlesinger. What is the name of this conglomerate that owns your company?

A.   North American Petroleum.

A surge went through Bert Klein. "Oh, Christ!" he whispered to Harry Wright. "He sandbagged Hawkes! Didn't even let his own witness know what he was going to do!"

What Klein said here of Hawkes and the witness was equally true of course for Klein himself, for he was just as surprised. "There's only one lawyer in the world as good at that as Joe Purcell," Bert said to Perry Muncrief, back at their motel quarters following the afternoon session in court, "and that's Max Aranow. They take a fact so apparently meaningless, so irrelevant, that the defense could investigate that witness and that situation sixty-five times before the trial ever started, and no one would think to check on that fact. Then in the middle of the trial, you find the moment and spring it on them and boom."

"But it *is* relevant," Muncrief objected. "North American Petroleum is the richest of all the defendants. That doesn't make Nance and Mid-Central exactly poor, but they're single-industry people. They don't diversify. If you have to single out a chief heavy among heavies, North American is it. They're the octopus—no matter what goes on, they've got a tentacle stuck into it."

"You'll make a lawyer yet," Klein said. "Joe's building to that. Plus the fact that North American's chief operating officer—what's his name? Harrison McKenna—was with the railroad division of the Department of Transportation when the jumbo tank car designs were approved. Now out of left field—I sound like Aranow—he brings in this great piece of symbolism. The oil company owned the publisher who was going to lift Janet Brophy out of having to drive a school bus. But before that could happen, the oil company's product exploded and killed her."

"It's beautiful," Muncrief marveled. "And you're right: no investigator would ever have thought of asking who owned Whitecliff-Hall."

Klein shook his head. "Always look for the odd, unrelated fact, I keep telling myself. Purcell told me once that Aranow had won five wrongful-death suits because he liked baseball."

"But the way you tell it, Joe lucked in with the way he got this conglomerate thing into the record today."

Klein looked at him. "Why?"

"Because," Muncrief said, "the way you tell it, Joe didn't make the point about North American till redirect."

"That's right. So?"

"So from what they teach me in law school, you can't address a point on redirect unless the other side mentioned it on cross. Joe hadn't brought out the owner of the publisher on his direct examination. He was gambling that Hawkes would refer to the conglomerate on his cross-examination. And Hawkes did."

"Maybe you *won't* make a lawyer yet," Bert Klein said. "Joe was lying back in the weeds, yes, and when he sprang that NAP thing it was with maximum effect. But he wasn't risking anything. North American's ownership of that publishing house is something Joe wanted to dramatize, yes, but he could have introduced it during his cross when Hawkes puts one of the oil company cats on the witness stand. Joe didn't have to use it today. He just saw the chance and grabbed it."

"You mean to say he wasn't setting a trap for Arthur?"

"I'm positive he was setting a trap for him. All I'm saying is, if the trap hadn't worked, it wasn't the end of the world."

"But you said Joe's own witness was screaming at him, she was so mad. Was it worth going through that to bait the trap?"

There was a scraping sound of a key at the door. "Here comes The Man now," Bert Klein said. "You mix his drink, I'll put the George Feyer Gershwin album on the record player. Then you can ask him yourself. I've got a feeling he's in a good mood."

The door opened and Joe Purcell came in.

At the record player, Klein said, "That was Shangri-la in the courtroom today. That one question you asked on redirect."

Purcell grinned. "Yes," he said. "Arthur didn't expect that."

With uncommon swiftness, Perry Muncrief had mixed Purcell's Scotch and soda. Now he came forward with it. "Bert was telling me about it."

Purcell took the drink. "I liked it," he said.

"But you risked so much. You even got your own witness mad at you."

"That was a risk I had to take."

"To make your point?"

"To make her point," Purcell said. "The way it wound up at the end, that was gravy. But I had two problems with this witness." He started on his drink. "One was to get anybody to believe her. We were talking here about how much money an author who's never been published was going to make from her books. My witness, this Schlesinger broad, gets on the stand and says the sky's the limit. That's great, except who in hell is going to believe it? She's obviously on Janet Brophy's side, and Janet Brophy's lawyer is the one who called her. The only way we could establish objectivity and credibility was to get her mad at me. Openly hostile. Visibly angry. Genuinely mad as a wet hen. So I did that and she did that and the whole courtroom felt it. The animosity was absolutely real."

"It was all of that," Bert Klein said. "You could feel it."

"That's a great cocktail piano Feyer plays," Purcell said. He sampled his drink. "You can hear him in person at the Stanhope."

"What's the name of that song?" Klein said.

"'Funny Face,'" Purcell said. "I love your funny face/Your sunny funny face." He grinned again. "Now, the question was, if I want to get her mad, how do I do it? The only way was to question her authority. And how do I do that? It's another piece of Catch 22. I want to question her authority, but if she's not an authority, how can I sell her as an expert witness to begin with? So I drag in this conglomerate thing."

"And," Perry Muncrief said earnestly, "the North American Petroleum connection made it irresistible."

"It was irresistible on its own," Purcell said. "The North American connection was a fun touch, and I had to be an idiot not to use it. But that publisher could have been owned by Hunt-Wesson Foods, and I still would have used the conglomerate business. And would have got pretty much the same effect from it. Number one, it was the way to challenge my witness. On top of that, we're going to be painting North American for the way it's diversified. Like the midget in the nudist colony, who walked around sticking his nose in everybody's business."

Klein and Muncrief began laughing. "Okay," Bert said. "You've given your two reasons." He was still laughing.

Purcell eyed him over his glass. "No," he said. "So far, I've only given you one reason. Reason number two, you saw for yourself in the court-room: how easy Hawkes was on the witness. He had to be. By the time I turned her over to him, she was on his side. Or close enough to being on his side that he wasn't about to antagonize her too, and undo all the nice work I'd done for him. Did you see how gingerly he treated her? It could have been a powerful cross. Instead, it was weak. What the jury carries away from her on the witness stand is her estimate of the earnings capacity for Janet Brophy. That's what I was going for. And that's why I'm pleased, because it worked out."

Bert Klein nodded. "I can see it," he said. "Hawkes might have been the one to bring up the conglomerate business, instead of you."

"No, you don't see it," Purcell said. "We were never in any danger Hawkes would have brought up the conglomerate business. Arthur doesn't think that way. It wouldn't have occurred to him to find out who owned that publisher."

"Then I was right the first time," Klein said. "Just before you got here, I was telling Perry this was something only you or Max would have thought of."

Purcell nodded, not altogether good-humoredly. "If you're going to be right the first time, then stay right," he said to Bert. "No, the power in the Hawkes cross would have come from the way he would have depicted that witness to the jury. The Jew girl from New York whose decisions dictate what books the children of Mundelein, Ohio, will wind up reading. Arthur's an expert at that."

Klein said, "That's strange. I wouldn't take Arthur for an anti-Semite."

"He's not. If we were in front of an all-Jewish jury in New York and I brought in an expert witness from Montana, Arthur would parade him as a WASP sheepfucker. It's not the affiliation: It's the technique."

"But I haven't seen any sign of that technique. Not in this trial so far."

"There will be. At one point I'm going to make him do it."

"Why?"

"Because it's going to serve my purpose, that's why."

"To have him destroy one of your witnesses?"

Purcell shook his head. "No. To have him destroy me. Or at least try to." He signaled Perry Muncrief for a refill. "Actually, research indicates that publishers are not owned by Hunt-Wesson Foods. Publishers by and large are owned by Saudi Arabia."

Klein said, "Isn't everything owned by Saudi Arabia?"

"You might have a point," Purcell conceded. "But who knows where it leads? We have to allow for the possibility that Saudi Arabia is owned by Hunt-Wesson Foods."

That evening, Joe conferred with the witness he intended to put on the stand the following day. Bert Klein insisted on being in on the conference. "This may be our most important witness of all," he said.

"Certainly the best-looking," Joe said.

"What makes you think that has anything to do with my interest?"

"Four pair of shoes. Perry told me you'd been collecting them."

"Damn him. I wanted to surprise you."

"Did you, now?" Purcell laughed briefly. "Let me see if I have it right. We know that in the case of four of the volunteer firemen who were killed in the fireball, all that was found of them was their shoes. Now Mr. Klein, soon to replace me as a full partner in the A&P, intends to get ahold of those shoes and take them into court and spread them out on the counsel table. In fact, let's assume he already got ahold of them, and intends to put on this display in court tomorrow morning."

"Can you think of any more graphic evidence? It'll be a blockbuster."

"Any time a judge grants a mistrial it's a blockbuster," Purcell said. "Bohr wouldn't even let me bring a copy of *Fortune* magazine into that courtroom. I couldn't even carry it under my arm. Too much of a chance it would inflame the jury. But you're going to march in there with the shoes from the four dead guys. And tell the jury what?"

"I just thought—"

"How do you identify the shoes?"

"The relatives."

"Only Brophy relatives are allowed on the stand. This is a specimen case, remember? None of those four guys are the Specimen."

"Seems to me that's arguable."

"That's your whole purpose," Purcell said. "You want to argue about it."

"You mean just for the sake of arguing?"

"That's exactly what I mean, and you know it."

"I could kill that Perry Muncrief for telling you."

"I know you could. But don't blame him. He doesn't yet know about trial tactics the way I do. I should add, or the way you do. He thought your idea about the shoes was a flash of inspiration—the most dramatic evidence of the trial—and he was just bubbling over with what a brilliant idea you had." Again, Purcell laughed. "So let's write the scenario: Into court you come with the shoes. Either Hawkes lets out a scream or the judge lets out a scream, whichever one sees the shoes first. We all go traipsing into chambers, out of hearing of the jury. Where'd those shoes come from? What was our purpose in bringing them into court? How do we intend to get that kind of evidence introduced?"

"You can find precedent for—"

"Bullshit. We argue all morning and the judge says no shoes. Meanwhile, here comes Hawkes moving again for a mistrial. Now we argue *that*. What time is it now? Lunchtime. So we go to lunch. Meanwhile, the witness we were supposed to put on the stand tomorrow morning has to wait till afternoon before she can get on. Ordinarily, we could get rid of her in one full day, but this way she doesn't start till afternoon, so we have to hold her over to continue the next morning. That gives her an extra night in Mundelein with nothing to do. Oh, says Bert Klein, if you're all alone in this little city, so frightened and far from home, why don't we try to think of something we just might be able to do together?"

"Well, I'm a son of a bitch," Klein said.

"Yes," Purcell said equably.

"You think I'm capable of that? Going to all that trouble to get ahold of the shoes of four dead men, just for a chance at a piece of ass?"

"Yes."

"I'm a son of a bitch," Klein said again.

"Yes," Purcell said, and they went to interview the witness.

Her name was Andrea Bascomb, and she was quite likely worth the shoes of four men, dead or alive. In her late twenties, she was the combination of beauty and brains that on the basis of infrequency alone could only give the equal rights movement a bad name. Slender but full-breasted she was, with luxurious black hair, huge green eyes, and legs from a Hanes commercial. Max Aranow had found her at the Wharton School of Business of the University of Pennsylvania. She was a member of the Mensa Society, whose sole prerequisite for membership was an IQ at the level of genius.

Upon her graduation from Wharton, she had become a manpower economist by profession. Her testimony in the Mundelein court tomorrow would provide evidence of the worth of Janet Brophy, had she lived the nearly 50 additional years the established mortality tables provided as her normal life expectancy. To support her testimony, Andrea Bascomb already had furnished the A&P a welter of charts, Labor Department indices, columns and columns of figures, graphs of this and tables of that.

Janet Brophy had been earning $9,000 a year as a part-time school bus driver. By the time she reached retirement age, given the foreseeable trend in inflation, that $9,000 as an annual figure would become at least $175,000. Of course, Andrea Bascomb's testimony would also have to take that projection back downward, through use of a mathematical formula that would reduce it to present value, since any jury award for damages presumably would be collected in present-day dollars, which then had the potential of being invested at interest by the beneficiary.

"I'll be making projections over the next forty-three years," Bascomb said, "so I'll be using the Labor index showing the trends of the past forty-three years."

"Good enough," Purcell said to her. "But what about her other potential earnings? You were in court today. You heard that testimony from the publisher, about Janet as a writer and composer."

"No reason not to ask me about those," Andrea Bascomb said. "The point will have to come out that if she became a writer, then presumably she'd give up being a bus driver. If you don't bring that out, the other side will." Obviously she had testified in other cases before this one.

"Yuh, I know," Joe said. "But those are good figures that publisher was talking about."

"Still only a potential though," Andrea said. "The established wage gives me a nice floor. The publisher gives you a sky without limit. You be the advocate. I'll be the witness." Andrea opened her notebook and turned to a column of numbers. "Do you like my figure here?"

"Yes, I do," Bert Klein said from the armchair.

"Pay him no mind," Joe said to her. "He's harmless."

She looked at Bert appraisingly. "Cute, though," she said.

"I think her testimony's going to run more than a full day," Klein said to Joe.

"If I were in your shoes—all five pair of them—I'd pay some attention to what we're talking about here," Purcell said to him.

"Of course," Andrea Bascomb said, "we've got the replacement value of her services to her family. Including the loss of fringe benefits. Her husband, for example, didn't carry any medical insurance. He and the children were covered by her policy from the school district."

Klein said, "What about the grandparents?"

"Covered by Janet's insurance?"

"No," Bert said, "won't Hawkes argue that they took her place in this way and that way, so there isn't that much in the way of Janet's services that were lost?"

"I don't think he can make that stick," Bascomb said. "The kids will need services after the grandparents are dead."

They kept it up along those lines till after one o'clock in the morning. Room service closed at 10:00 p.m., and Perry Muncrief, after an evening of data retrieval at the computer console in the A&P suite, had gone to bed.

"One of us has to go for coffee and sandwiches," Purcell said to Klein. "Guess who?"

"My shoes hurt," Bert objected.

"Maybe you can find another pair that fit. There must be some lying around."

"Funny," Bert said, and went out into the night.

Andrea Bascomb's testimony did take up the entire time in court the following day. Purcell found himself enormously grateful to Max Aranow for finding this expert. Not only did she know her stuff, but she could explain it. Not only did she explain it, she actually made a good deal of it interesting, and the jury followed her alertly.

In his afternoon cross-examination, Arthur Hawkes's tactic was to take the most interesting testimony first and dull it with repetition. Where one question about a certain figure would have sufficed, he asked six. The jury sensed the game, but began soon to weary of it. So the tactic was working. Some of the jurors may have been irritated with Hawkes on that account, but boring them obviously was worth the opportunity he had to blunt Andrea's sharpness, so he kept on.

Toward the end of his cross-examination, Hawkes started playing up the inflation factor. With mockery and doubt, he reached his final question:

Q.   One last thing, Miss Bascomb. We're told that a private in George Washington's army made thirty-five cents a day. At the growth rate you've used to project the Brophy income, what would that same army private be earning now?

A.   You mean per day?

Q.   Yes.

A.   Fourteen million dollars.

Q.   Fourteen million dollars a day. Can you imagine that?

A.   I not only can imagine it, Mr. Hawkes, I've heard that identical question from the defense lawyer the last seven times I testified in court.

Even Junior Bohr joined the laughter that swept the courtroom, and Hawkes reacted angrily. "Your Honor might admonish the witness."

"What for?"

"For the gratuitous extension of her answer."

"I didn't hear any extension, gratuitous or otherwise."

"All I asked her for was the figure. She answered, and then—"

"And then," the judge said, "you asked her if she could imagine it, so she answered that question too."

Hawkes blew a nonexistent cigarette ash from the tip of his tongue. "No further questions."

"We'll adjourn for the day," Bohr said.

Purcell was smiling as Andrea stepped down from the stand. "Good work," he said. "The only thing we regret is that you won't get the chance to stay over tonight."

Again, Andrea Bascomb looked at Bert Klein appraisingly. "That's all right," she said. "I am going to stay over."

13

It was 8:30 in the morning when the phone rang in the A&P suite at the Western Motor Hotel. Perry Muncrief took the call, then moved into Purcell's quarters and found him shaving in front of the bathroom mirror. "That was the judge's secretary," Perry said. "He wants you in his chambers no later than nine-thirty."

"Fuck him," Purcell said. "What is it that won't wait till ten?"

"She didn't say. She did say it was important."

"I was looking forward to breakfast," Joe said. "I think I've turned into Max Aranow. I get up in the morning thinking about food."

"She said make it earlier than nine-thirty if you can."

"Fuck her too."

But it was only 9:20 when he entered the courtroom, and there the sight that met his eyes was one of the strangest he could remember. The courtroom was empty—except for the jury box, where all nine jurors sat already in place, staring and immobile, as if some architect had taken a model of a courtroom and set a cardboard-cutout photograph of a jury within it, to see how it would make the place look.

To Purcell it looked like a moonscape. There was something so spare and forbidding about it that he did not even nod a greeting at the jurors, moving quickly to the right instead to reach the human environment of the judge's chambers, and he found that Junior Bohr's inner office held what by now had become its familiar complement of two people: Junior and Arthur Hawkes.

Purcell nodded at them. "'Morning, friends," he said.

"No friends in here," the judge said. "You son of a bitch."

Purcell looked at him, then at Arthur Hawkes. To Hawkes, he said, "What's he got the red ass about?"

"You don't know?" Arthur said.

"Would I ask if I knew?"

With his eyes Hawkes indicated a mimeographed document on Bohr's desk. To Purcell it looked to be about fifteen pages, stapled together.

"What's that?"

"Here." The judge picked up the document and almost hurled it at Purcell. The pages hit him in the arm and fell to the floor. He bent to pick them up and read the title page:

DEPARTMENT OF TRANSPORTATION
Materials Transportation Bureau
(49 CFR Parts 173,179)
(Docket No. HM-144; Notice No. 76-12)
TRANSPORTATION OF HAZARDOUS MATERIALS
Shippers; Specification for Pressure Tank Car Tanks

As a result of a series of serious railroad accidents involving pressure tank cars transporting hazardous materials, The Materials Transportation Bureau is considering amending Parts 173 and 179 of the Hazardous Materials Regulations to modify the specifications for uninsulated pressure tank car tanks (112 and 114 specifications) so as to improve design and construction of new and existing cars.

BACKGROUND

```
Petition for Advance Notice of Proposed Rulemaking * * *
to amend 49 CFR Part 179, Sub-part C; 49 CFR Part 173;
Docket No. HM-125, Notice 75-4; and Docket No. HM-109,
Amendment Nos. 173-83 and 179-52 was submitted to the
Bureau by...
```

That was all that appeared on the first page of the document, but it was all Purcell needed to read. He tossed the stapled pages gently back onto the judge's desk and said, "So?"

Bohr extinguished one Camel and reached for another. "You act," he said, seeming to pick his words with care, "as if you'd already read it."

"Sure I did," Purcell said. "Months ago. It's not exactly a new piece of material. Why? Is it something new to you? I would have imagined you'd seen it." He looked at Hawkes. "Certainly you saw it, Arthur. You must have."

The judge said, "Yes, as a matter of fact I did see it. And of course Arthur has seen it. And—" he dragged deeply at the new cigarette, his voice rising now "—as of yesterday's mail delivery the whole goddamn jury has seen it. All nine of them!"

Purcell stared from the judge to Hawkes and back again. "The jury— every one of them—they got this in their mail? How?"

Junior Bohr leaned back in his chair. "We thought perhaps you might be able to tell us."

"You thought *I* could tell you? Why me?"

"Who else stood to gain from it?"

"Gain what from it?"

"It's a Department of Transportation order," Bohr said, "specifying among other things—hold on." He was riffling the pages." Here: specifying that all jumbo tank cars be retrofitted with insulation to be made safer. At a cost—" He was quoting from the single-spaced page now: "'The minimum cost of implementing the requirements proposed in this notice will be one hundred million dollars.'"

"So?" Joe said. "We've been in there telling them for weeks the goddamn cars aren't safe."

"That's you who's been saying that," Arthur Hawkes said. "Not the government. And, as you just pointed out, in a courtroom. Not through the mails."

"All right," Purcell said. "Why doesn't somebody come out and say subornation? Why doesn't somebody say jury tampering?"

"I already said both those things," Junior Bohr said, "before you got here. Arthur said no. He said you weren't that unethical. I said it wasn't a question of ethics. All the mailings were anonymous, and you were too smart to let them be traced to you. Unethical is only when you get caught."

"Thanks for your support, Arthur," Purcell said.

"You're welcome," Hawkes said. "I also demanded a mistrial."

"Maybe *you* sent the letters, then. Make the judge think I did it and get your mistrial that way."

Hawkes shifted angrily in his chair. "I defend your ethics so you attack mine?"

"Like the judge said, it ain't unethical unless you get caught."

"All right," Bohr said. "Let's all simmer down here."

"How'd the news come to you?" Purcell said to him. "Or did Arthur Hawkes tell you?"

"I didn't get it from Arthur. One of the jurors called me at home last night."

"Which one?"

The judge started to reply, then thought the better of it. "I don't think you're on a need-to-know basis, with that question. Anyway, what difference does it make?"

"Maybe it doesn't," Joe said. "But you only heard from one juror. What made you say all nine?"

"Because I called the other eight."

"Speaking of ethics," Purcell said to him. "Good God, Junior."

"I told each one of them the same thing," Bohr said. "I said I'd heard from a juror who said he—" he caught himself "—or she, if it was a she, had received a document from the Department of Transportation in their mail. And I asked them, each of them, if they'd also received such a document. And every one of them said yes."

"What else did you say to them?"

"Don't you cross-examine me, you prick," Bohr said. "I asked them all to be here an hour early this morning and to bring it with them. I told them there was no point in their paying any attention to the contents, because it was highly technical, and they'd get an explanation of it here this morning."

"What made the first juror call you about it to begin with? Did he say?"

"I told you not to cross-examine me," the judge said, but then unexpectedly he laughed. "He thought *I'd* sent it."

And here, just as unexpectedly, Arthur Hawkes laughed too. "It ain't unethical unless you get caught," he said.

But just as suddenly the laughter ceased. "It never occurred to him one of the lawyers would send it," Bohr said. "And if they didn't send it, it had to be from the court. In fact, what he wanted to know was how fast I wanted him to get it read, because he was going to the movies last night."

"Well," Purcell said, "at least we've established it was a he."

"Don't you play scumbag gumshoe with me," Junior said to him. "I may have used 'he' just to throw you off."

"And you may have used the word 'order' just to throw me off."

"What do you mean, 'order'?"

"You called that thing a Department of Transportation *order*," Purcell said. He lifted the document from the desk again. "This is just a cockamamy preliminary proposal. Every time Ralph Nader yells, 'Unsafe,' some regulatory agency in Washington punches out a preliminary proposal to cover its ass. And what happens? Nothing!"

"The jury isn't sophisticated enough to know that," Arthur Hawkes said. "Whether you sent it or not, the damage has been done."

"I'm interested in whether the judge called it an order. When he was talking to the jurors."

"You can take a running hump for yourself," Junior said. "No, I didn't call it an order."

"Maybe you did and don't remember."

"No, I didn't, smart-ass. And the reason I didn't was that I didn't know what it was. Not till I read it this morning. If I used the word 'order' it was a loose, rogue word, and only in here just now in front of the two of you." He stubbed out his cigarette. "Let me have that again." He gestured to Purcell, and Joe returned the document. "See, this juror started to read it to me over the phone, and he read the heading and all the numbers and the rest of the fucking junk, and then he started in with this: 'As a result of a series of serious railroad accidents involving pressure tank cars,' and right there, when he got to tank cars, I stopped him. So at that point I had no way of knowing *what* it was—order or proposal or whatever."

"All right, Junior, you're clean," Joe said. "And Arthur Hawkes denies he had it sent. And—oh, shit, I know. That asshole in the bar. You know the one: Price."

Hawkes nodded. "Right. Maybe you shouldn't have hit him."

"Maybe I should have hit him harder."

"What is this?" the judge said. "Who'd you hit?"

But Purcell ignored him. Instead, to Arthur Hawkes: "He goes to Cuneo, and Cuneo's had a gun in his pocket for me from the word go. First he tries to get me on the Marlowe thing, and that doesn't work. Then he tries with that nutty business of having Price hold you up with the airline cases, and that backfires on him. So now he does this, figuring it'll look like I sent the letters, and Arthur will get a mistrial out of it."

"You're right," Hawkes said. "That's who it was. I hadn't even thought of that." He waved a hand at the judge. "Joe's clean too."

"That's a relief," Purcell said.

"You know who sent it?" Bohr asked.

"Yes," Hawkes said.

"Well, let's go after him."

"How will you ever prove it?" Purcell said. "The game isn't worth the candle. At least we've got the answer."

"As far as who sent the letters, yes," Hawkes said. "As for the rest of it, no. I still demand a mistrial."

"On what grounds?"

"The jury was reached," Hawkes said. "The fact is still in place. What difference does it make who did it?"

"Wait a minute," Joe said. "Reached with what?"

"With evidence of postaccident repair," Arthur said. "You know that's not admissible in a negligence case."

"What repair?" Joe said. "This is just a proposal. Nothing has been repaired. That's number one. Number two is you're right that it's not admissible in a negligence case. But you're overlooking—and I think it's an honest oversight on your part—that in a product liability action, it would be admissible. And this is a product liability case as well as a negligence case. There's new law on that. Am I right, judge?"

"I think you are," Bohr said. "If you think about it, Arthur, you'll see he's right."

"And there, if by now anybody needs it," Purcell said, "is the last and most obvious reason why I wouldn't have had any cause to send that stuff to the jury in the mail. Hell, I can tell it to them in court: have witnesses explain it to them, instead of banking on them to decipher something like this on their own."

"If you can do that, why haven't you?" Hawkes asked. "I've been in court every day. I haven't heard you even mention it."

"I haven't finished presenting my case, that's why," Joe said. "You got any hard questions?"

"I'm still moving for a mistrial," Hawkes said. "Bringing it up in court, even if you were entitled to—and I'm not all that convinced in that direction—is one thing. But the jury's already seen it in their mail. The well has been poisoned."

"Arthur has a point," Bohr said to Purcell. "I'm a son of a bitch if he doesn't have a point."

"You'd better believe it," Hawkes said. "And you'd better act on it."

"And you'd better not issue any goddamn orders or you'll be out of here feet first," Bohr said to him. He pushed the intercom, and said, "Lenore, see if there's a court reporter here yet. And if there is, send him in here. And send the jury in with him."

The voice of Lenore said back, "You mean all nine of them?"

"Christ, no," Junior said. He thought for a moment. "Well, I'll want to see all nine. But send them in three at a time."

"In any special order?"

"One-two-three's as good an order as any for the first batch. Then four-five-six."

"And then when they come out, seven-eight-nine?"

"That's it." Bohr released the intercom button. "Lenore has a mind like a steel trap." He swept cigarette ashes from his robes and straightened in his chair.

They came in, the court reporter and the first three jurors, Lydia Herbert, Rafael DeSabitini, and Gregory Sales. The reporter had his pedestal and his machine, and behind him came the bailiff with a rolling chair for him. He set up and nodded, and Judge Bohr began to question the jurors.

They all had received the document? Yes. Had they read it? Sales and DeSabitini had read it partway through, but Sales had found it too complicated, and DeSabitini said it was too similar to the jargon he had to listen to in court to hold his interest. Mrs. Herbert had not read it at all. "You said you'd explain it to us in court," she said, "so I said to myself why bother."

Bohr dismissed them and the next group came in: Grace Cutter, Lucas Pointer, and Jean Cartwright. From Pointer came the unmistakable odor of chicken manure, and the two women stood markedly away from him. An identical line of questioning from the judge, quite a similar range of answers from four-five-six.

And finally Hilda Graysmith, Leonard Still, and Mother Nine, George Proctor, as ever clutching his notebook. Again the same questions and more or less the same answers, except for Still. When the judge asked him if he'd read the document, he said, "No, sir, Your Honor, you told me I didn't have to, it was all right to go to the movies."

The last trio left, the court reporter with them, and Arthur Hawkes said, "He blew your cover, judge."

"The fucker," Bohr said. "Isn't it always the way? He's the one who's out of work. So he's the one who goes to the movies. Where does he get the money, if he's not working?"

"*Moment by Moment* is at the Gem," Joe Purcell said. "That makes it even stranger."

"All right," the judge said, "now to details. You tell me one more time you want a mistrial, Arthur, I'll slap your fucking teeth in for you. I've been up all night on this, and I've been in the books, and I've talked to a judge in Columbus on the phone. On the one hand I'm persuaded no one in this room had a thing to do with this, and I'm equally persuaded the jury was not prejudiced to any irreparable degree. Those horseshit government documents are so impenetrable nobody can understand them anyway."

"It says a hundred million dollars," Hawkes said. "It talks about serious railroad accidents. Is that impenetrable? Does that leave them free from prejudice?"

The judge fished for a cigarette, found the pack empty, and reached in his drawer for a new one. "Just shut your face and let me finish. I said on the one hand the jury was not prejudiced. Now what I'll say is on the other hand: They're not prejudiced *yet*. But if they hear anything more about this DOT order—or proposal, if I have to use the right word—then they can well remember that it came to them in their mail, and that I warned them off it and summoned them early and took those mailings away from them and had them in here, and they'll put two and two together and say to themselves, 'Hey, this was a vital thing, an all-important thing.' And then this episode *will* have influenced them."

He lit the cigarette, inhaled, and said, "So the ruling is no mistrial! But on the other hand, no use of this document, no reference to it the rest of the way. Okay?"

"No!" The word came simultaneously from Hawkes and Purcell. And behind it, again simultaneously, came their flow of protest. For Hawkes, the damage had been done. The government was telling the tank car manufacturers to spend $100 million to fix these defects, and the most unconscious juror of the nine had the wit to remember that figure and know what it meant. For Purcell, the most powerful weapon in his arsenal—use of the government's condemnation of the tank cars as unsafe—had just been taken away from him.

In the clamor, Judge Bohr put up a hand. "*Shut up!*" he said. "You bungholes are giving me a headache. I happen to have some law books that make me think I'm right, and I've got a judge in Columbus who thinks

I'm a fucking genius, and if you don't like it you can kiss my royal patootie. Now get the hell out of here. Tell the bailiff church'll start in ten minutes."

A simmering Hawkes and a swearing Purcell exited the judge's chambers and returned to the courtroom: Hawkes to be enveloped in conference by his undertakers, Steppenworth and Halsey; Purcell to rant to Bert Klein, who by then also had arrived.

Bert listened to the story, and when Purcell got to the final part, he began to laugh.

"I'm glad somebody thinks it's funny," Joe said.

"In a way it is," Bert said. "It came damn close, the way you tell it, to *both* lawyers moving for a mistrial at the same time over the same issue!"

"If I didn't have an obligation to nineteen different lawyers with one hundred and four different clients, all in this one case, I would have," Joe said. "Who do I put on for witnesses now? The Rockettes? I was saving my best for last, and that cretin Bohr cuts it clean out from under me."

"Tell me something," Klein said. "How sure are you the jurors didn't read that thing, and understand what they were reading?"

Purcell looked at him archly.

"They were bound to deny it, or say it didn't mean anything," Bert said. "They know the judge would be mad at them otherwise."

The trace of a smile appeared momentarily, but only momentarily, on Joe Purcell's face. "That's a very cynical thing, what you just said," he told Bert. "I'd be ashamed, if I were you."

"I have a hunch," Bert said, "just a hunch, that Arthur's two undertakers over there just asked him the same question I asked you. And Arthur doesn't seem very happy."

"It's the old saying, when a jury's told to disregard something," Joe said. "How do you un-ring a bell?" He saw the grin on Klein's face. "Don't spend your winner's share quite yet," he said. "The answer to that question is you hire Arthur Hawkes."

14

Hawkes had indeed un-rung a bell or two in his time, and as the remainder of the plaintiff's case unrolled in court, it seemed he was doing so again in this one. If in fact any bell had rung to begin with. Bert Klein's wishful thinking to one side, the more realistic view had to be that the jury, like

Hamlet's view of all the uses of this world, was just as weary, stale, flat, and unprofitable as Joe Purcell had first supposed. Joe put one expert after another on the stand, took nearly an entire day with one man on the subject of insulation alone, without making a visible dent in the jury's pallor.

There was a reason for the Department of Transportation not singling out this particular kind of accident. There was no precedent for the Fireball, whose chain of disaster began with a solitary tank car sitting stationary during a heat wave. The government investigation and findings on insulation went instead to moving trains, and couplers and punctures, and the weather had nothing to do with any of that.

In point of fact, the only bell Arthur Hawkes wished most devoutly he could un-ring was the bell attached to the telephone in his suite at the General Dexter. Day in, day out, the phone rang while he was there, the messages piling up when he wasn't. "I know why Max Aranow took you in as a partner," he told Joe Purcell. "It was so somebody besides himself could be there to take phone calls."

The day's courtroom session was over, and Hawkes returned to his hotel, replaced his shoes with slippers, ordered two gin rickeys from room service, and found himself reflecting that the things that mattered could be found only in the eastern half of the United States. In this, he was one with Max Aranow. "You remember Harry Ruby, the old songwriter?" Aranow had asked him on one occasion. "He wound up in Hollywood, and he said, 'Living in California will put ten extra years on my life. I intend to spend those ten years in New York.'"

The business with the gin rickey, for example. Hawkes could remember ordering one at a bar in the Beverly Wilshire and having the bartender gape at him and say, "You must be from the east."

"Chicago," Hawkes said.

"When you're in L.A., Chicago is the east," the bartender said. "Anyplace where the radio stations have call letters that begin with 'W' instead of 'K,' you know it's civilized. You're the only customer I've had in three years asked me for a gin rickey."

"You mean I don't have to tell you how to make it?"

"Hell, I'm from Baltimore," the bartender said.

Room service brought the drinks, and Arthur Hawkes signed for them, loosened his tie, and sank back on the couch with his feet up on the coffee table. Directly beside his left ankle was a chessboard, the pieces set up to show the situation following the thirty-first moves in the classic game between Johner and Nimzovich in Dresden in 1926. Few games, Hawkes reflected, had such an enduring influence—one could see its effects in the fifth game of the Fischer-Spassky match nearly half a century later. "Not only the strategy, but the combinations, in this extraordinary game were unique," Nimzovich would later write.

The same, Hawkes mused, might be said of the lawsuit now being litigated before Judge Bohr in the Mundelein courthouse up the street from the hotel.

Then the phone, beside Hawkes on the end table, began to ring.

It was Herman Metcalfe calling: the house counsel for Trans-Continental Insurance, the carrier that insured the N. Nance Company. And somewhat to his surprise, Hawkes was not annoyed. More than anyone else, Metcalfe had left him alone during the course of the trial so far.

"I hear it's going just fine," Metcalfe said.

"Purcell's winding down," Hawkes said.

"I mean, up till now," Metcalfe said. "We've arranged to get the newspaper every day, same-day delivery, so we've been following it."

"If you mean the Huntington paper, then of course everything's going just fine," Hawkes said.

"Well, one of our people was down there a day or two, just to sit in, in the courtroom. He said he called you to say hello. Harvey Sinclair was his name."

"He did call. I couldn't see him."

"He was there when they put that kid on the stand and had him sing."

"That was a well-coached kid," Hawkes said.

"From what Harvey says, that was the high point of their presentation," Metcalfe said.

"I don't know whether it was or not," Hawkes said. "This is a trial where not only the strategy, but the combinations, are unique."

"What was that?"

"Nimzovich," Hawkes said.

"Ah," Metcalfe said doubtfully. Then: "But that's not my main reason for calling. Do you know any publishers, Arthur?"

"What kind of publishers?"

"Books."

"There was one on the witness stand here just the other day. You should have called me then."

"Well, I've got something you're going to like," Metcalfe said. "A friend of mine who's an agent. Literary agent, except he's also a lawyer. And I told him a little bit about the situation down there, and he said that would make a great textbook for lawyers: the act of God defense."

"Doesn't he want to wait and see how it comes out? Maybe God loses."

"No, I'm not trying to sell you an agent, Arthur," Metcalfe said. "That's why I asked you if *you* knew any publishers. But finding a publisher is the least of my worries."

"When would I have time to write a book?" Hawkes said.

"That's the chief problem," Metcalfe said. "Because we don't want just *a* book. We want a whole series of them. We'd underwrite the cost, and of course we'd make it worth your while. But you see the idea, Arthur? A series of textbooks showing how to defend different kinds of cases. Written by the prevailing master of the art. And we'd give you all the help you'd need, do anything you wanted to handle the time problem so you wouldn't have to give up your practice or anything like that."

"And Trans-Continental would underwrite all this?"

"Not just Trans-Continental, Arthur. I've talked to some others— Aetna, the Travelers, you name it—and we're talking about making it industry-wide. If it's money you're thinking of, just think of a number. You can name your own price."

"I withdraw my penultimate question," Hawkes said.

"Your what?"

"My question. About when would I have time to write a book. Let alone more than one book. It isn't a factor."

"I don't understand."

"Everything I know about defense law can be told in maybe five paragraphs," Hawkes said. "I have just come to that realization."

"Ah, come on, Arthur," Metcalfe said. "Look at all the textbooks that already exist. Are you saying none of them's worth anything?"

"No," Hawkes said, "that's not what I'm saying. But you make my point for me. The body of knowledge already exists. The books are already there. Who needs another one?"

"Because there are no books by Arthur Hawkes."

"About how to defend a case like the Fireball?"

"Exactly," Metcalfe said. "I happen to think the greatest untapped resource the insurance industry can have is better representation in the courtroom."

Hawkes was starting on his second gin rickey. He put down the glass and said into the phone, "The greatest untapped resource the insurance industry can have is *no* representation in the courtroom. I could have settled this case for half a million dollars less than it's going to wind up costing you people to *win* it in court, *if* you win, but I didn't have the kind of settlement authority I needed. You people wouldn't give it to me."

"Oh, we've been all over that, Arthur," Metcalfe said.

"Not so you learned anything from it, we haven't. And besides, how could I write a series of bedside readers for the insurance industry? It's bad enough I have to represent them on a case-by-case basis." Hawkes sipped from his drink. "You know what I think of Communists."

"I know what you think of *what?*"

"Communists," Hawkes said. "The entire insurance industry is communistic. What do you do when you sell me a life insurance policy? You tell me how I don't want to leave my loved ones unprotected, how you don't want my wife to be left without anything so she'd have to accept support from the family. You talk about making sure I have money so I can retire and not be a burden on my children."

Metcalfe said, "That makes us Communists?"

"The whole idea in everything you say is to break up the family, so they can live apart and not be dependent on one another," Hawkes said. "Who wrote that prescription? Karl Marx, that's who. The blueprint for the Communist state was the breakup of the family."

"Oh, for God's sake," Metcalfe said.

"Another thing is the way you and your fellow travelers in the insurance lobby are running around the country getting laws passed putting caps on damages and doling out awards on the installment plan. Your ideal would be a world where no matter who is injured, or how badly, everyone would get the same fixed, predetermined, inadequate amount. Tamp everybody into the same mold. Forget about individual rights. Achieve maxijustice for the collective."

"What's wrong with that? Sounds Utopian," Metcalfe chuckled. "Just think how predictable our cash flow would be."

"When you're predicting your cash flow," said Hawkes, "remember one thing."

"What?"

"Aetna doesn't do very well in Poland."

There was a beat pause. "I think you're really serious about us being Communists."

"It's *res judicata,*" Hawkes said. "The only difference between you and the Soviets is you have salesmen who take commissions and make the product just that much more expensive. The product itself is the same."

"Then you can add one text to the series called *Behind the Iron Curtain with Fireman's Fund,*" Metcalfe said. "I just think it's unusual that there's never been a book by Arthur Hawkes. That's what I had in mind. That's why I called."

"And let me tell you something else," Hawkes said. "I have a problem with the Fireball."

"Something that came up? Something you haven't told us?"

"No. It's about Joe Purcell, about when he's at his most dangerous."

"When's that?"

"When he doesn't give a damn. He says this is his last case. He's leaving the law. He even stayed away from the courtroom so he could rehearse a musical comedy he's writing."

"You're overthinking," Metcalfe said to him. "Anybody else would be delighted if opposing counsel wasn't paying attention."

"I'm not anybody else," Hawkes said.

15

At the end of another week, Joe Purcell rested his case. Not with a bang but a whimper. His last witness was a computer expert who had programmed the software for freight classification in Chicago. Nobody could understand a word he said. Hawkes worked with him for a while on cross, and managed cheerfully to muddy things up even more, but even he let go of it at last:

Q.   You say then that the possibility of the car's being misdirected is of the distinct second order?

A.   Of the order of 6.2 over the distant ordinal. That is before we extrapolate the standard deviation. Are you interested in that?

Q.   No. I have no further questions.

MR. PURCELL: No questions. No further witnesses. The plaintiff rests.

In chambers, Hawkes then moved for a directed verdict to dismiss the case. It was pro forma. After the plaintiff rested, the defense invariably moved for dismissal on the grounds that plaintiff had not made a prima facie case. The judge listened to Arthur's argument, hesitated, looked to see the effect his hesitation was having on Purcell, grinned, and then said, "Motion denied."

Now it was Arthur Hawkes's turn to present his case for the defense. He began with a dull, nondescript expert witness:

Q. Mr. Oliphant, will you tell us your professional calling?

A. I am the director of the National Fire Inspection Laboratory.

Q. Is that a private company or a government agency?

A. Private, but we have government contracts.

Q. With what branch of the government?

A. The executive branch.

Q. I mean, specifically.

A. The Department of the Interior, for the most part. But we have supplied data for the Department of Commerce, and Labor, and Agriculture.

Q. Are you anything like the Underwriting Laboratories?

A. Who? I'm sorry.

Q. The Underwriting Laboratories. You know, when your wife buys a toaster, it comes in a box with those letters "UL" on the side. UL-approved, or whatever it says.

A. Not really, sir, no.

Purcell had his eyes closed, a wake-me-when-it's-over glaze to his face. The witness, Lester Oliphant, was another Castor—a replier: The more he told you, the less you knew. Hawkes was leading him now through the qualifying routine. The difference between his company and the Underwriters seemed to be that the latter specialized in investigating merchandise beforehand, the former after. Hawkes went to Oliphant's education, years of service, professional recognition.

Q. Am I correct also that you have served with the United States delegation to the United Nations?

A. Not the main delegation, no, sir. I did chair the multinational committee two years ago in its study of standardizing disaster and fire-fighting controls.

Q. You chaired a convention of many nations, is that correct?

A. Yes. There were 108 nations represented at our plenary session.

Q. I see. And where was this convention held?

A. Leningrad.

Q. Leningrad. In the Soviet Union?

MR. PURCELL: Plaintiff concedes the location of Leningrad.

THE COURT: It is like whales, is it not? Where many countries get together, in spite of widely varying political differences, and in the spirit of the common good they work together behind the scenes and behind the headlines to improve those elements that touch us all?

"I'm going to be sick," Purcell husked to Bert Klein. "Next, Junior narrates the documentary on whales." Again he closed his eyes.

Q.   Well, then, tell us, Mr. Oliphant, when you attend one of those conventions, is it just for cosmetic purposes—just for show—or do things get accomplished at such meetings?

A.   I thought the Leningrad session was especially fruitful.

There was a pause. Was Hawkes waiting for Purcell to object that this went too far afield, that it was Florian, not Leningrad, in focus here? Waiting for Purcell to object, or, more likely, hoping for it? Hawkes turned to glance at the plaintiff's table, but now Purcell's right elbow rested on the tabletop and his face rested in his hand.

Q.   Especially fruitful?

A.   Yes. This country and Norway had taken the lead in pioneering what we thought was an especially beneficial technique in forest-fire management.

Q.   What technique was that?

A.   Well, in layman's language, it is the idea that if you set forest fires on purpose, and let them burn themselves out, you produce a kind of survival of the fittest, where a new forest will grow, with strain and spacing that will make the next generation of trees more resistant to fire.

Q.   And this would benefit people everywhere?

A.   Obviously.

Q.   All right. But on the subject of forest fires, I have to ask just one more question. What is the most frequent cause of forest fires?

A.   Lightning.

Q.   Lightning?

A.   That's right.

MR. PURCELL: I hope this witness, for all his obvious expertise in this field, is not taking the witness stand here to denigrate our friend Smokey the Bear. I have always thought that was an enormous contribution to preventing forest fires.

THE WITNESS: Not at all. In fact, our organization had a great deal to do with bringing Smokey into being to begin with.

THE COURT: Didn't I read somewhere that Smokey had just died?

MR. HAWKES: Is everybody asking questions at once? I thought it was my turn.

THE WITNESS: Yes, Your Honor, and buried with appropriate honors.

THE COURT: I just hope there is a new Smokey on the horizon.

THE WITNESS: Yes, the education campaign is continuing.

THE COURT: Because if you are now telling us you are going around setting forest fires on purpose, I would not like the public at large, or even the jury, to get the idea it is all right to go around setting forest fires.

MR. HAWKES: With all due respect to the Court, I would like to know when I can resume questioning the witness.

THE COURT: You may proceed.

Q.   Thank you. Can we put this to rest, Mr. Oliphant, and consign it to the record that you are not advising anybody to go out and set a forest on fire?

A.   That is right. Setting forest fires is a job only for experts.

Q.   But the point you have already made here is that most forest fires are started by lightning?

A.   Oh, yes. By far.

Q.   Why would that be?

A.   Because of the frequency factor.

Q.   Can you explain that?

A.   Yes. It is generally accepted in our profession that lightning strikes the surface of the earth 1,800 times every second.

Q.   You say 1,800 times a second?

A.   For the entire surface of the earth, that is the accepted figure, yes, sir.

Q.   I am sorry. Brother Purcell and I grew up with the old math. Can you take that 1,800 times a second and translate it into a figure, say, for a 24-hour day?

THE COURT: I grew up with the new math and I cannot do it.

THE WITNESS: It would be more than 150 million times every 24-hour day.

Q.   We are not talking about 150 million fires set by lightning every day?

A.   Oh, no, of course not. We are simply saying that some part of the earth is struck by lightning 150 million times per day.

Q.   All right, then. Now, to be specific: Do you have any record of lightning hitting a railroad freight car?

A.   No, sir. Not in this modern era. There may have been a time, the old days of the mainly wooden cars, when that might have happened.

THE COURT: It hits 150 million times a day and never hits a freight car?

MR. HAWKES: I believe what he meant to say was, it never hits a freight car with a fire resulting.

THE COURT: I believe that's what you meant to say, Mr. Hawkes, not him. Perhaps you ought to let him clarify.

THE WITNESS: Oh, certainly, lightning will hit freight cars.

Q.   Including propane tank cars?

A.   Every kind of car.

Q.   But it doesn't start a fire? You have no record of lightning ever hitting any kind of freight car, including a tank car, and setting it on fire?

A.   That is correct.

THE COURT: I have to interrupt. It is not my place to act for counsel, but hearing no objection from Mr. Purcell, I still have to ask this question for my own information. Isn't it your contention that lightning hit this car at Florian?

MR. HAWKES: No, Your Honor. I think all sides are agreed the lightning touched in the air directly above the car, where vapor happened to be escaping at that instant, the point here being that lightning never touched the car itself. If it had, a built-in ground system, the very nature of the construction of the car, would have run it harmlessly off and away.

MR. PURCELL: Objection.

THE COURT: Take your hand away from your face, Mr. Purcell.

MR. PURCELL: Objection. Counsel is offering testimony.

MR. HAWKES: My statement was responsive to a question addressed to me from the bench.

MR. PURCELL: You've got a witness in the chair. Ask him.

THE COURT: I issue the instructions here, Mr. Purcell. And I do not know even what is at issue. My understanding had been that everyone accepted lightning did not hit the tank car itself.

MR. HAWKES: Yes, Your Honor. You are correct. And to clarify, I raised the question only to bring out how inherently safe the cars themselves are. After all, the manufacturer of the tank car is a defendant here.

THE COURT: And so I asked a stupid question. But perhaps it was not so stupid, because there is a distinction here, and it may be good that this exchange served to remind the jury of that distinction.

MR. HAWKES: I could not agree more.

THE COURT: Then your line of questioning is accepted and the objection is overruled.

MR. PURCELL: No, sir, I except. I perceive no distinction here. The car caught fire and the fire was caused by lightning. If that bolt of lightning hit the car itself or the vapor one inch above the car, why draw a distinction?

THE COURT: I think we have no quarrel here. It was an exercise in restatement and clarification, that is all.

MR. PURCELL: Not when counsel is using that distinction, abetted by the court itself, to preach how safe the tank car was. We have twenty-seven deaths and seventy-seven injuries here. If that is a safe car, I would hate to see an unsafe car.

MR. HAWKES: Now, I will move that the court strike that.

THE COURT: Yes, I will strike it. The jury is instructed to disregard the outburst from Mr. Purcell, and I am going to admonish you, Mr. Purcell, in no uncertain terms, that you cannot sit there appearing to be asleep and then conduct your lawsuit in this manner. If there is something you wanted to establish, you had your chance with your own witness and you will have another chance on cross-examination. That should be sufficient for any attorney.

MR. PURCELL: Mr. Hawkes testified it was a safe tank car. Who authorized him to testify? When did he take the oath?

MR. HAWKES: I responded to an inquiry from the court. I did not testify.

THE COURT: Mr. Purcell, I overruled you once on this, and in case you did not hear me I am overruling you again. Now, that is English. Do you understand English?

MR. PURCELL: Ordinarily, yes. But counsel made a speech here about a grounding system that runs off electricity. It was not the witness but the lawyer rambling on like that.

THE COURT: If he did, it was because I invited it. I have already acknowledged that. I think there is less here than meets the eye. We reclarified the situation. No one denies the car caught fire and lightning was the cause of it. Counsel for plaintiff has not been compromised. Any grievance he has can be ameliorated through cross-examination, and that is nothing more or less than standard procedure in any courtroom in this land.

MR. PURCELL: The court even informed the jury that I was asleep.

THE COURT: The court said you appeared to be asleep. I will state for the record that you are not asleep at this moment. Will you continue with your examination of the witness, Mr. Hawkes?

MR. HAWKES: By now I will have to have the last question read back, so I know where we were.

THE COURT: The court reporter will read the last question.

THE COURT REPORTER: Question: But it doesn't start a fire? You have no record of lightning ever hitting any kind of freight car, including a tank car, and setting it on fire? Answer: That is correct.

Q.   And you also said, I believe, that lightning causes most forest fires.

A.   Oh, yes. By far.

Q.   What causes most other kinds of fires, aside from forest fires?

A.   Lightning.

Q.   All right. Now: Did you come here today with a display to exhibit to this jury?

A.   Yes, sir.

Q.   So there will be no room for any dispute or doubt, will you confirm for the record who it was that asked you to produce this display?

A.   You did.

Q.   And what did I ask you to do?

A.   You asked me to get up a map with Florian, Ohio, at its center, and with a radius of 60 miles, and indicate in red dots on that map every place we had a record of a fire caused by lightning over a period of 5 years.

Q.   What period of 5 years?

A.   You said the most recent against which we had accumulated data. That would be for the 5 years ending last December.

Q.   And you have that map with you today?

A.   Yes, sir. It is rather large, so the graphics will be readily evident to the jury.

MR. HAWKES: It is at the counsel table over there, Your Honor. We would like to set it up on the easel now, and give Mr. Oliphant a pointer.

THE COURT: Well, put it on the easel. We will mark it for identification as an exhibit.

THE CLERK: Marked as defendants' number one.

THE COURT: Will you place it so Mr. Purcell and I can see it, as well as the jury?

MR. PURCELL: I can get out of my chair to come see it, if that will make it easier.

THE COURT: I am gratified.

MR. PURCELL: What? That I can get out of my chair?

THE COURT: There is no byplay called for here.

Q.   All right, we have it in place. Now, what we have here, Mr.

Oliphant—correct me if I am wrong—is a red mark for every fire caused by lightning within a 65-mile radius of Florian within—

A.   A 60-mile radius.

Q.   Excuse me. Within this recent 5-year period?

A.   That is correct.

Q.   That depicts every fire caused by lightning in that area in that period?

A.   Every fire reported. It goes to our reporting system, which is not perfect.

Q.   Your reporting system?

A.   Yes. Our sources are local police and fire departments, state and federal forest services, insurance companies, whoever—

MR. PURCELL: I didn't hear that very last part.

THE WITNESS: I said insurance companies, whoever else—

MR. PURCELL: Thank you.

THE WITNESS: Whoever else reports fires. Sometimes lightning sets something ablaze and nobody reports it. The damage is not that great. Other times it can set a fire somewhere and nobody notices it, or they do not know lightning was the cause. And I repeat, there is no way of knowing how many times lightning hit the earth in that area where no fire resulted.

Q.   So the depiction on this map is the very most conservative minimum number of lightning-caused fires, is that correct?

A.   Yes, sir. Absolutely.

Q.   And that is Florian at the center of the map, right? I see Kentucky over here down to the left and West Virginia over here down to the right. But you made Florian the center?

A.   Yes, sir.

Q.   Now, you said there would be red dots on the map, and I see some red dots, but mostly all I see is just a great ocean of red.

A.   They ran together, there were so many incidents.

Q.   All right. But there still must be an actual figure.

A.   Yes, sir, I have that. In that 5-year period there were 3,822 fires within a 60-mile radius of Florian, all verified as having been caused by lightning.

Q.   All right. Now, I do not want to be the instrument of any further silly argument. Let us all accept that the tank car in this accident at Florian was set afire by lightning, whether the car itself was hit or whether it was the air above the car. Except that we do know it was not the car that was hit and it was the air.

MR. PURCELL: Objection.

THE COURT: Will you state the grounds?

MR. PURCELL: Same grounds as before. If Mr. Hawkes wants to testify, let him mount the stand and take the oath.

THE COURT: I think it was a harmless remark. Everyone concedes it was the air that was hit, not the car.

MR. PURCELL: It was the car that caught fire.

THE COURT: Yes, and that is conceded too. Objection overruled.

MR. PURCELL: You are permitting one gratuitous, self-serving remark after another.

THE COURT: I have already stated, there is no damage. I have to be the one who measures colloquy in this courtroom.

MR. PURCELL: I heard no colloquy.

THE COURT: Then I will measure it whatever it is. Go ahead, counsel.

Q.   Your map shows 3,822 fires caused by lightning. Agreeing that this fire in this tank car was caused by lightning, how many of the remaining 3,821 fires shown on your map, all of them caused by lightning, occurred in a railroad freight car of any kind?

A.   None.

Q.   Could that have been because of a shortage of railroad cars?

A.   Certainly not in the area outlined by the map. There is an outsize abundance of railroad activity, compared to other places, within that circle.

Q.   Good. Then we can move on to something else—another area of your competence, Mr. Oliphant. Your organization issues an annual yearbook, is that correct?

A.   Oh, yes.

Q.   And who is the editor of the yearbook?

A.   I am in overall charge of it.

Q.   Now, I have a stack of them on the table over there, and I will introduce them as exhibits. These are the National Fire Investigation Laboratory yearbooks, Your Honor, for each of the past 12 years. And the witness will confirm that each one has an appendix section that goes to the techniques of fighting fires. Is that correct, Mr. Oliphant?

A.   Yes.

Q.   And can you tell the jury the purpose of such an appendix?

Mother Nine had his spiral-bound shorthand notebook out, preparing to take notes.

A.   Yes. One purpose is for review by existing fire departments. Sometimes accepted techniques for fighting fires are reviewed in the light of statistical experience, and we have the function of providing those statistics for such review. Insurance companies may also want to—

MR. PURCELL: I am sorry. The voice dropped. I did not hear it.

A.   Insurance companies, I say, also seek a statistical precedent, an experience background, because sometimes there are some areas where more fires seem to erupt than might be expected. And there is the interesting area also of what we call futures. If an area has a high fire experience and some municipality or private developer wants to build up that area, he may want to consult the yearbook ahead of time. Or if a town someplace is thinking of where to locate a new firehouse, we can supply a backlog of statistical information that might be helpful.

Q.   Well, I think this is an education for all of us. But now let me take it one step further. Do you just list fires, or do you also list the damage they cause?

A.   Oh, the damage, too, of course. That is more important than the fires themselves.

Q.   And why is that?

A.   Because there is a correlation. Put a good fire department down the block from a high-fire-risk enterprise and you have fewer problems than with a bad fire department situated a mile away from a lower-risk enterprise.

Q.   Then your investigation also takes into account the presence of any local fire-fighting machinery, whatever it may be?

A.   Oh, yes, it would have to do that. Fire-fighting competence is far more important than fires themselves.

Q.   Why is that?

A.   Because the bottom line is fire damage. A woman cooking lamb chops in one house may get an oven fire and have to call the fire department, and it may destroy the kitchen. Another woman cooking the same lamb chops will know how better to deal with it, or she'll have an extinguisher hanging on the wall, and we'll never even hear of it.

Q.   Then I'm correct in assuming you're trained professionally in that part of it too.

A.   That most of all. No man works for me unless he has been out in the field for a full year, working with various fire fighters and learning the techniques.

Q.   If you are impressing the jury one-half as much as you are impressing me, then I must compliment you all out as witnesses go. I know from your testimony that you can offer no direct experience in how to fight a fire in a tank car when that fire was caused by lightning, because your 5-year survey never recorded its having happened.

A.   Well, yes. But tank cars can catch fire for other reasons.

Q.   We know of evidence to that point. Suppose then that I set a tank car, of the kind involved in this case, on fire, and you as a volunteer fire department arrived on the scene and you had 15 minutes to do something about it. You know the situation, you know the fuel involved, you know the weather, you know everything there was to know that day in Florian. In your opinion, as an expert, is that a controllable fire?

A.   Yes. My opinion is that any department properly equipped and trained could control that fire, to the point where it offered no threat to anybody or anything other than the tank car itself. And I can cite precedents involving not just propane but other cargoes.

Q.   Other cargoes?

A.   Oh, yes, there is a whole variety of situations. Some are even classified.

Q.   Classified?

A.   Yes. Categories that I could give you.

Q.   But about a properly trained and equipped fire department—

MR. PURCELL: Just a minute. Is he going to permit his own witness to answer?

THE COURT: What is the interruption?

MR. PURCELL: He was about to answer as to other cargoes. I am concerned about what other things these freight cars might carry.

THE COURT: I don't know what you're talking about.

MR. PURCELL: Neither do I. The witness said they were classified. It could be nerve gas. We know that has been transported by railroad tank car.

THE COURT: Are you contending this is a nerve gas case? We all know what kind of case it is, and it isn't nerve gas.

MR. HAWKES: I am going back to this witness's statement, as a ranking expert in his field, that this fire could have been controlled with no damage other than to the tank car itself, all within the time that the Florian fire department was on the scene to deal with it. The man is a world-renowned expert in this field, and I do not propose to subject him to any more questioning on the subject. Period.

THE COURT: Then you are saying Mr. Purcell can now cross-examine?

MR. HAWKES: Mr. Purcell can do anything he wants.

Hawkes huffed to his seat at the right-hand counsel table. And Purcell got slowly to his feet and walked up to stand in front of the witness.

Q.   Mr. Oliphant, let's take last things first. You were talking about—

MR. HAWKES: Does the court want us to take down the exhibit?

THE COURT: What exhibit? You mean the map on the easel?

MR. PURCELL: You can let it stay there, Your Honor. It won't be the first time in this case the other side made it easier for us.

THE COURT: Hearing no objection from Mr. Hawkes, I will let the map stay.

MR. PURCELL: I am up here to cross-examine, not discuss maps.

THE COURT: I was exercising a consideration for your benefit.

MR. PURCELL: You say any properly equipped, properly trained fire department could have prevented an explosion.

A. That is right.

Q. You weren't there yourself, were you?

A. Of course not. I am citing many years of accumulated experience with this kind of fire.

Q. Tank cars?

A. It is a broader spectrum than that. It goes to pressurized contents of all kinds in all kinds of containers. There are very well-known procedures to utilize in such cases.

Q. Do those procedures include evacuating the surrounding area?

A. I would imagine so, in some cases, yes.

Q. You would imagine so. Have you ever heard of a case where such evacuation took place?

A. I believe so.

Q. Well, if fighting fires like this is such a simple thing, why would you evacuate the surrounding area?

A. I did not say it was a simple thing.

Q. But you did testify the explosion didn't have to happen.

A. That is right, I think.

Q. Then why evacuate the area?

A. It is a sensible precaution. But you see, it is—

Q. Just a sensible precaution?

MR. HAWKES: I think he did not complete his answer.

A. I was going to say, you are getting a little away from fire-fighting technique there.

Q. Well, then, why don't you bring me back to it?

A.   Is that a question?

Mother Nine's pen wrote in the notebook.

Q.   In the presence of a fire of this sort, isn't evacuating the area one of the first things you do?

A.   Well, we recommend it, yes. But that is like saying that when there is an earthquake you should turn off the gas. Precaution is one thing. The technique of engaging and controlling a fire is something else. Actually, when you come right down to it, you are dealing essentially with different personnel. Evacuating an area, for example. It is the role of firemen to fight fires and police to clear the area.

Q.   And the role of medical people to tend to the dying and injured?

A.   Exactly.

Q.   And there are techniques for fighting various kinds of fires? Separate techniques?

A.   Of course. A brush fire in a field is one thing. A fire on the eightieth floor of a skyscraper is not the same.

Q.   But there was a specified technique for fighting this fire in Florian, in the tank car?

A.   Oh, yes.

Q.   Then have you ever heard of this kind of a fire where a properly trained and equipped fireman was killed or burned or otherwise injured?

A.   I am sure it must have happened, yes.

Q.   Then with thanks again to Mr. Hawkes for leaving it there, let us look at your map on the easel. All that red—that is just fires caused by lightning alone, is that correct?

A.   Yes.

Q.   Did you bring with you any figures for the number of firemen who were killed, burned, or otherwise injured fighting any of those fires?

A.   No, sir.

Q.   Why not?

A.   Mr. Hawkes did not ask me to.

Q.   You did not discuss those figures with him at any time?

A.   It never came up.

Q.   Well, let's have it come up now. These yearbooks of statistics that you edit and bring out every year—they discuss casualties among fire fighters, do they not?

A.   I believe so. I believe it is not so much a discussion as the figures given in tabular form.

Q.   Not to be mysterious about it, I have read those yearbooks. We can now go through them together, or if you prefer I will just make a preliminary statement about them and you can verify it or not. If you do not verify it, then we will have to go into the books themselves.

MR. HAWKES: Wait a minute.

MR. PURCELL: I am leaving it up to the witness, Your Honor.

THE COURT: I think it is not an improper proposal. It gives us a chance to save time, hopefully, and certainly the books are in evidence, Mr. Hawkes. It is all right for a cross-examiner to settle for the shorter answer if he so desires.

MR. HAWKES: Often the short answer can be a summary giving off a misleading effect.

THE COURT: You can correct it if you wish, on redirect.

MR. HAWKES: No. Once it has been uttered, it leaves an imprint. The books are right here. Let us go through them one by one, if that is what Mr. Purcell wants.

MR. PURCELL: We may have to. I am trying to avoid it. I will make the statement that they will bear out what I am now going to say and then some. Mr. Hawkes may be opening a can of worms for himself, over and above his insistence on wasting time.

MR. HAWKES: I will be the judge of that.

THE COURT: No, I am the judge here. We have not even heard Mr. Purcell's statement. I will let him make it now, and if the witness wishes to agree with it, then we will see where we are.

Q.   Thank you, Your Honor. All I was going to say, Mr. Oliphant, was that your statistics in your yearbooks show consistently, year in and year out, that in the categories of fire fighters, professional departments against volunteer departments, it is the professionals who are killed, burned, or otherwise injured by an over-whelming proportion—better than 90 percent of the casualties. Would you agree with that statement?

A.   Yes, I would. But there is a reason for it.

Q.   The professionals are the ones best trained and best equipped, is that right? As opposed to the volunteers? And yet following all the correct techniques they still lose their lives?

MR. HAWKES: He is not letting him complete his answer.

A.   I was going to say, most fires that involve casualties involve professional departments. The professional departments are by definition situated in built-up areas, and the more built-up the area, the more fires. Also—

Q.   Go ahead.

A.   Also, it is a key variant that while volunteer departments in spread-out areas often reach a fire too late to have any real hand in keeping down the loss, it is a matter of geography that the professionals get there that much faster, and so are exposed to conditions that are not yet burned down or burned out, so the danger is that much higher. After all, a given number of those red points on the map could be a farmhouse with the roof on fire after a lightning strike, with perhaps only the farmer himself there to play a hose on it. Now, he is neither a professional nor a volunteer. In the first place, he is in no danger to himself. In the second place, we would not even learn of it to include it in the statistics except for the insurance claim he put in afterward.

Q.   The what?

MR. HAWKES: I am getting sick of this, and if he tries it one more time I am going to ask for a meeting in chambers.

A.   The insurance claim, is what I said.

MR. HAWKES: That is what I mean, precisely.

MR. PURCELL: Your Honor, if Mr. Hawkes wants to complain, I will do my best to give him something real to complain about.

THE COURT: You are threatening each other. It bothers me and it bothers the jury even more, because they are laymen and you are threatening each other over something which in this instance is a very narrow technicality.

MR. HAWKES: Every time the witness gets to that point, he makes him repeat. He suddenly loses his power of hearing. It is a New York lawyer stunt and you know it, Judge.

THE COURT: The court is not unaware of it, Mr. Hawkes.

MR. PURCELL: Just a minute, Your Honor. Are you condoning that New York lawyer characterization?

THE COURT: So far, I am letting you conduct your case, Mr. Purcell. Don't test me on this. And you, Mr. Hawkes, sit down. You proceed, Mr. Purcell, but be forewarned.

MR. PURCELL: I am not going to take that New York lawyer business. I was born and reared in the country. My middle name is Farnum, which was my mother's maiden name, and that is a name well known here, because she was descended from the Farnums who came from New England to the Ohio River Valley.

Oh, beautiful, Bert Klein said to himself. He is so great: he not only gets it in, but with *indignation!*

MR. HAWKES: Did you hear what he just said, judge?

THE COURT: I did indeed, and the jury will disregard it.

MR. HAWKES: That will not satisfy things. I want to move here and now for a mistrial.

THE COURT: The motion is denied. But as singular and irregular as it may have been, what Mr. Purcell just said, I will say it was also singular and irregular that you provoked him into saying it. You baited him and you know it. That does not mean I am excusing you, Mr. Purcell. To the jury I will point out again what the jury already knows—that both lead counsel in this case are from out of town, and from big cities. I do not care if Mr. Purcell had ancestors in Ohio, and I think this jury is too sensible to care about it either. Now, Mr. Purcell, you continue with your cross-examination, and I do not wish to hear how your maternal grandfather tended an open-hearth furnace in Florian. The jury is not stupid. If you try anything like that again, I certainly will entertain a motion for mistrial. But I think the jury's common sense will prevail this one time. That plus the open provocation which caused you to say what you did. But don't press it.

MR. PURCELL: Thank you, Your Honor. I did indeed speak in

the heat of provocation. I agree with you the jury should forget what I said, and I think they will. After all, this is not some backward Alabama town where all you have to do is say "New York" and they find against you.

THE COURT: I said don't press it. Ask your next question.

Q. Very well. I am sorry for the interruption, Mr. Oliphant. I really have very little else to ask. There was one thing. When you first took the stand, Mr. Hawkes asked you about your company, the National Fire Inspection Laboratory, and you said it was a private company.

A. That is correct.

Q. Which means you are not funded by public money?

A. No, we are not. As I said, it is true we do business with the government, various departments, for the census and all the other needs they have for our findings.

Q. But that would be like, say, Boeing or Lockheed doing business on government contracts? They still remain private companies?

A. Exactly.

Q. The Boeing Company may have contracts with the Department of Defense, but still it is a private enterprise, and doing business selling its planes to private companies, like American Airlines or United or Delta?

A. Yes, sir.

Q. And that is true of your company too?

A. By all means. The backbone of our business is our private subscribers.

Q. And who would they be?

A. Well, the manufacturers in the fire-fighting trade, the people who make the foam cans and firemen's coats and every kind of equipment. And private corporations, for their plant fire protection. And the carriers. And the—

Q. The carriers?

A. Yes, of course. Kemper, Sentry, State Farm, the Travelers, Transamerica, Farmers, the Prudential—

MR. HAWKES: Now one minute after he said he was going to stop this he has done it the worst of all. I move a recess and a hearing in chambers. In all my life in court, I have never—

THE COURT: Yes, Mr. Hawkes. We are going to have a recess.

In chambers, Junior Bohr lit a Camel and sank into his desk chair. In front of him, Arthur Hawkes stepped like an angry stork. The court reporter came in, bearing his console, and set himself up beside the desk. The door opened one more time, and Joe Purcell came in, bearing a slim magazine with a picture of the Grand Canyon on its cover. He seated himself on the sofa and opened the magazine to the page he wanted.

"Be sure you take all of this down," Hawkes said to the court reporter. "The plaintiff's attorney has introduced the presence of insurance into this proceeding. I repeat my motion for a mistrial. I have never seen such open-and-shut clear grounds for a mistrial. I can give you a list of citations longer than your arm. I can even cite some from memory, here and now. *Danforth versus Payne Brass*, for one. *Cordry versus Donaldson*."

"Now, Arthur," Purcell said.

"Don't now Arthur me," Hawkes said. He was inflamed but controlled. At the height of passion, he still remembered he was talking on the record. "For you to introduce—"

"Your own witness did the introducing," Purcell said. "And under direct examination by you. I introduced nothing."

"If he did introduce it, it was never done in a way to call attention to it," Hawkes said. "You were the one who made sure the element of improper emphasis was supplied."

"Really?" Purcell said. "I think you'll find *Danforth versus Payne Brass* silent on that point. Not to mention *Cordry versus Donaldson*. Actually, you cut me off at the best part. I was waiting for him to get to Fireman's Fund and Lloyd's of London."

"It's an edgy point," Junior Bohr said. "I know you can supply citations, Arthur—" The judge tilted his head toward the court reporter. "Make that Mr. Hawkes—supply citations, Mr. Hawkes, but they go to cases where the insurance company was identified as the defendant's own insurance carrier, and that of course is not permitted to be brought up in the hearing of the jury. If that is what had happened here, I think I would grant you the mistrial."

Purcell said, "I want to repeat, it was his own witness and I'm accused of being the one to introduce it."

"I think we both know what Mr. Hawkes meant by 'introduce,'" Bohr said. "You did everything possible to accentuate it, and on that basis I think Mr. Hawkes's objection was well founded."

"I say it justifies a mistrial," Hawkes said. "That's how far Mr. Purcell went."

"I don't think he did go that far," the judge said. "But he was right at the edge."

"Then, for the record, you're denying my motion for mistrial?"

"Yes, Mr. Hawkes. Motion denied. For your part, Mr. Purcell, I think you would be well advised to stay off that particular subject from now on."

"Your Honor," Purcell said, "I have only one other question to ask the witness."

"Does it deal with insurance?"

"Yes and no."

"What does that mean?"

"I want to read to the witness just one sentence from an article in this magazine," Purcell said. "This is the latest issue of *United Technologies Magazine,* which is put out for lay readers by the public relations people at United Technologies. They used to be an aircraft company—Pratt and Whitney, Sikorsky helicopters, so forth and so on—and they still are, but they've branched out. Now they have outfits like Carrier air-conditioning and Otis elevators, all under the same roof. To put it in context, I'll read you the section."

He cleared his throat, and read aloud:

- "'In the United States alone, cloud-to-ground flashes have compiled a frightening record of annual death and devastation.

- An estimated 400 persons killed and 1,000 injured, either directly or indirectly, such as by lightning-caused fires. Thunderbolts kill more people than hurricanes, tornadoes, or floods.

- Damage or destruction involving 18,000 homes and 12,000 other buildings. Lightning is the reason behind half of all home and farm fire insurance claims.

- 10,000 forest fires, more than from any other cause.

- An astonishing 85 percent of all cattle deaths.'"

Purcell looked up. "The sentence I want to read from that is the one that goes, 'Lightning is the reason behind half of all home and farm fire insurance claims.' I simply want to ask the witness if he agrees with that statement."

"Let him do it," Hawkes said huskily. "And you'll hear another motion for mistrial. Will you deny that one too?"

"Just a minute," Junior Bohr said. "You say that's the United Technologies magazine? I don't understand. What has lightning got to do with that company?"

"As I said, it's a lay magazine, Judge," Purcell said. "Sort of soft-sell public relations. There's a part further on where it says United Technologies takes lightning into account in designing its aircraft systems against being struck by lightning. It's the kind of article you could find in any magazine—even on the feature page of a newspaper."

"But you only want to read that one sentence. The one about insurance?"

"I can read the whole article, if you want."

"Once again your purpose is to call insurance to their attention," Hawkes said.

"It doesn't refer to the defendants' insurance," Purcell said. "It doesn't even refer to the insurance in a court case. This is no-fault insurance. You have a fire, you make your insurance claim. It doesn't go beyond that."

Junior Bohr was shaking his head. "No, Mr. Purcell, I think you should go no further with this line of questioning. I think you have adequately emphasized the idea that insurance exists in this world. I would advise you to leave it at that."

"Your Honor," Purcell said. "If you rule that way, then you are cutting off my line of reply to the main contention of the defense. The point is that this kind of thing is foreseeable: they claim nobody can seek recompense for an act of God, but their own witness just emphasized the fact that this particular act of God is known to cause fire. So you should make the tank cars fireworthy." Purcell pulled at his ear. "After all, Junior—I mean, Your Honor—" If the court reporter, an extra man imported from Cincinnati just for this trial, noticed the slip, he gave no sign. But Junior Bohr noticed it. "No, Mr. Purcell," he broke in. "I've made my ruling on this. We have heard the word 'insurance' one time too many already, and not to your disadvantage, either, no matter who introduced it or how it might bear on the jury. If you want to make the point of reply you just mentioned, you have every right to do so, but you are going to have to find another way of doing it. I don't want insurance pursued with this witness any farther."

"Are we off the record?" Hawkes asked. The judge nodded and the reporter stopped his stenotyping. "I'm not happy with this at all."

"Join the club," Junior Bohr said. He motioned dismissal to the court reporter and waited till he had left. "Joe," he said then to Purcell, "I'm fucked if I understand you."

Purcell stood up and headed for the door. He paused there and looked back at the judge and Arthur Hawkes. Then he grinned. "Nobody's perfect," he said.

Back in the courtroom, he swung in beside Bert Klein at the counsel table and told him what had happened. "At the end the judge said he was fucked if he understood me."

"What'd he mean by that?"

"I think it was just his cryptic way of saying that if I'd opened the cross-examination by reading from that article, I could have got away with it. And that way the jury would have heard it."

Klein put a palm to his chin. "Do you think he was right?"

"I don't know. But if I'd read from that article, then the word 'insurance' would have come from my mouth, and Arthur could have based his motion for a mistrial on that. It might have made things a little tougher for me in fighting it off."

"You're right," Klein said. "I gather it was tough enough for you in chambers the way it was."

"A little dicey at one moment, maybe. But I really didn't think any of Arthur's citations would hold up."

"Still," Klein said, "no reason to take that extra chance. And this way you still got the article on the record in chambers."

"You mean for when we appeal?"

Klein colored. "I mean *if* we appeal."

Purcell grinned again. "Well, when or if, it'll make damn good reading for a loser to take to the court of appeals. I played the righteous indignation for all it was worth. How he was robbing me of my only line of argument, and all the rest. It's what Max always says. If you have to lose a case, make the best record for when you appeal."

"I was watching the jury after the judge called the recess," Bert said. "They looked disappointed."

"Did they look like they understood why the judge called for the break?"

"Hard to tell. Not really they didn't, no. I think they were just enjoying watching you and Arthur fight."

"Good," Joe said. "That makes Arthur the heavy. He makes the motion and the judge clears the room. Entertainment's over." He tugged at his ear. "Except that maybe Junior's right. Why *didn't* I just read that damn sentence to that witness? I bet I could have got away with it. Damned if I couldn't."

16

Arthur Hawkes used fifteen expert witnesses—specialists in everything from heat transfer to fire-fighting technique—to offset the experts the A&P had called, and their testimony did just that. Purcell battled but did not shake them on cross-examination. The sum of their testimony was that the Jumbo Nellie Nellie was designed as a safe car, manufactured as a safe car, and in perfect condition in all respects at the time of the fireball. At three different points, from three different witnesses, Hawkes elicited testimony about the safety valve atop the tank car, so constructed and heat-resistant that it was found all but intact in the rubble of the explosion and received a clean bill of health from the government's investigators. Purcell did not even cross-examine on that point. Obviously, if there was the slightest chance of flawed design, manufacture, assembly into the tank car, or working condition, the valve company would be a named defendant. For Purcell to take up that part of it would only accentuate the absence of that defendant—something Hawkes had already pointed up in his opening statement to the jury. Purcell's sole consolation was that the defense case was unbearably dull. The defense experts took up eight full days on the witness stand. Mother Nine still kept to his dogged note taking, but even he looked bored. DeSabitini, the plaintiff's favorite, was beginning to seem weary. Juror number seven, the 64-year-old grandmother named Hilda Graysmith, lasted barely through the morning sessions, then slept through the afternoons.

One morning Hawkes called someone who promised to be more interesting, less technical, and certainly impressive by way of position held. He was the president of the N. Nance Company, manufacturer of the tank car—to be sure, of the entire Jumbo Nellie Nellie line. Trevor Peters was his name, a trim, twinkling presence with dimpled right cheek who woke number seven up when he smiled at her. She beamed right back.

And his testimony proved in all manner nontechnical. Following the barrage of testimonials to the perfection of his product, this smiling but earnest young man—he was barely into his forties—lent example to the acknowledged, world-class skill of Arthur Hawkes in one of the most overlooked techniques of trial advocacy—the ability to present witnesses in the optimum order of appearance. The crux of his testimony was contained in his replies to two successive questions by the defense counsel:

Q.   You manufactured this tank car in accordance with a design approved by the Department of Transportation?

A.   Yes, sir, that is what we did.

Q.   Could you have manufactured it any other way?

A.   No, sir. The approved form was the only way we were permitted to manufacture it.

And on cross-examination, Purcell followed the lead of Hawkes and stayed away from the technical side. For one thing, it could only be repetitive: experts from both camps had already specialized the subject to death. True, Purcell could accentuate a technical point to his own possible advantage here or there, but at this juncture it was not worth the risk of giving Hawkes the edge of having presented this witness in his more appealing form. Nor did Purcell want to put the jury back to sleep. It was most to his purpose to strike from a new direction:

Q.   Have you ever heard of a man named Albert Simon?

A.   Yes.

Q.   Did you know him?

A.   No. He died a few years before I came with the Nance Company.

Q.   But you know who he was.

A.   Yes. He was the controller of the Nance Company.

Q.   This approval you got for the design of the jumbo tank car, from the Department of Transportation. This approval came from the DOT in Washington, did it not?

A.   I believe so, yes. It was early 1966.

Q.   And at the time that approval came, do you know if it is true that your Mr. Simon happened to be in Washington on company business at that same time?

A.   I knew you would want me to check the record on that point, Mr. Purcell. You are right. Mr. Simon was in Washington at that time.

Q.   On company business?

A.   That is right.

Q.   Did that company business have anything to do with the Department of Transportation handling of your proposal to change the design of your jumbo tank car?

A.   Not to my knowledge.

Q.   Not to your knowledge, you say.

A.   Well, again, I was not with the company at that time. But I do know from the company records that Mr. Simon was in Washington for totally different reasons.

Q.   And those reasons were what?

A.   He was having meetings at the Interstate Commerce Commission.

Q.   I see. You're quite sure of that?

A.   Well, as I say, I did check back into the files on this point, and found the report he had filed.

MR. HAWKES: I have copies of the report here at the table if the court please.

THE COURT: Well, so long as it has come up we can have it marked. Mr. Bailiff, will you see to that? And what number do you have for it?

THE BAILIFF: I have 141.

THE COURT: To be marked as defense exhibit 141.

MR. HAWKES: Perhaps Mr. Purcell will stipulate 141 into evidence and allow the witness to summarize the contents briefly.

MR. PURCELL: Yes, I have no objection to that.

THE WITNESS: Well, briefly, at that point in time, there was a very heavy expansion of imports of middle-eastern oil, because of the demands of the war in Vietnam, and the crude product was being refined here in the continental United States, then transshipped across the Pacific. So a need was foreseen to build additional railroad tank cars to handle this extra traffic.

Q.   You couldn't just put the oil in a tanker ship at Saudi Arabia and carry it in an eastern direction through the Indian Ocean to Vietnam?

A.   Well, no. As I already said, the refining capacity was concentrated stateside. I believe also there were Defense Department considerations involved. They did not want to have to protect tankers in the Indian Ocean with the ships of the seventh fleet, just to prevent some military incident that might widen the conflict.

Q.   But at the same time, were we not also increasing our imports of oil from Indonesia?

A.   I believe we were. But it would still have to be refined here in the continental United States.

Q.   Couldn't they have refined it in California, then shipped it back to Vietnam in the refined state? That way they wouldn't have needed extra railroad cars.

A.   Well, I see what you are saying. But the answer there is no. I should have begun with this part of it, in answering you. The problem there, you see, was that the Indonesian oil is a very high-quality, low-sulfur product. And at that point the pressure was starting up for the first time from the environmental groups in this country to clean up the air. So there was a premium for the users of that clean Indonesian oil, particularly the utilities—the power companies—to put it into domestic use here, not just return it back to the Far East for our use there.

THE COURT: Even if you had refined it in California and return-shipped it back to Vietnam, then California would have had to get replacement oil from somewhere else, so you still would have needed the extra tank cars?

THE WITNESS: That is right, Your Honor.

THE COURT: And there was no Alaskan pipeline in existence at that time?

THE WITNESS: That is also correct.

THE COURT: I am just trying to speed this up, Mr. Purcell. It seems to me we are going very far afield from the subject at hand before us in this trial. If you could help the witness speed it up, it would be good. Can you do that?

MR. PURCELL: I will try, Your Honor. So, Mr. Peters, you say that your Mr. Simon was in Washington to talk with the Defense Department about the construction of additional tank cars?

A.   Not the Defense Department. The ICC. They were the ones involved in the question of what company would build what kind of rolling stock for the railroads.

Q.   And you wanted your share of that business?

A.   I would certainly think so. Our company is in business to build tank cars.

Q.   All right. I have not read Mr. Simon's report, but if you say that we have just heard a summary of what it was about, I will be ready to accept that as being so. I also think it gives all of us an interesting inside look on how the war in Vietnam tied us to greater dependence on mideast oil.

MR. HAWKES: Don't leave out the environmentalists.

THE COURT: Don't leave out the Norwegians and the British and the North Sea either. The only thing we are leaving out is the subject of this trial. Anytime you want to get back to that, Mr. Purcell, it will make us glad.

MR. PURCELL: I was about to do that, Your Honor.

Q.   Now that you've established, Mr. Peters, what it was that Mr. Simon was doing in Washington, did he go to any other government department while he was there? Other than the ICC?

A.   Not according to his report, no.

Q.   But you have no firsthand knowledge?

A.   No. I have said, that was before my time. But if he had, I'm certain he would have included it in the report.

Q.   You don't think it's possible he paid a visit to the Department of Transportation?

A.   Why would he have done that?

Q.   I don't know. I am asking you.

A.   I can't imagine why he would have done that.

Q.   Then let me assist your imagination. Mr. Simon was in Washington at the same time the Department of Transportation was issuing its okay for the design of your jumbo tank cars. Does that strike you as interesting?

A.   No.

Q.   Just a coincidence, then?

A.   I don't know how to characterize it, Mr. Purcell. I don't know that I'd even try. This was never one-on-one between Nance and the DOT. There are other companies that make tank cars. You might check their records and see if they had any of their people in Washington at that particular time. I can only tell you that there is no record in our files at the Nance Company indicating that Mr. Simon was in any way involved in that.

Q.   Doesn't the tank car industry—not just Nance, but the others—have a full-time lobbyist in Washington?

A.   Well, yes, we do. All large industries have lobbyists. There is absolutely nothing evil or wrong in it. I expect you trial lawyers have your own lobby, and a political action committee, and all the rest. When the Senate turned down the bill for no-fault automobile insurance, I would expect your people had done some lobbying to get that result.

Q.   Would you like to hear why that was a proper result?

THE COURT: The witness will not answer that question. I do not care whether the witness would like to hear it, Mr. Purcell. The court does not want to hear it. This is not an automobile case.

MR. PURCELL: He was being gratuitous, Your Honor.

THE COURT: I think you brought it on yourself. Let's say everybody agrees that lobbyists in Washington are a normal, natural part of the process by which the system operates in this country. I don't see why you even brought the subject up.

Q.   Mr. Peters, as I understand your testimony, you don't rule out that Mr. Simon could have spoken to someone at DOT while he was in Washington on that trip, right?

A.   About the approval of the jumbos?

Q.   Exactly.

A.   I don't rule it out but it would have been most unlikely.

Q.   Why? The DOT was in the transportation business and Nance was in the transportation business. Are you saying Mr. Simon didn't even know anybody at the department?

A.   I'm not saying that at all.

Q.   Then why is it unlikely?

A.   Because the approval of the jumbos was a matter of the design of the cars, and Mr. Simon was not a design man. He was controller of the company. He dealt solely in financial matters, not engineering matters. From what I hear, he didn't even know what a blueprint was.

Q.   Did he have to? You concede it's highly likely he knew people
at the Department of Transportation. He was in Washington at the
time this approval came down—you concede that too. You say he
specialized in financial matters. Here you got a green light to build
the biggest line of tank cars in the history of the world. Are you
saying that was of no financial significance to your company?

A.   I am saying simply that Mr. Simon had another reason for
being in Washington and that he would have been a very unlikely
person to involve himself in a design matter of any kind. And I think
there is no doubt on either of those points.

MR. PURCELL: I have no further questions.

THE COURT: Mr. Hawkes?

MR. HAWKES: Just one question, Your Honor.

THE COURT: Ask it. Then we will have a 10-minute recess.

MR. HAWKES: You were talking about the problems brought
on by the Vietnam war and the environmentalists, Mr. Peters, back
there at the time Mr. Simon was in Washington. Now, in this
report Mr. Simon made of his visit to the ICC, as they talked about
different kinds of tank cars, did they ever discuss the jumbo car?

A.   No. That just didn't enter into it. There was no added need
for those cargoes—liquid petroleum gas and the rest—brought on
by the war. The jumbos never even came up.

In the men's room down the hall, Purcell and Klein waited while two of
the jurors, Leonard Still, the unemployed bottling-plant worker, and
Lucas Pointer, the poultry wholesaler, relieved their bladders, then nodded cheerily to them and took their place.

"After all the years of medical malpractice cases we've had," Purcell
said, "I have become an expert at diagnosis."

"What brought that up?"

"I believe number eight has the clap," Joe said. "Did you see the way
he was standing, while he was going, bracing himself with his fist against
the wall?"

Klein began to laugh. "I missed it," he said. "I was thinking of that last
question Arthur asked."

"You mean the very last one? The one on redirect? Leave it to Arthur.
He doesn't miss a bet. He was going to get the environmentalists in there
just one more time."

"Is that why he did it?"

"It's why I would have done it," Joe said. He moved, zipping, to the washbasin. "This is coal country, don't forget. High-sulfur coal. It burns dirty, so the EPA puts out all kinds of restrictions and half the world around here is out of work."

"You didn't do so badly yourself," Bert said. "I told Perry Muncrief I wished he could come to watch you work on Peters."

"Why didn't you bring him along?"

"He's feeding transcript into the computer, that's why. It takes forever. I don't want him building a backlog and falling behind."

It was Max Aranow who had given Klein the go-ahead on a computer.

"Get a computer," Aranow had told him. "Not because any of your arguments impress me, but because they obviously impress you. Somebody on the jury will laugh in the wrong place and you'll tell yourself that would never have happened if you'd used a computer. It's not worth shooting our morale. Get a computer. Enjoy."

"I was just arguing the difficulties," Bert said.

"In the words of Winston Churchill," Max Aranow said, "'do not argue the difficulties...they can argue for themselves.'"

Now, as Bert Klein dried his hands at the basin in the men's room of the Mundelein courthouse, Joe Purcell said, "I was just thinking of something Max said. When he came back from a trip to Paris."

Still thinking Aranow-and-computer, Bert blinked. "Paris? What was he doing in Paris?"

"I suppose he was eating. They don't play baseball in France. Anyway, he went to the men's room at some restaurant, together with a couple of Frenchmen he was with, and they were fascinated the way he washed his hands *after*. In France they do it before. It's one of those things that the more you think about..."

They exited the men's room and returned to court. The witness waiting for them there was Winston McHale, of the Mid-Central Railroad. Red of face, downcast of mien, he took the stand and let Arthur Hawkes lead him where he would.

Hawkes led off with the lost tank car.

Q. The court has already heard these dates, but just to make certain, your records show that this tank car was filled at Whiting, Indiana, on what date?

A. February 27.

Q.   And delivered to Florian, Ohio, the Tri-State Gas siding there, on what date?

A.   April 29.

Q.   And those dates were in the same year, of course?

A.   What kind of a question is that?

Q.   I mean we are talking about a 2-month delay here, is that correct? Not a 14-month delay. Or a 26-month delay.

A.   Yes, of course. Two months.

Q.   And have you checked your records to see if there were other times, perhaps in other years and other places, when other tank cars operated by your railroad also failed to arrive within the normally expected range of time?

A.   Yes.

Q.   And were there any such occasions?

A.   Three, over a period of 20 years.

Q.   So we are talking about a total of four. Four in 20 years?

A.   Yes.

Q.   And what was the longest delay of the four?

A.   This one. The Jumbo Nellie Nellie at Florian.

Mother Nine was jabbing away at his notebook as McHale played his own gravedigger, and at their table, Bert leaned toward Purcell and muttered, "He's asking all *your* questions. What are *you* going to say?"

"All I can think of is role reversal," Joe murmured back. "He's killing him so I have to be nice to him."

But Hawkes, of course, was only doing the same thing with Winston McHale that Purcell had done in telling the jury about the Specimen's rape conviction, before the trial even began: preempting something the other side was bound to bring up by being the one to bring it up first—what trial lawyers called "drawing the sting."

Now he took McHale's figure of only four overdue tank cars in 20 years. How many tank cars had the railroad moved in those 20 years? McHale did not know the figure.

Q.   Didn't you tell me you were going to get that figure for me and bring it into court with you?

A.   Yes, but nobody could find it.

Q.   Could you give us an educated guess?

A.   Well, it would be in the millions.

Q.   Millions of tank car movements?

A.   Yes.

Q.   How long has the Mid-Central Railroad been in business?

A.   About 110 years.

Q.   About? You don't have an exact figure?

A.   I'm afraid not. For a while in the 1800s it was the same railroad but not with the name Mid-Central. It depends which year you count from.

Q.   And how long have you been serving the community of Florian?

A.   About that same amount of time.

Q.   Again, you're not sure?

A.   Well, I might have been able to get the answer on that one for you, but I didn't know you were going to ask the question.

Q.   But you've been serving Florian, and the entire area here, for over a century?

A.   Yes.

Q.   How would you describe the service?

A.   We've always tried to be helpful.

Q.   Can you give an example of that?

A.   Yes. The 1937 flood on the Ohio River. The big one. We used trains to carry food in and take people out.

Q.   Do you have any figures on that?

MR. PURCELL: Objection. Immaterial.

THE COURT: Sustained. What happened in the Ohio River area in 1937 just doesn't bear on what happened in Florian last year.

Q.   Then I will ask you this, Mr. McHale. What was the reaction of your railroad when you learned of the accident to the tank car at Florian?

MR. PURCELL: Object.

THE COURT: Sustained.

MR. HAWKES: If the court please, I am simply being prevented from asking one question after another.

THE COURT: You may ask other questions.

MR. HAWKES: I have no other questions, Your Honor. I should say I do have other questions, but none that you will permit me to ask. You may cross-examine, Brother Purcell.

"Jesus!" Bert Klein hissed. "I didn't know Arthur gave up that easy." "Too easy," Joe growled, and got to his feet.

MR. PURCELL: Mr. McHale, I'm correct, am I not, that you talked with your counsel here, Mr. Hawkes, before you took the witness stand?

A.   Yes.

Q.   And how long did that rehearsal last?

A.   Rehearsal?

Q.   Yes. Rehearsal. That was quite a little act the two of you just put on, don't you think?

MR. HAWKES: Objection.

THE COURT: Sustained. Ask something substantive, Mr. Purcell.

MR. PURCELL: It is substantive, judge.

THE COURT: Specific as well? Let me hear a specific.

MR. PURCELL: I refer specifically, just as an example, to the first question Mr. Hawkes asked of this witness about other tank cars. Maybe the court reporter can find it. It came at the part where Mr. Hawkes referred to a 26-month delay.

MR. HAWKES: There was no 26-month delay.

MR. PURCELL: You referred to the possibility of one.

MR. HAWKES: Your Honor, what is he trying to do here?

THE REPORTER: "And have you checked your records to see if there were other times, perhaps in other years and other places, when other tank cars operated by your railroad also failed to arrive within the normally expected range of time?"

Q.   Thank you. Now specifically, Mr. McHale, you rehearsed that question, didn't you?

A.   Can you be more specific than that?

Q.   Yes, I can. There's a phrase in there: "failed to arrive within the normally expected range of time." Am I right?

A.   Yes. What is it supposed to mean?

Q.   I was just about to ask you that.

A.   Maybe you should ask Mr. Hawkes. They were his words, not mine.

Q.   No, I am asking you. "Normally expected range of time"— what does that mean? If a freight train is an hour late showing up? Or 3 hours? Or a day? Or what? What constitutes a late train?

A.   Well, he did not say late train. He said delayed, not late.

Q.   Is there a difference? I think the jury would love to hear. I know I would.

A.   Well, you can say that all late trains must have been delayed.

Q.   Then can't you also say that all delayed trains must be late?

A.   Not necessarily. A train can make up time after a delay.

Q.   I am still trying to get a time frame here. You said you had only four delayed trains in 20 years.

A.   No, sir. I said we only had four delayed tank cars in 20 years. In the Florian accident, for example, as far as I know every train that car was attached to operated on schedule. It was the car that took 2 months to get there, not any train.

MR. PURCELL: Your Honor, I count four members of the jury who are laughing. My problem is, I don't know whether they're laughing at the witness or me.

THE COURT: Now all nine of them are laughing and you still don't know. Perhaps this will be a good time for the lunchtime recess. You can resume your questioning after lunch.

MR. PURCELL: I think I will have no questions of this witness after lunch.

"You were kind of hectoring him, you know," Bert said. They were driving back to their motel, for a quick bite there. Purcell had taken to doing this more often than not, to check his incoming mail.

"I shouldn't have asked him any questions at all," Joe said. "I let Arthur set me up."

There had been nothing from Marcy since her sudden departure the day after the audition. Five days later Purcell had mailed her a check for $5,000. Still no response.

Nor was there anything from her in today's mail. His secretary had, however, forwarded this month's statement from his bank. Joe opened it and looked at the summary. Marcy had cashed the check.

An elbow away, Bert Klein said, "Strike up the band, chief. I have a nice note here from Andrea. She's my new favorite."

"Andrea who?"

"Bascomb. You remember."

"Ah, yes." *Strike Up the Band.* Well. So Marcy had taken the money. What was it, should one suppose? A peace offering or severance pay? She had not been in touch with him. And he for his part had made no effort to get in touch with her. What would he say if he did? The only thing he could possibly say to her was the one thing he was unwilling to say: that he was giving up on the chance of having *The Last Laugh* staged, through the financing of Leonard Kinder.

It wasn't till they were in the car again, returning to the courthouse, that Joe remembered the other thing. "*Strike Up the Band,*" he said to Bert.

"That's what I said back at the motel," Bert said.

"I know. Did you ever see the show?"

"What show?"

"Ask a stupid question, get a stupid answer," Purcell said. "The Gershwins. Ira wrote the lyric, and one part of it nobody remembers. It's not from the chorus. It's from the verse, which nobody ever sings. Worse than that, this is from the second stanza of the verse, which nobody even knows exists. I guarantee you've never heard it."

"No," Bert said. "But I've got a feeling I'm about to."

"Just two lines," Purcell said, and sang:

We don't know what we're fighting for
But we didn't know the last time...

"You're worried about how the trial's going to come out," Bert said. "Aren't you?"

"Am I?" Purcell said, and they returned to court for the afternoon session.

It was again a tribute to Hawkes's skill in orchestrating the order of his witnesses that directly in the wake of Winston McHale he brought to the stand a gaunt but feisty figure—Kenneth Laurents was his name—who worked for the American Petroleum Institute. Laurents was a generalist with expertise on every aspect of moving LPG on the rails, from the design of tank cars to filling them to unloading them. To set the stage and get the jury alert, Hawkes began by deliberately baiting Purcell:

Q.   You were sitting here in the courtroom while Mr. Purcell was cross-examining the last witness?

A.   Yes.

Q.   Then it will be evident to you what Brother Purcell was trying to establish. Obviously he was—

MR. PURCELL: Object.

THE COURT: Sustained.

MR. HAWKES: Wait a minute. He objects and you sustain and neither of you even know what I was going to say.

THE COURT: In the sense that I cannot speak for Mr. Purcell, you may be right. Speaking for myself, I know what you were going to say.

MR. HAWKES: I have the right to frame a question.

THE COURT: You have repeatedly abused that right in the course of this proceeding. Every day it just gets worse. The only thing that has saved you is the court's dedication to impartiality. By which I mean Mr. Purcell is just as guilty as you are. Your reputation as trial lawyers precedes both of you into this courtroom. In fact, this court has had the singular experience of watching the two of you at work on a previous occasion. You are so accomplished at your craft that there have been times when this court was at the point of suggesting a slight change in ordinary procedure—namely, that in the interest of simplifying things and speeding them along, we have the witnesses ask the questions and you give the answers. Now, I want no more of this. Resume the questioning of the witness, Mr. Hawkes.

"Patient" might be the word to describe how Arthur Hawkes—and Joe Purcell, no less than his rival—listened to the judge's words. Both lawyers knew it would not change anything, that in addressing witnesses their questions would be more declarative, time and again, than interrogatory. *Unaffected*, certainly. Both lawyers knew it. And beyond question, Junior Bohr knew it too. Nor was there all that much he could do about it. He might temper things for an hour or two, but Hawkes and Purcell were bound to revert to normal.

The problem of the moment, as it confronted Arthur Hawkes, was purely tactical. In pursuance of his chess-playing Bristol Theme he had purposely left Winston McHale, the Mid-Central man, open to Purcell's savaging. There was no getting around the fact that the Jumbo Nellie Nellie had been misdirected in transit, that having left the loading track filled to wintertime level it was delivered for unloading at summertime temperatures. No question that in warmer months more space would have been allowed for vapor expansion. And no question that the railroad was manifestly at fault for the transit snafu, an open-and-shut demonstration of negligence on Mid-Central's part.

But only by the deliberate isolating of one of his pieces could Hawkes bring the next piece into play, in the person of his present witness, the petroleum-institute expert named Kenneth Laurents. And he played his next piece like the grand master he was. In just one hour of brilliantly crafted direct examination, Hawkes summed up his defense, tied a ribbon around it, and laid it in the jury's lap.

First, he underscored the point made with McHale, that the computer's misrouting of the tank car was a one-in-a-million event. Then the jury was reminded of the phenomenal record-breaking May heat wave, and how this "supernatural" ambient temperature caused the safety relief valve to open and vent propane vapor into the surrounding air. And at that instant the lightning struck, igniting the vapor. A few seconds sooner or later and nothing would have happened. Everything had to conspire in wildly perverse coincidence for this bizarre accident—this act of God—to occur.

Purcell glanced furtively at the jury. His worst fears were confirmed. They were all leaning forward, attentive and receptive. The defense bells were ringing loud and clear.

And then Hawkes, with true instinct, went for the frosting on the cake. Having knocked the railroad off the board, he took a shot at rehabilitating it. He shifted gears and tone.

Q. Just a few more questions on a different subject if you don't mind, sir. Do you happen to know the amount of heat generated by a bolt of lightning?

A. Well, current can surge through a thunderbolt with a power of a billion kilowatts. In everyday language, that is 60,000 degrees Fahrenheit.

Q.   And in everyday language, could you give us a picture of how hot that is?

A.   About five times hotter than the surface of the sun.

Q.   Do you know what the temperature was in Florian, Ohio, the day this particular tank car was delivered?

A.   I believe it was 99 degrees.

Q.   So the temperature in that bolt of lightning would have been approximately 59,900 degrees hotter than the prevailing outside temperature in Florian that day?

MR. PURCELL: Objection. How can he testify to that particular bolt of lightning?

THE COURT: Sustained. Rephrase the question.

Q.   Very well. The temperature in any bolt of lightning that happened to strike in the Florian area that day.

A.   Yes. That could be up to that figure.

Q.   Then if we assume that the tank car had been less full for summertime temperatures instead of wintertime, if lightning had struck that day, in your opinion as an expert could the heat of the lightning have caused the LPG to expand and open the relief valve with a result identical to what it actually was in this case?

A.   Yes, sir.

Q.   That tank car could have arrived in Florian the day it did, filled to summer level instead of winter level, and the same chain of events might have taken place?

A.   Yes, sir.

Hawkes waved an inviting hand to Purcell to cross-examine. Joe's first task was to appear to be glad of the opportunity:

MR. PURCELL: You agree, I take it, that there are different accepted filling levels for these tank cars, wintertime versus summertime? Cold weather versus hot?

A.   Yes. It's just that in this particular case it probably would not have made any difference. Not in view of how it happened. The accident, I mean.

Q.   Your answer was yes, am I correct? There is a difference in the filling levels?

A.   Yes.

Q.   And is there a reason for that?

A.   Not one that would have applied in this case.

Q.   I asked you if there was a reason for it.

A.   Yes.

Q.   Will you tell us that reason?

A.   It allows for more space for gaseous expansion in hot weather than in cold. But—

Q.   Just a minute. Please just answer my questions. The reason you've just given: It has to do with safety, does it not?

A.   Partially, yes. But it is a secondary matter.

Q.   Safety is a secondary matter?

A.   For all practical purposes, it would be in this case. The main reason the particular line of tank cars here are filled to lower capacity in hotter weather is because there is not as much customer demand for LPG in summer as in winter. So that is the real reason you find the cars filled to different levels at different times of year.

Q.   And safety has nothing to do with it?

A.   I didn't say that. I said safety was a distinctly second-order factor.

Q.   And in this particular case—

A.   In this particular case the level of filling probably made no difference.

Q.   Thank you for answering a question that wasn't asked. My question, if you will allow me to ask it, was going to be as follows: Could a summertime filling have produced a longer span of time, before the explosion—so more people could have been evacuated?

MR. HAWKES: Object. Speculation.

THE COURT: Sustained.

MR. PURCELL: All right. You maintain, however, that the extent to which you fill a tank car with hazardous material has very little to do with safety?

A.   Mr. Purcell, the world is filled with things classified as hazardous materials. They have to be transported from the producer to the consumer, so people can make use of them. Obviously the greater the volume, the more you can argue there's more of it. One gallon of liquefied petroleum gas is not as dangerous as 33,000 gallons. An empty tank car is one thing, a filled tank car is another. It is a matter of degree.

Q.   And the fuller it is, the more dangerous it is?

A.   It is a matter of degree. An empty tank car is an empty tank car.

Q.   And a full tank car is a full tank car?

A.   Yes. But the difference there is the extreme degree. In the case of the car at Florian, you are talking about the difference between cold-weather payload and hot-weather payload, and there the difference in degree is much smaller. So small in this case as to have been probably no difference at all.

Q.   And you say that in this case, leaving extra room for the gas to expand would have no bearing on the question of safety?

A.   That is correct. In fact, allowance is built in for extra expansion. That is what the safety relief valve on top of the tank car is for.

Q.   I know. You are saying the same chain of events could have happened just as easily in cold weather as in hot.

A.   When a fire is started by lightning, yes.

Q.   So lightning would be the first link in the chain?

A.   That's the assumption here, is it not?

Q.   Yes, indeed. But tell me, Mr. Laurents, does lightning strike as often in cold weather as in hot? Anywhere near as often?

MR. HAWKES: Objection. The witness is not an expert on lightning.

MR. PURCELL: You asked him the temperature of a bolt of lightning. If he could answer that question, he can answer this question.

THE COURT: Yes, I'll allow the question. You can go ahead and answer, Mr. Laurents.

A.   I just wouldn't know the frequencies there.

Q.   I'm not asking for scientific knowledge, Mr. Laurents. Just your own powers of observation. Are you apt to have more thunderstorms, more lightning, in summer or winter? Hot weather or cold?

A.   I think more of it with warmer weather, yes.

Q.   So if that tank car had been delivered on schedule, just a few days after it was filled back in February, the whole chain of events might never have happened?

MR. HAWKES: Calls for speculation.

THE COURT: Overruled. Witness may answer.

A.   It didn't have to happen when it did happen. If lightning was there, it could have happened and it did happen. If lightning wasn't there, I guess it wouldn't have happened.

Q.   But there was a greater chance of lightning in hot weather than in cold?

MR. HAWKES: He's badgering. Question's already been answered.

THE COURT: Yes, Mr. Purcell. Counsel is right.

Q.   Did your industry ever consider the fact that it ought to fill these tank cars to a lower hot-weather level no matter what time of year the cars are actually filled?

A.   I don't know why that would be relevant. The matter of degree is something I've already testified to.

Q.   Because tank cars get lost, that's why it's relevant. They lost one here. It showed up 2 months late.

MR. HAWKES: That isn't even a question.

THE COURT: Yes, Mr. Purcell. What answer was called for?

MR. PURCELL: The answer that the industry simply puts greed ahead of safety, filling those tank cars to the brim the way they do.

MR. HAWKES: That's awful.

THE COURT: We're going to strike everything you've said, Mr. Purcell, from the point of the last answer the witness gave. Don't do it anymore. That's not just a suggestion, it's a warning.

MR. PURCELL: I have no further questions.

MR. HAWKES: And no further answers either, I trust. No redirect, Your Honor.

The Bristol Theme had done all Hawkes could have asked it to do. Purcell had landed a light punch at the end of Laurents's testimony: if the Jumbo Nellie Nellie had been delivered on schedule in late February, the chance of a lightning strike at that time of year would have been far less than it was the first Monday in May. But—and this Hawkes would be entitled to argue to the jury in his summation for the defense—undoubtedly by the beginning of May another tank car might then have been on the siding in Florian, waiting to be unloaded, and the same accident could thus have happened regardless.

But over and above that, Hawkes had used the Bristol Theme to set a pretty trap. By letting the railroad take its pratfall for misdirecting the Jumbo Nellie Nellie, Hawkes was doing some misdirecting of his own. He was letting the full force of Purcell's assault land in the area of negligence. And no jury was going to come in with a slam-bang multi-million-dollar monster verdict because of a human mistake in a railroad switching operation. If Hawkes could not win the case outright, at least this way he could limit the award, keep it to hundreds of thousands of dollars rather than millions. And that would be as good as a win. The business of the wayward tank car took away from the focus on product liability, let alone conspiracy. If Joe Purcell wanted a mighty judgment, he would have to prove that what was unsafe was the Jumbo Nellie Nellie itself, not the time of year it happened to show up.

Worst of all was the way the act of God defense was taking hold. If the happenstance of that bolt of lightning was something beyond anyone's control, so was the record heat in Florian that day. The dim, recessed perception came upon Purcell that Hawkes had maneuvered him into the position where he was giving Arthur two acts of God for the price of one.

17

Of three defendant corporations in the Fireball lawsuit, two had by now been represented on the witness stand, in the persons of Trevor Peters, president of Nance, and McHale, the general freight manager for Mid-Central. All that remained from the defendant trio was North American Petroleum, and there was no question who would testify for NAP.

It had to be Harrison McKenna, for he would speak not only in his role as ranking vice president of the oil giant but as well in his earlier capacity as assistant secretary of the Department of Transportation. And once again, Hawkes in unfolding his game plan had chosen his witness well.

In contrast to Winston McHale, McKenna was in all ways an articulate, persuasive witness, made more credible by his looks, which were those of the handsome, silver-haired statesman—as indeed he had been, having served not only as an assistant cabinet secretary but as a candidate for the United States Senate.

"He looks like that guy who always plays the desk admiral in the old War World Two movies on television," Bert Klein said to Joe Purcell.

Purcell nodded. "Or the VD doctor in the training films."

On the witness stand, Harrison McKenna was explaining his early background as a railroad executive, prior to his joining the Department of Transportation as chief of its railroad division.

"Did you have a subspecialty?" Arthur Hawkes asked.

"Yes," the witness said. "If you mean freight as against passenger—"

"That's precisely what I mean."

"Yes," McKenna said. "Then I would say my subspecialty was freight."

Q.   And freight was a more important consideration, from the Department of Transportation's standpoint, than passenger traffic? At least while you served with the department?

A.   Yes, but not just while I served with the department. The prime function of railroads everywhere in the world has always been to carry goods, not people.

Q.   And that is still true today?

A.   More than ever. The airplane and the automobile and the bus have taken over from the railroads as people movers.

Q.   And you don't foresee a reversal of that? Because of the energy situation, hasn't there been a lot of talk about more railroad cars to attract more passengers?

A.   You have asked me two questions. The answer to the second question is yes. I happen to agree that there is no more economical means of moving people than by putting steel wheels on a steel track.

Q.   Even though you are now an executive of North American Petroleum? If you took all that gasoline away from automobiles and airplanes and buses, wouldn't that cut into your sales?

A.   What is right for this country is, in my judgment, right for its oil companies too. Oil profits are not the only thing in this world. But, to answer the first part of the two-part question you asked just a moment ago, I would not agree with the word "reversal." The railroads can end up carrying a greater percentage of passenger traffic than they do today, but on a volume basis you are not going to see fewer cars and buses on the road, or fewer airplanes in the sky. You are going to see more of them.

Q.   And so it follows that we are going to see more railroad tank cars too, to carry the fuel?

A.   No. Perhaps fewer tank cars.

Q.   Why? Wouldn't they be essential to feed this volume growth you speak of?

A.   Not necessarily. Pipelines and trucks and barges all are competing actively with the railroad tank car, and that competition is expanding.

Q.   I see. And are there other forms of competition?

A.   Of course. Alternative forms of energy. Nuclear, solar, hydro-electric, geothermal, wind power. Petroleum is simply something you burn in order to create heat. Heat creates energy. If you can create the energy some other way, by using some other fuel, then you don't need a railroad tank car delivering oil.

Q.   What about other factors? Conservation, for example.

A.   Certainly. Even something like the 55-mile-an-hour speed limit. The trend to more fuel-efficient automobiles. People turning down their thermostats for less heat in the winter and turning up their thermostats for less air-conditioning in the summer.

Q.   Such things reduce the cost to the individual, don't they?

A.   They do more than that. Many of them result in greater safety. Like the speed limit I just mentioned.

Q.   And safety is also a consideration for a large oil company like yours?

A.   Not just also a consideration. It is our first consideration.

Q.   These jumbo railroad tank cars we've been talking about, like the one in the accident at Florian. Were they designed and conceived with safety in mind?

A.   No question about it. And of course that ties in with the concept of fewer tank cars on the rails. The bigger the car, the more petroleum or petroleum product it can carry, the safer the operation.

Q.   Why is that?

A.   Because it means fewer cars overall. Fewer car movements, fewer couplings, fewer loadings and unloadings, actually—when you come right down to it—fewer trains. If one 747 can carry as many people as four smaller planes, you've reduced your risk of collision. The greater the capacity of the single vehicle, the fewer vehicles you need.

Q.   And back when the Department of Transportation approved the design for these jumbo tank cars—when you were director of the railroad division of the department—you therefore had considerations for safety in mind?

A.   It was one of the prime considerations, Mr. Hawkes.

Q.   I have no further questions at this time.

At the plaintiff table, Joe Purcell rose, but that was all he did. Ordinarily, he would approach the witness box, but with Harrison McKenna he simply stood in place, creating an almost deferential gap between himself and the witness.

Q.   Excuse me, Mr. McKenna, but a little bit ago, when Mr. Hawkes was asking you about alternative forms of energy, did I hear you mention coal?

A.   If I didn't, it was an inadvertent omission.

Q.   We are in the middle of coal country down here.

A.   I said the omission was inadvertent, Mr. Purcell. Of course you can include coal if you want to. I realize it is important to the people of this area.

Q.   And railroad cars carry coal, don't they?

A.   Yes, Mr. Purcell, they do. I will concede you cannot carry coal by pipeline.

Q.   And the more coal, the more railroad coal cars will be needed to carry it?

A.   I suppose that is conceivable. But my understanding is there is more rolling stock available to carry coal than the demand for such rolling stock. It is a holdover from the old days, when coal was a much more important product. If we begin using more coal, essentially what I am saying is the cars are already there. I doubt that additional ones will have to be manufactured.

Q.   But more of them will be moving on the rails, instead of being in storage somewhere?

A.   I suppose you can say that.

Q.   And that means more payloads?

A.   Obviously.

Q.   And your company—North American Petroleum—does the company have any financial interest in any coal operations?

A.   We are interested in all forms of energy, Mr. Purcell. They are interrelated. Coal beds, for example, are subject to new technology. They can be a source of petroleum. And we are a petroleum company.

Q.   Doesn't your company also own leasehold rights to underground steam wells in California?

A.   You are talking geothermal energy. Yes, that is correct.

Q.   Do you find any petroleum there?

A.   I said all forms of energy, Mr. Purcell.

Q.   That's right, you did. So even if it is not petroleum, but steam, say, or coal, that is being used you stand to make money nevertheless, is that it?

A.   The profit motive is not illegal in this country, Mr. Purcell.

Q.   Not even when it's 116 percent, am I right? That was North America's figure for the first quarter of this year?

A.   That profit came from the overseas area. We showed no profit on our domestic operations.

Q.   But you still made money? What difference does it make where it came from?

A.   The difference is the degree to which we are concentrating on developing energy here at home, so this country does not have to be forever dependent on OPEC oil.

Q.   So to hedge your bet, you are getting into things that have nothing to do with oil. In fact, you own a publishing house too, do you not?

A.   We have been diversified for many years, Mr. Purcell. That is not illegal in this country, either.

Q.   The list of North American Petroleum's various interests is quite impressive, nevertheless. At one point, you even had an interest in a beer company in Hawaii, if I am correct. Primo beer— do I pronounce it right?

A.   That was many years ago, Mr. Purcell. I might add that it was an excellent beer, in my judgment—the best I ever tasted, and I told my board of directors about it. We thought that with an infusion of capital we would get national distribution for it, because it was only a local product, out there in the islands.

Q.   And it didn't work out?

A.   That's right. In the end, we sold to a brewery. But so long as you have brought it up, I would like to expand on my answer, because it goes to two fundamental points.

Q.   By all means.

A.   The first point is that when you talk about an oil company diversifying, as a way to hedge against this country's being dependent on foreign oil, my point with the example of the beer company is that this process of diversification is not just something that came along with the Arab oil boycott and price hikes of the seventies. Our company had been involved in diversification for many years before that.

And the second point is that the acquisition of that beer company did not benefit us financially in any meaningful way. The idea that larger companies help smaller companies simply for the sake of profit is an inaccurate and unfair way to look at companies like North American Petroleum.

From his place at the counsel table, Purcell's vision took in the entire jury. What he saw resulted in high marks for Harrison McKenna. To a Dorothy Brewer, he might be the archvillain of all time—and, as a ranking officer of a huge, monopolistic, multinational oil company, easily painted as such. But if so, Purcell was botching it. What he read in the jurors' faces was that this was a quiet, authoritative, plausible, and in all ways a most effective witness.

Yet in the end result, this might prove not unsuitable to Purcell's purpose. He continued to take an even strain:

Q.   You realize, Mr. McKenna, that your appearance here is of double value. You were a railroad executive before you joined the Department of Transportation and have been an oil executive since you left the department. Is that correct?

A.   The facts are correct, yes, if you want to call that something of double value. I would regard it more as a logical single-line succession. The difference between a railroad that moves a tank car and the oil producer who fills it does not strike me as something all that unusual. In either position I would deal with tank cars.

Q.   No, no, I agree with you, sir. When I said double value, I was not referring to your different positions as an industrial executive. The second element I had in mind was that you were also chief of the railroad division of the Department of Transportation at the time the department approved the design of the jumbo tank cars.

A.   That is also factually correct.

Q.   What then can you tell us about the department procedure that resulted in the approval of this design? The government okay, in other words, that gave Nance the go-ahead to produce this tank car?

A.   Very little, I'm afraid. To say that I headed the railroad division of DOT at the time is not to say I was a specialist in structural design. I left that to the experts.

Q.   You were not aware that you were being asked to approve the construction of the biggest freight car ever designed before or since? Not only the biggest freight car, the biggest railroad car, in its overall dimensions, ever built, before or since? Not only the biggest railroad car but the heaviest railroad car? And you were completely unaware of this?

A.   You are overlooking something, Mr. Purcell. The jumbo tank car you refer to may have been exactly what you say it was in weight and overall dimensions, but it was evolutionary. The trend to larger tank cars was already in motion.

Q.   May have been? It still is, isn't it? Even to this day.

A.   It may well be. That does not change the fact that it was an evolving process. This car was not that much larger than some of its predecessors that had already been approved by the department. It was just not that dramatic an event.

Q.   You don't think that, as in the case of the straw that broke the camel's back, somewhere along the line those cars might just have become too big? Too heavy?

A.   Too big for what, Mr. Purcell. Too heavy for what?

Q.   For safety, Mr. McKenna.

A.   They have a record of millions of safe miles of operation.

Q.   Are you aware that just the weight of these cars has had the effect of flattening the rails they travel over?

A.   I don't understand. What has that got to do with anything?

Q.   You think it's just as safe for a train to go around a curve that has flat rails as narrower rails that are built up so the flanged wheels can get a grip?

A.   It is if the train makes allowances and operates at the proper speed. The Amtrak trains, on most of their routes, are now operating at slower speeds than in the past.

Q.   So it is just passenger derailments we keep reading about in the newspapers? Was that a passenger train that derailed in Canada, just outside Toronto, that caused the evacuation of a quarter of a million residents from the surrounding area for a period of four days? Or was it a freight train with tank cars carrying explosive cargo, like liquid petroleum gas, so the authorities couldn't take a chance on an explosion?

A.   I am not certain that train was trying to negotiate a curve at the time, Mr. Purcell. You have a way of setting up a premise and then switching it on me. It is not just the comparative flatness of the rails that can cause a derailment.

Q.   What are some of the other things?

MR. HAWKES: Objection.

MR. PURCELL: On what grounds?

THE COURT: I'll be the one to ask that question, Mr. Purcell, if you don't mind. Mr. Hawkes?

MR. HAWKES::   Materiality, Your Honor. The complete absence of it, I should say. Here's Brother Purcell making another one of his speeches, this derailment and that derailment, while the tank car we're talking about in this case didn't derail at all. It wasn't even moving. It had been standing in one spot for days, all by itself.

THE COURT: Yes, there is something to that.

MR. PURCELL: It doesn't have to be a derailment. My line of questioning deals with the design of these tank cars, and it was the province of the railroad division of the Department of Transportation to approve that design, and one of the things they had to consider was the safety of operation. And this witness was the director of that division of the department at the time they approved this tank car.

MR. HAWKES: A train can derail because some mentally imbalanced person jimmied open a switch or put a log across the tracks. Or does Brother Purcell blame that on the design of the tank car too?

MR. PURCELL: If it then explodes, I blame it on the design, but let us take the same mentally imbalanced person and say he set a torch to the Jumbo Nellie Nellie in Florian, and set it on fire intentionally. So what? If the car was insulated it would simply burn down and nobody gets hurt. What's wrong with making them fireworthy?

THE COURT: What I issued was a question, not an invitation for a full-scale debate. By now it is too late for me to rule whether derailment is material, since the two of you are standing there arguing it anyway. Mr. Purcell, I do agree with Mr. Hawkes that it is not necessary to hear any more on that subject. This is not a derailment case.

MR. PURCELL: I think that safety—

THE COURT: The whole world knows what you think, Mr. Purcell, and on a variety of subjects. My ruling here is that you should stick to the point.

MR. PURCELL: The point—

THE COURT: No more. The point is this one tank car at Florian and what this witness can attest to. Both sides have let this testimony go too far afield.

MR. PURCELL: Very well, Your Honor.

Q.   Now, Mr. McKenna, I was asking you about the procedure at the Department of Transportation for approving the design of a jumbo tank car. That approval would take into consideration the factor of safety? All kinds of safety?

A.   Yes, indeed.

Q.   And how does this take shape? Do you have hearings or what?

A.   Do you mean into the design of this particular model of tank car or design changes generally?

Q.   We can take them one at a time, if you want.

A.   Well, it was automatic to schedule a hearing in any case. But I think very few hearings actually took place.

Q.   Very few hearings into safety?

A.   Very few hearings, period. The purpose of a hearing would be to listen to conflicting views. If either the government or the industry had a question that needed to be asked, or if some qualified objection had come forward, then a hearing would be held. If there was no such element, then there would be no point in holding a hearing.

Q.   And in the case of this specific jumbo tank car design?

A.   I actually do not remember.

Q.   If I told you that no hearing was held, would you accept that as being the case?

A.   If you say no hearing was held, I will accept your word for it. A hearing would have been totally unlikely.

Q.   Why?

A.   For a number of reasons. As I say, hearings were the exception more than the rule. The department of course would study the proposal in advance, so that independent scrutiny was always on hand. But in this particular case, we are not even talking about a proposal that involved a new design. It was simply a modification of an already approved design.

Q.   A modification that produced the biggest, heaviest railroad car in history, is that right?

MR. HAWKES: Objection.

THE COURT: Sustained. You are supposed to be delivering a question, Mr. Purcell, not a television commercial. You have been repeating that biggest-and-heaviest business every five minutes.

Q.   All right, Your Honor. But speaking of commercials, Mr. McKenna, your North American Petroleum Company does advertise its products on television, does it not?

A.   Yes, of course.

Q.   And on the radio and in newspapers and magazines?

A.   Yes.

Q.   And on the sides of your railroad tank cars?

A.   We have our logo on them, yes. All freight cars have company logos on them.

Q.   But as a regular thing, those are railroad logos, aren't they? They advertise the name of the carrier, not the company whose product is being carried.

A.   It is common practice for oil companies to put their names on the tank cars they lease. I cannot remember when this was not the case.

Q.   Yes, but we are not talking about those friendly little black tank cars that we all remember. We are talking about the big white ones. The jumbos. Those are an exceptionally nice piece of advertising—free advertising—for you, aren't they? Sort of a moving billboard, you might say? And the white background makes the lettering stand out even more?

A.   Which question am I supposed to answer?

Q.   It was all pretty much one and the same question, I would say, and I rather think the thing speaks for itself. I won't take up any more of your time, Mr. McKenna. I have no further questions of this witness, Your Honor.

Purcell sat down. "Shit," he muttered to Bert Klein, "I stuck my foot in it and Arthur's going to cut it off."

Hawkes was indeed on his feet.

THE COURT: You have something on redirect, Mr. Hawkes?

MR. HAWKES: Just two or three questions, judge.

THE COURT: Yes. Go ahead.

Q.   That beer company interests me, Mr. McKenna. The one you said that North American Petroleum had an interest in.

A.   That was a long time ago, Mr. Hawkes.

Q.   Yes, but I believe you said it was the best beer you ever tasted.

A.   I thought it was excellent, yes. But I don't understand your drift, Mr. Hawkes.

THE COURT: Yes, Mr. Hawkes. Please.

Q.   I simply do not wish Brother Purcell's clever line of questioning to create the impression that you were a heavy drinker, Mr. McKenna, so perhaps you can verify that, just for the record and so the jury will know.

A.   No, in fact I drink very little. I grew up in an abstemious Scotch-Irish household, Mr. Hawkes, and to this day, the most I will have will be a single Scotch before dinner, cut with water. No ice. It is an old Scottish habit, and my doctor tells me he thinks it is a good idea.

Q.   And beer?

A.   Only with my meal, sir, and then only if the entree is lamb or beef. Particularly lamb. Again, it is an old Scottish custom.

Q.   Thank you. Now, you also said that in the progression of positions that you have held, you went from a railroad executive to become an assistant cabinet secretary in charge of the railroad division of the Department of Transportation, and from there to your present position with North American Petroleum, and you say you saw nothing unusual or illogical in that progression?

A.   Absolutely not. It is the most logical thing in the world. My specialty lay with tank cars, and those are the cars that more than any other kind of shipping unit won two world wars and have been characterized as the most important, the most vital individual shipping units we have ever had in this country.

Q.   And this vital link between railroads and oil was—

A.   The shipment of petroleum, Mr. Hawkes.

Q.   You saw no conflict of interest when you were at the Department of Transportation?

A.   No. The subjects were too close to being one and the same. Besides, we ship our oil by means other than railroads.

Q.   And you had no vested interest, therefore, in the particular design of a particular model of tank car?

A.   I have tried not to be vague in any of my answers, Mr. Hawkes, but—

Q.   Yes. I think everyone will agree you have been most forthright.

A.   —but in this case it is simply the truth to say that I have no recollection of that particular design modification, or the proposal of it. If it went through the way Mr. Purcell said it did, I will take his word for it. Obviously it did receive department approval. Otherwise the manufacturer would never have incorporated the change. I am not a specialist in tank car design in and of itself. But there were specialists at the department, as well as the manufacturer's own people and others throughout the industry. The Nance Company, you have to remember, is not the only manufacturer of tank cars.

Q.   And safety, you have said, was their prime consideration?

A.   Yes, and a prime consideration at the DOT too when the proposals and plans would come in. But as head of the entire railroad division, I had a wealth of other matters to attend to daily. And I cannot, as I say, testify here today, so long after the fact, that I involved myself directly with each and every structural design modification coming to the department from the various manufacturers of all the various kinds of locomotives and rolling stock. Just in the relatively brief period of time I was with DOT there had to be dozens of such proposals. And we had a subdepartment to deal with them.

Q.   Nevertheless, you were familiar with the world of tank cars and did have a point of view, overall, about them?

A.   Yes, indeed. I believe I have already suggested what that overview was, but I will say it again. It was, very simply, to get the safe and economical delivery of petroleum products to the people of this country. And I have already testified why the jumbo tank car was especially qualified in both those areas.

Q.   Especially safety?

A.   That is correct, and I have testified to the reasons.

At the plaintiff's table, Bert Klein whispered, "What were you worried about, Joe? What is it that Arthur was going to hurt you with?"

"Maybe he didn't notice it," Purcell whispered back.

"Just one more question, Mr. McKenna," Hawkes was saying now. "Mr. Purcell asked you about the advertising on the side of the jumbo tank cars. Those big white cars, as he put it."

"Son of a bitch," Purcell whispered. "He did notice it."

Hawkes was completing the question. "Those rolling billboards, as he suggested. Would you say there was anything unsafe about them?"

"Why, no," the witness replied. "If anything, they contribute to safety."

"Contribute to safety, you say?" Hawkes pressed. He cast a look at the jury. "How would your advertisement on the side of those cars contribute to safety?"

"Because of the white paint," Harrison McKenna said. "As Mr. Purcell pointed out, the old-time smaller tank cars were dark-colored. Dark colors absorb heat. But white reflects heat—keeps it away from the contents of the car—insulates it, you might say."

"I have nothing else to ask this witness," Hawkes said to Junior Bohr. From his place at the plaintiff's table, Purcell's line of sight traveled upward through Hawkes's shoulder blades as the latter faced the judge. Sighting therefore through the man's back, Joe still could see the amused look on Arthur's face.

Hawkes now was thanking Harrison McKenna as the latter left the stand. "Now, Your Honor," Arthur said, "we call as a witness Mr. B. J. Catchpole."

"Mr. B. J. who?"

"Mr. B. J. Catchpole. Correction. *Officer* B. J. Catchpole."

There was no missing this witness. Unlike the overwhelming majority of policeman-witnesses, who in their courtroom appearances inevitably showed up in civilian dress, this one wore the olive uniform of his calling, complete to a forest-green shield patch just below his left shoulder. "Florian Police," said the upper and lower arcs of the patch, the area in between taken up by what Joe Purcell took to be crossed ax handles flanked by a pair of dice.

Neither Purcell nor Klein had been present when Hawkes deposed this witness, leaving it to Harry Wright instead, and Wright had reported back—as indeed the deposition brought out—that this witness had no connection with the accident, having arrived on the scene only after the explosion. The deposition itself was barely five pages long and totally innocuous. Which of course was precisely what Arthur Hawkes needed.

"The son of a bitch *told* him to show up in that fucking uniform," Purcell husked to Klein as the policeman took the stand. "He's going to make an asshole out of him and he wants him suited up for it."

But if the uniform was Hawkes's idea, obviously it had not taken much persuading. A large man, Catchpole flashed a celebrity smile, first at judge, then jury, radiating large stained teeth as he took his seat in the witness box. His moment was at hand, to be strutted and enjoyed.

"You're the police chief at Florian?" Hawkes asked him now.

"Yes, sir."

"I may have put that question badly. Actually, Florian has only one police officer, and you're it, is that right?"

B. J. Catchpole uttered a mighty laugh. "Yes, friend, right you are. That makes me chief, don't it?"

Hawkes nodded. "And you were on duty the day of the accident at the Tri-State energy yard?"

"Yes, I was. Remember it like it was yesterday."

Q.   You knew there was a fire before the accident?

A.   No, sir, I sure didn't.

Q.   You didn't hear the fire siren go off?

A.   I heard the siren all right. But I didn't know where the fire was. The siren don't tell you.

Q.   And you didn't investigate?

A.   No, sir, I sure didn't. You only got one police officer in a spread-out area like that, he has to harbor his resources, as the saying goes. Can't be running to somebody's outhouse that starts to smoke or every little grass fire that comes along. It's first things first.

Q.   Well, where were you, actually, at the time the siren went off?

A.   Arlie's.

Q.   Arlie's? What is that?

A.   Little restaurant.

Q.   It's a bar, too, isn't it?

A.   That's right. Arlie's gives full service. Lunchtimes, anyway. They don't serve supper.

Q.   So you went there that day for lunch?

A.   That's right, friend. Even a policeman's got to eat.

Q.   Do you usually eat that late in the day? Around 2:30 in the afternoon?

A.   Well, I was finishing my lunch. Having a beer afterwards.

Q.   You drink while you're on duty?

A.   I'm always on duty. Twenty-four-hour call, except for 2 weeks' vacation or out sick. Then Lenny Joss takes over.

Q.   But you were drinking that day?

A.   Having a beer on a hot day. I wouldn't call that drinking.

Q.   I see. And that was what?—just one beer?

A.   Wouldn't have been much more than that.

Q.   Could it have been two?

A.   Could have.

Q.   Or three?

A.   On my pay, you don't see me drinking three beers.

Q.   There's never been a day when you had three beers?

A.   Not unless somebody else was buying.

Q.   Was somebody else buying that day?

A.   Not that I remember.

Q.   But you can't be sure.

A.   No, sir, I sure can't.

Q.   So for 20 minutes, from the time the fire siren sounded till the explosion, you just stayed there in this Arlie's bar.

A.   That's right, friend.

Arthur Hawkes turned and walked to the defense table, to examine a piece of paper there. "Stagey," Bert Klein whispered to Purcell. "He's just letting that sink in."

Purcell nodded. "And interesting," he whispered back. "Arthur used the word 'explosion.' I don't think he meant to do that. You're defending this one, you say accident, not explosion."

Hawkes moved back toward the witness stand. "And in all that twenty minutes, you didn't know where the fire was, or what was on fire?"

"Well, toward the end I knew."

"How did you find out?"

"Somebody—might have been Eddie Hewitt, as I recall—come in the bar and said the fire truck was over to the Tri-State yard. But I didn't know what was on fire, no."

"He didn't say?"

"Not as I recall, no."

"And you didn't ask?"

"No, sir, I didn't pay it much mind."

In the jury box, Mother Nine took up writing in his notebook once more. His was the only black face among the nine jurors, but all nine showed the same reaction to this witness: the silent agreement that B. J. Catchpole was so stupid that he did not know he was being patronized. Hawkes had served himself well, having this man appear in uniform— except that it might well have been Catchpole's own idea. Either way it played to Arthur's second line of defense, which by now was at least as effective, and nearly as important, as the front line that said his clients were not responsible for an act of God. The second line was to take that issue of responsibility and throw it back on the officials of Florian who could have acted—done *something*—in that 20-minute burn time between lightning strike and catastrophe. And now on the witness stand, the entire police department, in charge of the public safety, said that on a hot day you drank beer.

Q.   So you were still there, standing at the bar, when the accident happened?

A.   Not standing at the bar. Sitting down. One of the tables there, friend. Arlie's hasn't got what you'd call a bar.

MR. HAWKES: I have no further questions of this witness, Your Honor.

THE COURT: Mr. Purcell?

MR. PURCELL: Officer Catchpole, how far away from the scene of the explosion were you at the time it happened?

A.   Not far enough, friend.

This time when Catchpole laughed, gold glittered from a large left lower molar, and the courtroom laughed with him, even Hawkes and, to the tentative minimum, Halsey. Only Steppenworth failed to laugh. But Steppenworth never laughed.

Arlie's, as Catchpole described it now, was on Center Street, north of the tracks and the center of town. In the fireball's caprice, some buildings had blown up in an instant while adjacent structures stood unscathed. And Arlie's had been one of the lucky ones. He had heard the rumbling sound, Catchpole said, and directly afterward he, like everyone else, remembered hearing the staccato sounds of the propane bottles stored for retail sale as one after another they gave way and blew. It was that sound, Catchpole said, that caused him to get up from his table and go outside to have a look around.

Q.   And what did you see?

A.   Nothing.

Q.   Nothing?

A.   It was raining, friend. Raining very hard and all of a sudden, seemed like. But looking off to my right I did see something that looked like black smoke, down to the center of town more or less, across the tracks.

Q.   And what did you do then?

A.   Went back inside of Arlie's.

Q.   Went back inside of Arlie's? Why?

A.   To phone the fire department.

This time not everyone laughed, but some—including jurors four, five, and eight—did laugh outright, and others in the courtroom smiled. Catchpole smiled too, agreeably enough. No, he continued, he had not actually made the call, for he remembered that the fire truck was off answering an alarm somewhere else. And no, he had not made the connection that the smoke in the center of town had been caused by an explosion elsewhere. He had gone back outside and got into his car—a Plymouth that never started right, he said—and driven to the intersection of Center and Railroad, but when he looked west along Railroad Avenue to his right, and saw all the fires and debris, he had to get out of his car. Even then, he did not proceed toward the Tri-State yard. "I still didn't know that was where the blast come from originally," he explained now. "I remember somebody running past and yelling that the Texaco station had blew up, so I guess I thought that's what caused it all."

It was the second time in the course of the Fireball trial that the cross-examination was noticeably gentler than the direct. First had been the way Purcell savaged his own witness, the woman from the publishing house in New York. Now it was the opposite way, with Hawkes doing the savaging of this useless, near-irrelevant peace officer, while Joe played sun to Arthur's north wind. The difference was that in the earlier case the witness had resented it. B. J. Catchpole, in contrast, seemed unaware of the lawyer approaches, let alone any difference between them. He smiled and nodded cheerily for Hawkes, and then for Purcell, and now on redirect for Hawkes once again.

MR. HAWKES: Let's see if we have this straight. You knew the fire truck was at the Tri-State energy yard, but it never occurred to you there might be some element of danger in that—is that right?

A.   No, sir, that's right. A man doesn't think that way.

Q.   It never occurred to you that a fire in a place like that might have further consequences if it wasn't dealt with properly?

MR. PURCELL: Object. What does he mean—dealt with properly? Assumes something not in evidence.

THE COURT: Sustain.

MR. HAWKES: The thing speaks for itself, Your Honor. If it had been dealt with properly, the fire would have been put out.

THE COURT: That's for you to say in argument, not in conversation with this witness. You'll get your chance.

MR. PURCELL: He'll get his chance? He's been using the chance every five minutes.

THE COURT: That's enough from you too, Mr. Purcell. Counsel will resume the questioning.

Q.   You knew there was a fire at Tri-State, but you just didn't do any more thinking about it. Is that right?

A.   Right, friend. A man doesn't think that way. When something explodes, it explodes. A man don't think about it before it happens.

Q.   And after it did happen, you still didn't connect it in any way with the fire at Tri-State?

A.   No, sir. First I thought it was the middle of town, then I heard somebody say the Texaco station. What you're sayin' sounds right enough, but when he's on the spot a man don't think that way.

Q.   Especially if he's been drinking beer all afternoon?

MR. PURCELL: Object.

THE COURT: No. The witness can answer.

MR. PURCELL: How can you let him do that?

MR. HAWKES: We have a policeman admittedly drinking on the job, Your Honor.

THE COURT: I said I would overrule. Go ahead.

MR. PURCELL: This is two witnesses in a row who've been asked about their beer drinking. Neither one of those things had the slightest connection with the explosion. We're dragging everything in here but the cat and the kitchen sink.

MR. HAWKES: If the cat and the sink are material, I will use them too. I've been retained to defend this case, not follow the instructions and the preferences of opposing counsel.

THE COURT: You are at it again, gentlemen. We're going to stop it right now. I mean it. I say the witness can answer the question.

Arthur Hawkes drew a deep breath. "Thank you, Your Honor," he said. "Tell us, officer, do you think the same when you've been drinking as when you haven't been drinking?"

Again a mighty Catchpole laugh. "Depends," he said, "on what it is I'm thinking of."

He got a big laugh, and Judge Bohr, noticing the time, decided to adjourn at that point. Hawkes could resume his redirect questioning of this witness in the morning. The trial was nearing its close—Officer Catchpole was the last of the scheduled witnesses for the defense—and, not for the first time, Purcell had to envy the mastery of Arthur Hawkes when it came to organization.

Joe said as much to Harry Wright, who could not understand why Hawkes would want to prolong the testimony of Catchpole into another session tomorrow, or why he would schedule Catchpole as his final witness, or even, for that matter, what the real value of Catchpole was at all.

"The answer to all three of those questions," Joe told Wright, "is that Catchpole is the most perfect closing witness Arthur could have found. He's entertaining—good theater. He's a contrast to the technical testimony. He's walking proof that not everybody dies or gets burned in an explosion—whatever else he may be or not be, he's sure healthy; and he was there that day, and didn't get touched, and all the people he related to were the same as he was: right there in downtown Florian, and nothing happened to them." Joe sighed. "So his presence in Mundelein today is the perfect way to minimize what happened in Florian a year ago last May."

"Really," Wright said.

"But best of all, from Arthur's standpoint, is that he's stupid." Purcell's left foot kicked bitterly at an imagined obstacle. "He represents not only the incompetence in that horseshit town generally, but at the level of public safety. He's what passes for chief of police—so you can just imagine what they must have had for a fire department!" This time it was the right foot that kicked angrily at nothing. "They didn't put the fire out, Harry. How am I supposed to argue my way around that?"

"You'll think of something," Harry Wright said loyally.

"Mm-hmm," Purcell said. "But just in case I don't, if you think of something you'll let me know, won't you?"

"Whatever I can do."

"Okay. And speaking of whatever you can do, did you check the Specimen?"

"Yes."

"And."

"And? Oh. Good news—he'll be in town the rest of the week."

"All right. Might be good to have him in court one more time, before we close."

"The kids too?"

"I think so. The Specimen can bring them. Certainly the oldest one. He's the only decent witness we've had so far."

"That's the bad news," Harry Wright said. "Elliot's sick."

"Ah, damn," Purcell said. "How bad? Just a cold?"

"Maybe. Or maybe a touch of flu. Either way, he's running a fever."

"Damn," Joe said again.

"Maybe all isn't lost," Harry Wright said. "I know the family doctor. He might say it was all right to have him in the courtroom."

"No, it isn't all right. He may be a doctor, but I'm a lawyer—for the balance of this week, anyway. I can't lay it on a jury by draping a sick kid in front of them."

"Really," Wright said. "I hadn't thought of that."

Purcell got in his car to drive back to his motel. He himself had only one witness left to call, a rebuttal specialist in gaseous pressures who had arrived earlier today from New York and was quartered at the Western Motor Hotel now, awaiting an evening preparatory session with the A&P

lawyers. The kid had to get sick on me now, he said to himself. Sure. Why not? Everything else was going down the tubes, might as well have this too. "Damn!" he said again, and banged his hand against the steering wheel. "Pastime—last time. God*damn* it!" It was another part of what he had sung for Bert the day before, the way Ira Gershwin had rhymed it: "...intellectual *Pastime*...know the *last time*." And his own "Taxicabs in the Sky": "The *last time* I dreamed, the *pastime* that seemed to me extremely unfair..." "Ah, nuts," he said. "You derivative shmuck, Purcell."

He arrived at the motel in a black mood. Which would not be good for A&P morale, because Max Aranow was coming into town this evening and bringing Sheila O'Hara with him, leaving only Willie Blake behind to mind the store. And all would be quartered at the Western Motor Hotel.

Purcell's thought now for their morale was ironic: One of the reasons Max and Sheila were coming to town was for *his* morale. Not only had he run up the biggest pretrial and trial costs in the firm's history, but he found himself weathering one blow after another from the same lawyer, with the same judge, in the same courtroom that witnessed a Purcell defeat in the Marlowe case the time before.

And Max and Sheila would not be the only lawyer types descending on this unlikely Mecca as the Fireball trial reached the end. Through some arcane grapevine, a bus from Washington, a plane from Boston, another plane from San Francisco would be delivering this law student from Georgetown, that professor from Harvard, the other practicing attorney from the Pacific coast, perhaps a dozen all told, to a speck on the map called Mundelein—for the education, the satisfaction, the outright drama of being there when Joe Purcell and Arthur Hawkes clashed in their most eloquent hour: their final arguments to the jury. Others already had mailed their checks to the court reporter's office to order copies of the transcript, but there was no substitute for being there in person. The jungle telegraph of the law had delivered the news: The time was now.

18

The back row of spectator seats in the courtroom was against the wall, so there was no place for standees. But between the counsel tables and the front row of seats there was a space of perhaps eight or nine feet, room for three rows of folding chairs, and Toby Ball, the night watchman at the court house, stayed overtime that morning to set them up.

Max Aranow and Sheila O'Hara took seats in the front line of the temporary chairs, somewhat to the left of the table where Purcell, Bert Klein, and Harry Wright would be sitting. Perry Muncrief, the paralegal from Rutgers, had accepted with good grace that he must remain behind at the A&P motel headquarters. Indeed, he would be seated at the computer console, with a headset beside him, installed yesterday by the telephone company along with a private ad hoc telephone line, so that any calls from the courthouse, any request for data, would reach him instantly without having to be routed through the motel switchboard.

Max had seen Perry at work on the computer last night, and pronounced it good. In a dummy run, Aranow fired half a dozen questions at the young assistant, each dealing with some aspect, even curio, of testimony from the weeks of trial. Muncrief's fingers flew over the keyboard, and back chattered the desired answer. "I'll be damned," Aranow said. "I used to say I wouldn't have a high-technology specialist for a client, but maybe I'll change my mind. Tell me, do these things cheat?"

Perry looked at him. "Cheat?"

"Yes. I've heard of all kinds of marvelous crimes these machines can commit."

"Well, no," Perry Muncrief said. "Not the machines themselves. It takes a human being to do it."

"I was going to say," Max said, "the fact is I've never had a computer for a client either. But the way you make that thing work, I think the day is coming. A machine in St. Louis can sue another machine in Detroit."

"And you'll take the case?"

"I don't know who'll take the case. The only thing you can count on is that Arthur Hawkes will represent the insurance company."

As they seated themselves in the courtroom now, Max and Sheila could have chosen space directly behind Joe Purcell at the plaintiff table, but Max preferred the location a few chairs to the left, for it fronted him on the focal point of the arena: the crescent apron bordered by jury, witness box, and judge, within which the lawyers would stalk and prowl. And that left a space directly behind the nearly touching shoulders of Harry Wright and Joe Purcell, and that chair was taken now by the most appropriate occupant: Vincent Brophy, the Specimen. Harry Wright had put a folder of papers on the seat of that chair, to reserve it, and that was prudent, for by the time the bailiff intoned the "All rise" for the judge's entrance there was not an empty seat in the courtroom.

First on the witness stand was the same Officer B. J. Catchpole, held over from yesterday, but he could have spared himself the trip from

Florian. Evidently Arthur Hawkes had changed his mind overnight, for he had no further questions to ask of this witness. Neither did Purcell, and a vastly disappointed B. J. Catchpole was told by the judge he could leave. "We appreciate your testimony here," Junior told him, "and apologize for the imposition on your time, both yesterday and today." Bohr could be gracious, and in the presence of an extra-elite audience such as today's, he would be on his best behavior.

Now Arthur Hawkes approached the bench to consult with the judge. The latter listened, then nodded, and took from the desk shelf before him a white envelope. He opened it, drew out the folded piece of paper it contained, unfolded, read, and nodded again. To Hawkes he said, "You have a witness for the purpose of impeachment?"

"Yes, Your Honor," Arthur said. "We call Miss Tammy Waite."

"Spell." It was the voice of Bert Klein from plaintiff's table. "Waite," Hawkes said. "W-A-I-T-E."

As if with a single pair of eyes, both Purcell and Bert Klein looked to their left at Harry Wright. He shook his head, spread his hands, and shrugged—then blinked, rose, and headed for the phones.

The witness who came forward was dressed in a gray pantsuit that was wrinkled from travel. She was perhaps twenty-five years of age, thin of both face and body, her mouse-brown hair set in a pageboy bob that was wrong for what was basically a not unattractive face. She was not large, but her bones were.

She was a waitress, Tammy Waite testified, at the Kit-Kat Motel in Beech Grove, just outside Indianapolis. How long had she been employed there? Four and a half years. Was she working the day of the tank car accident at Florian? Yes. What hours? Four to midnight. Was she acquainted with a Vincent Brophy? Yes, that was him sitting there in the front row.

Purcell tilted his chair backward and, with his left hand back of his ear, gestured Brophy to bend to him. "Who is she?" he said in a low voice. "Did you know she was coming here today?"

"No," Brophy said. "But she's lying."

"Does she know you?"

"Yes."

"Then what's she lying about? That's all she's said so far." Joe moved forward again to take up with Harry Wright as the latter came back from the phone.

"Called Perry, and the machine doesn't have anything," Wright said.

"I didn't think it would."

"Neither did I. So I called Nero in New York and he was blank too."

"If he's blank, so are we," Joe said. He turned his head to pick up Hawkes's questioning.

Q.   Now, this Mr. Brophy we're talking about, Vincent Brophy, did he come into the coffee shop that night?

A.   Yes. About 11:30, 20 minutes to 12:00.

Q.   And will you tell us what happened then?

A.   He sat at the counter and he ordered the Salisbury steak and chocolate milk.

Max Aranow pressed a hand to his forehead in pain.

Q.   Well, that was some 19 or 20 months ago. Can I ask you how you happen to remember what it was he ordered?

A.   Because that's what he always had. Never any different.

Q.   You mean he'd visited the coffee shop before?

A.   Oh, yes.

Q.   Do you know how long he'd been coming to the coffee shop?

A.   Well, he always came.

Q.   Always? For how long a period?

A.   As long as I was there.

Q.   In other words, for at least $4\frac{1}{2}$ years?

A.   Yes.

At the plaintiff table, Joe Purcell doodled a hangman's noose on his pad. Bert Klein noticed it and pointed to his own pad: a grave and tombstone.

Q.   And was there any particular reason, that you know of, why he picked that particular coffee shop?

A.   Because it was there.

Q.   There? I'm sorry, I don't quite understand.

A.   The coffee shop was part of the motel. The motel was where he stayed when he was in town.

Q.   I see. And how long would he stay, as a rule?

A.   Just overnight. Just in and out.

Q.   Did this happen frequently?

A.   I don't know what you mean by that. By frequent.

Q.   Well, how often was he in town? As far as you know?

A.   He was in at least once a month. Sometimes two or three times.

Q.   But at least once a month?

A.   There may have been once, twice, when it was longer than that. But ordinarily, yes, at least that.

Q.   All right. Now, on this night of the accident at Florian, you say he came in about 11:30, quarter of 12:00?

A.   About that.

Q.   He has testified that he arrived at the motel about seven o'clock that evening. Have you any memory of that?

A.   Well, he would check into the motel at different times. Sometimes he would sleep or something for two, three hours. But he would always come in the coffee shop around 11:30.

Q.   And have his Salisbury steak and chocolate milk?

Max Aranow put his face in his hands.

A.   Yes. That way he could be done eating.

Q.   Done eating?

A.   By midnight.

Q.   Oh. The coffee shop closes at midnight?

A.   No. It stays open 24 hours.

Q.   Then what was so important about midnight?

A.   I already told you. I get off at midnight.

Joe Purcell looked to Bert Klein at his right. "Do you think we may be in a little trouble?"

"Does Howdy Doody have wooden balls?" Bert said.

Q.   So he was waiting for you?

A.   Well, he was doing both. Eating and waiting.

Q.   And was this something that happened regularly?

A.   Oh, yes.

Q.   Not just that one night?

A.   No. It had been going on.

Q.   For how long? From the beginning?

A.   Maybe not from the beginning. No, not from the beginning. Maybe for 2, $2\frac{1}{2}$ years.

Q.   Before that night of the accident at Florian?

A.   Yes.

Q.   And then at midnight, when you got off, you would what? Go out together? He took you out?

A.   You mean like a date or something? No, that wouldn't be the way. I mean, where would you go at midnight?

Q.   But you did go somewhere together?

A.   Yes. We went to his room.

Q.   I see. And when you got there, what would you do?

A.   I don't know how to answer.

Q.   It's a simple enough question. Just tell us what you did when you got to Mr. Brophy's room.

THE COURT: I'm sorry, Miss Waite, but an answer is called for.

A.   I know. I'm trying to think how it should be said. Well, we did what a man and a woman usually do when they get together.

Q.   Did you have sex?

A.   Yes.

Q.   And on the particular night in question did you have sex?

A.   Yes.

Q.   You remember that specifically?

A.   That we had sex that night? Yes. I would have remembered if we didn't. We always had sex.

Q.   I see. And were you in the habit of having sex with married men?

A.   I didn't know he was married.

Q.   Did you ever ask him?

A.   I don't remember if I did or not. The way he talked, you would say he wasn't married.

Q.   Did he ever discuss the possibility of you and he getting married?

A. Well, that's what I mean about the way he talked. He'd keep saying things like how somebody in his business, driving a truck from one place to another all the time, how somebody like that wasn't in any position to settle down or anything. So I took it from that he wasn't married.

Q. I see. And after the accident at Florian, did he continue to come to the motel?

A. Oh, yes.

Q. And you continued to see each other, the same as before?

A. Yes.

Q. And went to his room and had sex, the same as before?

A. Yes.

Q. And how recently did this happen?

A. The night before last.

Q. At the Kit-Kat Motel in Indianapolis?

A. Well, not Indianapolis. It's Beech Grove, actually.

Q. I see. And thinking back to the night of the accident again, when was the first night you saw him after that?

A. About ten days later.

Q. Ten days after the accident?

A. About that.

Q. And did you have sex then?

A. Yes.

MR. HAWKES: I have no further questions at this time.

At the plaintiff table, the three attorneys turned their heads to the Specimen, and Brophy leaned forward to huddle with them. "She's lying!" he said. "I told you she was a liar. They paid her to come here."

"That wouldn't make her a liar," Joe Purcell said.

"Well, she is a liar. She knew all along I was married!"

"Oh, sweet Jesus Christ," Purcell said in disgust. "Bert—enjoy yourself. She's your witness."

"I don't know what the fuck to ask her," Klein said.

"I don't either," Joe said. "But we can't just let her go."

"But I'm going into a minefield. What if I dig us deeper?"

"Nothing can dig us deeper than we already are."

Bert gave him a baleful look, stood up, and looked down at the notes he had scribbled during the direct examination of the witness by Arthur Hawkes. Then he looked up at the witness.

MR. KLEIN: Miss Waite, there was one question Mr. Hawkes asked you and I'm not quite sure you answered it. If I recall correctly, he asked you if you were in the habit of having sex with married men, and you answered that you didn't know Mr. Brophy was married.

MR. HAWKES: Objection. She already did answer that question.

MR. KLEIN: She didn't answer the question you asked, Mr. Hawkes.

Purcell turned to his left and winked at Max Aranow. Aranow grinned back. Nothing Bert said was going to save them; they both knew that. But his instinct for the courtroom was stunning. Just by the way he worded his opening question, just in his tone of voice, he had baited the great Arthur Hawkes into a clear mistake. And now Arthur had to extricate himself.

MR. HAWKES: Your Honor, nothing in the scope of this witness's testimony involves any question of her social attitudes or reputation. Be they good or bad, they have nothing to do with the testimony she just gave on direct examination.

MR. KLEIN: I just want to ask the same question Mr. Hawkes asked, so we can get an answer.

MR. HAWKES: You got an answer.

MR. KLEIN: It wasn't an answer to the question you asked.

MR. HAWKES: This bright young man, Your Honor, is so desperate in the face of this witness's testimony that the only thing he can do is mount a personal attack against her. I say that's improper. Her veracity, fine, if that's what he wants to challenge. But not her sex habits. That's something totally immaterial here.

THE COURT: I would like to have the court reporter read the question back, and the answer. The question the way Mr. Hawkes stated it and the way she answered him.

COURT REPORTER: "Q. And were you in the habit of having sex with married men? A. I didn't know he was married."

THE COURT: No, Mr. Hawkes, I don't think your question really was answered. And since you yourself were the one who first asked it, I see no reason why Mr. Klein can't pursue it.

Q. All right. Now, Miss Waite, were you in the habit of having sex with married men?

A. No. Not if I knew they were married.

Klein shot a look at Purcell. "Now what do I say?" the look said. Purcell turned a helpless palm.

Q. And you say you didn't know Mr. Brophy was married?

MR. HAWKES: Same objection. She's already answered it.

THE COURT: Yes, this time Mr. Hawkes makes his point. I sustain that one, Mr. Klein.

Q. All right. You didn't know Mr. Brophy was married. How long did that continue?

A. How long did what continue?

Q. The fact that you thought Mr. Brophy was unmarried.

A. I always thought that.

Q. Nobody ever told you he had a wife? Not even after she was killed in that explosion at Florian?

A. Well, about my thinking he was unmarried, before she was killed, that's what I did think. And when I saw him next, the first time after she was killed, he was unmarried then too. I mean, how can you still be married if your wife is dead?

Q. It didn't bother you that just 10 days after his wife died, burned almost beyond recognition, the victim of a horrible catastrophe that made page 1 in every city newspaper and the top story in the national news on television—that here he was, same as always, business as usual, wanting you to jump back into bed with him?

"Don't go too far, Bert," Sheila O'Hara mumbled.
"What difference does it make?" Max muttered. "The Specimen's had it. All Bert's got left is to try to take her down with him."

A. What he said was that he needed me more than ever.

Q.   Can you tell us how he told you about his wife? How he broke the news to you that he even had a wife?

A.   He didn't. I already knew.

Q.   How did you know? Television? The newspapers?

A.   No, they didn't have it. I mean, they had it, but not the names of the people who were killed. I mean, if it had happened in Indianapolis they would have, but it happened someplace else.

Q.   Well, if you didn't hear about it on television, or from the newspaper, and if Brophy didn't tell you, then who did?

A.   Mr. Carlson.

Q.   Mr. Carlson? Who is Mr. Carlson?

A.   He was from the insurance company.

Q.   An investigator, you mean?

A.   Yes. He came and asked me about Mr. Brophy.

Q.   He knew about you and Mr. Brophy?

A.   No. He was asking questions at the desk at the motel, and they told him I knew him, so he came to me.

Q.   When was this?

A.   About five days after she was killed.

Again, Purcell and Aranow exchanged a look. This time neither was grinning. Five days after the explosion would be one day after Brophy's lawsuit was filed. In just one day, Arthur Hawkes's bird dogs had found his trail.

Q.   I see. And what was your reaction? When he told you what had happened?

A.   I was sorry his wife had been killed.

Q.   What about when you learned he'd been married all along?

A.   Well, I found both things out at the same time. Mr. Carlson said the wife was killed, so I knew there was a wife and I knew she was dead, both at the same time.

Q.   You weren't angry at all?

A.   If she was alive and I found out, I would have been. But her being dead and all, no. That made it different.

Q.   Then what was it that made you decide to show up in this courtroom to testify against Mr. Brophy?

A.   They told me I had to. Otherwise I'd be supponed.

Q.   Subpoenaed?

A.   That's it.

Q.   Who told you that? Mr. Carlson?

A.   Yes.

Q.   He came to you just five days after the explosion and said you'd have to testify?

A.   Oh, no. This was only a couple of months ago, that he came back and said that.

Q.   I see. And did he offer to pay you to testify?

A.   Only my expenses. To travel from Indianapolis to here and back.

Q.   And your per diem—your hotel, and meals, and so forth, while you're here?

A.   Yes. And my time.

Q.   Your time?

A.   The time I had to take away from the job.

Q.   And what are they paying you for that?

A.   I don't know. They said that would depend.

Q.   Depend on what?

A.   On how long you had me on the stand asking me questions.

Q.   Uh-huh. And did Mr. Brophy know about this?

A.   No.

Q.   Just a minute. You've said you were in bed with him the night before last. But he didn't know you were going to be here today to testify?

A.   I wasn't sure I was going to be here. Mr. Carlson told me sometimes there are mistrials or cases are settled or all kinds of reasons why they end up not needing you in court. I didn't even hear till yesterday that I was supposed to be here today.

Q.   What about Mr. Brophy? Did he ever give you money?

"Don't go too far, Bert," Sheila muttered again. And Hawkes was on his feet objecting.

"Yes," the judge said, "I think there's no call for that question."

"Your Honor," Bert protested, "I think the nature of the relationship between this woman and this man is well within the scope here. Sex for money tells us one thing about a man. Sex for some other reason—affection or comfort or some physical problem at home—could tell us something else."

Junior Bohr seemed impressed. "Yes, I think perhaps something along that latter line might be admissible. I'm going to let this proceed, Mr. Hawkes, and we'll take it one question at a time."

"I'll try to choose the words with care, Judge," Bert said.

Q.   Did Mr. Brophy ever bring you a gift?

A.   Yes. Panty hose.

Q.   When was this?

A.   Oh, it was pretty regular. He used to have shipments of them on his truck, so he would liberate a pair for me from time to time.

Q.   Thank you. I have no further questions, Your Honor.

THE COURT: Redirect, Mr. Hawkes?

MR. HAWKES: Yes, Miss Waite. That last answer of yours to the final question from Mr. Klein. You said he would liberate these panty hose? What do you mean, liberate?

A.   Well, that was his word. He had these volume shipments, so he would take out a pair or two. He said they expected that sort of thing—that nobody would ever miss them.

Q.   And in that same answer you also said this happened regularly, did you not?

A.   Well, from time to time, yes.

"Score one for you, Sheila," Max said. "Bert did go too far. That's some Specimen. His record makes him a rapist, Hawkes makes him an adulterer, now Bert makes him a thief."

"No further questions, Judge," Hawkes said.

"Very good," Junior said, and discharged the witness. She did not look in the Specimen's direction as she departed.

"And the defense rests," Hawkes said.

Joe Purcell said, "Request a meeting in chambers."

"All right," the judge said. "We'll go inside. I think we're near enough to the noon hour to have the lunch break now. Reconvene at two o'clock."

Max, Bert, Sheila, and Harry Wright repaired to the General Dexter for lunch. The A&P's threesome were unanimous that Brophy was doomed. Not only that, his continuing presence in the courtroom would sink any chance Joe might have to salvage at least something from the wreckage.

Harry Wright had a different view. "If he's not in that courtroom, Arthur Hawkes will have a field day with it. He'll keep telling the jury how Brophy doesn't dare show his face."

"And if he does show his face?" Max Aranow said. "They'll never hear another word Joe says. Didn't you see them while that girl was testifying? They kept staring at the Specimen."

"Let's leave it up to Joe when he gets here," Bert said. "It's his trial."

"Why did he want to go into chambers with Hawkes and the judge?" Harry Wright asked.

"Joe's moving for a directed verdict in the plaintiff's favor," Sheila said.

"And he expects the judge to say yes to that? After what happened this morning?"

"You forget, Harry," Bert said, "all it is, is a formality. A base Joe has to touch. It's not a question of what he expects. The defense rested, so Joe made the motion, same as the one Arthur made when Joe rested."

Someone shifted the conversation to the subject of Felix Harding, the A&P's chief investigator, and for a brief time Nero was at least as unpopular as the Specimen. But then Purcell appeared, and now he seemed philosophical on the point. "After all," he said, "when you think it through, how did the defense even find out Brophy was in Indianapolis, let alone what motel he was staying at? Either they read it in the paper or they called up Brophy and asked him. It's a harmless enough question. So who told them about it? Brophy told them. So much for their detective work."

"And so much for ours," Wright said, as much in self-reproach as anything.

"Well," Purcell said, "if the other side could have thought to ask Brophy about it, I'm sure one of us could have thought of the same question. Nero could have thought of it. You could have thought of it, Harry. But most of all, I could have thought of it, and I'm the one who should have. I went right to the point of it when I talked to him down here, 'way back when. He told me he was in a motel in Indianapolis. I could have asked him what motel, and he would have told me that too. But I didn't. Nero had nine hundred thousand things to investigate—and without any backup corporate or insurance manpower or facilities—and he does one of the great jobs of all time, and here we're down on him for not thinking of the one question I should have thought of. If you want to get mad at somebody get mad at me. No, on second thought don't get mad at me. Let's forget it."

"Second the motion," Max said. "And to change the subject, we took a vote on whether the Specimen should show up in the courtroom the rest of the way."

"How'd it come out?"

"We decided to leave it up to you."

"If it's up to me, I say no," Purcell said. The waiter came for his order, and Joe ordered a double Red Label and soda. Was that all, sir? And the lentil soup, Purcell said. Aranow, the senior partner, beamed approval.

The beginning of the afternoon session in court would be—and was— a duplicate of the morning, with the judge opening another envelope, like the one that contained the name of Tammy Waite. This time however it was Joe Purcell, not Arthur Hawkes, who had supplied the envelope, with a witness for purposes of rebuttal.

Now Herman Molle took the stand.

He looked very much as he had looked the day he emerged from his basement apartment in the old brownstone on New York's West 22nd Street to attend Mr. Gutman's funeral. Even the clothing was the same— green sweater under jacket under overcoat—though in the warmth of the courtroom he consented now to set the last garment aside, for a few moments at least.

What differed here from the morning was that no Harry Wright went outside to the telephone. Steppenworth or Halsey could have gone for Hawkes, but neither of them made the move. They already knew who Herman Molle was: something had stirred in the memory bank of Arthur Hawkes. He flashed an index finger, and Halsey, dipping behind him, fished a worn list of names from a briefcase. There was Molle's name on the list, and next to it two symbols. The first denoted that the man was not someone of any substantive importance to the defense; the second that he was unreachable, with no telephone listed for his 1966 address. And there the trail had ended.

By the same token, there was not the alarm at the Hawkes table that there had been at Purcell's this morning. As unexpected witnesses went, Tammy Waite reigned at this moment, and would continue to reign, as undisputed knockout champ. No one, least of all Herman Molle, would touch that bombshell.

Still and all, Arthur Hawkes knew Joe Purcell too well to take something like this for granted. The preliminary qualifying out of the way, it took just one totally innocuous question to bring Hawkes to his feet:

Q.   Is it fair to say, then, Mr. Molle, that your professional life has been devoted to the study of pressure containers and particularly metallic stress and strain and what is called metal fatigue?

A.   I suppose so.

MR. HAWKES: He supposes so?

THE COURT: None of that, Mr. Hawkes. The witness has answered the question.

"Hawkes is edgy as a cat," Sheila whispered to Max. "He doesn't know where Joe found this dude."

There was confidence in Max's smile. "The difference between Joe and Hawkes," he said, "is that Hawkes is at his best only when the going is good."

THE WITNESS: I mean, I have been retired for several years.

Q.   But you were not retired in February of 1966?

A.   No. I was still active, but business wasn't very good.

Q.   But in 1966 you were still on retainer from the Nance Company?

A.   Yes. But they weren't sending me much business.

Q.   Any particular reason for that?

A.   I guess because they didn't have much business to send. They sent me the specifications for the new jumbo tank car they were going to be manufacturing. But I think that's about the only thing they manufactured from then on.

Q.   And why did they send you the specifications?

A.   Because they wanted my reaction to it. Like always before that.

Q.   And what was your reaction?

A. I thought it was a disgrace.

Q. A what?

A. A disgrace. It was a Coke bottle on wheels.

Q. A what?

A. Coke. Coca-Cola. Or call it any soft drink you like, except maybe Dr. Brown's, because Dr. Brown's stuck with the heavier bottles, for a long time anyway. Maybe they still do, but I haven't found out. I think I'd have to go down to Ratner's to get it. Delancey Street and Second Avenue. That's a sleeper jump from where I live.

The jury leaned forward, examining this newest specimen as if it were a bug under glass. Mother Nine had quit writing in his notebook altogether. Only Two, DeSabitini, seemed to be enjoying this. When Molle got to Dr. Brown's, Two nodded and smiled widely in appreciation.

Purcell shot a glance at Hawkes. Arthur was watching the jury too. So was Junior.

Q. All right. You say a Coke bottle on wheels. What does that mean?

A. I said all soft drinks. Except Dr. Brown's.

Q. Very well. Except Dr. Brown's.

A. I said a Coke bottle on wheels just to mean any soft drink bottle on wheels.

THE COURT: The Coca-Cola company will forgive you, Mr. Molle. Can we get to the point here? What does it mean?

THE WITNESS: They explode.

THE COURT: Coke bottles explode?

THE WITNESS: They were exploding back then, in the sixties.

THE COURT: Why would they do that?

MR. PURCELL: If it please the Court—

THE COURT: Continue your questioning, Mr. Purcell.

Q. Why would they do that?

A. Because they'd gone to the composition bottles. And that meant a weaker container, thinner, and the walls of the bottles couldn't always stand the pressure of the carbon dioxide inside. So the bottles here and there would blow up. Right on the grocer's shelves, they'd blow up. And people were getting cut and hurt and bringing lawsuits.

Q. Doing what? I didn't hear that last.

MR. HAWKES: You heard it.

THE COURT: Strike that last exchange. Just go on to the next question, Mr. Purcell.

Q. Well, what did they eventually do to these bottles to get them so they wouldn't explode? Do you know?

A. Yes. They reduced the level of carbonation. From that day to this, you haven't been able to get a decent bottled soft drink.

Q. But they did do something.

A. Yes. I just told you. With the exception of Dr. Brown's.

Q. So in this case you went back to the Nance people with your report, and you said this tank car is a Coke bottle on wheels.

A. Not in those words, I didn't.

Q. But the message was the same, essentially?

A. Not at all, it wasn't.

Q. But in technical language, it was.

A. Not in technical language either. My analysis and recommendation wasn't that they should do what the soft drink people did and reduce the pressure. You can't reduce the pressure of liquefied petroleum gas. Carbonation, yes. LPG, no. My recommendation was that they stay with the thicker container.

Q. By thicker, you mean insulated?

A. Yes.

Q. Insulated tank car?

A. Yes.

Q. And what did they do with your recommendation?

A. They invited me to Washington.

Q. For what purpose?

A. To testify at the Department of Transportation hearing.

Q. And did you do that?

A. Do what? Go to Washington? Yes.

Q. Testify at the hearing.

A.   There was no hearing.

Q.   There was no hearing?

A.   No. They met me at the hotel and took me to supper at a fancy restaurant, the Rive Gauche, and told me my recommendations would be taken under full consideration but that the hearings had been postponed, and they'd let me know if I was needed again.

Q.   Do you remember the date of this?

A.   The 17th of February, 1966. The hearings were supposed to be the next day.

Q.   And instead what did you do the next day?

A.   Went home to New York.

Q.   When you say *they* told you this, do you remember their names?

A.   Yes. There were two of them. Mr. Simon and Mr. McKenna. They had lamb, and it came in a pastry—an order for two, and they shared it. It was very pink. I had the sole. The thing I remember most was the asparagus. You could swear it was fresh, not frozen, and you wondered how they would get fresh asparagus in February.

This time, Purcell shot a look at Bert Klein. The latter nodded emphatic agreement. If only, the shared thought said, Max Aranow was questioning this witness. They would talk food for nine hours.

Q.   You seem to have a clear memory for the details of the occasion. Why is that, would you say, after so long a time?

A.   Somebody gives you fresh asparagus in February, you'll remember it too. It had to be hothouse.

Q.   Do you remember their first names? The two men with you?

A.   Albert Simon and Harrison McKenna.

Q.   And whom did they represent?

A.   The Nance Company, of course. The people who retained me.

Q.   You'd met them both before?

A.   No. Neither one of them. Simon was the one who called me at my hotel to make the date for dinner. So I met him over the phone.

Q.   And what was Mr. Simon's position? Do you know?

A.   He was an official with Nance. More in finance than in engineering. But exactly what his title was, that I don't remember.

Q.   Mr. Molle, the current president of Nance, Trevor Peters, testified here a week or so ago that Albert Simon was, back in 1966, the controller of the Nance Corporation. Do you have any reason to doubt that?

A.   No.

Q.   And Mr. McKenna? What was his position?

A.   Like with Simon, I didn't know exactly what his position was.

Q.   Did you know for a fact that he worked for Nance?

A.   No. I assumed it. That's the way it would be. Who else would he work for? I mean, Nance was my account. They were the ones who invited me down there.

Q.   And nobody told you that McKenna didn't work for Nance?

A.   No. I already told you.

Q.   Nobody told you that at that time, in February of 1966, Harrison McKenna was in fact assistant secretary of the Department of Transportation. That in fact he was in charge of the railroad division of the department?

A.   No. I thought he was with Nance.

Q.   Do you remember anything else about him? From that evening when you went to dinner?

A.   No. He didn't say much. He talked more to the waiter than he did to us. I thought he was a little strange.

Q.   Talked more to the waiter than he did to you? Why?

A.   I'll tell you why. He kept asking for some sappy Hawaiian beer to go with his dinner. In a fancy place like that. Primo. That was it. Primo beer.

MR. PURCELL: I have no further questions. Mr. Hawkes?

MR. HAWKES: No questions.

At the counsel table, Harry Wright said, "I don't understand Arthur Hawkes. Really."

"Why?" Purcell said.

"Because he didn't cross-examine."

"And get his head handed to him, like Bert did with their last witness? The Mole is a minefield." The Mole was the obvious nickname for Molle, equally for the sound of the name and the looks of the man.

"Arthur still could have attacked his credibility," Wright protested. "What kind of an expert is this seedy little guy? He hasn't even worked since the sixties."

"Nance hired him as an expert consultant," Joe said. "That's the kind of expert he is. And if he hasn't worked for a long time, maybe it's because he was blacklisted as a troublemaker. And Arthur knows I would have brought that out on redirect. Christ, I should have hit it on direct." He tugged at his ear. "No, Arthur played it smart. He just left him alone."

After recess, in the balcony corridor outside, overlooking the well of the courthouse, Bert Klein said, "It *was* a little odd. About Hawkes in there just now."

"His not cross-examining?"

"No, just that you got away with surprising him with that witness. He had the same information in front of him that you did. If you found the Mole in New York, he could have found him too."

Purcell shook his head. "The point is, Arthur had no reason to investigate in that direction. The Mole was a paid consultant for Nance. Paid consultants always go along with company decisions—or so Arthur's conditioned to think. If they have any reservations, they state them early and one way or another the thing gets worked out. But here was a case where they posted pro forma notice of a hearing, and one of the manufacturer's paid consultants is ready to blow the whistle on them, so they just canceled the hearing and figured he'd go away. Which is exactly what happened. But how would Hawkes ever find out about it?"

"Somebody at Nance could have told him."

Again Purcell shook his head. "You heard the testimony on that. It all happened in 1966. By now, none of the people at Nance who were involved are even around anymore. And it doesn't change Arthur's defense any. Anytime you have product liability, there's always somebody who'll testify that the company had been warned in advance. So Arthur will deal with this new business the same way he defends the case overall. In the final analysis, the Mole is a witness who saw there was something wrong with the product. They've already put on a sackful of expert witnesses, all of them saying there's *nothing* wrong with the product. No, the only lawyer here who screwed up on surprise testimony was me. That fucking waitress. The day I met him, I didn't trust that Specimen. I had every reason to check up on his story, and I didn't. So Arthur winds up with the same defense he's always had and I wind up in the shithouse."

Looking down from the balcony, they could see the gray-coated attendant at the newsstand as, with a practiced swipe of his hand, he ripped open the top of a carton of cigarettes. As if to punctuate Purcell's last words, ten packs of Salem Light 100s cascaded helter-skelter onto the floor in front of the counter.

Harry Wright said, "I know this is a dumb question. Really. But *why* was it so important? That Primo beer business?"

"Because," Bert Klein said, "after what McKenna said about the beer, and now the Mole testifying to it, that means perfect identification. If the Mole says it was McKenna at that dinner that night, the jury will know it was McKenna. And if the Mole's memory is believable about that, then it has to be believable about everything. A little thing like that—the brand name of a beer. Wouldn't you say, Joe?"

"That's part of it," Purcell said.

Klein stared at him. Part of it? What else was there?

He let the question go unanswered. What Purcell said next might be the answer to it—or might not. Klein could not tell which. "It was a fascinating thing, the way the Mole talked about the exploding Coke bottles," Joe was saying. "We're in an age of new law on this. This is the age of the container. You can't separate the package from the product."

"I have trouble with that," Harry Wright said. "In Kentucky there was a case like that a few months ago. Somebody won a case where a grocery sold them a bad can of baked beans—no, it wasn't baked beans, it was soup. Either way, food poisoning. And the grocery had to pay part of the damages."

"The grocery store is part of the commercial chain," Bert Klein said. "They make a profit from the sale. So why shouldn't they share the responsibility?"

"Well," Wright said, "I can see that once they hear about it they have the responsibility to take it off their shelves and not sell any more of it. But how can they be responsible for that first can? Are they supposed to open every can to make sure the contents are all right?"

"You're thinking from the store's standpoint," Klein said. "Think about it from the customer's. He's entitled to assume he's getting a safe product. If he doesn't, it's not up to him to have to prove who was at fault. That shifts the burden to the customer. The people in a better position to carry that burden are the people who are supposed to protect him. His money pays for that protection, and the store took his money."

"Well, maybe I'm making the wrong point," Wright said. "Really. I mean, there *was* something wrong with the soup. But in our case here there was nothing wrong with the propane in that tank car."

"That doesn't make any difference either," Klein said. "Even if the manufacturer makes his product with the best of care, he's still part of the commercial chain that brings the product to the consumer. And as a matter of social engineering, the law now provides that everyone in that commercial chain can be held responsible."

"Well, it didn't used to be that way," Harry Wright said.

"With this jury, it may not be that way now either," Joe Purcell said. His voice had the tone of someone who has just returned from somewhere else, rejoining a conversation rather than continuing it. Again, Bert had the feeling that he was talking almost to the point, but not entirely.

"We were called into a case in New Mexico a few years ago," Joe said to Harry Wright. "A dump truck on a construction site was backing up, and it ran over one of the workmen and took off his leg. So naturally they sued the contractor for the negligence of the driver. The defense was that the workman was the one who was really negligent because he walked into the path of the backing dump truck without looking where he was going. So they took depositions, and in comes the truck driver, a nice, presentable guy, with his wife holding his hand, and every time he talked about the accident he began to cry. You figure the jury's going to love this guy, and identify with him, so there's no way you're going to win the case."

"What happened?" Wright asked.

"We switched the theory of the case," Purcell said. "Instead of making it a negligence case we made it a product liability case."

"What was the defective product?"

"The dump truck."

"Why?"

"It didn't have an automatic backup alarm system."

"I didn't know dump trucks had to have a system like that," Wright said. "I thought that was just for heavy construction equipment."

"That's what the defense said." Purcell tugged at his ear. "But we found an expert witness—a safety engineer—to testify that it *should* be on dump trucks because dump trucks do exactly what the heavy construction equipment does. They work on construction sites, and by their very nature they have to back up, and they're blind in the back because of the dump bed. So it's a classic example of a vehicle that needs an alarm system. And when he testified, he brought a backup alarm unit with him and set it off for the jury. When they heard what it sounded like, they had no trouble understanding how the accident could have been prevented—and who was in the best position to prevent it."

"It was Joe who came up with that theory," Bert Klein said to Wright. "And it was beautiful. Not a damn thing wrong with the dump truck, yet now instead of having just one victim, we had two: not only the client who lost his leg, but this poor driver. He was also a victim of the corporate indifference of the construction company."

On the main floor below, the newsstand attendant bent down to pick up the last of the spilled Salem packs in front of his counter. A large woman, made larger by capacious jeans and plaid coat, took a step backward and fell over him, landing in a seated position heavy with anger and surprise.

"There's an example for you," Bert Klein said to Harry Wright. "You can take the lady's case. Mrs. Whatever-Her-Name versus R. J. Reynolds Tobacco. A great target defendant."

Harry Wright laughed, but it was a nervous laugh. The new movement in the law, under which parties ever more removed from the actual event could, in a society ever more complex, be held responsible for the consequences, was one with which he had not yet made his peace. His loyalty bound him without a moment's question to Joe Purcell in the Fireball case. But loyalty was one thing; logic was another. "If I was sitting on that jury and didn't know either lawyer," he had told his wife only last night, "damned if I wouldn't think Hawkes made more sense than Joe does." But he believed that only north-northwest. If only he felt more at home with the way the law was trending.

"You know," he said to Klein now, "you've almost got me believing what you just said."

"Believe it," Bert told him. "Right, Joe?"

"Right," Purcell said. "Especially if she develops a tumor on her ass. Everybody knows cigarettes cause cancer."

19

Joe Purcell's final argument to the jury the next day took the entire $2\frac{1}{2}$ hours of the morning session. Under the circumstances, it was an understated masterwork. He opened with reference to an ancient adage: "God couldn't be everywhere, so He created mothers," leading just as in his opening statement with Janet Brophy. This time, though, there was no loving husband he could refer to. He could talk about the children, and did; even throw in a line about not visiting the sins of the father. He could talk about damages and he did; of Janet's future potential; of what Elliot had been like on the witness stand.

He spoke of product design, conspiracy, corporate greed, and the appropriate nature of punitive damages. He quoted one witness after another from memory, and accurately so. He reviewed all the technical data, with special emphasis, time and again, on the fact that the Jumbo Nellie Nellie had been without insulation. Prohibited by the judge's ruling, in the wake of the jury mail episode, from alluding to any Department of Transportation proposal to retrofit and insulate the jumbos, he threw all the weight of the associated evidence at the jury and scored on the point even in the face of the proscription.

Yet no feeling of satisfaction came with it, certainly no feeling of confidence. The development with that waitress yesterday was so unexpected, so bizarre, that Joe had no feel for what he had accomplished this morning—if anything. And he was grateful and relieved when it came time for the noontime break.

Sheila went with Harry Wright to his home for lunch. Max, Joe, and Bert went to the General Dexter, but Bert did not stay long. They ordered a premeal round of drinks, and Max said, "It's fascinating. You'd think this would be a Cincinnati town, their being Ohio and all. But instead they root for the Pittsburgh Pirates. I was talking to number five in the men's room at the break. He said half the town here went into mourning when Roberto Clemente died."

"Didn't he die in that plane crash?" Joe said. "On that mercy mission somewhere?"

Bert Klein jumped to his feet. "I've got to get out of here," he said. His voice was low and tight, unlike anything Joe or Max had heard before. "I'm not going to sit here and listen to the two of you with that trivia bullshit of yours!"

He stormed off, almost knocking over the arriving waiter. "Will the gentleman be back?" the waiter said.

"I doubt it," Purcell said. "What was he drinking?"

"The same as you, sir. Red Label and soda."

"Leave it with me," Joe said.

"Bert's tense," Max said.

"He's worked hard," Joe said. "Too bad I couldn't give him a better case. He was great on that cross yesterday, up till the very end. I'm leaving the firm in good hands, Max."

"Maybe better hands than you realize," Max Aranow said. "You're right about his dying in that plane crash."

"Whose dying?"

"Clemente. Interesting that Five would bring it up. Let me tell you a thing or two about it..."

The afternoon session:

"Ladies and gentlemen," Arthur Hawkes said to the jury. "I want to begin by quoting to you two statements. The first of these you heard before this trial even began. You haven't had a chance to hear the second one yet."

"He's in good form," Purcell whispered to Bert.

"He sucks," Bert hissed back. Joe glanced at his young partner. He could see that Bert's intensity had moved him over the brink. He could no longer sit back and objectively admire the virtuosity of Hawkes. He was overtaken by personal dislike.

Hawkes was reminding the jurors of the day they were selected and sworn in, and of the man who was challenged off the panel by Brother Purcell because he'd been in a tornado and hadn't sued anybody. That tornado was an act of God, Arthur said, and so was what happened at Florian in the case of the Fireball.

The quote that they had yet to hear, he said, would come from Judge Bohr. "It will come in the judge's instructions to you before you retire to the jury room," Hawkes said. "You are permitted to deliberate only the facts, not the law. The judge will tell you what the law in this state is, and you must follow it. And when you come to consider the proximate cause of the accident at Florian, you must follow the instructions of Judge Bohr. And here is what he will tell you: 'When I use the words "proximate cause" I mean first, that there must have been a connection between that conduct of the defendant which plaintiff claims was negligent and the injury complained of by the plaintiff, and second, that the occurrence which is claimed to have produced that injury was a natural and probable result of such conduct of the defendant.' And, ladies and gentlemen, you must ask yourself what was the occurrence which they claimed produced the injury in this case. I will tell you what it was. It was a flash of lightning.

"So now you must ask yourselves one question and one question only: is a flash of lightning a natural and probable result of any conduct of any defendant in this case or in any case in all the world? If your answer to that one question is no, then under the law you must find for the defendants in this case. Unless you think that North American or Nance or Mid-Central stood up in the heavens and caused that lightning to strike where it did and when it did on that day, then under the law you must follow the judge's instructions and return a verdict in favor of the defendants."

Hawkes had been standing behind the defense table, but now he moved toward the jury. "Was that tank car, that Jumbo Nellie Nellie, built to U.S. government specifications? The answer is yes, and not even Brother Purcell could try to tell you otherwise. In fact, under existing regulations at the time, that tank car could not have legally been built any other way. And speaking of that tank car when the lightning hit, too often we have been a little casual with one another in this courtroom during this trial, and we have spoken of the lightning hitting the tank car. But the lightning didn't hit the tank car. Or, if it did, it caused no damage whatsoever. Tank cars do get struck by lightning, but if they're properly grounded—with a built-in lightning rod, so to speak— then the lightning is harmlessly diverted. And we know this tank car was properly grounded, and not even Brother Purcell has sought to assert otherwise.

"Brother Purcell claims that insulation would have prevented this accident, but you have heard expert testimony that insulation would not have prevented it. And so if insulation would not have prevented it, would *anything* have prevented it? Yes, indeed: a very simple thing, something as simple as a properly trained and equipped fire department. They are the rule, not the exception. They exist everywhere you go. Everywhere but the town of Florian on that day a year ago last May.

"I said that lightning did not hit the tank car. What, then, did it hit? We know that too: what it hit was the air above the tank car, and the vapor in the air that was being vented by the safety valve of the tank car. And that safety valve was in perfect working order, and not even Brother Purcell has tried to claim otherwise.

"Brother Purcell has made much of the evil of that huge corporation, North American Petroleum. But what are they guilty of in this case? They did one thing: they filled an order for propane at their refinery in Whiting, Indiana. And that is all they did.

"Brother Purcell has made much of the delay of the tank car in reaching Florian, with the temperature hotter that day than it would have been if the car had been on time. But what was the result of that added temperature? The result was that the safety valve operated, and operated perfectly. And then lightning hit and ignited the vapor, so there was a fire. I will be the first to agree with Brother Purcell that if the vapor was not there and the lightning did not hit it, there would have been no fire. But that gets us back to what the judge will instruct you on the law. And unless you believe that one or two or all three of these defendants caused that lightning to strike, then there is no proximate cause, and therefore—not under any opinion you may have of any fact in the case, but under the law, as the judge instructs you on the law—you must bring in a verdict for the defendants.

"The law gives you no options, no discretion, no flexibility. You are at liberty to do nothing but *follow* the law." Hawkes was not playing to any one or two jurors any longer. He stood a good seven feet away from the jury box and played to the ensemble. Intently, they watched and listened: "And remember that the fire, which did occur because the lightning struck, injured no one—didn't harm a single hair on a single head. And that brings us back to the nonperformance of the fire department. They didn't even have to put the fire out, for Heaven's sake! You've heard testimony to that effect. All they had to do was contain it, keep it at a certain level, and eventually, harmlessly, it would have burned itself out. But they didn't even know how to do that. God knows they were punished for their incompetence." Hawkes moved a few steps closer to the jury. "God also knows it would be unjust to punish the innocent for the incompetence of others."

"I don't want to be around when he gets to the Specimen," Purcell whispered to Klein.

"I think you'd better leave now," Bert whispered back.

He was wrong. "So Brother Purcell knows that he cannot win this case on the facts, and certainly cannot win this case on the law. So what does he do? He papers the whole thing over. Papers it over with a big sign consisting of a big ten-letter word." Arthur's hands went above his head and painted the word in huge airborne letters: "C-O-N-S-P-I-R-A-C-Y— conspiracy. All right. What is a conspiracy? By definition, it's two or more people getting together in an attempt to break some law. Can any of you sitting on this jury tell me of any law that was broken by any two or more defendants in this case? All through the trial I have waited to hear some- body explain that. How many witnesses did you hear from Mr. Purcell's side—was it sixty-eight of them?—some astonishing number like that— and did a single one of them offer a single shred of evidence in that direction?

"I will give Brother Purcell credit for one thing. He has moved heaven and earth to convince you that these companies are large companies. I think we all know that to be a fact. And Brother Purcell has had some success in his time, I give him all due credit, in having verdicts brought against big companies. You have to teach them a lesson, he says. Well, we all know who pays for big verdicts. The answer to that is: everyone. And even in a case like this, where Brother Purcell cannot show you a single thing that one of these defendant companies did that was wrong, what was it he was asking you to do this morning? Send them a message, he said. Big companies deserve to have to pay out big verdicts. Not because they did anything wrong, but because they're big."

Hawkes stopped, looked around thoughtfully at the spectators, then back at the jury. "I see a jam-packed courtroom here this afternoon. Not an empty seat. So maybe it is a good thing that Mr. Vincent Brophy isn't here, because he would have to stand instead of sit, and that might interfere with his idea of the pleasant life. Oh, what a loving, grief-stricken husband he was when he testified from the witness stand. What an honorable, faithful husband. Except that less than ten hours after his wife was killed, and as soon as ten days later, and as recently as three nights ago, he was lying in another woman's arms. And bringing her presents to keep her happy. And what did he pay for those presents? Nothing. Why pay for something when you can steal it? This petty thief, this despicable philanderer, was sitting here in court just yesterday morning. Then his true character was revealed. Somehow we haven't seen much of him since. Is it any wonder?"

There were three elements in Hawkes's defense, as propounded in his final argument: the act of God, the downright incompetence of the fire department, and the character of the plaintiff, Vincent Brophy. Of Brophy's four coplaintiffs, the four children, Hawkes said not a word. Instead, he stayed with Brophy for a time, then started working his way back the other way: back to the fire department and the hours, the days of evidence brought against them in this courtroom—and finally, inevitably, to the act of God: None of the defendants knew how to create lightning.

The organization was superb, the impact obvious. He even had a coda for a finish: "Ladies and gentlemen, first you have heard Brother Purcell's argument, and then you heard mine. Now, the way these trials are structured, the rule is that he gets another turn and I don't. You will hear another argument from him in this room tomorrow morning, but I am not permitted to respond. Brother Purcell knows what to do with an opportunity like that. But I hope in fairness you will remember what I have had to say this afternoon. He can speak again to you, but I can't. That's the way it is."

He thanked the jury and sat down. He had taken 1 hour and 54 minutes. Junior Bohr adjourned the case till morning.

Joe Purcell spent that evening composing a new song on the piano in the A&P suite at their motel. Perry Muncrief brought him two cheese-burgers at midnight.

"Did you get me a chocolate milk?"

"You didn't say you wanted one."

"I didn't."

"Do you want one now?"

"No, thank you," Purcell said. "What are you doing tomorrow?"

"I'll be here."

"What for? Come on into court, if you want to."

"Are you serious?"

"Yes." Purcell looked at him searchingly. "You sure Max or somebody didn't tell you to get me a chocolate milk?"

"Look," Perry said, "I'll go out and get you one. I'm happy to do it."

"Nope. Do we have any Scotch? The Chinese drink Scotch with their cheeseburgers."

"I didn't know they had cheeseburgers in China."

"They don't. No Scotch either. It's the Chinese in Hawaii who do it."

"I'd better stay here tomorrow," Perry said. "What if you need some-thing? I'm the one most used to running that keyboard."

"Too late," Joe said, and poured three ounces of Scotch into a tumbler from the bathroom. His mouth was crammed with cheeseburger. "Here's a go!" And he downed half the contents of the glass. "Too late," he said again. "There was a lot of Burton Lane in that song I was working on tonight. No, there's nothing for you to do here. Go to bed. And you can come in tomorrow with everybody else."

At a little after 3:00 in the morning, Purcell direct-dialed a call to Marcy in New York, not even knowing what he'd say if she answered. She didn't answer. A recording answered, saying her phone was no longer in service.

It was after five o'clock before he fell asleep. Bert arrived at 8:30 in the morning and shook him awake. Purcell opened his eyes and looked up. "What?"

"The judge wants you in his chambers."

"We went through that last time."

"He wants you again this time. Nine-thirty."

"Did we get lucky? Did Cuneo tamper with the jury again?"

"His secretary didn't say what it is."

"She never does. What time is it now?"

"You've got less than an hour."

"Christ. Do I have time for a shower?"

"If you crack ass, you do."

When he reached the judge's chambers, he found Hawkes and Junior already there, same as the time before with the jury business. "I feel awful," Joe said. "Does it show?"

"It's all right," Arthur Hawkes said. "We've got something to improve your outlook."

"What's that?"

"A settlement," Junior Bohr said. "Tell him how much, Arthur."

"A million five," Hawkes said.

"Shove it up your ass," Purcell said.

"Listen, Purcell," the judge said to him, "a judge has a duty to bring the parties together and encourage them to reach agreement out of court. And if you think I'm going to hear that trial again, you've got another goddamn think coming."

"My God," Arthur Hawkes said, "he doesn't know."

"What I know," Purcell said, "is that a million five doesn't even pay our postage in this case."

Hawkes and the judge were both laughing, the latter so hard he was coughing instead from untimely cigarette smoke and had to hold up a hand for inner and outer peace. "Shit," he said at last. "Harry Wright didn't get ahold of you?"

"Why should he?"

"Tell him, Arthur."

"It's the Marlowe case," Hawkes said. "They reversed the judge and upheld your appeal."

"Now Ohio's in line with the rest of the states in getting rid of the locality rule," Bohr said. "I think there were forty-six states ahead of us."

"And I cleared settlement authority this morning," Hawkes said. "We'll go a million five. That's over a million more than we offered first time around. I know there's been inflation since then, but not that much inflation."

"Take it, you limber prick," the judge said.

"I have to run it past my client first," Purcell said. "You know the drill."

"Good," Junior said. "We'll consider it done. Now you can never say you never won a case in Mundelein. And it's a nice going-away present for you."

"Hell," Hawkes said, "it's not just the last day of the trial, it's Joe's last day in the law business. I'm sorry about that witness, Joe, but I had no choice. I had to put her on."

Purcell shrugged. "Win some, lose some. I had my chance with my own witness in the afternoon."

"That little Molle guy?" the judge said. "He gave me the fucking willies."

"Appearances aren't everything," Purcell said.

"You want a drink?" Junior said. "To celebrate?"

"Yes," Joe said.

"All I have is bourbon."

"Then I'll have bourbon."

"Arthur?"

"Light, with water," Hawkes said.

"I'll have mine neat, like Joe," Bohr said. "I'm betting you can't stay away from the law, Joe."

"Try me and see."

"You'll be back sooner than you think," the judge said. "I don't know what that shit is you've got with the musical theater."

"I've got a roll of Clorets," Hawkes said.

Bourbon had never tasted so good as it did to Purcell now. He said, "Do I look any better?"

"No," Bohr said, eyeing him. "As a matter of fact, you don't."

When Purcell and Hawkes got back into the courtroom the place was filled once again. The only business of the morning would be Purcell's rebuttal, unless it was a short one, in which case the judge would have time to instruct the jury. Purcell told all hands about the Marlowe settlement, and there was glee in the A&P camp. Harry Wright had known about the appeals court ruling, but not about Hawkes's settlement.

Then the judge came in, convened the court, and nodded to Purcell. Joe walked in front of the jury, tugged at his right ear, looked down at the floor, and began to talk, in a quiet, gravel tone. "Roberto Clemente of the Pittsburgh Pirates," he said. And in the instant he said it, Bert Klein shot a look at Max Aranow. Max was already looking at him. Bert turned his eyes and saw Joe Purcell looking at him too, just for that instant. You went screaming away from the table yesterday, Bert told himself, because Max was talking that stupid baseball nonsense when he should have been concentrating everything on this trial—except that he *was* concentrating everything on this trial, and Joe picked up on it. And this was the last time the two partners would ever share that secret communication of theirs. Bert's throat went tight.

"Roberto Clemente," Joe was saying, and how Mundelein loved him and the Pittsburgh Pirates. And how Clemente died in the takeoff crash of an overloaded cargo plane carrying relief supplies to the stricken natives of Managua, Nicaragua, which had been devastated by an earthquake eight days earlier. And Arthur Hawkes would tell you the earthquake was an act of God, therefore nobody was at fault for overloading that plane and causing it to crash. "I am sick and tired of God being blamed for the recklessness of greedy corporations," Joe rasped. "Not to mention the negligence of the government—the Federal Aviation Authority, in that case—the government-controlled FAA tower that let that plane take off."

Instantly, Hawkes was on his feet, objecting. "Your Honor! The government is not a defendant here."

"Neither is Vincent Brophy," Purcell said. "But you've got him up for rape, adultery, and theft."

"Mr. Purcell," Junior said, "I like to see latitude in argument, but where's the connection?"

"The government is part of the conspiracy in the Fireball case," Joe said to him.

"Did we have testimony on that?"

"Yes, sir, we did. Yesterday."

"Well, proceed for now," the judge said.

The testimony of Herman Molle was what Purcell was reviewing now. Mr. Hawkes had said there was no evidence of conspiracy, but here was Harrison McKenna of the Department of Transportation—the same Harrison McKenna now with North American Petroleum, the same Harrison McKenna who had testified that at DOT if there was an objection to something like a tank car design, you had to have a hearing. But when Molle objected to the Jumbo Nellie Nellie, they canceled the hearing. No hearing, despite a registered expert's condemnation of the tank car design. And would McKenna say as much in writing? No indeed. He would bring Molle to Washington instead, tell him orally at dinner, and send him away. Thus leaving nothing in writing for the record.

And did anybody notice what Molle said about McKenna trying to order a bottle of Primo beer? North American Petroleum owned Primo beer. McKenna in his own testimony had related how he told his board of directors to buy the Primo company. And what was interesting about that? Simply that McKenna had testified he ordered *his* board of directors to make the Primo purchase "in the late fifties or early sixties"—half a dozen years before he officially joined NAP! "My" board, he called them. How could a man order "his" board to do something years before he was a member of the company? Unless, behind the scenes, he had controlled the board all along!

And what was it that particularly tied the oil company and the tank car company and the railroad together? The profit that each would derive from the design of the jumbo uninsulated car. The jury had heard the figures: leave out the insulation, even though you knew it was dangerous to do so, and you achieved profit at the expense of safety.

More than that, the jury had heard the testimony of Herman Molle. This was not a witness coming in to testify, as so many others had, on both sides, *after* the fact as to whether these tank cars were fireworthy. The record showed that this was the one and only witness who was on record foretelling, *before* the holocaust, the danger and the risk if the uninsulated jumbos went into manufacture.

"Why did they do it?" Purcell asked the jury. "Because they wanted to kill people? No. Because it was cheaper to risk killing people than to spend the money to make those tank cars fireworthy to begin with. The cost accountants knew this in advance. It was a question of safety versus profit. And they came down on the side of profit."

The jury, Joe said now, would remember the testimony of one witness. "And I remembered," Purcell said, "coming down here not long after the fireball happened, and I remember getting out of my car and walking over to the Mid-Central tracks and tearing my pants leg on a blackened railroad tie. Then I went to the site of the explosion and I saw the crater underneath where the tank car had been standing. And you have heard the testimony as to those railroad ties and that crater. And I thought about them, and I said to myself, 'We all know the upward force of that explosion—throwing a mushroom cloud like a nuclear blast against airplanes five miles in the sky.' And I thought of Eugene Meara—you remember him, the man from the Tri-State Gas Company, who testified that after the explosion they continued to sell off their reserve fuel and then the branch at Florian went out of business. And I said to myself, 'This is a very complicated picture, especially because Mr. Hawkes said—he said it just yesterday, in his final argument here—that insulation would not have kept the explosion from happening. And he had experts on the witness stand who told you the same thing.'

"And then all of a sudden, it wasn't complicated at all." Joe stopped, and touched his ear with his right hand, and now he chuckled and nodded at the jury. "It wasn't complicated at all, because we had the proof right in front of us that insulation *would* have kept that explosion from happening. Forget that mushroom cloud and the upward force of the explosion. Think of that railroad tie and that crater—the *downward* force. So savage it left absolutely nothing but powdered dust." He wagged an index finger. "And now what happens? Keep in mind the *downward* force of that explosion—and along comes Tri-State Gas, to ship what propane it had left to its customers. *Downward force*—but where did Tri-State find that reserve fuel? In its own *underground* tanks, some of them not ten yards from where the Jumbo Nellie Nellie blew up! What happened to those underground tanks, and all the propane in them, in that explosion? Absolutely nothing! Were those underground tanks insulated? You bet!" His voice was driving but measured. "With–five–inches–of–ordinary–dirt."

Silence fell on the courtroom. Purcell let it take hold, a long beat pause. Then: "Five inches of dirt. That was all the insulation they had. But it was all the insulation they needed. The heat around those holding tanks was hotter than the heat of the sun. And what happened to those tanks? Nothing. And now that railroad and that oil company and that tank car manufacturer send people into this courtroom to tell you insulation couldn't have prevented that fireball, and Mr. Hawkes tells you to believe them!"

Joe nodded heavily. "You have it in your power to send them a message to tell them how much you believe them. And to show every other company, every other industry what consequences they just might face the next time they put greed and profit ahead of safety. Five inches of dirt . . ." He went no further. He paused for a moment, looking down at the floor. Then he looked up again, nodded his thanks, and returned to his seat at the plaintiff table.

He had taken less than twenty minutes. The judge took a little over an hour to charge the jury, then for the third time in two days he brought out an envelope and opened it. Quickly he noted the contents, then handed the single sheet of folded paper to the bailiff, who read it aloud:

"Number Two!"

"Mr. DeSabitini," Junior Bohr said, "you are excused from the deliberations of this jury, with the gratitude and appreciation of this court. The juror so excused could have been any one of you, ladies and gentlemen, as you know. You all sat here these many weeks with that knowledge. Thank you again, Mr. DeSabitini. The other jurors will retire to the jury room to begin considering their verdict."

Purcell had a glimpse of Max Aranow leaving the courtroom in a hurry, and looked inquiringly at Sheila O'Hara. "Max is getting a plane back to New York today," she said. "He authorized me to take you to lunch."

"I ought to eat something," Joe said. "I had two cheeseburgers around midnight, and I don't remember the time before that."

They went to the General Dexter. "Can I have a drink first?" he asked. "And don't tell me I don't need one."

"I think you will need one," she said. "Me too."

"I may go on the wagon for a week when I get back to New York," Joe said.

"When are you leaving?"

"Maybe tomorrow."

"I am too," Sheila said. "Maybe we can go up together."

"If I had Max's energy I'd get out today," he said. "But I didn't know it was going to wrap up this early in the day. You realize I've committed my final act for the A&P?"

"No."

"Well, realize it."

"No," Sheila said again. "You're not leaving."

"Wanna bet?"

"Yup."

"Did Max put you up to this?"

"He sure did," Sheila said. Her voice was uncertain and there were tears in her eyes. "I told him let this cup pass from me, but he said no, he thought I was the best one to tell you."

"What's the matter?" Purcell said. "Is Max sick?"

"Does he look sick?"

"He never looks sick."

"That's because he isn't. But you have to stay because the firm can't survive with both of you gone. And Max is the one who's leaving."

The tears were rolling freely down her cheeks now. She was searching for a handkerchief. The waiter came with their drinks. Purcell said to him, "Bring me another one. Right now." To Sheila, he said, "How long have you known about it?"

She sniffed heavily. "About five weeks."

"Have the others known? Bert? Willie? Nero?"

She nodded, miserably. "We couldn't tell you. Not while you were on the Fireball."

"Screw the Fireball," Purcell said. "I was on my goddamn musical, that's what I was on. It cost me two years of work plus the only woman in my life, and now you lay this number on me. What gave Max the priority here?"

"It's important work," Sheila said.

"Really? I happen to think what I'm doing is important."

"The University of Pennsylvania is sponsoring it," she said, as though she had not heard him. "A nonprofit public-interest law firm, with Max to be the head of it, taking up where the federal government is canceling the legal service programs for the poor. I'm sorry, Joe."

"*I'm sorry, Joe!* That's a great line."

"I mean," she said, "sorry you had to hear it like this. But Max said there was no other way."

"And ran out on me."

Sheila blinked. "Oh," she said, "you mean in the courtroom just now? Oh, no. He wasn't running from you. He was running after number two. The juror. Wanted to find out how he thought it was going to go."

"It went right out the door with Two, that's how it's going to go," Joe said. "He was our best juror."

"Don't be angry at Max," Sheila said.

"And he goes right out the door after him," Joe said. "Sure."

"At his age he's earned the right to retire," she said. "You asked what gave him the priority. That has to be part of it."

"The hell with this," Purcell said, and stood up. "Order yourself some lunch. Eat some for me."

"Where are you going?"

"I wish I knew," Purcell said, and left her sitting there.

20

In what was now the nineteen months between the fireball and the end of the trial nothing much had changed. The afternoon flight from Huntington to New York still stopped at Pittsburgh. No ordinary vector would afford Max Aranow a view of Three Rivers Stadium, the airport lying too far south for that, but he chose a left-hand window seat anyway. What was denied him in Pittsburgh, he explained to his seatmate in the first class section, might be restored coming into LaGuardia. "Excellent chance we'll get Runway 31 there. That way we get to see Shea Stadium."

"I'll keep my fingers crossed," the seatmate said. She was Dorothy Brewer. At the conclusion of the morning session in court, Castor had driven them to the A&P's motel, where Max collected his luggage, then on to Sunrise, for Dorothy to collect hers. Hallie offered them a spot of lunch, and Max opted for a limburger cheese and onion sandwich, on the hunch the onions in the Sunrise pantry would be from Vidalia, Georgia. He was not disappointed. "You hear a lot about the Walla Walla onion and the Maui onion, but the Vidalia onion is the sweetest of them all," he said to Dorothy. "Tonight in New York I will take you to Mardigan's for the herring and a steak." Everything he said was non sequitur, therefore nothing was.

"If that's an offer, I accept," she said.

"You're not leaving for Europe tonight?"

She shook her head. "Not till tomorrow. I have some meetings in the morning with some very dull people. Lawyers. Present company excepted."

"You could include me," Max said, "except that I'm off for Ambler tonight. A Carey limo is picking me up. Probably the same one that's meeting us at LaGuardia. But I have to stop at my office after dinner."

"I thought you were quitting, Max."

"I am. But I have to stop by the office to pick up a box of cheese. From a client in Ladysmith, Wisconsin. Isn't that a wonderful name for a town? A case of clergy malpractice."

"What kind of malpractice?"

"Clergy. Doctors and lawyers can be sued for malpractice. Why not clergymen?"

"I don't know," Dorothy said. "It's just that I never heard of it."

"The clergy has heard of it," Max said. "The insurance companies make sure of that. In fact, the Episcopalians have their own insurance company."

"Does anybody ever win a case?"

"Not that I've heard of. Not in a courtroom, anyway. That's why the insurance companies make so much of it. They scare the preachers half out of their wits, so they all go running to buy the insurance."

"Well, what did you do for your client? Why did he send you the cheese?"

"We got a settlement from the insurance company."

"They didn't want to go to court?"

"They did want to go to court. The lawyer in Ladysmith called me up and said could he tell them Joe Purcell was going to take the case. I said sure."

"Did you tell Joe?"

"Hell, no," Max said. "Didn't have to. The lawyer in Ladysmith just passed the information on to the insurance company, and they'd lost four different kinds of cases in a row to Purcell and they weren't looking for a way to make it five. Especially this kind of a case, where losing it would set a precedent. So they settled. Very quietly, I might add."

"Clergy malpractice," Dorothy said, and shook her head. "What was it all about?" The stewardess set a goblet of white wine down on the tray before her and passed in two miniatures of Walker Red Label for Max. The wine shivered and spilled slightly, from the motion of the plane.

"Nothing that spectacular," Max said. "Woman goes to a minister for counseling and it winds up a seduction scene."

Dorothy set down her glass and spilled some more of the wine. "Joe would have just loved that case," she said, and laughed.

Max looked at her. "You know about that?"

"The complaint by that woman against Purcell? I got a copy of it in the mail. Came anonymously, with a note reminding me this was the lawyer who was going to be trying the Fireball, and saying it might make a good story for my papers."

"Did you say anything to Joe about it?"

"No. Just threw it in the wastebasket. Whoever sent it obviously didn't know I had a special reason for wanting to see Joe win the case. I did wonder about who'd send a thing like that."

"Did it have a Miami postmark?"

"I'm almost sure it did. It was Florida someplace. But how would you know that?"

"There's a private investigator down there who was a little unhappy with us," Max said, and told her about Victor Cuneo. "What you may not know is that the Marlowe woman withdrew her case against Joe. And what Cuneo may not know is that her original case against the hospital was settled out in our favor. Joe's appeal was upheld."

Dorothy frowned. "When did that happen? The *Beacon* should have had a story about it."

"Only a couple of days ago," Max said. "And it might be just as well you didn't have a story about it. At least not one that mentioned Purcell by name. That's all the jury would need to hear about. Hawkes would have yammered for a mistrial in the Fireball. He already tried it once. Another one of Cuneo's little stunts."

"Another one of his stunts?"

"The anonymous mailing business," Max said. "Everybody on the jury got one. Copy of a Department of Transportation proposal that the tank cars be insulated. One of the jurors went running to the judge about it and it damn near wrecked our case."

"That's right," Dorothy said. "If you make changes after the accident happens, the jury's not supposed to know about it. I had that explained to me once."

"The doctrine of postaccident repair," Max said. "And it's true that in negligence cases the jury's not supposed to know about it." He opened his second Scotch miniature and poured it into his glass. "But there's a fine line here between negligence and product liability. Some very recent law on this makes it admissible in a product case. See, in a negligence case, the focus is on the actor. And the law encourages the actor to make repairs so there won't be future accidents. The law wants you to fix that hole in the sidewalk so other people don't fall. But in a defective-product case it's different. Maybe the hole in the sidewalk wasn't caused by your negligence. That's up to the jury to decide, and it shouldn't be held against you that you took it on yourself to patch it up while you were awaiting trial. So the jury can't be told you patched it up." He swigged the Scotch. "But what if the focus is on the product and the issue in the case is whether the product was designed properly? Obviously it's relevant to demonstrate that if in fact this particular defendant had the technical knowledge and ability to change its design—to insulate the tank cars, to take our example—before the accident took place, yet failed to do so, then that failure to insulate constituted a design defect. And the law now says that this kind of thing you *can* set before a jury, and they can take it into consideration."

"In other words," Dorothy said, "it didn't make any difference that the people on the jury got that government proposal in the mail? Joe could have introduced it anyway?"

"Sure," Max said. "He had all kinds of experts up there on the stand saying six inches of insulation here, four inches of insulation there, would have prevented the fireball. And he used it in closing argument. You heard him in court this morning."

"But the government document. Why didn't he use that?"

"The judge wouldn't let him. That was the compromise between Hawkes asking for a mistrial and Joe wanting to get the DOT proposal into evidence. The judge said that so long as the jury had seen the document in an unlawful way—its coming to them through the mail instead of being introduced as evidence—it was tainted, you might say, and he wouldn't let Joe refer to it."

"But if the jury got it in the mail and read it, didn't that have the practical effect of being as good as introduced in evidence?"

"That's what Hawkes argued, when he wanted a mistrial. Joe argued back that there wasn't a soul on that jury with enough technical background to read it and understand what he was reading."

"My God," Dorothy said. "I never thought of that."

"Neither did Cuneo when he had it mailed to the jurors."

"Maybe Cuneo didn't have it mailed to the jurors."

"What does that mean? If he didn't, who did?"

"I did."

It was Aranow's turn to spill a drink. "*You* did?"

Dorothy waved an aimless hand. "It was whatever you called it—what doctrine—"

"Postaccident repairs."

"Postaccident repairs. My bureau chief in Washington got the document from the Transportation Department. Told me she damn near had to sleep with somebody to get ahold of it. Said you could never bring it up in court, but maybe we could be the ones to get it to the jury's attention anyway. I'm sorry, Max."

He nodded heavily. "I'm sorry, Max."

"I was looking for you to win it. There didn't seem to be any other way."

"There was another way. If we lose, it'll be because you prevented us from using it."

It was sinking in now. "Oh, my God," she said. "If it hadn't been for—"

"There are no ifs about jury tampering," Max said. But this rebuke, like the one directly before it, was delivered almost without rancor. Instead, the pug prizefighter's face seemed gentled by an inner amusement. "You say she almost had to sleep with the guy to get that document? Why didn't she just walk into the DOT, go up to the desk, and ask for it? Those things are all public record."

"Maybe she didn't know what document to ask for."

"She could have asked Purcell," Max said heavily. "He would have given her a copy."

There was a long pause. "Maybe it won't matter," Dorothy said finally. The ethics of jury tampering were not a factor for her. She was a patrician, not a criminal, and what she had done had been in a proper cause. "I thought Joe was magnificent in court today."

"You should have heard Arthur Hawkes yesterday."

"I didn't hear him," Dorothy said. "But you can't tell me he was good enough to convince all eight people on the jury."

"All he needs is six," Max said. "This is a civil trial."

"Six, then," Dorothy said. "Besides, Joe told me Hawkes didn't care if he won or lost."

"When did he tell you that? Were those the exact words he used?"

"More or less."

"Make it more."

"I can tell you exactly what Joe said," Dorothy said to him. "He said this jury could come in with all the money in the world and it wouldn't make any difference to the future of Arthur Hawkes."

"Ah," said Max. "Well, when he puts it that way, Joe's right. But he didn't mean what you thought he meant. What he meant was that if Arthur loses the case, it'll make him more right than wrong, and his clients may listen to him a little more closely next time. He asked for settlement authority this time, and the most they'd give him was three million dollars. These big companies think in the past. They all have their own hotshot lawyers, and they figure a pigsty jury in Mundelein, Ohio, isn't good for any kind of big money, so they'll pay three million for the nuisance, just to save trial expense. I think Arthur's secretly been looking for a way to lose big, just to convince his corporate clients that a decent offer of settlement can save them millions in court. In that Marlowe malpractice case against your hospital in Mundelein, maybe a hundred thousand more to sweeten the original offer to settle and I think Joe would have taken it and we'd never have gone to trial. As it is now, we win it on appeal and it costs the defense four times as much as their original offer. Arthur can do anything he wants to his clients except convince them of that one piece of arithmetic." Aranow wigwagged to the stewardess and waved an empty miniature of Scotch.

"We're coming into Pittsburgh, Mr. Aranow," the stewardess said.

"Then make it two," Max said. "We'll celebrate the landing." He turned back to Dorothy. "One of the reasons they don't listen to Hawkes is that he doesn't lose that often in court. And one of the reasons he doesn't lose is that he has no fear of losing because losing is not going to hurt him any. His reputation's safe by now, and for all time. But he *doesn't* lose. So he advises his clients of the risk and tells them to settle, and they don't listen to him, and that's what makes Arthur so relaxed in court, and that sense of confidence is what gets over to the jury. It's Arthur's secret weapon. And that's what Joe meant when he told you Arthur wouldn't care how the case came out." Max fastened his seat belt and sighed. "I just hope it's going to be Edam."

"Be what?"

"Edam. The cheese from that guy in Ladysmith, Wisconsin. Actually, it's not just a box. More like a crate, you might say. But it keeps, and the Edam from Ladysmith is better than anything you can get in Holland. Drop by the office with me after supper and I'll let you have a couple of rounds."

"Fine," Dorothy said. "Then I can compare them."

"With each other?"

"No. To the real thing. I'm going to be in Holland day after tomorrow. We have meetings in Amsterdam."

"Don't tell me you own the afternoon paper there too."

"In a sense I do own the paper," Dorothy said. "Not the newspaper—the paper it's printed on. We have timber holdings overseas. Norway. Sweden. Canada. So forth."

"Why do you meet in Amsterdam if you own timber? There's no wood in Holland."

"No," she said. "But Holland does manufacture chemicals and textiles, and we have an interest in them too. We're diversified."

"Diversified!?" Max said. "Good God, you're worse than North American Petroleum."

Dorothy laughed. "Yes and no," she said. "One major difference is we're a family-held company. North American moves stock on the big board."

"That is a difference," Max conceded. "It means nobody ever gets to look at your books."

"That's one of the advantages. What's that you put in the seat pocket?"

"A copy of *Trial* magazine."

"May I see it?"

"Why not?" There was time, Max reasoned, for him to sip one more Scotch before the takeoff from Pittsburgh to New York. And then a nap en route.

He did not wake until he felt the bump of the wheels touching down at LaGuardia. Then he came immediately alert and awake and said, "Jesus Christ, did I miss seeing Shea?"

"I don't know," Dorothy said. "I've been reading your magazine."

"Find anything interesting?" The tone of doubt held priority.

"Oh, yes," Dorothy said.

"You don't have to be polite," he said.

"You're accusing me of all kinds of things," she said. "First you accuse me of screwing up your lawsuit—and I can see now that maybe I did. But being *polite?* Not guilty, counselor."

"Guilty," Max corrected. "You claim you found something interesting in *Trial*." In reflex, he patted the pocket that held the little bottle. "What was it? The ad for the Animal Behavior Advisory Service?"

"No," Dorothy said. "The article by somebody named Colson."

"Bill Colson," Aranow said. "He was president of the trial lawyers, back in the sixties. I didn't read it. What was so fascinating about it?"

"Just that he listed the ten top qualities of a trial lawyer," Dorothy said.

"Ah, yes," Max said. "A trial lawyer is loyal, reverent, kind, trust-worthy—"

"Courageous," Dorothy broke in. "The article lists courage as the number-one trait." Max noticed for the first time that she wore reading glasses; as in the case of many persons, including, most of all, the hand-some ones, they enhanced her looks. "'The willingness to let a jury knock on the door and the "guts" to listen to the verdict,'" Dorothy read aloud. "'How many juries knock on how many doors? How many lawyers figure out a way to get out of the hotbox? Every lawyer I know is subject to anxiety, to stress, to waking up at five a.m. and considering momentarily an excuse to convince a client to turn and run. A good trial lawyer must be able to overcome the fear of failure. He or she must understand that anxiety and stress are normal conditions of the courtroom, and that the adrenaline should be running. A good trial lawyer must be willing to go into the courtroom and let the jury knock on the door.'" She looked up and smiled quizzically at Aranow. "Joe told me you're *never* in court to hear a verdict."

"Neither is he," Max said.

"I know. He told me that too."

"Look," Max said. "I hired him originally so I could have somebody to be in court when the verdict comes in. Eventually, he saw the wisdom of this, so we expanded the firm."

"But on a case as important as this one? And nobody there?"

"Who said nobody? We'll have four people. Bert will be there. Sheila will be there. Harry Wright will be there. Our paralegal—the boy, Perry Muncrief—will be there. Joe's already sung 'Camelot' to him. You know, the part at the end where Richard Burton meets the kid in the woods and tells him what it was like."

"What about the defense?" Dorothy said. "Won't Arthur Hawkes be there?"

"Not if the jury decides to take two weeks, he won't," Max said. "If he's still in town he will. But defense is something else. When they find the guy guilty of murder, he expects his lawyer to be there to catch him when he collapses. That's what the lawyer's paid for. Why should Purcell be there? To catch the Specimen when he falls? Hell, he'd let him fall. Probably kick him in the behind when he's down."

"Two weeks," Dorothy said. "You think it will take that long?"

"For the jury to come in? Who knows?"

"It's been a complicated case," she said.

"Ah," he said, "you noticed that."

"Don't patronize me," she said.

"I'm not patronizing you," he said. "I'm condescending to you. You're a newspaper publisher. English should not be a foreign tongue." He genuinely liked this woman, and she liked him, but he would neither forgive nor forget her meddling in the case of the Fireball, and a little civilized needling would continue to remind her of that. "But you can't tell about juries," he said now. "Ordinarily, you'd say this one would be out a long time, just because of the complexities and the equity on both sides. If they did come back in early, it would be to ask for more readings of testimony or instructions, not to deliver a verdict. On the other hand, I've seen cases where it didn't work that way. Just a couple of years ago, a lawyer out west brought a suit for civil damages against the state in the case of a battered child. Claimed the state owed protection to the baby. A little black baby, it was, and it wound up dying for having been beaten as often as it was. And the state offered twenty-five thousand dollars in settlement, and this lawyer felt it had to be worth seventy-five thousand. So he did just what Joe did in the Fireball. He never insisted on one precise figure. He just told the jury, 'Send them a message.' The jury was out long enough to elect a foreman. Then they came back in with a million-dollar verdict against the state."

Dorothy said, "You find that comparable to your case?"

"No," Max said. "I don't. People may have wondered about how fast I disappeared after the judge's instructions this morning. Actually, I didn't disappear that fast. I ducked outside and got to that juror who was excused: Mr. Rafael DeSabitini. Joe said he was our best juror, and Joe was right. And when we lose the case, he's going to be one of the three reasons we lost it. The luck of the draw, and losing him as a result."

"The three reasons? What are the other two?"

"Your little gesture was one of them. Sending that proposal to the jurors in the mail, so the judge said we could never introduce it. And the other one was Arthur turning up the adultery with the Specimen. I didn't tell Joe or the others, because I didn't like what DeSabitini said."

"What he said?"

"Yes, what he said. What he said was that he thought Purcell was the greatest lawyer he'd ever seen in a courtroom, including Arthur Hawkes, although he said Hawkes was very good. He also said this was the first jury he'd ever served on, which may have limited his experience—but surely not his enthusiasm." The plane, held to await gate space, began to move forward again. "But he said everybody on the jury hated the Specimen. *Hated* him. And he said they weren't about to give him anything. And if our best juror said that, you can imagine the rest of them." Max shook his head. "So maybe it *won't* take them that long to come in with a verdict."

"But look at what Joe did with that man from the railroad on the witness stand. He destroyed him. You think the jury isn't going to remember that?"

"Oh, yes," Max said. "Arthur Hawkes set Mid-Central up for that, so they could be the ones to take the fall. All of their negligence, losing that freight car the way they did, and Joe was never more brilliant. Except for one thing: that jury in Mundelein may never have heard of Nance and may never have heard of North American Petroleum, but you can bet they've heard of Mid-Central. The railroad's a pillar of that community. Among other things, it's the biggest taxpayer in town—which keeps everybody else's tax rate down. It's a stunt Arthur learned from playing chess. So how badly are they going to punish that railroad?"

The plane had drawn up to its ramp. They stood up with the rest of the passengers, Max disremembering to take the copy of *Trial* magazine with him, and outside in the terminal there was the Carey limousine driver to collect the luggage and escort them to the waiting car. "Mardigan's," Max said. "Forty-fifth and Second." He turned to Dorothy. "Let's make it a leisurely supper," he said. "My adrenaline doesn't last two weeks. Did you know that Joe was a Farnum? That he had people who used to live in Mundelein? I visited the museum there. A fascinating place, that museum."

21

"Your move, Mr. Hawkes." The words came from a bearded twenty-two-year-old stranger named Ginsburg. He was one of the young law students who had paid his way to Mundelein to watch the two attorneys in action at the conclusion of the Fireball trial. Meeting Hawkes in the corridor outside, he had petitioned him for a piece of his time.

"You want to pick my brains?" Hawkes had said to him.

"Yes, sir. But there is something else I can do."

"What's that?"

"Beat you in chess."

It was now seven o'clock in the evening. The board lay between them on the nice free-standing coffee table—nice because, unlike the furniture at Purcell's plastic motel, the table in Hawkes's suite at the General Dexter was not bolted to the floor.

The position, with Hawkes playing the black pieces, was:

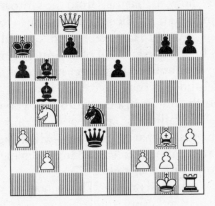

The young man was no liar. He was an accomplished chess player. It was Hawkes's turn to move, but by virtue of a rook over a bishop, the material edge, at this advanced stage of the game, lay with Ginsburg.

"As I see it," the law student said now, "you've pretty much got to move your queen. Otherwise I take it with my knight, and your checking me with your knight just leaves that threat in place."

"Right you are," Arthur said. "Right you are."

"If your queen checked me at bishop eight, it might be our most interesting situation yet."

"Right you are," Arthur said.

"Are you thinking of that?"

"I don't know." Hawkes's eyes were on the top of a lighted Christmas tree, as seen through his window in the storefront across the street. "Tell me something. Do you have a sense of how the Fireball case will come out?"

"You're going to win it," Ginsburg said.

"Am I, now?"

"Yes," the young man said. "You demolished his Specimen. I actually felt sorry for him."

"You felt sorry for Joe Purcell?"

"And his clients," Ginsburg said. "But juries nowadays are rebelling against the idea that society owes free protection to every plaintiff that comes along. You know, I went to Washington a couple of years ago and I heard Joe Purcell testify before the Senate against no-fault automobile insurance, and he was brilliant, and he won."

"Well, most insurance today is no-fault," Arthur Hawkes said. "Life insurance is no-fault. It's not your fault you die." He was not looking at the chessboard. "Joe was staking out one area to be exempted from that, and he made the point that it was just that one narrow area he was staking out."

"It isn't as simple as that."

"You're right. It isn't. It never is. And the Fireball, my young friend, is a perfect example of how complex the system is, a level of complexity they don't teach you in law school." The battle over, it was Hawkes singing "Camelot" to a youthful acolyte. "I'm not just talking about the social and economic conflicts in major civil litigation. I'm talking about the complexity which derives from mixed emotions about winning and losing."

Ginsburg looked at him. "You're not going soft, are you? Spare me the old bromide about there being no joy in depriving widows and orphans of just compensation."

"Fear not." Hawkes was smiling now. "Justice always prevails when I win. But that's not my point. The more I win, the less my clients listen to me." He had been rubbing two of the eliminated chess pieces together in his hand as he spoke. He tossed them into their wooden box and slammed the lid, as if to punctuate his speech. Then, in his most dramatic courtroom whisper, he said, "I almost want to lose sometimes, just to prove I was right."

Ginsburg laughed. "I know your reputation, Mr. Hawkes. You don't try to lose cases."

"I didn't say I tried to. I said I *almost* wanted to. There's a difference."

"Sure," the bearded young man from Columbia said. "And meanwhile you've got a chess game in front of you. Do you want to lose that too?"

"Ah," Hawkes said. "The chess game."

"Ah," Ginsburg mocked. "The chess game."

"Well, then," Arthur Hawkes said, "you're right. I've got to move my queen." He moved the black queen. "Queen takes bishop."

For a time, Ginsburg stared at the board. Then he said: "I'm sorry I upset you."

"You didn't."

"You can take it back if you want to."

"Thank you. I'm not in this game for charity."

"It isn't charity. If you make that move, then my pawn takes your queen, and the game's over."

Now for the first time, Hawkes looked directly at the board in front of him. "You're right," he said. "The game is over."

"You want to take it back?"

Hawkes shook his head. "No. That isn't the way the game is played. Go ahead and announce your move."

"Then pawn takes queen."

Hawkes sighed. "Right. So I have only one thing left to do. Knight to bishop six. Checkmate."

22

Max and Dorothy had dinner at Mardigan's, then an after-dinner drink at the Beekman Tower, that most remarkable of Manhattan observatories, where the height of the city in its late December dress was eye-level, and in the black nighttime current of the East River the moving finger wrote Pepsi Cola backwards.

As they talked, it grew past ten o'clock. "Lord a'mighty," Max said. "We've got to get over to my office. The cheese." He signaled for the check. "Where are you staying?"

"The Inter-Continental," Dorothy said. "But I can stop by your office with you. I'd like to see it. And I'm in no hurry."

"If I was staying at the Inter-Continental I wouldn't be in a hurry either."

"Why? What's wrong with it?"

"Nothing, probably. I've only been there once. For lunch. It was the Barclay then. I'll never forget that was frozen asparagus they served me. And in June, too. *June!*"

They went by cab to the office, its entrance just west of the subway stairs, on the north side of 53rd Street, and Dorothy made a mental note that before she left New York she must see the Christmas windows on Fifth Avenue. She made a note too, while Max was signing in with the night man in the lobby, of the wall directory: Aranow & Purcell, it said. 14th Floor. The entire floor, she told herself. But, when the elevator reached it and they stepped out into the reception area, she looked around and saw no identifying sign.

"I don't understand," she said to him. "You don't have the name of your firm."

"So?"

"So. So if I get off the elevator at your floor, how do I know I'm in the right place?"

"You don't," Max said. "Overall, in all the years we've been here, three of the biggest cases we ever had came from people who got off at the wrong floor. I think it was the atmosphere that got to them." He gazed about the reception area. "Nice. No?"

"No," she said.

"No?"

"Not really. The last time I was in a place like this was the waiting room of a medical lab. They were going to work me up for a GI series. Same business—the window on the wall over there, with the receptionist sitting behind it. Same frosted glass. You can do better than that, Max."

"Did Purcell get to you too?"

"What does that mean?"

"For years he's been telling me we looked like a dentist's office, with that receptionist in the cage," he said. "He wants the receptionist out here, with her own desk."

"I think he's right."

"Do you?" Max strode to the receptionist window, behind which, daytimes, sat the beauteous, black-haired, dark-eyed Rita Guitterez. "Look at that!"

Dorothy came over and looked. "So?" she said.

"So!" he said. "Do you want your clients getting off the elevator and looking at that phone console? What the hell do you think the name of our firm is? Atari Games? If Joe wants to change it, now's his chance. As long as I was here, it wasn't going to happen. But now I'm leaving. So you don't have to propagandize me."

"Oh, God," Dorothy said.

"What do you mean, Oh, God?"

As she stood in the well-lit waiting room of the A&P, Dorothy seemed to sag. "You and I are the same types," she said to Max. "You left it to Sheila O'Hara to tell him you were leaving."

"Sheila's good at that kind of thing," Max said. "And I'm not."

"Yes," Dorothy said. "You can be with Sheila for five minutes and sense how good she is. So you left it with her to confront him."

"And?"

"And I was with her for five minutes, so I left something else with her to confront him. Leonard Kinder isn't going to back Joe's show. He and Mary Ellen are getting divorced."

"And Joe doesn't know that?"

"Not as of today when I left. As I said, I left it with Sheila to tell him."

"Ah!" Max Aranow said. A great vibe hit him and suddenly he seemed three inches taller, and in that moment he crossed to her and kissed her bountifully upon the mouth. "I forgive you," he said. "I forgive you for everything."

"Whatever turns you on," she said.

"I wish I had known about Kinder before I called Marcy. We could have plugged that in to our plot. But it makes no never-mind. The point is that now Joe can lose the Fireball and he's still stuck here," Max said happily. "Any other questions?"

"Only one," Dorothy said.

"Ask away."

"Why are the lights on in here?" she said. "Do they stay on all night?"

Max Aranow did a take. "As a matter of fact, no." He looked around. "Something else for Purcell to worry about. I'll leave him a good-bye note: Do not leave lights on when nobody's here."

"Maybe somebody is here," Dorothy said.

"What makes you say that?"

"Look at that telephone console again," Dorothy said. "The one behind the window. When you showed it to me just now, there was a light on. Over one of those button-things or whatever you call them. As if somebody, somewhere inside, was using the phone."

Max went to the window and looked in. "Jesus," he said. "You're right."

"Which phone is it?"

"How the hell do I know? You have to have a degree from Carnegie Tech to understand that damn phone setup."

"Did the guard downstairs say anything?"

"Nope."

"Well, that doesn't mean anything," Dorothy said. "Maybe it's just somebody here, working late."

"If it is, that's another thing they didn't learn from Purcell." All the other doors leading off the reception area were unmarked. But only one of them fed directly into an office, and that office belonged to Max Aranow as senior partner. This time of night, as at almost all times during the day, it was locked. He tried it now. Still locked. He took out his key. "Come in here and sit down," he said to Dorothy. "I'll go prowling."

He opened the door, and his office was ablaze with light. Seated at his desk, two size-13 gunboat shoes comfortably upon the desktop, cigar in mouth, guest ashtray in hand, Willie Blake leaned back comfortably in Max Aranow's padded chair, the telephone receiver held to his left ear. No, not held to his ear so much as cradled there by his shoulder. Willie was neither talking nor, apparently, listening. More apparently, he was simply trying Max's office on for size.

"Jesus Harrison Christ," Max Aranow said. "Couldn't you wait for the body to get cold?"

Blake took his legs off the desk. But it was more a simple physical reaction than one of guilt. "We thought you'd be coming by the office tonight," he said. "Thank God you're here."

"You son of a bitch," Max said to him. "Did you get into my cheese?"

Willie regarded him with sudden fear. "Oh," he said. "What this must look like."

"Yes. What this must look like."

"It's like I just said," Blake said. "We thought you'd be coming by tonight. So they called, just on the off chance they'd get you. You weren't here. But I was."

"How'd you even get in here?"

"I stayed late doing some work," Blake said defensively. "I was on my way out—I'd already pushed for the elevator. I was going to turn off the lights and go home. I reached for the switch and the phone board lit up. So I reached in and answered it, and when I found out who it was, I decided to take it in here."

"Why in here?"

"Because yours is the closest office."

"That still doesn't answer my question. How'd you get in?"

"I tried the door, and it was open."

"It's never open. It was locked just now."

"I locked it behind me. That's reflex this time of night."

"How come it was open to begin with?"

"I don't know. Somebody was in here earlier and maybe forgot to lock it when they left. Maybe it was Rita. Who knows?"

"Where would Rita get a key?"

"She has the master key. Don't you know that? You're the one who insisted she ought to have it."

"All right," Max said heavily. "Then why would Rita have a reason to be in here?"

"To let the man in with your cheese," Willie said, and waved a foot at a bulky shipping carton beside his desk. "Look. It hasn't been opened."

Max turned to Dorothy. "See?" he said. "It makes all kinds of sense. He's at my chair at my desk in my office and I'm guilty of intruding on a private conversation."

"Yes," she said, and nodded, and smiled genially at Willie Blake. "I'm Dorothy Brewer."

"I'm Willie Blake. I've heard of you. Joe speaks very highly of you."

"And I've heard of you. He speaks very highly of you."

"See how he speaks when he hears you're the one who sent that DOT paper to the jury in the mail," Max said. "Damn it, where's the Scotch?"

"Max," Willie said. "This is your office, not mine. You find the Scotch." He sighed. "You're going to need it. We're all going to need it."

"Why?"

"Because the jury's in, that's why. What do you think this phone call is about? It's from Mundelein. They called here because they thought you might be here, like I told you." Willie Blake brought the receiver close and said, "Harry? You there?" He nodded at the evident response. "You been listening to everything I've been saying here in the office? All right. It doesn't make any difference. Anyway, Max just walked in." Again he nodded. "Of course I'll hold." Willie took the phone away from his ear, cradling it against his shoulder once again. This time he nodded to Max. "Harry Wright," he said.

Max was staring at him. "The jury's *in?*"

"That's right," Willie said.

"It can't be in," Max said. "It's too soon. They just came back to ask for more instructions, or to hear testimony read."

"No," Willie said. "They have a verdict. We're waiting now for them to round everybody up. They had to send for the judge and all the lawyers." He uttered a brief laugh. "All the lawyers except Purcell. Harry said they couldn't find him, and I asked him why they even tried. He wouldn't show up anyway."

"The Scotch is in the credenza," Max said. "With glasses."

"If you're asking me if I'll join you," Dorothy said, "the answer is yes. I like these high armchairs, Max. You're a man with taste."

"Maybe we could all use a drink," Max said. "It's Walker Red Label. I don't like the Black Label. Too smoky. But still, to its credit, at least it's Scotch. I won't have a bourbon distiller for a client. Brown and Foreman tried to retain me once, and I told them what they could do with their mash." He crossed to the credenza that held the whiskey. "We can toast the victory."

"The victory in the Marlowe case," Willie Blake said. "That's reason enough for celebration."

"Right," Max said. "We'll get a full one-third of that, and deserve it, too."

"Do you get a full one-third from the Fireball?" Dorothy said.

"What's one-third of nothing?" Max said.

"But suppose you won thirty million dollars," she said. "I don't mean in this case. But some other case. Would you take ten million dollars?"

"No," Willie said. "First the expenses come out, then you have to share it with all the lawyers who referred their cases to you, and if that still leaves you with too much, then you'd be expected as an ethical matter to hold down your fee to a reasonable figure. It would be very unusual for this law firm to take a ten-million-dollar fee from a thirty-million-dollar verdict. Right, Max?"

"This law firm isn't going to take *bupkus*," Max said. He began pouring the Scotch.

"Max," Willie said to him, "you've been drinking already."

"A touch or two," Max said. "One or two of those little miniatures on the plane."

"One or two?" Dorothy said.

"That's all," Max said. "And a before-dinner drink at Mardigan's and an after-dinner drink at the Beekman Tower. You know how—" He broke off.

Willie was clutching the telephone to his ear and his free right hand grabbed for the pen and the legal pad on the desk in front of him.

"Compensatory damages," he said, repeating aloud what Harry Wright was saying to him over the telephone from Mundelein, Ohio. At the same time, his pen wrote on the yellow page. "We find for Vincent Brophy and against the defendants and each of them and assess damages in the amount of four hundred dollars." Two generous beads of sweat formed on Willie's forehead. "Four hundred?—Come on, Harry, you're—"

"One-third of the burial expenses," Max Aranow said. "And I guess that's about right." He drank. "The great Specimen of all time."

"For Elliot Brophy, five thousand," Willie Blake recorded aloud. "For Katherine, five thousand. For Dexter, five thousand. For Louisa, five thousand."

"Oh, Jesus," Dorothy Brewer said. "The children. What did they do? Five thousand apiece—it's nothing. What's wrong with that jury?"

"They're afraid the father will get his hands on the money," Max said.

"Funny," Dorothy said. "Intellectually, I guess I knew the Fireball was a crapshoot. But somewhere, deep down inside, I had the feeling that Joe could work a miracle."

"There are no miracles in a courtroom. The last certified miracle this country has seen was the 1914 Boston Braves."

"But Joe Purcell—*losing?*"

"Hell, he lost the Marlowe case in your town. Are you forgetting that?"

"But won it on appeal."

"He won't appeal this one. The clients can't afford it. You think those kids are getting five thousand each? They're getting nothing, that's what they're getting. That twenty thousand is a drop in the bucket where legal expenses go, and they have to be paid off first. And that doesn't begin to pay what we're still on the hook for. Think seven figures, and maybe that'll give you an idea."

"Oh, my God," Dorothy said. "I didn't realize till this very minute how bad it actually could turn out."

"Finish your drink," Max said to her. "Willie, you're not—" But Willie held up a hand. It was a hand that shook. "Against the defendant Mid-Central Railroad," Willie was repeating now, but then said, "Are you sure of that, Harry? For the—all right." Again his voice took on the relay tone. "In the matter of punitive and exemplary damages—" And the pen fell from his hand.

"Oh, goddamn it, do it, do it," Dorothy Brewer said. She began to cry.

Max was pouring anew from the bottle.

Willie took up the pen again. There was a choked quality to his voice.

"—we find for plaintiffs in the amount of one hundred and four million dollars."

Only the voice of the relay robot in Max Aranow's office now: "—and against the defendant N. Nance Company and for the plaintiffs in the amount of two hundred and eight million dollars."

Max examined the label of the Johnny Walker Red. There was a slight smile on his face. His hand was very steady. Dorothy Brewer had taken her hands away from her face and was staring at him, almost without comprehension. "Shape up," Max said to her. His voice was cold. "Here comes your friend McKenna. See if this makes you happy."

And literally on cue, Willie Blake relayed it from the phone. "In the matter of punitive and exemplary damages against the defendant North American Petroleum, we find for the plaintiffs in the amount of six hundred and seventy-five million dollars." Willie shook his head, as if to clear it. "What's that, Harry?" He looked up at Max and Dorothy. "Sheila says to tell you it was eight to nothing. Unanimous."

"Ah, no wonder," Max Aranow said.

In a strained voice, Dorothy said, "No wonder what?"

"No wonder it didn't take them any time. We had a hundred and four cases, so they slapped the railroad for a million each. They hit the tank car manufacturer for two million each. And they made up the balance with the oil company."

"Balance? What balance?"

"To get it to a billion dollars."

"Does that add up to a billion?"

"With the compensatories it does." Max's hand swept down on the desk and removed the legal pad from under Willie's pen. "Let's see," he said, adding aloud. "Four hundred, twenty thousand, one hundred and four million, two hundred and eight million, six hundred and seventy-five million—no, it doesn't add up to a billion." His own pen showed the total: $987,020,400. "Oh, but sure, I see what they did. The other compensatories for the other cases haven't been decided yet. They're estimating a nice thirteen million for those, and my guess is that'll round out right about a billion. The newspapers tomorrow will be calling it the first billion-dollar verdict."

"Our newspapers certainly will," Dorothy Brewer said. "When Willie gets off that phone, I'm going to get on it. It'll be front page in every one of my papers."

"It was bound to happen," Max said.

"They're all going crazy down there," Willie Blake said, still holding the phone. "I told them you were here, and Bert and Sheila both want to talk to you. So does Perry."

"What about Harry Wright?"

"He's scared. He thinks the judge will reduce the verdict."

"On what grounds?"

"I'll ask him." Willie addressed the telephone: "What grounds, Harry?" He looked up. "He says same grounds as the Pinto case. Excessive award."

"Tell him not to worry," Max Aranow said. "This one's too excessive to be excessive. What's the judge going to do? Take a half billion off the award? He'll still have a half billion left. No, there's going to be no reduction."

Willie went back to talking to Wright. He looked up again. "They want to talk to you, Max."

Max waved a hand. "Tell them go celebrate. They don't need to talk to me. Hell, they'll be four days finding Purcell to talk to him." He turned to Dorothy. "You were going to get two rounds of the Edam," he said. "With this news, you get just one. You've been made happy in another direction. Let me get the box, and we'll take off." He went to the side of the desk to pick up the cheese, then headed for the door. Dorothy was waiting there.

Willie was still on the phone. "Look at him," Dorothy said. "He's crying."

"He cries at Mighty Dog commercials," Max said. "He's absolutely great in court."

They went into the reception area outside, and Max rang for the elevator.

"No," Dorothy said.

"What do you mean, no?"

"It's too pat. You said it was easy for the jury—one hundred and four cases, so they awarded a million to each, and built from there."

"That's right."

"But there weren't one hundred and four. It was one hundred and eight."

"That's before Cuneo had his boy Price take those four airline injuries out of the case," Max said. "If they'd stayed in, it would have been a hundred and eight, and the guy who sprained his shoulder would have been an instant millionaire with his pro rata share of the punitives. Justice does have a way of working, doesn't it?"

The elevator came, but again Dorothy balked. "I meant to call my papers," she said. "I was going to use the phone from here."

"Go ahead," Max said to her. "Just reach inside the window and push a button and hope. Joe was right. It *is* a dentist's office."

Dorothy went to Rita's window and leaned in to use the phone. After calling the paper she called Sunrise and arranged for Castor to drive into town and look for Joe and offer the whole A&P crowd the house for a victory celebration. While she was talking, Max prowled the reception area like a caged puma. Copies of the *Christian Science Monitor* were there as always. He began sorting them like a librarian. Finally, Dorothy hung up and turned to him. "I talked to Tom Glass in Mundelein," she said. "He already called the wire services. They broke in with bulletins on their A-wires. The first billion-dollar verdict." She paused. "But there's something missing."

"What?"

"We don't have quotes," Dorothy said. "How would you like to be interviewed?"

"Why me?"

"Your law firm won the case."

"I'm still not who you want."

"But nobody can find Joe Purcell."

"Just as well." He laughed. "We've ended the case the same way we began it. Nobody could find Joe Purcell then either."

"You've got a record verdict and the winning side doesn't want to talk about it?"

"Charge it off to modesty," Max said.

"And how about the other part?"

"What other part?"

"All of this tort reform and insurance crisis business that's going on now," Dorothy said. "Are you ready for what the press will do on this one? Another crazy jury with a lottery verdict, they'll say. Excessive—"

"How excessive?" Max cut in. "When you come right down to it, how excessive? This verdict was the system working just the way it's supposed to work. It nails corporate greed. No oil company or tank car manufacturer or railroad will ever again sit down and do cost-benefit studies on whether it's cheaper to kill and maim people than it is to recall a dangerous product. All the government safety agencies in Washington, at costs of many times the billion dollars, wouldn't do the job on North American and Mid-Central that the tort system did here."

Dorothy had reached into Rita's window for a notepad and a pen. "These are the quotes I was talking about, counselor," she said. "Keep talking."

"The jury spoke true," Max said. "And the judge knows it, which is another reason he's not going to reduce the award. More importantly, he knows that the tort system, with trial lawyers and juries and judges—the same adversary system that's been in place since the days of the thirteen colonies—not only provides us with a refined and beautiful and unique method of resolving human conflicts, but one that's remarkably cost-effective to boot. No multi-million-dollar studies, no governmental department with twenty thousand overpaid bureaucrats, just eight jurors delivering one-on-one justice with a shot heard 'round the world."

Dorothy looked up from her note taking. "Delightful," she said. "I'm enjoying every word of it. But doesn't the consumer lose? Won't he see this verdict on his heating bill?"

"First of all," Max said, "we're talking pennies, when it's spread out, against the greater cost that comes from blowing up whole trackside communities. The next one of those tank car explosions could have taken out downtown Boston. Now that's not going to happen because jumbo uninsulated tank cars are history. It's beautiful. The prophylactic effect of American tort law.

"And second, North American still has to compete with all of the other oil companies who *aren't* paying billion dollar verdicts. So they can't raise their prices on the basis of this verdict. It may cost their stockholders a few bucks in dividends and some of their executives may get a shorter bonus next year—your friend McKenna included, I suspect—but that's not going to cause many tears."

"Well," Dorothy said, "all well and good. But there are some state legislatures that don't agree with you. They've put caps on insurance awards."

"And Ohio isn't one of them," Aranow said. "At least not yet. Are you interviewing me or yourself? Yes, there are places where the insurance industry has used tens of millions of dollars for lobbyists and advertising and public relations campaigns to get the laws they want on the books. It's wonderful. Everybody pays premiums so Madison Avenue can tell them tort reform will cut down on their insurance costs. Where else but in America?"

"Well, they may not have the law in Ohio," Dorothy said, "but people in Ohio watch the same news programs and the same insurance commercials on television. And those people would include the people who were on the jury in Mundelein just now. Yet they gave you an award like this one despite all the advertising and propaganda. How do you account for that?"

"That," Aranow said, "would come down to Joe Purcell's theory of the case."

"You're being mysterious."

"*Mysterious?* How unmysterious can it be? You want to know how Joe won? Ask him, and he could tell you in three simple words."

"What three simple words?"

"Oil companies suck," Max said.

There was a pause. Then Dorothy said, "You want to be quoted on that?"

"I don't want to be quoted at all."

"What about Willie?"

"What about him?"

"You were rough on him in your office when you first went in."

"You're right," Max said. He went back to the door of his office, opened it, and looked in. From the doorway, he called, "Willie!"

Blake said, "Just a minute," into the telephone, and looked at Max.

"Don't forget to lock the door when you leave," Max said to him. "And turn off the goddamn lights."

23

"Don't feel badly, Arthur." It was Winston McHale, of the Mid-Central Railroad, on the telephone from St. Louis to Arthur Hawkes in Mundelein. "And don't think I'm angry."

"What about me?" Hawkes said. "Should I be angry?"

"You're being sarcastic with me, Arthur," McHale said. "What do I have to say to prove I'm serious?"

"Nothing," Hawkes said. "I know you're serious. If you're not, you should be. You were my primary client here and I got you off the cheapest. It doesn't even do anything conspicuous to your aftertax profits."

"But Nance and North American. They're sore. Right, Arthur?"

"Wrong, Winston. They're the two that had the most to do with the design of the Jumbo Nellies. All you did was run the things over your rails. They could have insulated them from the word go, but they made the conscious decision not to. As Purcell said in his summation, they were willing to take the chance and pocket the savings."

"But they'll pay for it now. Under the retrofit. And in today's dollars."

"And with today's revenues," Hawkes said. "The only thing they feel sorry about is their public image."

"We have that problem too."

"You do and you don't. Ford had the image problem with the Pinto, and that killed the Pinto. But nobody's going to kill your business in Mundelein or Florian. You're still the only railroad they've got. And Nance will still build the cars and North American will still peddle the oil. The only one who's angry is myself. If I could have settled the cases realistically, the jury wouldn't have gone runaway on the punitive side. There would have been no jury to go runaway."

"I don't understand," McHale said.

"Which word didn't you understand?" It was Hawkes-become-Purcell.

"The judge isn't going to let the verdict stand."

"Who told you that?"

"Ed Jamieson. He's our lawyer."

"I know who he is."

"He's here with me now, Arthur. Do you want me to put him on?"

"No."

"Wait a minute," McHale said, and Jamieson came on the phone. "Arthur, congratulations," he said.

"Jesus Christ," Arthur Hawkes said. And in a torrent of words, he launched the explanation of why Junior Bohr was not about to reduce the size of the verdict. It was the same explanation—almost word for word, if Hawkes had known it—that Max had pronounced to Willie Blake.

Jamieson heard him out. But what he said then came as a surprise. "Oh, I realize all that, Arthur," he said. "And I'm sure you're right. Winston didn't hear me right when I was talking to him just now. I wasn't talking about a reduced verdict from the judge. I was talking about an appeal."

Hawkes did a beat pause, and in something like disbelief he stared at the telephone receiver in his hand. Then he said, "What appeal?"

"The one you're going to file. I've seen the transcripts, Arthur. You were building to an appeal all the way."

"Listen," Hawkes said to him. "I was building to an appeal the same way I'll file for a new trial tomorrow morning: for form's sake, so you sons of bitches won't sue me for malpractice. The truth of it is, I was trying for a mistrial."

"I appreciate your problems," Jamieson said. He was being more than conciliatory. "Time and again you had the grounds and time and again that stupid judge wouldn't see it."

"That stupid judge isn't that stupid," Hawkes said. "And Joe Purcell never gave me that last inch."

But Jamieson was persistent. "I can understand your mood at the moment, Arthur. But tomorrow morning you'll see it differently. You established all kinds of grounds for an appeal."

"There isn't going to be an appeal," Hawkes said again. "I don't think you people appreciate the cost."

"The cost of a new trial?" Jamieson said. "I think between us the defense can handle that."

"Plus two hundred and fifty thousand dollars?"

"I know your fees, Arthur. Yes. Plus two hundred and fifty thousand dollars." Jamieson laughed hollowly. "People don't realize how much of their insurance premiums go to pay lawyers like you. But we happen to think it's worth it."

"You didn't hear me," Arthur Hawkes said tiredly. "I said a quarter of a million dollars."

"I did hear you. I heard you perfectly."

"Maybe you heard me, but you didn't let me finish. What I was going to say was: a quarter of a million dollars—*per day*. That'll be more or less the legal interest that will accrue on a billion-dollar verdict. And that's just till the appeals court rules, which might take two years, and we'll probably lose the appeal. Is anybody going to spend two hundred and fifty thousand a day betting against that parlay?"

"Well, now, Arthur, you're talking negatively," Jamieson said. "And that's understandable at this moment. Tomorrow morning you'll feel differently."

"So will you," Hawkes said. "If you think out what I just said."

"I think we ought to sleep on it."

"Do you? If so, there's a little something extra you can sleep on while you're at it."

"What's that?" Jamieson asked.

"The jury," Hawkes said.

"What about them?"

"The score."

"The score?"

"Yes, the score. Eight to nothing, that's how we lost it. It could have come in seven-one or six-two. But it came in unanimous. And not just as to fault, but as to amount as well. A billion dollars, and not one single son of a bitch in that jury room arguing for one penny less than that."

There was colloquy at the other end of the phone, and then Winston McHale came on the line. "Ed told me what you just said, Arthur. It's still going to be all right. Don't feel badly."

"I'll try not to."

"Ed says he still remembers that chess problem you showed him. What was it, Ed? Oh. The Bristol Theme. He explained that's why you didn't jump in to help me when Purcell was kicking me around about losing the tank car."

"The reason I didn't jump in to help you," Hawkes said, "was that you were beyond help."

"I thought you were throwing me to the wolves."

"You threw yourself. But it didn't affect the outcome that much. You certainly couldn't call it willful negligence, and he wasn't after negligen-ceanyway. He won this on defective design. Don't you remember the day of the explosion—" the trial over, Hawkes was no longer referring to the fireball as an accident "—when you called me, and then I called you back, and you read me back those specifications that said 'noninsulated'—no insulation. Tell you the all-out truth, Winston, that gave me a queasy little feeling that we might encounter a little trouble, just here or there along the way."

24

When the judge excused number two, and Rafael DeSabitini rose to leave the courtroom, Purcell had noticed the way Max Aranow rose too, to follow him out. No news from Max since then, and no news was bad news. Or so Joe by now had convinced himself as he sat alone at a very tiny table in the disco at the South Point Holiday Inn. The girl kept bringing him bar Scotch and he was beginning to like it, but not enough to persuade himself that he hadn't botched the case, particularly the summation.

This for Joe Purcell was the worst time of any trial—the interminable wait for the verdict. Some lawyers used this time to review the high spots and recount them to a partner or spouse or friend or whoever would listen and applaud the advocate's brilliance. But the Purcells sat in solitude and gnawed away at their own guts, hour after hour, remembering what should have been said but was forgotten, what should have been left out, how this or that should have been handled but wasn't, how now he thinks he spent all of his closing argument looking at just the two jurors in the middle and forgot to look at the others, and oh, my God, why didn't I draw the sting on Brophy? How could I have let Hawkes savage him so mercilessly with no defense? Why didn't I tell the jury in advance to watch for the attack on the Specimen—that this was the tactic of a desperate defense lawyer who could not defend on the merits and would try to distract them with irrelevancies—that this was not a case about the sins of a weak man whose wife had been killed—that this was a case about an outrageously defective design of thousands of jumbo tank cars which would continue to kill and destroy everything in their wake like great white sharks (that's the metaphor I should have used) until some jury in some town stopped them by returning a verdict that would send a loud and clear message.

The cocktail waitress brought another Scotch and Joe began to enjoy the lights and music of the disco at the Holiday Inn in South Point, Ohio—

the place where he and Ruth Marlowe had spent the night. He had made Bert be the one to make the phone call to her when the news of the million-five settlement came in. Why? He tried to picture in his mind's eye what she looked like in bed that night, but he couldn't see her.

And then Joe thought of Marcy and how very much he missed her. And then he thought of Max and how much he owed him. He owed a lot of people a lot of things. He ought to get in touch with Arthur Hawkes: do *something* with him. Maybe take him to the movies. Purcell grinned. *Moment by Moment* was still showing at the Gem. And do something for Bert and Sheila and Harry and Perry: a staff party, to celebrate—what? No matter. You had the party anyway.

He went to the phone booth, these things in mind, and when Sheila O'Hara answered the phone in the A&P motel quarters, Joe said without preamble: "Did Max ever get back to you with DeSabitini's reaction?" Then in the same breath, he said, "Good God, what's all that noise? What kind of a party are you having?"

"Joe!" Sheila screamed. "Where are you? We've been searching all over for you."

"Why didn't you ask the bailiff? I called him before I left my room and told him I was going to the bar at the Holiday Inn—to call me here if the jury comes in tonight."

"Joe, you don't know."

"Know what?"

"The jury came in over an hour ago."

Joe felt it. It was an indescribable sensation that started deep in his loins and his pulse quickened and every nerve in his body began to tingle and he could feel the blood rushing to his brain. It was his body beating his brain with the news that we've got a winner. It was match point at Wimbledon and a service ace. It was coming down the stretch at the Kentucky Derby a full length ahead. It was a grand slam in the bottom of the ninth, or hearing your name announced for an Oscar, or being told by your doctor that the tumor is benign and you're going to live.

And then, seconds later, the intellectual function, the understanding, the logical analysis. Joe knew he had a winner because the noise of celebration at the other end of the phone sounded victory, not defeat.

"We won?" Joe said into the telephone. "We won?"

"*You* won, Joe. Not we. *You—won—the—Fireball.*" Sheila was now crying. Bert Klein grabbed the phone. "You creamed them, Joe. It's an all-time world record."

"How much? Tell me." Joe was laughing, with tears now streaming down his face, and all he could hear was hysterical shouting and whooping noises coming from the A&P headquarters.

Now Harry Wright was on the phone. "Joe, this is Harry. Have they told you how much? Do you know the verdict?"

"Harry," Joe said, pulling out his handkerchief to wipe away the tears. "Please, for Christ's sake, tell me."

"Joe, are you sitting down?"

"Harry!"

"Joe, when you add it all up, the compensatories and the punitives, it comes to right at one billion dollars, really."

Silence.

"Joe, are you there? Are you okay? I didn't say million with an 'M.' I said billion with a 'B.' Joe, did you hear me?"

Now it was Sheila's voice. "Stay where you are, Joe. You said you're at the Holiday Inn at South Point, right?"

"Right."

"Good. Dorothy Brewer's chauffeur is trying to find you. He just called a second time and gave me his mobile phone number. I'll call him and have him come get you."

Ten minutes later Castor drove up to the front entrance of the motel and jumped out of the car with unusual energy and an even more unusual dazzling grin on his face. "Mr. Purcell, *sah*, and I do mean *Mistah*," beamed Castor. "You are the man!" Castor bowed ceremoniously as he opened the back door on the passenger side for Joe. In the darkness Purcell could barely make out two figures, both on the driver's side of the spacious rear section, facing each other, one on the jump seat.

The door closed behind him and Joe eased into the right rear corner. A gloved hand from the figure on his left thrust a glass in front of his face and a woman's voice said, "Johnny Walker Red Label and soda."

The man in the jump seat laughed as he opened the door of the portable bar that nestled between the two rear-facing jump seats. "And lot's more where that came from," he said, the interior bar light revealing an almost full bottle of Red Label, a silver ice bucket, and three splits of Schweppes club soda.

Castor, in the driver's seat, flipped on the courtesy light and, still beaming, looked over his right shoulder to see if Joe recognized his fellow passengers. Joe did. It was Mother Nine and his wife, Mr. and Mrs. George Proctor.

"Mr. and Mrs. Proctor," said Joe, and that prompted a raucous laugh in the front seat.

"Call me Ellie," said Mrs. Proctor. "Ellie Castor Proctor."

"Ellie's my sister," said Castor, still guffawing, and he started the engine. "Puttin' more miles on this old Lincoln tonight than I usually do in a month, and enjoyin' every one of them. Already made one run from the airport to Sunrise and now gotta go back to the airport, but first we'll drop you off at Sunrise, Mr. Purcell."

"Why am I going to Sunrise?" asked Joe.

"Orders from Miz Brewer and Miz Sheila."

"Oh, is the party moving out there?"

"Sorta," said Castor, and he flipped off the courtesy light as he pulled into traffic.

"Castor's taking us to the airport after he drops you off," said Ellie. "George is going to be on the *Today* show tomorrow morning. From New York. But we in no hurry 'cause we got a Lear jet charter and it ain't goin' nowhere until we gets there."

"The *Today* show?" Joe asked.

"George was the foreman of the jury," said Ellie. "You *do know* what happened, don't you?"

"Just that we won big."

"Big?" Ellie Proctor said. "Billion-dollar verdict and all you can say is *big? Today* show could have put him on from Charleston. Or even here from Huntington. But they want him in New York. That's so the big interviewer can talk to him face to face, that's how big it is."

From the front of the car came the sound of a ringing telephone. "That'll be for you, George," Mother Nine's wife said to him. To Purcell she said, "We left word at our house to relay the calls to the mobile phone."

Castor handed Proctor the phone. "I made him take those notes all the way through the trial," Ellie said to Purcell. "I figured to myself, how are seven whites gonna elect a black man foreman? And I answered myself, if he takes notes, they'll elect him, because it's going to be a complicated trial and a long trial, and the man who has it all down in writing has to be foreman."

"In the second hour," said George Proctor into the phone. He put his hand over the mouthpiece. "It's *Good Morning America*. They want me on their show too."

"I don't even know the details of the verdict," Purcell said.

"Four hundred dollars for your Specimen," Ellie said. "Five thousand apiece for each of the kids. Nothing, except that with the punitives, everybody gets well, including them."

"Who took the worst of the punitives?"

"I'll give you three guesses. One of them's got to be right."

"I'll try it in one guess. North American Oil."

"You got it in one. Six hundred and seventy-five million."

"Number two is Nance."

"Right on. Two hundred and eight million."

"And last the railroad."

"Bingo! Hundred and four million. Hundred and four cases, hundred and four million dollars. That's why it didn't take that long. George just told them, the bigger they are, the bigger the message it takes to learn them."

"Okay," said George, still on the phone. "I'll see you in the morning. Bye-bye." He clicked off and passed the phone to Castor. "I told them I was doing the *Today* show in the second hour. So they're going to put me on in the first hour and then limo me over to NBC."

"I wonder if Junior will handle CBS," Joe muttered, half to himself, and he leaned forward to pour another drink. "Can I fix anyone a drink?"

"I'm driving," said Castor. Mother Nine and Ellie ordered plain club soda.

"I guess I ought to be thanking you, Mr. Foreman—thanking you very much on behalf of a lot of grateful people."

"Well, don't mention it," said George. "It took us over a hundred years to thank you and your kin."

"What are you talking about?"

"Didn't your partner tell you? He knows about the Farnums who moved back to Connecticut. He spent half his time in the library while he was down here."

"What George is saying," Castor put in, "is that most every black in this part of Ohio owes the Farnums for helpin' our slave ancestors. George is a direct descendant from Martin Sweet, who died in the cause of the slaves, and you're a Farnum."

"You only had one problem in that whole trial," Ellie Proctor said to Purcell. "And that was that George would be the one who bought the bullet and got removed from the jury. His seat was number nine, and if he turned out to be the ninth man in the draw, he's gone. But it was eight to one that wouldn't happen, and it didn't."

"I'm a son of a bitch," Purcell said. "And all along I thought I had all sorts of problems."

"Don't get the wrong idea," said George. "I couldn't have done it without you. I mean, persuade those white folks."

They arrived at Sunrise. Again, still chuckling, Castor jumped out and ran around to Joe's door, opening it with all of the mock ceremony of a royal footman. Before getting out Joe leaned over and kissed Ellie on the cheek. "Thank you so much," he said warmly, clasping George's hand at the same time.

"Main thing was how good a job the jury thought you did," Ellie said to him. "George is going to say so on the *Today* show. Aren't you, George?"

He nodded, and saluted Purcell with a half wave. "And on the *Good Morning America*. I'll tell everybody."

Castor helped Joe out of the car and closed the door behind him. He turned and looked back at Joe. "See, Mr. Purcell," he said, "ain't nobody can take nothing away from you." He raced around the front of the car, jumped in, and gunned the black Lincoln into the night.

As the red taillights disappeared, Joe noticed that fog was rolling up the west bank from the river. He shivered slightly, then turned and walked slowly toward the massive front entrance. All was cold and dark and silent.

Purcell mounted the steps between the huge white pillars. Before he reached the front door it swung open and there, silhouetted against a soft glow of interior light, was Hallie.

"Congratulations, Mr. Purcell."

"Thank you, Hallie," said Joe, removing his belted Burberry trench coat. Hallie took it from him while closing the door behind him. "Is Mrs. Brewer still up and about?"

"Miz Brewer left for Europe this afternoon."

"Europe?"

"Yes, sir."

"Now I'm really confused. How about my crew? Miss O'Hara, Mr. Klein, Mr. Wright—have you heard from any of them?"

Before Hallie could answer Joe heard the faint sound of a piano playing "We Have Met Before," the love song from his musical.

Hallie smiled. "Only one here, Mr. Purcell, is the piano player in the drawing room. I've laid out some supper and set up the bar. The east bedroom is all ready for you—including kindlin' and wood for the fireplace. If you need anything else you know how to ring me in my room."

As Hallie spoke Joe had already started down the hall toward the closed double doors of the drawing room. The piano continued playing a simple, almost childlike, arrangement. Joe stopped, his hand on the doorknob, listening. It's perfect, he thought—exactly how that tune should be played.

Then suddenly it occurred to him that there was only one person in the world who would play that tune that way.

25

At some point, in between kisses, Joe learned that Max had been playing Cupid between trips from the library to the courthouse. He had chartered a jet for Marcy, and Castor had picked her up at the airport. Dorothy had flown to New York with Max, and between them all of the logistics had been worked out. Yes, Marcy said, she found out about the verdict after landing in Huntington. No, Max had called her from Mundelein after the jury went out and had told her she had to be here, with Joe, because the case could go bad and you would need me and I need you, darling—"God, how I've missed you."

"Marcy," Joe said. "I've decided. First thing in the morning, I'm going to call Leonard Kinder and tell him that the deal's off. You're the only one who can play that part. I wrote it for you."

"Joe, don't—"

He stopped her, first by putting his hand gently over her mouth and then by drawing her slowly to him and this time there was a softness and tenderness in Joe's embrace and kiss and Marcy felt her body relaxing, as if she were melting in his arms.

After a very long time, Joe said, "Listen lady, you're more important to me than all the hit musicals in the history of Broadway. Besides, I've decided it's not ready. I'm going to shelve it for six months or so and then rework the weak parts."

"Joe, let's go to London," Marcy said suddenly.

"Tonight?"

"No, I'm serious." She went back to the piano where she had left her purse and removed an envelope. "Look at this. Max mailed it to me a week or so ago."

It contained a full-color brochure complete with Coldstream Guards and Big Ben, announcing the American Trial Lawyers' Mid-Winter Convention in London. Stapled to it was a note on white message pad paper imprinted From the Desk of Max Aranow.

Then, in Max's handwriting:

London is a great place to pick up the pieces. Joe needs a week or so off. Go see some musicals and, it shouldn't be a total loss, the grilled dover sole at the Connaught Grill makes the eyeballs revolve in the head.

"I love it," said Joe. "We'll fly over on the Concorde and stay at the Connaught. The Grill there does a chocolate souffle. It's absolutely aphrodisiacal."

"I don't need an aphrodisiac, do you?" said Marcy. She passed him one of the two snifters of Remy Martin she had poured and loosened Joe's tie and began to undo the top buttons on his shirt.

The phone on the bar rang. Marcy crossed to pick up the receiver while Joe finished removing his tie and tossed it on top of the piano. He sat down and began to play "We Have Met Before," trying to copy Marcy's simple, endearing arrangement.

"It's Sheila, calling from the motel." Marcy brought the Panasonic portable phone to Joe. "I'll go up to the bedroom and start the fire. Bring the bottle of Remy with you when you come up."

She kissed him lightly on the lips, executed a graceful twirl, and danced out of the room.

"You copied that move from Rita Hayworth in *Cover Girl*," he called after her.

Marcy popped her head back through the door. "Frankly, I was thinking more of *un*cover girl."

Joe took a long drink of his cognac and then remembered Sheila on the phone. "Hi," he said. "What news?"

"Joe, I'm sorry. It's bad news. I got so tied up with the good news about the verdict, I forgot to tell you."

"Don't tell me, let me guess," said Joe. "Hawkes filed a midnight motion for new trial and—" Joe looked at his watch "—at exactly one-fifty-three a.m., Judge Junius Bohr, Jr., granted it and we start all over at ten o'clock tomorrow morning."

"No," Sheila said, "but you may think it's worse than that. Dorothy Brewer told me not to tell you until the trial was over. Leonard Kinder called her. He backed out of the deal on your show. His wife has gone to Vegas to file for a divorce. The marriage is kaput, so he's not interested anymore."

Joe began to laugh into the receiver.

"Joe, are you okay? Did you hear me?"

"Sheila, I heard you," said Joe, "and I love you and I'm going to sleep for a week and then go to London. What extravagant present can I bring back for you?"

"I've always pictured myself driving a white Rolls-Royce convertible with red leather seats."

"I can't afford the overweight on the plane. Tell me you'll settle for three Liberty silk kerchiefs and a two-pound crock of Stilton cheese from Fortnum and Mason."

"No deal," said Sheila. I'll get a reputation for being an easy settler and the insurance companies will eat me up alive."

"I'll throw in a full five-ounce bottle of Joy perfume."

"I hate haggling," she said. "You've got a deal."

"And one more thing," said Joe. "Order some new letterheads. I think Aranow, Purcell, Klein, O'Hara, and Blake has a ring to it. What do you think?"

"Oh, Joe, are you serious?"

"I never joke about letterheads," he said.

"You big turkey." Joe could hear that Sheila was now sobbing. "Every time I think I'm a grown-up trial lawyer, you do it again. You make me cry."

"Good-night, pussycat," Joe said. He clicked off the portable phone and walked over to the bar and put it back in its cradle. He picked up the bottle of Remy Martin, turned off the lights in the drawing room, and started to mount the stairs. As he reached the landing he noticed that the door to the east bedroom was ajar. He could see the flickering glow of the fire and hear the flames crackling. He pushed the door open and stood in the doorway.

Marcy was propped up in the four-poster bed against several down pillows. She was wearing a pale blue lacy negligee for which every living part of her magnificent body had been molded.

She looked at Joe. He was slumped against the doorjamb, with the bottle in hand, his shirt half unbuttoned, hair mussed, and a full day's growth of beard. Marcy smiled, swung out of bed, and moved slowly toward Joe. She began to undulate her hips seductively. It was showtime. They were both performing for a vast nonexistent audience. It was the love song, and the imaginary orchestra, just right, neither too loud nor too soft, gave Marcy her cue. She began to sing, ever so quietly:

Sometime in the springtime,
In my dreams I've seen
Your face at some familiar door somewhere...

Marcy turned and silently crossed back to the bed. Joe watched her go. Then he followed through the familiar door.

Epilogue

One hundred and thirty-seven days, four hundred and twenty-one pages of brief, and eleven hours of oral argument later, Judge Junius Bohr, Jr., denied all defense motions for a new trial and affirmed the verdict in its entirety. Despite the protestations of Arthur Hawkes, the three defendant corporations insisted he appeal. Fourteen months later, after one hour of oral argument by Hawkes and Purcell, the Supreme Court of Ohio unanimously affirmed the lower court decision, having taken direct jurisdiction because of the importance of the case. In a 21-page opinion, the court went to the unusual length of praising the trial judge for his unerring handling of so complex a trial. In Philadelphia, Max Aranow had the final page of the opinion framed in walnut and mailed it to Junior Bohr. In the same opinion, trial counsel were referred to as being "competent." In New York, Joe Purcell had that page framed and mailed it to Arthur Hawkes.

In the ensuing six months, all of the remaining cases were settled, in the total amount of $14,625,825, bringing the overall award, before interest or taxable costs, to $1,001,646,225, a record for a civil jury trial to that time.